A
Night
with a
Rogue

Also by Julie Anne Long

The Runaway Duke
The Secret to Seduction

A Night with a Rogue

2-in-1 Edition with

Beauty and the Spy and *Ways to Be Wicked*

JULIE ANNE LONG

FOREVER

New York   Boston

Copyright © 2021 by Hachette Book Group
Beauty and the Spy copyright © 2006 by Julie Anne Long
Ways to Be Wicked copyright © 2006 by Julie Anne Long

Cover design by Daniela Medina
Cover images © Trevillion; Shutterstock
Cover copyright © 2021 by Hachette Book Group, Inc.

Forever
Hachette Book Group
1290 Avenue of the Americas, New York, NY 10104
read-forever.com
twitter.com/readforeverpub

Beauty and the Spy and *Ways to Be Wicked* originally published in 2006 in mass market by Warner Books.

First 2-in-1 Edition: July 2021

Forever is an imprint of Grand Central Publishing. The Forever name and logo are trademarks of Hachette Book Group, Inc.

The publisher is not responsible for websites (or their content) that are not owned by the publisher.

ISBN: 978-1-5387-0383-0 (mass market)

Printed in the United States of America

CW

10 9 8 7 6 5 4 3 2 1

Beauty and the Spy

For Karen—for the times we nearly drove off the road because we were laughing so hard about something we could never, ever explain to anyone else; for Fritos on Christmas Eve; for the millions of little things that make up the language of sisters.

And I do not look like a yam.

Acknowledgments

My gratitude to Melanie Murray, an editor so completely wonderful that I killed off a (fictional) wife just to make her happy (teasing, M); to Diane Luger and Mimi Bark for yet another gorgeous cover; to Geoff Hancock for my new, daily view of hummingbirds and roses, which has done miraculous things for my peace of mind; to the Divas (http://www.fogcitydivas.com) for friendship, laughter, and advice about certain, shall we say, *intricacies* of publishing that have nothing to do with writing; to Elizabeth Pomada, for helping to launch me on this thrill ride in the first place; to Ken and Kevin and Melisa and Karen for being so brilliant at just being there; to all the readers who've sent warm, funny, touching notes or stopped by to say hello at signings—I'm so delighted and honored that you enjoy my stories, and I hope you always do.

Prologue

Years later, Anna would remember how big the moon had been that night, swollen and slung low like a pregnant woman on the brink of birth. The hard white light of it penetrated the shutters in her bedroom and kept her tossing and turning, and there was too much room in the bed to thrash. For Richard had been to visit, and Richard had left, as he always did, and tonight the bed seemed emptier than ever for it.

She tried soothing herself with thoughts of mundane things: Susannah, just three years old, was getting the last of her teeth, and was fussy and feverish with it. *I must tell Richard,* Anna thought, so he could exclaim over it and make Susannah giggle, for she loved her papa. She was such a funny little thing, bubbling over with laughter so easily, already exhibiting a taste for luxuries. Yesterday she'd taken one bite from a cake and then handed it back to Anna. "It's broken, Mama," she'd said sadly, as though she couldn't possibly eat something that wasn't whole.

Then there was Sylvie, four years old now, who was proving to have her mother's quick tongue and temper and her father's intelligence. "I'd really rather *not*," she'd loftily said to Anna just this morning, when she'd been told to pick up her toys. Anna smiled, remembering. Sylvie would be a...*challenge*. And Sabrina, who leafed through books intently and couldn't keep her jam-sticky fingers away from the pianoforte; who always seemed to know when her mother was feeling sad, and brought her little offerings, flowers, and leaves. It unnerved Anna, how much Sabrina noticed. Her daughters were miracles, all beautiful, all made of the best of her and Richard. Her love for them frightened her with its exquisite, terrible totality. Like her love for Richard.

Ah, but thinking of Richard would not bring sleep; instead, her senses surged with a hunger that his absences kept honed. His light eyes with the lines raying from the corners, the way her body fit so perfectly against his—he still took her breath away. An arrangement born of economics and necessity—he'd needed a mistress, she'd needed money—had bloomed into a surprising, abiding love. Together they'd built a semblance of family life here in Gorringe, a town, legend had it, named by a duke who'd gone mad searching for a rhyme for "orange." It appealed to Richard's perhaps overly developed sense of the absurd and to Anna's desire for a quiet country home, and it was a mere few hours' coach ride from London where Richard, a much-beloved member of the House of Commons, spent most of his time.

There had never been talk of marriage; Anna had never expected it, or pressed him for it.

But lately she'd begun to suspect that Richard, having survived battlefields, had grown too accustomed to danger and was no longer capable of living without it. He'd told her over dinner once, while the girls slept, that he suspected one of the country's most influential politicians, Thaddeus Morley, had amassed his fortune by selling information to the French. And Richard, a patriot to the bone, intended to set out to prove it.

Anna had seen Morley precisely twice, and she had been struck by his stillness and sheer presence—he held himself like a man carrying a grenade in his pocket. The populace thought highly of him; he had risen from humble origins to a position of prominence. Anna knew a little something about what it took to rise so high from humble beginnings. She suspected he was a very dangerous man.

"If anything ever happens to us, Anna…" Richard had murmured against her mouth the other night, as his fingers had worked busily at the laces on her dress.

"Hush. Nothing will happen to us, except perhaps some marvelous lovemaking tonight."

He laughed a little, applied his lips to her neck. "If anything happens to us," he insisted, "I want the girls to have the miniatures of you. Promise me." He'd commissioned three exquisite miniatures of her, brought them with him during this all too short visit.

"Of me? Why not of their handsome father?"

"Of you, my love. Of their beautiful mother." He'd had her stays undone by then, and then his hands had covered her breasts—

Bam, bam, bam.

Anna shot upright, her heart clogging her throat. Someone was throwing a fist against the door downstairs.

In one motion she swept from her bed and thrust her arms through the sleeves of her robe; her trembling hands tried once, twice, three times before she finally managed to touch a light to a candle. Cupping the tiny flame with her hand, she moved into the hall. Susannah was whimpering, startled awake; Anna heard the whimpers become choking sobs.

The maid, a girl with eyes and a mouth too sultry for her own good, stood at the top of the stairs, dark hair spilling like two shadows down the front of her, hands twisting anxiously in her nightdress. She'd come highly recommended from the agency, and yet she'd proved nearly as hapless as she was handsome.

"Please go see to Susannah." Anna was amazed to hear her voice emerge so gently. The girl jerked as though shaken from a trance, then glided into the nursery. Anna heard murmuring, heard Susannah's sobs taper off into hiccups.

Somehow Anna's bare feet found each stair without stumbling, and then she was at the door. She threw the bolts and opened it.

A man stood heaving before her, hunched with exhaustion, breath bursting from him in harsh white puffs; a thick scarf coiled around his neck and a heavy overcoat protected him from the weather. Behind him Anna saw the dark outline of a coach against the star-spattered night; two spent horses bent their heads in their traces.

The man straightened: the white glare of the moon showed her the long nose, kind eyes, and small, ironic mouth of James Makepeace, Richard's friend from London. The whole of his message was written on his features.

"It's Richard." She said it before he could, as if doing so would somehow protect her from the blow.

"I'm so sorry, Anna." His voice was still a rasp, but it ached with truth.

Her chin went up. The deepest cuts, she knew, brought a blessed numbness before the agony set in. "How?"

"Murdered." He spat the word out, like the foul thing it was. "And Anna…" He paused, preparing her, it seemed. "They're coming to arrest you for it."

The words sank through her skin, cold as death.

"But...that's...*madness*." Her own voice came faintly to her through a burgeoning fear.

"I know, Anna. I *know*." Impatience and desperation rushed his words. "It's impossible. But witnesses claim to have seen you arguing with him at his town house yesterday; others have sworn they saw you leaving it shortly before he was...found. You can be certain clues will be discovered that point to you, as well. If he's gone this far, I'm sure he'll be thorough."

No word had ever sounded more bitterly ironic than that last one.

"Morley," she breathed. "It was Morley."

James's silence confirmed this. Then he made a strange, wild little sound. Almost a laugh.

Anna jumped at the crunch of approaching hooves and wheels, and the flame of her candle leaped tall, nearly flickering out. In that instant, Anna saw silvery tracks shining below James Makepeace's eyes.

His low, curt voice cut through her numbness. "The hackney you hear approaching is one I hired for you. Anna, please—you need to leave *now*. They know to look for you here. Take it anywhere but London—I've paid the driver well enough not to ask questions. But don't tell him your name, for God's sake."

"How...how was he..." She stopped, shook her head; she didn't want to know how Richard had been killed. She wanted to picture him in life, not death. "The girls—"

"I'll take them. I'll make sure they're cared for until...until it's safe for you to return, Anna. You've my vow."

"But I can't...they're...they're so small..." Such futile words, and not really what she meant to say. *Richard is dead.*

James Makepeace seized her cold, cold hand in his gloved fingers and squeezed it hard. She sensed that he wanted to shake her instead. "Anna...*listen to me*: a woman with three children...you'd be dangerously conspicuous. They'll find you, and who knows then what will become of the girls? You're a brilliant scapegoat; the public will tear you to pieces. I swear to you if there was some other way..." He threw a quick glance over his shoulder, turned back to her, and she could see him struggling for patience.

He'd risked his own life for her.

Would it be better to flee without her girls, if there was the slimmest chance to reunite with them later?

Or for her girls to grow up knowing their mother had hung for their father's murder?

Anna made the only sort of decision one could make in the frantic dark: she gave a quick shallow nod, acquiescing.

James exhaled in relief. "Good. I swear to you, Anna, if I could hide all of you, I would. I just...there wasn't time to make other plans."

"You've risked so much for us already, James. I would never ask it of you. I cannot thank you enough."

James ducked his head, acknowledging the gratitude he heard in her voice.

"How did you...how did you *know* this?"

He shook his head roughly. "It's best I not tell you. And forgive me, Anna, but I must ask one more thing: Did Richard say anything, *anything* to you about where he kept some very important"—he chose his next word with care—"documents?"

"I'm sorry?"

"Richard said he'd found the perfect hiding place for them, a place no one would think to look, particularly Morley. He said it had something to do with 'Christian virtues.' Richard was amused by it, actually. Found it ironic." James's mouth actually twitched. A grim little attempt at a smile. "Richard was... Richard was clever."

"Oh, yes. Richard was clever." Anna felt a helpless, selfish rush of anger. When would love become more important to men than glory? How could one woman and three little girls ever compete with the glamour and excitement of capturing a political traitor? The thought itself was probably traitorous. "I'm sorry, he said nothing to me of it."

They stood facing each other. Frozen on the brink of a life without Richard, and hating to move forward into it.

"I loved him, too, Anna," James said hoarsely.

Loved. Past tense.

Anna stepped aside to allow him into the house. And then she became a whirlwind in the predawn darkness.

James Makepeace waited while Anna dressed herself in dark mourning, covered herself in a heavy cloak, twisted up her hair, and pulled a shawl around her head. She woke the girls, Susannah and Sylvie and Sabrina, kissed and held their little bodies to her, breathed in their hair, felt the silky skin of their cheeks, murmured quick desperate promises they couldn't possibly understand. She bundled them with clothes and the miniatures.

Anna gazed down at those miniatures briefly and felt hot furious tears pushing at her eyes. Those miniatures meant he had known, damn him. He had known they were in danger. Had known that something might become of Anna, or of him.

She would love him for all time. She wondered if she would ever forgive him.

"For you," she said to James, thrusting a simple but very fine diamond necklace into his hands. "It should help with ... well, it should help the girls."

James took it without question. Closed his fist over it, as though sealing a bargain.

"How will I ..."

"Send a letter when you can, Anna, but wait a few months for the uproar to die. Leave the continent if you can; I doubt any place in England will be safe when word spreads. Godspeed."

And then Anna looked one last time at the house that only hours earlier had been the source of her greatest happiness, her greatest love, her only love.

She prayed for her girls. For Richard. For justice.

James helped her into the hackney. The driver cracked the ribbons over the backs of the horses and the hackney jerked forward and took Anna Holt away.

Chapter One

Susannah Makepeace had a new dress, and Douglas was being particularly charming, and together these two things comprised the whole of her happiness.

She sat with her best friends on a low hillside at her father's country estate, the young ladies scattered like summer blooms over the grass, the young men sprawling as they plucked tiny daisies to make chains. The day was warm, but a frisky breeze snaked around them, lifting the ribbons of bonnets and fluttering the hems of dresses. Douglas cast a furtive eye toward Susannah's ankles and she drew them quickly under her skirt with a teasing frown. He winked at her. In two weeks' time, when he was her husband, Douglas would be privy to the sight of every inch of her. The thought made her heart jig a little.

Like the breeze, their conversation meandered: friends and balls and parties were touched on, laughed about, abandoned, taken up again. It was summer after all, or very nearly, and summer was about gaiety. And they were between

London balls. God forbid there should be a lull between entertainments.

"Did you notice how George Percy dances?" Douglas mused. "His arms hang as though they're inserted on pins, and he rather...*flails*...like"—Douglas lurched to his feet—"like this." He flopped about like a marionette, and everyone laughed.

Behind them, their chaperone Mrs. Dalton *tsked* in disapproval.

"Oh, come now, Mrs. Dalton, you must admit it's a *little* funny," Douglas cajoled, which earned him a *hmmph* and a reluctant, tight-lipped smile from the matron, who was the latest in a series of Susannah's paid companions. She drove her needle back into her sampler, no doubt stitching something meant to be inspiring but that always sounded admonishing instead, such as THE MEEK SHALL INHERIT THE EARTH. Susannah often felt that Mrs. Dalton's samplers were a silent attempt to rein her in. *You'll have to try harder than that, Mrs. Dalton,* Susannah thought cheekily. Susannah Makepeace hadn't become the belle of the season because she was *meek*. Nor, for that matter, was meekness the reason Douglas Caswell, heir to a marquis, had proposed to her.

Amelia Henfrey, Susannah's best friend, clapped her hands together in sudden inspiration. "You're so funny, Douglas! Now do Mr. Erskine!"

Susannah cast a sharp glance at Amelia, wondering if she was flirting. Amelia had a head full of golden curls and blue eyes very nearly the size of dinner plates, both of which had been the subject of any number of amateur odes this season. She did a surreptitious count of the flounces on Amelia's dress, and was a little mollified to discover that it featured only *one,* while her own new dress boasted three.

As for her own eyes—to Susannah's knowledge, no poems had been written about them. They were hazel, a kaleidoscope of greens and golds that, Douglas had once declared in an

ardent moment, "fair dizzied" him. He claimed her eyes had
mesmerized him into proposing, that she'd given him no choice
in the matter, really. Douglas could be very clever that way,
which was part of the reason she loved him.

Amelia, despite the golden curls and limpid eyes, wasn't
engaged to anyone at all. But as they were both heiresses,
Susannah silently and magnanimously allowed that Amelia
would likely make a match as spectacular as her own.

And besides, Amelia is good, Susannah conceded. She
never said an unkind thing, she had a smile for everyone, she
never misbehaved. *While I am…*

Not wicked, *precisely,* she confessed to herself. *But not*
good, *either.* She charmed and sparkled and said witty things,
but she knew very well she was being charming and sparkling
and witty while she was doing it, which felt somehow wrong.
She was often plagued with an indefinable restlessness, an ache
really, that beautiful dresses and nonstop gaiety couldn't fully
assuage. And she frequently secretly suffered from envy and
entertained observations that she dared share with no one, since
she was certain they would do nothing to add to her popularity.

She had one of those thoughts now: *Amelia is dull.*

She batted it away. Amelia was her best friend, for heaven's
sake. Susannah reached for her sketchbook and began quickly
charcoaling in the stand of trees at the edge of the park in an
attempt to distract herself from any more heretical thoughts.

"Erskine?" Douglas was rubbing his chin in thought at
Amelia's suggestion. "The chap who laughs too loud at everything, bends double when he does it?"

"Remember how foxed he was at Pemberton's ball?" Henry
Clayson, one of the sprawling lads, contributed lazily.

"Pemberton's ball? Was that where I wore my blue satin?"
Amelia categorized all of the events in her life by what she
wore during them.

"Yes," Susannah confirmed, because, quite frankly, so did Susannah. "And where I wore the silk with the matching—"

"*Tell* me we aren't now discussing ball gowns," Henry Clayson groused.

Susannah playfully tossed a daisy at him. "Let's discuss horses, then. Have you seen my new mare, Henry?"

Douglas sat down proprietarily next to her, a silent message to Henry Clayson: *She might toss daisies at you, but she belongs to me.* Susannah smiled to herself.

"Susannah's father is forever buying her new *everything*," Amelia said wistfully. "My father buys *one* new gown and tells me I'm in grave danger of being spoiled. And my mother never can persuade him to loosen the purse strings."

And there it was, that unwelcome little tightening in Susannah's chest: envy. It seemed extraordinary to envy the fact that Amelia's father *refused* to buy her things. It was just that . . . well, Susannah's mother had died so long ago and James Makepeace had left the rearing of his daughter in the hands of governesses and housekeepers and redoubtable matrons like Mrs. Dalton, who were charged with ensuring that Susannah acquired a full complement of ladylike accomplishments. Susannah could play the pianoforte and sing; she could draw and paint better than passably; she could certainly dance; she could sew. And miraculously, she'd escaped becoming *too* spoiled and willful, primarily because it had always seemed more effort than it was worth to seriously misbehave.

But that was the very root of her envy: though Susannah had grown up in a beautiful house surrounded by beautiful things, she would have traded most of it—well, perhaps not her new mare, but maybe the pianoforte and a few pelisses—if her father had seemed to care even a little about how much she spent on clothing. Or, frankly, about what she did at all. Oh, he'd been pleased enough about her engagement to Douglas, as any sane father would. But he was so seldom home—his antiquities-importing business often took him away—and she rather suspected her father considered her part of the furnishings. He…*maintained* her the way he did the big clock in the library or his best musket. He was as distant and impersonal—and as necessary to her well-being—as the sun.

And so whenever Amelia and Douglas and her other friends spoke of their parents, Susannah felt a tiny clutch of panic. This talk of parents was a language she could never hope to share with them.

All Susannah had of her mother was a fuzzy memory—of being awakened in the middle of the night amidst frantic whispers and movement, of a woman's dark hair and dark eyes and soothing voice—and one tangible thing—a miniature portrait of a beautiful woman: curls, large pale eyes with a bit of a tilt to them, a soft, generous mouth, cheekbones delicately etched. Susannah's own face. On the back, written in a neat, swift hand, were the words: FOR SUSANNAH FAITH, HER MOTHER ANNA. The miniature was the only image of her anywhere in the house.

When Susannah was small, she'd wanted to keep the miniature on her night table, but her father had gently asked that she keep it in a drawer, out of sight. Susannah had decided then that her mother's death had shattered her father's heart so completely that any reminder of her—including his daughter—pained him.

But just last week she'd found him in her bedroom, holding that miniature in his hand. Susannah's breath had suspended; the hope had been piercing: perhaps they'd finally speak of her mother…perhaps, little by little, her father's heart would thaw, and they would become close, and then he would complain about how much she spent on pelisses.

But then she noticed he was looking at the *back* of the miniature. And he'd murmured "Of course." Not "Alas!" or "Oh, me!," which would have seemed more appropriate for someone with an irreparably broken heart, but "Of course." And those two low words had thrummed with a peculiar excitement. They had, in fact, sounded rather like "Eureka!"

James had looked up then, and Susannah watched a startling desolation skip across his features.

"I beg your pardon, my dear." And with that, he'd drifted out of her room.

Douglas leaned over her now to reach for the sketchbook. The sun had turned the back of his neck golden, and Susannah was sorely tempted to run her finger along the crisply cut line of his dark hair. *Soon I can touch every bit of him.* She wondered what sort of message Mrs. Dalton would have stitched if she'd known *that* particular sentiment. But the thought made the tightness in Susannah's chest ease; surely being the wife of a marquis-to-be would make envy and restlessness a thing of the past.

Douglas suddenly paused his sketchbook-leafing and frowned, shading his eyes with his head. "I say, Susannah, isn't that your housekeeper coming this way? At rather a fast clip?"

Mrs. Brown, a large woman who typically moved as if every step required careful deliberation, was indeed taking the green so quickly she'd gripped her skirts to free her ankles.

Later Susannah would remember how, little by little, everyone went very still, transfixed, as though the housekeeper's mission was apparent in her exposed ankles.

And as Mrs. Brown's grim face came into view, Susannah slowly rose to her feet, her heart beating swiftly and unevenly.

She knew before Mrs. Brown spoke the words.

❧

The earl's pen continued to fly across the bottom of a sheet of foolscap when Kit appeared in his office doorway. "Good morning, Christopher." His tone was abstracted. "Please sit down."

If Kit hadn't already known the summons from his father meant trouble, the "Christopher" would have confirmed it. He settled resignedly—and a little gingerly, since he'd been out very, *very* late the night before, and it was very, *very* early now—into the tall chair situated in front of...the prow of his father's desk. The thought amused him. It was a bloody great ship of a desk, of oak so polished the earl could watch himself at his daily activities: Thinking profound thoughts. Affecting the course of history with signature.

Berating his son.

For the life of him, however, Kit could not come up with a reason for this particular summons.

"Good morning, sir."

His father looked up then, eyebrows aloft at his son's formal tone, and then he leaned back in his chair to study Kit, twirling his quill between two fingers. Outside his father's great office window, London went about its business on foot and horse-back, in barges and hack—business his father, who oversaw the budget for intelligence affairs and was often the last word on the assignments of His Majesty's agents, so often indirectly, secretly influenced.

"Just because you think your superior officer is an idiot, Christopher," the earl began wearily, "doesn't mean you should *call* him one."

Ah, *now* he remembered.

"But, father, that idi—"

The earl moved his head in the slightest of shakes, and Kit stopped. Truthfully, though he'd *thought* "Chisholm is an idiot" any number of times, he'd never said the words aloud...until last night, apparently. Which was a bloody miracle, really, since Kit had an innate tendency to frankness that only years of

militarily honed discipline had managed to keep in check. And
frankly, Chisholm *was* an idiot.

But he was just as appalled as his father that he'd said the
word. It must have been all that ale. Well, that, and the brandy.
And... hadn't there been whiskey, too? Fragments of last night
were returning to him now, out of sequence, but unfortunately
all too clear. He recalled that the evening had begun at White's
with a few fellow agents, his best friend John Carr among them.
Naturally they had begun drinking, which they seemed to be
doing more and more in the five years since the war had ended.
It was boredom, he supposed; Kit had become accustomed to
living his life at the fine edge of danger, to subtlety and strategy
and purpose; life in the wake of war lacked a certain... piquancy.

At some point in the evening, his superior officer Chisholm
had appeared at White's, and then...

His father idly tapped his quill against the blotter. *Tap, tap,
tap.* The sound echoed in his head like cannonfire. Kit was
tempted to lean over and seize the bloody instrument of torture
out of his father's hand and snap it in two.

"Chisholm is *not* an idiot, Christopher."

"Of course not, sir," Kit agreed.

Mercifully, the tapping stopped. A silence.

"He is an *ass,*" the earl clarified, finally.

"I stand corrected, sir. I should have cleared the word with
you first."

And now his father was struggling not to smile. He sobered
again quickly, however, and resumed studying Kit in a way that
made him a little apprehensive. And after ten years in service
to his country, after dozens of narrow escapes and heroic suc-
cesses and employing his astonishing aim more times than he
preferred to count, *very* few people could make Kit Whitelaw,
Viscount Grantham and heir to the Earl of Westphall, apprehensive. He thought he'd better speak.

"Sir, I know what I said was inexcusable, and I hope you realize it was uncharacteristic—"

The earl snorted. " 'Uncharacteristic?' Like the incident with Millview?"

Kit paused. There *had* been an incident with Millview, hadn't there? Lord Millview. An incident so…objectionable…the earl had in fact threatened to reassign Kit to a government post in Egypt as a result of it, a potent threat indeed, given Kit's passion for London. Kit had questioned Millview's, er…parentage.

"I apologized for that," Kit said stiffly. "We'd all been drinking, you see, and…Well, I apologized for that. And I intend to apologize to Chisholm, too."

"Don't you think you've been doing rather a *lot* of apologizing lately, Christopher?"

Kit knew better than to attempt to answer a rhetorical question. His father was about to answer it for him, anyway.

"*I* do," the earl said. "And you've acquired quite a reputation for womanizing, too."

Have I, really? Part of Kit was impressed. The other part was appalled that he actually had a "reputation," let alone one with a name.

"Notice, at least, it's *woman*izing, sir," he attempted feebly. "Not *women*izing. Just one woman."

"One woman at a *time*. And the latest is married."

"She *isn't*!" Kit feigned shock. Though he'd awakened in time for this meeting only because said married countess had been hissing at him to get dressed and leave *now,* before her husband came home from the bed of *his* mistress. The countess wasn't terribly interesting, but she *was* beautiful, spoiled and difficult, which had made the pursuit, at least, interesting.

The earl ignored this; for some reason, he began marking off a list of sorts with that deuced quill. "You've distinguished yourself in battle, Kit. *Tap.* You saved the life of your commanding officer while you were wounded. *Tap.* Served bravely and well by all accounts." *Tap.*

Kit listened, puzzled. He'd merely been himself on the battlefield and in assignments beyond; none of those things had ever seemed particularly heroic to him.

Ah. Then he grasped his father's point: *You aren't exactly making me proud* lately, *Christopher.*

Kit redefined heroism then and there as managing not to squirm while waiting for his father to reveal his bloody agenda.

"To the matter at hand. Though you've distinguished yourself in many ways, as you know, Kit, in the wake of the war, we've less and less call for the sort of work agents do. In fact, I was informed this morning that James Makepeace is dead, and we don't intend to replace him. So I've decided to—"

"James Makepeace is *dead*?" Nothing like a bit of startling news to burn away the fog of a pleasant debauch. Why Kit had seen James just last—

And suddenly all the little hairs on Kit's arms rose in portent.

"How did James die, father?" He managed to ask this calmly enough. He suspected he knew the answer.

"Cutthroats. He was robbed; pockets were empty. It's a shame, and I'm sorry for it. Now, on to the business at hand. As I said, there's less and less call for the work agents do, so I've decided to send you to—"

"Sir, I think James was murdered because he was pursuing a suspicion about Thaddeus Morley."

It was a blurt, really. And once the words were out of his mouth, Kit realized how mad they sounded, particularly in the bright daylight of his father's office, instead of the soft lamp-and-smoke haze of White's, where James had first told Kit the tale. Certainly the expression on his father's face confirmed this.

But murder cast the tale in another light altogether.

A week ago, Kit had arrived at White's to find James Makepeace sitting alone, staring at a glass of whiskey as though wondering what one actually *did* with a glass of whiskey. The alone part wasn't unusual; James was often alone. The whiskey, however, struck Kit as odd; James was employed by the Alien Office, and on the occasions Kit had worked with him on matters of foreign intelligence he'd never before seen James take in anything more controversial than tea. In fact, James Makepeace's most striking characteristic had always seemed...well, his striking *lack* of characteristics, apart, that was, from quiet dignity, rare flashes of dry wit, and an unswerving competence that inspired trust, if not warmth. He owned a town house in London, Kit knew, and a country home; he had a daughter. That was the extent of Kit's knowledge of the man, but he had long ago decided he'd liked him, partly, he suspected, because James was difficult to know. This intrigued him, and so little else did anymore.

So Kit had wandered over, thinking perhaps if James didn't plan to drink his whiskey, he'd do the job for him. But when James greeted him with, "Tell me Grantham, what do you know of 'Christian virtues'?" Kit had, half-jokingly, smoothly turned on his heel and began walking back the way he'd come.

But then James had...laughed.

If one could call the bleak little sound he'd made a laugh. Which drew Kit back to him out of perverse curiosity.

"Don't worry, Grantham, I'm the very last person to lecture someone about morals," James had said then, which was interesting enough. But then he added, "I've a story to share concerning Christian virtues...and a certain Mr. Thaddeus Morley."

And James, who had lived in Barnstable so many years ago like Kit and his family, and knew a little of Kit's past, knew Kit could no more turn away from a discussion of Thaddeus Morley than a hound could from a hare.

So James had told his story, and Kit had listened, more entertained than convinced. And then John Carr and a few of his other friends had swept Kit away before James could finish his mad tale, but not before Kit could finish James's whiskey.

His father was grim-faced, displeased at the interruption. "James was pursuing a suspicion about Morley? The Whig MP? What *sort* of suspicion?"

"It was last week...James told me he believed Morley was involved in the murder of Richard Lockwood some years ago. He said..." Kit paused, willing the returning fog in his head to move aside so James's words could return accurately. "He said that Lockwood had been gathering evidence—documents, apparently—proving Morley had sold information to the French to finance his political career. And so Morley arranged to have him murdered."

For a moment, his father said nothing. And then, like a man slipping into a coat, he donned the expression of exaggerated patience that Kit had known and loathed deeply since he was a child.

"Christopher, you know full well that powerful men provoke jealousy, even myths, and Morley has perhaps drawn more than his share because of his humble beginnings."

Kit sucked in a long impatient breath. "Sir, James told me that Lockwood hid the evidence incriminating Morley in a place that had something to do with...Christian virtues. Some place...'whimsical.' That was the word he used—'whimsical.' But Lockwood never told James precisely where. And he was murdered before this evidence came to light."

The earl burned a dark frown into his son. Kit met it levelly.

And then all at once the earl's face cleared, as though he'd reached some sort of satisfactory conclusion. "Was James drunk when he told you this? Were *you* drunk?" Fatherly suspicion lit the earl's face and he leaned forward, forehead furrowed in scrutiny, and gave a sniff. "Are you drunk *now*? Did you drink your breakfast, Christopher?"

"Oh, for God's sake, father. No, I did not drink my breakfast." At the moment, the very idea of food or drink, in fact, made Kit's stomach lurch beseechingly. "And I've never seen James drunk in my life."

"Hmmph" was the earl's grunted opinion of James's alleged sobriety.

"And the very last thing James told me, father," Kit continued doggedly, "was that he thought he finally knew where to find those documents incriminating Morley. And now he's dead. That's two deaths now. Two murders. Both former soldiers, both of whom were ostensibly investigating Morley."

"Two deaths seventeen years *apart*, Christopher." And then the earl slapped two exasperated palms down on his desk, which made Kit's brain shrivel in pain. One of his eyes rolled up into his head. *Shouldn't have had the bloody whiskey, too.* "I fail to see the connection. And James most certainly wasn't *authorized* to pursue any sort of suspicion about Morley, if indeed, that's what he was doing when he was murdered. *Furthermore . . .*" the earl drawled, "witnesses put Lockwood's mistress at the scene of his murder, and then his mistress disappeared—never to be seen again. London was in an uproar for months. Sketches of her in the newspapers, a mad search for her all over the country . . ." The earl gestured broadly, illustrating the mad search, perhaps. ". . . and then the whole thing inevitably died away. It's really a very simple, if somewhat sordid tale, *and* a testament," he concluded, in a return to what appeared to be the day's developing theme, "to the potential danger of mistresses."

The potential danger of mistresses? Kit was briefly

distracted as he considered these. Last night, the countess had been in danger of wearing out his—

"And let me ask you this, son, Why would James Makepeace choose to confide his...delusion...in *you,* in particular?"

Bloody hell.

And as Kit knew he couldn't answer the question without incriminating himself, he remained stubbornly silent.

And finally his father leaned back in his chair and sighed a long-suffering sigh, the sound of confirmed suspicions. "Christopher, just a few days ago, Mr. Morley asked me—very delicately, mind you—whether he'd done something to earn your dislike."

This was a surprise, and yet not a surprise. "His impressions are unfortunate, father," Kit said stiffly, "but I can assure you I've done nothing to inspire them."

But Morley, Kit was certain, knew precisely what he'd done. It went back to an evening nearly two decades ago, to a party at his father's house in Barnstable, to a rivalry between two friends that had almost turned deadly. To a beautiful, reckless young woman. To the first time Kit had met Thaddeus Morley.

And the last time he'd seen Caroline Allston.

A stalemate's worth of quiet ensued, and a breeze nudged the curtains at his father's window into a languorous motion that set Kit's stomach pitching and rolling again. With effort, he kept his eyes focused on his father's face, rather than closing them, which is what he very much would have preferred to do. So like his own face, the earl's was, but gentler, its lines more harmonious and pleasing. Handsome, everyone said. His son, with his grandfather's arrogant arch of a nose and long angular jaw and his mother's disconcertingly vivid blue eyes, had never been directly accused of being handsome. "Unforgettable," however, applied.

Or so he'd been told by any number of women. In tones ranging from infuriated...to satiated.

"Father," he tried again quietly, because it simply wasn't in his nature to surrender, "What motive could James Makepeace have possibly had for telling me such a story? Doesn't this at least warrant—"

"Christopher." His father's voice was terse now. "Leave it."

"Why?" Kit almost snapped the word. "Because investigating Morley would be awkward for you politically?"

Oh, *that* was a risky question, and Kit immediately regretted asking it. His throbbing temples were allowing unfortunate words to get through. He seemed to recall champagne now, too. Hadn't the countess poured some into her navel, and then hadn't he—

"That *should* matter to you, son," the earl said quietly.

Kit fell silent, chastened. His father did deserve his loyalty; his father, in fact, unquestionably had his loyalty. And he knew he could never fully explain his feelings about Morley to his father. Just as he would ever have the words to explain Caroline Allston.

"Well then," his father said crisply. "We've wasted enough time with this nonsense. To the business at hand, Christopher, in light of recent events, I've decided to send you to Egypt, as we previously discussed."

Kit's lungs froze. He parted his lips a little; nothing emerged.

His father stared back at him with a sort of detached interest. A scientist, awaiting the results of an experiment.

"You've…" Kit finally croaked. The rest was too horrible to repeat.

"…decided to send you to Egypt?" his father completed gently. "Yes. Today. A ship leaves in two hours. I've arranged for your trunks to be packed."

Kit had lost use of all of his faculties. His limbs had turned to marble. He certainly couldn't form a sentence. He stared at his father, waiting for shock to ebb so he could strategize.

The earl was still watching his son, but his face had gone steadily more pensive.

"Or..." his father mused.

Kit clung to that "or" the way a sailor clings to the splintered mast of a wrecked ship. He waited. He tried a bit of a smile, as though nothing had ever mattered to him less than what his father was about to say next.

"...you may repair to Barnstable immediately to work on your folio."

The smile vanished. "My *what*?"

"Your folio. Your nature folio." Said with deceptive innocence. "Like the work undertaken by the recently departed Mr. Joseph Banks. There's a recognized need now to document the flora and fauna in the English countryside, and the Barnstable region has heretofore been neglected. We've been looking for just the man to do it, and I think that man is *you*. You will take notes, make sketches. And you'll live at The Roses while you do it. It was your mother's favorite of our homes, as you recall, and it's been all but neglected in recent years."

Had his father just suffered a stroke? "Banks was a *naturalist*," Kit explained slowly. "I'm a *spy*."

"Yes, well, that's what you became after you shot your friend over that wild girl years ago and I packed you off into the military—"

"It was a *duel*," Kit muttered. "I was *seventeen*."

"—but when you were a very young boy, Christopher, you wanted to be a naturalist."

Kit couldn't believe his ears. "Yes. For about five *minutes*."

But the earl appeared to have drifted into some kind of reverie. "Don't you remember? Up trees, following squirrels and deer, bringing home snakes, nests, things of that sort. Always observing. Swimming at the pond. Making little sketches. Your mother thought it was adorable. And wasn't there a rare mouse in the region?"

"Vole. There's a rare *vole* in the region," Kit said testily.

"You see? You know all about it," the earl said delightedly, as if this proved his point.

All at once, with a sinking feeling, Kit comprehended. "Ah," he said flatly. "I see. I'm to be exiled regardless."

The earl gave him a smile that managed to be sunny and evil all at once. "*Now* you're catching on."

"You can't...*exile* me simply because I called a man an idiot."

His father regarded him in placid silence.

"Or for calling a man...a bastard."

Serene as a lake, his father's silence.

"Or for...womanizing?" Kit faltered.

"Oh, I can," the earl disagreed cheerfully. "For all of them. I warned you once before, Christopher. You now have two choices: you may travel to Barnstable and begin work on the folio, or you can leave for Egypt. Choose."

His father, Kit realized, was deadly serious. And when his father was deadly serious, no amount of reasoning could penetrate his resolve, which was how Kit had found himself installed in a military academy with head-spinning speed after his duel so many years ago. Kit stared at the earl, and his mind's eyes drew him a painfully vivid picture of the hard-won countess, and all of the myriad, glorious pleasures and comforts of the *ton,* shrinking inexorably from view as his ship drifted from English shores.

And as for Barnstable and The Roses...well, Barnstable was just a few hours' hard ride from London, but it might as well have been Egypt, simply because it wasn't London.

"You *need* me here. I'm the best agent the crown has."

He was absurdly gratified when his father didn't disagree

with this patently unprovable statement. But he also didn't relent.

"Egypt or Barnstable, Christopher. And if you choose Barnstable, I want you to make a thorough job of that folio. Every plant, every creature... I want them carefully, lovingly documented. You have one month in which to accomplish it, after which we shall review your continuance in his Majesty's Secret Service. If I hear of you womanizing, if I hear of you doing *anything* other than working on your assignment, if I see you in London during that time, if I hear of you being anywhere *near* London... I will personally escort you on to a ship bound for Egypt where you will then take up a quiet little government post. Do I make myself clear?"

Silence fell like a gavel.

Kit decided he could at least do this with a little dignity. "I choose Barnstable," he said quietly.

"Good. I should miss you if you went to Egypt."

And then his bloody father actually *smiled*.

Kit would not be softened by fatherly expressions of affection. "If I complete the assignment to your satisfaction before a month is over?"

"You may return," his father said placidly. "*If* you're confident you've completed it to my satisfaction. You can take a day to prepare for your journey. And now, you may go."

Kit pushed back his chair and stood—all gingerly, of course.

"And son..." His father's voice was idle in a way that told Kit his next words were in no way meant idly. "I don't need to tell you again to leave the issue of Morley alone, do I?"

His father knew him too well. "Of course not, sir. I thought it was understood."

"You always were a clever boy, Christopher."

Chapter Two

The large ormolu library clock measured off seconds of incredulity.

"With...without resources?" Susannah repeated, just in case she hadn't heard her father's solicitor correctly.

"Penniless." Mr. Dinwiddy mercilessly enunciated each syllable. "That's what 'without resources' means, Miss Makepeace."

Bewildered, Susannah swiveled her head about the library, as if searching for help, for some clue to the man her father had been.

His throat had been cut, they said. Such a violent, dramatic punctuation mark to a life so quietly led. And all morning Susannah had graciously accepted murmured condolences from mourners, wishing she could summon tears, or a smile— but there was only this dull grief that cast a strange haze over her senses. Grief over the loss of a man who had never been anything but kind to her. And grief over the fact that she would now never truly know him.

She doubted it was the sort of grief that a daughter ought to feel for a father, the kind that welled up out of a broken heart. And so mingling with the grief was guilt and, if she were being perfectly honest with herself, anger, too. She'd *wanted* to know him. She'd *wanted* to love him.

He hadn't allowed it.

"Miss Makepeace?" Mr. Dinwiddy's voice came to her.

She swiveled back to him. "Penniless? But...I don't understand. How—that is to say—"

"The goodwill of shopkeepers and merchants has enabled your father to purchase almost everything in this house—including your clothing—on credit for years now. The servants have been paid, but no other creditors have—and *I* will not be," he added ruefully. "Your father's properties and furnishings will be confiscated immediately to satisfy his debts. I suggest you vacate the premises as soon as possible."

Penniless. The word throbbed in her head, and she couldn't get a proper breath. She stared almost unseeingly at Mr. Dinwiddy, and her mourning gown—beautifully cut and very dear, and apparently unpaid for—suddenly seemed sewn from lead.

Somehow a fly had found its way into the library, and it was orbiting Mr. Dinwiddy's shiny head. Susannah watched, half-hypnotized.

Mr. Dinwiddy's face was impassive. And then his head creaked to a tilt, and his expression became oddly... considering.

"Have you any relatives who will take you in, Miss Makepeace? No others are mentioned in your father's will."

"I don't...I'm not..." A strange ringing in her ears frightened her. *Am I going to faint?* She had never before fainted in her life, though once or twice she'd feigned light-headedness at a ball in order to get a moment alone in a garden with Douglas. And because it clearly made Douglas feel manly.

The fly decided to settle above Mr. Dinwiddy's right ear. Mr. Dinwiddy swiped a palm over his perspiring dome, disturbing it; it resignedly resumed its lazy circling. The solicitor cleared his throat. "Perhaps, Miss Makepeace, you and I can come to... an arrangement."

" 'Arrangement'?" Hope animated Susannah briefly. "Arrangement" seemed a better word than "penniless."

"I have a home in London in which you may live in exchange for..." He paused. "Entertaining me... once or twice a week."

Susannah frowned a little, puzzled.

Mr. Dinwiddy waited, his eyes tiny and bright behind his spectacles.

When the meaning of his words at last took hold, she leaped to her feet and backed away as though the solicitor had suddenly burst into flame.

"You—how—how *dare* you!" she choked out. Her face burned.

The solicitor shrugged. *Shrugged!*

Susannah drew a long shuddering breath and drew herself up to her full height. "I assure you I will be *well* cared for, Mr. Dinwiddy. My fiancé is the son of Marquis Graydon. And once I tell him of your... your... *suggestion,* no doubt he will call you out."

"Oh, *no* doubt." But the solicitor sounded more weary than sarcastic. And then he rose from his chair with a leisureliness that shook Susannah's confidence to the core.

"Good day, Miss Makepeace. You may wish to keep my card"—he extended it; Susannah jerked her head away and balled her hands into fists, as though she feared one of them might betray her and reach for it—"in case you find your fiancé other than... gallant."

"But...but...Mama *said* you would understand, Susannah."

Douglas stood before her, his fingers curled whitely into his hat, his face drawn with distress. And usually when Douglas showed any signs of distress, Susannah would comfort him, place a soothing palm against his cheek, perhaps, for that was the sort of thing fiancés did for one another. But now—

"Pardon us, miss! Step lively, now!" boomed a cheerful cockney voice. Two stocky, booted men were staggering across the marble floors bent under the weight of the pianoforte. Susannah stepped aside; briefly she saw her own reflection, distorted and pale, in the instrument's polished surface, before it vanished out the door, forever.

Douglas threw a quick, longing look over his shoulder toward the door. He'd done that a few too many times in the last five minutes.

"Douglas—" She heard the plea in her voice and stopped. She was *damned* if she would beg. She'd never begged for anything in her life.

Damned. Now there was a word she had never before included in her vocabulary.

But one needed the fortification of such words when one has just been jilted.

Susannah's mind reeled with the sheer *speed* of the spread of the news—*Susannah Makepeace is penniless*—as if the fly orbiting Mr. Dinwiddy had in fact been a spy for all the mamas in the area. Douglas's own mama had leaped so quickly into action she might as well have been whisking him away from the plague.

"*Whoop!* Lift yer feet for me, miss, there ye are luv, my thanks." Two more men were rolling up the soft parlor carpet as merrily as if they were playing with a hoop and stick. They hoisted the great tube of it up under their arms and wended their way toward the door, and the carpet's heavy fringe trailed across the curve of a bulbous cream-and-blue Chinese vase, like fingers dragged against the cheek of a lover. The vase wobbled threateningly on its pedestal once, twice...it stilled. Susannah exhaled. She was glad it hadn't broken.

She might need to hurl it at Douglas.

"It's...it's for the best, Susannah." Quoting his mama again, no doubt.

"How, Douglas? Please explain to me *how* it can possibly be for the best? Or perhaps"—she added bitterly, and she could not recall saying *anything* bitterly before in her life—"you should have your mama come explain it to me."

They stared at one another wretchedly as cheerful cockney voices drifted in from the courtyard, where the crewmen were loading carts with the things she'd taken for granted since she was a girl. Carpets, chandeliers, candelabras, books, settees, beds.

Her life.

"Don't do this, Douglas," she cried softly, despising the hint of plea in her voice. "I love you. And you love me, I *know* you do."

Douglas made a little sound in his throat then, and took a sudden step toward her, his hand outstretched in...in what? Supplication? Comfort? Farewell? Whatever it was, he apparently thought better of it, for he dropped his hand and shook his head roughly, as though clearing his mind of her. And then he turned abruptly and went the way of the pianoforte and the parlor rug, smashing his hat down on his head as he went.

He never looked back.

Susannah stared after him. She could feel what surely must be the jagged edges of her heart clogging her throat, and her hand went up to touch it there.

"Make way, miss, thank ye kindly!"

A man was marching down the stairs, his arms piled high

with her beautiful gowns. The silks and velvets and muslins slipped and slid in his grasp, and suddenly, to Susannah, they all seemed like kidnap victims struggling to escape.

"Put...those...down. *Now.*"

The glacial ring of her own voice strengthened her—she hadn't know she'd had such a voice at her disposal, and it certainly seemed to give that big man pause. He froze midstep and stared at her wide-eyed.

"But miss, we've orders to take all of—"

She seized the heavy vase from its pedestal and hoisted it slowly, meaningfully, over her head. The man's eyes followed it up there warily.

"You have until the count of three." Every word chiseled from ice.

He raised a brow and took the tiniest step forward, daring her. Susannah brandished the vase warningly.

"One..." she hissed. "Two..."

"Susannah?"

Susannah turned her head swiftly. Amelia stood in the doorway, her dinner-plate eyes bulging with astonishment.

There was a rustle from the stairs.

Susannah swiveled. *"Three!"* She drew the vase back.

"All right, all right, no need to take on so, miss." Surrendering, the man lowered his bundle of dresses to the stairs; the fabrics settled there with a sound like a collective sigh of relief. "I'll just move on, shall I?" He lifted his hands placatingly.

Susannah lowered the vase and hugged it to her chest, and the man, seeing that whatever demon had possessed her a minute ago had now vacated, clambered confidently down the remainder of the stairs until he stood before her.

"And I'll just take that, too, shall I?" he said gently.

Susannah sighed and handed the vase to him, and he took it out the door, whistling, the very picture of no hard feelings.

She sank down on the stairs and covered her face in her hands, breathing hard, horrified and strangely exhilarated all at once. Her father's death had unleashed a veritable Pandora's box of emotions, all of them interesting, none of them pleasant.

She'd just threatened a man with a *vase* over *dresses*.

Amelia was silent, and at first Susannah thought she might have left. But then she saw the toes of her friend's shoes through cracks in between her fingers: blue kid walking boots.

"Do you suppose it was pride, Amelia?" she finally asked, pulling her hands away from her face.

"Pride?" Amelia was staring down at her, looking distinctly nervous.

"As in, 'goeth before a fall,'" Susannah quoted bitterly. It seemed as sensible a reason as any for the sudden collapse of her life.

Alarmed, Amelia unconsciously touched a hand to her blond curls. "*Were* you proud, Susannah?"

"Yes," Susannah said emphatically and a little cruelly, in case Amelia felt a little *too* proud of those blond curls and those blue kid walking boots. Amelia's hand flew from her hair and began to fuss with her skirt instead.

There was a silence. "What are you going to do?" Amelia all but whispered, finally.

"I—" Susannah stopped.

The servants had been tendering their notices for days now. Good servants were hard to come by, and they'd all found new jobs easily enough; one by one they'd bid her fond but pragmatic farewells. *They* were all on to new lives in new places. But as for Susannah...

Well, she knew how to run a large household. That was, she knew how to instruct *servants* how to run a big household. She wasn't qualified enough to be a governess, really, unless one wanted one's daughters tutored in dancing and the number of flounces considered most stylish in 1820. In short, she hadn't the faintest idea what she would do.

Of course, there was always Mr. Dinwiddy's offer.

Susannah was suffused with a fresh wave of hate.

Until a few days ago, her life had been one long sunny afternoon, a song in a major key. And now . . . soon she wouldn't even have a place to live. Her palms went clammy, and she rubbed them against her skirt. Pride might very well have led to her fall, but it was the only remaining timber of her life, and she clutched it to her. Damned if she would give Amelia any sort of reply.

Damned. She was growing fond of that word.

"And Douglas . . . ?" Amelia added carefully, when Susannah remained silent.

Something in Amelia's tone made Susannah look intently at her, and for the first time ever she found the face of the eminently transparent Amelia Henfrey . . . closed.

So this is why she came today. She knows. She just wanted to make certain. Susannah wondered if Douglas's mama had sent a note to Amelia's mama: *There's a position opening up . . .*

Before she could reply, Mrs. Dalton appeared, dressed for traveling in sensible dark clothing. She was the last of the current household members to leave and she, too, had acquired another young lady to oversee and plague with her dutifully judging presence. "This is for you, Miss Susannah, as a farewell," she said briskly, handing over a sampler.

Susannah read it: CHARITY BEGINS AT HOME. "Thank you, Mrs. Dalton," she said, with the irony the gift deserved.

Mrs. Dalton nodded modestly. "And this arrived for you, too, Miss Susannah, in the post. From a Mrs. Frances Perriman in Barnstable." She extended a gloved hand holding a letter.

Susannah had no idea who Mrs. Frances Perriman in Barnstable might be, but the letter was indeed addressed to Miss

Susannah Makepeace. And Susannah felt so alone in the world that she decided that Mrs. Frances Perriman, whoever she was, was her new best friend.

She reminded herself that the last shining thing in Pandora's box was Hope.

She gave Amelia another deliberately enigmatic look, and split the seal on the letter.

Dear Miss Makepeace,

I hope you will forgive the presumption, as we have met but once, and then when you were only a little girl. But I am your poor deceased father's cousin, and I have heard of your new circumstances. I would like to invite you to stay with me, if you haven't another situation, and I've enclosed enough fare for a mail coach...

And so it appeared that she did have a family, of sorts.

"I shall be living with my aunt in Barnstable," she told Amelia triumphantly.

C✦

Thaddeus Morley pushed aside a heavy velvet curtain and gazed out onto St. James Square, watching for the hackney that would bring his visitor. He saw only a few pairs of fashionable men and women promenading beneath a sky sullied with the smut of London's daily life, and the statue of William the III, snowcapped with bird droppings.

He dropped the curtain and let his hand fall to his side. His cat immediately drifted over and bumped its head against it. *Perhaps he smells the blood on them.* His mouth twitched in

self-mockery at the thought. *Such* melodrama. In a moment
he'd be muttering "Out, *out,* damned spot" like that barmy
Lady MacBeth.

Besides... there had only been *two* deaths.

Still, blackmail letters arrived nearly as often as ball invitations lately.

He smiled again. Perhaps a good meal would steady his
thoughts; he seemed a trifle prone to hyperbole today. There
had only been *two* blackmail letters.

Nevertheless, one would have been too many.

"Puss, puss, puss," he crooned, running one of his broad,
blunt-fingered hands—hands that betrayed to the world that he
was but one generation away from the peasantry—over Fluff's
silky body, to make him arch and purr. Something about the
arching and purring suddenly brought to mind Caroline, the
author of the first blackmail letter, and an unexpected sweep of
regret and irritation stilled his hand.

One night, years ago, at a party held by the Earl of Westphall, he'd collected Caroline, much the way one might gather
up useful things in preparation for a journey. He recognized
darkness and weakness and need in other people, and sank
into it, like a tree sinking roots deep, deep below the surface of
the ground in search of water. He'd seen it in Caroline. It was,
in fact almost integral to her astonishing beauty. And once...
well, once he had felt a twinge of something when he was with
Caroline. "Perhaps this is love," he'd thought wonderingly.

More likely it had only been gas.

But Caroline—perhaps inevitably—had left him almost two
years ago. He hadn't kept her chained, after all, and any wild
creature might venture out when the door is left open. She'd
chosen to wander out of doors with a handsome American
merchant.

Perhaps she'd left the merchant, too. Something had clearly

gone wrong with him, or she wouldn't now be resorting to blackmail.

Morley thought she of all people would have understood why blackmailing him would be a terrible mistake. How ferociously, ruthlessly, quietly he had fought for everything he now had. How ferociously he would fight to preserve it.

But then again, Caroline wasn't clever, and rarely thought past a given moment. He'd run her aground soon enough.

The bell rang. He waited for Bob's heavy boots to come up the stairs to his sitting room. He called all of the men Bob; it seemed simpler; it reminded them of their place and imposed a sort of anonymity. This particular Bob had proved his competence and discretion for many years now.

Morley leaned hard on his cane for balance and turned from the window. He said nothing, simply looked a question at Bob.

"Nothing, sir. Searched every bloody cranny, opened all the upholstery, opened up every drawer, went through every bit of furniture. Went over the whole place, stables and outbuildings, too. And you *know* I'm a professional." He puffed out his chest a bit.

Relief was perhaps an overstatement for what Morley felt, because he'd been certain all along Makepeace had been bluffing. Blackmail was usually a desperate act; Makepeace had been crippled by debt. And he'd been neatly, thoroughly, remorselessly dealt with before he could become any more of a nuisance.

Plink. The sound of a chess piece knocked from the board. That was Makepeace.

"Very well"—he turned back toward the window—"thank you, Bob." A dismissal.

But Bob, irritatingly, cleared his throat. "Sir . . . there's something else you should know."

Morley turned around again, waited, grinding the tip of his cane into the plush carpet beneath his feet in impatience.

"The girl...Makepeace's daughter—"

"Yes?" He didn't like to spend more time than necessary in the presence of men like Bob; it reminded him too much of his own origins, which pulled at him, sometimes, like a great wave coming to take him back out to sea.

"She's the image of Anna Holt."

The jolt through his body was extraordinary. For a moment he couldn't breathe.

"Were like seein' a ghost," Bob added, with an illustrative shudder.

"Are you sure?" Morley hated the uncertainty in his own voice.

"I'm a *professional,* sir." Bob sounded wounded. "I've a memory like a trap, you know. And I saw Holt often enough when I was following Lock—"

Morley lifted a hand. He didn't like to be reminded of... well, he thought of them as previous chess moves. Maneuvers planned and executed, literally.

"And anyhow, there were letters."

"Letters?" Morley repeated sharply. "What do you mean?"

"Letters to James Makepeace. They all said just one thing: "'I beg news of the girls.'"

The girls. Morley had forgotten about the girls. He'd known about the daughters, of course, but they'd been so small, seemed so unimportant in the scheme of things. They'd disappeared along with their mother. Morley had always assumed they were together, Anna Holt and her daughters.

Apparently not.

His mind was moving quickly now. "Where did the letters originate?"

"Couldn't tell you, sir."

"Were they signed?"

"No, sir."

"And did you burn them?" Morley asked.

"Of course." Bob almost sounded wounded by the question. "Went right up in flames, sir."

Morley's thoughts tumbled through the past. "Where is she now? The girl? Susannah?"

"Barnstable, heard her say. She was going to stay with an aunt. Pretty thing. She tried to brain me with a vase," he added, half-awed, half-resentful. "Wanted her dresses, so I left her to them."

The girl *must* be one of Anna Holt's and Richard Lockwood's daughters. But how had she come to live with Makepeace? In his methodical fashion, Morley swiftly riffled through potential scenarios in his mind.

There were two possibilities that he could discern: Perhaps Makepeace had been bluffing in the letter he'd sent, and knew nothing at all about Morley's past or Richard Lockwood. Perhaps he'd adopted the girl. Perhaps the entire thing was a coincidence.

He dismissed this out of hand; he didn't believe in coincidences.

The other possibility was that Makepeace had known all along that the girl was Richard Lockwood's daughter, and very recently had come to some sort of conclusion, or come upon some clue, some exceedingly damning evidence.

But Makepeace had been an agent of the crown. And Morley found it difficult to believe that an agent of the crown would have resorted to blackmail if he'd truly uncovered any evidence. Although desperation and debt could play havoc with a man's sense of reason.

"Is she married? The girl?" he asked Bob. "Has she any other family?"

"No, sir. Watched her bloke jilt her outright, in fact, sir. Right there in the parlor. He can't marry a penniless girl—he's an heir. She went to live with an aunt."

"What a shame." Morley did feel an errant stab of sympathy. The horror of losing all he'd acquired woke him less and less often at night as the years went on, but Caroline's letter, and then Makepeace's letter, had introduced sleeplessness again. Blackmail was not a lullaby.

It was entirely possible James Makepeace had bequeathed the evidence to the girl, if the evidence did indeed exist, and she had managed to keep it about her person, which would explain, perhaps, why they had found nothing in Makepeace's homes. And now that Susannah Makepeace was penniless... perhaps she would resort to her father's means of obtaining an income.

Or, if she was feeling civic-minded, would somehow get the evidence into the hands of people who would know precisely what to do with it.

Morley began to concoct still more scenarios in his head, but stopped himself. He could truly make this complicated, if he liked, but he lacked the fervor for complications that characterized his youth. He was tired, and he rather intended to spend his dotage peacefully—in Sussex, gardening—rather than at the end of a rope, swinging. He'd discovered a passion for gardening, in fact, along with large houses and fine furniture. This was odd, since he'd once considered gardening a sort of farming. But wealthy men could afford to tenderly tend frivolous plants; in a way, cultivating roses was the ultimate expression of Morley's rise in the world.

Sometimes when he was gardening, he'd pull a weed out by its roots, only to watch it sprout again some weeks later, threatening to strangle all he'd carefully tended.

And he knew, suddenly, that the solution was elegantly

simple. Susannah Makepeace was a weed. And if her sisters were to sprout up, too...well, they were also weeds.

"Mr. Morley? What should I do about Susannah Makepeace, sir?"

"Why, whatever you do, Bob...you should make it look like an accident."

And because Bob was a professional, he understood his orders. He puffed out his chest again. He did enjoy a new challenge, and Mr. Morley paid well to keep his own hands free of blood.

Chapter Three

∽

Two days later, Susannah arrived at the door of Mrs. Frances Perriman's cottage. She would have arrived a good five hours earlier, except that the mail coach in which she had been traveling had tipped over. *Keeled* over, in fact, like a felled elephant, with a groan and a crash, just as everyone had finally tumbled out of it to go into the inn for a meal.

All the weary travelers, who by this time heartily loathed the sight and smell and sound of each other, had gazed back at it stupidly, almost unsurprised. Almost perversely pleased that this particular instrument of torture had been felled.

The horses had been alarmed but unhurt, and it had been determined that the wheel or something or other on the coach had broken. Susannah had heard faint murmurings about it, but she'd been too exhausted to care about the details. And besides, she'd needed all of her resources to locate another conveyance to Barnstable. Someone who would take her there out of sheer kindness, or in exchange for a pair of slippers or gloves. Which was really all she had in the form of currency, anyway.

As the coach driver refused to hire out his horses as mounts, the passengers descended en masse upon a poor farmer who had innocently arrived to fetch his nephew for a visit. A lot of frantic negotiation ensued among the passengers. Some waved bills, some plied charms, Susannah had nearly sprained her eyelashes in an attempt to beguile and disarm him.

In the end she'd been triumphant. The farmer agreed to take her a few miles out of his way to deposit her at the door of Mrs. Frances Perriman, and Susannah had needed to remove his nephew's hand from her thigh only once. Gently, but firmly.

The sheer, chaotic, exhausting indignity of it seemed rather a metaphor for her new life.

And now she stood at the threshold of a little cottage just after midnight, and Mrs. Frances Perriman held up her candle and gazed and gazed at Susannah with what could only be described as bemused wonder, as though a large exotic bird had flown off course into her parlor.

Finally, recovering herself, she flung open her arms. Susannah stepped into them, as that's what seemed required.

Frances was about Susannah's height, but considerably rounder, with the same mild brown eyes and the long nose that seemed to be Makepeace hallmarks, and she was soft and smelled of lavender. Susannah's vision blurred with fatigue and—for heaven's sake, *tears*. Astonished, she quickly dabbed them away, and lifted her head up to take in the softly lit room with a glance: small and worn, though some effort had gone into making it other than plain: wallpaper in a pattern fashionable more than a decade ago, a few pictures upon the wall, one small vase filled with flowers. Her beauty- and luxury-loving heart clenched.

"I'd begun to worry, Susannah, and Mr. Evers finally went home to his family when your coach never arrived at the inn."

"There was a bit of an accident, I'm afraid, hence the delay. I came in with a farmer who was kind enough to bring me."

"Well, I'm glad to find you sound, and there *is* kindness in the world, then. Anyhow, welcome, my dear. It's not the grand place you've no doubt been accustomed to, but I do hope you'll feel at home. Would you like some tea? Or shall we get acquainted in the morning?"

"I can't thank you enough for having me Mrs. Perri—"

"Aunt Frances," her aunt interrupted firmly. "Call me Aunt Frances. And say no more of it, my dear. I'm happy for your company."

Susannah managed a weary smile. "I think I'd make a better impression after a night's sleep, Aunt Frances."

"And you must by all means make a good impression," her aunt said with mock severity and a pat to reassure Susannah she was teasing. "Let's pack you off to bed, then."

Within minutes, Susannah found herself tucked into a small bed in a small room up a flight of creaking wooden stairs, an ascent that couldn't be more different from the marble steps she'd taken to her rooms since she was a little girl. A single rose in a vase next to the bed breathed its fragrance into the room. It mingled with the smells of aging wood and clean linen. The sheets were worn, but deliciously soft from age; her quilt had a patch, she noticed, and smelled, like her new aunt Frances, of lavender. The room was dense with summer heat, but she saw no fireplace. She parted the blinds to peek out, saw stars strewn thick as salt against the blue-black summer sky. Sleepily, Susannah decided she'd spent her life tripping gaily from star to glittering star; perhaps it had only been a matter of time before she slipped and fell into the blackness between. It was almost a relief to have finally done it.

Her first thought upon waking and looking about was: *Good-ness. I must have drifted off in the servant's quarters.*

And then she recalled where she was. She sat bolt upright, sending her pillow cartwheeling to the floor.

Light was pushing through the blinds, and Susannah slipped out of the little brass bed to open them all the way. A wash of sun and green instantly swamped her eyes: the *country*. The country used to be a place to retreat to between parties and balls, a place to wait impatiently for the season to begin. She'd used the country much the way one used the withdrawing room at a ball, to sew up a trodden hem, or pat your hair into place before you reentered the festivities, refreshed.

It was to be her view every morning from now on, this end-less green.

It was silent, apart from a bird trilling a maniacally cheerful scale over and over and over again.

She fished a dress out of one of her trunks and pulled it over her head: the three-flounced summer walking dress in blush-colored muslin. She dispensed with drawers for now, a nod to the heat and to the fact that no clucking maid was about to object. She rolled on stockings, however, because she liked her garters; they were pretty, and they cheered her.

She twisted her hair into a quick knot. Out of habit, she seized her sketchbook, and then all but tiptoed down the stairs, discovering that the third one from the top creaked. Soft, snuf-fling snores came in intervals from behind Aunt Frances's door, but the house was quiet otherwise: no maids about starting breakfast or getting in wood or coal for fires.

The house was so *tiny*. The sort of house a gardener would live in, she imagined, with its faded wallpaper and scrubbed wood floors, its plain, serviceable furniture. The settee in the par-lor was a faded ruby and sagged in the center; there was a large nick in the surface of the small table, which supported the small vase of flowers, a vase lacking any sort of pedigree, no doubt, unlike the one she'd threatened to heave at a cockney workman.

Panic squeezed her lungs. She desperately needed to step outside, if only to remind herself that the world was indeed bigger than this little house.

So she pushed open the front door. It was just past dawn, and the roses lining the front of her aunt's cottage were in full exuberant bloom. They were the brightest things as far as Susannah's eye could see; they reminded her of young ladies in ball gowns, with their delicate flounces and rich color—everything else around her was green, green, green. That tiny pressure began somewhere in the center of her chest again, and she knew it might very well blossom into despair if left unchecked, so Susannah reflexively opened her sketchbook.

With sweeps of charcoal, she captured the roses, their contrasts in texture and color, the tiers of petals, the red shading into crimson at their tips; the tiny stalks topped in yellow fuzz springing from their hearts.

Finished with the roses, she lifted her head. Outside her aunt's gate, a tree-lined path wound tantalizingly off into two different directions; to the right, where it surely lead to the town of Barnstable; to the left, where it appeared to lead into a wood—the trees were taller there, the greenery denser.

Something reckless in her reared up. *I shouldn't walk alone.* Mrs. Dalton certainly would have frowned upon it, as would have all of the duennas who preceded her.

Which seemed an excellent reason to proceed.

Overhead, the birches and oaks and beeches had latticed together, creating a romantic sort of arch. It could hardly be dangerous, could it? She entered into it, hesitantly, and then more boldly, and followed it furtively, promising herself with each step that she'd turn back after just a few more. There was something about paths, however: they drew one forward as surely as a crooked finger, and on she went, over soft dirt and leaves crushed to a fine powder by the passage of other feet over the years.

And she thought, perhaps, if she kept moving, she could outpace the feeling of being dropped outside the comfortable confines of society. Of exile.

A hot spark of green, very like light glancing off an emerald, tugged her eyes off the path. She braved a few steps into the trees toward it.

The spark of green expanded into a pond as she approached, luminous as stained glass. Not an emerald, perhaps, but pretty enough, and the dense smell of wet dirt and green things was strangely agreeable. From where she stood, she could see the tip of what appeared to be a faded wood pier; something pale glared atop it. She squinted. It looked like—could it be—

Good heavens, it rather looked like a pair of feet.

She craned her head to the left, and stood on her toes, and—

Clapped a hand over her mouth to stifle a yelp as she ducked back against the nearest tree.

The feet were attached to a man.

More specifically: a rangy, breath-catchingly *nude* man.

Susannah peeped out from around the tree. Just, she told herself, to prove he wasn't an apparition.

He wasn't. His torso was a perfect "V" of golden skin and muscle; his slim hips, whiter than the rest of him, tapered to thighs and calves that could have been turned on a lathe, and these were dusted all over with fair hair that glinted in the low sunlight. The hair on his head was cropped short and beacon-bright, but the features of his face were nearly indistinct from where she watched. Given the glory of the rest of him, they scarcely seemed to matter. The man's beauty was, in fact, an *assault,* and a peculiar tangle of shock and delight and yearning began to beat inside her like a secret, second heart.

And then the man stretched his arms upward, arching his back indolently; exposing the dark fluffs under his arms, and this, somehow, seemed more erotic and intimate than the rest of his naked body combined. Susannah had seen paintings and statues of naked men, for heaven's sake, but none of them had ever sported fluffy hair beneath their arms. In fact, the sheer easiness with which this man wore all his raw beauty frightened her a little. He was like someone too casually wielding a weapon.

She fumbled her sketchbook open.

Quickly, roughly, she sketched him: the upraised arms, the curves of his biceps and legs and the planes of his chest, and when he turned, the darker hair that curled between his legs and narrowed up to a frayed silvery-blond line over his flat stomach. Nested right between his legs were, of course, his... *male* parts... which looked entirely benign at the moment, really, at least from this distance. She sketched those, too, as she intended to be thorough, hardly thinking of them as anything other than part of her drawing.

A squirrel rippled by and stopped to stare at her, its tiny bright eyes accusatory. It chirped once; Susannah frowned at it and put a finger to her lips.

The man bounced lightly once on his toes and then dove; the smooth water shattered.

He surfaced an instant later, sputtering happily, his arms rising out of the pond in rhythmic long strokes that took him away from the pier, and then he rolled over and did it on his back, his pale toes kicking out of the water, playful as an otter. And Susannah's knees locked; she toppled over with a little grunt.

She fumblingly righted herself again, and to avoid any further toppling, braced a hand against the oak tree, and while he swam the length of the pond she took the opportunity to refine her drawing, quickly roughing in the trees behind him and the pier beneath his feet.

The man finally pulled himself from the water onto the pier again. Dazzled, she watched water run in clean rivulets down the muscles of his back and buttocks. He shook himself like a great cheerful animal, diamond droplets flying from him, exhaled a satisfied-sounding, *"Ahhhh!"* and then strode off the pier and vanished from her sight.

For a moment, Susannah remained very still, staring at the place he'd been, feeling light-headed, oddly elated. *Perhaps he does this every morning.*

The thought filled her with an entirely improper hope.

The magic of the moment finally began to ebb a bit and sense seeped in; she worried about her aunt waking and finding her gone. She pushed herself upright, and found herself eye-level with a pale, heart-shaped scar gouged into the oak. Inside it, the words KIT AND CARO had been carved; they were now swollen with age. Susannah traced the heart with her finger, half enchanted by it, half sorry for the wound to the tree.

And this was when two hands—*smack, smack*—landed on either side of her face, flat against the tree's trunk.

Her heart turned over like a great boulder in her chest—*thunk*—and lay still.

There passed an intolerable moment, during which no one moved or said a thing. And then a masculine voice drawled virtually into her scalp, fluttering her hair and causing gooseflesh to sweep up her arms. "Do you think it's *fair* that you have seen every inch of me, and I have seen none of you?"

Oh no, oh no, oh no. Her heart had recovered. It was now drilling away inside her chest like a woodpecker.

The warmth of the man's body behind her was as penetrating as a sunbeam, though not one bit of him actually touched her—she pressed herself closer to the oak tree, to make bloody sure of that. But his scent immobilized her as surely as a net: sun-heated skin and the faintest tang of sweat, and something else, something rich and complicated and fundamental that started a primal buzz of recognition in her blood and made her peculiarly aware of how very *female* she happened to be.

This wasn't the groomed-for-a-ball brew of starch and soap with which she was familiar. This was stripped-to-the-essence *male*.

She lost her tenuous grip on the sketchbook; it flopped to her feet.

Susannah slid her eyes sideways. They saw long elegant fingers and a sinewy forearm covered in that silver-gold hair. When his hand shifted a bit she saw a small birthmark in the shape of a gull in flight on the vulnerable skin below his wrist.

She made the subtlest of attempts to crane her head to try to get a closer look at his face.

"Oh, I wouldn't turn around if I were you." Still amused.

Oh, God.

And when, at last, her throat was able to release words, the ones that emerged appalled her even as she said them: "*You* were bloody quiet."

There was a shout of surprised laughter; the man's hands fell away.

And not being a fool, Susannah bolted around the tree, crashing through the young bushes for the path. She didn't dare look back.

⌒

Oh, it really had been too bad of him. For he was of course completely clothed; he would never creep up behind a young lady in any other state. Actually, he couldn't recall ever creeping up behind a young lady at *all;* he wasn't mad, just a rascal.

But she *had* been spying, whoever she was. She'd thoroughly deserved to be shocked.

Kit had arrived in Barnstable, hot, sticky, and resentful from his long trip from London, his thoughts ricocheting between James Makepeace and Morley and the countess. He'd decided to stop at the pond before he headed for the house and rousted all the servants, who would be flabbergasted by his presence and would need to be reminded of what they were actually paid to do. The thought hadn't improved his mood, but the swim had. It was odd; he hadn't known how heavily he carried his life until he plunged into the pond again, and emerged feeling as though years had been rinsed away.

His mother had called this estate "The Roses." Which had always amused him, because there might be all of ten rose-bushes on the small property, and it didn't even boast a green-house. He'd been raised here, however, in Barnstable, and the orderly grounds surrounding the house always interested him much less than the woods bordering it, filled as they were with haphazard shadows and light and surprising wild things. They'd been wonderful for make-believe and exploration when he was very young; for trysts when he was a little older. And for duels.

Since his mother's death a few years ago, his father spent almost all of his time in London, visiting this particular estate only every now and then. Kit had visited it rarely since he'd disappeared from the town so many years ago so swiftly—and under a veil of mystery, to boot. The Roses didn't even have a bailiff, merely a small staff of servants charged with keeping the place from crumbling.

Kit smiled a little as he bent to retrieve the abandoned sketchbook; the irony of a spy being spied *upon* didn't escape him. He leafed through it idly.

Imagine that . . . she'd not only been spying . . . she'd been *documenting* her findings.

He bit back a laugh when he saw himself, arms stretched skyward, penis dangling modestly—he *had* been swimming, after all. But it was a beautiful drawing. She'd roughed in the pier beneath him and the trees behind it, too, and she'd caught him perfectly, the mindless contentment of the moment, the strength and confidence of his body, a hint of pleased-with-himself arrogance in the arch of his back. There was nothing tentative or miss-ish about the drawing; it was, above all things, honest and surprisingly accomplished. He was flattered, but he felt oddly exposed, which had nothing to do with the fact that he was naked in the sketch. She'd captured something essential about him.

He slowed his leafing to examine the other drawings: a young man—this one fully clothed—stretched out on a spread of grass, the smile on his face soft and intimate. Irrationally, Kit felt a little pang of envy. The artist and her model clearly knew each other well, probably cared for each other. Another page was covered with roses, tenderly rendered in skillful strokes. A house filled another page, a great estate that looked somehow familiar; the view of it was distant. There was a simple stand of trees. A group of young ladies, the ribbons of their bonnets undone, their sweet faces bland and open.

There was an almost offhand passion, a skill and singularity to these sketches that mere drawing lessons could not impart. Much to his surprise, Kit found himself moved by them.

His father had been right: Kit *had* wanted to be a naturalist at one time. He'd been fascinated by Joseph Banks, his travels with Captain Cook, and his discoveries of flora and fauna. But he'd never been able to draw the things he saw in quite the way he saw or felt them, and he'd found it maddening. It was as though nature had gently manacled him in this way: *No, you shan't be allowed this gift along with all the others.* He'd been so accustomed to excelling at everything he tried; his attempts at drawing had humbled him. He supposed he'd *needed* humbling at that age.

He studied the drawings again, paging back to the beginning. Who was the artist? The line of her body was slim and softly feminine in a way that spoke to every one of his senses. Her hair, a rich mahogany had smelled wonderful, though he'd be hard-pressed to describe just exactly what it smelled *like*...fresh, he would have said. Or clean. Or sweet. But none of those words really seemed to apply, precisely. How he loved discovering the unique smell of a woman...a good place to start discovering it, he knew, was the nape of the neck. But there were other delightful places, too.

He smiled, a wicked, private smile, which faded when he remembered he was not to be discovering the smells of females while he was in Barnstable.

You were bloody quiet, she'd said. As though he'd *thwarted* her.

He gave a bark of delighted laughter. It rather sounded like something he would have said.

❧

This is going to be fun.

Kit stabled his horse, badly startling the pair of lethargic stable boys who looked after four geldings, a beautiful, enormously pregnant mare, and a smug-looking stallion who lived here at The Roses. She would bear watching, that mare; she would foal any day, he was certain.

Then he crept around to the back of the house and entered very stealthily, pushing the kitchen door open only enough to allow his lean body through. The kitchen was empty; there wasn't a soul in sight. He imagined the maids were all out dallying with the footmen; he could hardly blame them, really, given the weather and the continued absence of the Whitelaw family, but he would have to impose some semblance of order today.

He stood still for a moment, listening for voices. And then he heard them, lifted in a lively cadence, coming from the large sitting room, the one dominated by an enormous portrait of the Whitelaws featuring a small, half-scowling Christopher, none too pleased at being forced to hold still long enough to be captured for posterity. Knowing from childhood where to find carpets to stifle his footfall, which tiles or patches of floor were likely to squeak, Kit crept toward the room, sidled against the wall, and peered in.

Mrs. Davies the housekeeper and Bullton the butler were sprawled on a pair of settees, their backs to him, teacups lifted to their lips.

"My *dear* Mrs. Davies, *will* you be attending the assembly tomorrow night?" Bullton's imitation of an aristocratic accent was cuttingly accurate. He thrust his pinky out sideways and took a sip.

"*Hooo* my, I jus' *cannot* decide 'ow to wear me 'air, or what *gown* to wear, Mr. Bullton. I must 'ave me *maid* choose it for me, the way she does everything *else* for me, as ye ken I canna think for meself."

They laughed merrily together and clinked teacups.

"Hello," Kit said pleasantly.

They both shot nearly straight up into the air in a blur of scrambling limbs. He watched with some regret as the china cups flew up with them, their contents arcing up in graceful streams and landing on the carpet.

It had been worth not writing ahead to warn them of his arrival, he decided.

"Yer . . . yer *lordship*!"

They bowed and curtsied and bowed and curtsied and then

bowed and curtsied again, as if bowing and curtsying would make up for the fact that their feet had been up on his mother's ancient French furniture.

"'Tis I!" he said cheerily. "How goes it Mrs. Davies? Bullton?"

"It goes...it just...we were..." They stammered over each other.

"Just about to rally the staff to make ready for my visit?" he suggested politely.

"Our apologies, sir. If we'd known you'd be *paying* a visit, sir—" Bullton had admirably gathered his composure; he was dignified and apologetic now. *Good man.*

"Didn't know myself, Bullton, Mrs. Davies, and for that I apologize. But if you'd begin airing the rooms, getting some food in—well, you know your jobs. I needn't tell you."

"Yes, sir. No, sir. That is, of course, sir." Another jumble of overlapping words.

"You'll want to see to that stain straight away, Mrs. Davies," he said mildly.

"Y-yes, my lord." Her eyes rolled down to the carpet, and her expression went tragic. Ever since Kit could remember, Mrs. Davies had treated the carpets as though they were her own children. Even the best housekeepers become a little lax in the absence of any sort of lord of the manor, he suspected.

"And is there really an assembly tomorrow night in Barnstable, Mrs. Davies?"

"Y-yes, my lord."

"And where would that be held, if you please?"

"The town hall, sir. Everyone in the town is invited."

That is, everyone except *servants,* Kit knew.

"Well, then." He regarded them sternly, almost broodingly for a moment, long enough for them to begin fighting not to squirm. "I fully expect there to be an assembly of *servants* here tomorrow evening. And get in a little—what's your poison, again, Bullton?"

"Wh-whiskey, sir?" Bullton said a little faintly, hope beginning to glimmer around the corners of his mouth.

"I expect you to get in a little whiskey, then, for it. Mrs. Davies, I trust your household funds will cover it?"

"Oh, yes, sir." Mrs. Davies had relaxed a little, too. And then she hazarded a question. "Will *you* attend the assembly in town tomorrow evening, sir?"

"Of course, Mrs. Davies," he said breezily. It had been many, many years since Kit had set foot in Barnstable, and with any luck, his legend would have grown.

The two servants smiled in earnest this time, and he grinned back at them. The villagers would be every bit as surprised to see the viscount as they had been, and Mrs. Davies and Bullton would almost prefer to witness *that* than have an assembly of their own.

"And will you be here long, sir?" Mrs. Davies asked.

"At least a month, Mrs. Davies. I've a special project here to complete, you see."

He could see her working out in her mind how to break the news to the maids and footmen, who would now actually need to behave as though they were working.

"I'll be out of the house much of the time," he assured her, and she smiled sheepishly at him, knowing her thoughts had been read.

"And your father is well, sir?" Bullton asked carefully.

"He won't be coming, Bullton."

Bullton tried and failed not to look relieved. "Very good, sir. It is a pleasure to see you, sir," he said finally.

"I'm sure it is, Bullton." Kit was struggling not to laugh. "And that will be all for now, thank you. The stain, Mrs. Davies?"

"Oh!" she dropped as though shot down behind the settee to

attend to it, and Kit strode up to his chambers, to see if spiders had knit coverlets over the entire room in his absence.

❧

Susannah didn't stop running until she was at the very threshold of her aunt's garden, and then she stopped to compose herself and get her breath. Something savory was cooking, and the smell was winding its way out of the cottage and out into the yard invitingly. *Nothing like fleeing from the naked stranger you'd been spying on to build an appetite.*

Feeling tentative and a little embarrassed, she poked her head into the kitchen, which must also be the dining room, as there was no dining room to be seen. Whereas in her old home, the kitchen was an enormous galley beneath the house, and the dining room was a good acre or so away from it. And at her father's town house in London—

"Good morning, Susannah." Aunt Frances turned. "I thought perhaps you'd changed your mind and fled back to London."

Is that an option? But Aunt Frances seemed so kind, and so prepared to overlook the fact that her niece was wandering into the kitchen from *outside the house* just after dawn, that she smiled. "Good morning, Mrs.—Aunt—Frances."

"Do sophisticated young ladies take morning walks alone these days?"

The question seemed innocent enough, though Susannah suspected Aunt Frances was more shrewd than she was naive. "I…well, your garden was so pretty that I—" She was about to say, *wanted to sketch it,* but she realized with horror she'd dropped her sketchbook. *Damn.* "That I was drawn to it for the fresh country air."

She would desperately miss her sketchbook, for more than one reason. She almost squeezed her eyes closed with mortification, remembering: *You were bloody quiet.* What if he was a neighbor? What if he paid social calls? Would she recognize him *clothed*? Would he recognize *her*?

Her aunt turned then and looked more directly at her, gazed for a long disconcerting moment. "Aren't you pretty?" she concluded delightedly, with a tilted head. "And your dress..." The delighted expression slipped a little, and then became officially worried, complete with a furrow between her eyes.

"Oh, Susannah," she said impulsively, seizing her by the hands. "I'm terribly concerned you'll find it very dull here, a fashionable young lady like you. Perhaps it was impulsive and selfish of me to invite you to live with me. I just...well, I'm about all the family that James had, and though he seemed to do quite well for himself...well, word does travel, bad news rather more quickly than the good, it seems, the way a storm does. I heard about your...circumstances. And I know a bit about the...ways of the world." The last four words were delicately tart.

Susannah was both touched and a little startled by this effusiveness. "You knew I was engaged to be married," she guessed carefully.

"Yes, that's what I meant, my dear." She patted Susannah's cheek. "And as you came to me straight away, I must assume that you no longer are, which is what I feared might happen to you...well, mamas of marquises-to-be can be so devastatingly practical, can't they?" Again, acerbically delivered.

It was wonderful to have someone so completely, frankly on her side. An entirely new feeling, really. "Yes," Susannah managed, feelingly. *"Practical."*

"His loss, my dear," Aunt Frances said briskly. "More fool he. And life *does* goes on. As does breakfast. There's fried bread, and sausage in honor of your first full day here, and tea. Will you get the plates down for us?"

Susannah welcomed the subject change, but she twirled about, bewildered. She felt a little abashed. It seemed her aunt had actually *cooked* the meal. No one else was about to set the table, either, or to—

"They're in the cupboard, dear," her aunt said gently.

"Of course," Susannah said weakly. She reached up tentatively, and saw that "plates" meant exactly that: four plates. Plain stone crockery, the color of an old bone.

A flush of shame blazed over her skin. How many times had she seen a servant reach into a cupboard?

Suddenly, those four plates seemed bald evidence of her plummet from status, and the life ahead of her came rushing at Susannah the way the hard ground rushes up to meet someone falling from a great height.

With hands that shook a little, Susannah selected two of the plates and laid them on the table, hoping her aunt thought the flush in her cheeks was due to the warm day.

"Thank you again, Aunt Frances, for inviting me to stay," she said bravely.

"I'm happy for your company, Susannah." Her aunt's tone was crisp. "Say no more of it, I beg of you. There's an assembly tomorrow night, and I don't mind telling you, you've made quite a celebrity of me, as a new face in the neighborhood *will* set everyone to talking. They're all dying to get a look at you. And you're welcome to come, if you feel up to it, my dear."

This cheered Susannah just a little. She didn't mind being looked at. Being looked at was one of the things she did best, in fact. And an assembly . . . well, gaiety and motion had always kept the restlessness that forever danced on the edge of her awareness at bay. Perhaps she could forget everything for an instant, the loss, the humiliation, the grief—

Wait.

"Do they...do they know how I came to live with you, Aunt Frances?" she ventured cautiously.

In other words: *Do they know I've been jilted? Do they know I'm penniless?* Susannah knew very well what it meant when *people* were "set to talking." She'd been one of those "people" not too long ago. Having a good laugh at the way George Percy danced, for instance. It occurred to her that she might wish to take a night...or a fortnight...or a year or two...to assimilate her new status here in the cottage, before she threw herself upon the mercy of the villagers. She knew precisely how juicy a piece of gossip she represented. They'd feast on her like a swarm of mosquitoes.

Aunt Frances's brown eyes were sharp and knowing and sympathetic. "They know that your father died, and that you came to live with me, and anything else they might know they learned from someone other than I. But I think a better question is...how much do you care, Susannah?"

A breeze kicked up the curtains at the window then, and the room, with its plain wood floors and whitewashed cupboards and fireplace, was suddenly awash with light, and a faint scent of roses came in to mingle with bread and sausage. It occurred to Susannah then that most anything could be beautiful when viewed in the proper light.

And so pride hiked her chin. "Why, I find that I don't care very much at all."

In that sunny, airy moment, it was almost true.

Chapter Four

Kit had forgotten what a miser the Grantham country manor was—it hoarded heat in the summer and cold in the winter, and by nightfall, stepping into his chambers had been like stepping off a ship docked in the East Indies. But he'd learned not to be fussy about where and how he slept; in the military, you took sleep when you could, the way you did food, grateful for any crumb of it. He stripped off all of his clothing and heaped it over a chair; his pistol, locked, went on the table next to his head. He cut a slice of cheese from a wedge on a plate and devoured it. And then he settled the knife down again, too, next to his head, because he rather liked having a buffet of weapons to choose from, should the need arise.

He flipped open his one indulgence brought from London—fine bedsheets, which were almost as good as a breeze on a night like this—and climbed beneath.

But before he doused the lamp, he impulsively reached for the sketchbook again, trying to piece together the story the drawings told. The artist had led a benign, genteel life, he concluded from the pages, filled with pretty houses and friends. But then, suddenly, like an exclamation point: a naked viscount!

He grinned and set the sketchbook aside, doused the lamp, and closed his eyes.

❧

The light in the room hadn't changed when he opened his eyes again; clearly he hadn't been asleep long. But there was a different quality to the silence now...as though something new had been introduced into it.

His senses sang a warning. Holding his breath, he scanned the room through slit eyelids.

And saw a tall shadow next to the bureau.

In one swift motion, Kit seized the knife, rolled from the bed, and clamped his arm around the throat of the intruder from behind.

"Move and your blood will be *everywhere*," he murmured.

A male hand clawed vainly at Kit's arm. For a long moment, the two men stood locked together in a knot of tensed muscles, their breathing rasping the air.

"Ease up, Grantham," the intruder finally choked out.

Kit's grip slackened a fraction. *"John?"*

A silence.

"K-kit?" John Carr choked out.

"Ye-e-s," Kit confirmed incredulously.

Another silence.

"Are you *naked*?" John Carr sounded horrified.

Kit pushed John Carr away with a snort and jerked his trousers from his chair. He thrust his legs into them and then lit the lamp next to his bed, and the light swelling into the room revealed his best friend since childhood standing in the center of it, rubbing his throat ruefully.

"John Carr. Thought I smelled goat."

His friend gave a short hoarse laugh, hoarse because a powerful forearm clamped across the windpipe could do that to a voice. "Christ. So you're a pirate now, are you, Kit, with that bloody great cutlass or whatever that is? *'Move and your blood will be everywhere,'* " he imitated.

"It's a *cheese* knife, John. And it's a hot night. A man can sleep naked in his *own room*." Apparently, he couldn't be privately naked anywhere in Barnstable today. "How did you get in?"

"Window open just a hair in the nursery, and you know that tree outside of it—"

"Ah." He nodded appreciatively. Kit did know the tree. Very cooperative tree, that one. He'd shinnied up and down it to go in and out of the nursery window numerous times as a boy when he was supposed to be sleeping, or being punished for some other childish transgression. John had come in and out of that window numerous times, too. In due time, they'd both been caught at it and thrashed, naturally, because Kit's father had always been one step ahead of him.

There was a silence.

"John, why the *hell*—?" Kit made a sweeping gesture, indicating the absurdity of the question.

John Carr, dressed in boots and dark trousers and a dark coat of light wool—the better to blend into shadows and scale trees, presumably—pulled out a chair and straddled it backward. "You weren't supposed to be here."

Kit didn't honor that with a reply, so John tried again. "I'm on assignment, Kit."

"You're on assignment. In my bedroom. In Barnstable."

"Yes."

Kit stared at his friend. John had always been the handsome one: tall and hard, dark-haired, dark-eyed. His features achieved that magical balance of rugged and refined guaranteed to set feminine hearts aflutter.

But most people began babbling when faced with a few moments of Kit's silent blue stare.

John stared levelly back at him.

And suddenly, foreboding prickled at the back of Kit's neck. "You'd better tell me."

John lowered his head briefly, deciding. Then he lifted it again, his expression carefully bland, which Kit disliked immensely. Kit and John never used their spy faces with each other. "I'll tell you what I can."

"Am I under investigation?" Kit heard the incredulous tension in his own voice. "Does my father know?"

"Why would he know? Because he's omnipotent?" A whiff of rivalry hung about those words. John's father was a baron who enjoyed gardening; he was *not* one of the most powerful peers in England.

"He'd definitely like us to think so," Kit said mildly.

John couldn't help but grin at that. "All right, I'll tell you why I'm here Kit, but I must ask you not to repeat it. To anyone, including your father. I could be seriously reprimanded. Or worse."

Kit shook his head impatiently. "Talk, John."

"It's about Morley."

Kit went very still; oddly, he was unsurprised. And then he padded over to his bureau, blew dust off a pair of glasses, which made John snort a laugh, and poured two brandies. He slid one across the table to John. "Go on."

"We've intercepted a letter to Thaddeus Morley written by a woman who says she will 'tell all I know, all you've done,' if he doesn't send money to her. In other words, she's blackmailing

him. We need to find her, because she might very well be able
to prove Morley sold information to the French. But so far, she's
remained one step ahead of us."

"Who is 'we' John? And what the hell does this have to do
with me? Apart from, shall we say, my 'interest' in Morley?"

John curled his fingers around his brandy a little too casually.
"I can't tell you who 'we' is. But that woman is Caroline Allston."

The sound of her name after so many years wasn't quite as
dramatic as a sword drawn from its sheath, but it wasn't comfortable, either. Kit watched John's hand go up almost absently
to rub his shoulder, where a round scar marked his skin. Kit had
put it there with a pistol shot when they were both just seventeen years old.

Caroline's legacy.

"Again, What does this have to do with me, John?"

John took another sip of brandy, and there was an odd lilt to
his voice when he spoke. "She's sent a letter to you, too, Kit."

The muscles of Kit's stomach tightened. He was stunned.
"Ah," he said.

John continued quickly. "To your London town house. I
intercepted it. In the letter, she asked for your"—he paused, and
cleared his throat; his voice had gone strangely husky—"for
your help. Said she was in trouble, and she hoped to come to
you. I suppose the letter was meant to prepare you for her . . .
visit."

Help. Caroline needed his help.

"When was this letter sent?"

"A week ago."

"And you're here at The Roses because . . ."

"She never arrived at your town house. And The Roses
would be the ideal place to meet her, or hide her . . ." John took
a sip of his brandy, lowered the glass. "If you were inclined to
do so, that is."

The lamplight guttered in a wayward breeze; the liquor glowed on the table between them, but their faces were momentarily cast in shadow.

"I haven't seen or heard from the woman in almost two decades, John," Kit said finally, managing the words blithely. "I've scarcely given her a thought. But you've only to ask me, not crawl about my bedroom. Or my town house, for that matter."

"Orders, Kit."

"From whom?" he demanded swiftly. A fruitless question, he suspected, but it was worth a try, anyhow.

John shook his head. "You know I can't tell you. And I didn't know you'd . . . that is, I wasn't told you'd be here. It's possible she would have come here without your knowledge, looking for you, if she didn't find you in London."

"Possible," Kit said, in such a way that made it sound *highly* improbable.

John said nothing; he merely looked about the room idly. He probably knew Kit's room as well as he knew his own. Kit considered whether to tell John about James Makepeace. Part of him resented the fact that he wasn't allowed to investigate Morley. He wondered, too, how it was that his father didn't know about the investigation. And it was maddening, God help him, to think that John might very well bring Morley down before Kit could have a chance to do it. The unworthy, competitive part of him was tempted to stay silent.

But this was John . . . his best friend since childhood, the brother of his heart, and Kit was a patriot. If Morley had sold information to the French . . .

"John . . . there's something I should tell you. You've heard that James Makepeace was killed?"

John ducked his head in somber confirmation.

"A few weeks ago, James told me the most extraordinary

tale, which I took only half-seriously at the time, I confess. And Morley was . . . shall we say, the hero of it."

John raised his brows. "Go on."

"Do you remember a politician named Richard Lockwood? Murdered some years ago?"

"I believe it happened about the time we were . . ." John hesitated as he was much more of a diplomat than Kit ever was. "Sent off to the military academy."

"The year I shot you, you mean," Kit said with blunt mischief.

"The year you *missed* me," John countered, predictably.

Once started, the two of them could go on like this forever.

And so Kit told John the whole story: of Lockwood and Morley and Christian virtues, of the allegedly whimsical hiding place of the allegedly incriminating documents.

John drummed the table a few times in thought. "Are you sure James wasn't drunk when he told you all of this?"

"When have you ever seen James drunk?"

"Were *you* drunk when he told you this?"

"Why," Kit said irritably, "does everyone think I'm bound to be drunk?"

John smiled crookedly. "You often *are* bound to be. But why do you think James told you? Was it a whim of the moment, or do you think he *planned* to tell you?"

"Difficult to say, really. Perhaps because he thought he was in danger. Perhaps because, of all the people he knew, I might be disinclined to let the matter rest, should anything become of him."

A diplomatic way of admitting he was dogged to a fault. To his credit, John didn't snort.

"Do you believe him, Kit?"

"He wasn't raving, if that's what you're asking."

"Do you suppose Caroline knows anything about the Lockwood murder? Her letter . . . it said, 'all we've done.'"

"It's why I told you about James. It might be a mad tale, then again, I can't help but think it's somehow related to Caroline and Morley. But I suppose it will be up to you to discover that."

John smiled crookedly, damn him, because he knew precisely how much it would bother Kit to not be able to pursue this particular mystery. "What would you have done if James hadn't been killed, Kit?"

"Press him for more information, of course. Tell me why you've begun investigating Morley," Kit demanded swiftly.

"Excellent try. But you know I can't."

Kit swore colorfully under his breath.

John laughed. "But you've helped, truly. This was worth crawling in the window. And I'm getting a little old for that sort of thing."

Kit twisted his mouth wryly. The brandy was warming the pit of his stomach, but his mind was uncomfortably alert now. "To James," Kit said, lifting his glass.

"To James."

They drank together, and for a moment indulged in separate thoughts.

"Kit . . ." John's voice was careful; Kit looked at him expectantly. "You do know that if Caroline helped Morley sell information to the French . . . that makes her as much a traitor as Morley. And now . . . she's attempting to find you."

But Kit had already arrived there in reasoning: If the Earl of Westphall's son was known to be consorting with a traitor, a political cataclysm would ensue. Lives would be ruined. His own, for instance. His father's, in particular.

No doubt, some people would like to see that happen.

He wondered, for a moment, if either he or his father were carefully being set up to take a devastating fall.

Kit leaned casually back in his chair, his well-trained

features entirely neutral. He clasped his hands behind his head in a luxurious stretch, the picture of nonchalance. He suspected that John knew it was a performance, because it was precisely what John would have done in the same circumstances.

And then, instead of saying anything further, he tipped the brandy decanter again into John's glass, and then into his own, and raised the full glass to his friend. "So where did you end up when we parted ways the other night? Lady Barrington's town house?"

John's smug grin confirmed this. "More specifically, her bed."

"Congratulations," Kit said in all sincerity, and they lifted their glasses to each other again. Lady Barrington had been John's particular quest for some time now.

John bolted the last of his brandy and plunked it down, gestured with a jerk of his chin for Kit to fill it again.

"What *are* you doing here, Kit?" John asked, as if the thought had just occurred to him. "I had no idea you'd even left town."

"Thought I'd work on my folio."

"Your *what*?"

It *was* rather amusing to spring that word on people. "I thought I'd take some time away from the noise and bustle of London to document the flora and fauna of Barnstable."

He was rewarded when John's jaw dropped.

Kit allowed his voice to drift philosophically. "Nature is endlessly exciting, John. All that death and sex and violence..."

John clapped his mouth closed. He looked worried. "But... you're a *spy*. And you... you *love* London. I mean... the countess."

Kit burst into laughter and gave the table a hearty slap.

John scowled at him. "Tell me the truth."

"All right. The truth is... my father sent me here to work on the folio project. Under threat of Egypt if I don't complete it in a month."

"So you've been exiled," John guessed.

"One might say that. In a manner of speaking."

"Hmmph."

" 'Hmmph'?" Kit repeated indignantly. "What the devil do you mean by that?"

"Well...you have seemed a bit...off, Kit."

"Off? And what the devil do you mean by *that*?"

"You drink too much," John said, and it sounded unnervingly like the beginning of a list. "More than I've known you to in the past, anyhow. You're argumentative...more so than usual. You're irritable. You've spent an inordinate amount of time in pursuit of a married countess, which seems to me an elaborate way to avoid matrimony."

" 'Avoid matrimony'?" Only John Carr could get away with saying such a thing. "And what about *you*?"

"*I* am saving myself."

"For *what*?"

John smiled enigmatically. He allowed Kit to glare at him for a moment.

"I suppose I've been a little...bored," Kit finally muttered.

"We've all been 'a little bored.' But only one of us called Chisholm an idiot, and that was you."

Kit admitted the truth of this with silence. For a man who prided himself on control, his behavior had reflected little of it lately. His restless mind craved challenges, his restless body craved action. *Purpose*. He took a deep breath, released it, confused, irritated. He was not, in other words, happy.

John looked up toward the ceiling. "I suppose the countess will be...lonely now that you've gone."

At this, Kit laughed an oath. "You wouldn't *dare*."

He wasn't terribly worried, however. John might very well be the handsome one, but they both also knew Kit was, and always had been, just slightly better at everything else—shooting and running and riding and swimming and... well, at *fascinating* people. Simply by virtue of being his own idiosyncratic, stubborn self. Perhaps it was because he tried a little harder.

No, he decided cheerfully. *I'm just better at everything else.*

Détente regained, another companionable quiet passed.

"You can trust me, John," Kit said, finally, a little gruffly. "I won't say anything to my father about what you've told me. Or to anyone else."

"I know," John said after a moment. His words were shaded with something peculiarly like sadness. "If you hear from Caroline..."

"I'll tell you straight away, John. And now that your glass is empty... you'll see yourself out?"

"You're tossing me out?" John Carr feigned incredulity.

"I want my sleep. And visit your mother while you're in Barnstable, or I'll tell her you were in the neighborhood and didn't stop by. And go out the door."

"Bastard," John muttered glumly. Kit laughed.

❧

When John was gone, Kit resumed his chair, poured another brandy, then thought about what John had said and poured it back into the decanter. He stared out the window into the darkness, listening, thinking. How silent it seemed here; within a few nights, he knew he'd realize what a racket nature could make, birds, chittering squirrels, crickets. The sounds would come in through his flung-open windows, as lively as London, in its way. His chest was already sticky from the night's heat; he absently rubbed the back of his neck, where a bead of sweat trailed.

And then Kit crouched next to the bed and pulled out a chest he'd kept here since he was a boy. He lifted the lid, and ruffled through the strata of his past—rocks and bones and leaves and books, his first pistol—until he'd found the letter.

" 'I'm sorry,' " was all it said. But he would have known the writing anywhere. He'd exchanged secret notes with her for two feverish years; they'd hidden them in the trunk of a tree near the clearing where he'd aimed a pistol at his best friend. Caroline had been a terrible speller, Kit recalled. But "I'm sorry," *that* she'd spelled correctly.

He remembered the morning of the duel vividly: the bruised dawn sky, the tribunal of birds, a half dozen or so, clinging to the winter-stripped trees, staring down at them. John's white breath hanging in the air, a ghost of the words he had just spoken: "She's not worth it, Kit." It had been both a plea...and a taunt.

Oh, but she had been. At least from a seventeen-year-old's perspective. She'd encouraged Kit to touch her bare breast, and sometimes he thought it was the single most important experience of his life.

And so Kit, who had always been the better shot, had aimed for John's shoulder, and their fathers had packed them immediately off to the military, where their friendship and John's shoulder had recovered nicely in the absence of the fever that was Caroline.

The letter had been posted from a town called Gorringe about seventeen years ago, shortly after his duel with John. A town, legend had it, named by a poetry-minded duke who'd apparently gone mad from searching in vain for a rhyme for "orange."

And now she was in trouble. This was no surprise, really, as Caroline had *always* been in some kind of trouble. She'd *courted* trouble. And everyone in Barnstable had known and disapproved of her.

Or known and wanted her.

And she'd disappeared the night she'd met Thaddeus Morley at a party held by Kit's father.

Why had he kept the letter? Proof that he *had* won her, he supposed. At least insofar as Caroline could be won. And, he thought, no doubt John would have found it, if Kit hadn't been asleep in this room tonight.

In short, John might very well be keeping things from Kit. But Kit had also kept things from John.

Again, Caroline's legacy.

Caroline couldn't remember a time when she didn't... *want*. Like an itch she could never reach, like a word that lived forever on the tip of her tongue, like a burr clinging to her soul, an indefinable want had driven her from the cradle, and every decision she'd ever made had been in an attempt to appease it.

Consequently, her life had been anything but dull.

For instance, she was fairly certain that Thaddeus was trying to kill her, a result of... well, a perhaps not very good decision she'd made a little while ago. She'd needed money; Thaddeus had buckets full of the stuff, some of which one might fairly say she'd helped him acquire. So she'd dashed off a sentimentally worded letter of blackmail.

Shortly after that, someone had tried to stab her, and she'd just barely squeaked away with her life.

She'd moved on to another town, her money dwindling.

And then someone had *again* tried to stab her. Thank heaven she had good vision and reflexes. She'd been moving from town to town ever since.

Ah, well. She should have known that Thaddeus would never do anything by halves.

She peered at the teeming crowd in the coaching inn, awaiting her tea. She was dressed all in black as befitting the widow she wasn't, but the discreet little veil clinging to her hat only heightened her mystique, she knew. The veil bared only her lips. Those red, inviting lips.

And then, out of desperation, she'd even dashed off a letter to Kit Whitelaw, telling him she was in trouble. Telling him she was coming to him. But she'd run out of money, and she hadn't been able to reach London, so she might never know if Kit had grown into the sort of man he'd promised to become when he was seventeen.

At eighteen, Caroline had raked up a rivalry between Kit and his best friend until it blazed like a cheery autumn bonfire, and she'd warmed herself over it. It had eased that everpresent want in her, much the way her father lifted his war-wounded legs up onto the stool in front of the fire every night to soothe the ache in them. That and a bottle or two each night had always seemed to take the edge off the pain for him. Swinging a heavy hand at his daughter seemed to help, too. She'd learned to dodge him.

And she'd been dodging most of her life, it seemed, from the results of her decision and impulses, which ensured that she didn't need to think or feel any one thing for very long, because that would be uncomfortable, indeed.

And now . . . and now she couldn't seem to stop moving.

When she was younger, Caroline would sometimes look in the mirror and wonder at the cruel joke of her face: that flawless white complexion, lips so naturally red, huge dark eyes like pools that might be either treacherously deep or innocently shallow; to find out, one would have to risk wading in. Waves and waves of silky dark hair. What was the use of such a face when her father was a drunkard who'd sold off all their belongings; when she hadn't any decent clothes; when she was trapped in Barnstable, wild with boredom, reminded daily of her social inadequacy. God knows she wasn't about to marry the son of a farmer or mill owner, and God knows she was never deemed fit to marry the sons of the gentry, let alone the son of an earl.

But oh, how willing they were to dally with her. Given a little encouragement. Kit had needed a good deal of encouragement, he had a very defined sense of right and wrong. But not even Kit would resist her, in the end.

Kit's ardor in particular had been dangerous. She'd almost felt something in her thawing when she was with him, and it had hurt, hurt, as though she'd been clawing her way through ice to get to him. She'd enjoyed handsome John Carr's attentions, too, but he wasn't nearly as dangerous as Kit. In part, because his father was only a baron. But mostly because he'd never really come close to touching her in any way besides physically.

Oh, but Kit had. Kit was another one who never did anything by halves.

And then one evening, at the annual party the Earl of Westphall held to demonstrate his largesse to the locals, Thaddeus Morley had appeared. Twenty years her senior, powerful in a quiet way that gave her shivers, she'd made another of her decisions: She'd cast her fate into his hands. And for a time, life had been exciting and interesting. And oddly comfortable. They'd suited, she and Thaddeus.

"Thank you," Caroline said softly to the innkeeper, accepting that cup of tea, stealing another glance about.

Men either looked at her with awe, with fear, with desire, or some combination thereof. The ones who had tried to kill her hadn't really looked at all. This being hunted business wasn't pleasant, but then danger and controversy kept the want at bay, too.

But now she was out of money, because she'd spent the last of it on these widow's weeds—her disguise—and a small pistol. And she needed money, since her blackmail scheme had failed. Thaddy had loved her once, or as much as he could love anything besides a cat, but she should have known he wouldn't let something as impractical as love interfere with ambition. Especially given how he'd come to be who he was. The blood and sacrifice involved. His own, and that of others.

Often Caroline wanted things simply because other people had them. For instance, that handsome, fair-haired young man having supper with what must be his wife and her mother at the table in the corner, who'd glanced at her more than once—the last time lingeringly. The wife was a blond thing, bland as blancmange, and her mouth had moved almost continuously, yap yap yapping while the husband's eyes drifted...and found Caroline's.

He froze, stared. The way they always did. She allowed him a moment of feasting before she returned her attention to her tea.

He was probably bored with his wife. But he'd married her no doubt because she was respectable, and they no doubt enjoyed a comfortable life. Possibly he even loved his wife, or at least tolerated her.

Caroline decided then that she wanted him.

And since she also wanted some money rather desperately, perhaps she could kill two birds with one stone.

Luck was on her side; the young man rose, and walked in The General direction of her table, heading toward the bar. Caroline casually stood just as he passed her.

"Second room to the right. In five minutes. Five pounds," she murmured.

Before she turned to head up the stairs, she caught a glimpse of his expression: Shock and lust. Fear and fascination. One after the other. And this was how she knew she would soon have enough money to keep moving, which was all that mattered.

Chapter Five

∼

The Assembly decorating committee had clearly undertaken their responsibilities with zeal, but not even a galaxy of candles or a meadow's worth of flowers could disguise the fact that the Barnstable Town Hall wasn't Almacks. A buffet stretched out along one end, ratafia and sandwiches; an orchestra sawed away in the corner, pianoforte and strings. Susannah wondered if they were capable of sawing out a waltz. Not that *she* would be waltzing, of course. She was in mourning, and besides, she doubted there was anyone in attendance with whom she *wished* to waltz.

She took in the room with an expert glance—dresses, fans, slippers, coats—and felt a moment of swooping disorientation: every dress on every maiden had last been fashionable just after Waterloo—five entire years ago. In her own beautifully made, utterly current dress, mourning shade though it was, she might as well have dropped into their midst from another planet. At the moment, a goodly number of Barnstable's denizens were caught up in the patterns of a quadrille; the rest of them would awake with cricks in their necks from pretending they weren't trying to get a look at Susannah—the young men, in particular. So as she stood at Aunt Frances's side she smiled, a general sort of smile, warm and dazzling, the kind that had begun so many friendships in her old life.

Odd, but she could have sworn that everyone in the hall took a tiny collective step back.

Aunt Frances gave her arm a bolstering little squeeze. "Here comes Mrs. Talbot," she whispered. "You will hate her." She smiled cheerily at the woman in a Turkey red dress and matching turban bustling toward them.

Once curtsies and introductions were exchanged, Mrs. Talbot lowered her voice confidingly. "I've had it on good authority that Viscount Grantham is here tonight. He's a thoroughly disreputable character, Miss Makepeace. Disappeared from Barnstable years ago under a cloud. Went on to make his fortune in smuggling. I can't think who might have invited him, but he *is* the local aristocracy, so of course he's welcome here. Perhaps he'll dance with my daughter. She's very pretty, you know." She mopped Susannah with an accusatory head-to-toe glance, her face anxious and hard, then snapped open her fan with a flourish, a warrior putting up a shield. "A pleasure to meet you, Miss Makepeace," she concluded, managing to make it sound as though she meant entirely the opposite, and away she sailed, the red turban listing perilously atop her head.

"She's only *one* person," her aunt whispered apologetically. "She despairs of getting her daughter married, and I fear the strain has begun to show. I assure you, the viscount isn't quite as—oh, look, here are Meredith and Bess Carstairs," Susannah and her aunt smiled for the Carstairs sisters, a pair of pretty brunettes with almost perfectly spherical faces, on which their features were arranged neatly, symmetrically, like roses painted on china plates.

"Do be careful of the Viscount Grantham, Miss Make-peace," the sister named Bess urged in a low dramatic voice. "He's here tonight. There's a scandal in his past so terrible no one will speak of it. I hear he's wanted for piracy."

"You don't say!" Susannah beamed, happy to be included in gossip.

The Carstairs sisters reared back a little. One would have thought she'd thrust a lantern in their faces. Their uniformly pretty faces suddenly became wary, as though they'd begun to suspect she might be an alien species who'd dressed as a human in order to attend an assembly.

After a few more mild pleasantries, they made polite excuses and went in search of their partners for the next dance, a reel.

Susannah gazed after them, puzzled.

"Just give them time to know you, Susannah," her aunt soothed with a pat. "They are unaccustomed to your...polish. I'm certain you will all eventually be great friends."

Susannah was not. She looked out across the wooden floors of the hall, at the smiling dancers lining up for the reel, and despite their woefully outdated clothing, envied them their comfort with each other. The music began, sprightly if a trifle slipshod, and so did the familiar, almost soothing, rhythms of the reel: the dancers bowed and curtsied, they approached and parted—

Which was when she saw him.

Across the hall, hands clasped behind his back, eyes slightly narrowed, as if to more clearly focus the beam of his gaze on his intended target: her. No one was speaking to him, perhaps because he was the sort of person whose mere physical presence enforced a respectful, perhaps nervous, distance. His clothes were beautifully made and clung to his body as though they felt privileged to do so, and much to her approval, they were utterly current. It was difficult to tell from this distance whether he was handsome, though he was certainly tall.

The scandalous viscount, she thought, with a little thrill.

The dancers approached each other again; he disappeared from view. When they parted once more, she noticed he hadn't moved an inch from his observational stance. It occurred to her then that he was gazing at her as though he had come to the assembly to do expressly that.

And…hmmm. Wasn't there something familiar—

Oh, no. Oh, no, oh, no, oh no.

Kit had seen her almost the moment he'd arrived with Frances Perriman. She was too well dressed to be a local, and the black of her mourning dress suited her; her face was a pearl in the gentle light of dozens of candles. The way she held herself spoke of sophistication and breeding, of confidence in her own appeal, and there was something restless about her…her foot was tapping—that was it. Interesting. He wondered why she would venture out to an assembly if she were in mourning, and considered that perhaps the locals of Barnstable had become more forgiving and welcoming since he'd left.

This, however, seemed unlikely.

He'd watched her address the two pretty Carstairs sisters, who all but radiated dislike. Then again, she did rather put them in the shade, even dressed like a crow, and London polish *could* seem a bit like glare here in the country.

Ah, here was Mr. Evers, the owner of the Barnstable mill and the font from which all local gossip sprang. He was attempting to skirt Kit the way a cat might a sleeping watchdog—on his way to the punch bowl, no doubt. His vivid berry-colored nose told Kit it wouldn't be Mr. Evers's first trip to the punch bowl this evening.

"Evers!" Kit said quickly, politely. He stifled a laugh when Mr. Evers came to an almost guilty stop and bowed, the flap of hair remaining on his head flopping forward with him. Kit's reputation had never really recovered from the events of seventeen years ago; it had, in fact, blossomed luridly since then. In truth, this didn't bother him. He found it afforded a sort of camouflage, and he was not adverse to camouflage.

"Hello Grantham. You're in the neighborhood, then?"

Kit regarded him in friendly, but utter, silence.

"Of *course* you're in the neighborhood," Evers muttered, catching on. "Why, here you are."

"That I am, Mr. Evers!" Kit said cheerfully. He knew he was being a rogue, but he wasn't in the mood to make anything easy for anyone today. "And how do you fare? Your wife? The mill? All in good repair?"

"Good, good, all good, can't complain."

Evers looked hopeful that this would be the end of their exchange. Which, given the mood Kit was in, all but guaranteed that it would not be. "And the punch, this evening, Mr. Evers?"

This topic Evers warmed to. "Very good batch, Grantham," he confided. "Might want to get some yourself before I—before it's gone, that is."

"I might, at that," Kit agreed. He dropped a confiding arm over the man's shoulder. "Mr. Evers, I wonder if you would mind enlightening me about something."

Evers looked a little flattered. "I will try, sir."

"Who is the young woman with Mrs. Perriman?"

Evers lit up, and Kit knew his question would be spread to everyone in the assembly hall within the hour. Not that he minded, terribly. It would rather add to his legend here in Barnstable.

"Her name is Miss Susannah Makepeace, Grantham."

Kit could have sworn time stopped the moment the words

left Evers's mouth. All the little hairs on his arms rose in attention.

"Seems her father died—James, hailed from Barnstable, don't know if you recall—and now here she is in the country, living with her aunt," Evers continued. "Quite the London miss, ain't she? All the lads are quite terrified of her. Been gawking all night, but won't asked to be introduced."

So the minx with the sketchbook *was* James Makepeace's daughter, though nothing at all about her suggested him; she must favor her mother in looks. Kit was almost sorry to find her here: Barnstable wasn't the place for such a vivid creature.

Then again, he was inclined to believe that fate had played a hand in exiling both he and Susannah Makepeace in Barnstable. For he was now certain of one reason James Makepeace had chosen to share his tale with him.

No matter what, Kit was unlikely to ever, as his father had so tersely suggested, "leave it."

"Thank you, Evers," Kit said distantly. "You've been very helpful."

❧

Susannah's charm continued to glance off the denizens of Barnstable much the way an unsuspecting bird glances off a clean windowpane. They visited for introductions, eyed her with wariness, wandered off again.

"Give them time," Aunt Frances soothed. "You are the most interesting thing to happen to Barnstable in a good long while, and it makes them feel important to pretend that you are not."

Susannah offered up a weak smile, wondering how long Aunt Frances intended remain at the assembly. She'd been in constant motion since her father had died, buffeted by events, too proud to allow the weight of them to drag her under. But she suddenly pictured that patched quilt on her bed, and wondered how it might feel to crawl beneath it, close her eyes, and linger for days.

Another dance concluded; dancers milled about in search of new partners. Susannah glanced across the room, half in hope, half in terror. The scandalous viscount was no longer watching her.

Relief mingled with a peculiarly acute disappointment. Perhaps she would never retrieve her sketchbook, but then again, perhaps she would never need to revisit her humiliation: *"You were bloody quiet."*

Remarkably the orchestra began to scrape out…could it be a *waltz*?

Susannah succumbed to the temptation to close her eyes briefly, imagining her life hadn't changed at all, that this was Almacks and not a town hall, that everyone sought rather than shunned her company. When she opened them again, she was eye level with a white shirtfront.

Slowly, slowly, she tilted her head back.

And her heart bounced into her throat.

"Good evening, Mrs. Perriman." The scandalous viscount bent his long frame into a bow. "I just paid this bloody awful orchestra to attempt a waltz so that I may dance with your niece. Do you mind?"

Oh, God. His voice was a lovely thing, refined, low and confiding. A *London* voice.

And it was the voice that had mused into the nape of her neck yesterday.

Aunt Frances's mouth dropped open; for a moment it hung that way, as if the hinges had snapped.

Shock iced Susannah's hands. Up close the man was imposingly tall. Imposingly…*male*. The ice gave way to heat, which begin at Susannah's collar and slowly spread upward. Two competing desires began a violent tussle inside her.

Spinning on her heel and fleeing was one of them.

"We thank you for the offer, but Miss Makepeace is in mourning, Lord Grantham." Aunt Frances had gotten her mouth closed, and this was very elegantly, and not impolitely, said.

The viscount's eyes—blue eyes, *unreasonably* blue eyes—glinted down at Susannah with an unholy and decidedly ungentlemanly amusement. "But you'd *very* much like to dance, wouldn't you, Miss Makepeace?"

And God help her: that was the other desire.

Later, much later, she would admit to herself that there really had been no contest.

"Please forgive me, Aunt Frances. I'm sorry, so sorry, *truly* sorry..."

The grinning viscount quickly proffered his arm, and he led Susannah, still trailing abject apologies, out to the floor.

⟡

She lifted her hand to fit into his, the most familiar gesture she'd made in days, comforting somehow even as she reeled in shock at what she'd just done. As she did, the sleeve of his coat slid back, and Susannah saw it. Between the start of his glove and the cuff of his shirt: a birthmark in the shape of a gull.

She promptly stumbled.

The viscount placed his other hand on her waist just in time, effortlessly steadying her, and eased her into the dance. "Yes, 'tis I, Miss Makepeace. The last time we met, I believe you said...what was it...what was it....oh yes: *'You were bloody quiet.'* And then you went bounding off like a deer through the underbrush. Do I look different in my evening clothes? I imagine I do." His eyes glinted an almost intolerable amusement down at her.

Speechless. Then the words staggered out of her mouth. "You—how *dare*—you are—"

"Your sketches of me are quite good, by the way," he added. "Unflatteringly *accurate,* in some respects, but quite good. And I've always been a strong proponent of accuracy."

"I—" she choked. Her face, from the feel of things, was the color of Mrs. Talbot's turban.

"The way I see it is this, Miss Makepeace: you can either pretend to be horrified and make a scene—but I *do* know you'd be pretending—or you can laugh, which is what you'd prefer to do. Either way you'll still be the talk of the assembly, and the good people of Barnstable won't like you any more than they do now."

"How *dare*—" she began again, her tone indignant, because of course she knew she ought to feel indignant.

His eyes widened in mock fear.

Dash it, anyway. "No, I suppose they don't like me," she admitted, genuinely puzzled. "And people usually do, you know."

He laughed then, surprised, a rich sound that unfortunately made heads all over the room swivel toward them. And there they remained, riveted by the sight of Susannah Makepeace in her mourning gown waltzing with the scandalous viscount. "Do they, now? I suppose you make certain of it."

"It's easy, you see," she confessed. "Or, it usually is." This conversation was rapidly running away with her, and it was both terrifying and exhilarating.

"For you, I suppose it is. But perhaps you needn't try so hard."

"I wasn't *'trying,'* " she objected.

"No?" He sounded as though he didn't believe her at all. "Well, perhaps they don't like you because you're more handsome than the lot of them."

Finally the viscount seemed to be doing the sort of flirting she recognized. She dimpled a little.

"Comparatively, anyway," he added, sweeping the room with a dispassionate gaze, as if to ascertain the truth of that statement.

Her dimples vanished.

"And you've a certain amount of sophistication," he assessed thoughtfully.

Tentatively, her lips began to lift again.

"A modicum." He said it firmly, as though correcting himself. He glanced at her. "Why are you glowering at me?"

Accuracy, indeed. Flirtation wasn't about *accuracy,* for heaven's sake. *Everyone* knew that.

Her silence didn't seem to bother him. "Your drawings are brilliant Miss Makepeace. You're quite talented."

"My *drawings* are brilliant?" *What about my smile? What about my eyes?*

"Yes," he said. "Detailed, accurate, yet still singular and strangely"—he looked upward for a moment, seeking a clean slate for his thought, then returned his eyes to her—". . . passionate."

He all but purred that last word, his eyes dancing with mirth, and for the life of her, she didn't know what to say. Susannah studied him warily instead, since his face was the one part of his body she hadn't yet sketched in vivid detail. His features were too strong, perhaps, to be considered classically handsome; his face a bit too long and angular, like a diamond, his nose slightly arched. Light brows, light lashes, and those disconcerting eyes. But in the midst of all those angles, his mouth was a work of art, wide, sensitively curved, indisputably masculine.

And of course, the rest of him was beautifully made, too. Almost overwhelmingly so.

God help her, she could feel color setting fresh fire to her cheeks at the memory.

"I'd like to make you an offer, Miss Makepeace."

Her head went back and her eyes flew open wide; on the heels of her last thought, his words were genuinely shocking. "I *beg* your pardon, sir?"

"Of *employment*. Don't look so hopeful." He was laughing silently again.

This man was absolutely, dizzyingly, *maddeningly*—

"Employment?" She said the word as though she'd found a tiny sharp bone in her soup.

"Yes. I'm a naturalist by avocation, and I've been commissioned to complete a folio—a study of the flora and fauna of this region. I've need of an accomplished artist to assist me with it. I'll pay you well. Good heavens, you should see your face. You'd best change your expression quickly or everyone here will think I've gravely insulted you."

Humiliation had so completely snarled Susannah's thoughts she simply couldn't transform them into words. He wanted her to *work* for him. Like a maid, like a governess, a cook, a—

"How, Miss Makepeace, do you suppose your aunt accommodates one more person in her cottage? She isn't rich. And yet you don't look underfed."

He might as well have kicked her in the ribs.

Susannah thought of the patched quilt that covered her at night, her aunt's faded, sagging furnishings, the humble breakfast, the lack of a maid to poke up the fires.

Shame pooled, molten, in the pit of her stomach. She turned her face away from the viscount's direct blue gaze and swallowed hard.

For a moment, mercifully, he didn't speak.

"Forgive my gruff ways, Miss Makepeace." His voice was gentle, conciliatory; it curled deliciously around her, like rich smoke. "I lack experience with the tender sensibilities of young ladies."

Susannah cautiously returned her eyes to his face and narrowed them a little, not certain she wished her sensibilities to be considered tender. He seemed to enjoy that, for his eyes glinted at her again. Such a blue, his eyes were. Like the center of a flame, as though some internal furnace lit them. She was tempted to hold her hand up to them, to see if she could feel heat.

He must have considered himself forgiven, because he kept talking. "Talent is like…money in the bank. You should spend it wisely, of course, but not to spend it at all is simply foolish. I have need of your assistance; your aunt, I'm certain, would be happy for the money. We can be of use to each other. Will you help me?"

"But…work?" she repeated faintly.

"Perhaps you'd prefer to cast about for other employment, Miss Makepeace?"

There it was, that word again. "No," she said vehemently.

"No? Good. I'll speak to your aunt, then, assure her of your safety, and make everything proper, etcetera."

"But—" she began. She gave up. "What is your name?" she asked suddenly, instead. "Your full name?"

"Christopher Whitelaw, Viscount Grantham. Kit, to *you*, Miss Makepeace."

And then he smiled a smile that made Susannah remember that he'd made a fortune in smuggling, and was wanted for piracy. Perhaps he'd also had an affair with the queen. For it was just that sort of smile: crooked, slow, unnervingly inclusive and intimate. It knew things, that smile. She felt shy suddenly; she was acutely aware of how substantial he was, how hard the muscles under his shirt and trousers were. Douglas seemed unfinished in comparison, a sapling.

Though she of course had never seen beneath Douglas's clothes.

"My aunt—" she faltered suddenly.

"Is not anywhere near as shocked as she seemed, I assure you. She's known me since I was in short pants, and I doubt I've truly surprised her. She's sturdier than you might think."

Susannah couldn't help but smile at that, thinking of him in short pants. "Did...did you know my father, then? He hailed from this region as well."

"He was older than I, so we didn't spend much time together when I was growing up in Barnstable," he said easily. "But I knew him in London. We were both soldiers at one time, and we shared a common acquaintance, a Mr. Morley. Perhaps you've met him?"

"No, sir, I am afraid I haven't. Are you involved in imports and exports, too?"

"We did have some business together, your father and I. Which is how I came to know him."

She almost said, "I wish *I'd* known him." She was quiet, instead, and focused on the row of buttons climbing up the viscount's dazzlingly white shirt, thinking about the quiet enigma that had been James Makepeace. His kindness, his detached bemusement. His violent end, which had, in a way, violently ended a way of life for her, too.

And suddenly her feet were heavier, and the waltz was an effort.

Susannah looked up again to find the viscount watching her, those vivid eyes softer. "He was a good man, Miss Makepeace. I'm sorry for your loss." Almost excruciatingly gentle, his voice.

"Thank you." And she felt tears burning the backs of her eyes for her father. "Am I horrible to dance?"

"A little," the viscount said lightly, which instead of making her *feel* horrible, comforted her somehow.

"I intend to get roaring drunk in his honor at first opportunity," he added after a moment.

She wasn't at all sure what to say about this, although it did sound like something of a tribute.

The dance ended then, and she was certain the orchestra all but mopped their brows in relief. The viscount released her hand.

"It's settled then? As of this moment, you are in my employ?"

"I—"

But she said the word to his retreating back, because his question had only been rhetorical, after all. It was clear he'd been certain all along of getting precisely what he wanted.

Chapter Six

$\mathcal{J}$t...did what?" Morley fixed Bob with a pleasant gaze.

Bob flinched. He knew from experience that Morley was at his least pleasant when he...seemed pleasant. "Tipped over, sir."

"Tipped...over..." Morley repeated musingly. He knelt to waggle his fingers at Fluff, who trotted over urgently, as if it had been far too long since he'd been petted. It had been about five minutes.

He scooped the cat up.

"In the yard of the coaching inn," Bob explained hurriedly. "I replaced the linchpin with a short 'un, ye see, which works a treat nearly every time. When the coach came to the turn on the road just past West Crumley, it *should* have made a right nice accident—arms, legs, trunks, everywhere." Bob's mouth twisted wistfully. "Why, just last year a mail coach on the way to...on the way to..."

He trailed off at the look of frozen politeness on Morley's face.

"I'm a *professional,* Mr. Morley," Bob muttered defensively. "Deuced timing, is all."

"You also aren't the *only* professional in your...field, Bob."

Bob said nothing. He shifted his sturdy legs, one then the other, as though attempting to extricate himself from something sticky.

Morley sighed. "She's in the country now. Surely there are any number of ways one can...experience misfortune in the country? I can think of dozens. But I pay *you* to do the thinking, Bob."

"I'll see to it, sir."

❧

The viscount had been efficient: he'd spoken to her aunt; somehow managing to explain his need for artistic assistance without mentioning how she'd demonstrated her skill. This proved that he had at least *some* diplomatic skills. And now Susannah was to meet him at eight in the morning. It seemed a barbarically early hour, but she'd heard before how everyone who lived permanently ("permanently" rather sounded like one has been sentenced) in the country was up with the light.

And so had she been. She'd rubbed the kernels of sleep from her eyes and splashed water over her face, managed to butter a slice of bread for breakfast, and then dosed herself with strong tea (her aunt's one indulgence seemed to be excellent tea). The night before, Aunt Frances had been kind enough to pack her a lunch, too, in a basket, in case the viscount neglected to feed her. She found the basket on the shelf leading out on to a mud porch, hooked it over her arm, and plunged into the bright, uncompromisingly green, birdsong-filled day.

If Aunt Frances was aware that going out to "work" constituted a cataclysm for Susannah, she'd said nothing of it—she in fact seemed so pleased about the whole thing that Susannah entertained a fleeting suspicion that she had conspired to get her to Barnstable precisely because she'd needed a wage earner under her roof. She *had* mentioned something about extra sausages and beef for meals, now that there would be a little more money.

Susannah dismissed that unworthy thought. Aunt Frances couldn't possibly have known that her niece harbored any particular income-producing talent.

Beautiful clothing had always been her battle gear, so she'd dressed with particular care this morning. Laying her mourning dress aside, since it was her only one and she had no wish to ruin it, she'd chosen the soft pink muslin trimmed in an even paler shade of ribbon, with two flounces, as it suited the weather as well as her complexion. An admiring glance or two from the intriguing viscount would at least make the day more tolerable.

She found him waiting for her at the end of the path that led to the pond, wearing snug fawn breeches, Hessians, a white shirt open at the throat, and an impatient expression. He, in other words, had *not* taken particular care with his dress. But still, somehow, he managed to look as though he had. The man seemed to confer elegance upon his clothes, rather than the other way around.

"Good morning, Miss Makepeace," he began pleasantly enough. But then he paused and swiftly appraised her, from her bonnet to her boot toes. "Your gown…" he began, and stopped, seeming at a loss. And then for some reason an amused furrow appeared between his brows. "…suits your coloring."

Susannah decided she might as well treat this as a compliment. She dipped her head demurely and looked up at him through her lashes, which had never failed to disarm any male within five feet of her. "Thank you, sir." Soft as a dropped handkerchief, her voice.

The amused furrow deepened and became *be*musement, as though she hailed from some exotic land and her customs were foreign to him. "That wasn't a compliment, Miss Makepeace. It was an *observation*. A demonstration, if you will, of the sort of thing we'll be doing today. Observing. Now show me your shoes."

Grrrr. While irritation and chagrin wrestled for control of her tongue, she lifted one foot out in front of her. Like a bloody child. Or a high-stepping horse. She couldn't seem to help it: he had that sort of voice. A taken-for-granted-that-no-objections-would-be-brooked sort of voice.

The viscount examined her brown-kid, rosette-topped half boots critically. "Not Wellingtons, by any means, but sensible enough for traipsing through the woods. Good choice."

Good *choice*? Did he really think she would wear dancing slippers out to the wood?

"Are you quite certain about that, Lord Grantham? Perhaps you need to inspect the *rosette* more closely, to ensure it meets your approval."

She dropped her foot again, stared up at him.

Well. She could tell from his crooked smile that her sarcasm, for some reason, met with his approval.

"As much as I would enjoy inspecting your…*rosette* more closely, Miss Makepeace"—and the smile spread, becoming that intimating, preternaturally confident smile of the night before—"I'll forego that pleasure for the moment. And I suppose we can avoid the water today. In honor of the rosette."

The wit-scrambling smile had her staring back at him blankly. Still, she had a concern.

"Water?" The word came out a little more faintly than she would have preferred. But really: did he intend to drag her through a *swamp?*

He was laughing again, silently. "Let's get started, shall

we?" He made a startlingly fast turn and began covering the ground with strides so long she had to scramble after him to keep up. "And mind the snake," he called over his shoulder.

"Sna—"

A bright, slender *S* of a creature whipped across her path and vanished into the grass. She bit her lip against a shriek.

"Don't worry, Miss Makepeace," came the viscount's voice again. "It was only a little grass snake. *Those,* at least, aren't poisonous."

Somehow, she could tell he was smiling from the back of his head.

Kit wondered whether he was taking his resentment toward his folio assignment out on Miss Makepeace, and forgave himself if that was the case. He was enjoying keeping her off balance; it was like idly prodding a pianoforte in different places just to hear what sounds would emerge. He knew from experience that surprising people was the quickest way to take their measure, for they had no choice but to respond with their true natures.

So far, he admitted to himself, the sounds she made weren't entirely boring.

Wicked of him to tempt her to waltz—he'd seen the longing all but vibrating in her posture from across the room last night—but then, he'd been feeling more wicked than usual all day. And besides, he'd seen so much of death in war that the very ritual of mourning—the clothing, the sequestering, the denial of pleasures—struck him now as shockingly extravagant, given how capriciously, terrifyingly short life could be, and how splendid it often was to be alive. The impulse to waltz struck him as infinitely braver and saner than the inclination to languish. Better to celebrate the lives of the dead by living thoroughly.

He suspected Susannah Makepeace might even become truly interesting...given a little encouragement.

She was pretty. Not in the usual way, the way the Carstairs sisters were pretty, the sort of beauty that would become indistinct with age. But...well, Miss Makepeace's eyes seemed filled with colors, and with a spy's impulse toward investigation, he had an urge to get a look at them in the full light so he could see how many and which ones. And her mouth...it was plush, her mouth. Pink as the inside of a seashell.

The softest, softest shade of pink imaginable.

The sort of mouth that made him feel restless and ill tempered, given that Susannah Makepeace was no doubt the veriest babe when it came to matters of passion, naked sketches notwithstanding, and that a dalliance with her would take unfair advantage of her status, which was no status at all, really.

Egyptian sand dunes undulated threateningly in his imagination, and Kit lengthened his stride: the sooner he completed some sort of folio, the sooner he could resume his life in London and return to the countess's practiced lips and arms.

A wedge-shaped shadow floated across the ground at his feet then; he looked up for its source.

High overhead, against the brilliant blue sky, a small kestrel was circling, wings tipping into the wind. Kit dropped his gaze, swept it along the trunks of trees, and saw the telltale signs: bark nibbled away in rings at the base of young trees. Circling kestrels plus nibbled bark usually equaled voles. Voles ate the bark; kestrels ate the voles. It was a very sensible, no-nonsense arrangement, but then nature was like that.

And damned if the thrill of discovery, of tracking, didn't stir in him. Just a yawn and a stretch, really...but a stir, nevertheless.

If he didn't know better, he would have sworn he was excited over *voles*.

❧

Unfortunately, the dreamlike—or was it nightmare-like?—sensation hadn't yet ebbed. Susannah was accustomed to music, and comfort, and the company of gorgeous friends. Instead she was kneeling in a meadow next to a small hole in the ground, and a tall viscount, who by all the laws of nature, should be admiring *her*...seemed enthralled by what appeared to be a nest of baby mice.

He had a dent of concentration between his eyes, a pencil between his fingers, and he was scratching things into a small bound book.

The sun was seeping through Susannah's bonnet, baking her head; she could almost imagine it swelling, swelling atop her neck, like a great loaf of bread. She now regretted wearing the blush colored muslin, as she was certain perspiration was darkening it even now.

She gazed down at the little creatures. Again: mice were as shriek-worthy as snakes. Or so she'd once thought. Certainly, if she'd encountered one in the presence of Douglas, she would have shrieked a little for his benefit. But these lot, six or so, were scarcely the size of the first joint of her thumb. Vulnerable babies, and, astonishing though it was to think it...charming. They were sleeping in a little heap. Her impulse was to apologize for staring and leave them to it.

"Voles," Kit whispered. "*Long*-tailed voles." He sounded as though he were sharing an exquisite confidence.

Susannah looked at them a moment longer, indulging him. And then:

"I heard you made a fortune in smuggling," she whispered. Which to her, seemed a much more pressing topic than voles.

"Did you?" he murmured. Still looking at the voles. Still writing in his book.

She'd wanted an affronted objection. She'd wanted to startle him the way he so excelled at startling her. Perhaps he *had* been a smuggler, then. Perhaps he still *was*. Perhaps this was how Aunt Frances managed to acquire her marvelous tea.

She tried again: "I also heard that you are wanted for piracy."

He stopped writing then, but only to look out across the meadow with a pleased, contemplative half-smile on his lips, as though he was imagining what it would be like to be a pirate, or fondly remembering a piratical moment.

He never did comment; silence went by, and he bent his head over his book again. He'd missed a few whiskers when he'd shaved this morning, she saw; they glinted gold on the underside of his sharp jaw. He wasn't wearing a hat. By the end of the day, his face would be darker than the pale gold skin that covered the rest of his body.

"Did you happen to hear the one about the opium dens?" he whispered.

"No!" She started guiltily from her thoughts of the rest of his body.

He looked mildly disappointed. "I was fairly certain that one wouldn't take."

Her mouth dropped open; she closed it hard again. "Why do they—why do you—"

He was laughing silently now. "Draw the voles, Miss Make-peace. You're in my employ now, or have you forgotten?"

She *had* forgotten. She felt the heat of a blush layering over her already sun-warmed cheeks; she really wasn't sure how employed artists were supposed to behave. Like a governess?

Like a cook? No doubt deference was involved, not questions and flirtation.

She lowered her head to the task, and was soon enough submerged in it, in the strange deliciousness of drawing. She sketched the textures of their fur, shaded in the soft shifting colors of their overlapping bodies, their tiny toes and noses. And those tails, of course, where they showed. For these were, after all, special, rare, long-tailed voles.

She put the finishing touches on a vole toe and looked up from her drawing; she was surprised to find his eyes fixed on her hands. He was frowning in concentration.

A shadow, like a flying platter, darkened them briefly, and was gone.

"A kestrel. Looking for a meal," the viscount murmured.

Susannah was tempted to throw her body over the nest.

He looked up from her drawing into her face then, his expression thoughtful. For a brief, giddy moment she thought he was about to compliment her bonnet, or at the very least, her drawing. She smiled softly, in case he needed a little encouragement.

"You don't appear to be terribly grief-stricken over your father's death, Miss Makepeace," he said.

Susannah's breath left her in a cough of shock.

But the viscount's eyes remained on her levelly, for all the world as though it had been a perfectly reasonable thing to say. Granted, there hadn't been a shred of accusation in his words; he simply wanted to *know,* and so he had asked.

She supposed she could be missish and protest the question. But again, she found it oddly liberating, this forthright way of his. This…reckless…brand of honesty. She *wanted* to answer his questions. She wanted to know the answers to them as much as he did.

"I grieve for my father," she kept the words cool, because he deserved the coolness, she decided. Her voice was still a little unsteady from shock. "But we weren't close, Lord Grantham."

He said nothing for a moment. And then:

"Kit," he corrected. With a crooked half-smile.

Susannah frowned at that, which made his smile complete. He waited, his blue gaze steady. Confident she would say more.

And she couldn't help but say more into that silence. "I saw him seldom, as he was away so often for his business. I wanted very much to know him, but he was nearly a stranger to me, which I shall always regret deeply. So, yes, I do grieve him. But perhaps not to the degree I would have should we had enjoyed a warmer relationship. And perhaps not to the degree *you* find appropriate."

A droplet of sweat made the meandering journey from the back of her neck to the crevice of her bosom while the viscount took this in. She watched something shift in his expression, something difficult to interpret.

And then he gave a short nod, as though she'd given the correct answer.

Susannah felt pique. Both for him, for what seemed to be condescension. And for herself, for feeling gratified by his approval.

"He was difficult to know, your father," Kit offered mildly, surprising her. "I liked him, but I believe he invited very few people into his inner world. So he wasn't a stranger only to you, Miss Makepeace. It was, in fact, difficult for me to imagine how he acquired a daughter at all."

What a fascinating thing to say. "Do you suppose he had an inner world? My father?"

"Don't we all?" The viscount sounded surprised.

She glanced around them, at the little tree-ringed meadow they occupied, home to the voles. No houses were visible from where they crouched, nor was the pond. It occurred to her that they were very alone, she and the viscount, and yet she'd been far too absorbed in work to worry about impropriety. What on earth would Mrs. Dalton say?

"What of your mother, Miss Makepeace? What became of her?"

Susannah was still feeling light-headed from the abrupt questions and her own ascent into bold honesty. But this conversation seemed to have acquired its own momentum. "My mother died when I was very young, Lord Grantham. I remember only..."

She stopped. She'd never before told anyone of that night. Partly because the memory was so faint, like something from a dream rather than an actual memory; she'd jealously guarded it, as though sharing it would somehow wear it away further. And partly out of pride: she didn't want to be pitied for having only one paltry memory.

But his voice and demeanor were easy. Not probing, or demanding, or sympathetic; rather, conversational, as though nothing she could say or do would ever shock him.

And suddenly it seemed safe to tell him.

She took a deep bracing breath; oddly, her heart was knocking. She turned away from him to speak. "I remember...oh... waking in the dark. A lot of rushing about and whispering. Someone...crying. A woman leaning over me...she had long black hair that tickled my cheeks." Susannah gave a short laugh; self-conscious, and rubbed the back of her hand against her cheek. "Her eyes were dark. Her voice was..." she cleared her throat. "Her voice was soft."

Susannah risked a glance back at the viscount. His expression was abstracted; he seemed to be picturing this along with her. "This woman with the dark hair was your mother?"

"This may seem odd, but..." Susannah hesitated. "I'm not certain it was. I have a miniature of her, and she didn't look like that at all. She looks like me. I look like *her,* that is."

"What was your mother's name, Miss Makepeace?"

"Anna."

"Anna," he repeated softly. "Rather like Susannah, isn't it? Perhaps you'll show the miniature to me one day."

This suggestion puzzled Susannah. Was he flirting, now? It was entirely possible, since the viscount didn't seem to flirt in any of the ways she recognized. "Perhaps," she agreed, cautiously.

His mouth twitched a little at that. And then, abruptly, he lowered his head to the voles again.

Finished with one specimen and on to another, Susannah thought acerbically.

She found, however, that she wasn't through with the conversation.

"Did . . . did my father ever speak of her to you? My mother?" She tried to make the question sound casual, yet she could hear the faint note of hunger in it.

The viscount looked up, surprised. "No." The word was gentle. "Did he never speak of her to you?"

Susannah paused. And then she gave her head a coquettish toss, as if nothing had ever mattered to her less. "Apparently my father never spoke to anyone of anything, Lord Grantham."

The viscount didn't smile. "And no one else spoke of your mother to you, either?" Still gentle.

The lightness proved difficult to sustain. "No." Odd how the admission shamed her.

Pride kept her gaze even with his.

He watched her a moment longer, his expression difficult to read. Then he inhaled deeply, exhaled, and ducked his chin briefly into his chest in thought. And raised his head again, eyes glinting.

"I thought we'd address the White Oak next, Miss Make-peace, since you ignored it a few days ago in favor of sketching *another* magnificent specimen."

Susannah gave a start, and blushed, and wanted to shake

him, and all of this was somehow easier than the gentleness and the honesty. She felt her equilibrium restored, somehow. Oddly, Susannah suspected this was why he'd said it.

"May I see your work?" he asked, laughing silently at her flustered face. Mutely, she handed the sketchbook to him.

He studied her sketch of the voles. And for a time, a long time, it seemed, his face revealed nothing at all, which in itself seemed revealing. And then steadily, slowly, she watched his expression go sterner. A wall going up, overcompensating for some softer feeling.

At last, as welcome and startling as sun breaking through clouds: awe struggled through.

"How do you do it?" he demanded brusquely. It sounded like an accusation.

"'It'?" she repeated, afraid she sounded stupid. Still, she didn't know what he meant.

"Capture them so...precisely the way they are. Their... *vole*ness." He rapped the drawing with the back of his hand and looked intently into her eyes. As though much hinged on her answer to this question.

"I..." she hesitated. "I've never really thought about it," she admitted almost shyly, hating to disappoint him, because he clearly considered this significant. "It's as though..."

He waited. So she thought about it. She didn't know quite *how* she did it—captured voleness, that is. But she did know she'd always turned to her sketchbook in order to escape from or capture something, whether it was a thought or an impulse she needed to stifle, or something she needed to understand, or...Perhaps it was because—

Oh, but this was going to sound foolish.

"It's as though I can stop being *me* for just a moment, and I feel what it feels like...to be a vole. Or a rose. Or—"

She was going to say, "or you."

She wouldn't presume to know what it felt like to be him. But she thought of him on the pier, gloriously nude, stretching his arms toward the sky... and it had been as though his own pleasure in the moment had become her own pleasure. As if every bit of his pleasure, his abandon, his beauty, had infused her drawing.

"No," he said suddenly. Softly but firmly. As though he'd just had a revelation of his own.

"No?" She was crushed. And here she'd really given it some thought.

"No, I don't think you ever stop being *you* when you draw, Miss Makepeace... not even for a moment. I suspect you are entirely yourself when you draw." One of his fair brows went up along with the corners of his mouth, daring her to challenge his conclusion.

And his eyes still held hers relentlessly. His fair lashes darkened to gold at the tips, she could see now, and a trio of lines rayed from the corner of each of his eyes; they deepened when he smiled. There was a tiny divot, a scar, near the corner of his mouth; fair whiskers sparked in the hollows of his high-planed cheeks. The terrain of his face seemed utterly suited to the man, with its unforgiving angles and unexpected softness combined. She had an impulse to trace a finger over the slopes and corners of it, the way one would follow a map to see where it lead.

"Oh," she said faintly, at last. Imagine, she, who could always effortlessly talk of small things, could only say "Oh."

She suspected no talk was small for this man.

But the questions and challenges he'd hailed upon her like a shower of bright, sharp jewels since they'd met had ceased long enough to allow her an insight of her own: he hailed those questions and challenges so she would *not* be able to see into him. So that she would forever be dodging, rather than looking.

Oh, but that's a mistake, Viscount Grantham, she thought.

It only made her desperate to know what he was so determined to hide... or protect.

Her eyes lowered then to his softly smiling mouth, drawn to it as though his secrets could be found there, or perhaps because it was the most forgiving aspect of his face; certainly at the moment it was easier to bear than his searching eyes. And there her gaze lingered... a little longer perhaps, than it should have. Because she *was* a woman, after all. And it was a splendid mouth.

She watched the smile fade from it.

Cautiously, she returned her eyes to his. What she saw there landed as cleanly as a lightning strike at the base of her spine.

The blue had darkened nearly to black. There was a thrilling tension in his face; his eyes skimmed her mouth, hovered... considering. A delicious, breath-stealing heat unfurled through her limbs.

And then his face changed abruptly: hard, slit-eyed and predatory, he sprang to his feet with such shocking speed that she stumbled backward.

Someone had been watching them.

He'd sensed it like a shift in the wind; even after years away from this land, anything that didn't belong rippled his awareness. And so when instincts had tugged his eyes away from Susannah Makepeace's... promising... mouth...

He'd seen on the outskirts of the wood... a man.

Who'd run when Kit sprang to his feet. Disappearing from view with remarkable speed.

Frustration bit into him now like a tether. He supposed he could give chase, for he could run like a bloody deer, and he knew this terrain better than anyone; he'd have the advantage over the intruder.

But he suddenly felt distinctly uneasy about leaving Susannah alone.

Kit lowered his pistol; he'd retrieved it from his boot without thinking, a reflex. He swiftly scanned the perimeter of his property, the place where the man had been standing. He saw nothing else untoward. Trees, grasses, flowers, squirrels. No men.

Poachers weren't entirely out of the question, but everyone in the region by now would know the lord was back in his manor, and he sincerely doubted even a desperate poacher would risk a daylight foray—though a stupid one might. He hadn't seen the long dark shadow of a musket in the man's hand, but he'd investigate the area later, look for footprints in the earth, for traps, any clues to the man.

For if someone had wandered innocently on to his land... they wouldn't have run.

He thought of John Carr; dismissed that possibility. And then he wondered whether his father was actually having him watched. Now, *that* seemed possible.

Bloody hell. And there he was, naturally, gazing into the eyes of a female.

He turned to find Susannah still on the ground, leaning back on her hands. Frowning a little. Not as rattled as she might be, given the fact that he'd just leaped up and drawn a pistol.

"I didn't know naturalists took pistols out with them. Did you intend to challenge the voles, then?"

He couldn't have said it more dryly himself, and for a moment, he wasn't sure what to say, which was a rare enough occurrence. Point to Miss Makepeace.

"It's not a dueling pistol," he said, before realizing too late how absurd a defense this was.

"Ah."

"I thought I saw a poacher," he clarified coolly.

"I've never known anyone to hide a pistol in his boot. While he was out drawing voles."

"Haven't you?" he said absently. And then, remembering his manners, he extended his hand to help her to her feet. She accepted it with alacrity. She'd removed her gloves to sketch, and what a soft little paw she had; he was tempted to linger over it for a moment, as he would any small pleasure, and allow his imagination to complete for him how soft the rest of her would be. In fact, a moment ago . . . a mad, mad moment ago . . .

Well, it was probably a very good thing he'd seen the man when he'd had.

Irritated with himself, his father, Miss Makepeace and the world, Kit released her hand abruptly. She wasn't a siren. He wasn't a boy. He was just a bored, restless spy.

"No," she replied firmly. "I haven't."

One didn't really expect such a display of spine from a young woman in blush-colored muslin. He wondered if she understood just how narrowly she'd escaped being kissed.

"And how would you know what a naturalist would choose to take out with him, Miss Makepeace? Odd, but I don't recall seeing any voles in your sketchbook before today. Naked viscounts, however, I *do* recall."

His words painted her face red as surely as if he'd dipped her in the color, and effectively silenced her, which had been his intent. He wanted to be able to look at her for a moment with a spy's eyes, and not a man's eyes.

For not only did she not in the least resemble James Makepeace—but the mother whom she presumably *did* resemble was entirely a mystery to her, if she was to be believed.

And he did believe her. It ached in her, he'd heard it in her voice: this void where her parents should have been. The twinge of guilt he felt about interrogating her was nicely fought back by his desire to get at the truth. It was all too odd, the deaths, the watching man, the mystery of James Makepeace's life.

"Perhaps," he suggested casually, "you should ask your aunt whether she thinks you inherited your talent for drawing from your father or your mother."

He probably couldn't overtly interview Frances Perriman about James Makepeace, however desperately he wanted to do it. But he could subtly urge her niece to do it for him.

Susannah still looked becomingly flustered; she fumbled her sketchbook closed. "It would be interesting to know." Polite and cool.

He preferred her sarcastic, or blushing, or proud, he decided. Anything other than polite. "Do you ride, Miss Makepeace?" he found himself asking suddenly.

"Yes, quite well." Then, as an afterthought: "Thank you." Chin angled high, like a flag carried into battle.

Ah, that was better. "Please meet me at my stables tomorrow morning. We shall ride out in search of ferns."

She did brighten a little at that. And oddly, though it was a small thing, it pleased him to please her.

Chapter Seven

The day's heat gave way to a cool evening, and Susannah watched as her aunt swiftly and capably stacked wood in the fireplace, as competent and unself-conscious as a chambermaid. Susannah recalled the years of mornings she'd awakened to the familiar sound of a maid lighting the fires, of rolling over to see a white mobcap bobbing atop a girl busy with the coals, of waiting until the heat filled the room before she left the cocoon of whatever soft bed in whatever great house she'd been visiting.

As Aunt Frances stooped lower to arrange the logs, her knees against the hearth, she reached a hand behind her to touch the small of her back. An increasingly familiar dual shame swept through Susannah. Shame that no servant was about to do something as simple as light a fire for the two of them.

Shame that she didn't know the first *thing* about lighting a fire.

She felt...useless. This was another new sensation; it had never been necessary to be strictly useful before.

"I'll do it," she faltered. "I'll...I'll take care of the fire."

Her aunt turned around, surprised. "Well, it's done, my dear. But you can do it tomorrow night, if that would make you happy."

Aunt Frances was a wry one.

"Ecstatic," Susannah confirmed. They laughed a little together, less shy then they had been.

"Perhaps we can divide up the chores. I'll do the budget..."

There was a budget?

"...And you can light the fires. Your back is better for it, no doubt, Susannah." Her aunt was teasing, she could tell, but... *was* her back better for it? What sort of back would she have if she knelt to stack wood morning and night, and cleaned, and cooked? Broad as a horse's? What sort of hands would she have? She'd always been so careful with hers, keeping them smooth and white, her nails tidy and pink and even. And yet she supposed hands were *meant* to be used. To lift and carry and build. Knit things. Wield firearms, steer plows.

A basket of knitting and mending sat next to a chair near the fire; the beginnings of a scarf spilled out of it. Aunt Frances clearly made thorough use of her hands. Susannah discreetly looked down at her own. At least she *could* sketch with hers—well enough to bring extra sausages and beef into the house.

The evening yawned, intimidating as a chasm, and they couldn't very well go to bed right after supper...or could they? She wondered what the Carstairs sisters and the rest of Barnstable's denizens were doing this evening. No one had come to call or sent an invitation since the evening of the assembly.

"They won't be able to stay away forever," her aunt had said, "as you are the most interesting thing to arrive in Barnstable in ages." Until they *did* come calling, what did one *do* with an aging aunt before one went to bed?

She could stitch a sampler, she supposed. Her needlework

was better than passable. What would the sampler say? I'M BORED! perhaps, or: SAVE ME, PLEASE! The thought amused her darkly. She could create a whole gallery of frustration, hang it in frames across these bare walls to cover the fading wallpaper.

She watched Aunt Frances moving about the little room, lighting a lamp here and there, and together with the fire the lamps conspired to fill the room with a comforting glow, casting the shabby furnishings into a more flattering light.

Douglas had always admired her hair by firelight.

That thought would get her *nowhere*.

Still, her mind began to worry the image of Douglas like a tongue searching out the space once occupied by a tooth. Oddly, Douglas drifted out of focus; a more vivid, more complicated man usurped him tonight. And even though Douglas had betrayed her, Susannah felt a bit of a traitor for this.

"There you are my dear—now we can see each other, and we shan't freeze," Aunt Frances said as she settled her comfortable girth on the settee. "Do you sew? Or perhaps you'd like to read to me while I do finish my scarf?"

"What do you enjoy reading, Aunt Frances?"

"Oh, novels, my dear. And nothing but. All sorts, but I particularly like horrid novels."

"Do you?" Susannah had always been too busy socializing and sleeping off the effects of the socializing to do very much reading, but *horrid* novels sounded intriguing. "What are they like?"

"They all have a ghost, and include dark and stormy nights, and secrets and the like. They're delicious, actually. Oh, and I'm a great admirer of Miss Austen, too. Very funny and romantic, Miss Austen is. All about lost love, and found love, and betrayal, and unrequited love, and such. And everyone lives happily ever after." She pronounced those last three words weightily, and gave Susannah a meaningful look.

Aunt Frances wasn't terribly subtle.

Odd to think of her as a romantic, this stout matron with the long face and merry eyes.

"Were you ever married, Aunt Frances?" Susannah broached tentatively. She hoped it wasn't a sensitive question. Perhaps Aunt Frances knew firsthand of unrequited love, which was how she'd guessed Susannah's own circumstances.

"Was I ever married?" Aunt Frances gave her thigh a gleeful little slap. "Good heavens, look at your sympathetic face, my dear. Of course I've been married. I've been *thoroughly* married. Wore three good husbands out, Susannah. Put the last one in the ground a year or so ago. Rather liked having this little place all to myself for a time, but then it does get to feeling a bit lonely come the winter evenings. I suppose I could acquire another husband, but in truth, Miss Austen's stories are all I need in the way of romance these days. And I suppose *you'll* have to do for company."

She winked at Susannah, and plucked up her knitting. "Will you sew and chat with me, or will you read aloud?"

"Perhaps we can do both. Chat *and* read."

"We've many dozens of evenings ahead of us in which to do both, Susannah. I think you might enjoy a little tale to take your mind off of things, for just this evening."

Those "many dozens of evenings" ahead of her sounded a bit like an advancing enemy army. Then again, her aunt had spoken of acquiring husbands as though one bought them at the milliner's shop. It should take at least a few of those evenings to discuss all of those husbands.

"Very well. Do you have a favorite novel?"

"Oh...let's start with *Pride and Prejudice,* shall we? If Mr. Darcy doesn't make you forget all about that young fool you left behind, my dear, I'll eat my knitting."

Miss Austen was funny and romantic, her aunt said. Why

did the viscount suddenly spring to mind? He was funny, perhaps. Irritating, certainly. But romantic? Not in the way Douglas had been, all charm and compliments and calculated grace. Though his *gaze* had been somehow more intimate, more physical, than the one kiss she'd shared with Douglas. That was certainly romantic in another way.

And then there was the heart carved into the tree. That heart was virtually branded upon her imagination now.

Susannah opened *Pride and Prejudice* a little tentatively, and read the first sentence to herself. " 'It is a truth universally acknowledged, that a single man in possession of a good fortune, must be in want of a wife.' "

Susannah blinked. Those words were fairly *embossed* in irony.

She thoroughly approved.

So she read that sentence aloud, and the one that followed it, and the one that followed that, while her aunt's clicking knitting needles and chuckles marked off the time. Aunt Frances had a way of kicking her ankles a bit when she heard something she enjoyed. Susannah would see them flying up out of the corner of her eye each time she read a particularly acerbic line.

And before she knew it, she'd turned more than a dozen pages, the lamps had burned low, and an entire evening had passed.

She couldn't truthfully say she'd been bored.

Only dozens and dozens and dozens more evenings to go.

❧

Two diffident stable boys, gangly with youth, cast furtive glances up at Susannah from beneath their caps when she arrived at the stables, then quickly turned and pretended to be busy pitchforking straw into stalls. The viscount, towering and impatient in his shirtsleeves, turned, saw her... and slowly took in her willow green riding habit and the hat with the plume in it. Beginning at the top, with the hat.

All right: She knew she was a little late this morning, but the riding habit she'd finally chosen brought out the green in her eyes, made them *glow,* in fact, subduing the golds and blues in them. And she knew the plume of her hat was a little worse for wear ever since the carriage had tipped over in the yard of the coaching inn, taking her trunk down with it, but it was still pert enough. And she was virtually certain the lunch basket she'd hooked over her arm was a fetching addition to her ensemble.

Why, then, did the man look so bloody *amused*?

He turned away from her again. "We had a choice of four geldings or a stallion, Miss Makepeace, and I've saddled a fine gelding for you, because I'm afraid the mare is ready to burst. She should be foaling any day now." He outlined the star between the horse's eyes with his finger; his voice, and the gesture, gruffly tender. For some reason it made Susannah's breath catch.

"She's lovely." Susannah tugged off one of her gloves to touch the mare's velvety nose. She'd left her own mare behind.

Thank goodness, then, she'd threatened a man with a vase, in part to rescue her riding habits.

It occurred to her that evenings full of Jane Austen were only going to encourage her predilection for irony.

"Come," the viscount said, and cupped his hands for her boot and boosted her up on to the saddled gray gelding as if she weighed no more than the plume in her hat. Happiness surged; Susannah intended to enjoy this ride even if it *was* in the name of employment, and she did ride beautifully. He swept his eyes over her posture and apparently approved, because he swung himself swiftly into the saddle of his gelding and kneed it into a slow trot out of the stableyard. Susannah adjusted her basket over her arm and urged her own mount to follow.

The gelding lurched forward for a few bizarre little hopping steps, then gave its head a dramatic toss and stopped so abruptly she nearly toppled from the saddle. Susannah was thrown forward; she pulled the reins tight in her fists, balanced herself by gripping the saddle.

She was mortified. Any casual observer would have thought she'd never before sat a horse. She murmured to the gelding and soothed him with little pats, and though its ears switched wildly to and fro, and its haunches twitched, she managed, through the sheer force of her charm, to persuade him to break into some semblance of a trot.

Dear God, it was as though an invisible rope was tugging him forward.

What on earth was troubling the poor creature?

The viscount glanced over his shoulder; Susannah saw the quick bright flash of his blue eyes as he took in her scarlet face— Susannah suspected her face was destined to be scarlet anytime she was in the vicinity of the viscount—and his fair brows leaping upward in a question. She gave him a winning unconcerned smile. The gelding danced sideways like a drunk staggering out of a pub and nearly bounced her from the saddle again.

The viscount was out of his own saddle and next to her in just a few long strides, and his hand went to her horse's bridle. Good lord, but the man was quick.

"I'd like you to dismount, Miss Makepeace."

Disappointment roiling sickly in the pit of her stomach, her face hot, Susannah swung her leg around the calf block, and the viscount lifted her down from the gelding as swiftly and matter-of-factly as if she were a stack of plates on a high shelf and set her aside.

"Lord Grantham, I assure you I—"

He put up a hand. His face was distant; he was as tense as a cocked pistol.

The gelding, on the other hand, was considerably calmer now. Its ears continued to switch forward and back like a weathervane in a breeze; it rolled its eyes at Susannah one more time, then hastily ambled over to join Kit's horse, its gait perfectly smooth, as if it couldn't *wait* to get away from her. As if she were a bloody *wolf,* for heaven's sake.

Puzzled, Kit took Susannah in: chin up, fair cheeks flushed in embarrassment, the very fetching riding habit—he did like the green—the plume, the basket on her arm, the—

He could have sworn that the lid of the basket had just... bumped up. Just a little.

He hadn't been drinking the night before, he'd had a decent night's sleep...there was nothing, really, he could point to that might cause him to hallucinate.

It happened again: the lid...bumped up. As though something alive was inside it...and trying to escape. A leather loop loosely latched the basket.

"Put the basket down, Susannah." He said it quietly.

"I thought we were going to—"

"Put the basket *down.* Do it very carefully. But do it now."

What she saw in his face made the high color leave her own. She did it: she lowered the basket to the ground; he could see her hands trembling now.

"Now come stand next to me. Quickly."

She took a tentative step forward, clearly not eager to get closer to his stern expression. His arm shot out impatiently and curled her swiftly the rest of the way into his side, and he held her fast. To her credit, she didn't even gasp.

"What—"

"Hush," he said abruptly. He kept his arm tightly around her.

Kit didn't see a long stick anywhere within reaching

distance, and swore softly. It would have made a useful tool in this circumstance. And for God's sake, it might only be a squirrel or a mouse, something benign or inconsequential, and then wouldn't he look foolish?

The lid of the basket bumped up a little again.

Kit wasn't conditioned to think things might be "benign" or "inconsequential." They so seldom were, at least in his world.

So he lashed out a foot and toppled the basket over.

And an adder nearly as thick as Susannah's arm darted out.

Kit swiftly lifted Susannah up into his arms as it whipped past; she ducked her head in his chest.

Fortunately the adder's retreat was hasty and complete.

"It's all right," he said softly. "You're all right. It's gone."

Susannah said nothing for a time; just breathed swiftly in and out. She was warm and lithe in his arms; the faintest scent of lavender, and that mysterious sweetness of her own, the scent he'd discovered at the nape of her neck the day he'd caught her spying on him, rose up to him, released by the heat of her skin.

"It was a snake." Her voice, a trifle unsteady, was muffled against his shirt.

"It was, indeed," he said softly. Her breath had found a gap between the buttons of his shirt; it washed over his skin in a very nearly hypnotic rhythm. In...and out. In...and out. In... and—

He put her down so quickly she nearly staggered.

"Thoughtful of you to bring a specimen along *with* you to sketch, Miss Makepeace," he said abruptly, to disguise the fact that he felt a little unsteady, too.

To his astonishment, she actually managed a weak smile.

Surprise: again, a useful way to take the measure of a person.

He looked at her carefully. Her eyes were a little too bright, and her face was a little pale, but she wasn't wobbling on her legs, or shrieking. And the sheer surprise of that adder could have stopped the heart of many a stout man.

"Was *that* one poisonous?" she wanted to know. Her voice was a little threadbare.

"Yes," he told her, gently. "It was. Not very poisonous, but...yes, it was. And that's what was troubling your horse." Both horses had wandered a few feet away from them, and were now nipping contentedly at the short meadow grass. "Did you perhaps put that basket down outside, Susannah, or open it before you left the house this morning? Did you ever leave it unattended?"

"No, I never did. Aunt Frances packed my lunch last night, and put it on the shelf on the mud porch, just as she did yesterday. Perhaps...perhaps the adder found its way in last night, somehow?"

"I suppose it's possible..." *Not bloody likely, however.* "But...well, adders are very shy. They—" A cascade of boyhood memories crowded into his mind, and he knew that taking the mystery out of something could take away the fear of it. "Shall I tell you about them?"

Susannah nodded, albeit cautiously.

"Well, this one looked like a female adder—she was a little brighter in color than a male. Almost green." Almost *too* green, in fact, he realized suddenly. The ones in the Barnstable region tended to be lighter in color.

"She was pretty," Susannah said bravely. "Very shiny. Lovely marks."

"She *was* pretty, wasn't she?" he agreed enthusiastically. "*Big* for an adder, too."

"W-was she?"

"Oh, yes! And you'll notice she blended quite well into the grass, as adders are designed specifically *not* to be seen. When I was a boy, I eventually became quite good at spotting them," he added proudly. "And adders are not any fonder of people than people are of adders, which is why it would be unusual for her to enter your house. And did you know adders have their young this time of year? And adder venom can make you quite ill, but in most cases, it won't kill you, unless you're already frail, or you're a dog. And as you are neither…"

He trailed off when he realized Susannah was watching. Head tilted, wearing a slight smile. In his experience, women did that sort of thing when they were about to say something disconcerting.

"This makes you happy, doesn't it? Adders and voles and…" She swept her hand about, indicating the universe of greenery surrounding them. "Studying them. Knowing about them."

He stared at her. *No,* he wanted to bark incredulously. *Are you mad? This is exile.*

Except… he was a proponent of accuracy.

He turned abruptly and walked a few paces away from her and gathered the reins of their horses. Susannah's mount, a considerably calmer beast now, came docilely. He led them to where she stood.

"Will we need to draw adders as part of this folio?" she wanted to know, when he still didn't speak.

The devil in him made him say it. "To be thorough, it would be nice to have at least one proper adder in the folio."

There was an eloquent pause.

"Perhaps I can draw it from memory," Susannah suggested testily.

"Perhaps we'll be lucky enough to see another."

She scowled, which made him laugh, which teased her scowl into a smile again. "If I must, I must," she said dramatically. "After all, you do keep Aunt Frances and I in sausages. But I seem to be having rather a run of *luck* lately."

"A run?" Kit gave the basket another nudge with his foot;

nothing else slithered out; he picked it up, inspected the inside more closely. Finding no other living things, only lunch and a sketchbook, he presented it to her. She took it very, very gingerly. "Did something else happen, Miss Makepeace?"

"Well, there was . . . my father dying, you see. That was rather a significant something." Said with admirable dryness. "And then there was—" she stopped, and he had the distinct sense she was skipping over something. "And then there was the mail coach tipping over in the inn yard—"

Kit frowned. "The mail coach *tipped over* in the inn yard?"

"As I was traveling to Barnstable. Something to do with the wheels, I believe? I was too tired to pay much attention to the cause."

A peculiar apprehension crawled up Kit's spine. Mail coaches didn't typically just . . . *tip over*. The idea of it was as discordant as an adder in a basket. A linchpin would have had to come loose enough for a wheel to shake off completely, or an axle would have had to snap. And the roads weren't rough enough at this time of year to snap an axle, unless the axle was already severely compromised.

Oh, bloody hell. Perhaps he simply saw patterns of nefariousness everywhere now; the price—the reward?—of life as an agent of the crown. But an adder in a picnic basket? A tipped coach? A watching man? He'd found crushed twigs yesterday when he'd investigated the place he'd seen the man standing; he'd seen part of a footprint pressed into some old leaves. And that was all.

A chilly little wind of suspicion ruffled his instincts. And his instincts had kept him alive again and again in situations that rightly should have finished him off. Well, instincts, and his impressive complement of practical skills with weapons.

But thirty days and a folio were all that stood between him and Egypt.

Again: *bloody hell.* Surrendering to his instincts might very well get him exiled for good. They had work to do. He drew in a deep breath, exhaled his exasperation.

"Well, they say bad luck comes in threes, Miss Makepeace, so I think you've had your run of it."

"*Do* they say that about bad luck?"

"Well, *I'm* saying it now."

She pondered this, head tilted back. "Because I'm not certain whether to count my father's death and the loss of my home as one thing, or two."

How on earth to respond? "Fives, then," he amended. "Bad luck comes in *fives.*"

This inanity, remarkably, made her smile again. And granted, it was just a slow, wry curve of that lovely mouth. But for some reason it pleased him beyond all proportion.

Which led him to this swift and startling realization: he rather liked Susannah Makepeace. It shifted his balance, a little, this realization: he couldn't recall the last time he'd simply . . . liked a woman. For years he'd seen them only in terms of . . . challenge. They were a necessity, a palliative, a diversion. Not something simply to enjoy, the way one enjoyed . . . well, a summer day. The kind with a soft breeze and something cool to drink.

"Do you feel equal to drawing today?" he asked, uncomfortable, suddenly, with the fact that he was comfortable.

"Oh, for heaven's sake. It was only an adder."

It was a passing good imitation of nonchalance. They smiled at each other, both enjoying her bravado, and then he cupped his hands for her boot and lifted her up to the gelding again. *Ferns,* he told himself.

Chapter Eight

❧

Morley cradled Fluff in the crook of one arm and combed his fingers through the soft hair on his belly. Fluff regarded Bob through sleepy, contemptuous gold eyes.

"When I said 'make it look like an accident,' Bob, I meant of the *permanent* variety. I didn't mean make her a little *ill* for a little while." Two days he'd waited for news of Susannah Makepeace's demise. And now *this*?

"T'was a right large adder, Mr. Morley—"

"Which would have been splendid, had it been possible to *frighten* the girl to death. You might as well say, 'it was a right large *apple,* Mr. Morley,' for how much true danger an adder presents."

This blisteringly icy stream of sarcasm made Bob blink. "I'm a London man born and bred, sir. What would I know of the country? And it was right difficult finding that bloody snake, too," he added on a mutter. He'd needed to buy the adder, in fact, from an odd old woman, a witch, some whispered, who specialized in the sales of crawling things. Bob was proud of the snake, the basket, creeping in at dawn to do it, the whole plan, in fact. Proud of the mail coach. Timing and stealth and skill had been required, knowledge and expertise gained only through years of experience.

Bloody difficult to make things look like an accident.

"And Caroline? What of her?" Morley demanded.

"Can't be everywhere at once, sir."

Bob was getting cheeky. Then again, he wasn't accustomed to failing, and perhaps it was taking a toll on both of them.

"Caroline Allston is not inconspicuous, Bob."

"But she *is* clever, Mr. Morley."

"No, Bob," Morley explained, strained patience weighting his words like lead. "She is *not* clever."

Beautiful, wily, unpredictable as an animal. All instinct. But *not* clever. Not his Caroline.

His Caroline. Odd, but it was how he used to think of her. How he still thought of her, even as they now attempted to hunt her down.

There was a long silence, during which Morley consulted his watch and Bob scuffed his feet nervously on the carpet.

"Sir, you know I'm a *profess*—"

"Then get it *done,* Bob."

Morley turned and lowered Fluff to the ground. The cat stretched and flicked his tail, unhappy at the interruption in attention.

Morley realized Bob was still standing there, when in essence his words had been a dismissal. "Yes?" he made the word a hiss of impatience.

"*Must* it be an accident, Mr. Morley?"

"Lost faith in your own repertoire of nefarious skills, Bob?"

Bob looked at him blankly.

"Can't do it?" Morley translated, keeping his sarcasm checked with some difficulty.

"It's just that she's never alone, sir. Always with that great fair-headed geezer."

This was new. "And who would this 'great fair-headed geezer' be, Bob?"

"Not certain, sir. They appear to be wandering about and... and"—his brow wrinkled—"*drawing* things." His tone said everything about how he felt about the peculiar habits of the gentry. "Looks like a farmer," he further illuminated. "Dresses like one, anyhow."

"Bob. Just go ahead and get it done. In your own inimitable, skillful, professional manner. And find out who the 'geezer' is, if you would. It might be important."

"Really, sir? It needn't be an accident?" Bob had brightened; his eyes were alight with new plans. "Because you see, after one too many accidents..."

"Accidents cease to look like accidents. I understand. Use your own excellent judgment, Bob. Please report back only when you've succeeded... or if you've new information."

Bob clicked his heels, his confidence restored now that his options had expanded. "You can count on me, sir. I'm a professional."

A little more than a week of riding through meadows and trudging about the woods had yielded sketches of the White Oak, some squirrels, and a few ferns, but the woods were filled with wild medicinal herbs, too, Kit knew, and it would take days to document them.

One month, his father had said. *Thorough,* his father had said. As if Kit would ever do any other kind of job of it. Every sketch in that book kept Egypt at bay.

He led their saddled geldings from the stable. "Today we go in search of Hellebore," he announced to Susannah.

Her vivacity instantly dropped several degrees. "Tell me 'Hellebore' isn't what it sounds like."

He grinned at that. "Fear not, Miss Makepeace. Hellebore will never creep into your picnic basket. It's an herb. A medicinal—some would say poisonous herb—that grows wild in this area. It's been used as a purgative and to bless cattle, among other things. And in...magic spells."

Speaking of magic spells, she was wearing the green hat again, which made her eyes glow a nearly mesmerizing shade. He knew now that her eyes were in fact hazel, which wasn't in and of itself a magical thing, but he couldn't help be fascinated by their ability to take on the color of things near them.

He cupped his hands for her boot and lifted her into the saddle, and Susannah hooked her leg over the calf block, settling into the saddle, taking the reins up in her hands. "Perhaps we should cast a spell upon—"

The gelding beneath her reared with a scream, his forelegs flailing the air. He heard Susannah gasp as she pulled the reins tightly in her fists. The horse came down hard and bucked out twice.

And launched into a headlong run.

Sweet Lucifer.

Kit vaulted into the saddle of his own horse and kicked it into a gallop. That gelding intended to unseat Susannah, and in single-minded horse fashion was heading straight for a tree branch in order to accomplish it.

Her hat flew from her head, a bright disk of green hurtling through the air, and she was leaning over the pommel now, clinging to the horse's neck, struggling to regain her balance and losing the battle for it. He saw her slip, and his heart flew into his throat. Bloody *sidesaddles.*

Kit kicked harder, harder, urging his horse to stretch out in punishingly long swift strides until he finally drew flush with Susannah.

To his horror, Kit saw her saddle slip roughly sideways, as though the girth had loosened. Susannah looped her arms around the frenzied horse's neck, clinging desperately now; the reins had become nearly useless to her.

Harder. He kicked his poor horse harder, goading it and goading it, cursing the fact that he couldn't bloody *fly,* until he finally drew past Susannah's gelding. And then he yanked his horse up short to a rearing halt and threw himself out of the saddle just as Susannah began to fall. He lunged for her, pulled her into his arms the moment the sidesaddle slid completely beneath the gelding's belly.

But the shift in gravity and the weight of their two falling bodies was too much for her gelding; it lost its footing. Kit flung Susannah aside just as the horse came down on him.

Blinding pain in his shoulder.

Blackness as his breath left him.

And then mercifully, quickly, the horse righted itself, thrashing its way to its feet.

Kit lay stunned, flat against the earth. He struggled to inhale, and couldn't. He choked, wheezing; in a moment there was breath in his lungs again. With great difficulty, he levered his torso upright.

Pain.

"Susannah...," he gasped, turned his head, which sent a cloud of tiny dots swaying and bobbing before his eyes. He saw her through them, whole, sound, her face stark white above the green of her habit, the sky oddly brilliant behind her, her shoulders heaving with terrified breathing.

Pride and masculinity forced him to get all the way up on his feet as she rushed for him.

I am not going to faint. He took a step, but moving made him nauseous.

Now, vomit, on other hand—that I might just do.

He knew more than a little about pain; so he closed his eyes, took a deep breath, exhaled, did it again, to steady himself.

"Kit." She was next to him now. "God, please don't move. Are you—"

Well, then. At last she'd called him Kit. "You're all right?" His voice was a little wheezy, barely a voice. He opened his eyes; those black dots were still everywhere.

She squeaked. "Am *I* all right? Am *I*? A *horse* fell on you."

He winced. "Only part of a horse." His voice was steadier now. "His shoulder and foreleg. Not the entire horse. Your voice hurts," he added absurdly. "Too squeaky."

"But are you—" Still squeaky. She stopped, adjusted her tone. "You're hurt, you *must* be." Her hand reached out reflexively.

"Careful of the shoulder," he heard himself say calmly. "Best not touch it."

Those black dots were floating like a flock of tiny birds before his eyes. His voice sounded distant in his own ears. *I am not going to faint.*

"Your face…"

"Was already like that before the horse fell on me, Miss Makepeace."

"Don't jest," she said curtly. "I can see it hurts. Breathe through it, through the pain. Deep breaths. Is anything broken?"

Kit wiggled his fingers, then raised his elbow a little, all of which hurt like the very devil, but the fact that all of those parts still functioned was a very good sign indeed. Tomorrow was going to be *deeply* unpleasant.

"Just sprained and bruised, I think. I hope. My arm took the brunt of it. And ... my ribs might be a little bruised. I'm bloody lucky. He wasn't on me long."

"Lucky?" Susannah repeated incredulously. "I would say you've inherited *my* sort of luck." And then she looked at him closely; he saw her face go worried at what she saw. "Kit ... are you sure ..."

He could only imagine how white his face must be. He felt bleached clear through, strangely hollow. "It's just ... my body seems to want to go into shock. Struck my elbow in just the right place. Or wrong place. Happens that way."

"Breathe," she said gently. "I'll catch you if you fall, if you insist on standing."

He gave a faint laugh. But it was sensible advice, and some-how, he liked hearing her give it. So he did it, took more deep breaths, exhaling the pain with each one. A fine cold sweat gathered on his brow and over his back, but the black dots slowed their frantic dance before his eyes. He was more certain now that he wasn't going to faint in front of her. He thought he might like to lie down, however. And he was *positive* he was going to drink quite a bit the moment he returned to the house. Bloody hell, but he'd need a sling, at the very least.

What on earth had possessed a perfectly amiable horse to try to kill its rider? It couldn't possibly be another adder.

Kit's curiosity overcame his pain. He held his injured arm close to his side, gingerly, and slowly went to the gelding. The animal was still a little wild-eyed, and he tossed his head at Kit's approach, but he didn't try to bolt. He was clearly much happier with Susannah out of the saddle. Feeling much more himself.

"Ho, my lad," Kit said soothingly, reaching his good arm up to touch him. "What's got into you, eh? Shall we take a look?"

Susannah touched the horse, too, gently, calmingly on the flank.

"Poor beast. It was the saddle, I think. The moment I settled into it, he desperately wanted me *out* of it. And then the saddle itself…it felt as though it came loose. I tried to hold on, I did, and you…" She paused. "Thank you," she said simply. "You saved my—"

Kit gave a short, nonchalant, heroic shrug, which hurt, but it cut off her words. And then he used his good arm to try to pull the saddle from the horse, but the hefty leather of it was awkward. Susannah quickly took the other end of it. They deposited it on the ground, and Kit flipped it over with the toe of his boot. Then he slowly knelt, mindful of his throbbing limbs. While Susannah watched, he ran his hand across the underside of the saddle skirt, searching carefully, feeling over every inch of where it might touch the horse.

He stopped when something pricked his finger.

It was a small twig with an end so sharp it nearly looked deliberately sharpened, and it had somehow lodged between the panel and the skirt of the sidesaddle. The added weight of a rider would have driven it right into the haunch of the horse. Not deeply enough to cause much damage, or a great wound… just deeply enough to cause great pain to the horse.

And possibly kill the rider, should the horse have succeeded in bucking the rider off.

A horrible little coincidence, perhaps. Any number of odd little things could find their way into a stable. Perhaps a saddle had been dropped to the floor of it, and the twig had become lodged there, or…

"Here's the culprit," he said lightly, holding the twig up. But he didn't drop it to the ground; he pocketed it.

Kit was having a difficult time stringing his thoughts together; pain had set up an annoying buzz in his mind. He took in another breath. He'd need a drink *soon*.

He examined the girth of the saddle, and saw that it had

snapped entirely where it joined the leather beneath the flap, a place one wouldn't normally notice as they cinched the saddle around the belly of the horse. He supposed he could shout at the stable boys, but it wasn't entirely their fault. He ran the girth through his fingers; the leather was somewhat brittle with age.

Brittle enough to break?

Susannah had been using this sidesaddle for days.

He looked closely at the snapped ends. The break looked almost...too clean.

A chill settled into his gut. He couldn't shake the unreal sense that a knife had assisted the girth in breaking.

The watching man.

The mail coach, the adder...

The twig, the girth...

And this was a sidesaddle. No man was about to get into a sidesaddle.

Only a woman.

He looked up at Susannah, who was still quietly watching him. Behind her he could see the woefully crumpled green plume of her hat on the ground, fluttering in a breeze, and her hair was a little wild from her ride, spilling about her face. He'd never before seen it down, and his gut clutched in response. Lovely hair. So many subtle colors in the strands. Mahogany, and chestnut, and sable, and...

She suddenly seemed so...crushable standing there. Eminently fragile. How easily she could have been gravely injured today. What a near thing, what a very near thing, it had been.

An irrational fury, almost a panic, made his breath come short again.

How do you tell a woman who has just lost everything in her life that he suspected someone was trying to kill her?

You didn't say anything of the sort until you were entirely sure.

Susannah's gelding was nosing about for grass now next to his own mount, who was doing the same thing. Their reins trailed the ground. Susannah's poor gelding looked considerably more sound than Kit felt. *Glad I provided a soft place to land,* Kit thought mordantly.

"You're not in the army now. You don't have to endure the pain if you don't want to. There's a little something called laudanum that might help."

Susannah was trying a joke, but it didn't register, as his thoughts were elsewhere entirely. He would begin, he decided, by inspecting the saddles and having a chat with the stable boys.

"Yes." His voice was distant. "Or whiskey."

He wasn't certain whether walking or riding back to the stables would jar his body more, then decided it wouldn't make a difference; it would hurt like the very devil regardless.

"Thank you again for saving my life," she said gravely.

For some reason the tone made him smile. "It's the least I can do for a valuable employee, Miss Makepeace. You're certain you're sound?"

"The horse," she emphasized, "fell on *you*. Not me. You flung me out of the way."

He couldn't smile at that. *But it could have been you,* he thought. *It could have been you.*

The thought kept him from speaking.

He gathered the reins of his horse in his hand, and Susannah followed suit. He'd decided to walk, and slowly at that. Out of the corner of his eye he saw the hat again, a shade that had never grown in nature. "Willow," he knew it was called; fashionable in London just now, or so he'd heard. No actual willow tree was ever this color, but it did make Susannah's eyes glow that remarkable, mesmerizing shade of green. And for that he would forgive it anything.

"Your hat," he said.

"Oh." Susannah strolled over and plucked it up, gave the irreparably crushed feather a disconsolate stroke. "I did like this hat," she said.

"So did I," he said, unthinkingly.

Her eyebrows arced with astonishment. "A *compliment,* my lord?"

"An observation, Miss Makepeace," he corrected hurriedly.

But for some reason his answer made her give him a slow, softly radiant smile, as though he were her prize pupil. And oddly, for a moment, just that moment, nothing hurt at all.

Chapter Nine

⌒

Pettishaw, a relatively new MP, was droning on and on about the need for parliamentary reform. The faces around him were arranged in varying expressions of attention; some were even nodding. In agreement? Morley wondered. Or fighting off sleep? Difficult to know, really. The beauty of the House of Commons, Morley thought, was that someone would ultimately say something hopelessly rude and direct to shut Pettishaw up. A man was given but few opportunities to prove his oratory talents, and if he demonstrated that he had none, he was heartily discouraged from then on from orating at all. They could be an unruly crew, the Commons.

Morley's own voice was deep and pleasant; it carried enough warmth and inflection to keep the listener awake, and he had a knack for eloquently persuading while never veering into floridity or drama. In other words, he'd never been told in rude and uncertain terms to shut up. His political talents, in fact, had been compared to those of Charles Fox, only Morley was better looking and he hadn't Fox's bad, if colorful, habits of gambling and womanizing.

Morley's leg ached; it often did in session, because these rooms seemed to hold the damp and release it just to plague him. He was grateful, in a way, because the ache reminded him of how he'd come to be here. He was grateful, too, for the scars that scored the length of it—great, ugly rippling scars, like calcified flame. Women often mistook the limp and the scars for a war wound, and he never disabused them of the notion. It *was* a war wound, as far as he was concerned. At least of a sort.

And he'd seduced more than a few of them based on that alone.

For some reason, however, he'd told Caroline the truth of it.

It had become useful, another tool. Morley was accustomed to thinking of everything in terms of how it served him.

Like Bob. Who was hopefully serving him by spending the day in Barnstable finishing the job he'd been assigned, so Morley could continue to sit in the Commons, taking for granted voluble politicians and the faultless reputation he'd earned.

His father had been a farmer. More truthfully, a peasant. His family had been large, and they'd eked out a living on a patch of land scarcely the size of four handkerchiefs sewn together, or so it seemed now from a perspective of years. But then industry had moved in, and the spinners and button-makers and poor farmers like his father had lost their livelihoods to machines that did the work faster if not better, and to landowners who built factories on all of the handkerchief-sized patches of land. His father had taken his family—his mother and brothers and sisters—into London to look for work.

Unfortunately, *everyone* who had lost their livelihoods— and they were legion—had migrated to London from the country, looking for work. Or to other factory towns. Consequently, no work was to be had. The Morley family then set out to slowly starve in St. Giles, which is where Thaddeus had made so many interesting and ultimately useful friends.

And then came the fire.

It killed everyone in the Morley family's lodging house—his entire family, in fact—except for himself, for some reason known only to the fates. He'd been gravely injured, his leg blackened and blistered, but the wealthy building owner, stricken with conscience, perhaps—the building had been a disaster, after all—or perhaps wishing to buy his way into heaven, paid for Thaddeus's care, and then, discovering he was a bright boy, paid for him to go to Eton.

And then he'd grown bored of the largesse, and completely forgot about Thaddeus Morley. Leaving Morley floundering.

But only briefly.

Because he had wit, intelligence, charm, a handsome face, a sympathy-eliciting limp, and a great, helpful, deeply buried seam of rage that ran like lava through his soul and fueled his enormous ambition. He wasn't overly burdened with scruples; living in St. Giles taught one the frivolousness of scruples. He used them selectively. A connection with a few old friends involved him briefly in the distribution of smuggled goods, and he invested his earnings wisely, and earned his way into Oxford.

And after Oxford, nothing would satisfy him other than a parliamentary seat. Where he would set out to attempt justice for people like his family.

And . . . well, perhaps exact just a little revenge, as well.

But getting there had been like climbing the face of a cliff with bare hands. To be elected to the House of Commons, he desperately needed money to campaign. And he'd thought he'd found the support he needed when the Earl of Westphall invited him to a party over the winter holidays. The earl had, for reasons of his own, regretfully declined to contribute any funds to Morley's election. However, the Westphall party *had* yielded Caroline Allston. And so, in retrospect, Morley did have the Earl of Westphall to thank for his entire political career.

He remembered his first sight of Caroline Allston—he'd been astounded to find such a creature in a town like Barnstable—and knew instantly she was another person who would need to scale the faces of rock cliffs with her bare hands. Her beauty was wasted in the country town; Morley knew how to make *excellent* use of it.

He remembered those blue eyes of the earl son's, Kit Whitelaw, Viscount Grantham, burning into him that evening. Even at seventeen, the boy had possessed an unnerving intensity. The hurt and longing in them as he'd watched Morley and Caroline. Clever boy. He'd known.

His leg twitched violently, suddenly. Morley covered it with his hand, soothing it like a restless pet, willing the pain to subside. He remembered a time when Caroline could tell from a glance at his face when the pain in his leg became unbearable. Without saying a word, she would knead the pain away, and chatter to him about something else as she did it.

Pettishaw was still droning on. Morley glanced about the room; Groves, an MP who hailed from Leeds, intercepted the glance and rolled his eyes. Morley gave him a faint, commiserating smile.

His arrangement with Caroline had at first been simple: She warmed his bed in endlessly original ways, he paid for her keep. She was grateful and young and excited by him; they both recognized the value of their alliance.

But Morley saw everyone and everything as useful or not useful; sentiment (for people, anyhow, cats were another story) had been burned out of him in the fire.

So when Morley saw Caroline's effect on other men, his busy mind went to work. At a private dinner he'd strategically introduced her to a naval captain he'd met socially, who, as it turned out, became garrulous after he'd made love, as most men did. Garrulous, and particularly careless after too much wine, and hence, helpful beyond words.

Soon after that, Caroline had gleefully gifted Morley with the most marvelous information. Numbers and types and names of ships, and the numbers and types of guns they carried. Where and how they would be deployed. The officers who commanded them, and the names of other officers aboard. Snippets of information, mostly, and a document here, and a document there, things Caroline purloined when the captain was sleeping. But useful and very *valuable*—to the right people.

French people.

And the sale of this information was how he'd financed his campaign. And how he'd been elected. And how he'd built his wealth. And why he still sat here today, with a reputation for calmly crusading for the rights of children and workers, for tasteful dress and a moderate lifestyle. He'd been faultless ever since.

Almost faultless.

He glanced around the chambers now, and thought: *Surely these men are plagued by more ghosts than I? Surely they have more blood on their hands, having aimed rifles and cannons at flesh-and-blood men during war, with the goal of taking as many lives as they possibly could?*

And his own hands might even have remained entirely clean, if bloody nosey fellow MP Richard Lockwood hadn't happened to meet that particular naval captain socially, too. Or if the naval captain hadn't innocently, and with great enthusiasm, told Lockwood all about his encounters with a beautiful woman introduced to him by Thaddeus Morley. The topic had been mistresses, apparently, and the naval captain had been eager to brag, since Lockwood had such a splendid mistress of his own in Anna Holt, who had just been installed in her own home in the town of Gorringe and now needed a household staff.

"Asked a lot of questions about you and the girl, Lockwood did," the naval captain had told Morley cheerily. "Perhaps he's casting about for a new mistress. What became of her, by the way?" he asked hopefully.

"Found a wealthier protector," Morley had lied mournfully. Caroline hadn't yet left him at the time; her departure with the handsome American merchant was still two years away. But he'd tucked her back into her quiver, to be used again when the time came, and made certain she wasn't seen publicly.

Perhaps Lockwood hadn't reckoned on the strength of Morley's sense for things dark, for self-preservation.

It had almost been child's play to discover what Lockwood had been about, and to put a stop to it. It wasn't a pleasant business; he hadn't taken pleasure in it, but it had needed to be done, and he'd undertaken it like a job, planned it and executed it. And he'd thought it *had* been done . . . certainly, he'd begun to ease into complacency in the ensuing years.

And then Makepeace's letter had arrived.

Well, if his political career was to be bookended by murders, perhaps it couldn't be helped. He'd been seeing more of Bob lately than he preferred, but he was looking forward to their next visit more anxiously than he preferred.

❧

By the time he saw Susannah home and returned to the house, Kit felt . . . well, exactly as though a horse had fallen upon him. Pain sang a nasty chorus all up and down his nerve endings. He could scarcely tell where it began and ended.

Bullton stopped in his tracks when he saw him enter the house.

"Sir?" Bullton's face was eloquent with the question.

"A horse fell on me, Bullton."

"Ah. Whiskey, sir?"

Good man. "If you can spare yours, Bullton."

"And a doctor?"

"I don't think so. But I'll let you know. If you'd help me with the stairs?"

"Of course, sir."

"And I need a pen and foolscap, if you will."

"You'll be writing your will, sir?"

"I do appreciate the attempt at wit, Bullton, and rest assured I am laughing on the inside. Laughing on the *outside* rather jars everything at the moment. No, I'll be writing . . . some important correspondence." He knew just how to word it, too, to avoid arousing the suspicions of anyone who might want to intercept it—particularly his father.

"Very good, sir. Foolscap and a pen it is."

The two of them, Kit and Bullton, got Kit's aching body up the stairs, and then they got him out of his shirt and into a sling. The arm felt better when the muscles and tendons were relieved of the need to move at all. Some bolted whiskey helped with the rest of the pain; Bullton imbibed, too, as Kit hated to drink alone. Kit gingerly prodded his ribs, took in a few deep testing breaths. They weren't broken, he warranted. He knew from experience that broken ribs were excruciating and unmistakable. If he could move without stifling screams, no doubt he was only severely bruised.

"How is your penmanship, Bullton?"

"Fair, sir."

"Fair as in 'maiden fair,' or fair as in 'only passable'?" Kit was feeling a little drunk now, and it wasn't unpleasant.

"The former, sir. If you don't mind my saying so."

"Not at all, Bullton, not at all. I admire a man who isn't afraid to admit to his talents. Take a letter for me, if you would then, and let's have a little more of that whiskey while we write it, shall we?"

A bottle of whiskey later, the letter read:

Dear sirs,

I am writing on behalf of my neighbor, who was traveling your coach line en route to visit her aunt in the town of Barnstable when your conveyance apparently "tipped over" in the yard of the coaching inn, leading to a ride with a randy farmer, irreparable damage to her favorite hat (a very fine green one), and immeasurable overall distress. I am tempted to bring my considerable influence to bear in order to exact retribution and to discourage other passengers from riding your line, but I may settle for a full accounting of the precise cause of the accident and an assurance that it will not happen again. Rest assured, the information you impart will remain confidential. Your hasty reply is appreciated.

Christopher Whitelaw, Viscount Grantham

"Terrible thing, about the hat, sir." Bullton hiccuped mournfully. They were at the stage in their second bottle of whiskey where everything seemed either beautiful or tragic, or some combination thereof.

"It was, oh, it was, Bullton." Kit's voice sounded a little despairing. "It was a fine hat. Had a plume…Made her eyes *so* green…"

"Very good color—green," Bullton agreed wistfully.

"Particularly for eyes," Kit mused. "But I'm partial to hazel. Hazel is green with blue and bits of gold in it," he explained to Bullton.

"Are you, sir? Are you really partial to hazel?" Bullton solemnly wanted to know.

"Very, very partial," Kit said dreamily.

"I'm an admirer of brown eyes," Bullton confessed.

"Doesn't Mrs. Davies have brown eyes, Bullton?"

"Brown as a spaniel's." It was Bullton's turn to sound wistfully dreamy.

This struck Kit as very funny, and he laughed, which turned out to be a mistake, because the whiskey hadn't entirely vanquished the pain in his ribs. And then he groaned, but groaning also hurt.

"All right, sir, time to rest," Bullton ordered. "No traipsing about in the woods tomorrow."

"You are very strict, Bullton. But you are no doubt correct. Get my boots off, will you, good man?"

Bullton tugged and tugged and tugged, then staggered backward and toppled to the floor with a Hessian in his arms as though it had been shot out of a cannon, which struck Kit as very funny again. He laughed, forgetting what happened the last time he laughed, and as a result, was soon groaning again.

"*Christ.* You really must stop being funny, Bullton."

"I will try sir, but there's another boot, yet."

Bullton got the other boot off, and Kit laughed again, then groaned, and then laughed because he was groaning again, which made him groan some more. Finally, the whole business wore him out.

"Thank you, Bullton. Good night. Dream of spaniel eyes," Kit murmured.

"Good night, sir. Dream of hazel."

Chapter Ten

⁓

It was Aunt Frances's turn to read this evening, so Susannah settled into her chair near the fire and took up her sketchbook, idly drawing while she listened. Aunt Frances had a habit of licking her finger before she turned a page, which had definitely taken getting used to. But now the little smacking noise measured off their evenings as surely as a ticking clock, and Susannah had begun to find it soothing. They were both deeply involved in the story; Susannah vicariously enjoyed proud Elizabeth Bennett's heartbreaks, the sweet idiocy and hope of love.

Behind her, a fire she had built—she'd stacked the wood and lit it—crackled away. She was bloody proud of that fire.

The viscount had vigorously rebounded from being fallen upon by a gelding, and apart from a sling and a tendency to wince a little when he moved too quickly, showed no signs of permanent damage, either to his wits or his person. She'd trailed him as usual—on foot—for the past few days, adding a new fern and several more trees to her sketchbook, and nothing at all to her storehouse of knowledge about his past. But he *did* talk: about squirrels and birds and ferns and trees and the like, with an enthusiasm and reverence and a sort of abstracted, increasing delight, as though he was discovering something he already knew. It was contagious, this joy; it found its way into her drawings.

"With the Gardiners they were always on the most intimate terms. Darcy, as well as Elizabeth, really loved them; and they were both ever sensible of the warmest gratitude toward the persons who, by bringing her into Derbyshire, had been the means of uniting them."

Aunt Frances sighed with pleasure. "I always hate to read the last sentence of a wonderful book, don't you?"

Susannah gave a start. She hadn't heard that last sentence at all, truthfully.

"Everything is wrapped up rather neatly, isn't it?" she said, diplomatically. She would peek at it when Aunt Frances wasn't looking.

Susannah glanced down at her sketchbook and discovered, with some surprise, the reason she hadn't heard the last sentence: the viscount's face, rendered in pencil, now occupied the corner of the page. He looked amused in her drawing, but there was something wistful in the lines around his eyes, and his mouth, that lovely mouth, was somewhat tentative, quirked into a smile at the corner. She ran her thumb lightly across the face, gently traced his lips with the edge of her fingernail.

Then feeling a little abashed, she turned the pages quickly to the safer-looking ferns and trees.

"How goes the traipsing about with the viscount, Susannah?"

She wondered if it was a coincidence that her aunt had transitioned from talk of a happy ending to the viscount.

"Oh, it goes very well. He is all that is . . . gentlemanly." She tried to keep the regret from her voice.

"Oh, I sincerely doubt *that*," he aunt said, amused. "I'm certain he is *some* that is gentlemanly. But I also know he wouldn't lay a hand upon you, Susannah, no matter what some of the neighbors might say. His father bred him too well."

Odd, but she found her aunt's firmness of conviction along those lines a little disappointing.

"Is there really a scandal in his past, Aunt Frances?" She asked it tentatively. She wasn't positive she wanted to know, since the wondering about it had been both such a pleasure and a torment.

"Well . . . there *was* a little something, when he was a boy. His father packed him off into the army rather abruptly one day, as I recall. Or perhaps it was the military academy. Just a lad at the time, he was. One day he was here—the next, or very near it—poof! Gone! There was something about a girl, too, I believe, but I can't recall her name."

Caro, Susannah almost supplied. She was surprised when she stopped herself. Odd, but somehow, it would have seemed almost like . . . like a betrayal of him.

"It's too long ago, and it scarcely matters now, does it?" her aunt continued. "He's served his country, which in my book redeems him, more or less, no matter what he's done. But you know how rumors are . . . people *will* cling to one, and tend it until it grows like a great weed in all directions. He was a good lad for the most part, even if he was full of oats. He's a good man, too, I warrant. I know, because it's in the eyes," her aunt said sagely, pointing with two fingers to her own brown ones. "And he's in Barnstable so seldom, but he never fails to call upon me when he is. And as far as I'm concerned, that is the mark of a gentleman."

Susannah rather thought so, too, and it warmed her heart to think of Kit sitting in the parlor with Aunt Frances, gripping a cup of tea, having a chat about—

About what? Horrid novels?

"The viscount thinks I'm very talented at drawing." Susannah offered this almost shyly. She'd never discussed her "talent" with anyone else before.

"Well, how about that?" Aunt Frances looked pleased. "Talented, are you? Not just a young lady who draws like any other young lady?"

"That's what he says. Do you suppose I got my talent from my father?" She remembered Kit suggesting this question; it had seemed important to him.

"Well, you might very well have at that, Susannah. Lord knows no one in the Makepeace family has a whit of artistic talent."

Susannah frowned a little. That sentence hadn't made a whit of *sense*.

"But . . . you *do* think I might very well have gotten my talent from my father?" She said it almost gingerly, in case this was the first sign that Aunt Frances was actually losing her mind, and she would have to begin making plans to live somewhere else.

"Well . . . yes, dear." Her aunt, for her part, looked a little troubled now, too. "That *is* what I said."

They stared at each other with wary politeness.

Aunt Frances's knitting needles slowed.

An uneasy silence slunk by.

And it had started out as such a *benign* discussion.

"James," Susannah tried carefully, "my *father*. I might have gotten my talent from *him*? Is that what you meant?"

Her aunt's needles froze completely. "Oh—oh my. Oh my *goodness*."

Aunt Frances sat straight up and pushed her spectacles up on her nose. Susannah paused in her lunging, sat back in her chair again. She didn't look ill; on the contrary, she looked alarmingly lucid.

"Aunt Frances? Are you—"

"Good heavens. Susannah—surely you know?"

Susannah almost closed her eyes. *No more revelations, please.* But she had to ask.

"Know *what,* Aunt Frances?"

"That James wasn't your father, dear."

It was Susannah's turn to go perfectly, perfectly still. "I beg your pardon?" She said it so faintly they were barely words.

"I said, James wasn't your—"

"I heard you," Susannah said abruptly. "I'm sorry. That is to say . . ." She shook her head roughly. "I *beg* your pardon?"

"Oh, my dear. My poor dear." Aunt Frances sounded truly distressed; she had her hands fisted against her cheeks now. "I'm so sorry to startle you. I had no idea you didn't know."

Susannah couldn't move, or think properly. *James wasn't your father.* Those four words had become the entire contents of her mind.

"But surely . . . surely that's the sort of thing a solicitor would at least mention, Susannah? As he read the will to you?" Aunt Frances peered with frowning concern into Susannah's face. "I suppose not," she concluded after a moment, from Susannah's dumbstruck expression.

"But *how* . . . *why* . . . I mean, *what* . . . ?" But no question seemed quite adequate or appropriate at the moment, so Susannah stopped trying to ask one.

Fortunately, Aunt Frances was able to collect herself enough to launch into a coherent tale. "My dear, I will tell you all I know, which I heard from another member of the family, so it's thirdhand, my dear. Almost twenty years ago now James went to a town called Gorringe. And apparently he returned with a little girl, who *may* have come from Gorringe, but no one knows, really."

"*I* was that little girl?"

"Perhaps. There was speculation in the family that perhaps James had a mistress who died, and this was her child, which in truth cheered his mother no end. Because, you see, James wasn't one to take much notice of women . . . he rather liked vases and art, I hear."

"Yes," Susannah said softly, remembering all of the vases and carpets and art coming in, and then going out, of the door. "He did. But . . . why? I just don't understand."

"I'm sorry, dear, but I've told you all I know. And I honestly don't know anyone who can tell you anything further, either. James was always the family's enigma. He seemed to prefer it that way. He kept *everyone* at a distance."

"But . . . what about my mother? I've a miniature of her, and I look just like her, I *do*! They weren't . . . weren't they . . . were they married? Wasn't he *ever* married?"

"Married? Good heavens, I don't think so dear. Well, I suppose anything's possible, really, but no one knew of a marriage, if he in fact was. But perhaps your mother was married to someone *else*," she added, hating to shock Susannah any further, perhaps, with the suggestion her mother had been a fallen woman.

"Someone who would have been my father."

"Well, undoubtedly, dear," Aunt Frances said hurriedly, reassuringly. "Perhaps you were orphaned, and James took you in."

"Then . . ." Susannah felt the world slipping out from beneath her yet again, as another realization took hold. "You . . . you . . . aren't really my aunt, then, are you?"

She dropped her eyes to her lap.

There was a silence.

"Oh!" Aunt Frances said softly. There was a moment of quiet, and then Susannah heard Aunt Frances pat the settee. "Come here, my dear."

She lifted her eyes, struggling to maintain a stoic expression.

She raised up and went to the settee, curling her feet up underneath her.

And then Aunt Frances gestured coaxingly to her own plump shoulder with a tilt of her head and a lift of her brows. Hesitating an instant, Susannah gingerly laid her head down upon on the curve of it. She was a woman grown, but this was the sort of solace she'd never before known, this leaning her cheek against another woman's shoulder. It was so curiously comforting she felt again the tears pushing against the back of her eyes.

Aunt Frances stroked her brow soothingly, with a cool, rough hand. "There now. I am sorry to shock you after such a pleasant evening, my dear. But isn't it better that you know, somehow?"

"I suppose it is. It explains a good deal, Aunt Frances. There were never any pictures of my mother about the house. I thought perhaps...perhaps her death wounded him too grievously to think of her. A romantic notion, I know."

Aunt Frances nodded, approving of the romantic notion.

"And he..." Susannah swallowed over a knot in her throat. "Well, he never really seemed to care for me. Oh, he was kind enough," she said swiftly. "But...not fatherly. He was so seldom home, and didn't seem to have need of my company."

I sound pathetic, she thought, and despised the sound of it. She'd never before indulged in being pathetic. It involved relinquishing one's pride for a moment, and admitting to herself that she liked the stroking hand on her brow. *Just this once,* she thought. *And then I shall buck up.*

"Oh, I'm certain he cared for you," Aunt Frances said stoutly.

"Do you really think so?"

"He did keep you very well all of these years, Susannah, did he not? And made certain you were raised not wanting for anything."

Except a mother and a father, Susannah thought, traitorously. "He did." She couldn't deny it. But the sense of unreality was profound. She'd thought she'd lost everything but her sense of self: she'd at least known, despite the defection of the rest of her life, that she was Susannah Makepeace, daughter of James.

And as it turned out, she'd lost that, too.

"I wonder why James never told you," her aunt mused.

"Perhaps he never thought it . . . important." It seemed inconceivable to her that someone wouldn't think family was important. It was the only thing she'd ever really lacked, and, as it turned out, the only thing she'd ever really wanted. Perhaps he'd meant to tell her, some day. *No one really intends to get one's throat cut,* she thought. "Perhaps he thought keeping it a secret would ensure my good marriage."

"Or perhaps he was hiding something," her aunt added with acerbic practicality.

Susannah thought about this, about the gentle cipher who had been her father.

And then she thought of the adder hiding in the benign-looking picnic basket. What did one ever really know about anyone?

But then . . . something twitched inside her . . . it felt like hope again. And little by little, whatever it was began to blossom.

She'd always thought she'd had no family, no mother or brothers or sisters or cousins.

But now . . . her family could be anyone at all; she could be related to dozens of people, or none. Her life, her future, which had just a few minutes ago seemed as limited as this little house, now seemed as large as all the possibility in the world. She didn't know at all where to begin investigating it, but her imagination had already gone to work on it. She might be the bastard daughter of a prince. She might be . . . a peasant. She might be—

"Perhaps I have a family after all," she said to Aunt Frances.

"You do in me, Susannah. One can be an aunt in spirit, you know."

Susannah was moved, too overwhelmed with impressions and revelations to speak. She hadn't done a thing to warrant such kindness, such warmth or acceptance, from Aunt Frances. She hadn't charmed her way into Aunt Frances's graces, or earned them with her status or money. She simply had to *be,* and Aunt Frances had taken her in, without question.

"Thank you, Aunt Frances." It was really all she could say. She quietly vowed to endeavor to live up to such acceptance. "One can be a niece in spirit, too."

Aunt Frances chuckled, her shoulder shifting up and down with it.

But maybe that was the point of acceptance: one didn't have to live up to it, or earn it. Susannah sensed that her entire life, she had tried a little too hard, no matter what she did.

Possibly because she hadn't a family, she'd needed everyone else to love her.

Perhaps you needn't try so hard, Kit had said to her. He'd seen it in her from the very beginning, her need to dazzle. And so, it seemed, had the denizens of Barnstable.

"Well, the Bennett girls went through their trials, didn't they dear, but it ended well for all of them, didn't it? Even, in a way, for that Lydia chit, isn't that so?"

"It did, at that." Susannah smiled a little. Miss Jane Austen certainly knew how to end a story.

The next morning, Susannah arrived at the stables to find the viscount stroking and murmuring to the pregnant mare.

The mare jerked her head away from him, tossing it high.

And then a low moan came from her, a sound so very nearly human the breath froze in Susannah's lungs.

Kit turned and saw Susannah. His face was granite-colored with a terrifyingly contained anger. She took an unconscious step back.

"Go home." He bit the words off, turned back to the mare.

Susannah's hand flew up to cover her stomach with shock; his words had entered there, two swift darts.

"Something's wrong with the mare … she's … tell me what is wrong." Her voice was a shred of sound; it had taken all of her courage to speak to the cold wall of his back.

The mare groaned again and jerked her head high then her eyes rolled whitely in pain. And then the horse shifted and leaned into Kit, who pushed back, attempting to keep her upright, murmuring soothing words that contrasted starkly with his expression.

He finally looked again at Susannah.

"She's in foal, but she should have dropped it by now, which means the foal is presenting wrong. She's in tremendous pain. And the stable boys who should be caring for her are …" He stopped. "Nowhere to be seen."

He drawled these last words, and the hairs rose on Susannah's neck. Kit's fury was nearly acrid; she could feel it in her own throat. She imagined it blackening and curling the leaves on the trees black for miles around. The stable boys would be hung, drawn, and quartered when they returned, she was certain. If they dared return.

"What will happen to her?"

"She will die. And the foal will certainly die. Painfully and slowly, unless I shoot her." He tossed the words out casually, hard as little rocks.

"But … can't you do something?" Helplessness swelled in her, and oh *God,* she was tired of feeling helpless.

The mare's legs began to fold; Kit threw his body against her again. He seemed determined to keep her upright. And then he turned again and something he saw in Susannah's face made his angry mask slip.

"It's ... it's my arm ... I can't turn the foal and brace the mare with just one arm. She could crush me, or the foal. I need to keep her upright."

Susannah understood now: His own helplessness in this circumstance was killing him.

"I'll help. Let me do it. Please." The words sprung from some place deep and instinctive; she was just as astonished that she meant them.

Kit made a short disdainful sound. "You'll thrust your hand into the womb of a horse and turn a foal, Miss Makepeace? Because that's what's required. And we might not save her, even then."

His fury was contagious; she'd caught it now. She yanked the sleeve of her riding habit up and held her arm out, glared at him, breathing hard now. "Tell me what to do."

He began to turn away from her again.

"Tell. Me. What. To. *Do*. Damn you," she added, fervently.

His head went back at that, as though she'd struck him with a glove. A mere instant later, the hard white mask was gone, and the Kit she knew glimmered through. "Hold out your arm," he demanded.

She did, as her reflexes always seemed to obey him unquestioningly. He scooped a handful of lanolin from a bucket, vigorously rubbed it up past her elbow and guided her arm toward the mare's uplifted tail. His voice was even, clipped, the voice of someone accustomed to issuing orders and hearing them unquestionably obeyed.

"You'll need to insert your arm into the mare. I'll steady her, and tell you what to do. And she might kick, and I'll try to protect you from it. But mind yourself."

She pushed her hand, slowly, tentatively, into the darkness of the mare, felt the straining muscles close around her arm as the mare shifted her legs, saw her elbow vanish. Somewhere above her, Kit murmured reassurances to the mare, leaned his body against her when she moved her haunches and tossed her head again, with a sound that was half-groan, half-whicker.

And then for Susannah the sounds of the mare faded, and the stable around her faded, and her world was the wet heat of the horse and Kit's calm voice from above. Her fingers, with scant room to maneuver, fumbled, carefully fanned out, attempting to translate what she felt. Her breath caught.

"A muzzle," she breathed. "I feel a muzzle." She moved her fingers over the dip of a nostril, a pointed ear, a lip.

The foal *nipped at her finger.*

"Oh! It's trying to bite me!" She half-laughed, half-gasped.

"It's alive, then." Kit's voice came to her, even, nearly emotionless. "Do you feel the legs?"

Susannah moved her hand up around the face of the little foal, felt knobby little legs pushed up there, too.

"Yes. I feel a leg...near the foal's face."

"Now feel carefully...is it a foreleg, or a back leg? Is the joint above the ankle a knee, or a hock?"

Susannah felt a knobby knee, not a hock. "Foreleg."

"Good. Very good. Now we need to turn its head so that it faces us, and its legs need to be toward us, too, which is how a foal is normally presented in the womb. Feel up around its head, if you can, and...guide it toward you."

"Will it hurt the mare?" Stupid question. Everything was hurting the mare now. Susannah shook her head once abruptly, as if to retract the words, and Kit didn't respond.

She did as told, fumbled up over the length and curves of the foal's head, felt bristly little eyelashes, a short coarse mane. Gently, gently, she pulled it toward her.

It wouldn't budge.

"Try harder, Susannah," Kit said from above, his voice a little taut. "You won't hurt it."

Susannah drew in a deep breath, closed her eyes, prayed, and gave a harder pull, put her muscle into it.

"Kit, she—he—oh, it's *moving*…"

"All right." She felt Kit's voice as surely as a steadying hand on her back. "She'll push, Susannah—you'll feel her push—and when she does, we hope to see the foal's forelegs."

Susannah waited, and then the mare pushed.

A small hoof emerged. And then another…and then the forelegs, up to the knees.

The mare pushed again: most miraculously of all, the small muzzle began to emerge.

"Kit—"

Kit dropped his control as if it scalded him.

"Bloody fantastic, yes, *yes,* you've done it Susannah, that's exactly right, we have it now…we need to grasp the legs, and tug now…I'll tell you when…"

Susannah slowly, carefully withdrew her arm, and gently seized a hoof scarcely larger than a teacup. When the mare heaved again, she pulled, along with Kit, inexorably, guiding, guiding—another heave—

An entire little foal fell into her arms, wet and warm, all legs and nose and wriggling life, and Susannah tumbled back with it into the straw.

"By *God,* Susannah!" Kit sounded ecstatically.

It was only then that Susannah became fully aware of her body and her surroundings again, the tang of straw, the powerful earthy smell of blood and horse, her aching arm and shoulder and back. Sweat glued her hair to her face, her riding habit to her spine. She released the little foal gently, it struggled to its feet, collapsed again, wobbled up onto its four new legs. The mare turned around to nose it, welcoming her baby into the world.

Susannah felt wobbly herself; she straightened with some effort to her feet, feeling Kit's arm beneath her elbow guiding her.

Kit knelt to do a quick examination, the little foal tripped and righted itself a few more times, getting accustomed to the fact that the world was hard and flat and large, not close and warm and wet.

"She's sound...a beautiful little filly." And then Kit rose to his feet, too, and turned to Susannah. The corner of his mouth tilted.

Susannah rubbed her sleeve against her cheek. She felt dazed and light and unaccountably happy. A peaceful sort of happiness, as though she'd finally momentarily satisfied an appetite she hadn't known existed.

They heard voices then, boy voices laughing and swearing, the sounds of scuffling feet.

The stable boys had returned.

When they saw Kit they froze, turned into stone as surely if he were Medusa.

Kit regarded them for a time, expressionless, terrifyingly expressionless, and Susannah felt her own heart knot.

"You *did* know this mare was due to give birth any day?" Kit asked almost pleasantly.

Eyes bugging with fear, they remained silent. One of them darted a look toward the bonnie little foal.

"Answer me."

Susannah risked a sideways glance at Kit. How could one person imbue so much menace into two little words?

"Y-y-es, sir." One of them was brave enough to get the words out.

There was another long silence, broken by the slap of the

mare's tail against her rump, the rustle of little hooves in the straw.

"They could have died," Kit said, almost musingly, "while you were gone. This mare, and her foal. Alone. And it's your responsibility to care for the horses, is it not?"

Susannah was certain the expressions the two boys wore were similar to those turned up to the executioner's ax. They said nothing; no doubt their vocal cords had turned to stone.

"Go," Kit finally said, his voice low and contemptuous. "And don't come back."

They spun on their heels and ran.

Behind Susannah, the mare nudged the little filly, a twin of her mother down to the star between her eyes. She was twitching her miniature tail, learning all about balancing on four legs, and breathing air, and her mother's teats.

Kit stared after the stable boys for a moment, silently, then turned back to the mare and foal. He watched them, quietly, and Susannah watched him.

"I'll have to keep an eye on them for a few days." Kit ran his hand thoughtfully along the sweat-darkened flank of the mare. "But I think they'll do well enough." She could hear the relief in his voice. The warmth.

He turned back toward her and his expression was . . . tentative, almost awkward. As though he couldn't decide what to say.

Susannah doubted *that* happened very often.

"It was a brave thing you did, Susannah."

Something unfamiliar in his eyes warmed Susannah clear through, and at the same time made her feel strangely bare. "I wasn't trying to be brave."

Kit's lovely mouth lifted at the corner. "Which is what *makes* it brave." His expression was still difficult to read. He seemed so somber, almost shy, if she didn't know better. Humble? No, *that* couldn't be. But the warmth in it was unmistakable. "You'll be a little sore tomorrow." He absently reached out and kneaded her upper arm.

Susannah closed her eyes to slits; the kneading felt wonderful. It was almost more intimate than a kiss, but then again, almost nothing seemed intimate in comparison to having one's hand thrust up a horse, and Susannah, at the moment, didn't care.

Kit abruptly dropped his hand. She opened her eyes fully again.

And they stood again quietly together for a moment, simply looking at each other. A peculiar peace stole over Susannah, a lovely, dreamy sort of fullness.

He cleared his throat. "Well, I think we can forego riding and drawing today, Miss Makepeace. *Again.* I'd like to watch these two"—he gestured with his chin at the horses—"for a time. I'm afraid your riding habit is quite ruined."

Susannah looked down; it most certainly was. "I've more of them at home."

For some reason this made him smile and shake his head slowly back and forth.

Susannah rubbed her sticky hands against her already ruined skirt and took another look back at the little filly, trapped and twisted only moments before in her mother's womb, now thirstily taking her first meal. She smiled, felt her heart squeeze sweetly. She would sketch the mother and baby, tomorrow perhaps.

"What will you name her?" she asked.

"I was thinking 'Susannah.'"

That had certainly been quick out of his mouth. His eyes glinted devilishly.

Susannah tipped her head to the side, pretending to mull this. "Perfect," she pronounced finally. "It's the perfect name for such a beautiful creature."

And then she spun prettily, casting a saucy look at him through her lashes over her shoulder, and headed up the path for home.

And as she walked, she cherished the last expression she'd seen on his face. It hadn't been amusement, for a change. Or indifference. Or impatience.

It had been something else entirely.

And a strange, sweet hope bucked inside her.

Chapter Eleven

$\mathcal{S}$leep that night was a deep, endless black well, and Susannah didn't so much fall as plummet into it. It felt natural to wake with the light now, to birdsong and the first sense of the day's weather filling the room. She felt rested to the depths of her soul, a different kind of rest than she'd ever before felt.

Warm again today. What a streak of weather they were having. Susannah lifted herself out of bed, startled to find her arms and back so stiff, and then remembered why: the little filly. *Susannah*. She smiled. She might not have much of a family, but there was now a new little filly named for her. She supposed it was something.

Today...today she'd wear the buttercup-colored muslin, the one that found the gold in her eyes, made them glow almost amber. She knew the viscount would notice. Oh, he'd never *say* anything quite so frivolous. But she knew...she knew he would notice.

He'd liked her hat. The green one. Goodness knows what other remarks were lurking in his full and enigmatic mind, if *that* was the one that slipped out when a horse fell upon him.

Her heart gave a sharp, sweet, peculiar leap.

She slipped the dress on; tightening the laces was a little more difficult this morning, with her stiff limbs, but she got it done. She put the miniature of her mother into an apron pocket; thinking she might show it to Kit. He'd asked, after all; for some reason she wanted him to see it.

She'd just begun her descent when her aunt's voice sang up the stairs.

"Susannah...I have a *surprise* for you..."

Oh, no. She wanted her tea and fried bread as well as something heartier this morning, and she knew they had sausages because the viscount's money had allowed them into the budget. She didn't think she'd ever be able to look at a picnic basket again without flinching. And after the revelation about her father a few nights ago...

No more surprises, please, Aunt Frances.

So she slowed her pace. As she rounded the bed of the stairs, she froze. Her heart clogged her throat.

"Douglas."

She was suddenly very glad she was wearing the buttercup-colored muslin.

"Hello, Susannah." His face was aglow with the sight of her. "You look..." His eyes took her in like a man starved.

"...wonderful," he concluded softly.

At first, she couldn't speak at all. Her heart was kicking like a parade drum. "Thank you, Douglas," she said finally. "You look very...fine, as well."

Oh, and he did. She'd nearly forgotten how handsome Douglas was—could it really have been only a few weeks since she'd seen him?—with his dark hair and fine features, those clear gray eyes that she knew as well as her own.

There could only be one reason he was here. A frisson of anticipation made her breath catch.

Aunt Frances stood next to Douglas, her hands clasped in front of her, her delighted, curious gaze darting from Susannah to Douglas and back again.

They stared at each other for a moment longer before Susannah considered she should probably descend the remaining steps. It *was* lovely to see him, but a bit jarring, too, like... finding a teapot in the bathtub. He didn't seem to belong here, in this small house, in the country.

"He doesn't want *tea*," her aunt said meaningfully. "He wants to go for a *walk*."

Meaning: He wants to be alone with you. Rather urgently.

There was now little doubt in Susannah's mind what Douglas had come for.

For days now she'd felt as though she'd been stretching to reach something up on a high, high shelf, something she couldn't quite see, something she couldn't even identify, something she suspected might have great value, if only she could reach it.

But if Douglas took her away from Barnstable, she could stop stretching. And oddly, at that thought, relief and regret seemed of a piece.

"Leave your coat here, Douglas," she said softly. "My aunt won't mind, and it's already very warm. We'll go for a stroll."

Aunt Frances took Douglas's coat, and her eyes widened and rolled exaggeratedly at the fineness of it, which made Susannah bite back a smile. And then Aunt Frances winked, which thankfully Douglas either didn't notice, or graciously pretended not to notice.

Susannah took Douglas past the roses, and out the front gate, and through the path in the woods, and the silence between them was almost comical in its awkwardness. It had been quite some time since they'd walked together, and then, they'd usually done it arm in arm. They walked side by side, instead; the distance of inches between them felt like miles.

Douglas cleared his throat. "So this is where you live, now?"

"No, I live in a barn, Douglas."

"You live in a *barn*?" And then he saw her expression. "Oh! Ha-ha!" he laughed nervously. "Sorry. I suppose that question *did* sound a bit barmy."

"I'm sorry, too. I should not have made a joke."

How clumsy they were with each other. How nervous and polite. And here Susannah had almost begun to suspect she'd forgotten how to be polite in the way one was polite in the *ton*.

"And how do you find life in Barnstable, Susannah?" Douglas tried again. Very politely.

She considered this question. "Lively." Also very politely.

"Is it?" Douglas looked dubious. They were quiet a while longer, and Susannah heard around them the sounds that had become so familiar: the rush of leaves and rattle of twigs above her as squirrels and birds leaped from branch to branch.

And then suddenly Douglas stopped and whirled on her, and Susannah jumped.

"Oh, enough politeness. Susannah, I miss you terribly."

"Do you?" The words emerged a little breathily. His sudden stop and his words had her heart bumping hard.

"Oh, yes. Nothing is the same, you see." His voice was rushed and ardent. "I haven't laughed quite so much since you've gone. No one *dances* quite the way you do. And no one"—he gathered her hands in his and pulled her into his chest—"*looks* at me quite the way you do...with those...those eyes of yours..."

He trailed off into silence. And then Douglas dropped his gaze to her mouth; it hovered there.

Douglas was going to kiss her.

She was going to let him.

And when his mouth touched hers, it was that same, just-slightly-more-than-chaste kiss she remembered, the kiss that had so intrigued her before with its hint of *more*.

But then, well . . . it *became* a little more.

His tongue crept out to touch her bottom lip, and he pushed himself closer to her. Through his snug trousers, through her fine dress, she could feel part of him stirring against her in an unmistakable, very masculine way.

Hmmm. Douglas was most definitely taking a *liberty*.

She opened her lips a little, partly out of curiosity, partly because it seemed . . . well, the *polite* thing to do. But she couldn't seem to lose herself in the moment; perhaps his mind had been filled with her since he'd jilted her, but her life had become filled with other things. Viscounts and voles and foals. Art and talent and bravery. Things that imposed a distance Douglas would have to cross before she felt comfortable kissing him again, let alone being pressed up against his significant arousal.

Confused, she turned her head abruptly away from his with a shaky little laugh.

Douglas took a deep bracing breath, collecting himself. But he didn't apologize, and he refused to relinquish her hands, even when she gave a little tug.

"Susannah . . . you must know the reason I came."

"I think I have an inkling, but I'd like to hear it from you." She smiled up at him, teasing.

"Well, it's this," his tone was eager, "I thought perhaps I'd buy a home in London for you to live in—"

So it *was* happening. Again, relief and a peculiar regret mingled. How strange it would be to slip back into her old life once more. How odd to treat Barnstable like a dream.

"For *us* to live in, you mean?" she smiled up at him.

Douglas smiled indulgently and lifted her hands, one then the other, to his lips, and then at last released them. "Well, I suppose on occasion I will stay there with you. But I'll of course be expected to live with my wife most of the time."

She stared at him, puzzled.

And then suspicion seeped in and leeched all sensation from her limbs.

"*But* you'll be expected to live with your wife?" she repeated on a nervous laugh.

"Well, yes, of course," Douglas continued, sounding conciliatory. "Amelia. Amelia Henfrey. We're to be married in a month's time, and I'll be expected to live with *her,* naturally. But you do know, of course...Susannah, I would much rather be with you, and I *will* be with you as often as possible."

He smiled down at her winningly, bent to kiss her again.

Susannah jerked her head sideways.

And even over the roaring starting up in her ears, and the hideous rush of pain that gathered around her heart, somehow she got the words out, all in the right order.

"Just to be very clear, Douglas: Are you asking me to be your mistress?"

His brows dipped in genuine confusion. "Well, yes, of course. You know I can't be expected to marry a penni—"

Susannah's hand sailed upward, hard.

And then they stood utterly still, while Susannah watched in awe as the angry red outline of her fingers rose on Douglas's cheek. She looked down at her own numb and stinging palm as though it belonged to someone else entirely.

An unbearable silence skulked by.

"Susannah," he said quietly. "Please lis—"

She couldn't stop the words; they bubbled out like lava. "Who do you think you *are,* Douglas? Do you have *any idea* what I've been through? My arm was up to here"—she thrust out her arm and pointed to her elbow—"*here,* inside a *mare* yesterday—"

"A m-mare?" Douglas flinched backward defensively.

"A *mare,* you *ninny,*" she repeated ferociously. "I've dodged danger, I've had everything I've ever known taken from me...

and do you have any idea what that's *like* Douglas? But I've a sense of myself now. I'm strong, I'm resourceful. I'm *talented*. It seems"—she took in a deep breath, and managed, with a little dignity—"I also have a temper. And I suspect that *I* am more *man* than you will *ever* be."

"Susannah—"

"I want you to go. Go *now*. I never want to see you again."

"But—"

And oh, despite herself—and later she would despise herself for it—she waited, for hope, bloody hope, clung more tenaciously to life than a cockroach. "But *what,* Douglas?" *Say something to make it better, Douglas. Change everything back to the way it was.*

"But—my coat—"

And of all the things he could have possibly said then, perhaps this was the very best, for he had never sounded more hapless and contemptible, and contempt went a long way toward balming her pride, which was so swollen and throbbing it threatened to strangle her.

And yet, even as she stared with contempt into his once-beloved gray eyes, now clouded with genuine hurt and bewilderment, she knew it would have been impossible to change things back to the way they were. And it was her fault: *She* had already changed irrevocably.

"Have your *wife* buy you a new coat, Douglas. Give my regards to Amelia."

$\mathcal{C}\!\sim$

She'd heard of blind rage before. Until today, she hadn't been convinced it existed. Her hands went up to her face in horror, reliving the last few minutes: Douglas's last memory of her would be of her shrieking like a fishwife, her face contorted with fury.

Susannah bent down, scooped up a small stone and hurled it as hard as she could at nothing in particular.

A moment later she heard a dull thud followed by an indignant: *"Ow!"* Oh, dear God.

She squeezed her eyes closed. *Please, no.*

When she opened them again, Kit Whitelaw was standing before her, rubbing his chest and frowning darkly.

What had she come to—*battering* men? She put her hands up to her cheeks. "I'm so sorry—are you—did I—"

She stopped abruptly when a grin slowly spread across his face. "Your arm is good, but your aim needs work, Miss Makepeace. You missed. Care to try again?" He hefted her missile in his hand, then held it out to her invitingly.

She spun on her heel and stormed roughly in the direction of her aunt's house. A moment later, she heard the hurried crunch of footsteps behind her.

"Before you do yourself or anyone else an injury, Miss Makepeace, perhaps you'd like to tell me what's troubling you."

She whirled on him. "If you *must* know, my fiancé— *Douglas*—"

Kit's expression went from teasing to opaque in a blinding instant. "Lovers' quarrel, Miss Makepeace?"

"We aren't *lovers,* it wasn't a *quarrel,* and it's been over for some time. That is, more accurately, he's no longer my fiancé. When my father died, Douglas promptly jilted me, because his *mama* told him to, as the heir to a marquis couldn't *possibly* marry a penniless girl. And today he returned to inform me that he intends to marry my best friend, and to ask me to be his mistress."

This recitation seemed to strike the usually glib viscount dumb. Susannah was strangely gratified: So it *was* every bit as bad as she'd thought it was.

Kit remained thoughtfully quiet for some time. "Do you plan to cry?" He sounded curious.

"No," she said incredulously, as if the very idea was an insult.

He studied her carefully, the tiniest of furrows between his eyes. Then he fished about in his pocket, came up with a handkerchief and held it out to her.

She promptly burst into tears.

"I'm not dis-dis-*traught,* mind you," she choked out. She lowered herself fumblingly to a tipped log.

"Of course not," he agreed equably, calmly. He settled down next to her, stretching his long legs out.

"I'm bloody *fur-fur-ious.*"

"As anyone would be."

"It's j-j-ust ... *everything* that has h-happened, you see ..."

"There's been a good deal."

"He's a bloody *c-c-cad.*"

"The very bloodiest." Kit reached down, selected a twig thoughtfully from the floor of the woods. "Shall I call him out for you?" He said it idly, twiddling the twig between his fingers.

The sobs stopped almost immediately. Susannah slowly turned eyes round with astonishment on him. "You'd d-do that for me?"

Kit rolled and rolled the twig, as though he intended to start a fire with it. "Perhaps I'd only make him bleed a little."

She gave a short laugh, half-bitter, half-startled, and dashed her knuckles roughly across her damp cheek. "You could do that? Not kill him, I mean ... only wound him a bit? Wouldn't that be ... well, difficult?"

He turned away from her for a moment. "Oh, yes," he said, finally. His smile was faint, a rueful, grim thing. "I could do that."

He turned back to find Susannah watching him speculatively,

as if weighing her options. "He isn't worth the danger to you," she decided.

This made him smile. "Your concern for my safety is flattering, Miss Makepeace. But why you'd believe he'd pose any sort of danger to *me*..."

She turned away and unfurled the crumpled handkerchief in her fist; her thumbnail began worrying the embroidered initials on it, CMW, tracing them over and over. Only an occasional forlorn hiccup remained of her storm of tears.

"How do you know that *I'm* not dangerous?" she said suddenly, and slanted him a look from between her lashes.

A little burst of admiration warmed him; he felt like applauding. *Well done, Miss Makepeace. All is not lost if you can still flirt.* "Oh, I've no doubt you are," he assured her. "With stones, at least."

She smiled, a little. And then she sniffed, and dabbed with quiet dignity at her eyes. They said nothing for a time, simply sat together, fingers of sunlight piercing the trees and enclosing them in warmth and swirling dust.

A squirrel chittered irritably overhead, sounding for all the world as if it were shaking its tiny fist at them.

"I slapped his face," she confided suddenly, in almost a whisper. Sounding half-ashamed, half-thrilled.

"Hard?" Mildly said.

"I'm afraid so."

"Good. Then you left him in no doubt as to how you feel about his...proposal."

"No," she said sadly. "No doubt."

She fell silent again, and he honored it. Odd how peaceful the aftermath of a storm of tears could be.

Susannah smoothed the sodden handkerchief out in her lap, over and over, as though preparing to lay a table on it. "Have you ever been in love?" she asked softly.

He almost laughed. Oh, how like a woman to ask such a question. Flippant words poised to leap from his tongue.

But then he turned and took in her mottled, flushed cheeks, her eyes still brilliant with tears. She was trying to discover, he realized, how much he knew of broken hearts.

He inhaled deeply, exhaled. All right, then.

"Yes," he told her gently.

Her eyes widened; she was seeing him anew, perhaps. And then she looked swiftly away, as if it was difficult to see him this way.

"Do you love Douglas?" He was surprised to find himself asking it, but suddenly it seemed imperative to know. He'd been prodding at this young woman for days, teasing her, unfolding her, in part for his own entertainment. And discovering, to his surprise and discomfiture, there was much more to her than he'd suspected.

But he'd never really given any thought to the content of her heart.

"I do," she said softly. "I did. That is, I thought I did. Which, I suppose, amounts to the same thing, doesn't it?"

He was struck silent by the bravery of her words. "Perhaps it does," he agreed softly.

He thought about the poor young buffoon who'd just been slapped and sent packing, a young man who thought the solution to his own misery was to keep Susannah—who loved friends and gaiety, who was more passionate and brave and unique than even she knew—in a house in London and attend her only every now and then. Like a pet parrot.

He must have tensed, for the twig he'd been twiddling snapped between his fingers.

Kit released the pieces of it to the floor of the woods, and then searched for words, something of comfort and use to her. God only knows, he wasn't any good with diplomacy, or soft platitudes. He only knew how to offer his own truths.

"I know it's difficult now, Susannah...," he began hesitantly, "but try...try not to think too badly of Douglas, if you can bear it. Young men are so often at the mercy of their parents and society. I expect he thought he was making things better for both of you. And...well, he may always regret the loss of you."

She lifted her head and gazed at him, studying him like a map. He submitted to it without blinking, lost momentarily in the lovely complexity of her eyes. All those colors. Like the pond dappled in morning light, those eyes were, the shifting play of green and gold; tears had made spikes of her chestnut lashes. It was all he could not to brush a thumb across them, taste the salt of them, to run the cool back of his hand against her flushed cheek, soothing it. He wondered why it had begun to seem more unnatural *not* to touch her...than to touch her.

At that thought, something kicked sharply inside him, once. And then it unfurled, slowly, slowly, filling him with an ache both unutterably sweet...and as old as time.

It occurred to him then: *She might very well be right. She might just be a little dangerous after all.*

"Who is Caro?" she asked suddenly.

Hell. He narrowed his eyes at her by way of reply, and she smiled, amused at him and pleased with herself for the ambush.

"Do you want to know the worst of it?" She paused, and took in a steadying breath, released it. "When Douglas appeared this morning, I thought...*at last,* I *have* someone. I'll have my old life back. I'll have a family. Did you know that all I have of my old life are my clothes? And those only because I threatened a man with a vase for them."

"They're excellent dresses," he assured her gently.

She smiled at that, and shook her head much the way he shook his head at her every time she showed up for a day's work exquisitely groomed. "They certainly are," she agreed with him, in the spirit of accuracy. "Anyhow, when Douglas came today, I thought...well, he'll propose, and then I suppose I'll finally have a family of my own. Because a few days ago my aunt told me that my father...wasn't even my real father."

"James wasn't your father?" The quick intensity in his voice made Susannah start a little.

"No. I asked about my...my talent, as you suggested. And my aunt...well, all Aunt Frances knows is that my father went away one day, and when he returned, he had a very little girl with him: *me*. He never explained it to anyone, he never married as far as anyone knows, so you see, I've no idea at all who I truly am. And now..." She made a sound; it was almost a laugh, except laughs were seldom so ironic and heartbreaking. "I have no one."

But Kit felt the hair on his arms lifting. He knew, somehow, the answer to his next question. "Susannah, the name of the town where your father found you...do you know it?"

"Gorringe. Named, apparently, by a duke who—"

"—was looking for a rhyme for 'orange.'"

She looked at him in surprise.

He wasn't surprised.

He shifted his gaze into the leaves overhead instead. It was like looking up at a collection of puzzle pieces, the sharp-edged oak leaves bunched thickly but still cut through with light, and he thought the metaphor apt: For all he had was a collection of facts and coincidences, and he couldn't quite make them join; there were gaps between all of them. There was a girl sitting next to him who had lost everything twice over now. James had not been her father, and he had been killed after mentioning Morley to Kit. And now it seemed as though someone was trying to either kill Susannah, or at the very least, thoroughly frighten her.

And Caroline had written him from Gorringe, shortly after she'd disappeared, no doubt with Thaddeus Morley.

"Here is my mother," Susannah said shyly. "You wanted to see her. I thought I'd show it to you today."

Very gently, she settled the miniature of her mother into his open palm.

A beautiful woman. It was Susannah's face, or very nearly.

Kit needed to look away from her to make his decision; up into the trees again.

It was maddening. The answer hovered on the periphery of his vision, but it dodged away every time he spun to face it. Excitement and an overwhelming frustration surged.

Perhaps he *was* going mad. Perhaps his suspicion of Morley *was* unreasonable. Perhaps his instincts weren't instincts at all, but the delusions of a man too long immersed in the necessary, disciplined paranoia required of a spy.

And perhaps pigs fly.

The threat of Egypt hung over his head like the sword of Damocles. But when he looked again at Susannah Makepeace, he knew he didn't have a choice.

"Let's forget about drawing today, Susannah. I'll take you to Gorringe instead."

Chapter Twelve

ॐ

It was two hours to Gorringe over extravagantly rutted roads, which Kit suspected might be as effective as moats for keeping visitors away from the town. The journey might have gone more quickly on horseback, but he wasn't sure his ribs and arm could withstand the ride, and he preferred the relative shelter of a coach to making open targets of both himself and Susannah, since he was convinced someone was determined to hurt her. He was armed with a pistol tucked into his boot, another inside his coat alongside a sheathed knife, and the supreme confidence that he could best almost anyone—or two, or three—who attempted to accost them, despite the fact that his arm was freshly out of a sling.

At last, a short stone bridge arcing across a stream took them into the town, and Gorringe bloomed into sight before them.

Gorringe was a lovely surprise. Small, clean whitewashed houses, huddled together like gossiping neighbors along a cobblestone road that clattered very agreeably beneath the carriage wheels. Flower boxes burst with bright summer blooms; a few shops—a bookshop, a tavern, a cheesemaker—appeared on the main road. Against all odds, Gorringe seemed a neat and thriving little town, very self-contained and peaceful in its way.

"Does anything look familiar to you?" he said to Susannah. She'd gone very still, tense. She gripped the edge of the seat.

"I wish I could say yes," she answered hesitantly. "It's lovely, isn't it? It looks as though one could be happy here."

The wistfulness in her voice cut him. He'd always had the luxury of knowing he was part of an ancient lineage, that he had cousins and uncles and aunts spread all over England. Many of his ancestors were complete reprobates, but those were offset by numerous noble Whitelaw achievements and a sprinkling of genuine heroes. He had two sisters, who both loved and annoyed him and were loved and annoyed by him in turn, a father, and a whole treasury of memories of his mother.

A flash of jeweled colors winked on the edge of his vision, and this was how he found the church: It presided over the small homes from the center of town, solemnly medieval and yet surprisingly elegant, inset with stained-glass windows. The windows were a bit of a surprise, as so many had been destroyed years ago, when the church was eager to eradicate all traces of popery. Hence, images of the Virgin Mary and the saints were scarce. Perhaps these windows had been spared because their subject matter was more neutral.

"I thought we'd begin with the church. They may have records of your birth, Susannah, if you were born here."

She didn't answer him. He could see the anticipation in the set of her jaw, in her pale lips. Her fist was closed possessively over the miniature of her mother. He said nothing more; he knew she was too tightly wound to welcome reassurances right now.

They proceeded up a path that cut through a tidy churchyard featuring headstones both ancient and new. Susannah glanced at them and quickly glanced away: her mother, or her real father, could very well be beneath one of them.

Kit secretly loved churches. The pews of this one glowed darkly, seasoned by centuries of prayer and polished by centuries of shifting bums, and the stained-glass windows threw brilliant green and red and blue shapes down onto the floor. He'd been right: These *were* simple windows: three of them on either side of the room, roses and lilies twined around the borders of each. The words FAITH, HOPE, and CHARITY, were etched in extravagant Gothic lettering across each one.

"Hello." A politely cautious voice came from the apse. "May I help you?"

The vicar shuffled toward them. His head was tiny, his neck fleshy and boneless-looking, like a turtle's, and his vestments swamped him. When he was near them, his chin moved up and up and up, as though some internal machine was slowly levering it. His gaze finally arrived on Kit's face.

"Good afternoon, my lord," he said pleasantly. "You *are* a 'my lord,' aren't you, son? I'm the Vicar of Gorringe, Mr. Sumner."

The vicar had clearly reached that satisfying stage of life when he didn't particularly care what he said to anyone. Kit, personally, was looking forward to that particular stage.

"We are visitors to your fair town, Mr. Sumner. I was just noticing your windows—they're splendid."

"Aren't they? They aren't original, you know. A . . . generous benefactor donated them some years ago, along with our mausoleum behind the church. I suppose he believed he'd be buried there, but God had other plans for him, as He so often does. Is there something I can help you with today?"

Kit had noticed the special warmth given to the words "generous" and "benefactor."

"We rather hoped you might be able to assist us with a

query. I've been known to be a generous benefactor, on occasion. I might even require a mausoleum some day."

"I'll certainly try to help, sir."

Susannah, in a mute form of blurting, thrust out her hand with the miniature in it. Kit supplied the question: "Do you know this woman?"

Hesitating a moment, the vicar gently took the miniature and gazed down at it for an inordinately long time, perhaps leafing through decades of memories.

"Time does get to blurring, you see, at my age." His eyes peered up at them serenely. "Things, and places, and people all run together..." He drifted off, gazing toward the windows.

There was a long silence. Acting on a suspicion, Kit leaned forward and gave a discreet little sniff. Wine had most definitely been part of the vicar's midday meal.

"All run together...?" he prompted politely, before Susannah's head shot from her neck like a cannonball out of impatience.

"Er, yes. All run together. But I aver, you're the *spit* of your mama, young lady."

The expression on Susannah's face was glorious. The words lit her from within like one of the stained-glass windows. Kit felt again a tiny, sweet clutch in his chest.

"You knew my mama?" Hope made Susannah's voice weak.

"Pretty, pretty thing, she was," the vicar mused dreamily. "Had a daughter baptized here. We didn't see much of your mother in church, otherwise, I'm afraid, and I cannot quite recall her name. It's been some years, though sometimes it feels like only yesterday. But then, of course it wasn't yesterday, at all, was it, because look at you—all grown." He beamed at them.

Kit hoped for the parishioners' sake that the curate gave the sermons, not the vicar. He hoped there *was* a curate.

"Anna," Susannah said excitedly. "Her name was Anna!"

The vicar frowned. "No, that wasn't it."

"But—" Susannah glanced at Kit, who widened his eyes and gave a slight shake of his head, and she wisely decided not to argue the point. "But you *do* remember her? What was she like?"

"A pretty, pretty thing." The vicar sounded surprised to have to say it again.

Kit intervened quickly. "One more question for you, sir: Do you by any chance recall a woman by the name of Caroline Allston?"

He felt Susannah's eyes on him, quite as intense as a pair of torches.

"Caroline Allston...Caroline Allston..." the vicar mused. "Can't say that I do. Was she pretty?" he asked hopefully.

"Very." Well, it was true, wasn't it? And "pretty" did seem to be the thing that branded someone into the vicar's memory. "Dark hair, dark eyes, fair skin. Very difficult to forget once you saw her. Was perhaps about eighteen years old when she first lived in Gorringe."

"Miss Allston does sound pretty, sir. But no, I cannot recall anyone specifically by that name. You're welcome to look at the records, as you don't look the sort to steal them."

Damned with faint praise. The vicar led them back to a room that housed the church records: shelves of books recording births, deaths, marriages, and baptisms—any occasion the church at Gorringe had marked.

"I'll leave you to it, then. I ask that you come to see me before you leave so that I may lock up after you."

❦

"When were you born, Susannah, do you know? How old are you?" Kit was tracing a finger over the spines of the registries, looking for likely years.

Susannah didn't speak for a moment. Her mind was obsessively playing and replaying his words of five minutes ago. And finally she could contain them no longer.

" 'Was she pretty?' " She mimicked the vicar's creaky tones. " 'Very,' " she answered, in a very good imitation of the viscount's own baritone.

Kit snorted a laugh.

But really, Kit had waxed almost lyrical about Caroline Allston—*Caro,* no doubt. Susannah wondered if Caro was carved on the viscount's heart the way it was on the oak, scarred and thick with age.

"I'm twenty—at least I thought I was," she said coolly, though why she thought she was entitled to coolness was beyond her understanding.

"And what day do you normally celebrate your birthday?" he said, as though her tone hadn't changed at all.

"The twelfth of August."

"Soon, then," he said cheerfully.

Ah, now he was trying to distract her. And she did love birthdays. Thought this pending birthday might be a trifle less climactic than her others, given that she'd held a grand party and received the gift of a horse for her last one.

Something occurred to her that swept petty jealousy right from her head.

"What if my name isn't really Susannah?" The thought horrified her. "What if my father—that is, James Makepeace—changed it? What if my name is Myrtle, or Agnes, or—"

"Something splendid or exotic, like Alexandra, or Katarina?"

Suddenly she felt strangely light-headed. "I could be anyone at all," she murmured, half to herself. "Anyone."

She felt oddly formless, unanchored, as though she could drift away or be absorbed into the air like vapor if she didn't soon find some bit of information, an actual name, or a mother, or a date of birth, to serve as ballast.

"Are you going to faint?"

Kit was watching her intently; he sounded more curious than concerned. As though she were a mystery to analyze, rather like voles. She had to admit, however, that she found this approach bracing. It made every surprise or upset or triumph seem merely part of an interesting puzzle, and it sobered her rather quickly.

"No."

He regarded her solemnly another moment, ascertaining the truth of this. Then he gave her the sort of smile she could make a crutch of forever: reassuring, warm as an arc of light.

Someday she might not blush when he smiled at her. Today would not be the day.

They returned to working in silence for a time, paging through the registries, running their fingers along the names. Fortunately Gorringe was a small town. Unfortunately, a good half of the women in the town seemed to have been named Anna, and they all seemed to have been abundantly fertile. None yet had given birth to a Susannah.

"There *are* other names in the world," Susannah groused. "Mary—perfectly acceptable name. Martha. There's another one."

"Myrtle," Kit suggested absently from over his book.

"Precisely," Susannah agreed. "You'd think these people would have heard of one or two of them."

The faded writing and poor light in the room taxed their eyes as they pored over the lists of names, whole lives, hundreds of them, summarized by three or four simple notations: birth, marriage, more births, death. Despite the business at hand, Susannah's thoughts were evenly divided along two tracks, when really they should have been focused on the one.

And then, because she couldn't help it:

" *'Difficult to forget,'* " she mimicked. It was a spot-on imitation of Kit's low, refined voice.

Kit looked up from his work and stared at her. "*Is* something troubling you, Miss Makepeace?" he asked mildly.

Oh, she hated that mild tone. "*Who* is Caro? And why did you ask about her?"

He returned his head to the book he was perusing. "You ask that almost as though you expect me to answer it." He sounded amused, distracted. Dismissive.

And this infuriated her. "You know everything about me—"

"Correction: We know nothing at all about you."

"You know what I mean! And *I* have a reason. You are simply secretive because... you are *afraid* to be otherwise. You hide from *everything*."

His head slowly, slowly lifted up.

I take it back! she wanted to say immediately, because his expression frightened her. His eyes fairly glittered, hot and blue; he was furious, this time at her. But something taut in his face made her think that she had somehow hurt him, too. Perhaps even... unnerved him. As though she had somehow unwittingly reached a place in him he didn't know how to defend, and so he could only offer up this silence.

She couldn't look away. He *wouldn't* look away.

When he finally spoke, she flinched. But his words weren't the kind she'd been expecting.

" 'August of 1799,' " he said. " 'Born to Anna Smith: Susannah Faith.' "

Her heart nearly stopped. "What? *Where?* I... I exist!"

She forgot she was frightened of him and scurried over to his side, and his posture eased as he moved aside to allow her to read the entry. "Who was my father?"

He paused a beat. "No father is listed, Susannah," he said gently.

She disliked the gentleness, and the implication. *Perhaps you were born on the wrong side of the blanket, Susannah.* "Perhaps my father was killed in the war!" she said indignantly.

She doubted anyone had ever said that sentence quite as hopefully. Kit looked at her askance.

"Susannah Smith...Susannah Smith..." she tried out the name. "It's rather nice, don't you think? I wonder who my father was?"

"One hopes his last name *was* Smith," Kit said dryly. Clearly he was slightly less romantic and optimistic than Susannah. "It rather sounds like an alias. Now on to the deaths."

"But we've only just discovered I was actually born! Can I not savor it a moment?"

"And also have you home in time for your supper, Susannah? I think not. I won't have your aunt worrying about you. Deaths it is."

Twenty minutes later they'd discovered that no Smiths had expired in Gorringe, at least none that were recorded in the church registry.

Susannah was giddy with possibility; her name was a brush she could use to paint her whole life over. "What if...what if they're still alive? What if...James Makepeace kidnapped me, and my parents couldn't meet the ransom, and—"

"Then Makepeace decided to keep you, as, after all, he'd always wanted a daughter with very expensive tastes, and your parents gave up, because they couldn't afford to keep you in dresses?" Kit suggested. "One thing at a time, Miss Makepeace. We know that you were born here; it appears as though your parents neither married nor died here, though we can explore the cemetery if you wish. But we can move on to our next task: Trying to find someone in the town who may have known Anna Smith. I know just the place to start."

⌒

This tavern was thick-timbered, dark, scented with a few hundred years of wood and cigar and cooking smoke. Two men were leaning across the table over a rough-hewn chessboard and chess pieces smooth with use and age. It looked the sort of establishment that welcomed both men and women; it probably served a decent supper, Kit surmised. As it was the middle of the day, a few men were sprinkled about the tables enjoying a lunch of sausages and potatoes and ale. They looked up and continued looking, though not in any hostile sort of way, when Susannah and Kit walked in.

Kit steered Susannah directly to the bar. "Good afternoon, sir."

"Good afternoon, to you, sir," the barkeep, a wiry man with thinning hair, volunteered cheerily. "Name's Lester. What can I do for you today? Good meal? Ale's good. My brew is famous."

"Good afternoon, Mr. Lester. I am Mr. White. I was wondering whether you knew this woman, sir. She lived in Gorringe some years ago, 1802 or so. We think her name is Anna Smith."

He held out the miniature, and the barkeep perused it with the squinting frown specific to those who would soon need spectacles to read anything at all. "Anna Smith…Anna Smith…*Frank!*" Mr. Lester bellowed. Kit winced and Susannah jumped a little. "He's hard of hearing, ye see," he apologized to the two of them. One of the men playing chess turned slowly around.

"D'yer ever know an Anna Smith? 'Round about…'oh-two, ye said?"

"Wasn't she the gel what 'ad a brother come to visit now and agin? Fine cattle—remember that 'orse, Bunton?"

The other man lifted his head from the chessboard. "Oh,

that *was* one fine animal! Nivver saw the likes in these parts. And he come in that fancy contraption sometimes—"

"That open coach, like—a broosh?"

Ah, men, Kit thought, amused by his own gender. *Can't remember a man's name, or a woman's name, but they'll remember a man's horse and barouche for decades.*

"I recognize 'er face, guv—'ard to forget a face like that, ye see—but I saw 'er but a few times. Kept to 'erself, like. Dinna know who else might have known 'er. She lived 't the end of town. But you know who did know 'er?" He paused and glanced sideways at Susannah, then gave Kit a long meaningful look, which Kit interpreted correctly: He didn't want to repeat it in front of the lady. Intriguing. Kit nodded almost imperceptibly, giving permission to say it.

"'er name's Daisy Jones," he said sotto voce.

Good Lord. Kit was impressed. "*The* Daisy Jones?"

The man nodded vigorously. "Lived 'ere in Gorringe before she made a…a…name fer 'erself."

"Who on earth is Daisy Jones?" Susannah was impatient.

The men ignored her. "Last I 'eard she was in London."

"Oh, she's still in London, all right," Kit confirmed. The men exchanged wicked, manly grins and Frank turned back to his chessboard.

"*Who* is Daisy Jones?" Susannah tried again, the irritation amplified.

Kit pretended not to hear her. "And did you by any chance know of a woman named Caroline Allston? Was here about fifteen years ago? Dark hair, dark eyes, pretty—"

"Difficult to forget," Susannah interjected crossly. "Once you see her—don't forget to tell him that."

The barkeep gave Kit a commiserating look that said: *Women.* "Can't say that I did, guv. Sorry about that. *Frank!*" he bellowed again. Kit winced.

Frank turned around again at a leisurely pace.

"D'yer know of a woman name of Caroline Allston?"

"She was *very pretty*," Susannah supplied, loudly, for Frank's benefit.

Frank ruminated on this for a time. "Can't say as I did, guv," he said. "'Nuther cove were in 'ere t'other day askin' the verra same question."

Kit was fairly certain he knew the answer to this question, but he thought he'd ask it, anyway. "This cove—do you remember his name?"

"Didna say, guv. Handsome, though. Fine figure of a man."

The men at the other tables broke into jeers of laughter at this. " '*Fine figure of a man!*' " they bellowed, slapping their tables.

"I'm only *sayin'*," Frank muttered defensively.

John Carr, Kit thought with resignation. He'd somehow followed Kit's leads about Lockwood to Gorringe.

"Thank you, sir. You've been most helpful." Kit proffered a few coins to the barkeep.

The man waved the coins away. "Oh, no need, no need. But I'll take yer money if I can give yer wife and yerself some lunch."

Wife! The word was so jarring that Kit pulled back his handful of coins in confusion.

Susannah was smiling, pleased at his discomfiture. "Give the man his money, dear."

❧

Clunk. Clunk.

Two plates of sausages and potatoes and two tankards of foaming ale were deposited with some ceremony on the table in front of each of them. Susannah stared at her plate, then gave the sausages an experimental poke with her fork. She'd never before eaten in a pub; she'd never before been treated to a tankard of ale, for that matter. She peered into it. It was certainly pretty: dark golden, with a pale silky head.

Kit was watching her poke at her meal. "You put them in your *mouth*," he explained. "I recommend cutting them into pieces first." In direct contrast to his recommendation, he stabbed his sausage with his fork and bit off the end of it.

She gave the sausage another halfhearted poke.

"You're not hungry, Miss Makepeace?" he asked, when he'd swallowed.

"It's just..." She couldn't eat until she knew. "Confound it, who is Daisy Jones? You *must* tell me. If she knew my mother..." *And who is Caro?* But she hadn't the courage to ask that question yet again.

Kit took a long quaff of his ale, as if fortifying himself, and leaned back in his chair, studying her, his face lit with some secret amusement. She heard the click of chess pieces being knocked off the board behind them in the silence that followed.

"Daisy Jones..." She could almost hear Kit sorting through a selection of words in his mind. "...Is an opera dancer." He was struggling not to smile.

Susannah narrowed her eyes at him. "No, she isn't. She's something much worse, isn't she? I can tell."

"Or much better. I suppose it all depends on whether you're a man...or a *clergy*man." He was laughing silently now.

"It's not funny! If my mother was the friend of an opera dancer..." She trailed off when a suspicion struck. "Are *you* friends with opera dancers?"

"It's difficult *not* to be friends with opera dancers. Opera dancers are very friendly."

She almost laughed. But then she thought of what he might

do with opera dancers . . . and an astonishing pair of feelings reared:

Jealousy that someone else would be able to freely touch him.

And an extremely perverse wish that she might, for even a moment, be an opera dancer, so that she could freely touch him, too.

Oh God, she now knew it was almost certainly true: Her mother must have been an opera dancer. For no one but the daughter of an opera dancer would have those sorts of thoughts. She'd almost certainly inherited her "passion," such as it was, and all these wayward impulses, from her mother.

"What if my *mother* was . . . was an opera dancer?" she said in a whisper.

Kit stopped chewing. "Well . . . would it matter to you? Would you still want to know about her?"

She thought about this. "Yes. It would matter to me—how could it not? But yes, I would still want to know."

"All right, then. Eat your lunch." He resumed devouring his own.

She watched him eat for a moment, fascinated. There was nothing fastidious about the way he ate; it was purposeful and practical and astonishingly fast, but not the least bit untidy. He ate as though it were his last meal.

"Would you be shocked?" she asked him.

"If you ate your lunch? I might be."

"If my mother was an opera dancer."

"On the contrary. I'd be *delighted*." He looked up and smiled at her expression. "Come now, Miss Makepeace. Very little shocks me."

"Except the word 'wife,' " she said tartly.

He stopped chewing; regarded her across the table with that vivid blue stare. His expression was difficult to read, but it was definitely not what she would have called warm. More...considering. Specifically, as though he were considering whether or not to spear her with a fork.

It's your fault! she wanted to blurt. He was forever coming at her with all his little challenges and feints, which worked to shake her more controversial thoughts loose, and then out they came.

She supposed, however, if he could do that so easily, she was engaged in far too many controversial thoughts.

No doubt because her mother *had* been an opera dancer.

"Are you going to drink your ale?" he said finally.

"Some of it," she said airily. She lifted it up, took a long sip, and then coughed until her eyes teared.

With dignity, she brushed her hand across her eyes, then pushed the ale across to the now smiling viscount. And then she cut the sausage in half, and deposited half on his plate. He looked as pleased as if Christmas had just arrived, which for some reason pleased her just as much.

❧

It had been some time since Kit had done anything quite so ordinary as promenade on a beautiful day with a pretty girl.

"Give me your arm," he said to Susannah.

"Why, your *lordship*—" she teased.

He frowned darkly at her, which made her bite back a smile, and she tucked her gloved hand into his arm. He felt faintly ridiculous and smug all at once; it seemed right, oddly peaceful—a pub lunch with a lovely girl, a stroll after it. The crowds were thickening at this end of the street; a summer fair was in progress, and stalls offering ribbons and sweets and games were lined up on the cobblestones, cheerful attendees jockeying to get a look at them. He wished they had time to linger, to poke about. It had been ages since he'd lingered any-where purposelessly, ages since he'd wanted to, really.

Their carriage was just coming into sight when Kit saw the man coming toward them, head lowered, moving at a casual clip like everyone else in the crowd, his head turning about aimlessly, admiring booths, deciding where to linger, perhaps.

As he drew closer to Kit and Susannah, he glanced up from underneath his hat, slipped his hand inside his coat.

And the world narrowed to a glint in the man's hand.

Kit twisted his body in front of Susannah before the knife struck. He flung his arm up to block the blade, felt the bite of it through his coat across his forearm and bicep, and kicked out, hard, catching the bastard in the knee. But the knife flashed up again as the man crashed to the ground, and Kit dropped and half-rolled to the side to duck it.

In the moment he'd looked away, the man had slipped off into the crowd, dodging, weaving neatly and quickly, never really breaking into a run, never causing more than a head or two to turn in his direction. In other words, he wasn't new to this sort of thing. He was a professional.

Kit sprang upright, reached out for Susannah, closed his hands over her arms and pulled her soft body into his chest so tightly he could feel the hammer of her heart against his ribs. She was white-faced, but not in shock; the color was even now returning to her cheeks.

"Are you all right?" he demanded quietly.

He wasn't, quite; his arm was already hurting like a bastard now. *Same damn arm.* He was fairly certain it wasn't a seri-ous wound; his coat had taken the brunt of the strike. Still, he would need to see to it.

A couple strolling toward the festivities gazed at them with some concern. "He's had a bit too much ale," Susannah whispered to the woman, who looked amused and sympathetic, and turned her head discreetly away.

"I think you're bleeding," she said to Kit, sounding faintly accusing.

"It's only a—"

"You're *bleeding*." She sounded furious now, near tears. "We'll go to the tavern. We'll see to your arm there."

He half-smiled. "Yes, sir."

"Don't you *dare* make light of this. You make light of *everything*. You could have been *killed*. And it's because of me, wasn't it? I know that now. It's because of me."

Her voice trailed off. She jerked her head, not wanting him to witness her tears yet again; she tried to pull away from him. He released her.

"Yes," he told her gently. "I think it may very well be."

"You could have been *killed*." She said it again, softly. Her hand rose up; for one astonishing moment, he thought she meant to touch his face. Perhaps he looked alarmed, because she dropped her hand to her side again, curled it into a fist instead, lowered her head, took in a long breath, steadying herself. He watched, admiring every bit of it.

"Thank you for saving my life again," Susannah said with some dignity.

He couldn't help it: He did smile then, though the burning pain in his damned arm made it a little more difficult than usual. "Not at all, Miss Makepeace. Or whoever you are. It's always a pleasure to save your life each and every time. You're having a very eventful day, aren't you?"

She smiled a little thinly. "You're not a naturalist."

"I am," he disagreed, startled.

"But that's not all you are."

"I was a soldier," he allowed.

"But that's not all you are."

He hadn't yet outright lied to her. And for some reason, though he could easily, colorfully lie in the name of an assignment, it seemed important not to ever directly lie to her.

"No," he admitted.

She gazed up at him and said nothing more, knowing, perhaps, his limits. She seemed entirely composed now.

Perhaps she was growing a little too accustomed to danger.

With this thought a sizzling fury jagged through his veins, hampering his breathing.

"All of it. The coach...the adder...the horse...Why does someone want to kill me?" She sounded a little awed.

He almost smiled again. Almost. Fury and pain weren't conducive to smiling.

"I was wondering the very same thing. You must be tremendously important, Susannah, if someone wants to kill you." He thought he'd try for a joke.

"I thought that went without saying." Almost breezily said.

And damned if she didn't actually look a little amused.

Kit looked down at her, and felt another sharp little poke in the vicinity of his heart, an uncomfortable reminder that he did indeed have one. And with a breathlessness that had nothing to do with the fact that he'd just been rolling on the ground with a knife-wielding attacker, he realized the fact that Susannah was still warm and breathing and smiling up at him made him light-headed with a quiet elation.

I'm probably just losing blood.

And again, the puzzle pieces were before him, but he couldn't quite make them fit. He suspected that it would now be more dangerous to stop searching than to leave it.

Damn his father and Egypt, anyway. Someone had just tried to thrust a knife into Susannah Makepeace. And it *wasn't* a coincidence, he was certain, that someone had done the very

same thing to James Makepeace, not to mention Richard Lockwood fifteen years ago.

"I don't know who's trying to kill you, Susannah. But they'll
certainly have cause to regret the attempt when I find out. And
I will."

$$\mathcal{C}\!\!\sim$$

"Back so soon, Mr. White?"

Susannah spoke before Kit could. "We were wondering if
we might trouble you for a basin of water and a room for just an
hour or so?"

Somehow taking charge of this situation at least helped her
feel a little less helpless, and not as though someone had been
trying to kill her since she set foot in the county, and not as if
this man had spent the past several days saving her life.

"Just an *'hour or so,'* eh?" he said to Kit, with a wink, who
gave him a rakish smile and a return wink, as he held the slit
edges of his sleeve discreetly closed. Susannah could feel heat
in her cheeks, which probably did nothing but convince the barkeep of what they were about to get up to, but she held her head
haughtily as he led them to a room. He left them with a basin of
water and another wink.

Kit stripped off his coat and shirt with unself-conscious
alacrity and twisted around to look at his arm.

She'd seen him completely undressed before, but that
had been at a safe distance. From a few feet away, his beauty
stunned. There wasn't a spare ounce of flesh on him; hard, distinct muscles were cut in his back and chest and arms, and of
course he was covered all over in that smooth, pale gold skin.
She saw scars on him now that she was closer, a long white line,
puckered at the edges scored a shoulder blade; a roughly round

patch of skin, thick and white, on his back, closer to the top of his trousers. War had done that to him, no doubt. A bruise turning greenish spread over his chest, where the horse had fallen on him; and a new angry red line slashed across his forearm and up over his bicep.

What a sharp knife it must have been to cut through his coat and shirt and skin. How much more easily it would have sliced through her.

He might be a quicksilver man, maddeningly glib, unnervingly skilled, but that angry red line proved he was as vulnerable as any other human being, as temporary. He'd flung his body in front of hers, to take the knife meant for her, but in the end blood flowed in his veins the same as anyone's, and could be spilled just as easily.

Well, nearly as easily. She'd watched him spin and kick and duck, and she simply couldn't imagine Douglas, for instance, doing that. And if she'd been promenading with an actual naturalist, no doubt she'd be dead by now.

He looked up, startled, and then a little abashed, as though he'd just recalled she was there. "It's *blood*," he half-warned, half-apologized. "I'm sorry, I didn't think. I shouldn't have—"

"*Your* blood," she said. The words came out through a knot in her throat.

He regarded her levelly for a moment, a tiny crease between his brows, as though he was worried yet again that she might faint. And then he reached for the basin of water, and took the hem of his shirt in his teeth.

"Then again," he said, and tore a bandage from the hem, "you're *accustomed* to seeing me in the undress, aren't you, Miss Makepeace?"

Wicked man.

"One *time* does not make one accustomed." That was certainly an understatement.

He opened his mouth and for a moment it seemed as though he intended to say something typically Kit, but he stopped himself and looked back at her instead, his eyes suddenly guarded. And the fact that he had stopped himself made her profoundly aware that they were in a room together, alone, and one of them was without a shirt, and that he had realized the implications of precisely the same thing.

"Give the water to me," she tried, casually. "I'll do it. I can see the wound better than you can."

He looked almost as uncertain as she felt. "It's blood," he warned again, weakly.

"I had *this hand* inside a horse the other day." She lifted it up.

His eyes brightened at the comparison. "I hope I'm an improvement."

"Somewhat. At least it's your *arm* we're interested in."

He snorted a short pleased laugh and sat down on the bed. When she drew near the rich musk of him wrapped around her again: shaving soap, ale, and that delicious, darker, something— *him.* It might as well have been opium for what it did to the run of her thoughts.

Focus. She took up one of the rags he'd made, and there was silence for a time, apart from the quiet dip of a rag into the water, and the trickle of water back into the basin, which was pinkening now with his blood. He held obediently still, like a little boy, his eyes calmly fixed on the white wall ahead of him, and he didn't flinch at all. Perhaps it hurt very little compared to whatever had put the other scars on his back.

She bathed him, but the rhythm of the rag dipping into the water slowed, as she wondered why everything he did— blinking, breathing in and out—seemed more significant when *he* did it than when any other human did.

A minute, perhaps more, passed before she became aware

she'd stopped swabbing altogether, and had been standing very still instead, watching the fair, fernlike trail that traveled from his flat belly up between his ribs rise and fall, rise and fall, with his quickening breathing.

He turned his head, slowly, slowly lifted his eyes up to hers.

This ... *this* was desire. Not the near-chaste kiss pressed upon her earlier today by another man, but this thing that made a tyrant of her senses, that made it seem absurd to stand this close to him and not taste the smooth curve of his shoulder, not trail a finger along the hair that began between his ribs and disappeared into his trousers. This thing that sealed the two of them in heated, fraught silence; that suddenly made thought seem pointless, even frivolous beyond words.

But in this moment it didn't matter at all to Susannah whether Kit had made love to one woman or a million, it didn't matter at all to her whether he saw her as just a body from whom to take pleasure. She didn't care whether he was here for her sake, or for the sake of Caroline Allston. She wanted him with an incinerating ferocity, because in a sense it was all she had to give to him.

His eyes read hers. His chest expanded, sank, with a long, unsteady breath.

I'm lost.

"Thank you," he said softly. And turned away from her. And stood.

"Use this piece to make a bandage"—he gestured to a shred of his shirt—"and wind it snugly, but not too snugly, or my circulation will be impaired, and my arm will fall off. And that would be inconvenient, to say the least."

A familiar glib lilt to his words. The moment was gone as if it had never been.

He *was* a bloody gentleman, then. The mad longing slowly released its grip on her, leaving behind a shamed empty fluttering in the pit of her stomach. Perhaps later she would feel grateful to him, but now she simply felt ashamed: not for having wanton thoughts, but because she'd so brazenly given him an opportunity, one that he clearly wanted, and he'd chosen not to take it.

She wound the bandage as instructed, her hands shaking a little. "That should keep your arm on," she told him, trying again for bravado.

"I'll apply a little salve of Saint-John's-wort when we return home," he told her. "Wards off fever."

What do you have for warding off another kind of fever?

"I'll remember that for the next time I'm accosted by a knife-wielding attacker."

"That's enough," he said coldly.

She froze as though he'd slapped her.

Kit thrust his arms almost angrily in the remains of his shirt, and then his coat. "We'd best hurry home."

⌒

It was late afternoon when the carriage took them home, more subdued, more edified, than when they'd originally set out. Kit assured her that his coachman and footmen were as bristling with weapons as he was, and they were as safe as they could hope to be at the moment.

"Should I tell Aunt Frances about . . . today?"

Kit turned to her, all solicitous politeness. "What would you like to do?"

Susannah thought about it. "I shouldn't like to worry her, or make her afraid for me. I shall continue in your employ."

He nodded, as though anything she might have said would have suited him.

And then the silence in the half-dark of the coach grew thick and uncomfortable, and then Susannah's thoughts began to blur and she began to drowse.

"I fought a duel over Caroline Allston when I was just seventeen."

She was fully awake now. She watched him quietly for a moment, assessing his emotional temperature.

"With my best friend," he added. His voice was strained, as though he'd been rehearsing the words in his head for some time. She heard the wry shame in them.

"Did you kill him?"

He smiled faintly. "No, he walks among us still. And he's still my best friend."

"And you don't know what became of Caroline?"

"No. She disappeared the very next day."

"And you've reason to believe she might have been in Gorringe?"

"Yes."

She'd noticed how succinct he became with issues that actually revealed him.

"Did you love her?" she asked, almost gingerly.

"Oh, I thought that I did, yes. But then again, I was just seventeen." He said it lightly, as though being seventeen precluded it being love.

She considered teasing him: *So that's your scandal?*—but something told her to refrain.

And then he gave her his usual cocky smile, and she thought she understood better the origin of that smile now. He was a very good discoverer of secrets, true. But he was also very good at keeping a smoke screen around what she now suspected was his own secret: his heart was as breakable as her own. Had in fact been broken before.

She smiled back at him, shook her head, didn't push for

more. Somehow she knew it was the only way more would be forthcoming.

And she was asleep soon thereafter.

❧

He watched her sleep with some complex emotion; it seemed to have tiers and facets, and the moment he managed to get one facet in focus, another one winked into prominence. He'd begun to suspect he was a romantic, despite everything, and the thought irritated him and amused him. It was a tremendously inconvenient thing to be, and not at all what one expected to find lurking in the heart of a spy.

Today...how easy it would have been to slide a hand over the small of her back, pull her forward into his bare chest, and touch his lips at last, at last, to that soft, soft mouth. He was, in fact, dangerously close to *needing* to know how her mouth would feel against his. He'd watched the pulse beating in her smooth throat, and for an extraordinary moment he'd had every intention of pressing his mouth against it...after he'd tasted her lips, of course. And from there...

This bloody folio assignment. His bloody, bloody father. A month away from a painstakingly wooed and won countess was simply too much to ask of a man in his prime.

Susannah was a beautiful woman, a soft and sensual woman just coming to understand the depth of her own passion and strength, and it was a breathtaking thing to witness. But he understood his own role in fomenting the heat he'd seen in her eyes today and rued it a little. He wondered if, in doing so, he'd done her a disservice, for who or what in a town like Barnstable could ever satisfy it? She would be a delightful interlude, at best, but truly he wanted nothing more than that. Indulging himself even a little would only hurt her, as she was so very nearly innocent. She'd already known too much of hurt.

Best to cast his lot in with the countess, who knew very well how to play the game. Best to impose a distance comprised of politeness and gallantry for the duration of his folio assignment. He would do his best to discover why someone intended to kill her, and then he would resume his life in London.

Still, there was something he'd wanted to know for some time now, and he found he couldn't deny himself this particular opportunity. Very gently, almost stealthily, he leaned forward and rested the backs of his fingers against Susannah's cheek.

He regretted it instantly. For her skin was every bit as soft as he'd dreamed.

Chapter Thirteen

Kit arrived home to a letter from his father, and in the mood he was in—the arm *did* hurt, Saint-John's-wort salve notwithstanding—every word of it seemed sarcastic.

> *Dear Christopher,*
>
> *I do hope you're enjoying your stay in Barnstable. I'm eager to review your findings. Would you be so kind as to send a sampling of your notes and your sketches to me posthaste?*
>
> *Warmly,*
> *Your Father*
> *Earl of Westphall*
>
> *P.S. I've booked passage for you on the next ship to Egypt. It leaves at the beginning of next month.*

Bloody, *bloody* hell. Thanks to the fact that someone was trying to kill Susannah Makepeace, all he had were some sketches of voles, a few ferns, and a tree or two. Oh, and of course, there was a wonderful sketch of him naked on a pier. They'd barely scratched the surface of Barnstable's flora and fauna. He didn't know whether to be amused at how well his father knew him; incensed that his father clearly didn't trust him; or ashamed that the mistrust was *warranted,* given that he'd spent the day in Gorringe with the daughter of a dead spy, for reasons both altruistic and selfish. And, coincidentally, related to Morley.

Another indication of how well his father knew him. And now when he knew something was genuinely amiss—as evidenced by someone lunging at Susannah with a knife—he couldn't tell his father about it.

He couldn't complete this assignment on his own; his pride simply wouldn't let him submit his own merely adequate drawings. And…well, he wanted to make a success of this, for if Susannah's drawings were to become known, perhaps she would have a life outside of Barnstable.

And a woman like Susannah deserved to have an interesting life.

Now all he needed to do was keep her alive long enough for her to *have* an interesting life.

She'd left her sketchbook behind in the coach again. He leafed through it, but he could never seem to do it casually. The near effortlessness, the grace and precision of the drawings still awed him a little, it was like watching someone he knew wave a wand to conjure something—and so little awed him anymore. Her drawings had been brave and passionate long before she knew that she was. The clues to her were there for anyone who'd known to look for them.

He stopped his leafing when he saw a drawing he hadn't seen before.

Me, he thought, surprised.

It wasn't an overly handsome drawing, as he wasn't an overly handsome man, and his pride did twinge a little. But somehow, she'd seen intensity in the set of his jaw, wit and steel shaded with vulnerability in the cast of his eyes; she'd made a downright poem of his mouth.

When had she drawn this? More importantly: How had she…*seen* this? It was almost more uncomfortable than being sketched in the nude. Somehow it revealed as much about Susannah as it did him.

He liked the way she saw him.

Sunset was streaking the sky in citrus shades now, and dark would fall hard in less than an hour. He thought of Susannah alone in the cottage with Frances Perriman, and of a twig and a sawed saddle girth, of a nondescript man artfully lunging from the crowd with a knife in his hand.

And he collected blankets, a bottle of brandy, a lantern, a box of matches, and loaded his pistols with fresh powder and shot. He loaded a musket, too, because one could never be too prepared. He was downstairs in minutes.

"But you've just arrived home, sir." Bullton looked confused. "And you're going out again? Is there an assem…" He trailed off when he noticed Kit's bundle and his clothing. "Will you at least take some dinner?" he asked in resignation.

"I'll stop in the kitchen, Bullton, and take some food out with me. But I've…work to do outside tonight."

Bullton stepped aside, and Kit stepped into the kitchen for some bread and cheese and cold chicken. He pumped a flask of water for himself.

And then he was out of the door and down the pathway. He knew just where to set up a little camp that couldn't possibly be seen by anyone in the cottage, but which would afford him the ideal view of it. The pain in his arm would ensure he stayed awake; the brandy would keep the arm manageable.

But no one else would be able to get near her.

And if anyone tried, by God they'd rue it.

〜

He'd waited, listening to crickets, to deer picking through the underbrush, to the first birdsong. When dawn began to light the sky, he took himself wearily to the pond for a quick swim, rinsed his mouth with water from his flask. His eyes felt as though they'd been plucked and replaced with two musket balls. He swiped a hand over his bristly face; the shave would have to wait.

He was standing at Mrs. Perriman's gate, rumpled, weary, but strangely satisfied when Susannah ventured out the door, basket on her arm, looking posy-fresh in pale, striped muslin. The sight of her was bracing. He was suddenly glad she'd threatened a cockney workman with a vase for her dresses.

She saw him and stopped. "You look as though you engaged in a debauch last night," she said lightly. "You've rings beneath your eyes, and..." She trailed off, and her gaze became something uncomfortably like concern.

"You're familiar with the look of debauchers, are you, Miss Makepeace?" Which effectively disconcerted her, displacing her concern, as he'd intended. "The arm is still attached. We'll see what today brings, however, as fate seems determined to separate me from it. Are you ready to put in a day's work?"

"Are *you*?"

"I've no choice," he said grimly. "Duty calls. And I've your sketchbook."

"Oh." She looked uncomfortable. "I didn't mean to leave it."

He would have teased her about the drawing, but he couldn't bring himself to do it. It seemed somehow as intimate to her as his revelation about Caroline was to him, and suddenly, he felt a little shy.

So he shrugged, and handed the sketchbook to her.

"Are we riding or walking today?" she wanted to know.

"Walking. Today I thought we'd finally sketch the Hellebore."

"And do you have your pistol?" She'd asked it almost matter-of-factly.

"Wouldn't dream of going anywhere without it." And he wasn't the least bit wry about it.

"Well, then. Shall we?" She squared her shoulders. A soldier in striped muslin.

C

He wasn't in the mood for conversation—he wasn't certain he could string words together at all, weary as he was, though his thoughts were certainly active enough—and Miss Makepeace was quiet, too.

She was working up to something, however, he could almost feel it.

"Will you take me to London?"

Ah. And there it was.

"You're not one for circumspection, are you, Miss Makepeace?"

"No, but *you* are."

"You wish to get a late start on the season, is that it?" He said it over his shoulder, and he saw a little shadow pass over her features. He silently cursed himself. He doubted voles and adders made up for Almacks.

"I wish to see Miss Daisy Jones," she said.

So did he, for that matter. He *wanted* to take her to London.

He wanted to talk to Daisy Jones, both to attempt to unravel the mystery behind Susannah Makepeace's life...and behind the reason someone wanted her dead.

But of course, if his father knew of his presence in London, Kit wouldn't be in London for very long. He'd be waving good-bye to London from the deck of a ship bound for Egypt or some other godforsaken place that lacked countesses and gentlemen's clubs.

"I'll think about it," he told her gruffly, and kept walking. On past the white oak, beyond the pond, deeper into the wood, where trees prevented the worst of the heat from beating down on them. He could scarcely think now. There was a clearing, mossy, where hellebore grew, and by God, despite everything, he still wanted to document the hellebore.

Then he heard a little shriek, and spun. He watched Susannah stumble, her arms windmilling slightly; she fell on her rump hard before he could catch her.

Kit dropped to his knees next to her, his heart in his throat. "Good God. Are you hurt?"

She laughed up at him. "It's all right...I merely stumbled over a stone. And I'm not made of glass. Just clumsy."

He wasn't amused. "Forgive me, but I'm a little sensitive to *shrieking,* Miss Makepeace, given the events of the past few days." He thrust out his hand.

She ignored his outstretched hand in favor of propping herself up on her elbows and throwing her head back to study the sky, as if surprised to find such a thing above her. Her hair was coming a little loose of its pins; her dress had hiked up a little, too, revealing a hint of long calves, lyrically curved, tapering into slim ankles. All of it covered in pale stocking. Susannah the siren.

"That cloud?" she said suddenly, gesturing skyward with her chin.

"Yes?" He crouched next to her, ready to help her up when she was ready to be helped up, and tilted his head back to see what she saw.

"Looks like a unicorn."

He studied it: That white, spiraling, vertical puff was the horn, he supposed; the wisp behind *could* be a tail.

"So it does."

She lowered her head and gave him a wry look. She knew he was humoring her.

The next thing he did was absently, and truly almost innocently done, born of the playfulness of the moment, perhaps, or simply because the purity of the line begged for it. He reached out and drew his finger lightly from her ankle right up the curve of her calf.

When his finger reached the crook of her knee he stopped. Astonished to see it there.

Silently, a little frantically, he considered excuses: *An insect was crawling up your stocking, Susannah. I was checking to see if you were injured, Susannah. I was—*

"Don't stop." It was her voice. Husky, abstracted.

And the words roared like a brushfire over his senses. He briefly closed his eyes. When he opened them again, the very quality of the day had changed: thickened, slowed, enclosed the two of them.

He slowly lifted his head. He found a dare in Susannah's eyes, and a heat easily the equal of his own, and the sweetest sort of anxiety. She wanted this, or thought she did, and was afraid she'd be rebuffed again.

And yet he wasn't sure she truly understood what it was she wanted.

He was all too sure what *he* wanted.

A breeze, mindless of the significance of the moment, gaily tossed a streamer of her hair across her forehead.

Just a little, a voice in his head urged him. He could show her just a little of passion, he reasoned; he could show her gently, skillfully, give her just a taste. Because lord knew what would become of her, and what sort of man would ultimately have the taking of her. He was certain he could give her pleasure, and she deserved that.

He was distantly amused, even a little alarmed, at how reason and lust had conspired to make his desire to crawl beneath Susannah's Makepeace's skirts seem noble.

And so he did it: He drew his finger as slowly as he could bear along the length of her practical stocking, up over the curve of her calf, and he could feel the warmth of her skin beneath it, hear the stuttering catch in her breath, and her mounting excitement flowed into him. He reached her garter, a surprisingly plain one, given that this was Susannah Makepeace: a pink ribbon, no satin rosettes, just a bow. And with his finger he leisurely traced, once, twice, again, the satin of it, deliberately postponing for both of them the moment when he would touch the skin above it.

Her eyes fluttered closed.

"No," he commanded softly. "Open them."

She did, but her lips parted slightly with breathing that was growing ragged with anticipation. Slowly, slowly he uncurled his fingers and laid his open hand against the top of her thigh, over her stocking, just below her garter. He left it there, resting at that threshold between stocking and skin, for as long as he thought they both could withstand it, and smiled down, a crooked, slow smile. A silent declaration to her that he would be leading every moment of this interlude, that he would determine the start and finish of it.

At last, he slid his hand smoothly upward to touch the skin of her thigh. His smile vanished.

The vulnerable, silken heat of her skin...quite simply, it undid him.

Kit understood then that he'd been fooling himself, had been fooling himself for days. It was she who owned both this moment...and him.

And when he eased his body down alongside her, her hand rose up as though the air had become as viscous as honey, and she cradled his lowering face as though they'd been lovers forever.

Forever. He found himself wanting to stretch each second, to heighten each moment, to make distinct memories of them all: *Now I'm touching her skin...now I'm kissing her lips...* His lips touched hers, just a brush, once, twice, over the full softness of her lovely mouth, discovering what she knew of kissing. With devastating instinct, she echoed him, dragging her lips softly across his, with his, until the desire in him was coiled so tightly his limbs trembled from it.

"Susannah." A ragged whisper. She sighed a warm breath out against his lips and brought her other hand up to hold his face; in her hands he could feel her tension and urgency. And he'd meant to linger over this kiss, to take it deeper with delicacy and finesse, and then to end it, but he found he could not. His desire was suddenly untenable; he was convinced only the taste of her could ease it. He touched an impatient tongue to her lips and coaxed them open. When she parted her mouth he sought her tongue, and discovered, with a low sound in the back of his throat, the hot, silken sweetness inside her mouth. Her tongue tentatively moved, tangled with his. *Oh, God.*

"Like this?" she whispered.

"*God,* yes," he breathed.

She smiled against his mouth.

"No smiling," he murmured. "Only kissing."

Their mouths moved languidly over each other at first, nipping, delving deeply, retreating. And gradually it built to urgency. He rose up over her to take his kisses deeper still, to taste the contours of her mouth, teeth clashing against her teeth, and still it never seemed enough. The sensation was like soaring in place; Kit couldn't feel the ground beneath him, or the air above him; he was aware only of the sweetness of the woman joined with him, and distantly he marveled, he'd never felt quite so lost. He tucked his hip in firmly against hers, astounded at how painfully aroused he was.

"Sweet," he murmured, moving his lips from hers to kiss and nip beneath her chin, to draw his tongue down the cord of her throat. Her breathing was rushed, and with the rise and fall of her chest he could see the tight darkness of her nipples beneath the fine fabric of her dress. "Sweet," he sighed again, moving his mouth to breathe against her breast; he touched his tongue to her nipple through the fabric. She caught her breath at the sensation, arced up a little to meet him. And as she did, his fingers, five feathers, began to stroke the tender skin inside her thigh.

At first she tensed; the muscles of her thigh quivering, uncertain. But then her legs parted a little more for him.

"Stockings, but no drawers?" he teased, breathlessly. He nudged the neckline of her gown lower with his teeth, exposing her breast, distracting her as his hand glided farther up her thigh, to come gently to rest against the damp, silken curls at the crook of them.

"Too warm for...drawers...but I liked the...garters..." She gasped out the words, and he gave a short laugh before he took her nipple into his mouth. Puckered velvet, it was, the palest, most delicate pink, like her lips; her breast could fill the palm of his hand. He knew because he skimmed his palm over the other one.

"*Kit,*" she rasped. "*God.*"

"One and the same," he murmured. He heard her gasp something, either a tortured laugh or a word, which may have been "beast," but she stopped abruptly when he took her nipple into his mouth again and drew slow circles around it with his tongue. Her softly sighed *"oh,"* her back arching up to meet him, her fingers combing over his head, made him wilder than he thought he could bear.

But he would bear it. Today was for her, and today was all there would be.

He settled for tucking his hips closer to her, his aching erection brushing against her. His fingers stroked lightly over the curls between her legs, twining in them. And then he returned his lips to hers, gently, because he wanted to watch her eyes when he slid a finger lightly along her cleft.

He felt her body go taut when he did; she drew in a sharp breath.

His hand stilled. "No?" he said softly.

"Yes," she disagreed on a whisper, touching his face.

He kissed her softly, as his finger slid lightly again, and then again, and at last her legs slipped open wider still, inviting him in. Desire clawed him, a great bird of prey clinging to his back, he could scarcely breathe. With his fingers, he circled her gently, slowly at first, and then insistently, listening to the pulse of her breath, to her soft murmurs, to learn the rhythm she wanted, until her desire drenched his fingers. He touched nearly chaste kisses to her mouth as his fingers played over her, and watched, triumphant, as her pupils grew large, her beautiful, complicated eyes opaque, her breathing become a quiet storm.

"Kit?" she whispered urgently. "I—it's—"

"I know," he sympathized hoarsely. "Move with me now."

And she began to move her hips in time with his knowing fingers, colluding with him in her own pleasure, and he moved his own hips against her, craving his own release even as he knew he must deny it. He covered her mouth with a kiss, a deep kiss, tangling his tongue with hers, and oh the taste of her: honey and velvet, rich as plums. He moved his fingers in time with his tongue, knew by her escalating breathing, the rhythm of her hips, that it would be soon.

She took her lips from his, her head thrashed to one side. *"Please..."*

"Hold on to me, Susannah." She was utterly focused on her own journey now, and God, how he wanted to go there with her.

At last, her fingers dug into his arms and she bowed up with a soft cry, pulsing against his hand.

And somehow, this seemed nearly as precious as the beat of her heart, and the pleasure he took in her release was so acute it might well have been his own.

Kit gently took his hand from her, breathed in deeply, breathed out again, steadying himself, willing his own need to ebb, and tried desperately to knit back together the frayed ends of his senses.

For so long now, part of the pleasure in making love to a woman had been the mechanics of seduction. He'd always been the master of each step of it, and this, too, had been part of the pleasure for him.

But ... this pleasure was different. It was in Susannah's breath, warm against his neck in the aftermath of her release. The flush in her cheeks and creamy throat. In the scent of her hair. In her lovely eyes going opaque from desire, her hands in his hair. In—

"Did we just make love?" Susannah wanted to know.

In questions like that.

He smiled faintly. "Very nearly."

"There's ... more ... for you, I know." She said it shyly, and reached out and tentatively covered his subsiding arousal with her hand. He sucked in a breath and clutched her wrist to stop her. And then he rolled over on his back to look at the sky, a distance away from her.

The sky looked different, somehow. Probably the whole world looked different now.

"It's just..." He faltered, after a moment of silence, for he was afraid he'd hurt her with his words. "There will be no going back for you, then, Susannah."

But was that what bothered him precisely? Now that the fever of the moment had passed, a strange panic was welling inside him, and he didn't know how to identify it. He had a tremendously ungentlemanly impulse to run like the devil.

She was quiet next to him for a moment; a bird trilled its song into the silence and the trees shook their leaves into a welcome breeze.

"Perhaps...perhaps I don't want to go back," she said. Oh, and already he heard the hurt in her words.

He rolled over on his side to look down at her for a long moment. "Susannah," he murmured. He traced her lips, swollen from kisses, with his finger, and then kissed them gently. He stroked her hair away from her face, avoiding looking into her questioning eyes. He brushed his lips over her cheek, her brow, then plucked a leaf from her hair, and tenderly straightened her bodice, all while she silently watched him, studying his face, well aware he was refusing to look directly at her.

Finally, he levered his tall frame to his feet, and his arm, which for the past half hour he hadn't felt at all, was throbbing.

"Come. I'll walk you home. I find...I find my arm is aching." He reached his hand down; after a moment's hesitation, she took it, and he helped her to her feet. She brushed the leaves from her dress. They set out for home, not touching.

The walk was silent; he left her at her aunt's gate with a bow. It was a strangely formal thing to do, and he saw Susannah flinch a little. But for some reason he needed to impose a distance.

"Hellebore tomorrow then?" she said brightly. Tinsel bright. It rang falsely in the still of the day.

He'd done this to her, he'd put that falseness in her voice. Still, there was nothing he could do to make her feel any more certain, because it was possible no one had ever felt as uncertain than he did at the moment.

"My arm." He shrugged apologetically. "Perhaps a day of rest . . . ?"

Coward.

He'd never before been one for lying. But then again, he'd never before been afraid of the truth before.

Susannah's brightness faltered. "All right. I do hope it feels better soon."

"So do I." He tossed the words out lightly, but they sounded awful, jarring, instead. He could have kicked himself.

I never should have touched her.

Funny, but a mere half hour ago it didn't seem that he'd had any choice at all.

He gave another short bow, and left her staring after him at her aunt's gate, and noticed as he backed away there was one last tiny leaf still clinging to her hair.

Susannah stood at the gate flanked by her aunt's roses, and watched Kit disappear down the path. A leaf clung to his bright, close-cropped hair. It added a little whimsy to what was otherwise an almost cruelly dignified departure.

She remembered traveling down that very same path on her very first day in Barnstable, lured by recklessness, a little bit of despair, a need to test the boundaries of her new life. She'd discovered him on the other end of it, stark naked, arms up in the air, roaring a satisfied *"Ahhhh!"* to the elements. He wasn't precisely a pot of gold at the end of a rainbow. Perhaps a treasure chest instead. The kind one finds at the bottom of the ocean, filled with rubies and doubloons, guarded by snapping crustaceans and darker things that perhaps no one had yet discovered or named.

She considered whether to regret taking that path that morning. She couldn't quite decide yet.

But she'd certainly got what she'd thought she wanted, hadn't she?

The taste of him lingered on her lips; she could smell him on her clothes. It was almost as though he stood there with her still. She put her fingers up to her lips; they felt chafed and tender and thoroughly, properly, used for perhaps the first time ever. A white heat of desire threaded through her veins again; it stole her breath. She closed her eyes.

She knew now what his beautiful mouth could do. It could prod her with sarcasm and truth and wit. It could devastate her with tenderness; it could relentlessly build a storm of pleasure in her. It could own her until that storm broke over her.

Oh, and after that, too. Because she couldn't imagine now ever drinking her fill of him.

She wondered, however, if Kit had taken his fill of *her*. He'd rolled over, been distracted and silent and pensive. Bloody *polite,* in fact—which is how she'd known something was terribly wrong. Perhaps she'd been too innocent, or too eager, or too dull for a man like him, a man who'd fought a duel over a woman when he was scarcely yet grown, who'd seen war. Who'd befriended opera dancers. And she—well, before Kit, she'd been kissed by Douglas, twice, and pressed up against his erection once. It hardly counted as worldliness.

No, she'd seen it—Kit's narrow face, homely and beautiful all at once, had been brilliantly open to her in that moment when his mouth had touched hers. He'd been trembling, too. They'd been equal in that moment. Both in want...and wonder.

She'd almost be willing to wager the remainder of her wardrobe upon it.

She'd hoped to give herself to him, but that would have been more of a gift to herself, she understood now. She knew now what she really needed to give him: time.

To decide what it was he wanted from her, if anything at all.

And for some reason this seemed riskier, more terrifying, than giving him her body.

Kit stopped in to see to the horses. Since he'd sacked the stable boys, it was his job now until he could find someone else to do it. Susannah the new little filly gamboled over to see him, and he had a thought: *I'll give Susannah to Susannah when she's grown.*

Moving slowly with the horses, breathing in their animal scent, spending time in the simplicity of their presence, soothed his thoughts, calmed his body; he returned to the house in a slightly easier frame of mind.

He nodded to Bullton as he made his way up the stairs.

"If you'll pardon my saying so, sir, you've a leaf clinging to the back of your head."

Kit halted and swiped an alarmed hand over his hair; a tiny maple leaf fluttered to the ground. He gave Bullton a sharp look, but when Bullton wasn't full of whiskey, he was a butler to his toes, which meant he wasn't about to let judgment or amusement or anything of the sort show on his face.

Kit collected his dignity quickly, began again to head up the stairs, and Bullton bent to pick up the leaf.

"It's a *green* leaf, sir. A very fine color. Green."

Kit stopped and turned swiftly. Bullton's face was entirely enigmatic.

Bullton might just make a wonderful spy, Kit thought admiringly.

"And you've a letter, sir."

"Oh. Thank you, Bullton." Kit accepted the letter and took the stairs slowly, splitting the seal on his way.

Dear sir:

In response to your inquiry regarding the accident in the coaching inn of May the twenty-third.

The conveyance in question was determined to have been in excellent repair. The cause of the accident has been traced to the linchpin on a forward wheel, which was of a size and width inconsistent with the other linchpins, which subsequently unbalanced the wheel and caused it to loosen. This in turn led to the unfortunate incident in the inn yard. A comparison with other coaches in our fleet reveals that this is a singular incident, as no other linchpins of this sort occur anywhere on any other coach.

We regret to inform you that we have been unable to trace the offending linchpin's origin, but we will redouble our efforts to ensure that such an accident does not happen again. In the meantime, we will be happy to sack the employee of your choice, should you feel it necessary, and reimburse you for the cost of the irreparably damaged hat. Do buy another green one.

Yours sincerely,
M. Rutherford

Kit couldn't help but laugh, pleased with M. Rutherford, whoever he might be. Some harried bureaucrat placating a spoiled aristocrat with thinly disguised irony and steeled patience. Kit didn't blame him in the least for the tone, nor was he the least bit embarrassed by it. His petulant, whiskey-inspired letter had accomplished precisely what he'd wanted to accomplish, and he knew he wouldn't have received such a timely response without acting the part of the put-upon viscount.

He had his answer now, but he'd already known it, really: The shortened linchpin meant the coach Susannah Makepeace had taken to Barnstable had been cleverly, subtly, deliberately sabotaged.

He was seized by a sense of helplessness that infuriated him. Susannah was wrong: Her luck wasn't bad, it was extraordinary, considering someone was methodically attempting to kill her, and with yesterday's knife, had at last abandoned any pretense of subtlety.

He'd been lucky, too: He'd been able to keep her alive. But he didn't know how long his own luck would hold.

Oh, he'd been right, he was so seldom wrong, after all. She most definitely had an instinct for passion, an instinct that matched his own, that had nearly caused him to lose his head. Well, now he knew her skin was petal smooth; he knew the rich wine of her mouth; he knew the feel of that delicate, puckered nipple rubbed against his cheek—

Kit swiped two frustrated hands down over his face, rubbed his eyes. God, he needed a shave; it was a wonder his whiskers hadn't cut Susannah's tender skin.

There was a reason, after all, that he'd cultivated the countess so carefully, and it wasn't as though she wasn't skilled at what he'd... well, cultivated her for. Mistresses most definitely had a purpose. Perhaps he could sneak in a visit to the countess,

to remind her of his existence and to take the edge off this foolish, misguided—boundless—want for Miss Makepeace.

His father would see him in Egypt if he saw him in London,
that much was clear. But even if he wound up in Egypt, maybe
he could make a gift to Susannah of the truth about her past.
Maybe, maybe he could save her from whatever forces wanted
to prevent her from having a future. Maybe he could make sure
she *had* a future.

For Susannah, then. For Susannah he would risk Egypt. He
would take her to London.

Chapter Fourteen

❧

"*Susannah!*" her aunt sang. "I have a *surprise* for you."

Dear God, please *no,* she thought. And to think, she used to like surprises.

She hadn't slept much the previous night, having spent the evening reliving her interlude with the viscount until sleep dragged her under for a few inadequate hours. Feeling decidedly surly, Susannah hurled herself out of bed, padded to the top of the stairs, and peered down. Then reared back, alarmed.

The viscount stood in the parlor, hat in hand, dressed for traveling. He looked like a gentleman caller. Except, of course, he was not: He was her employer.

Her employer, who'd had his hand between her thighs only yesterday.

A rush of heat nearly buckled her knees as her body remembered precisely how that felt.

As deuced luck would have it, Kit had been looking up at the stairs just as she was peering down. His face split into a grin.

She flew back into her room, her heart thumping. She'd been

certain she wouldn't see him today, or perhaps even the following day. Perhaps not ever again, given the nature of their leave-taking yesterday. She heard her aunt make a scandalized noise, which Susannah suspected was all pretense, because it was difficult to maintain a true sense of scandal in the face of the viscount's cheery insouciance.

"Come down when you are able, Susannah," her aunt called up. "Viscount Grantham would like a word."

Her aunt sounded quietly thrilled. *This isn't a Jane Austen story, Aunt Frances,* she thought. *He isn't here to confess our indiscretion yesterday and make an honorable woman of me.*

Then again, perhaps he was. This was, after all, a man who loved surprises.

She dressed, as quickly as her shaking fingers could manage, and presented herself in the parlor after a few minutes. Her aunt had pressed some tea on the viscount. He stood and bowed when she entered, as proper a gentleman as she'd ever encountered.

"I need to present my folio findings in London, Miss Makepeace, and I am here to request permission from your aunt for your company. You will, of course, be well-compensated for your time. And we shall, of course, be accompanied by the appropriate number of servants."

This was to reassure Aunt Frances of the propriety of their excursion, doubtless.

But there was nothing at all proper about Susannah's thoughts at the moment. In fact, Susannah could not help but translate "well-compensated" in a distinctly *improper* way.

She imagined Aunt Frances interpreted "well-compensated" as more beef and sausages.

"Well, if you have need of her, my lord," Aunt Frances finally conceded, "by all means, you must take her. I shall get on without her for a day or so."

Poor Aunt Frances. Susannah's arrival had meant one awkward moment after another for her.

Kit thanked her somberly. "I shall wait while you pack the appropriate number of dresses, Miss Makepeace. The coach will be brought round to the road below."

He'd kept conversation minimal and bland during the hours of their trip to London. Susannah had attempted, with strained lightness, with idle questions, with looks between her lashes to scale the slippery walls of his breathtaking politeness, but she was no match for him. At last, she fell silent. Kit spent the remainder of the trip poring over books, for all the world as though he fully did intend to report to his father.

The carriage they rode in was older—the Whitelaw family didn't keep their finer equipages at The Roses, after all, and the four geldings seemed surprised to find themselves actually pulling a coach again—but he'd been able to obscure the coat of arms on it with a clever piece of painted board. The full complement of servants he'd promised Susannah's aunt was comprised of a driver and two footmen.

He was entirely alone with her niece, whom he intended to surprise with the purpose of their visit to London, and who, he trusted, would not convey the particular lack of appropriate servants to her aunt.

It was late afternoon by the time they reached London's East End. The White Lily Theater wasn't shy about announcing itself: An enormous sign painted with a lush, almost lurid flower—no actual lily had ever looked like this—hung over the entrance, which was flanked by two Grecian columns. Shiny *new* Grecian columns.

"You couldn't have drawn it better yourself, Susannah," Kit told her, gesturing to the sign with his chin.

She was enough of an artist to look insulted by that.

And then, as she began to understand why they were at the White Lily, he found himself turning away from the soft, glowing gratitude dawning on her face.

He pushed open the door to the theater and jaunty, nearly frenetic pianoforte music—played with much enthusiasm and a heavy hand—burst out, as if frantic for escape. A stage hugged the north end of the theater, and tiers of seats climbed up to the balconies and then to the ceiling. All of the seats were empty. From the looks of things, the establishment could comfortably accommodate several hundred people. The architecture roughly approximated classical, a florid sort of classical, with pillars propping up the corners, urns tucked into niches, and great heavy velvet curtains roped in golden cords lining the stage. Maidens in togas with breasts exposed and lasciviously grinning cherubs gamboled across the ceiling.

A tall, fair-haired man stood in the center of the aisle facing the stage, on which a row of heavily-painted girls, clad in what appeared to be modified shifts, appeared to be stumbling about. The man was marking time with his walking stick.

"All *right* girls! And one, and two, and *kick* and *slide,* and four, and turn, and—no, *no, NO!*"

These last three syllables were punctuated by the vehement thump of walking stick against floor. "Josephine!" the man barked, and the pianoforte music crashed to a discordant halt. And then he heaved a gusty, long-suffering sigh. "We open tomorrow *night,* ladies."

The girls stood in a dejected row, toeing the stage sheepishly with their bare feet.

"General," drawled the man who stood with his hands folded over the top of his walking stick, "would you please show the ladies—once *again*—how it's done?"

Hmmm. There *was* someone sitting in one of the chairs, but when he rose up, his head reached only a little higher than Kit's hip. The General, it seemed, was a dwarf. His face was darkly handsome, slashes of brows, a stern chin, dark eyes, and like his friend, he was clearly a bit of a dandy: His waistcoat was an unsubtle purple and metallic gold brocade, and a ruby stickpin gleamed dully from the complicated folds of his cravat. He strode down the aisle to the stage and hefted himself up.

"Josephine, if you would?" His roundly elegant voice filled the theater.

The music started up again, and The General, with a complete absence of irony, perched a hand on his hip, tilted his head coyly, and began to dance.

"And a one, and a two and *kick* and *slide,* and four, and turn, and *kick,* kick, back and *dip...*"

With accomplished precision The General danced for several bars, then stopped abruptly, waved a hand at Josephine for silence, and turned to the row of dancers.

"*Do* you ladies have it now?" He sounded as exasperated as the fair-headed fellow.

"Yes, General. Sorry, General." Sheepish feminine apologies. The General hopped down from the stage and rolled his eyes in exasperation at the other man as he came back up the aisle, which is when he noticed Kit and a gaping Susannah standing in the entry.

"Tom," The General nudged his taller friend. "We've visitors."

The man with the walking stick turned, and Susannah drew in a sharp breath. Kit could hardly blame her—the bastard was devilishly handsome. No, not *devilishly...* he was more like Pan, broad across the cheekbone, narrow at the chin, his nose and lips finely etched but unmistakably masculine, damn him. A fashionably unruly mop of red-gold hair dropped rakishly over one eye, and his eyes were pale, almost silver, in the theater's dim light. He was dressed as festively as The General, his waistcoat striped in silver. He radiated impish well-being.

"Good afternoon!" He swept a low bow to them. "Mr. Tom Shaughnessy here. I'm the owner of this fine establishment. The General here"—The General bowed, too—"is my partner and choreographer. And you would be...Mister? Sir? Lord?..."

"White. Mr. White." Kit bowed low in return. Mr. Shaughnessy stood back, rubbing his chin. "You look familiar, Mr. White."

"No, I don't," Kit said meaningfully.

Mr. Shaughnessy's brows rose. "Oh, of *course* not." He grinned, pleased. "My mistake. And what have you brought to me today, Mr.... White?" He swept Susannah with a thorough, appreciative, professionally speculative gaze. "Let me assure you, our girls are well-cared for and *completely* free of disease—except for poor Rose, of course, and we'll have you right as rain in no time, won't we Rose?" He called up to a girl on the stage and smiled encouragingly, sympathetically. "You'll choose the right fellow, next time, yes?"

He turned back to Kit and Susannah, cheerfully oblivious to the fact that one of the girls onstage was now a brilliant scarlet. The other girls were watching her curiously.

"Crikey, wotcha 'ave, Rosie?" one of them murmured.

"That's very, er...*reassuring,* Mr. Shaughnessy," Kit replied, "and I've heard...impressive...things about your establishment. But I didn't bring my"—he cleared his throat—"wife... to you. We are here on a personal matter. We were hoping to have a word with Miss Daisy Jones."

"Ah, my Miss Daisy Jones. *Daize!*" Mr. Shaughessy turned and bellowed in The General direction of the back of the theater. *"Visitors!"*

He turned to face them again. "Good heavens, my apologies,

Mrs. White, Mr. White. No offense meant. But my *deepest* congratulations on your wife, sir." He mimed tipping his hat to Kit, raised his brows again in appreciation. "She'd do quite well, here."

"No offense taken, sir," Susannah assured him, with coyly lowered lashes, which earned an appreciative grin from Mr. Shaughnessy. Kit fought a scowl, but still. The man was so bloody ingenuous he found it difficult to be genuinely annoyed with him.

A brassy woman's voice boomed from the back of the hall. "Do you *'ave* to bellow now, Tom, I was in the middle of me—"

The woman froze when she saw Susannah, and clapped one hand theatrically over her heart.

Kit suspected the gesture was genuine enough. Her handsome, round face had gone pale, turning the two perfectly circular spots of rouge on her cheeks into beacons. She was draped in some sort of toga made of purple satin and feathers, and bits of sparkly paste jewels clung and twinkled everywhere on her, including her hair. She was a flaming, buxom, constellation. Apparently she was preparing for, or just recovering from, a performance.

"Ye look jus' *like* 'er, dear, ye do," she breathed.

She stared at Susannah another moment. Then she became brisk, speculative. "We best talk in me room." She transferred her gaze to Kit, and it widened, became sultry. "'Aven't seen you in—"

"Ever. You haven't ever seen me, Miss Jones," Kit amended quickly, earning him a lifted eyebrow and a smirk from Miss Jones. "Allow me to introduce myself: I am Mr. *White,* and this is my...this is my...friend."

"Pleased to meet ye, Mr.....*White.*" Daisy Jones extended a hand theatrically, and Kit bowed over it. Miss Jones was a pioneer of sorts, and though he'd never personally partaken of her particular charms, he'd been an enthusiastic audience member on more than one occasion, and had once even sent flowers to her. For one did want to encourage pioneering in the arts.

They followed Miss Jones, who, though past her prime, still had a marvelous derriere. It swung like the deck of a ship in a storm, and Kit was nearly hypnotized by it as he followed her. At the end of a warren of halls they came to a closed door, and Miss Jones flung it open and gestured for them to precede her.

⁓

It was like entering a giant…*mouth*. The walls were papered in vivid pink, in a pattern that Susannah was certain had never seen the inside of a London town house. Two settees upholstered in matching pink velvet lolled across the room like enormous tongues. A number of chairs also covered in velvet and plump enough to accommodate Miss Jones's majestic derriere were scattered about, as though she received hordes of visitors nightly. Mirrors took up almost an entire wall, and a variety of strategically placed lanterns set the place aglow.

"I've me own room to dress in now, ye see." She waved her arm about proudly. Then she stopped and stared at Susannah fondly, then clapped her hands on Susannah's cheeks. "I simply canna believe it. Now—forgive me, but I jus' 'ave to—"

She seized Susannah and pressed her into her enormous, muskily perfumed bosom, and Susannah felt a feather climb into her nostril. When she was finally able to squirm out of Daisy's grasp, she sneezed discreetly into her hand.

"Yer the spit of Anna, ye know. She was just *beautiful,* and of course she didna last long 'ere at the White Lily. She was snapped right up. She talked me into retirin' a bit wi' 'er out in that little godforsaken town named by a duke who—"

"Gorringe," Kit and Susannah said simultaneously.

"Gorringe. And I thought I'd get me a respectable life of sorts, too. But I was so bored I thought I'd *die*. Spent most of me time at the pub. So bored I dreamed up me *act* there, ye see, so I suppose it wasna complete loss. It's a popular act, ye see."

She smiled meaningfully up at Kit, who smiled back at her, while Susannah tried with difficulty not to mind. Daisy leaned toward Susannah. "You see, dearie," she confided, "I was the first one to get up onstage and give the audience a real close look at my—"

"Was her name really Anna Smith?" Kit interjected hurriedly, leaving Susannah in suspense.

"Smith?" Daisy looked bemused. "Why d'yer think 'er name was Smith?"

"The church records in Gorringe," Susannah told her. "Her name was recorded as Anna Smith."

"Well, I suppose she wanted to live quiet like, an' a name like Smith. I knew 'er as Anna 'Olt. Now which one are ye?"

Susannah noticed that Kit had gone completely still, for some reason, at Daisy's words. She frowned. "I beg your pardon, Miss Jones?"

"Are ye Sylvie, Sabrina, or Susannah?"

"But I don't under..." Susannah stammered. And then suddenly she did, and tiny little moth wings of excitement fluttered inside her.

"Anna had *three* daughters," Daisy Jones leaned forward again and explained slowly, as though reciting the beginning of an arithmetic problem. "Which *one* are ye?"

Susannah's mouth dropped open, and then her hands went up to her face. She spun to Kit. "Sisters! I have *sisters*! I have sisters?" She whirled back to Daisy to confirm it.

And when Daisy nodded, Susannah impulsively seized the laughing Miss Jones in a hug.

Where a day or so earlier she was a cipher on the tablet of time, she was now Susannah, last name of Holt, possibly, and—very likely—had two sisters.

"Oh, ye poor thing, ye didna know? I suppose that's possible, ye were all so very small when Anna left, and the three of ye were split up."

"But... what was my mama like? What became of her? My sisters? My father? I'm Susannah. That's which *one* I am."

Daisy laughed at Susannah's enthusiasm. "Well, me dear, ye'd be the baby, then. Ye mama was in the chorus 'ere at the White Lily until yer papa clapped eyes on 'er, and then it was *all* over for 'er: a little 'ouse in the country, tha's what she wanted, and babies, and yer papa. And Anna—oh, she was the sweetest, funniest, lass, and *oh,* she'd a temper—a fiery one, my *goodness.* She was honest as the day is long. Spoke the truth as she saw it."

Susannah was silent, astounded to hear her mother described after so many years, to feel her come into view. She *must* be alive. She... *felt* alive.

"Yes, she was me dear friend," Daisy sighed. "And she never done it, ye know. I'm certain of it."

"Done it?" Susannah immediately regretted the question, because the answer was bound to be something frankly prurient, which would have been both fascinating and appalling.

"Why, murdered yer papa, lass."

Chapter Fifteen

❧

Daisy Jones looked horrified when she saw the look on Susannah's face. She turned to Kit beseechingly. "She didna know?"

He shook his head once, curtly. Kit was still oddly tense; Susannah had the sensation his every muscle was knotted in preparation to bolt from the room.

Daisy took a deep breath, and began in a gentle voice. "'Is name was Richard Lockwood, Susannah. Beautiful man, devoted, loved yer mama, loved ye and yer sisters very much. 'E was a politician, very important, very rich. As I said, clapped eyes on Anna one night 'ere at the White Lily and, well... 'E never married anyone else—nor did 'e marry 'er. But 'e set 'er up in 'er own lodgings 'ere in London. And after yer two sisters were born, 'e moved 'is family to Gorringe, because Anna fancied a country life, and because 'e got it in 'is 'ead that Gorringe was a funny place, what being named by a rhyming duke, and all. 'Ad a sense of 'umor, did yer papa.

"But then yer dear papa—" Daisy gentled her voice,

remembering. "'E was murdered, Susannah, and it was spread about in all the papers that Anna killed 'im. Crime of passion, they said. There were witnesses, they said. As fer me, I never believed a word of it, an' still don't. 'E was in London, and Anna was in Gorringe with ye girls at the time, I'm certain of it. And she never would 'ave..." Daisy paused, and her face went rueful and dreamy. "If ye'd seen how they loved each other, Susannah...real love, Susannah. Not just...passion."

She paused and peered into Susannah's face with concern. "Ye've gone a bit peaky, luv. Do you need to lie down?" She patted the big tongue of a settee invitingly, sympathetically.

"Why does everyone think I'm bound to faint?" Susannah protested, though, admittedly her voice *was* thin. Her mother was an opera dancer, a mistress, and an accused murderess. And it seemed tragic love affairs ran in the family. If ever she were entitled to faint, now would be the time.

She wondered why Kit had gone so still, so silent. Perhaps he regretted ever associating with her. Perhaps he was cursing his folio assignment, thinking to himself: *Bloody* voles *got me involved with the daughter of a murderess*. Perhaps he was regretting he'd ever touched her, tainted as she was with the scandal of murder, and wanted to wash his hands of her as soon as he could safely deposit her at home.

Which made a different kind of fear arrest her breath.

And then Kit moved, and such was his stillness the moment before that Susannah jumped. He lifted the pitcher on Daisy Jones's vanity, sniffed it, splashed a little into a glass. He handed it to her.

"Drink." A soft command.

It was brandy. It went down hot and smooth, and quickly buffered the jagged ends of her emotions.

Susannah realized then that Kit had quietly seen to her needs in just this way from the moment she'd arrived in Barnstable, from tempting her to waltz at the assembly to risking his own life to keep her alive. He might never touch her again, but he would never let anything harm her.

And then he was still again, as still as a sentry; his entire being seemed both utterly absorbed and utterly remote at the same time, preternaturally alert, leaving Susannah to ask questions.

"What became of my mother, Miss Jones? Do you know?" she asked when the brandy had worked its magic.

"That's just it, ye see. *No* one knows. She disappeared right after yer father's death."

"But...my father...that is, James Makepeace, I mean...do you know how I came to be with him?"

"Well, I was in London when the uproar over the murder happened—yer real papa, Richard, was a popular man with the people, young lady, and *'andsome*! I don't mind saying. And then a few days after 'e was killed I was 'ere at the White Lily when Makepeace came to me, all in a tizzy like. 'E was a theater buff, Makepeace was, and a friend of Richard's. 'E told me 'e had ye three girls. 'E swore me to secrecy. And keeping a secret for Anna's sake—well, that was no burden to me. So James kept ye, and I found a home for Sylvie—"

"Like a puppy?" Susannah tried not to sound bitter. Kit's hand dropped onto her shoulder, just the barest hint of a touch.

"What did I know of babies, my dear?" Daisy said gently. "I'd have taken the lot of ye, luv, for Anna's sake, but I was poor as dirt, then. It seemed safer for Anna, and all of ye, somehow, to split you girls up; for the papers had it that Anna had disappeared along with her girls. And if I'd been discovered with three little girls...if *James* 'ad been discovered with three little girls..."

Susannah could imagine the fear of the time. The loyalty and love that had kept her mother's secret.

"I'm sorry, Daisy," Susannah said softly. "You lost her, too."

Daisy's eyes were a little moist now and she touched a finger to the corner of one, to keep a tear from racing down to smear the rouge.

"And so... well, I was discreet. A French dancer name of Claude took a shine to Sylvie and offered to care for 'er, and so... off she went. No doubt raised French, more's the pity," Daisy added sadly.

"What about Sabrina?"

"I don't know, luv. I'm sorry, I just don't know. James knew of a vicar's family who may 'ave taken her on, but I never knew for certain."

"I was very fortunate, given the circumstances." Susannah took refuge in formality, as she didn't know quite what to believe yet, or how to feel. It was a little like falling off a cliff, and being thrown a rope... only to discover the rope was actually a snake.

"Did you ever hear from Anna Holt again?" Kit finally spoke. His voice was taut and strange, abstracted. As though he were working a problem out in his mind.

"Never heard from 'er, I swear to ye. No one knew where she went, she was never found, and the 'ubbub eventually died. But Anna would *never* willingly leave her babies—*never*. And I would swear on all that I 'old dear—my gorgeous bosom"— Daisy swelled up to display her assets matter-of-factly—"and my new town house, which my gorgeous bosom bought for me—that Anna didna kill yer father."

"I don't think she did it, either." This came from Kit, low and emphatic, and so quietly, surprisingly cold and furious the hair stood up on the back of Susannah's neck. She turned to stare at him. But her mind and heart were too crowded, too confused for her to speak; she needed to let all she'd heard settle in.

"You said James was a theatergoer, which was how he knew you," Kit prompted Daisy Jones.

"Yes. James was a lover of..." Daisy paused delicately. "Costume. And spectacle. But particularly...costume."

She exchanged a meaningful look with Kit, which bewildered Susannah.

"And you have no idea how James came to have the children?"

"No, but ye might talk to—" Daisy stopped abruptly.

"To whom, Miss Jones?"

"Well, ye do know James was a good man, Mr. White..." she began hesitantly.

"I knew him," Kit said softly. "I agree." It sounded like permission for Daisy to continue.

"Ye should have a word with Edwin, then," Daisy said. "Edwin Avery-Finch. 'E's a gentle sort, Edwin is. 'E was James's..." She paused again, selecting a word, it seemed, to Susannah. Since delicacy didn't seem to come naturally to Daisy Jones, Susannah found these pauses to choose words intriguing. "...Very good friend," Daisy finally completed. "'E sells antiquities. West of Bond Street, 'is shop is. 'Asn't been in the theater since James...well, since James was done in."

"Thank you, Miss Jones," Kit said.

"Oh, by *all* means, Mr. White." Now that the interview was over, Daisy was all winsome prurience again. "It would be my *pleasure*." She winked at Kit, then folded Susannah into her fragrant bosom.

"I hope ye find Anna, my dear," she said into Susannah's hair.

"So do I, Miss Jones." Her voice was somewhat muffled against Daisy's chest. "I want to clear her name." Daisy finally relinquished her, and Susannah gulped in a breath.

"May we speak to you again about this, Miss Jones, if the

need arises?" Kit asked. "We need to be somewhere else at the moment."

"It would be me *pleasure,* Mr. White."

❧

He'd all but dragged her out of the White Lily by the elbow, such was his speed. Past the handsome Mr. Shaughnessy and The General and all the rehearsing girls, into the waiting unmarked coach. He thumped the roof to get it moving, and hauled her so quickly up to a room at an inn not more than ten minutes from the theater that her feet nearly left the ground, all the while ignoring her protests, her requests for explanation, until Susannah at last gave up. He closed the door, locked it, all but flung her into a chair, and spoke before she could take a good look around.

"I have something to tell you, Susannah. And you need to be sitting for it."

"I never would have guessed it."

He didn't respond to her sarcasm. In fact, he still wasn't entirely here with her, she could tell; his eyes still had that remote, abstracted light to them, as if he were reading something written inside his own head.

"I think James Makepeace was murdered. And I think the same people who murdered him killed your real father, Richard Lockwood, and are now trying to kill you."

And to think, this time last year she was choosing her new dress patterns and swooning over Douglas.

She doubted anything would ever again make her swoon.

"And why do you think this?" she asked. The very steadiness of her voice seemed almost absurd, given that they were discussing her own possible murder.

She looked about the room while Kit took a deep breath,

organizing his thoughts, no doubt. One large bed, a little elderly, judging from the person-length dent in the center of it. A bureau, against which Kit now propped his long frame. A pair of lamps. It all looked clean enough. It was suspiciously close to the White Lily Theater, too, and Kit had seemed to know precisely where he was going. She didn't want to think of the opera dancers he might have pressed into the dent in that particular mattress. "Friends," he'd called them. Opera dancers. *Friendly.*

"Let me tell you what I know now," he began. "Richard Lockwood was murdered fifteen years ago. Officials intended to arrest his mistress for it. But she disappeared, and no one knew what became of her, and no thought was given to what became of her three little daughters—it was assumed she'd managed to escape with them, I suppose. But today we learned from Miss Daisy Jones that your mother was not Anna *Smith*—she was in fact Anna Holt, Richard Lockwood's mistress. Lockwood was your father. *And* you have two sisters. You, for some reason, wound up in James Makepeace's safekeeping. And now James is dead, too."

"But...why do these murders have anything to do with *me*?"

"Well...Richard Lockwood was investigating a politician named Thaddeus Morley—"

"Oh! You've mentioned Mr. Morley. People think very highly of him, do they not?"

Kit's face darkened subtly. His mouth parted as though he intended to comment, but then he shook his head roughly and continued. "Richard Lockwood was gathering evidence to prove that Morley had acquired his fortune in part by selling information to the French, but he was killed before he could present his proof to anyone. And I believe he was killed because Morley was somehow warned."

Susannah pictured this...her father, a politician, attempting to prove the guilt of an alleged traitor.

And then...*Wait.*

"How...how on earth do *you* know all of this?"

Kit studied her, as though gauging the current state of her internal fortitude. And then exhaled resignedly. "I'm a spy."

Blue eyes unblinking, face unreadable, he awaited her response. She stared at him, and suddenly:

"I *knew* it!" she said triumphantly.

This made him smile at last. "You didn't *know* it."

"When you're always so prepared for disaster, and so good at warding it off, and armed to the teeth, and unnervingly observant, you had better either be a spy or a criminal. I knew you couldn't simply be a soldier. I've danced with a soldier or two. They hadn't your..."

She wanted to say "confidence." Or "presence." Or "air of danger." But that would probably amuse him and embarrass *her,* so she stopped speaking.

He was trying not to look impressed, anyway. "You know so much about spies then, do you? You are simply very perceptive, which I believe is part of being an artist. I disguise it very well."

"*Am* I an artist?" She was momentarily diverted. She was growing accustomed to considering herself talented, but "artist" was a new and very distinct definition of herself: Susannah Makepeace/Lockwood/Holt, artist. A wanton, brave artist with a temper. She was coming into focus as a person, a bit at a time.

"A gifted one," he confirmed, and she knew it wasn't flattery, because he'd probably never said a deliberately flattering thing in his life. "You don't seem terribly shocked to hear that I'm a spy." He sounded almost affronted.

"What could shock me anymore?" she said with a faked insouciance that made him snort. It seemed the lesser of revelations at the moment, truthfully. "But how did I come to be with James Makepeace? And how would James know about Richard Lockwood, and Morley, and the French, and the documents, and all of that?"

"I don't know how you came to be with James, Susannah. But James must have been the one to warn your mother to flee. He was a spy, too."

Susannah gaped. "He *can't* have been."

Kit's mouth quirked wryly. "Not every spy is required to defend maidens. In fact, we *seldom* are. James was a... courier, not a warrior. I worked with him a few times. He was a liaison of sorts in any number of important situations, worked through the Alien Office, which is related to Bow Street, which is probably how he learned both of Richard's murder and the intent to arrest your mother for it in enough time to warn her. But the night he told me of his suspicions about Morley, he never mentioned you at all, Susannah. I imagine it was force of habit: He would never have wanted to compromise your future by exposing you to the truth. You *were* engaged to an heir, were you not? James Makepeace had protected you from the truth his entire life."

But how different her life would have been if not for James Makepeace.

"He risked so much for me," she mused softly. "And for my mother and father. If anyone had discovered he was harboring the daughter of an accused murderess..."

Kit nodded once, as though completing the sentence in his head. "As I told you before, I considered James my friend, though I confess I don't believe I truly knew him. James was a kind man, a gentle man, Susannah, and a brave one. And I don't think it's a coincidence that both James and Richard Lockwood were murdered while they were allegedly investigating Mr. Morley."

"But why would they"—it was so strange to say "they," such a nebulous word; who were "they," anyway?—"or he, want to kill me, too?"

Kit pushed himself away from the bureau and stood tensely

in the middle of the room. "*Think,* Susannah. Could you possibly *know* something significant?"

He rubbed the back of his head impatiently, and Susannah was briefly distracted. Anyone would have thought his hair crisp to the touch, because it was so short and so fair it shone nearly metallic in the light, but it wasn't: it was silky. She remembered the surprise of it beneath her fingers in a moment that had already teemed with new sensations: the breeze on her bare skin, then his breath, then his lips, then the scrape of whiskers, and then... oh God, the velvet heat of his tongue curling around her nipple. She'd combed her fingers through his hair then, finding it unexpectedly soft.

Everything about Kit Whitelaw was unexpected.

Blood instantly stormed the surface of Susannah's skin, and what could only be described as lust gave a great demanding thump inside her.

All because he'd rubbed the back of his head.

Kit must have seen something in her expression then, for he went utterly still for an infinitesimal moment, his pupils flaring hot. As though he could read the precise memory in her eyes.

And then, damn him, a mere instant later, he turned his head casually and continued talking, as though nothing about her had ever affected him at all.

"Susannah, did you see or hear something, anything that might incriminate Morley? Do you *have* something that might make Morley think you're a danger to him?"

"I don't think I've ever seen Mr. Morley before in my life. I rarely ever saw my father... that is, James Makepeace. The only thing I came away from my old home with was all of my dresses and a miniature of my mother. It was the only thing I have of her. The only image of her anywhere in the house."

"May I see the miniature again?"

Susannah had examined the image so closely so many times

it was a miracle she hadn't worn away the image with the sheer force of her longing and wondering. Before she handed it to Kit, she looked down at it one more time, at that sweet face, the humor lighting her pale eyes, and thought: *No. This is no killer.*

Kit took it from her.

"For Susannah Faith, from her mother, Anna," Kit read aloud from the back of it. "Could it be code, or . . . does it open?" He began to peer more closely at it, rub his thumbs at its edges.

Susannah squeaked, and he looked up at her inquiringly.

"Please don't hurt it."

Kit restrained his eagerness with some effort, and returned the miniature to Susannah, who received it in cupped hands like a tiny baby, and looked down at it again.

"Kit . . . even so . . . even if the miniature was somehow a clue, how would Mr. Morley know I have it?"

"I don't know, Susannah." He fell silent. "Did your father— James, that is—know you owned this?"

"Yes. In fact, shortly before he died I saw him looking at it and . . ." She trailed off, as something occurred to her. "He said, *'Of course,'* Kit."

Kit frowned. "I beg your pardon?"

"I found him in my rooms a few weeks ago . . . he was looking at the miniature." She flushed, feeling a little foolish. "But he was looking at the back of it, not at her face, which seemed wrong to me. And then he said, *'Of course.'* He sounded . . . pleased. Rather excited, in fact."

"He'd realized something, perhaps." Kit fell silent, thinking. He dropped his body into the chair, stretched out his long legs. "Why did you come away from your house with only your dresses and the miniature, Susannah?"

"Because the men stripped the house of everything else. Apparently nothing else was paid for."

"What were they like, these men?"

"They were all almost offensively cheerful. They rather looked alike, too. The one I threatened with a vase was stocky, had only one eyebrow, blue eyes . . . Oh! I just realized. I . . . I must have my *mother's* temper! Miss Jones said my mother had a temper." The thought cheered Susannah, perversely. It was nice to know she had somebody's *something*.

But Kit's face was grimly speculative. "My guess is those men searched your home on Morley's behalf. But again . . . I'm not certain I can prove it."

"But my father *was* penniless when he died . . . the solicitor told me so. And how would Mr. Morley know if my father . . . *knew* something?"

"I don't know." Kit slumped in his chair, rubbed his hands over his face in weary impatience, then flattened them on his thighs, as if to deliberately stop them from moving.

Susannah watched him. She'd never seen him quite like this: edgy, weary, stripped of dazzle.

Kit thought for a moment, and then brightened. "*But* . . . if they searched everything they wouldn't be trying to kill you if they'd found what they were looking for. So we still have a chance."

"Ah. So it cheers you that they're still trying to kill me?"

"Yes. Because I so enjoy endangering my own life on your behalf, Miss Makepeace."

"I think you *must*."

The corner of his mouth twitched upward. "I wouldn't do it otherwise."

"Because it would be more inconvenient to dispose of my corpse than to prevent my becoming one?" she quipped.

"That's enough." And again, he said it so coldly, so sharply, that warmth started up in her cheeks. She would have apologized, but she simply didn't know what line she had crossed.

Kit stood and began to pace. Pacing seemed unlike him,

too. He'd never seemed one to waste motion. She watched him for a moment, back and forth, back and forth...until he paused, and quite sensibly, lit a lamp, and then another. The room filled with light.

"Kit..." she faltered. "Why are you so certain Mr. Morley is guilty of these crimes?"

"I'm *not* certain."

"Please don't be oblique. You seem convinced of it."

He hesitated. "Instinct." He said it lightly, offhandedly.

But the hesitation told Susannah that her own instincts were correct: there *was* something more here. Something deeper, something older. Something she preferred not to hear, but needed to know. "It has to do with Caroline Allston, doesn't it?"

She made the words sound as casual as she could, so he wouldn't feel cornered, and wouldn't be stubborn, and wouldn't be glib.

What a delicate thing it was to manage a man.

Well, *this* man.

Kit abruptly stopped pacing, and turned and leaned up against the bureau again, folding his arms over his chest, staring back at her, his expression studiedly neutral. She met his eyes bravely. She was learning there were many types of bravery in the world. Patience—particularly patience with Kit Whitelaw—was another form of bravery, too.

And then, at last, a faint, appreciative smile curled his mouth.

He was funny that way—he loved to be challenged. He loved to be caught out. She suspected he was rarely *truly* challenged.

"I couldn't help her." His voice was soft, as though the words had traveled a distance of years. "Caroline."

"Why did she need help?" Her voice was conversational. To make it easier for him.

It was another moment before he spoke again. When he

did, he looked away from her and spoke...well, to the lamp, it seemed. "Caroline was the daughter of a Barnstable squire. And the man was...well, he drank too much, he gambled away their money...Caroline used to try to keep him in liquor so that he would drink himself into a stupor, because that way he wouldn't be able to hit her." Kit gave a humorless laugh. "He had hands like mallets—put bruises on her. I used to steal my father's liquor, so she could give it to her father. Until my father caught me and thrashed me. Thought I was stealing it for myself. Not that I *never* stole it for myself..." he added, with a swift glance at her. In the spirit of accuracy, no doubt.

"I'd expect nothing less of you," Susannah teased gently. But her stomach contracted, hurting for him.

A little of the tension left his posture; his arms unfolded. He was more comfortable now that he'd committed to wading deeper into his story.

"Caroline was...well, she was beautiful. There's no other word for it."

"So I've heard." She couldn't resist saying it.

Kit's brow arched upward, appreciating her sarcasm, as usual. "And...she was manipulative. That, I can see now. But back then...well, John and I—John Carr, my best friend—we were mad about her, and she knew it, too. She played us against each other. Still, there was something about Caroline that made you...want to protect her, no matter what." He looked directly, almost defiantly, at Susannah. "I wanted to marry her."

It sounded almost like an accusation, or a defense.

And she wondered at the tone: Did he think she would judge him for not marrying Caroline? Or did he think that perhaps she, Susannah Makepeace, aspired above her own social station, as Caroline had?

"If I'd the courage, I would have married her. But my father would have killed me, and so..."

"You were only seventeen," she said gently.

"One can breed at seventeen, Susannah," he said bluntly. "It's been done. People marry at seventeen all the time. My parents married at seventeen."

She flushed a little. "But you also were the son of an earl."

"Still am," he said half-whimsically, half-bitterly. "So, in short, I could have saved her, but I didn't. Because I was seventeen and the son of an earl and afraid of my father."

"What of John Carr?"

He paused. "Oh, he would have married her, too. He wanted to, just as desperately. His father didn't like the idea any more than mine. And she preferred me. We both knew it."

He looked directly at Susannah then again. Assessing her reaction to these words.

"I am the son of an earl," he repeated, by way of explanation. "And John is the son of a baron."

"No," Susannah said almost without thinking. He looked at her, puzzled, and she felt compelled to finish her sentence, even as her face grew warm. "It's because you are"—she faltered—"you."

He looked startled. And as she'd said a very good deal more than she'd intended to with that one little sentence, she spoke hurriedly. "Go on."

"Well, when my mother was alive, my father used to hold yearly parties at The Roses, and all the local villagers were invited. This particular year, Mr. Morley attended, too—I believe he was trying to get elected, and wanted my father's support. I remember when Morley first laid eyes on Caroline..." Kit stopped, gave a short humorless laugh. "I was so envious he could appear...unmoved."

This, Susannah thought, wasn't easy to hear, either.

"Caroline spent most of the evening speaking to him. It was very nearly unseemly, and she knew precisely how it affected

me. And John. Morley looked up at me ... And he ... *smiled*.
And Susannah ... everything the man is was in that smile. It
was like he ..." Kit paused. "He hated me. He didn't know me,
but he hated me.

"And then I turned my back ... and they were gone. Caroline
and Morley. And John turned to me and said ..." Kit turned
away from Susannah, as if to spare her the sight of him saying
the words. "He said, 'She's just a whore, Grantham.'"

He let the ugly words ring in the room for a moment. Susannah heard them as he must have heard them, a proud young
man in love, about to lose everything he wanted to a man he
couldn't hope to compete with: Morley.

"And so naturally, I had to call John out." Kit's tone was
mocking, but she still heard the twinge of shame in it. "Despite
the fact that he was my best friend. And John and I dueled, and
I shot him, and our fathers sent us into the army. But the night
of the party was the last time I ever saw Caroline. And Morley
was gone the next morning, too. And I do believe that's the end
of the story. He took her away."

"And that's why ... that's why you dislike Mr. Morley." She
said it slowly, as the understanding dawned.

Kit frowned. "What do you mean?"

"Because he took Caroline away, when you could not.
Because he saved her ... when you could not."

Kit stared at her, the sort of stare that should have frightened
her but didn't now, because she was growing accustomed to it.
And then his expression went ...

Well, oddly, he looked *bored*.

And suddenly he was all swift, abrupt motion. "I'll step into
the corridor while you get into your night rail and beneath the
blankets, Miss Makepeace. We've a Mr. Avery-Finch to visit in
the morning. I'll sleep in the chair."

He'd waited a suitable amount of time in the corridor while she
fumbled her way out of her clothes and into her night rail. Then
he entered the room again, doused the lamps, and stretched out
in the chair without saying a word.

Susannah could not have said how much time passed in the
dark, but neither of them slept. The events of the day, of the past
few weeks, the danger and the sweetness and the discoveries,
milled about in her head, colliding and creating more questions. And she dared one.

Her heart began to pound a little harder with the boldness of
what she was about to say. "You'll sleep badly in the chair, Kit.
Would you like to sleep next to me? I promise not to thrash about."

She tried to make her words light. Tried to make them sound
like a practical suggestion, and less like the wanton invitation
they disguised.

There was a long quiet so thick Susannah could have
grabbed fistfuls of it.

"No, Susannah. I will sleep even more badly next to you."

His voice was night itself: ironic, dense with meaning, a
little dangerous. He might as well have slipped a hand beneath
her nightdress for how it made her feel.

"Good night, then," she said. Her voice trembling. Doubting
she would sleep at all. Wondering why, for heaven's sake, he
refused to touch her now, as surely they had gone beyond honor
and propriety. Wondering if it was all for the best. Wondering
that her body seemed to have a reason all its own, that had nothing at all to do with her rational mind.

And knowing he was very likely right not to touch her,
which didn't make it any easier. And trying to be grateful for
what he was offering her: safety and the truth about her past.

And not to want anything beyond that.

"Good night, Susannah. We'll visit Mr. Avery-Finch in the morning. I shan't let anyone murder you this evening."

"Thoughtful of you," she murmured.

❧

His eyes had finally adjusted to the dark. He could see her breasts lift and fall gently with her breathing. She'd thrown off her blanket. He watched now. Feeling like an adolescent. Just as ridiculous, just as enthralled.

He imagined going to her, lying next to her on the bed, pulling her into his arms, waiting for her to stir awake. He imagined the feel of the fine, fragile fabric of the night rail against his hands—it would be warm, fragrant from her—and the whisper of sound it would make as it slid over her body when he lifted it from her. He imagined his hands gliding over the curve of her shoulders and hips; over the petal skin of her breasts, and her softer-still nipples. He imagined her lithe body rippling beneath his touch as he discovered her again, and thoroughly this time, he imagined his mouth finding, tasting every bit of her, the hollow of her belly, the musk between her legs, her soft cries of pleasure as he did. He imagined the slow final taking of her, moving inside her as she clung to him—

Oh, God.

He wanted. He wanted. He wanted.

Breathe through it, he told himself mordantly. *As you would any pain.*

And over the years, he'd become a walking weapon; he knew just what to do with his hands and feet, with sword and pistol, to preserve his own life or save another, and he'd done it again and again in service to his country. He knew he was remarkable; he had enough clarity to see it and was arrogant enough to be proud of it. Still, no matter how he hated to admit it, he knew he was far from infallible. Ah, but fate, with characteristic ironic humor, had thrown yet another endangered female into his all too fallible hands. And this one—

He half-smiled in the dark. *Mr. Morley saved her when you could not.*

She'd said it so casually. When, in fact, it rather unlocked more than a decade of his life.

This one . . . *saw* him. Clearly and fully, in a way he'd never before felt seen. He found himself offering up his secrets to her; she seemed to know them anyway. He knew he surprised herself even as she surprised him, with the depth of her passion, her strength and resilience. Her wit. And oh God, her beauty burned in him.

Yes, he knew he was remarkable. He knew he was fallible. And he knew, sitting there in the dark, that he was afraid now in a way he didn't fully understand, perhaps more afraid than he'd ever been before.

❧

Bob arrived with a limp.

"That great geezer she's always with nearly killed me. Fought like the bloody devil. Knew what he was about, he did. A *real* fighter."

Bob sounded irritated; he wasn't paid enough to deal with someone who actually *fought back*. Let alone competently.

"So she's alive," Morley said flatly. It had been a little more than a week since he'd had the pleasure of Bob's company. He supposed good news was too much to hope for.

"Yes," Bob said. He didn't sound the least bit apologetic.

"And I know his name now, too," he added. "Heard it in the pub there in Barnstable. Getting mighty sick of Barnstable, Mr. Morley. There's a chap what's always at the pub. Mr. Evers. Right boring chap. You said to come if I had news."

"Well?" Morley was impatient. "The name?"

"It's Grantham. And he's a *viscount*."

Morley's heart balled into such a tight fist that he coughed.

"Merowr?" Fluff questioned from his feet.

"A *viscount*," Bob repeated, marveling. One didn't expect a viscount, after all, to be able to fight like the devil.

Oh, Morley thought, *I really could do without nasty surprises for a day or two.*

He suspected his heart was not at all what it used to be. He could have sworn it had taken more than a second there to continue ticking. But it was ticking now, and so was his mind.

"Heard it in the pub," Bob said again, when Morley didn't say anything. "Local lord."

Dear God, what on earth was *Grantham* doing with Makepeace's daughter?

"Sir?"

Morley supposed he had been silent overlong. "Interesting," he said, sounding offhand. Just to interrupt the silence with a word. Just to make sure Bob noticed nothing amiss.

Maybe, Morley thought, it was a harmless courtship. Grantham hailed from Barnstable, too, and it was entirely possible their paths had innocently crossed. She was pretty, Susannah Makepeace, if she looked at all like Anna Holt. Grantham was a womanizer; that was well known. Perhaps he was merely passing his time in a way any young rake would find agreeable.

But it was another bloody coincidence in a series of bloody coincidences.

Then again . . . well, he really didn't believe in coincidences, so why bother with the word at all?

He had to admit, however, it was looking worse and worse.

That night, years ago, at the Earl of Westphall's with a single smile, he'd made certain Grantham had known what he was about to do. Perhaps that had been a mistake: allowing his triumph to show, his contempt, his hatred for all the things the lordling had represented, the things that had been denied Morley. He'd forgotten that boys became men, often with long memories.

Morley considered the pieces before him on the chessboard, the people in play.

And with a little thrill, a daring strategy occurred to him.

He couldn't kill Grantham—he could simply imagine the magnitude of the investigation that would ensue, and the difficulty involved in killing him, regardless—but he could play upon the things he knew about him: a taste for heroics, for honor...and for women. One woman in particular, in fact. He might be able to trap him neatly. Possibly discredit him; at the very least, he might be able to distract him from Susannah Makepeace long enough for Bob to do his job, or extract a little information.

"Find Caroline," he said to Bob, "and bring her here."

"*Bring* her here? She's right dodgy now, sir. Can't get close to her. Can't say as I blame her, either, sir."

"Tell her...it's all been a mistake. All is forgiven."

"Beggin' your pardon, sir: She might not be clever, but she isn't *stupid*. You may have to tell her yourself. After all, she knows *you* won't..." Bob drew a finger eloquently across his own throat.

Bob was right. Their only chance of corralling Caroline involved Morley himself.

He would have to meet her.

And then his heart moved again, and it wasn't a dangerous clench this time, but something unexpected.

"Where did you last see her, Bob?"

"A coaching inn outside of Headley Meade. A few days ago."

Headley Meade. Only an hour or so away from London.

"Think you can find her again?"

"Of course, sir. I'm a prof—"

Morley sighed heavily. "Then arrange a meeting as soon as you can."

Chapter Sixteen

〜

*M*r. Avery-Finch's shop was ripe with the must of age, and stuffed and stacked full of dully gleaming, hopelessly breakable objects: vases and tea sets, plates and pillars, statues and paintings, trunks and chandeliers and plump stools, arranged, it seemed, for maximum precariousness. Some shopkeepers hang a bell upon their door, Kit thought, to alert them of entering customers; Mr. Avery-Finch probably just waited for a potential customer to send something crashing to smithereens.

It wasn't all fine stuff; the fine mingled with the much less fine, but only an educated eye would be able to discern it. He wondered whether this arrangement was carelessness or a device to discover just how much a customer really knew about antiquities, and how much money could then be extracted from them.

Susannah looked afraid to move, burdened as she was with skirts. Kit picked a path between a reproduction of Venus de Milo and a gilded chest, and thought perhaps he would need a compass to find his way back to the door.

"Good afternoon! And what can I do for you, sir?" A man who could only be Mr. Edwin Avery-Finch stood before him, and bowed.

When he was upright, Kit was struck silent.

It was his eyes. Mr. Avery-Finch looked like many Englishmen in their middle years: a palm-sized scrap of hair remained on his scalp; his chin had gone soft; he was dressed well but not ostentatiously.

But his eyes were astonishing. Dark, bleak, and set into hollows carved brutally out by grief.

"Mr. Avery-Finch, I presume? I am Mr. White."

Bows were exchanged. Precise, careful bows, so as not to upset the stacks of things. "Good afternoon, Mr. White. Something for the lady today? I have a very fine Louis the sixteenth settee in the back. Perfect for one of your country homes."

Kit almost smiled. Mr. Avery-Finch had sized them up very neatly and quickly: wealthy, profligate. But the man's cheerful voice was almost in macabre contrast to that grieving face.

"Mr. Avery-Finch," Kit said gently, "Miss Daisy Jones sent us to you. We understand you were close to Mr. James Makepeace."

Mr. Avery-Finch went very still. Before their eyes, the false cheer drained from his face, leaving it gray and empty.

"Yes." His voice was graveled with emotion. "I was."

Kit knew then that "friend" did not begin to encompass what James Makepeace was to Mr. Avery-Finch. And suddenly, in the form of this plain little dealer in antiquities, James Makepeace was no longer a cipher, but a person who had been loved.

"We're investigating his death." *And his life, apparently.*

Mr. Avery-Finch said nothing. Stood motionless, as though the mere mention of James had clubbed him senseless.

"I'm sorry for your loss," Kit said quietly. "He was my friend."

"Were you . . . perhaps in the same line of work as James, Mr. White?" Mr. Avery-Finch ventured gingerly.

"Would that be . . . importing antiquities?" Kit said just as gingerly, making it sound like a question.

Mr. Avery-Finch smiled faintly. "You are, aren't you?" He had guessed correctly that this was a sort of code for "spy."

"And you are . . . ?" Mr. Avery-Finch directed this question to Susannah.

"I was his daughter, Mr. Avery-Finch. My name is Susannah."

Mr. Avery-Finch's eyes widened, and he stared at Susannah, but not in surprise. More in . . . speculation. Studied her, as though taking inventory of her features. His mouth parted, as if he intended to say something. He stopped himself.

"Perhaps we should have a seat and a chat in my back parlor. I'll just hang the sign on the door, now . . ."

Mr. Avery-Finch expertly picked through his delicate stock and turned the door. "I can make tea," he offered over his shoulder. "Goodness knows I've no shortage of teapots." He gestured, albeit carefully, about the crowded room.

Susannah laughed and Mr. Avery-Finch smiled a little, pleased that his small joke could lighten things.

"Miss Makepeace knows that James is not her father," Kit said once they were all arranged on settees and clutching cups of steaming tea. He thought he might as well begin that way.

Mr. Avery-Finch stared back at Kit, cautiously, consideringly.

"It's all right, Mr. Avery-Finch. Your confidences could not be safer with me. I do not think James's death was an accident, which is why we are here."

"I just wish he'd come to me before he . . ." Mr. Avery-Finch's voice broke. "James was in debt, you see. He had such a weakness for fine things, and a better eye for them than anyone. It was how we met—he came into the shop nearly twenty years ago." He offered a weak smile. "He was practical in so many ways, James was—he actually had quite a head for figures—but he couldn't seem to stop acquiring things he could not afford. He adopted them, like children. Seemed to need them. And . . . well, I had no idea how desperate he'd become for money."

"How desperate *had* he become?" Kit asked. He sniffed the tea. It wanted sugaring, he suspected, but Mr. Avery-Finch hadn't thought to supply any. He took an experimental sip, anyway.

"He told me over claret—James loved his claret . . ." He smiled a little, looking into Kit's and Susannah's faces, hoping they shared this memory, too. Susannah could only give him a weak smile of encouragement. "He told me he'd sent a letter to Thaddeus Morley."

"A blackmail letter?" Kit guessed bluntly.

"Well, what other sort will get you killed?" Mr. Avery-Finch said with startling tartness. "Yes, the bloody fool, that's what he did. He should have asked me for help. I'm not a rich man, but I could have found a way . . . together we could have found . . . have found a way . . ."

Kit waited quietly for Mr. Avery-Finch's grieving rage to ebb before he asked another question. "Why did he send the blackmail letter to Mr. Morley in particular?"

With this question, Mr. Avery-Finch suddenly seemed to find the teapot fascinating. He stared at it as if he were counting the painted flowers that sprawled over it.

Susannah spoke softly. "If there's anything at all you can tell us, sir . . . I would be so grateful. For you see, I have no family at all now . . . and if you perhaps know anything about them . . ."

Mr. Avery-Finch's face spasmed in sympathy then. And after a moment, he nodded, as if giving himself permission to speak.

"It was for Richard, you see, that James did it. Took on you girls."

"Richard Lockwood?" Kit said quickly.

Mr. Avery-Finch looked up at Kit, his expression wry now. "Mr. White, why don't you tell me what you *already* know about Richard and James, and I shall endeavor to supply you with new information."

This was a reasonable request, Kit decided. "We know Richard Lockwood and Anna Holt had three daughters, of whom Susannah is the youngest. We know that Lockwood was murdered, and that Anna Holt was accused of the murder, but disappeared before she could be arrested for it. No one seemed to give any thought to what became of the girls; I suppose it was assumed they were with their mother. And shortly before his death a few weeks ago, James told me he suspected Thaddeus Morley was involved in Richard Lockwood's murder. We learned yesterday from Miss Daisy Jones that it was James who took on Anna's three daughters."

"You know rather a good deal, Mr. White." Mr. Avery-Finch's mouth twitched, and he sat for a moment, thinking. "I will tell you this: James and Richard were dear friends. Met at the theater. Shared a love of spectacle, a similar sense of the absurd. They shared a love of antiquities, too, Richard and James. Yes, they became good friends." There was a touch of wistful envy in Mr. Avery-Finch's voice. "Richard confided in James...knew James was very good at"—he looked at Kit directly, almost challengingly, in the eye—"keeping secrets."

He would have to be, Kit thought. "James shared secrets with you, however," Kit guessed.

"Of course," he said. We were—" He stopped himself,

glanced at Susannah, then back at Kit. "Very close." A faint smile touched his lips.

"What about Mr. Morley? Was he acquainted with Richard, too?"

"Well, Richard was Mr. Morley's political rival. Richard never liked or trusted the man—I thought it was snobbery, at first. Richard was from a fine family, and Morley was not, and as my family origins are hardly lofty, I was inclined to sympathize with Morley. But then I had an occasion to meet Mr. Morley and...well, I didn't care for him, either. It's difficult to say quite why." He looked at Kit to see whether he understood.

"Sometimes these things are instinctive."

"Yes," Mr. Avery-Finch agreed, sounding relieved. "And James told me all about how Richard had undertaken his own investigation into Morley, and had apparently actually found something desperately incriminating. When Richard was murdered, I was inclined to believe him. That's when James rushed to take you girls, Susannah—so the authorities couldn't take you away."

"Did James tell anyone else besides yourself, Mr. Avery-Finch?"

"James was close to two people, Mr. White. You're looking at one of them. Richard was the other. He did not share confidences lightly."

"And James was close enough to Richard to risk his life by warning Anna and taking on three little girls?"

Mr. Avery-Finch looked up, surprised. "Close? James was in love with Richard."

In the silence that followed, one could almost hear the dust settle on the stacks of china and tea trays.

"More tea?" Mr. Avery-Finch took a delicately ironic sip of his own.

"I'm sorry, my dear," Mr. Avery-Finch turned to Susannah,

though he looked a trifle more mischievous than sorry. "Do I shock you?"

"No," Susannah said quickly. Her eyes seemed to have frozen into a wide position, however.

Liar, Kit thought.

"Your father, Susannah, was a very handsome man," Mr. Avery-Finch explained. "I liked him, too, you know, but I was never invited into a friendship with him the way James was. And yes, I will confess that I was somewhat jealous of their friendship, but...well, James did spend most of his time with me, so I didn't fuss, and Richard was passionately in love with your mother, Miss Makepeace, you should know that. What he felt for James was... was friendship only. Truly. But James loved him very much."

Mr. Avery-Finch's voice trailed away, as though the magnitude of this revelation had tired him. And then for a disconcerting moment he peered at Susannah as though she were somehow a window through which he could see the past. "You're the spit of your mother you know, my dear," he said finally. "Except for this." Startling her, he reached out and pinched Susannah's chin gently between two fingers. "This square little chin. That was Richard's."

Susannah's eyes flared with poignant astonishment and then a soft pleasure. And when Mr. Avery-Finch took his fingers from her chin, she surreptitiously replaced them with her own, wonderingly. Kit felt again that strange kick in his breastbone again. As though his heart beat in tandem with her own.

Mr. Avery-Finch cleared his throat. "Forgive me, as I am rambling now. So yes, James kept *you,* Susannah, for Richard's sake. And he found homes for your sisters, for Richard's sake. And he was silent all of these years, for Richard's sake. And he warned Anna to flee...for Richard's sake. He kept quiet, too... for the sake of you girls, thinking perhaps he'd find Anna, or Anna would return. She never did."

"And you haven't any idea where Anna might have gone?" Kit asked. "Or the other girls?"

"Nary a clue, and I *am* sorry. I can imagine what it must have been like for her...to lose everything she loved...all at once."

His voice didn't quite break. Englishmen, on the whole, Kit reflected, were made of stern stuff, regardless of whether they fought on battlefields or sold teapots. Mr. Avery-Finch took a deep breath, and another sip of tea. "Louis the sixteenth," he said, gesturing to the teapot. "I'll give it to you for a very good price, if you'd like it."

"Thank you, Mr. Avery-Finch. I shall take it under consideration," Kit told him solemnly.

"I knew..." Mr. Avery-Finch continued once the tea had restored his composure. "I knew if ever a chance came to get justice for Richard, James would take it. But his debt rather interfered with his plans, and addled his thoughts, I believe. Though his profession called for a unique sort of...discretion, shall we say, dishonesty didn't come naturally to James, and when he tried to kill two birds with one stone—that is, get justice for Richard and pay his debt— well...the bird killed him instead, didn't it?" His mouth twitched at his own morbid joke. "He rather went about things backward, didn't he? He blackmailed first, and then set out to find proof."

"Pity they don't teach the proper way to blackmail at Oxford."

"Isn't it?" Mr. Avery-Finch concurred on a murmur, and took another sip of tea.

"Mr. Avery-Finch, did James ever mention anything to you about the nature of this proof Richard Lockwood had collected...anything at all about 'Christian virtues'?"

"'Christian virtues,' Mr. White?" Mr. Avery-Finch's eyebrows lifted ironically. "No, I'm afraid the two of us did not spend much time reviewing Christian virtues. Are they important to our discussion?"

"James told me that Richard had been clever about hiding his proof of Mr. Morley's guilt. Apparently the hiding place had something to do with 'Christian virtues.'"

"Well, that *does* sound like Richard. He was fond of being clever. I wish I could provide some enlightenment with regard to that, sir, but I cannot. Perhaps James was protecting me from what he knew. Perhaps I should even now fear for my life, given what I *do* know. But I rather find I don't care much what becomes of me, these days, so it's all the same."

Kit didn't know what to say; he couldn't very well pat the man's hand, and he knew words were all but useless when it came to easing grief.

"We shall get justice for James, Mr. Avery-Finch, and for Richard and Anna. And I will do everything I can to see to your safety."

Mr. Avery-Finch's shoulder merely went up in a slight shrug.

It was certainly an extraordinary amount of information to take in all at once, for anyone. "Are you all right?" Kit asked Susannah.

For a time, she didn't answer. "It's very sad, isn't it?" she said finally. "I suppose I'm glad to know that even if James Makepeace didn't love me, he did love my father. They were lovers, weren't they? James Makepeace and Mr. Avery-Finch?"

He could only answer honestly. "Yes. I believe they were."

More silence. "I suppose I'm...I suppose I'm glad that someone loved him. My father. James Makepeace, that is. And that someone truly knew him. And misses him with his...his whole heart."

With his whole heart. Every day he was discovering ways in which she was remarkable.

"So am I," Kit told her softly.

He held out his arm and she took it. He scanned the street with his grimly talented eyes, ready to duck, or dodge, as necessary. Their unmarked carriage was only a few feet away, but a few *fraught* feet, given that someone was trying to kill Susannah and his father would love to send him to Egypt should anyone sight him in London.

"Your mother and father loved you, Susannah." His voice was a little rough with the sentiment; he certainly didn't say such things easily. But he wanted her to believe that someone had once loved her with a whole heart, too.

She simply smiled a little, and her fingers went up to touch her chin again.

Which is when Kit saw a handsome, tall, very familiar figure approaching them.

"Mr. White," John Carr tipped his hat as he passed Kit on his way into Mr. Avery-Finch's shop.

"Mr. Carson," Kit said politely.

"Heard Egypt is quite fine this time of year," John said over his shoulder.

"You wouldn't *dare.*"

John Carr merely laughed and continued past them.

"Mr. Carson?" Kit said sharply, suddenly.

John Carr stopped, turned an expectant face toward Kit, flicked a glance at Susannah that widened into deep appreciation, and then looked back at Kit, his eyes glinting a merry question.

Which Kit didn't answer. Instead he gestured with his chin to Mr. Avery-Finch's shop. "See to his safety, will you? Hire a runner?"

John Carr's face became somber, and he nodded shortly,

then turned with soldier precision and continued toward the shop.

Susannah was gawking. "Who on earth—"

"Someone I shot once, long ago."

"Someone he *missed* once, long ago," came John's voice over his shoulder, as he vanished into Mr. Avery-Finch's shop, to pursue his own line of questioning.

Kit watched him with an inevitable and utterly unworthy sense of competition rising. "On to Miss Daisy Jones to inquire about the miniatures, then back to Barnstable," Kit said.

Susannah was still staring back at the shop doorway. "Was that John Carr? Your best friend?"

"Yes. Handsome, isn't he? Fine figure of a man."

"Was he? I hadn't noticed."

"You're a poor liar, Miss Makepeace."

She laughed, a sound that delighted him beyond reason.

When Kit and Susannah entered the White Lily Theater, Daisy Jones, Tom Shaughnessy, and The General were onstage arguing fiercely, three sets of hands gesticulating wildly. Daisy was perched on a swing dressed as a mermaid, and every time she made a point she flapped her tail vehemently. It was a magnificent tail, purple, and covered all over in some sort of sparkling net that was meant to look like scales, perhaps. A billowing red wig flowed from her head down over her...primary assets... and Kit saw the brilliance of the act: when she swung backward and forward, that red wig might just fly up and—

Good heavens. Kit rather hoped he'd be in London to see it.

The General finally flung both hands up in disgust,

flounced off the stage, and stalked, muttering to himself, up the aisle. "*Mumble mumble* not bloody *Shakespeare,* for God's sake. Bloody *mumble mumble* thinks she's bloody Nell *Gwynn.*"

He stopped abruptly when he saw Kit and Susannah. He bowed low, and pivoted back toward the stage. "*Madame* Jones," he drawled with exaggerated politeness. "Visitors."

Announcement made, he continued stalking and muttering toward the back of the theater. "Bloody fat spoiled *mermaid,*" was the last thing Kit heard as he disappeared.

Tom Shaughnessy looked up from Daisy, whom he now appeared to be placating. "Ah, if it isn't Mr. White, and the charming and beautiful Mrs. White," he boomed. He swung gracefully off the stage. Today he was wearing fawn trousers and a bottle-green waistcoat, and his red-gold hair was a masterpiece of calculated messiness.

"Mr. White, if you'll give me a hand with our fair mermaid?"

Daisy hopped up off the swing and shimmied in her tail toward the edge of the stage, and Tom Shaughnessy and Kit each took an arm and swung her down. Her long red wig remained in place due, perhaps, to some cleverness of glue.

"We've just a quick question for you, Miss Jones, if you've a moment. We're terribly sorry to interrupt," Kit said.

"An interruption is what we needed, Mr. White," Tom Shaughnessy said smoothly. "I'll just gracefully retreat, shall I? To allow you to speak in private?" Mr. Shaughnessy bowed low, managing to make the simple gesture downright sultry, for Susannah's benefit, Kit was certain, and backed away. She dimpled, watching him go.

Kit cleared his throat, and she twitched her eyes away from Mr. Shaughnessy almost guiltily.

He turned toward the sparkly mermaid in front of him. "We've just one question, Miss Jones, and then we'll leave you to your rehearsal. Do you happen to know whether Anna Holt's other daughters—Susannah's sisters—had miniatures with them when James brought them to you?"

"Miniatures?" Miss Jones's red eyebrows met in a "V" of thought. "Yes, of Anna, now that ye mention it. The girls each 'ad miniatures of Anna, and little bundles of clothes. I remember thinking 'ow lovely it was for them to 'ave miniatures of their mama… and 'ow dangerous it would be if anyone discovered them."

"Do you recall whether anything had been written on the back of the miniatures?"

"I only saw Sylvie's miniature, Mr. White, but I do believe it said…it said…'To Sylvie 'Ope, of 'er mother, Anna.'"

"Sylvie Hope?" Kit wasn't sure whether this was significant, couldn't have said whether it was a clue yet, but he added it to his collection of information, to revisit later.

"Thank you, Miss Jones."

"Any time, as I said." Daisy swept Susannah into a mermaid hug, and then thrust out her hand for Kit to bow over, and swiveled in a very determined fashion back toward the stage.

"Tom! General!" she bellowed. "We are *not* finished 'ere. I need 'elp into me swing."

"Alert the bloody *navy*!" The General bellowed from somewhere in the back of the theater. "Tell them to bring a bloody *whale* net!"

⌒

It was the kind of establishment he hadn't visited in years, but astonishingly he wasn't entirely uncomfortable in it.

That realization, however, succeeded in making him feel a little uncomfortable.

Dark, the sort of dark that simply defeats lamplight, Morley thought. The darkness came from the floors, stained with a century or so of spilled spirits, food, blood. From the ceilings, low and permeated with smoke. The air itself was thick and fetid with food and smoke and customers, none of whom appeared to have washed any time recently, and none of whom appeared to have all of their teeth. Morley was certain he knew a few of them personally. Had perhaps even run through the streets of St. Giles with a few of them.

Bob had chosen the meeting place. Had gotten a note to Caroline, somehow.

It was a dangerous place for a woman, but then, Caroline wasn't an ordinary woman. She had an instinct both for getting into trouble and getting out of it, like a cat. Had about the same quotient of defenses as a cat, too. He wasn't concerned, but again, he felt it: a tiny, not unpleasant clutch of anticipation in his chest.

She appeared from the shadows. "Hello, Thaddeus. You've been trying to kill me." She extended her hand.

"Hello, Caroline." He kissed the hand. "You've been trying to blackmail me. I'd rise, but the leg, you know."

She clucked in sympathy.

"Why don't you have a seat?" He pulled out a chair. She gazed down at it fastidiously, and then resignedly settled into it.

"I needed the money, Thaddeus."

It wasn't an apology. He almost smiled. "You could have simply *asked* me for the money."

"Really, Thaddeus? For some reason I didn't think I'd find you in a charitable mood." She said it ironically. "And I *really* needed the money."

She was right, of course. One didn't reward the sudden defection of a mistress by giving her money, unless one was stupidly sentimental or desperate. And he was neither.

"What became of the American merchant?" he asked her.

"Is this a trap?" she asked lightly instead of answering.

"With your desirable self as the bait? Will your little man sneak up and stab me between the shoulder blades?"

He didn't respond to that. "Would you like something to drink, Caroline?"

"Here? I think not. Liable to catch all manner of diseases. Not up to your usual standards, Thaddeus."

"But private."

Dressed all in black, Caroline was nearly invisible, but for the striking luminosity of her skin. Her eyes had it, too, that luminosity; like water at midnight, mysterious, fathomless. Making love to her had been maddening: delicious, always elusive. Like making love to the moon.

If the moon had adventurous sexual tastes, that was.

He couldn't help himself, he needed to ask. "Why did you leave me?"

She shrugged.

And he supposed that was as accurate an answer as he could expect from her. He almost understood: her life had begun in turmoil and upheaval, it was her native state, the only state in which she felt comfortable.

Whereas Thaddeus, as he aged, was discovering a taste for consistency and peace. He resented the events of the past few weeks; this need to kill people made him weary.

"I simply cannot allow you to threaten me, Caroline."

"Well, I *know* that now," she said whimsically. "Your little man with the knife rather drove the message home. Why did you want to see me tonight, Thaddeus? To tell me simply that you 'cannot allow me to threaten you'?" She imitated his grand tones.

He couldn't help but smile a little. "I need your help, Caroline."

She laughed. "Well, *that* sounds rather more like you, now. I should have known you wouldn't beg to have me back." The tone was ironic.

But would you come back? No, he would never beg. He wasn't even certain whether he wanted her back. Despite the fact that of all the people who had entered his life ... perhaps she had understood him the best. There was both profound safety and profound danger in that.

"It's simple, really," he told her. "I need you to seduce Grantham and find out what he's doing with Makepeace's daughter. Find out whether it has anything at all to do with me. Then come back here and tell me all about it, so that I may decide what to do next."

"Grantham? Kit Whitelaw, you mean?" she was startled.

He nodded.

Her face was expressionless for a moment, frozen in pure surprise. "Kit," she repeated softly. Her eyes distant, face unreadable.

"What makes you think I can do it, Thaddeus?"

"He still hates me after all of these years, Caroline. And it's because of you."

This pleased her. She smiled, small white teeth shining in that dark pub. "Do you think so, truly? But he's a grown man now."

"Yes. A grown man with a weakness for women and who, no doubt, will find it difficult to keep away from you."

She simply nodded; this was true of most grown men, anyway. "He isn't married? Kit?"

"No."

"And who is Susannah Makepeace?"

"I think she's one of the daughters of Richard Lockwood and Anna Holt."

Caroline jerked back at those words. "With Kit?" she said softly. "She's with Kit? But why?"

"I don't *know,* Caroline," Morley explained, impatiently. "It's what I need you to discover. But he's a spy now. He's not a..." He searched for adequate words. "... Soft man. Or an easy man. He is, in fact, a clever and dangerous man."

And all at once he could see that Caroline understood the assignment wouldn't be as simple or pleasant as it sounded. He could see her mulling it. She fussed with her gloves in silence. Looked about the pub, made a face at the quality of the clientele, returned her eyes to him.

"How would I do it? Gain the information you need?"

"Tell him you're frightened of me. You need his help. He won't be able to deny that sort of plea."

"Will you stop attempting to kill me if I agree to help you?" she asked.

"Will you stop giving me reasons to attempt to kill you?" he asked, almost whimsically.

She half-smiled, but didn't answer. He took it as an agreement.

"How ... how is your leg these days?" she asked after a moment.

"Hurts. Talks to me during Commons sessions. Swears at me, more accurately. Drowns out the more boring speakers."

She laughed. "It's damp in those chambers. Perhaps the baths ..."

"I may go when the Commons adjourns."

She nodded. "You really should. It helped before, did it not?"

She knew him so well. And suddenly it was strangely difficult to speak, so he simply nodded.

"All right, Thaddeus. I'll do it."

He cleared his throat. "Where are you staying this evening, Caroline?"

"With you?" she suggested lightly.

He took her hand, held it in the dark of the pub. Her fingers curled into his, and it was familiar, painfully sweet. "I'm old, Caroline."

"We shall see," she murmured.

Chapter Seventeen

꧁

"Susannah?"

Susannah stared out the window at her aunt's roses, many of which were beginning to wilt, at last defeated by the heat. Rather like her spirits.

He'd kept his conversation neutral and bland the entire long, *long* ride home from London. And when they'd arrived home, he'd helped her down from the carriage, a proper gentleman. And helped her with her trunk, a proper gentleman. And then he'd bowed, and touched his hat, and smiled pleasantly, and left her. Proper, proper, proper.

It was like being *assaulted* with manners. What was the *matter* with him?

"Susannah?"

They were brilliant manners, too, shiny and impeccable and as inviting as a suit of armor. He'd scrambled into them in order to keep her at arm's length from the moment they'd arrived in London. It was only in the dark she could get him to speak about himself. As though things said into the dark counted for nothing. He was like a child covering his face with his hands and thinking he could not be seen.

And he wouldn't touch her. No, he'd slept in a chair.

And she needed to know: *Why* wouldn't he touch her? Was it her questionable birth and decidedly unusual history? The fact that he was a viscount, and would never dream of marrying a woman of her status—or rather, lack of status? That she no longer held any appeal, now that he'd touched her once?

No appeal? Well, *that* much, she was certain, wasn't true.

He cared for her; she knew he cared for her. He desired her; she knew he desired her. She knew it as surely as she knew that female adders were shy, and that long-tailed voles were rare in this region, and that the insides of a horse were warm and wet.

But he wasn't being forthright, which was entirely unlike him. Which could only mean . . . he either didn't know what he intended to do about her, or he felt that telling her the truth of how he felt would be much too devastating for her, and he wanted to spare her feelings.

Odd, but her feelings at the moment did not feel *spared*. More raw, jangled, crowded, frustrated . . .

Perhaps he was simply afraid.

Kit Whitelaw? *Afraid?* Afraid of what?

"Susannah?"

She slowly turned her head to look at her aunt. "Mmmm?"

"Did you know that was the third time I'd said your name, my dear?" Her aunt's voice was gentle.

"Was it? I'm terribly sorry."

"Is aught amiss? You seem distracted. Was London unpleasant? Do you miss your friends?"

Startling to realize that she hadn't even given a thought to her "friends" while she was in London.

What would Aunt Frances say if she said, *Oh, Aunt Frances, something* is *amiss. I'm in love with the viscount, and he*

*won't touch me, whereas the other day he touched me at length,
with his hands and mouth, and I thoroughly enjoyed it.*

"No," she said softly. "Nothing is wrong."

Her aunt frowned a little then, and came to her, sat down
next to her in the window.

"The viscount...he didn't..." She delicately trailed off, to
give Susannah an opportunity to complete the sentence in any
way she chose. Her aunt's face was taut with concern.

"No." Even she could hear the leaden disappointment in her
voice.

Aunt Frances burst into merry laughter. "Oh, all right. As
long as nothing is *wrong* then, my dear." The words were ironic.
"What is this clinging to your skirt?" She plucked something
from it. "It sparkles."

Susannah looked at it. "Must be a mermaid scale," she murmured. Then frowned faintly and returned to gazing out of the
window, her thoughts pulling her there like a magnet, her mind
so powerfully full of other things that she forgot her aunt again.

"I *do* know a thing or two about the...difficult sex, Susannah," her aunt coaxed. "If you've a question or two. And by
that, I do mean men, my dear."

Her aunt's voice registered as a low murmur beneath the
insistent clamor of her thoughts, and the sudden clang of her
decision.

He was afraid that someone was trying to kill her; he'd
probably kill her for leaving the house alone, because "don't
leave the house" were the last words he'd said to her as he left.

But finally she knew what she had to do. She stood up and
seized her sketchbook.

"Susannah."

Her aunt said the word almost sharply, which made Susannah stop and turn around suddenly. Her aunt studied her quizzi-
cally, taking a moment before she spoke.

"My dear, I know I am not your aunt by blood...but I truly have no wish to see you...hurt."

Susannah paused, abashed.

"Oh, Aunt Frances...," she said impulsively. "Thank you for caring. I'm so sorry. I promise...well, you have my solemn vow that I will not...I will do my best not to ever disappoint or shame you."

"That wasn't my concern, dear," her aunt said gently. "I'm certain you won't. But I do thank you for the solemn vow."

Her aunt *was* a wry one.

Susannah smiled a little. "Well, it's my concern," she said simply. "And I do mean it."

Her aunt studied her for a moment, her brown eyes thoughtful. She was clearly searching for words.

"When I said I had no wish to see you hurt, Susannah," she ventured, "I didn't mean you should never...take a risk. And risks would not be called *risks* if there were not some chance of hurt. Nothing in life worth having is easy, Susannah. And—oh, never mind, my dear. You're young yet, but I know you are sensible, so I've no need to issue warnings and spout platitudes and the like. And, as you say, I have your solemn vow. Go enjoy...'sketching.' But be home for dinner, if you would."

"*Do* you think I'm sensible?" For some reason this surprised Susannah.

"Yes." Her aunt sounded surprised that Susannah was surprised. "I do."

How about that? Among all of the other things she now knew she was...she was sensible, too.

Susannah smiled brilliantly at her aunt and pushed the door open, and all but raced down the path, despite the heat.

She was almost certain she knew where she'd find him.

$\backsim$

He was on the pier, roughly whisking a towel over his bare chest. He'd already slipped into his trousers, but his feet were bare and the lowering late-afternoon sun gilded half of him, leaving the rest of him in shadow.

All the way there she'd rehearsed in her head what she might say to him, how she would ask it, what she might do if his answers broke her heart. But then he turned suddenly and saw her. And his face, unguarded, told her everything she needed to know, and questions were no longer necessary.

"Oh, Kit. It's all right," she said softly. "I love you, too."

He stared at her, caught. And then he laughed a short laugh, which was no doubt meant to sound incredulous or devil-may-care, but which failed miserably.

Susannah approached him as carefully as one would a deer or squirrel, and his eyes tracked her, never leaving her face. She stopped when she was close enough to feel the heat of his body, stopped just short of touching him.

And then she did touch him: slowly, very lightly, she placed one hand against his ribcage.

"Truly," she said gently. "And I'm not going anywhere. I do promise."

She could feel his heart jumping beneath her palm, in time with her own, feel the lift and rise of his ribs as his breathing quickened. Awe, and then a fierce longing, tightened his features. He slowly lifted his hand and dragged the back of it softly against her cheek, across her lips. She kissed his fingers. She saw his eyes go nearly black.

"You have me at a disadvantage once again, Miss Make-peace," he murmured. "I am only half-clothed."

"Well, then…" Her eyes never leaving his face, and with a

bravado she didn't entirely feel, Susannah fumbled behind her neck for the laces of her gown.

"No," he said sharply.

The word seemed to stop her heart.

"That is," he said swiftly, "*I* want the pleasure of it, Susannah. That way, you can always blame me later, rather than yourself."

Her heart sputtered into life, into hope, again. And she lifted her eyes.

Kit was smiling down at her, but his smile was tense and rueful, his face more intent than she'd ever seen it.

More deftly and quickly than she preferred to think about, he reached behind her neck and loosened her laces. She nearly smiled. She felt the dying breeze of the day wash over her bare back.

He slipped his fingers inside her dress, touched her skin very gently and exhaled a soft shaky sigh, almost of relief. He combed his fingers over her shoulder blades, down either side of her spine, the rough pads of his fingertips and the exquisite lightness of his touch turning every cell of her skin to glowing cinders, her legs to liquid. Susannah closed her eyes, wanting only to feel, wanting to heighten the pure exquisite pleasure of his hands on her skin.

And then his mouth was warm against her ear. *"Susannah,"* he breathed there, her own name as sensual as his fingers. It traveled along the fuse of her nerve endings and lit a furnace inside her. Her lungs labored to breathe. She flattened her hands against his chest, savoring, at last, at last, the warm strong beauty of it. His skin was satiny over the rigid planes of his muscle, and again, this softness juxtaposed with strength... this was Kit.

"I like that," he murmured against her throat, where his mouth had traveled from her ear. He opened his lips against the soft skin there, put a hot kiss there. "Touch me anywhere you please."

"If you insist," she said. She was trying for insouciance, but the words were a squeak.

And he laughed, bloody man.

She indulged all of her weeks of stored longings and dragged one finger around the contours of his muscled chest, tracing a broad figure eight, then drew it down between his ribs, down the pale line of hair that led to the bulge in his trousers, stopping short of it, and was rewarded when he sucked in his breath. She opened her hands then and clasped them around his slim waist, let them wander down to cup his firm buttocks through his trousers. He mumbled some unintelligibly pleasured sound.

"Do you think it's *fair*," Susannah managed to breathe, arching her neck so he could place another kiss at the base of her throat, "that I have seen all of *you,* and yet you have seen none of—"

"Oh, I'm *keenly* interested in justice, Miss Makepeace." His hands left her back and found the sleeves of her gown, began to ease them down.

"No." She said it suddenly.

He stopped. The look in his eyes made her almost regret saying the word.

"*I* want to do it. That way I have only myself to blame."

He paused, and what he saw in her face made him slide his hands to her waist and rest them there. Honoring her need to make this decision for herself.

And before his eyes, with hands that trembled, Susannah tugged her bodice lower, slowly, slowly, until more breeze than muslin covered her skin, until at last the tops of her breasts were bare. Kit's eyes never left her face; they dared her, gave her strength. She took in a long unsteady breath and pushed the bodice of her dress with her hands until it drooped to her waist.

She watched his eyes slowly drop from her eyes to her lips ... to her ...

"God," he murmured with reverent enthusiasm.

She almost laughed, but he found her mouth again with his, and then his warm hands were on her bare waist, on her ribs, gliding up, up, up with torturous leisure, until his hands filled with her breasts, and his touch, his lips, became tender beyond words. She nearly sank to her knees. His thumbs traced her nipples into peaks, until at last she needed to take her lips from his and lean her head forward to touch his chest, shivering with helpless pleasure.

His hand moved to cup the back of her head then, so he could once more take a kiss as deeply as he could; his other hand pressed against the small of her back, bringing her into the heat of his chest. The sensation of his skin against the hard tips of her breasts was unlike anything she was sure heaven had to offer. She moved her hands down, felt the hard, thick length of his arousal beneath his trousers, dragged her hands over it. He muttered something like *"mmm,"* which she took to mean to do it again. So she did it again, and again, until his hands went down to cup her buttocks and roughly pushed her up against him. She looped her arms around his neck and pushed herself closer still.

She wanted desperately to crawl inside him.

"Making love to you, Susannah," Kit murmured against her lips, as his hips moved against hers, "would be a rare honor and pleasure."

"I want you to make love to me." Her voice was shaking now.

"Do you know what that truly means?" His hands had slipped lower now inside her dress, and his finger had found the crease of her buttocks to delicately trace. He looked intently down into her eyes.

"Yes."

"You *do* know? You know that I will be inside you..." He kissed her, this one languid, thorough, incinerating. "And that I will move inside you..." He kissed her again, the same way, until her thoughts were glittering fragments. "...Until we are both mad from pleasure?"

"I want you inside me." She was nearly weeping with the truth of that.

He abruptly swept her up in his arms, carried her from the pier to where the small wood shelter sat. He pushed the door open, lowered her to the ground. And then, with his usual unself-conscious speed, he stepped back and quickly stripped off his trousers. She saw the thick curve of his arousal arching toward his belly, the hard contours of his thighs, the uncompromisingly masculinity of his whole bare body only a foot away from her, and was jarred suddenly: *This is real. This is happening.*

She pulled her gown from over her head, mimicking his quick boldness, hoping it would be contagious. Still she stood, shivering and a little shy, a little uncertain suddenly, in her bareness. He bundled their clothes together on the ground, making a soft place for them, and this too, made it seem shockingly real.

"Come here," he demanded in a whisper. She stepped forward, and he gathered her into his arms, pressing her against the warmth of his body, and his strong hands moved down her back, clothing her in a soft trail of heat, dissolving her shyness.

His lips against her skin were tender and reverent. They knew her secrets, made her feel vulnerable when she wanted strength, wanted to believe she had a choice in this surrender, when there never had been any, really. His mouth traveled, tasted with lips and tongue, her throat, her temple, the bones at the base of her neck. And when they returned home to her lips she gratefully, greedily drank him in, meeting the searching heat of his tongue with her own.

His hands, deliberate now, on a mission not to reassure but to arouse, roamed her body with shocking skill; his fingers knew where to stroke and linger, how to tease soft moans from her, to make her beg. He found and savored the curves of her breasts, the peaks of her nipples, cupped and explored the warmth between her legs, until she was supple and boneless, clinging to him. And then wantonly nearly climbing him.

Time dropped away. They sank together to their knees, mouths joined, his fingers twisting in her hair and plucking out pins as it loosened; he pulled her head back to take his kisses deeper, his fingers roving her hair. Her hands on him were careful, tender, over his bruises of his chest, over his arm where the knife had slashed him. Kit closed his eyes when she touched him, as though he could hardly believe the wonder of it, and then folded his arms around her and pulled her down over him, lowering himself to his back.

"Now," he urged on a soft rasp against her mouth. "I need you, Susannah. Please let it be now."

"Yes." A breath of a word.

He rolled over with her in his arms, covering her. She cradled him with her thighs, pulling him closer, and he lifted his torso up, fitted himself to her, slid into her waiting heat. There was a quick bite of pain; Susannah took her lower lip in her teeth to stifle a gasp. But then came the extraordinary feel of him filling her, and in so doing somehow touching her body everywhere. She watched Kit's eyes close when he was deeply seated; the intensity of his pleasure seemed akin to pain.

He was still, hovering over her; for a moment they savored together the miracle of being joined at last. He opened his eyes. So blue. Smiled down at her, crookedly, with quiet, rueful amazement. Pulled back, and thrust forward again, dipped to touch his lips to hers. He was shaking; she could feel his lean body quivering, saw the sweat gathering, gleaming over the lean muscles of his arms and chest.

"I want to go slowly for you," he whispered raggedly. "God, I want to. I'm just not sure I—"

"Hush. It's all right." She covered his lips with a finger. "It's all right."

He sighed then, and began to move in her, his cadence even, purposeful. She arched to meet each stroke, taking him as deeply into her body as she could; reveling in the pleasure she was giving, in the dark desire she saw in his eyes. And she reveled, too, when control was lost to him. He turned his head away from her when the rhythm of his need took him over, escalated, drummed through her body, his hips quick and fierce. When he turned toward her again, she saw the singular mission in his eyes, the unconscious total pleasure, and from the rush of his breathing knew instinctively it would be soon for him. She dug her fingers into his shoulders, holding him fast.

"Oh, God, Susannah. Oh, God."

His long body went still; she felt his release shudder through him. Felt the almost tangible peace it instantly brought. A gratitude, a tenderness she could scarcely bear, filled her; she touched his lips. He kissed her fingers gently.

"Thank you," he whispered. His chest moved with ragged breathing still; Susannah touched her finger to a bead of perspiration traveling the seam between his ribs. Then touched her finger to her tongue, tasting the salt of him.

"Think nothing of it," she murmured.

He gave a short laugh. Pulled away from her. Eased down next to her, and wrapped her loosely with one arm, flung the other arm out above him. He sighed the long sigh of the replete.

And they were quiet for a time, the sweat cooling on their bodies.

"In case you were wondering," he volunteered lazily after a moment, "we just made love."

"Is that what you call it?" She rolled her eyes upward, studying her view, saw his half-smile and closed eyes. "Your armpit is very handsome."

This made him laugh. "Only an artist would think an armpit is handsome."

"But it *is* . . . the line of it is, anyhow. The muscles and shadows and hair . . ." She traced the muscles and shadows and hair with her finger as she said the words, and her voice drifted.

She sat up suddenly and reached for her sketchbook and quickly rendered him, that arm stretched over his head, his bare chest, and long legs, his lolling, spent manhood resting in curling hair, his wonderful face reflecting smug satisfaction, easy intimacy.

"You're a very good model," she told him approvingly. "You hold cooperatively still."

"I don't think I could move if you pointed a gun at me," he murmured.

She kissed the birthmark in the shape of a gull on his outstretched wrist, then leaned down and kissed his nipple, tracing it with her tongue, tasting it the way he'd tasted hers. His hand trailed down her back as she did; she saw unmistakable signs of stirring below.

"You're moving *now*," she teased.

He gave a short, very distracted laugh. "Siren," he said absently. Clearly enjoying the run of her tongue over his chest.

"I think I shall torture you," she whispered. She dragged her tongue down the seam between his ribs, then her lips skimmed his stirring shaft, which all but leaped to attention.

"Or I you," he whispered. He sat up suddenly, swept her into his lap so that she sat across his thighs, and breathed into her ear, touched his tongue there, traced the whorls of it. A silver-hot shiver of sensation coursed through her body.

"Do you like that?" he murmured.

"I don't know," she half-gasped. "It rather takes . . . everything over."

He dragged a single finger down her throat, over the fine bones of her chest, touched it to the stiff peak of her nipple. "Proof that you most definitely like it," he confirmed in a sultry whisper. She laughed a little, then stopped abruptly, because she needed all of her faculties to enjoy what he'd begun doing to her breasts with his hands.

And then they were quiet, and with a tacit sort of agreement, everything was soft as breath, delicate. With lips, and fingertips light as air, with breath itself, she caressed him, and he caressed her. She breathed into his ear, tasted the cord of his neck while his fingers gently, maddeningly, softly, played along her spine, her waist, her belly, the nest of curls between her legs, her throat, her breasts, as though he was bringing music from the most delicate of harps. Until every cell of her vibrated with desperate need. His breath was hot, then cool, in her ear. She finally gave up exploring him and submitted, hooking her arms loosely around his neck, selfishly wanting just to take the pleasure he could give.

He knew so much more than she did. But she would learn. She would learn.

"Kit," she finally gasped urgently against his neck, when it became untenable. She needed him to ease her need. She would beg him, if necessary.

It wasn't necessary.

"It's all right," he murmured to her. "It's all right." He cupped her buttocks in his hands, lifted her up, and guided her down over his shaft with a long sigh. When he was deeply inside her, their eyes locked.

Susannah's breasts slid against his chest, both of their bodies sweat-sheened, as she rose up again, knowing instinctively what to do. He smiled faintly, guided her down again. Which is when she saw his eyes go black again with desire and she exulted. She loved this power to give and take, this humbling exchange of strength and vulnerability.

"There's a place inside you, Susannah...," he said hoarsely. "Guide me. You'll know it when you feel it. I'll hold on to you."

So she lifted up again...and slid down again...and oh, he was right. There *was* a place.

She moved up over him again, with a sultry smile, enjoying this new knowledge, feeling that mysterious need escalating... she held it at bay for as long as she could. Which, as it turned out, wasn't very long at all. For her body took over, found the cadence it craved, and she began to ride him in an instinctive rhythm that grew ever swifter, and he held her, his hips thrusting up to meet hers.

The world became the harsh roar of their breathing, incoherent sounds of pleasure, softly groaned words of urging. Susannah could feel her release pushing, pushing at the seams of her, roaring through her veins like a river of stars, until it flooded its banks and burst from her in an exultant cry. The unthinkable pleasure of it rocked her, shook her like a rag; she trembled and trembled from it.

Kit held on to her, his own hoarse cry following, and she could feel his seed filling her as she breathed her exhaustion against his neck. Felt his chest heaving against hers as they clung together.

And then sank down to his back, bringing her down with him, holding her loosely. His chest rose and fell rapidly, as did her own. He shifted her to make himself more comfortable. They didn't speak until their breathing settled, became more even.

"You will be my wife," he ordered quietly, finally. As though issuing an answer to a problem.

"All right," she murmured with sated equanimity.

A silence. *We're in a shack on a pile of clothes,* Susannah thought, sleepily marveling.

"My father will like you," he said musingly.

"I intend to like him, too."

"He won't like that you have no *money*—"

"Nobody seems to," she said happily.

"But he will like *you*."

"Naturally."

He laughed at that. "Because 'it's *easy,*'" he said, quoting her words to him the night of the Barnstable assembly. He did a passing good imitation of her voice, too, high and fluty, and she gave him a little swat.

"It *is* easy, usually. *You* seem to like me well enough."

He grunted a laugh.

"May we live in London?" she asked

"Most definitely. Unless you'd like to stay here among the voles and adders."

She tensed.

He was laughing now, shaking beneath her. "There are no adders here at the moment, sweet." She batted him a little again, settled back down, and when he grunted, shifted her head to the shoulder that wasn't bruised.

"And Aunt Frances?"

"Can come to live with us, if she'd like."

"And we can have friends?" Susannah pressed. "In London?"

"I'm a viscount. I can buy you all the friends you want. How many would you like?"

She laughed again. He pulled her close, squeezed her a little with one arm as she lay across his chest. His eyelids were sleepily at half-mast. His body, however, was tense, at odds, with the soft satiety of his face.

She lifted her head up and studied him, her hair trailing

down over him. She traced his lips, his cheekbones, his chin with a single finger. Hers to touch from now on.

"Nothing will happen to me," she said softly.

For she knew this was what was bothering him. What made him snap at her when she jested about her death. This astonishing man with the breakable heart.

He opened his eyes wider, surprised at her insight. Drank her in with that vivid blue. But said nothing.

"Nothing will," she insisted. "You are Christopher Whitelaw, spy extraordinaire."

Then again, it was easy to be certain of the world when one had just been thoroughly made love to.

He smiled a little, and still he said nothing. But his hand began slowly roaming over her body softly, possessively, over the curve of her buttocks, her shoulder blades, up through her hair. More of a claiming than a caress. Making sure of her. Memorizing her.

I love him.

He hadn't yet said he loved her, but surely he must. Everything he did, the way he felt, spoke of a love so large it almost seemed wrong to confine it to a single word.

And oh, she did love him. It was beautiful and terrible, enormously comforting and terrifying, battle and peace all at once. What she'd felt for Douglas was a mere cinder of affection in comparison.

His hand ceased its roaming and he lifted his head up suddenly to look at her, as if he had an urgent question. She prepared herself for it.

"Do you think I'm handsome?" He sounded a little worried.

She almost laughed. Because, no, she didn't think he was handsome.

"I think you are beautiful," she told him emphatically, and quite truthfully.

He looked smugly satisfied with that answer, dropped his head again.

She could hear the sounds of the woods now as they lay quietly, and it was almost as natural now as his breathing. The pungent smell of crushed leaves, the soft sounds of wind shaking branches, the rustle of unseen creatures who made their homes in the woods... for her they would always be inseparable from the scent and feel of Kit.

"But we can stay in Barnstable, too, can we not?" she said suddenly. "Quite often?"

"Would you like that?"

She was surprised that what she was about to say was true. "I think I would."

"So would I." He sounded surprised, too.

c⁓

Kit managed to escort Susannah home in time for dinner, and Kit insisted upon formally asking for her hand from her aunt, who did a marvelous job of feigning astonishment while Susannah rolled her eyes from behind Kit's back. Aunt Frances's delight, however, wasn't feigned, nor was her relief, which she gave vent to when Kit was once again on his way.

"A countess!" Aunt Frances said, when Kit departed. "You'll be a countess, my girl. Someday, anyhow."

"And a wife!" Susannah was beside herself. "Of Kit!" This was the best part, as far as she was concerned.

"Kit, is it?" her aunt teased. "He's a good boy. I knew he would make an honest woman of you, Susannah."

Susannah was amused at the idea of Kit being a "good boy," but then she heard the rest of the sentence, and wondered if her aunt knew just how wanton she had been.

Her aunt read the abashed question in her face. "You've leaves in your hair, dear."

Susannah felt the scarlet flood her cheeks. "Aunt Frances! What you must think . . ."

"I think it's been some time since I've had leaves in my hair, but rest assured, I've had them. I'd worry a good deal more if you came home with leaves in your hair and no viscount in tow to ask for your hand."

"Perhaps the neighbors will return to visit you, Aunt Frances."

"Oh, I don't intend to wait for them, Susannah. I'll pay visits and spread the news myself, my dear. Would you like to come along when I do?"

"I believe I might."

She did wonder how she would be received when she didn't try so very hard. And she rather relished the opportunity to begin again.

Kit actually whistled on his way back home. He was off to fetch his lantern, brandy, water, tea, a blanket, and something to gnaw on. And then he'd return to guard her.

He wanted her in his bed tonight and always, but he supposed he would need to at least *pretend* to care about the proprieties. He would marry her with unseemly haste, anyway, as soon as a special license could be obtained; until then he'd keep her close.

He was happy. It wasn't an easy happiness, surrounded as it was by the fringed ends of their pasts, a countess who would pout when he abandoned her in favor of his *wife* (he loved that word), a disgruntled father, and all the violence and mystery that had characterized their time together. But in a way, that's precisely what made the happiness more precious, more complete. If not for those things, he might not have allowed Susannah to know him. If not for these things, Susannah would not be who she now was. She might be married to that poor young buffoon Douglas, forever ignorant of her own passion and strength, and he might still be bedding a married countess and drinking too much and never allowing anyone to touch him deeply again.

There were different kinds of fear, he knew. Battle was only frightening before and after, never during, because during battle one only did one's job. It was after when the pain set in; it was before when anticipation did things to one's mind.

And that was love, too.

He glanced about, and it occurred to him then: everything that made him what he was had begun here in these woods, tracking adders and voles and the like: his ability to draw connections and conclusions. His patience and agility and precision. A vision that allowed him to see the layers of complexity in the most deceptively simple things.

His first taste of passion. His ability to love.

He glanced up at the trees overhead, and the late afternoon light pouring through them reminded him of the stained-glass windows in Gorringe. *Faith, Hope and Charity,* he thought. "The greatest of these is love," the verse sometimes read. "Love" and "charity" were interchangeable words, some thought.

But they were all...

Bloody hell. They were all Christian virtues.

Kit stopped in his tracks. He gave a short laugh, wondering whether anyone had ever before used the words "bloody hell" and "Christian virtues" before in the same sentence.

The windows and the mausoleum at the Gorringe church had been donated by a generous benefactor. He would bet his left arm—the battered one, anyway—that Richard Lockwood had been that generous benefactor.

And finally, all the pieces slid into place.

"Of course," James had said, looking down at the back of the miniature.

And what did the back of the miniature say? "To Susannah Faith." *Faith,* a Christian virtue. Sylvie's second name had been "Hope."

He was willing to wager that Sabrina's middle name was "Charity."

Each of those miniatures had been a tiny clue. The whimsical Richard Lockwood had used his daughters as signposts to the location of the documents.

Tomorrow. He would go then tomorrow. He *must* go tomorrow. For Susannah's sake.

And…well…

Honestly, he wanted to beat John Carr to it.

Chapter Eighteen

❧

usannah spent a quiet evening beneath Aunt Frances's roof. They'd begun another book, this one a horrid novel, and she'd had a little trouble sleeping due to the ghost, as well as heated thoughts of Kit. But she woke at the usual time, and when she wandered out with her sketchbook at the usual time, she found the viscount waiting at the gate for her.

My fiancé, she revised, in her thoughts.

She stopped for a moment and just looked and looked at him. Delighted that he simply existed. Savoring the joy that flared hot and bright in her chest all over again, that made the ground beneath her feet and the sky above her feel one and the same.

She walked to meet him, and when she reached him, he stretched out an arm and pulled her against him, and she put her face up. He kissed her, sweetly and simply, because they could share any manner and any number of kisses from now on, from sweet to incendiary.

His face was chilled against hers, as though he'd been out of doors already for a good length of time. He tasted a bit of tea,

but his mouth was cold, too. Again, the skin beneath his eyes
looked faintly bruised. He wanted a shave.

She studied him critically.

And then a realization struck.

"You've been guarding me," she said, breathlessly. "At night.
Watching the house. It's why you look so…" She trailed off.

"Very handsome?" he completed winsomely.

Susannah's heart almost couldn't expand enough to accommodate the awe that filled it then. She wouldn't gush, however,
and make this tender, gallant man uncomfortable.

"Tonight," she said firmly, "I will let you in after Aunt
Frances has gone to bed, and you will sleep on the settee, if
you really must guard me. And you can be gone before Aunt
Frances comes down. I will not have you going without sleep."

He thought about this, and then nodded once, agreeing,
looking half-pleased to be ordered about. He extended his arm,
and she took it.

He led her up the tree-lined path, this time not into the
woods, but to the modest grounds of The Roses. Susannah
looked about at the fountains and shrubbery. "I had no idea you
had anything so ordinary as *roses* growing here," she teased.

He didn't laugh. He turned to her, and she saw the change
in his posture, the look on his face, the intent, and was already
lifting her face up to his as he reached for her. She met his lowering mouth with her own, and he groaned low in his throat and
pulled her closer, closer to him, as though he could press her
into his body and protect her from harm forever. Her body softened against his, and her hands slid up his chest to clasp around
his neck. The kiss was deep and hungry, the one he'd wanted to
give her this morning, but thought would perhaps be improper
to do right outside of Aunt Frances's cottage.

He lifted his face from her to breathe. "There's something I
need to tell you, Susannah. Today—"

He stopped and looked. There was a speck hurrying toward them from a distance, which turned out to be Bullton, who, as he drew closer, proved to already be reddening in the heat. Butlers spent most of their time indoors, after all.

"Is something amiss, Bullton?"

"Sir. You've ... Well, you've a ... visitor, sir."

Who could fluster Bullton so completely?

Bloody hell, it must be my father.

He'd forgotten to send any notes at all to the Earl. Kit braced himself, began to mentally compile excuses for his woefully thin folio, began to compile explanations for a mad dash to Gorringe, and looked up.

A slim, petite woman, dressed head to toe in mourning, stood diffidently in the garden. Her hair was gathered into a knot beneath a big black hat, from which hung a veil. And then, her gloved hands rose slowly, and she lifted her veil, turned her face up to him.

Kit froze, because that's what one did when one saw a ghost.

Unthinkingly, he dropped Susannah's arm. And with every step the ghost took toward him, the years dropped away.

She held out her dark-gloved hand to be bowed over and Kit, almost reflexively, lightly took her fingers. But she gripped his hand when he did that, and turned it over. Looked down at it closely instead. And smiled softly.

"Oh, Kit," she murmured. "It really is you."

And Caroline Allston kissed the gull-shaped birthmark beneath his wrist.

⟡

He didn't exactly *snatch* his hand away, but he did take it from her quickly. Caroline always did have a way with dramatic gestures, and it was easy to be caught up in them.

Recovering, he glanced at Susannah, the woman he'd just kissed within an inch of her life. She stared at Caroline with the same affection and admiration she reserved for adders.

Caroline wasn't any less beautiful for her years; she still had a remarkable face, dominated by those dark eyes, soft and deep, those feathery brows, the brows of a baby, almost. Those naturally red lips that had so fascinated a seventeen-year-old boy. It was still a delicate, passionate, wanton face. And yes, for all of that . . . still a vulnerable face. It made one instantly want to protect her, when really, one probably need protecting *from* her.

"Caroline . . ."

"Allston," she completed. "It's Allston." With no explanation of the mourning dress.

"Hello, Caroline. Allow me to introduce my fiancée, Miss Susannah Makepeace."

He reached for Susannah's hand proprietarily, tucked it into his arm. Susannah seemed to have gone into rigor mortis, however; her arm was decidedly stiff. He glanced down at her, meaning to reassure her, but she was studiously avoiding his eyes. Her eyes were instead still fixed on Caroline, as if she stared at Caroline just hard enough, she'd evaporate like a mirage.

Caroline was staring at Susannah, too.

"Congratulations on your engagement." Caroline managed to make the words sound ironic.

"We thank you. How many years has it been?" Kit strived for joviality. He wasn't entirely certain how to address a former lover, current alleged traitor.

"Seventeen," Caroline said. "Seems like only . . . yesterday."

The word "yesterday" was fertile with innuendo. It made it sound like it had indeed been only yesterday, and *goodness,* what they had gotten up to then!

How very, very like her. It was the sort of thing she'd done so many years ago, lobbing innuendo between John Carr and himself just to watch how they would volley it, just to see them bristle like fighting cocks. Could it be that she had remained entirely unchanged for seventeen years? Or perhaps it was something about *him* that launched Caroline into her games.

"To what do I owe the pleasure of your visit, Caroline?" His voice was decidedly cooler now that he'd recovered his composure.

Her face crumpled a little, and he saw in her face that girl who had tried so hard to be brave years ago, and whose only defense was lashing out in the only way she knew how. And his immediate impulse was to go to her, to make it better in the way he'd never been able to do for her before.

"I'm... I'm in trouble, Kit. Really in trouble. I didn't know whom else to turn to, I swear it. And you always... you always tried to help."

It was the word "tried" that embedded itself in him. *Tried.* He'd always *tried* to help. Tried and failed.

She must have seen the change, the softening in his face; her voice steadied, found dignity. "I beg a word, Kit. And forgive me, Miss Makepeace," she added gently. "For intruding on what must be a very happy time, indeed. I am more sorry than I can say."

Kit glanced down at Susannah, who had her teeth bared in a facsimile of a smile. She tried again to tug her hand away from him. Kit clamped it tightly with his arm. *You're not going anywhere, Susannah.* In a way, she was his talisman.

Kit didn't know whether he could or should trust Caroline. The anguish on her face seemed real enough and, as it had so many years ago, the need in her spoke to something in him that wanted to make everything right for her.

But beneath it was a very unsentimental curiosity: He wanted to hear what she had to say. She was integral to this mystery now, and he wanted very much to unravel it. And for some reason, it seemed inevitable that she should appear.

He softened his tone a little; it was still, however, implacably polite. "Anything you need to say to me you can say before my fiancée as well."

"Kit . . ." Caroline sounded desperate now. "You . . . might not wish Miss Makepeace to hear what I have to say. I think only of . . . protecting her."

Worse and worse. But Caroline was very likely right about that. He didn't want Susannah at all tainted or implicated by the presence of a suspected traitor. He wondered if John Carr was still in the vicinity somewhere, watching him; whether Caroline managed to arrive undetected. The whole mourning kit . . . veil, the black gown . . . he supposed it was a disguise.

For a wild moment he considered whether John Carr had found Caroline and sent her to him. Whether even now the king's men were descending upon Barnstable to arrest Kit for consorting with a traitor.

It might just be the one way that John Carr would finally, at last, win.

The thought made Kit furious with Caroline. It couldn't be true, he didn't believe it, but he knew, in that wild moment, that Caroline's legacy was deep indeed. That years ago she had seen something simple and good—the friendship he shared with John—and set out to ruin it, simply because she could. Simply because the ability to do so was one of the powers her beauty conferred. Perhaps the only power she could lay claim to.

"Kit . . . he's trying to kill me," she said softly. "Morley."

Ah. The magic word: *Morley.*

Kit simply waited.

"I know I've . . . made some rather . . . unwise decisions," she continued, smiling nervously at her own expense, "but I swear I never meant to hurt anyone, least of all you. And I'm tired, tired of running, Kit. I'm so frightened."

He said nothing. There was a part of him that couldn't

believe that Caroline Allston was standing in his garden. Another part of him, a primitive childish part that he wasn't proud of, that was glad, *glad* she'd come to him.

"Did you receive my letter?" she asked, when still he said nothing.

He felt Susannah tense next to him.

Which letter was Caroline referring to? The one that John Carr had intercepted, or the letter sent so many years ago: *"I'm sorry."*

He nodded slowly, regardless.

"Kit...for the sake of long ago...will you help me?"

Susannah was stiff with uncertainty, stunned, radiating hurt. He wanted to tuck her away some place where nothing of his past or of hers could touch her. But that would solve nothing; it seemed his past was somehow entwined with Susannah's, and before they moved forward into a future together, he would need to methodically unravel the knots.

"Susannah...," he said, regret and decision heavy in his voice.

"I'll go home right now," Susannah said quickly, too brightly. "To Aunt Frances. I'll leave the two of you to become reacquainted."

"No, you won't."

"I'll go to Aunt Frances and—"

"No," he said firmly. "You won't. You'll stay here in this house. It is *your house* now, too. We'll go inside. And I shall speak to Miss Allston privately while you wait for me."

"I would like to go to Aunt Frances." The words were cool; the two spots of color in her cheeks were not.

Kit turned and looked down at Susannah. She steadfastly refused to meet his eyes, focusing on the roses beyond his shoulder. He took her stiff hand and lifted it to his lips, while Caroline's eyes followed it there, her expression enigmatic.

"It will be all right, Susannah," he said softly.

Susannah's expression told him that she didn't believe him. And she didn't precisely jerk her hand away from him, but she didn't want to be touched by him at the moment, either, that much was very clear. He might as well have been gripping a leather-bound copy of Marcus Aurelius instead of a hand, for how yielding it felt.

"Of course it will," she said. "Of course it will. Because you're always *accurate,* aren't you?"

Her irony landed with the grace of a crowbar, but he hadn't the time or patience to placate her now. Potential disaster, in the form of Caroline, stood before both of them. Potential answers. Potential truth.

"Thank you for understanding," he said to Susannah, which would have to suffice for now. "Shall we go inside?"

And so sandwiched between his past and his future, Kit led two beautiful women into the house.

He'd taken one look at that woman...and he'd gone as white as a blank page of her sketchbook. As white as the day a horse had fallen on him. And then he'd dropped her arm, as if he couldn't possibly touch *her* and look at Caroline Allston at the very same time.

And oh, but that woman was beautiful. An intimidating, thorough, *fascinating* sort of beautiful. A *complicated* beautiful. Complicated, she knew, appealed to Kit. "Difficult to forget"? Susannah gave a short bitter laugh, as she waited in the parlor. "Difficult to forget" didn't by half do Caroline Allston justice.

And Kit—the man who was her very heart—was shut in the library with Caroline Allston right now. And it did feel that way: As though her heart had been scooped out, and a high cold wind was whistling through the place where it had once been.

Here she was in a parlor filled with shining, stiff, glamorous furniture; alone with a giant painting featuring the Whitelaw family. Kit's pretty mother, his handsome father, a pair of little girls who fortunately looked more like their mother than their father, slightly demure, slightly mischievous. Kit's little face was sullen, poking up out of some sort of ruffled suit. It made her smile faintly.

Susannah reached up to touch that image of him, wishing she could have known him then. Wishing she could have known him always. Wishing she could have been the one over whom he'd shot his best friend, the one whose name he'd carved into a tree. Known him when he was just learning how to love, so she could be absolutely sure that he loved her.

He does love me, she'd thought confidently only yesterday. *He must.* She'd thought it again, only an hour ago, as they'd kissed shamelessly in the rose garden. *He* must *love me.*

But what did she really know of the shades of love? That extraordinary-looking woman in the other room had been his first love. And she needed him now. Perhaps Kit would see an opportunity to redeem himself.

Well, I love him. And that would have to do for now, she thought. Her love for him would have to suffice in place of certainty. Until he was ready to say it to her. If he ever did.

And she stared up at that big painting, and ordered her heart not to break.

❦

He directed Caroline into a library chair and waited while Mrs. Davies, she of the spaniel-brown eyes, settled the tray of tea down with a rattle between them. Mrs. Davies wasn't nearly as gifted at inscrutability as Bullton was. She slid her speaking eyes toward Kit as she left the room, and her disapproval was very nearly palpable.

He watched Caroline remove her gloves, finger by finger, and ball them into one fist. And then she unpinned her hat, a great black thing heavy with feathers and a veil, and sat it next to her on the settee, where it crouched like a familiar. Her hair was still black and glossy, she wore it coiled loosely against her long white neck. Soft hair, he remembered. It had been like smoke and silk in his fingers when he was seventeen.

"I *am* sorry, you know," Caroline said quietly.

And for a moment, the two of them were seventeen and eighteen years old, and Kit had just had his heart broken.

Had her heart broken even a little? Had she run off to punish him, or to save herself? He'd been so sick with misery then, with outrage, that it was a marvel now that he could regard her...aesthetically. Nothing at all moved in the vicinity of his heart.

"That night...you did leave with Morley?" How odd it would be to know for certain after all of these years.

Caroline hesitated. Then nodded slowly.

"Did he touch you or force you, or—" The old rage began swinging up.

"*I* suggested it to him, Kit."

Kit took this in. He remembered Morley's inscrutable face, the contempt floating just below the surface of it. That smile he'd sent toward Kit. Why *wouldn't* Morley have accepted Caroline's suggestion? Any sane man would have had difficulty denying it. Caroline at eighteen had been glorious.

"Perhaps you had no choice," he said gruffly. It was his pride speaking. His guilt.

"That *was* my choice." Caroline gazed back at him levelly.

Unspoken: It was her choice, because Kit couldn't, or wouldn't, marry her. Though he most certainly had been willing to touch her.

"And yes...yes, he did...touch me, Kit. That night. And many, *many* others, too. In many...*many* ways."

She drew the words out, drawling them, so that he could feel and picture each one thoroughly. And she smiled a little as she did it, enjoying his discomfiture. How very like her. Always wanting men to froth with jealousy over her. Never happy when the waters were calm, the skies blue. She had a talent for it, Caroline did, stirring those darker feelings.

He said nothing.

"I was very young then, Kit. And...I left Thaddeus two years ago."

"Thaddeus," Kit repeated flatly. It sounded downright wifely when she said it that way.

"Yes, that *is* his given name, Kit," she said ironically. "But...after I left him—"

"Why did you leave him?"

She shrugged lightly.

And somehow, that shrug seemed unspeakably cruel. He wondered if Morley had loved her, too. And whether that had anything to do with why he wanted to kill her. Kit could almost sympathize.

"You left because of a whim, Caroline?"

She looked up at him, puzzled. A look that said, *Well, you have met me, haven't you?* Caroline was all but comprised of whim. And devoted to self-preservation.

"After I left him, times became hard, Kit, for me. So... I wrote to Thaddeus asking for money, thinking perhaps he might help me. And now he wants to kill me."

"Really." It was Kit's turn to drawl ironically. "Just like that, Caroline? A simple request for money and a well-known politician becomes murder-bent? Odd, but Morley doesn't strike me as an irrational man. Quite the opposite, in fact. He has managed to remain a politician for many years, and has likely only methodically killed a few people in the process. Only a few that I'm *aware* of, that is. Perhaps you know of more?"

Caroline flinched at this; he saw her skin draw tight around her eyes, suppressing some emotion. Shock, perhaps, that he would respond so coolly. Then she looked down at her folded hands in her lap, like a chastened child.

"Perhaps you threatened him for money, Caroline?" Kit suggested with gentle irony. "Now would be the time to tell me."

She lifted her head up and smiled impishly. "Well, it seemed a good idea at the time. My judgment never *was* the soundest, and well you know."

He sighed. "What, precisely, did you threaten him *with*, Caroline? Do you know something incriminating?"

She was silent. "He forced me to help him, Kit."

For some reason, Kit couldn't imagine anyone forcing Caroline to do anything she didn't want to do. Not even Morley. No doubt she'd gone into whatever it was thinking it would be a grand adventure. "Help him with what?"

She shook her head roughly.

"Help him with *what*, Caroline?" he repeated relentlessly. "And *how*, precisely, did he force you?"

He could almost see her mind working behind those mirrorlike dark eyes.

"Please don't make me tell you," she said finally, softly. "Kit...I'm just...I'm just so tired of running. I'm frightened. Please..." She leaned forward and placed her hand on his knee. "*Please* help me."

He looked down at the hand, and then into her face. The look he saw there promised things, and it would have buckled his knees if he'd been seventeen. At seventeen, he would have, in fact, had his trousers unfastened by now. He wasn't entirely immune to that look now; he *was* male, after all, and she'd had three decades to perfect it. But beyond a fluttering of flattered masculinity, he didn't feel much beyond curiosity. He stared at her the way he might a puzzle made for children. The sort of complication she presented had lost all appeal, regardless of its package.

He lifted her hand from his knee, very gently. He handed it back to her as though handing back his entire past, everything he'd once felt for her.

And the look on her face then was pure shock: shock that anyone would refuse her. Then confusion and panic; she hadn't anything left to her besides her looks and wiles.

"I can't help you," he said gently, "if you don't tell me why you think he's trying to kill you, Caroline. And Caroline... even if he *made* you help him, you'll be implicated, too, in whatever he's done. Unless you tell me. And maybe then... maybe then there will be something I can do to protect you."

She tried again: lips parted, she fixed him with a gaze that would have had a priest rending his vestments and leaping upon her. She clearly knew that men were simpletons, for the most part, and that her powers were potent.

Kit waited it out. He was excellent at waiting, when strategy called for it.

Caroline frowned a little, and the gaze went away, like a curtain being drawn, and she looked uneasy. Ah, at last. She was beginning to realize, he thought, exactly how much trouble she was in, and beginning to understand that Kit wasn't a seventeen-year-old hothead ruled by what swung between his legs. He sighed. He tried for the element of surprise.

"Caroline, there's a rumor that Morley sold information to the French. Do you know anything of this?"

"Is he being investigated then?" she asked almost eagerly. "Have you any proof?"

Interesting eagerness. Interesting question.

And then, with a mental *click,* he felt another piece of the puzzle slide into place, and he had an interesting realization.

He took great pains to disguise this realization with a carefully concerned countenance.

"What were you doing in Gorringe, Caroline?" He asked it casually.

"Gorringe?" she looked startled.

"The letter. The *'I'm sorry'* letter. You sent it from Gorringe. Many years ago. A year or so after you left with Morley."

"Oh," she said faintly. "I'd forgotten."

To him, it was the verbal equivalent of her earlier shrug. She'd *forgotten.*

But Kit was now certain he knew precisely what she'd been doing in Gorringe all those years ago. *He forced me to help,* she'd said. He doubted much forcing of any kind had been involved. Caroline had always had a taste for mischief; no doubt she'd thought the whole business exciting.

Ironic to think that Caroline had been a spy, too, long before Kit ever was.

He stared at her, his face revealing nothing, because he was trained to reveal nothing. He watched Caroline desperately, silently trying to gain a purchase on his inscrutable mood, to know what he was thinking, or how he felt.

This was what he was thinking and feeling: Caroline had helped shatter the lives of happy people, and deprived Susannah of a family, and assisted a traitor. And pity, the strongest emotion he'd felt for Caroline since she'd arrived today, was beginning to give way to the conviction that she was, in a way, an accessory to murder. A murder almost two decades old.

Caroline's life had begun difficult, but her own decisions had ensured it remained so. And very likely, finally, he realized there had never been anything he could do to help her, no matter how desperately he'd wanted to.

She cleared her throat. "Perhaps I should leave now, Kit," she said, briskly. "I'm sorry to have troubled you."

"No," he said softly. Placed a gentle but restraining hand on her arm. "I should like you to stay. I shall do everything I can to help you, Caroline."

It was a lie. But he didn't intend to let her get away now.

Susannah didn't turn around when Kit came into the room almost an hour later, but he was certain she'd heard him; he could tell by how her spine stiffened.

He sat down quietly next to her on the settee, didn't speak for a moment. He followed her eyes to the painting.

"How do you like my portrait?" he asked conversationally.

She thought about that. "You don't look happy in it."

"The painting was my father's idea. I remember those sittings well..." His voice drifted, he smiled ruefully. "My father is forever making me do something I don't want to do. Something I don't want to do...and then later I'm glad of." *Like the damned folio.*

Kit realized, irritated and amused, that his father was probably smarter than he was.

Well, if somebody *had* to be smarter than he was, he supposed he was glad it was his father.

"You have two sisters, too," she said softly. "Are they alive?"

"Yes." He wasn't about to regale Susannah about the mixed blessings sisters presented. Hopefully they would find her sisters, and she would discover those blessings for herself.

"Perhaps we can write to find my sisters. Daisy Jones said

Sylvie had gone to France. Sabrina might very well still be in England. And maybe my mother..." She trailed off.

"We'll do that right away," he promised her.

She smiled a little.

He reached for her hand, which was cold, but soft, unresisting now. He brought it to his lips and held it there for a long time, turned her palm up and placed a kiss in it, folded her hand over the kiss.

"I need to go somewhere, Susannah, and I meant to tell you earlier."

"With her?"

"No."

He saw the relief on her face; had she really thought he would leave her?

"Where will *she* be when you go?" she wanted to know.

"The two of you will come along with me." He'd decided this was the only way it could be.

"*Wonderful.* Just the three of us. How very cozy."

Kit smiled crookedly. But he didn't want to leave Susannah alone at all. And he wasn't about to allow Caroline to leave The Roses now that she was here. And he wasn't going to arm Bullton with a rifle and tell him to watch Caroline, nor did he think it fair to leave Bullton in charge of guarding Susannah.

His only option, unattractive though it might be, was to bring both women along to Gorringe. And quickly.

Where was bloody John Carr when he actually needed him?

"Susannah, listen to me: Do you want this to be over? Do you want to be safe?"

"No, I rather enjoy dodging for my life, and wondering when you'll next be stabbed or crushed on my behalf."

He smiled again, pleased with her the way he always was when she was sarcastic.

"How can you *smile*?" she wanted to know, irritated.

"You forget, my dear, that danger has been a way of life for me."

She pondered this. "Wouldn't you rather just be a naturalist?" she said weakly.

He didn't answer; he just looked at her for a long moment. And then he leaned forward and touched his mouth to hers.

Her lips were obstinate at first, but then they softened beneath his, and her hand went up to cup his face—he loved it when she did that—and she parted her lips. For a short, dizzying moment, they feasted tenderly on each other. It was incomparably sweet.

And when he was finished kissing her, she looked down and ran her tongue over her lips, tasting them, took in a long breath. He knew her head was spinning like his own.

"Where do we have to go?" she asked finally, composure regained.

"Do you remember when I said there were some papers incriminating Morley? I think I know where they are."

"Where?"

"Do you recall the stained-glass windows in the church in Gorringe? The vicar said they weren't original—he said they were donated by a 'generous benefactor,' along with the mausoleum behind."

" 'Faith, Hope, and Charity,' " Susannah mused, and then her eyes flew wide. "Oh! I see it now! The *windows* were 'Christian virtues'! It's something to do with the windows!"

"Yes. And I think that generous benefactor was your father. Richard Lockwood."

"Good heavens," Susannah was impressed. "He *was* clever, then."

"Too clever by half. Too whimsical by half, perhaps. He might have been a little more direct—no doubt we all would have appreciated it—but where would the fun have been in that?" Kit said wryly. "I believe the documents he collected—if they exist—might be hidden in the mausoleum in Gorringe."

"But if he'd been more direct," Susannah said, defending the father she'd never known, "perhaps Mr. Morley would have found and destroyed the papers by now."

"Clever, aren't you." Kit's mouth twitched.

"I get it from my father, I believe."

"Perhaps," he indulged. "But you're right, of course, about Morley. The fact that he seems to be trying to kill you ... I think it means he hasn't yet found the documents. I believe James threatened him with their existence, *then* set out to actually find them, which, as Mr. Avery-Finch told us, is a rather backward way to conduct blackmail."

"And then Mr. Morley searched my home for them, but didn't find them."

Kit nodded. "He probably thought it would be easy enough to eliminate you, just in case you had the documents and intended to use them, since he believed you hadn't any other means of income. He clearly hadn't reckoned upon *me*."

"I imagine you come as a bit of a surprise to most people."

He shrugged modestly. "Then again, the papers may *not* exist, Susannah ... but it's the best hope we have for bringing Morley to justice."

"What if you're wrong? About the mausoleum, that is? And the rest of this?"

"I so seldom am." He gave her a confident smile.

Which caused her to roll her eyes.

"But we do need to look for those documents *now*. Today. Because if they are what they seem to be ... then we might be able to arrest Morley. And stop the, shall we say, inconvenience of frequent attempts on your life."

"And clear my mother's name perhaps?"

"And clear your mother's name. I hope."

"And save Caroline, somehow, as well." Susannah said the words flatly. "Because you must by all means save Caroline."

Kit hesitated. He didn't know how to tell Susannah what he suspected; he thought perhaps he wouldn't tell her just yet. For the moment, he needed her relatively calm and enthusiastic. "Perhaps," he said.

Susannah was quiet for a moment. "She's very beautiful."

"Yes," Kit agreed simply.

Susannah turned her head away from him, studying the portrait again. She seemed to be struggling with something; he saw the passage of thought over her features.

"How would you describe me, Kit?" she asked finally.

"I'm sorry?" It wasn't the last thing he expected her to say just then, but it was very near it.

"How would you *describe* me? It's just . . . I've never heard you do it. I've heard you call Caroline 'difficult to forget.' Dark hair, dark eyes. But . . . what do you see when you see *me*? How would you describe me?"

She said it urgently, as if she couldn't possibly exist until he'd delineated her in words.

Kit was startled by the request. He would describe a vole, an adder, a fern, a horse. He knew the facts of them, their colors, their habits, the connections between them.

But how would he describe Susannah? He tried to think, but images and feelings tumbled together, defying single words: wit and complicated eyes and a green hat and exquisite breasts and—

For some reason the only image that lingered was Susannah with her arm buried up to the shoulder inside a horse. It seemed important, that image.

He realized he couldn't describe her any more than he could describe his own . . . *viscera*. She lived inside him now.

"I can't do it," he said softly, almost to himself, his voice frayed. "I can't describe you."

He saw the bitter disappointment flood her face. Then watched her struggle to disguise it.

He stood up then, feeling strangely agitated. "How can I possibly describe"—he made an abrupt, sweeping gesture—"everything, Susannah? Because that's what you are. You are...everything."

She gazed back at him, stunned.

"Does that satisfy you?" he asked quietly.

He knew it didn't. He was embarrassed by the inadequacy of it. Still, he couldn't bring himself to say the words to her.

"I'll have the coach brought round."

And then he left her, very quickly, as though the enormity of the love he saw in her face and the enormity of all that he felt drove him from the room.

Chapter Nineteen

Kit halloed for the vicar when they arrived at the Gorringe church, but there was no response. Perhaps the vicar was napping off his noonday wine.

Very well, then. He'd conduct his own tour of the church grounds. He led Susannah and Caroline around back.

The mausoleum was easy enough to find: a somber granite block, glowing white in the sun, guarded by suitably solemn carved seraphim holding trumpets aloft. Kit was amused; it wasn't grand, but the thing was so ostentatious as to be nearly mocking, perhaps more evidence of Lockwood's famously whimsical sense of humor. Or perhaps he really *had* intended to be buried in this mausoleum, and had wanted to do it in style, and add his family members to it, as well, as the years went on.

As Robert Burns had said so well: The best laid plans of mice and men...

It was locked. He'd been prepared for this eventuality. He fished about in his pack, came up with a length of wire, poked it in and jiggled it about. He pocketed the lock, as he didn't intend for them to be locked inside, and pushed the door a little. It gave, and the trapped must of years rushed out at him in a cloud of agitated dust.

He coughed and waved his hand.

It was dim inside, despite the brilliant day behind him. He produced a lamp and lit it—Kit was, of course, prepared—allowed the light to pulse into a glow, and he studied the inscrutable interior, which, unlike the door, yielded nothing. He gestured for the women to precede him inside, and they both did so gingerly. And once they were inside, Kit retrieved his pistol from inside his coat, kept it in his hand.

He hesitated to close the mausoleum door behind him, yet he didn't want to call attention to his presence. He compromised by wedging his tinderbox there. He entered, holding his lamp aloft, and waved it around.

The light found it: a box. He gave it a tug from its slot.

Susannah and Caroline leaped back, squeamish.

"It's not a body," he assured them. "No one has ever gone to their eternal rest in this particular mausoleum."

There was a sturdy lock on the strongbox; a few more minutes of fumbling with and swearing at the lock, and it sprang open.

Dust flew out like a genie escaping a bottle, and when it cleared he saw a stack of documents. He settled the lantern on one of the empty spaces above him, and began to leaf through them, his fingers careful; many of them had gone brittle with age.

The first was a letter, sent to a French operative whose name he recognized—they'd apprehended him years ago—in a code he recognized. How on earth had Richard Lockwood acquired this—bribery? Lockwood had indeed been playing a risky game, if he'd undertaken this investigation alone. The next document was a letter in French agreeing to a meeting with

Monsieur Morley at an inn near the London docks. Not terribly incriminating, in and of itself, but perhaps useful as part of a story. Another sheet of foolscap below that appeared to be a list of the names of ships. He recognized the names.

There were drawings of guns. And letters describing meetings.

"Sweet Lucifer," he breathed. It was true. It was all true. Morley was a traitor, and in his hands he held enough to hang him.

And then the thick dusty hush of the mausoleum was interrupted by a sound he knew too well, inches behind him: the *click* of a pistol.

And he turned around to discover Caroline Allston pointing one at Susannah's temple.

"Give me the documents, Kit."

He took in the situation with one glance. It would have been a simple thing to snatch that toy from Caroline's delicate little wrist, except—

"This is a dueling pistol, and it'll go off like"—Caroline snapped her fingers—*"that* if you so much as nudge me."

Except for that.

"Then perhaps you hadn't better do"—Susannah snapped her fingers—*"that."* Her voice was shaking, but it sounded more like fury than fear.

"Susannah," Kit said softly. "She's right. Don't move."

Susannah went obediently quiet. Kit could have reached out and crushed Caroline's windpipe between two fingers, such was the force of his fury at the moment. Fury with himself, as well. He'd known Caroline was capricious, and willful, and reckless.

But he'd never for one moment thought of her as violent.

His own prejudice, his own sense of honor, had clouded his judgment here, and now she was aiming a pistol at Susannah's temple.

His voice was a gentle thing. Breeze gentle. "Put the pistol down, Caroline. You don't want to do this."

"No?" She sounded half-amused. "You don't intend to 'help' me, Kit. It's my guess you intend to see me hang. I think I *do* want to do this."

"Why do you think I'd like to see you hang?" Again, gently, gently. So as not to jar her mood any further than necessary.

Caroline all but rolled her eyes at him. "Oh, you needn't speak to me so very *gently,* Kit," Caroline sounded amused again. "I'm not *mad.* Perfectly sane."

"Caroline, if you just hand the gun to me…"

She snorted. Held very still. As did Kit. The air itself seemed to congeal.

"She was kind, Susannah," Caroline said slowly. "Your mother."

Susannah's eyes slid to Caroline's face. Kit watched the comprehension begin to dawn there. She was beginning to realize what he'd realized today in the library.

Caroline smiled a little. "So few people really are," she continued. "They pretend to be, because they think that's how they're supposed to be. But your mother was truly kind. And I was a *terrible* maid."

"How do you know my mother?" Susannah said hoarsely.

Caroline's exquisite face registered nothing, but her eyes briefly reflected a boundless, startling sadness. "I *am* sorry," she said.

Susannah choked it out. "It was you that night…your hair…I remember. It was *you.* It must have been you."

"I was a maid in your home in Gorringe, Susannah. Morley had suspicions about Mr. Lockwood, and he knew that Anna Holt was hiring a staff for her country home in Gorringe, and he arranged for *me* to be part of that staff. And after that, it was a simple thing to just listen, as no one pays any attention to a

maid. I might as well have been a flea. Your father told your
mother everything. And so...I listened, and confirmed Thaddeus's suspicions. I imagine Thaddeus did...well, the rest."

The rest, of course, being to arrange for the murder of Richard Lockwood and to blame it on Anna Holt.

Caroline turned to Kit. "And *that's* what makes me think
you intend to see me hang, Kit. Because I realized today, when
you wouldn't allow me to leave, that you probably already knew
all of this. And because you are always loyal to the people you
love, so hell-bent on righting wrongs. But you never really loved
me; it was all tied up with your bloody sense of honor—the
wanting to marry me, the wanting to help me. All tied up in
your sense of right and wrong. But you *do* love Susannah. And
because of that, letting me walk away today would be wrong."

Kit was silent. *So Caroline was an expert on love, was she?*
he thought snidely.

She was, however, altogether correct.

He said it quietly. "You shattered their lives, Caroline.
Three little girls. A woman, their father. You were playing at
spy with Morley...you may have been young, but I think you
knew exactly what you were about."

"Well, I suppose I thought of it as an adventure, then...I
didn't think much of it beyond that. And I *did* say I was sorry,
and I am. But that doesn't mean I intend to hang for it, for pity's
sake. So kindly hand those documents to me. I intend to burn
them."

"Caroline, even if I did hand them to you, even if you do
burn them, you'd never really be free of this. I would make
bloody certain of it."

Kit could hear Susannah's breathing; it had grown more
rapid. Her face, even by the warm lantern light, was pale as the
marble walls. He wanted to reach for her, touch her, comfort
her; he didn't dare. He instead looked his love into her eyes, and

a faint smile touched her lips. As though she was reassuring *him,* for God's sake. She could teach a few men a thing or two about bravery.

Or perhaps it was just that she put a little too much faith in him. After all, he'd been doing nothing but saving her life for days now.

"And how do you suppose you'll get away?" he asked Caroline, almost conversationally. "You've only the one bullet in that pistol, if it's even loaded. You can't kill the both of us."

"Oh, someone followed us here. A man of Morley's, right scary little man. I imagine he'll be here shortly, and then off we'll go. This will be over sooner if you hand the documents to me now."

There was a faint scuffing noise, and Caroline and Kit swiveled. It was the toe of Susannah's boot moving a fraction of an inch.

"I'm terribly sorry, but I...but I think I might faint," Susannah whispered.

Kit felt a rush of concern and then...

No. If Susannah hadn't yet fainted—over adders, mad horses, and lunging men with knives—she wasn't about to do it now.

He waited, senses on alert.

Caroline shifted a little uneasily, and Kit watched the gun barrel nuzzle more deeply into Susannah's temple, and he felt it as surely as if it were pressed against his own skin.

"Really," Susannah said, again sounding desperate. "And I think I may very well be sick all ov—"

Caroline took the minutest step back in alarm, and in that instant Kit lashed out and seized Caroline's wrist, yanking it skyward, and the pistol fired into the mausoleum ceiling.

Chips of marble came showering down. Kit swept an arm across Susannah's waist and pushed her aside. He seized the petite Caroline's wrists in his own and twisted them behind her back.

"Susannah...pull the string from my knapsack. There's a knife in there...use it to cut it free."

For someone who'd just had a pistol pointed at her temple, Susannah managed to do this with admirable dexterity, and Kit bound Caroline's wrists.

"For pointing a gun at Susannah, Caroline...I'll see you hang."

The three of them swiveled toward a creak as the door opened fully. A lantern entered. Kit spun, pointing his pistol at the door. "Don't move another inch or—"

"Oh, spare the blustering, Kit, for God's sake. It's only me."

John Carr was holding the lantern, and a pistol, and a knapsack filled with helpful things.

Kit lowered his pistol. "*Now* you arrive, John."

John Carr paused in the doorway, took a look around, the blasted ceiling, the marble fragments on the floor, the broken-open strongbox. "Bloody hell. *Again* you beat me to it, Grantham. How the dev—"

"I'm just better, is all, John."

John shook his head, swearing softly, and Kit laughed.

"Found the documents, then?" John asked. "They do exist? I followed the trail here, at last."

"They're over here," Kit jerked his chin toward the strong-box. "And look who found *me*."

"Hello, John," Caroline said pleasantly. "It's been some time, hasn't it?"

John spun toward her voice. And went utterly, almost eerily, still. Merely regarded Caroline with an expression impossible to decipher.

His stillness was only seconds shy of troubling Kit when John finally spoke again.

"Are the documents what they're purported to be?" John turned away from her, said the words coolly.

"Have a look for yourself." Kit motioned with his hand, and John strode past the bound Caroline and the quiet Susannah, not meeting the eyes of either of them, focused on his goal. He leafed through the documents, skimming the words; his face grew steadily grimmer.

"I came upon a nasty little character named Bob lurking about, knocked him out, tied him up," John said absently, as he read the documents. "I do think he'll be useful when it comes to . . . proving Morley's transgressions. You may want to send someone for him." He continued reading.

"We've enough there to hang him, I suppose," Kit said. "Morley, that is. With the testimony of Mr. Avery-Finch, if he agrees to testify."

"Yes, it looks that way," John said slowly, as he turned the last of the documents over. "So why don't you let Caroline go?"

Kit wasn't certain he'd heard him correctly. "I beg your pardon?"

"You have enough here to hang Morley," John said calmly. "So let Caroline go."

Kit stared at John's handsome face. The words were disorienting, as though someone else had borrowed John's mouth to speak them. "John . . . are you mad? Tell me you're jesting. She's part of all of this . . . she helped all but destroy Susannah's family, she helped murder a man, she held a pistol to Susannah's *temple,* in case you're wondering why I've bound her wrists." He gave an incredulous laugh. "She was instrumental in obtaining the very information you're holding there. She's a traitor to England, John, as surely as Morley is."

The traitor to England lifted her delicate brows at this description, but otherwise remained silent.

John said nothing. Merely stared levelly back at Kit.

Then comprehension set in, and Kit's world tilted on its axis.

"You never were investigating *Morley,* were you?" he said softly. "This entire time... you were looking for Caroline... for yourself, weren't you?"

John kept his gaze level with Kit's, not speaking.

But finally, he squeezed his eyes closed. He opened them again, and pride and a plea for understanding were taut in his face.

"I wish I could explain it to you, Kit, but I'm not sure you'd understand. I just... never could forget her. I thought of her so often... more than I could ever confess to you. I was ashamed of it, if you must know. I knew it was a foolish obsession and yet... well, I finally surrendered to the urge to look for her. I began with Morley. I intercepted his mail."

"No one assigned you to do that," Kit said, half-wonderingly.

"No."

"If anyone other than me had learned you were doing that, John..." The risk had been extraordinary, the consequences grave, disastrous for John.

"I know." John's mouth twitched ruefully. "Are you beginning to see now? It was a risk I was willing to take. For her."

Kit opened his mouth to speak, and John waited. But no words came.

"And then... well, once I began with Morley... I started with you, too, Kit. And I don't expect you to forgive me, but I honestly couldn't explain this to you. I didn't think you'd understand. *I* didn't even fully understand. But somehow I knew she would come back to you. Because it was always, always you." He gave a short laugh, a little wondering, a little bitter. The sound of acceptance. "And I thought if I could help her... perhaps she would turn to me instead. I just couldn't let the two of you meet again. God, I wanted a chance with her." John looked uncomfortable. "Most of your mail is fairly dull, you know." He tried a joke.

"Sorry to bore you," Kit said dryly.

"But damned if she didn't try to reach you. I was right." John gave a humorless laugh.

"Ah, must be your spy instincts," Kit said. Again, dryly.

"I thought... with the information you gave me—the story Makepeace told you—perhaps I would be able to find those documents before you did... and if anything among them pointed to Caroline, I would destroy it, and just leave enough to hang Morley. And then... perhaps when I found her..."

He looked at Caroline now, who was regarding him with utter astonishment. "I'd take her away where no one could ever hurt her again." He said this with quiet, almost deadly, conviction.

John turned to Kit again. "And again... she came right back to you, Kit." He sounded half-amused. "Here she is."

"But John..." Kit was staggered. "She isn't..."

He was about to say, *She isn't worth it.* The very same words John had said to him that morning seventeen years ago, when they'd faced each other over pistols. Bitter words, Kit saw now. Words of self-defense. The loss had somehow been greater for John. Had always been greater for John.

And Kit couldn't bring himself to say those words about any woman.

"I *can't* let you do it, John. I can't let you take her. She helped *murder* a man. Two men, if you include what became of Makepeace. Her actions may have led to the deaths of English soldiers, John. Surely this *matters* to you."

"I don't care, Kit." John sounded weary and bemused and faintly awed by his own confession. "I'm more sorry than I can say, and I know it's all true of her, but when it comes to Caroline... God help me, but I don't care."

"John—"

John's voice rose, tense, impassioned now. "Kit, I have only ever truly wanted one thing, so help me. And I don't know whether or not it will make me happy. I'm not sure that I *care* whether it does." He gave a short, wondering laugh. "But I do know that I want Caroline. Know this: I love you as a brother. And if you've ever loved me—and I know what I've done is nigh unforgivable—let me win *just this once*. For God's sake."

Another fragment of marble *chink*ed to the ground. No one moved.

"Don't throw everything away, John," Kit pleaded softly.

John Carr said nothing.

"She doesn't love you, John." Kit could hear the resignation creeping into his own voice. John heard it, too.

A ghost of a smile touched John's face. "Oh, she will, one day. I mean...look at me."

Kit smiled faintly, too; he couldn't help it. But his heart was breaking again. He thought again about all the kinds of love there were in the world. Love, it turned out, was a constant surprise, in its mutations and permutations.

Susannah spoke, her voice a soft note in the tense silence. "Kit...I think you should let her go."

Kit jerked toward her. "This woman, Susannah...what she did to your family..."

"I know what she did, but...but nothing can undo that now. Hanging her won't bring either my father or James Makepeace back. Mr. Morley...isn't he the one truly at fault? Don't we have enough to bring him to justice?"

Kit's sense of justice, his patriotism, his need to put things right, his sense of right and wrong—all were at war here with something that adhered to no laws. He thought of the words of Pascal: *The heart has its reasons which reason knows nothing of.*

"I don't know if it's the right thing to do, Susannah." He said it quietly, almost desperately.

"Perhaps not everything can be either right or wrong. Perhaps you must simply choose."

And so, a moment later, he chose. He did it out of love, and not patriotism, knowing that no matter what he chose, John Carr was lost to him.

Kit turned to Caroline. "Will you go with him?" he said gruffly.

"Hmmm..." Caroline looked up toward the ceiling. "Goodness...the gallows, or handsome John Carr. Let me think...let me think..."

Kit sighed, and gestured with his chin toward John, and Caroline went to him. John quickly worked the bonds loose from Caroline's wrists.

"Good knots," he complimented Kit, quietly.

Kit said nothing.

When Caroline was free, she turned to look at John, and he fixed his eyes on her face for a long moment, absorbing her. Neither said a word.

Caroline broke their gaze, finally, and turned to Susannah.

"Your mother...well, your parents talked often of Italy. I truly don't know where she might have gone that evening...but she might have tried to go there."

Susannah gave a shallow nod of thanks.

Kit looked at his best friend in the world, the man who'd known him from boyhood, the brother of his heart, his rival. Bloody handsome John Carr.

"You'd better leave, John. Before I change my mind."

John Carr lifted a hand to Kit, smiled crookedly. Then turned and pushed the door to the mausoleum open. And walked away from Kit forever.

Caroline was behind him, but she paused in the doorway. She looked at Kit, uncertain; she appeared to be deciding whether she should speak.

"Thaddeus has . . . a cat," she faltered. "Will you see that someone . . . that someone takes his cat?"

She lifted her chin. Daring Kit to mock her. Still, she kept her eyes fixed on him, waiting for an answer.

And Kit gazed back at her, stunned. *How about that? She does love Morley.*

But Caroline wasn't burdened with a sense of honor; she traveled lightly, burdened only with her own sense of self-preservation, living from moment to moment. It wasn't love the way Kit understood it.

He found himself nodding just once, curtly.

"Good-bye then. Good luck to both of you." Caroline gave an ironic curtsy, turned to leave again.

"Caroline," Kit said sharply.

She stopped and turned, lifted her soft brows inquiringly.

"Endeavor to be worthy of him."

She laughed, as though he'd just said something tremendously witty, and shook her head wryly.

And was gone.

⟡

He didn't want to speak during the ride home. Silently, he led Susannah into the house, past the servants, up the stairs, into his chambers, where she'd never before been, and sank down on the edge of his bed. And Susannah could see in his posture that every fiber in his body, in his soul, was achingly weary.

"I'm sorry about John," she said softly.

"Come here," he said softly in return.

She drifted over, and stood between his legs, and he looped his arms around her. He looked up. She could peer right down into the nostrils of his arrogantly arched nose, right into those beautiful blue eyes fringed by those gold tipped lashes.

"I love you, Susannah."

"I know." It didn't seem nearly as important anymore to hear him say the words aloud; she knew he simply lived his love for her every moment.

"But I should have told you before now. When Caroline pointed a pistol at you, I—"

He stopped abruptly, turned his head.

"Hush...," Susannah murmured, and cupped her face in her hands, pressed her lips against the top of his head. "It's all right."

"It's not all right." He sounded irritated. He looked up at her again. "It's just that I—"

"Perhaps you weren't sure you loved me, and needed to be cert—"

"Susannah." He sounded amused and impatient. "Please stop defending me. It wasn't any of that... it was..." He paused, searching for words to describe an amorphous terror. "It was as though if I'd said the words aloud... you'd just disappear. And I couldn't bear it. I couldn't bear the thought of loving you as much as I do... I love you so much... and then losing you."

He sounded ashamed. As though he thought he wasn't entitled to ever fear.

She didn't know what to say. Probably nothing at all would be best.

"In summary," he concluded wryly, "I was a dreadful coward, and I love you."

"Well, that's quite an astonishing confession." Her voice was husky. "From a man who's been crushed by a horse and stabbed in my defense, and shot at by the French, and God knows what else. But you can stop confessing now. I love you, too."

"I know," he said on a sigh, looking dazed and pleased, and

his hands wandered lower, until they were looped beneath her behind. He pulled her into him, held her close.

He was just about eye-level with her breasts, and so he pulled her in closer, and pressed his lips to one, over the soft muslin. And his hands wandered up beneath her dress, lifting it until his fingers found the silky insides of her thighs. He leaned backward onto the bed, bringing her with him.

"Hush, now," he ordered on a whisper. "Lie still."

He tipped her to the bed and then knelt over her, reached behind her back and gently, deftly, unlaced her gown, eased it over her head, placed it carefully aside. Next, he applied himself to her garters, untying them, adding them to the dress, rolled her stockings down, still deftly, while she quietly submitted.

And when she was entirely bare, he sighed, and lay alongside her. He kissed her mouth, softly. His lips found her brows, her temple, the pulse in her throat; his hands pulled the pins from her hair, stroking it out until it fanned over his pillow.

And this is how he made love to her: The overwhelming, aching tenderness, the desire and reverence, in his every touch, more eloquent, more profound, than words could ever hope to be. Susannah closed her eyes and only once murmured his name, floating in the center of a bliss that had edges of flame. His hands, his mouth, seemed everywhere, everywhere, from her shoulders, to her breasts, to the round curve of her belly, relentlessly knowing, sure and delicate, setting slow fire to every cell of her until she arched and rippled beneath his touch, until she was nothing but a creature made to be touched.

And then his mouth moved between her legs, and he parted her knees so he could taste the silkiest, most sensitive part of her. Her fingers gripped the coverlet as his tongue dipped, and circled, and savored, loving her, until her blood roared in her ears, until she was nearly sobbing from the pleasure of it, until she splintered into light and sensation.

Then, at last, off came his clothes, which he did as deftly as he did everything else, and his beautiful body hovered an instant over her. She surrounded him with her thighs, pulled him to her with her arms, took him into her body. This joining always seemed never to last quite long enough to Susannah, because she could never fully be part of him, but the finite nature of it made it all the sweeter. And this was slow, slow, too, and his eyes never left hers; he burned his love into her with his eyes. He moved, inexorably to his own release, which came for him with a sigh of her name.

He kissed her. He turned over gently, with her in his arms. They held each other, face to face.

"*That's* how much I love you, Susannah," he whispered.

They lolled together, until Kit remembered that Aunt Frances would worry, and so they dressed, somewhat haphazardly and quickly, and made their way down the stairs.

Bullton was hurrying toward him again. This was becoming unnervingly familiar.

"Sir—" he began desperately.

He didn't need to say anything more than that. Because Kit heard the sound of an all-too-familiar throat clearing in the portrait parlor.

"Sir, he has . . . he is . . . ," Bullton whispered desperately. Then gave up trying to explain. "Well, perhaps you best go to him, sir," he said resignedly. "And you'll see."

Because, of course, it was the very worst thing Kit could possibly imagine happening, the earl was standing in the middle of the room holding Susannah's sketchbook, which she had of course left in the portrait parlor.

He seemed riveted by a particular page. Frozen in place, in fact, staring down at it.

When at last he slowly lifted his head, his expression was... well, indescribable, really.

Though "priceless" did go some way toward describing it.

Kit almost squeezed his eyes closed. One never, never, *never* wants one's father to get a good look at one's face in the aftermath of lovemaking. But that's precisely what that particular sketch afforded.

He glanced at Susannah, whom he'd tried to hide behind him. Her hair was sliding out of the pins on one side. She looked beautiful and, unfortunately, entirely wanton.

A cripplingly awkward moment staggered by, while Kit grappled with what he should say to his father. He mentally packed his trunks for Egypt, hoping Susannah wouldn't be disappointed to find herself living in the desert rather than on Grosvenor Square.

"Is this the artist?" his father asked, eyebrows raised in Susannah's direction.

"Yes," Kit confessed.

A silence as vast and arid as the Egyptian desert yawned while his father stared at the two of them.

"We're going to be married," Kit offered tentatively.

"Good God, I should *think* so," the earl said fervently. "Who is she?"

Kit went mute again.

"Well?" the earl gestured with his brows.

At last Kit found his manners, or some vestiges of them. "Father, allow me to introduce to you Miss Susannah Makepeace, my fiancée. This is my father, the Earl of Westphall."

Susannah paused, and then—because what else could one do under the circumstances?—she curtsied.

Kit almost laughed.

"Makepeace, eh? James's daughter?"

She hesitated, but apparently decided her real story would have to wait. "Yes, sir." Susannah's voice was remarkably steady.

"And did you make these sketches?"

Her face was a brilliant, flaming, summer-sunset scarlet, but her composure held up admirably. "Yes, sir."

The earl stared at both of them again for some time, clearly struggling with a number of diverse thoughts, among them, judging from the twitch of his features, hilarity and horror.

He cleared his throat. "They're really quite good."

Kit was in awe. The earl had clearly chosen the most benign thing from the myriad things he'd *wanted* to say, or could have said. *My father, the diplomat,* Kit thought. *I really should take lessons.*

"She's very talented," Kit said quickly.

Kit realized too late how this must sound, given the sketch his father had no doubt been reviewing. He nearly slapped his forehead.

The earl just sighed.

"Miss Makepeace, it is a pleasure to meet you. I should like to speak to my son alone now."

Susannah shot Kit a sympathetic look, and looked relieved to be leaving the library. Kit was tempted to pull her back by the elbow.

❧

"I'm sorry about the folio assignment, father," Kit began quickly. "I'll complete it, I promise you. Rather a lot of things... came up. That you will find very interesting."

"You were seen in London, Kit."

"By whom?" he said swiftly. *Bloody John!*

"Miss Daisy Jones said a Mr. White had come inquiring. I knew it was you."

"You conducted your *own* inquiry?" Kit asked. So his father *hadn't* thought he was mad when he mentioned Makepeace. It was a little mollifying.

Wait. Or maybe... "How do you know Miss Daisy Jones?"

His father just smiled enigmatically. "Did you find what you were looking for, Kit? What you should *not* have been looking for, I should say?"

"Yes, and it's true, sir. Everything Makepeace said was true. I'll show the documents to you, if you'd like to see them. Correspondence, lists of ships... and Morley is mentioned specifically. Lockwood really did gather valid evidence. It looks bad for Morley, sir. I spoke to an antiquities dealer who might be persuaded to testify."

The earl went still. After a moment, his face reflected a deep sadness. "It's a shame. All of it. He wasn't a bad politician, Morley. An intelligent man. A waste. A pity. A murderer."

"And a traitor, sir. He was a traitor."

"It was dangerous, what you did, Kit. Going about this alone. You could have been killed."

"I could have been killed any number of times in my life," Kit said wryly. "There's still time."

"But I *expressly* told you not to go anywhere near London." His father's tone had the ring of pyramids now.

"I swear to you, sir, I'll finish the folio assignment. I..." He paused when he realized this was true. "I *want* to finish the assignment."

The earl sighed again. "There was no assignment, Kit."

A silence.

"I beg your pardon?" Kit said flatly.

"There *was* no assignment. It was just..." The earl turned

away from him and rotated to look about the grand room, stopping to admire the portrait of his family. He smiled softly up at it, perhaps remembering the sittings. "I was worried about you, son. You seemed so . . ." His father paused. "Lost. Wallowing in various pleasures, but finding no *real* pleasure. A little too reckless. Unhappy without realizing it. And it had gone on for too long. It's the sort of thing a father notices."

Kit knew he should have been touched. But—

"And so you threatened me with *Egypt*?"

The earl looked placidly back at Kit. "I thought perhaps you could use a little time away from the *ton* to clear your head. Perhaps even rediscover an earlier, less dangerous passion. And I knew you wouldn't take any time away if I put it quite like *that* . . . and so, I invented an assignment. And . . ." The earl paused again, sounding bemused. "Once more, you've greatly exceeded my expectations. Then again, you never did do anything by halves."

His father gave him one of those sunny but evil smiles. The smiles that said, *I will always be cleverer than you, as long as I'm your father.*

Kit was speechless. His bloody father had *tricked* him.

Kit didn't know whether he wanted to throttle the man, or fall to his knees and thank him abjectly.

But he did know when he'd been bested.

"And it's good work, Christopher. Are your notes as good as these drawings?"

"What do you think?" All arrogance.

His father smiled. "Well, then, you *should* complete the folio. It bears publishing, you know, as good as these drawings are. We'll just . . . exclude a few of them."

"The voles?" Kit suggested innocently.

His father finally laughed. Then he glanced down at the sketchbook, and up at his son again, and shook his head slowly, to and fro. It took every fiber of Kit's self-control not to blush, and he could not remember ever blushing in his entire life.

"What is she like? Susannah?"

Damn. How Kit hated these kinds of questions. Whenever Susannah filled his thoughts, words seemed to flee. He thought of her, and it was just...

But his father must have read the answer on his face, and he gave a soft laugh. "Never mind, son. The sketches speak for both of you. And I'm more glad for you than I can say."

Epilogue

❧

$\mathcal{S}$he was trimming limp roses from their bushes when the breeze sprang up, a small surprise from the north; she closed her eyes briefly, let it trail around her neck like a damp silk scarf. The moist *sirocco* winds blew across Italy early in the fall, reminding her that she was not a native, would never quite feel like a native, even after seventeen years. The weather inside her was English.

Italy was beautiful, and she had known safety and anonymity here, but any place that wasn't home would always feel like a prison.

The pain had become an ever-present dull hum over the years; she'd learned to accommodate it the way one did an amputation. She'd known laughter again; she'd even known the faint rush of attraction again; she still turned heads, even as her middle years approached. Her very small circle of acquaintances knew her only as a widow, quietly committed to her mourning.

She'd risked two letters, two selfish letters, in the early years.

She hadn't signed them; even still, she knew sending them had been tantamount to aiming a gun at James—or at herself. But the longing and pain had been so fierce then she sometimes thought she would have happily died, happily sacrificed James or anyone else, for one scrap of knowledge of her daughters. James had replied only once: *they are safe.* He was right to discourage her from writing, of course. No doubt it had cost him not to ease her pain. But he'd been protecting them still.

But year after year, hope bloomed and died and bloomed again, like the roses she now pruned to make way for new growth. She would see her daughters again, and the truth would some day be known: this hope kept Anna Holt fiercely alive.

Ways to Be Wicked

This one's for you, Melis.

Acknowledgments

My gratitude to the Fog City Divas
for perspective, support and laughter,
to Melanie Murray for patience and insightful editing,
and to Steve Axelrod, for being the fount
from which all wisdom and sanity springs these days—
and for cheerfully grousing about bad coffee
by a hotel elevator in Reno.

Chapter One

⟡

Ironic, Sylvie thought, that the pitching and rolling of that wretched wooden ship should set up a corresponding pitching and rolling in her stomach, given that motion was more native to her than stillness. She in fact leaped, stretched, and pirouetted every day, achieving semiflight with no ill effects apart from sore muscles and the perversely gratifying jealousy of all of the other dancers in Monsieur Favre's corps de ballet. Sylvie Lamoreux was, in fact, the darling of the Paris Opera, object of desire and envy, the personification of beauty and grace—not accustomed, in other words, to losing the contents of her stomach over the side of a ship.

She supposed it had a little something to do with control. When she danced, *she* commanded her body. Well, and Monsieur Favre had a bit of a say in it, too: "I said, like a *butterfly*, Sylvie, not a cow. Look at you! I want to moo!" Or "Your arms, Sylvie, they are like timber. Lift them like so—ah yes, that is it, *mon ange,* you are like a dream. I suspected you could dance." Monsieur Favre was a trifle prone to exaggeration, but if she was his best dancer, he had helped make her so, and confidence was marvelous armor against sarcasm.

She'd rather be at Monsieur Favre's mercy any day than that of a bloody wooden ship, heaving this way and that over the choppy waters of the Channel.

He would not be pleased to find her gone.

The letter in her reticule said very little. But what it did say had launched her like a cannonball across the Channel to England for the first time in her life. For two weeks, Sylvie had furtively planned her journey, hurt and fury, poignant hope and a great inner flame of curiosity propelling her. She hadn't told a single soul of her plans. This seemed only fitting, given the magnitude of the things that had been kept from her.

Odd to think that a few mere sentences of English could do this. The letter had begun with an apology for bothering Claude yet again. *Yet again*—a little flame of anger licked up every time Sylvie thought of these words. It was not the first such letter sent, in other words. Or even the second, it would appear. And then, in the next sentence, it begged information about a young woman named Sylvie. *For I believe she might be my sister.*

The signature at the bottom said, "Susannah Whitelaw, Lady Grantham."

My sister. Sylvie had never before thought or said those two words together in her life.

To Sylvie the letter meant a past she'd never known, a future she'd never dreamed, and a store of secrets she'd only half suspected. Her parents were dead, Claude had told her, God rest their souls; Claude had raised Sylvie as her own. And if not for the fact that Claude had decided to holiday in the South as she did every year at this time, with a kiss on both cheeks for Sylvie and instructions to mind her parrot, Guillaume, Sylvie might never have seen the letter at all.

Sylvie had left Guillaume the parrot in the care of Claude's housekeeper. He would be in danger of nothing but boredom, as he spoke two more languages than the housekeeper, which was two fewer than Etienne.

Etienne. Sylvie's thoughts immediately flew from him as though scorched. And then flew back again, guiltily.

He was generous, Etienne, with ardor and gifts. He flirted as only one descended from centuries of courtiers could flirt; he moved through the world with the confident magnanimity of someone who had never been denied anything. He made heady promises she hardly dared believe, promises that would give her the life she had worked to acquire, that she had dreamed of.

But his temper . . . Sylvie would never understand it. Her own was a starburst—quick, spectacular, gone. His was cold and patient, implacable. It waited; he planned. And his retaliations always came with chilling finality and a sense of righteousness.

She'd last seen Etienne a week ago in the mauve predawn light, an arm flung over his head, his bare back turned to her as he slept. She'd placed the letter on her pillow, telling him only that she was sorry, but that she would see him again soon.

He loved her. But he used the word so easily.

But just as she knew Etienne would have tried to dissuade her from leaving Paris, she knew he would try to find her. And his temper would have been waiting all the while, too.

She did not want to be found until she'd learned what she'd come to learn.

The ship had released the passengers, and at last Sylvie's feet pressed against England. She allowed herself a giddy surge of triumph. She'd made it this far, entirely on her own. But she could still feel the sea inside her stomach, and color and movement and noise came at her in waves: men swarming to unload the ship, the early morning sun ricocheting hard between smooth sea and blue sky, gulls wheeling in arcs of silver and white. No clouds floated above to cut the glare or soften the heat. Sylvie took her first deep breath of truly English air. It was hot and clotted with dock odors, and made matters inside her stomach worse instead of better.

So be it. She would *will* her stomach into obedience. To date, there had been nothing Sylvie could not make her body do if she willed it.

She nodded to the man who shouldered her trunk for her and briskly turned to find the mail coach that would take her to London. She had never before traveled alone, but she had contrived the perfect disguise, her English was passably good, and she was not a child needing coddling or protection from a man. Besides, after Paris, a city as intricate, beautiful, and difficult as the ballet itself, no city could intimidate her. Great cities, at their hearts, were all the same.

She glanced up then and saw just the back of him, through the crowd, the broad shoulders, the way he stood. The sight of Etienne slammed hard, sending a cold wave of shock through her confidence. *It couldn't be. Not yet. Not so soon.*

But it was not a risk she was prepared to take. She swiveled her head, saw the mail coach, and made her decision.

⁀

Tom Shaughnessy was alone in the stagecoach mulling another failed trip to Kent, when a woman flung herself into his lap, wrapped her arms around his neck, and burrowed in, crushing her face against his.

"*What* in the name of—" he hissed. He lifted his arms to try to pry hers from about his neck.

"Hush," she whispered urgently. "*Please.*"

A man's head peered into the coach.

"I beg your pardon." He jerked his head hurriedly back, and vanished from view.

The woman in his lap had gone completely rigid, apart from her rapid breathing. And for a moment neither of them moved. Tom had an impression of rustling dark fabric, a lithe form, and the scent of spice and vanilla and roses and...well, female. This last made his head swim a little.

Startling, granted. But not precisely unpleasant.

Apparently deciding a safe interval had elapsed, she took her arms from about his neck and slid from his lap into the seat a distance away from him.

"And just when I was growing accustomed to you, Madame," he said wryly. He touched her arm gently. "Allow me to intro—*ow!*"

He jerked his hand back. What the *devil*—?

His eyes followed a glint to her lap.

Poking up from her neatly folded gloved hands was a...was that a *knitting* needle?

It was! She'd jabbed him with a damned *knitting needle*. Not hard enough to wound anything other than his pride. But certainly hard enough to make her...er...point.

"I regret inserting you, sir, but I cannot permit you to touch me again." Her voice was soft and grave, refined; it trembled just a bit. And, absurdly, she did sound genuinely regretful.

Tom glared at her, baffled. "You regret inser— Oh! You mean 'stabbing.' You regret...*stabbing* me?"

"Yes!" she said almost gratefully, as though he'd given her a verb she considered useful and fully intended to employ again in the future. "I regret *stabbing* you. I regret sitting upon you, also. But I cannot permit you to touch me again. I am not..." She made a futile gesture with her hand, as if she could snatch the elusive word from the air with it.

She was not...what? Sane?

But he could hear it now—she was French. Which accounted for the way her syllables subtly leaped and dipped in the wrong places, not to mention her unusual vocabulary choices, and perhaps even the knitting needle, because God only knew what a Frenchwoman was capable of. And apart from that tremble in her voice he would have assumed she was preternaturally self-possessed. But she was clearly afraid of something, or someone, and he suspected it was the man who had just peered into the coach.

He looked at her hard, but she kept her head angled slightly away from him. She was wearing mourning; he could see this now that she wasn't precisely on top of him. Her hat and veil revealed only a hint of delicate jaw and gleaming hair, which seemed to be a red shade, though this might perhaps be wishful thinking on his part. Her neck was long; her spine as elegantly erect as a Doric column. She was slim, but the gown she wore gave away very little of the shape of the woman inside it. The gown itself was beautifully made, but it fit her ill. Borrowed, he decided. He was accustomed to judging the fit of female clothing, after all, and this dress was not only too large; it had been made for someone else entirely.

Since he had done nothing but gape for nearly a minute, she seemed satisfied he didn't intend to reach for her again and slid the needle back up into her sleeve. For all the world like a woman tucking a basket of mending under a chair.

"Who is pursuing you, Madame?" he asked softly.

Her shoulders stiffened almost imperceptibly. Interesting. A further ripple in that self-possession.

"*Je ne comprende pas, monsieur.*" Delivered with a pretty little French lift of one shoulder.

Balderdash. She understood him perfectly well.

"*Au contraire,* I believe you do *comprende* my question," he contradicted politely. His own French was actually quite good.

All the very best courtesans were French, after all. Many of the dancers who passed through the White Lily were as well, which is why he knew all about the caprices of Frenchwomen.

The veil fluttered; she was breathing a little more quickly now.

"If you tell me, I might be able to help you," he pressed gently. Why he should offer to help someone who'd leaped into his lap, then poked him with a knitting needle eluded him at the moment. Curiosity, he supposed. And that delicate jaw.

The veil fluttered once, twice, as she mulled her next words. "Oh, but you already *have* helped me, monsieur."

And the faint but unmistakable self-deprecating humor and—dare he think it?—*flirtation*—in her words perversely charmed him to his marrow.

He opened his mouth to say something else, but she turned decisively toward the window, and an instant later seemed to have shed her awareness of him as neatly as a shawl or hat.

Damned if he wasn't fascinated.

He wanted desperately to gain her attention again, but if he spoke she would ignore him, he sensed; he suspected that if he so much as brushed the sleeve of her gown his hand would be swiftly "inserted" as neatly as a naturalist's butterfly to the mail coach seat.

He was watching her so intently he was startled when the coach bucked on its springs, taking on the weight of more passengers: a duenna ushering two young ladies, both pretty and diffident; a young couple glowing with contentment, as though the institution of marriage was their own marvelous, private discovery; a young man who looked very much like a curate; a plump prosperous merchant of some sort. Tom made his judgments of them by their clothing and the way they held themselves. At one time, each and every one of them, or someone of their ilk, had passed through his life, or he through theirs.

The little Frenchwoman widow might as well have been a shadow of one of the other passengers; with her slight build and dark clothing, she all but vanished against the seat. No one would trouble her or engage her in conversation if she appeared not to welcome it; she was a widow, and ostensibly still inside a bubble of grief.

Tom doubted it. He knew a costume when he saw one.

People wedged aboard the coach until it fair burst with heat and a veritable cornucopia of human smells, and the widow finally disappeared completely from Tom's view. When they were full, the coach lurched forward to London.

And as Tom was a busy man, his thoughts inevitably lurched toward London along with the coach: his meeting with investors regarding The Gentleman's Emporium was one line of thought. How he was going to tell Daisy Jones that she would *not* be playing Venus in the White Lily's latest production was another.

Ah, *Venus*. The concept was so inspired, so brilliant, such a delicious challenge for his partner's formidable talents that The General had very nearly entirely forgiven Tom for promising a particular earl a production involving damsels and castles... inside a week. A frenzy of choreography, carpentry and epithets had resulted in a production comprised of a brilliantly constructed little castle, scantily clothed damsels, and an inspired, prurient song regarding lances. It had been a roaring success, and The General had all but refused to speak to Tom for weeks afterward.

Tom had known the damsels would be a success. The inspirations that dropped into his mind suddenly and whole, like a bright coin flipped into a deep well, invariably were. The production had since become one of the staples of the White Lily's nightly offerings. But the reason audiences returned to the theater again and again was because they could count on Tom

Shaughnessy to surprise them, to feed their ceaseless appetite for novelty, and Tom knew he would soon need another small surprise to keep his audiences from becoming restless.

But Venus... Venus hadn't been a coin-dropped-in-the-well sort of inspiration. The theater itself had given it to him, just the other night: Tom had swept his eyes across the gods and goddesses who gamboled across the murals covering the theater walls... and the image of Botticelli's Venus, rising from her shell, had risen up in his mind. Venus would be a *tour de force,* a masterpiece, and the enormous profits he anticipated, along with the backing of a few key investors, would make his dream of The Gentleman's Emporium a reality.

Now all that remained was the delicate task of informing Daisy Jones that she would not be the one rising from the shell.

Tom smiled at the thought and glanced up; the curate sitting across from him gave him a tentative little smile in return. Very much like a small dog rolling over to show its belly to a larger, more dazzling dog.

"Exceedingly warm for this time of year," the curate ventured.

"Indeed. And if it's this warm near the sea, imagine how warm it will be in London," Tom answered politely.

Ah, weather. A topic that bridged social classes the world over. Whatever would they do without it?

And so the passengers passed a tolerable few hours sweating and smelling each other and exchanging pleasant banalities as the coach wheels ate up the road, and there was seldom a lull in conversation. And for two hours, Tom heard not a single word of French-accented English in the jumble of words around him.

When the curate stopped chatting for a moment, Tom slipped a hand into his pocket and snapped open his watch; in an hour or so, he knew, they would reach a coaching inn on the road to Westerly in time for a bad luncheon; he hoped to be back to London in time for supper, to meet with investors, to supervise the latest show at the White Lily. And then, perhaps, enjoy late-night entertainments at the Velvet Glove in the company of the most-accommodating Bettina.

And then in the lull a pistol shot cracked and echoed, and the coach bucked to a stop, sending passengers tumbling over each other.

Highwaymen. *Bloody hell.*

Tom gently sat the curate back into his seat and brushed off his coat, then brushed off his own.

Brazen coves, these highwaymen were, to stop the coach in broad daylight. But this stretch of road was all but deserted, and they'd been known to stop the occasional coach run. A full coach was essentially fish-in-a-barrel for highwaymen. Which meant there must be many of them, all armed, if they were bold enough to stop a loaded coach.

Tom swiftly tucked his watch into his boot and retrieved a pistol at the same time; he saw the curate's eyes bulge and watched him rear back a little in alarm. *Good God. No man should be afraid to shoot if necessary,* Tom thought with some impatience. He tugged the sleeve of his coat down to cover his weapon; one glimpse of it might inspire a nervous highwayman to waste a bullet on him.

"Take off your rings and put them in your shoes," he ordered the newlyweds quietly. Hands shaking like sheets pinned to a line, they obeyed him, as no one else was issuing orders in this extraordinary situation.

Tom knew he had only a ghost of a chance of doing something to deter the highwaymen, no matter their numbers. Still, it never occurred to him not to try. It wasn't as though Tom had never taken anything; when he was young and living in the rookeries, he'd taken food, handkerchiefs, anything small he could fence. But he had ultimately chosen to work for everything he owned; he found it satisfied a need for permanence, a need for... legacy. And damned if he was going to allow someone to take anything he'd earned if he could possibly avoid it. Even if it was only a few pounds and a watch.

"Out, everybody," a gravelly voice demanded. "'Ands up, now where I can see 'em, now."

And out of the dark coach stumbled the passengers, blinking and pale in the sunlight, one of whom was nearly swooning, if her buckling knees were any indication, and needed to be fanned by her panicking husband.

The air fair shimmered with heat; only a few wan trees interrupted the vista of parched grass and cracked road. Tom took in the group of highwaymen with a glance: five men, armed with muskets and pistols. Clothing dull with grime, kerchiefs covering their faces, hair long and lank and unevenly sawed, as though trimmed with their own daggers. One of them, the one who appeared to be in charge, gripped a knife between his teeth, Tom almost smiled grimly. *A showman*. Excessive, perhaps, but it certainly lent him a dramatic flair the others lacked.

Tom's innate curiosity about any showman made him peer more closely at the man. There was something about him...

"Now see here..." the merchant blustered indignantly, and promptly had five pistols and a knife turned on him. He blanched, clapped his mouth shut audibly. Clearly new to being robbed at gunpoint, he didn't know that etiquette required one to be quiet, lest one get shot.

And then Tom knew. Almost a decade ago, during a few difficult but unforgettable months of work in a dockside tavern, Tom had spent time with a man who drank the hardest liquor, told the most ribald jokes, tipped most generously, and advised young Tom which whores to avoid and which to court and imparted other unique forms of wisdom.

"Biggsy?" Tom ventured.

The highwayman swiveled, glowering, and stared at Tom.

Then he reached up and plucked the knife from between teeth brown as aged fence posts, and his face transformed.

"*Tom? Tommy Shaughnessy?*"

"'Tis I, in the flesh, Biggs."

"Well, Tommy, as I live and breathe!" Big Biggsy shifted his pistol into his other hand and seized Tom's hand to pump it with genuine enthusiasm. "'Avena seen you since those days at Bloody Joe's! Still a pretty bugger, ain't ye?" Biggsy laughed a richly phlegmy laugh and gave Tom a frisky punch on the shoulder. "Ye've gone respectable, 'ave ye, Tommy? Looka tha' fine coat!"

Tom felt the passenger's eyes slide toward him like so many billiard balls rolling toward a pocket, and then slide back again; he could virtually feel them cringing away from him. He wondered if it was because he was on a Christian-name basis with an armed highwayman, or because he had "*gone* respectable," implying he had been anything but at one time.

"Respectable might perhaps be overstating it, Biggsy, but yes, you could say I haven't done too badly."

"'Avena done 'alf bad meself," Biggsy announced proudly, gesturing at the characters surrounding him as though they were a grand new suite of furniture.

Tom thought it wisest not to disagree or request further clarification. He decided upon nodding sagely.

"'Tis proud I be, of ye, Tommy," Biggsy added sentimentally.

"That means the world to me," Tom assured him solemnly.

"And Daisy?" Biggsy prodded. "D'yer see 'er since the Green Apple days?"

"Oh, yes. She's in fine form, fine form."

"She's a grand woman," the highwayman said mistily.

"She is at that." Grand, and the largest thorn in his side, and no doubt responsible for a good portion of his fortune. Bless the brazen, irritating, glorious Daisy Jones.

Tom gave Biggsy his patented crooked, coaxing grin. "Now, Biggsy, can I persuade you to allow our coach to go on? You've my word of honor not a one shall pursue you."

"Ye've a word of honor now, Tommy?" Biggsy reared back in faux astonishment, then laughed again. Tom, not being a fool, laughed, too, and gave his thigh a little slap for good measure.

Biggsy wiped his eyes and stared at Tom for a moment longer, then took his bottom lip between his dark teeth to worry it a bit as he mulled the circumstances. And then he sighed and lowered his pistol; and with a jerk of his chin ordered the rest of the armed and mounted men accompanying him to do the same.

"Fer the sake of old times, then, Tommy. Fer the sake of Daisy, and Bloody Joe, rest 'is soul. But I canna leave everythin', you ken 'ow it is—we mun eat, ye ken."

"I ken," Tom repeated, commiserating.

"I'll leave the trunks, and jus' 'ave what blunt the lot of ye be carryin' in yer pockets."

"Big of you, Biggsy, big of you," Tom murmured.

"And then I'll 'ave a kiss from one of these young ladies, and we'll be off."

Clunk. Down went the wobbly new missus, dragging her husband down after her; he hadn't time to stop her fall completely. Never a pleasant sound, the sound of a body hitting the ground.

Biggsy eyed them for a moment in mild contempt. Then he looked back at Tom and shook his head slowly, as if to say, *what a pair of ninnies.*

"All right then. Who will it be?" Biggsy asked brightly. He scanned the row of lovely young ladies hopefully.

Tom thought he should have known his own formidable charm would get him only so far with a highwayman.

The crowd, which not a moment before had been mentally inching away from him, now swiveled their heads beseechingly toward him. Tom wasn't particularly savoring the irony of this at the moment. He wasn't quite sure how to rescue them from this particular request.

"Now, Biggs," Tom tried for a hail-fellow-well-met cajoling tone, "these are innocent young ladies. If you come to London, I'll introduce you to ladies who'll be happy to—"

"I willna leave without a kiss from one of *these* young ladies," Biggsy insisted stubbornly. "Look a' me, Tom. D'yer think I'm kissed verra often? Let alone by a young thing wi' all of 'er teeth or 'er maidenhe—"

"Biggsy," Tom interjected hurriedly.

"I want a *kiss*."

At the tone, the men behind Biggs put their hands back on their pistols, sensing a shift in intent.

Tom's eyes remained locked with Biggsy's, his expression studiedly neutral and pleasant, while his mind did cartwheels. *Bloody, bloody hell. Perhaps I should ask the young ladies to draw straws. Perhaps I should kiss him myself. Perhaps we—*

"I will kiss him."

Everyone, highwaymen included, pivoted, startled, when the little French widow stepped forward. "You will allow the coach to go on if I do?" she asked.

Ze coach, Tom thought absently, is what it sounded like when she said it. Her voice was bell-clear and strong and she sounded very nearly impatient; but Tom caught the hint of a tremble in it again, which he found oddly reassuring. If there had been no tremble, he might have worried again about her sanity and what she might do with a knitting needle.

"My word of honor," Biggsy said almost humbly. He seemed almost taken aback.

Tom was torn between wanting to stop her and perverse curiosity to see if she intended to go through with it. She hadn't the bearing or voice of a doxie. *I am not . . .* she had struggled to tell him. She was not someone who suffered the attention of gentlemen lightly, he was certain she meant to say. Not someone who was generally in the habit of leaping into the laps of strangers unless she had a very good reason to do so.

He hoped, *hoped* she didn't intend to attempt anything foolish with a knitting needle.

Biggsy recovered himself. "I'll take that, shall I?" He reached out and adroitly took her reticule from her. He heard her intake of breath, the beginning of a protest, but wisely stopped herself. Ah, she'd good judgment, too.

Tom saw her shoulders square, as though she was preparing herself for a launch upward. She drew in a deep breath.

And then she stood on her toes, lifted her veil, and kissed Biggsy Biggens full on the mouth.

And a moment later, Biggsy Biggens looked for all the world as blessed as a bridegroom.

Chapter Two

⌒

The configuration inside the coach on the way to the coaching inn was this: Tom at one end; the other passengers all but knotted together for protection.

And then the widow.

All was silence. He and the widow might be the hero and heroine of the hour, but no one wanted to acknowledge it, no one wanted to *touch* them, and certainly no one wanted to know either of them.

Once all of the passengers tumbled out of the coach in the inn yard, where they would be served a dreadful lunch before continuing on to London, Tom saw the widow glance furtively about.

And rather than follow the rest of the travelers inside, she made her way surreptitiously, but very purposefully toward the stables. She rounded the corner and disappeared from view; he picked up his pace and stopped when he saw her snug against the side of the building, half in shadow, her shoulders slightly hunched.

A wrench of sympathy and respect for her privacy made him pause. She was attempting to discreetly retch. He'd been within whiffing distance of Biggsy's breath; he could only imagine what it must have been like to taste it.

She whirled suddenly, sensing him there, swiping the back of her hand across her mouth; he took a step back, safely out of knitting-needle range. She stood very still and regarded him through that veil.

Wordlessly, cautiously, he reached into his coat, produced a flask, and held it out to her.

She looked down at the flask, then up at him. Two cool movements of her head. But she made no move to accept it from him.

"Or perhaps you prefer the taste of highwayman in your mouth...Mademoiselle."

Her chin jerked up a little at that.

After a moment, with a sense of subtle ceremony, she slowly, slowly lifted her veil with her gloved hands. *Ah, a woman confident of her charms.* This heightened Tom's sense of anticipation, which surprised and amused him. He wasn't precisely jaded, but surprise when it came to a woman was something he felt so rarely anymore. *Veils,* he noted to himself silently. *Must use more veils at the White Lily Theater. Perhaps a harem act...*

Still, nothing could have prepared him for the shock of her face when she finally tilted her head up to look at him.

He felt her beauty physically, a sweet hot burst low in his gut. A jaw both stubborn and elegant in its angularity, lifted now in pride or arrogance or defense; an achingly soft-looking mouth, the bottom lip a full curve, the one above it shorter, both the palest pink. Eyes very bright in her too-white face. They were pale green, her eyes, intelligent and very alive, with flecks of other colors floating in the irises. Two fine, straight chestnut brows slanted over them.

Her eyes met his, and with great satisfaction, he saw that impossible-to-disguise swift flare of her pupil. It was always a good moment, a delicious moment, the recognition of mutual attraction that passed between two beautiful people. Tom smiled at her, acknowledging it, confident and inclusive, inviting her, daring her to share it.

But she turned her head away from him slowly—too casually—as though the pigeons listlessly poking about in the stableyard were of much more interest to her than the man standing before her with a flask outstretched.

When she returned her gaze to his she reached out her hand for the proffered flask, as though the pigeons had cemented her decision. She lifted it fastidiously up to those soft lips and took a sip.

Her eyes widened. He grinned.

"I wonder what you were expecting, Mademoiselle. Whiskey? Do I strike you as the whiskey sort? It's French—the wine, is. Go ahead and swallow it. It wasn't cheap."

She held it in her mouth for an instant; at last, he saw her swallow hard.

He bowed, then, and it was a low, elegant thing, all grace and respect. "Mr. Tom Shaughnessy at your service. And you are Mademoiselle . . . ?"

"Madame," she corrected curtly.

"Oh, but I think not . . . For I have splendid *intuition*." He used the French pronunciation. The word was spelled just the same in English and in French, and meant precisely the same thing: a very good guess. "And *I* think you are a mademoiselle."

"You presume a good deal, Mr. Shaughnessy."

"I've always had luck with being presumptuous. One might even say I make my living being presumptuous."

She scanned him, a swift flick of her green eyes, up and down, drawing conclusions about him from his face and clothes and adding those conclusions, no doubt, to the impressions she'd already gleaned from his acquaintance with the highwayman. He saw those green eyes go guarded and cynical. But oddly...not afraid. Yes, this was a mademoiselle, perhaps. But not an innocent one, either, if she could draw a cynical conclusion about the sort of man he was. It implied she knew rather a range of men.

"It was brave, what you did," he said.

"Yes," she agreed.

He smiled at that. He could have sworn she almost did, too.

"Do you have any money?" he asked. A blunt question.

Again, that stiff spine. "I do not believe this is business of yours, Mr. Shaughnessy."

"A knitting needle and widow's weeds are all very well and good, but money, Mademoiselle, is everything. Have you enough to continue on to your destination? The highwayman took your reticule, did he not?"

"Yes, your *friend,* Mr. Biggsy, took my reticule. I might not have been so brave had I known the price of my bravery."

"Were you perhaps clever enough to sew your money into your hem?" he pressed. "Or into your sleeve, along with your weaponry? If one travels unaccompanied by a maid, one best be resourceful in other ways."

She was silent. And then: "Why are you interested in my money, Mr. Shaughnessy?"

"Perhaps, as a gentleman, I'm merely concerned for your welfare."

"Oh, I think not, Mr. Shaughnessy. For you see, I, too, have *intuition*. And I do not believe you *are* a gentleman."

As dry and tart as the wine he'd just passed to her. And just as bracing. Perhaps even—and this surprised him—a little stinging.

"All right then: Perhaps I'm concerned because you are beautiful and intriguing."

She waited a beat, studying him with her head tilted again.

"'Perhaps'?" she repeated. And up went one of those delicate chestnut brows, along with the corners of her mouth. As though she had struggled against her nature, and her nature had won.

A little thrill of pleasure traced his spine. Ah, there *was* a coquette in there; he had sensed it. But it was like viewing her through a fogged windowpane; he wanted somehow to rub away the fear and mistrust to bring the real woman, the vibrant, no doubt interesting woman, into view.

Her color looked better now; there was a healthier flush in her cheeks. Then again, good French wine will do that for a person.

"I can help you," he said swiftly.

"I thank you for your...*concern*...Mr. Shaughnessy," she all but drew quotation marks around the word, "but I do not wish assistance from...you."

As in, *you would be the last man in the world I would turn to, Mr. Shaughnessy.*

And given the circumstances, he could hardly blame her. He respected her wisdom in deciding not to trust him—this was not a foolish woman, despite the fact that she'd kept her money in her damned reticule—even as he felt the disappointment of it keenly. For she was right, of course. Gallantry played a role in his offer to help her. But it wasn't the primary role by far. And Tom was certain he wouldn't trust himself if *he* was a woman. In particular, not after he'd exchanged warm reminiscences with a gun- and knife-wielding highwayman.

"Very well, then. Let me just say that I do not 'regret' the fact that you...'inserted' me, Mademoiselle. Or...'sat upon me.'"

She studied him for a moment, head tilted slightly.

"Do you mock my English, Mr. Shaughnessy?" She sounded mildly curious.

"Why, yes, I believe I do. A little. *Un peu*." He was surprised to feel a little bit of his temper in the words.

To his astonishment, she smiled then. A full and brilliant smile, a genuine smile, which scrunched her eyes and made them brilliant, too, dazzling as lamps. It was the kind of smile that made him believe she laughed often and easily, in other circumstances, the kind of smile he felt physically again, as a swift and strangely sweet twist in his gut.

He was suddenly desperate to make her do it often.

But finding himself uncharacteristically speechless, he bowed and left her.

His mind oddly both full and jumbled, following the rest of the decidedly less-interesting guests into the inn for luncheon.

If not for the fortifying dose of surprisingly good French wine provided by Mr. Tom Shaughnessy, Sylvie would still be trembling now. All of her money was gone, the letter from her sister was gone, and a sort of delayed fear had overtaken her at lunch. She'd been able to push it away the way she did any sort of discomfort in order to take her through her encounter with the highwayman.

But now she could scarcely choke down the watery soup and indifferent bread and tough grayish meat. *Peh*. The English knew nothing of cooking, that was certain, if luncheon was any indication.

She peeked up from her silent meal—no one attempted to engage her in conversation, nor did she feel equal to making an attempt of her own. Mr. Shaughnessy seemed to have thawed the curate and the married couple, and the four of them appeared to be laughing together over some English witticism.

She jerked her head away from them, focused again on her gray meat.

She could not recall the last time she'd needed to look away from a man to recover her composure. Certainly Etienne was handsome, admired and swooned over by all the other dancers in the *corps de ballet*. Desired by all of them. But the sight of Etienne had never stopped her breathing.

And when she had seen Tom Shaughnessy, it was as though someone had taken a tight little fist and rapped it between her lungs.

In the full sunlight, Tom Shaughnessy's eyes had seemed nearly clear, like a pair of windows. Silver, she would have called them. His face could only be described as beautiful, but it wasn't soft: it was too defined; there were too many strong lines and corners and interesting hollows, and there was a hint of something pagan about it. His surname and his wavy red-gold hair implied Irish ancestors, but his complexion, a pale gold, suggested that something a bit more exotic also swam in his veins: Spanish blood, perhaps. Or Gypsy. This last would not have surprised her in the least.

And then there was that smile. It blinded, the smile. She considered that perhaps that was its purpose; he used it as a weapon to scramble wits and take advantage of a moment. It made a dimple near the corner of his mouth. A tiny crescent moon.

And his clothes—a soft green coat no doubt chosen for its unorthodox color, a dazzling waistcoat, polished boots and brilliant buttons—all might have looked just shy of vulgar on someone else. On him they seemed somehow as native as wings to Mercury's ankles.

And she'd seen as they had all stood in the hot sunlight next to the mail coach a glint in his sleeve, and looked more closely. He'd tucked a pistol in his sleeve, had cupped the barrel of it in his fingers, prepared to slide it out and use it. Somehow she had no doubt he knew precisely *how* to use it.

And every other man in that clearing had seemed prepared to allow the highwaymen to have their way with them.

He was armed in too many ways, it seemed, Mr. Shaughnessy—with those looks, and a charm that won and disarmed too easily, and clothing that was just a little too fine and a little too deliberately new, and with a hidden pistol, with dangerous friends. If a man was thusly prepared for danger, he could only be dangerous in some way himself.

But she *should* have choked down more food. She didn't know where she'd next acquire another meal, and even if she didn't feel hungry now, she was human, and her body, accustomed to rigorous activity, would no doubt eventually expect a good meal and begin demanding it with growls and aches.

In her trunk there were things she could sell if necessary, a few pieces of fine clothing, gloves and shoes, she supposed. She wouldn't know where or how to sell them, but she would discover how to do it if she needed to. She had always done what she needed to do.

She wondered whether anyone in England would find a use for ballet slippers.

When the mail coach finally lurched to its stop at its London destination, all the passengers hurriedly dispersed into the arms of waiting loved ones or into other coaches as quickly as ants fleeing a magnifying glass, without turning back. Shedding the dread of their earlier experience, and filled with a tale to tell. Sylvie imagined she would be the topic of conversation over dinner tables throughout London tonight.

The thought made her feel just a little lonely. But only a little. She truly didn't know what it was like to sit at a table with a large family and talk of the day, and it was difficult to miss what one has never truly known.

Though it had never been difficult to imagine it. Or, on occasion, to long for the things she'd imagined, when the life she shared with Claude, who was kind, was so small and careful and often fearful, as money had always been scarce.

She had memories of being shuttled away in the dead of night in a coach, bundled with other little girls. A strange man, a kind man with a kind voice, had attempted to soothe and hush them. She remembered she'd been crying. And then she had thought she should not cry so that she could hold the hands of the little girls with her, to keep them from crying and from being afraid.

And so she had stopped crying.

She had seldom cried since that evening.

My sisters, she thought. *They were my sisters.* They must have been. And yet the memory of that evening, and all that had passed before it, and the people in them, had become indistinct, wearing away in patches, it seemed, until she had begun to believe she had dreamed them.

And Claude had never done anything to discourage the idea. Sylvie could scarcely remember now how it had happened, but she had gone to live with Claude. And Claude had told her only that there had been an accident, and that her mother would not be coming home. She never mentioned sisters, which had made it easier to believe the other girls might have been just a dream.

Sylvie put her hand over her heart. She had suspended the miniature of her mother from a ribbon, and it hung there beneath her dress now, where it was both protected and, in a way, protection, a talisman. And soon, hopefully, it would be proof to Susannah, Lady Grantham, that they indeed shared a mother.

Sylvie stood next to her own trunk in the inn yard now, a little island of dark clothing amidst a swarm of people going purposely about their business. *So this is London.*

To be fair, one could tell very little of the city from the yards of coaching inns, she knew. It rather looked like any large city, cobblestones and storefronts; when she craned her head, she could see the tall masts of ships at harbor through the gaps in the buildings. The smells were city smells, the smells of thousands of lives lived close together: food spoiling or being cooked, coal smoke rising, the warm beasty odors of horses and other animals.

Despite herself, a little excitement cut through the trepidation. She'd done it. She was standing in London, she'd managed to cross the Channel entirely on her own, and soon, perhaps, she would learn what she'd come to learn.

"If you crane your head about like that, Mademoiselle, it will become obvious to the less savory among us that you're new to London, and no doubt someone will attempt to rob you—or perhaps kiss you—again."

She started and turned to find Mr. Shaughnessy before her, hat in hand. He bowed low. "Is someone meeting you?" he asked, when he was upright again.

"Yes," she said swiftly.

Up went one of his brows, betraying his doubt of this. "Very well, then. But you should *always* appear as though you know precisely where you are going, Mademoiselle. And if you do find yourself longing for my company, you can find me at the White Lily."

A grin flashed, and then he was gone before she could say another word, melting confidently into the crowd as he jammed a hat down on his bright head.

❧

Sylvie glanced about; her eyes met the eyes of a portly fellow standing near a hackney, the driver. She saw him assess her, her clothing and bearing, and make a decision in her favor.

"Need a coach, Madame?"

He said it politely enough, and there was nothing prurient or predatory in his gaze. Regardless, she was armed with a knitting needle and extraordinary reflexes, should the need to defend herself arise. And she hadn't really a choice.

"Yes, please. To ... Grosvenor Square."

His eyes flared swiftly, almost imperceptibly. "Shilling," he said shortly.

Quick thinking was clearly necessary. "My sister is Lady Grantham. She will give the shilling to you when we arrive."

The man's expression changed then ... but peculiarly. Not into the sort of expression someone of his station typically donned when the aristocracy was mentioned. No. Gradually, before Sylvie's puzzled eyes, it became harder. Then sharply curious. And then finally, inexplicably ...

Amused?

"Your sister is Lady Grantham?"

"Yes." She frowned.

"Lady Grantham is your sister, is she?"

"I believe I said 'yes.'" She'd clenched her jaw to steady her nerves.

He paused and appraised her again. "An' look, ye've a trunk and everythin'," he said almost admiringly. He shook his head to and fro in apparent wonder.

Sylvie knew her English was quite good, but perhaps an entirely different dialect was spoken in the heart of London, the way those who lived in Venice spoke their own version of Italian. Perhaps this London dialect was one in which the inflections meant entirely the opposite of what one might expect.

"An' she'll pay me when we arrive, like?" he said, sounding amused. For all the world as though he was humoring a madwoman. "Lady Grantham?"

"Again ... yes." Regal now, and cold.

He regarded her a moment longer. And then shrugged good-humoredly and smiled, as though he'd resigned himself to some odd fate.

"All right. Let's go see your *sister,* Lady Grantham, shall we?"

And still, despite his acquiescence, his tone could not be construed as anything other than ironic.

Chapter Three

❧

$\mathcal{G}$rosvenor Square turned out to be comprised of rows of imposing edifices, homes several stories high built snugly together, as if symbolically to prevent interlopers such as herself from wedging between them.

"Go on, now. Go see to your sister. Shall I bring your trunk up?"

"Perhaps not just yet," she said.

"Of *course* not," he said.

More irony. *Oh,* but the man was grating.

Sylvie ascended the steps, not faltering, but conscious of the curtains at windows along the row of houses parting, then dropping when she turned her head swiftly at the movement.

Though the temptation arose, she knew turning on her heel and fleeing was no longer an option. Her journey *must* end here.

On the imposing door, a snarling brass lion held a loop of metal in its teeth; Sylvie took a deep breath for confidence, took the knocker in her hands, and rapped hard twice.

Her breath came short now. What if the woman who lived in

this house had nothing at all to do with her? Would she be kind? Would she be stunned to discover her sister was a ballerina, someone who had occupied a twilight world where she was admired and envied by women like herself—but only from a distance? And, not infrequently, courted and pursued by their husbands?

But Etienne had promised to buy her a home. He owned many homes, homes she had never seen, homes, she was certain, many times the size of this one.

Moments later, the door opened; a butler stared at her. His face was bland, as impassive as the walls of the home itself, his hair and skin were a matching shade of gray-white, no doubt the result of a life spent indoors.

"May I be of some assistance to you, Madame?" A neutral sort of politeness, the sort at which servants excelled, and he'd employed it because he hadn't the faintest idea who she was and to which social stratum she belonged. She saw his eyes flick up, note the hackney at the foot of the steps. Flick back to her. Searching for clues as to whether he should warm the temperature of his voice.

He doesn't know who I am, Sylvie reminded herself. *Doesn't know I'm a dancer, with a lover, who fled across the Channel.*

"Is Lady Grantham at home, please?" She tried not to sound defensive. She also tried not to sound French, but this was virtually impossible.

The impassive expression changed not a fraction. "The viscount and Lady Grantham are away, Madame. Would you care to leave your card?"

"A-away?" Perhaps he meant they'd…gone to the shops or for a stroll, she thought desperately. Though, somehow, given the tenor of her journey thus far, she suspected this was optimistic bordering on the delusional.

"By *away,* I mean they've gone to France, Madame."

Something that might have been the beginnings of a frown shadowed the place between his eyes.

Suddenly the ramifications of the viscount and Lady Grantham going to France struck.

"Did they perhaps go to visit…Lady Grantham's sister?"

"'Sister,' Madame?" It was almost sharply said.

And then his face, in a heartbeat, went from bland to cynical and wary.

"I am Lady Grantham's sister," Sylvie said with some dignity.

She heard the sound of a cleared throat eloquently from the street. The hackney driver.

"Of *course* you are, Madame." Sylvie blinked; his words were all but chiseled from scorn. "You and every other opportunistic female on the Continent. Ever since the trial. It's not an original idea, though I must admit your widow's weeds are a new approach."

"T-trial?" "Trial" was seldom a good word in any language.

"Come now, Miss. Mr. Morley's trial. What a sordid business it was, what with him involved in the murder of Richard Lockwood, and Anna Holt blamed for it, and out it came that Lady Grantham—the wife of a *very* wealthy viscount, mind you—had two sisters who disappeared when she was very young, and she doesn't know what became of them. Oh my, the letters we've received, the young ladies who've appeared on the doorstep… the story seems to have inspired every opportunist on the Continent. You're not the first to think of it, Madame. Quite a nuisance, it's been, the flocks of young ladies and the pleading letters. Posing as a widow, however, is a novel approach, I will say that for you, Madame. And you've shown a certain amount of daring—or would it be stupidity?—in telling such a story when my employers have begun to prosecute the transgressors. They are, in fact, offering a rather large reward for the apprehension of them."

Sylvie's hands were now clammy inside her gloves, and despite the sun beating at the back of her neck, the black of her gown soaking in every ray of it, a sick, icy feeling suddenly made her even more aware of how empty her stomach was.

"But...I had a letter. From Lady Grantham. Susannah. I brought it with me, you see, but the highwayman...the high-wayman...he took it..."

She trailed off when the butler's expression grew more and more incredulous. "Lady Grantham's sister is in France," he said sternly. "Lady Grantham has gone to France in search of her."

"I have come from France. *I* am French," Sylvie said indignantly.

"So are thousands and thousands of other people, more's the pity."

Sylvie's patience slipped and her hand darted into her bodice, fishing for her miniature.

The butler's eyes bulged like hen's eggs when she did, and then he flung an arm over his face. "Madame, I assure you that exposing yourself won't convince me to—"

She finally retrieved the miniature on its little black ribbon. "Please look," she said, struggling for calm.

The butler kept his arm up over his eyes.

"I have a miniature," she coaxed softly.

There was a silence. From the foot of the stairs, the bloody hackney driver began to whistle a mocking little tune.

"A miniature *what*?" the butler ventured nervously. Only his lips moved from beneath his arm.

It would have been a simple enough thing to say, "a miniature of my mother, Anna, whom I suspect is also Lady Grantham's mother." But the devil in Sylvie was stronger, as was the coquette. "Why don't you have a look, monsieur?"

Ah, so he was a man after all. He slowly pulled his arm away from his eyes. And he looked. She bit back a smile.

He recovered his composure quickly enough when he saw the miniature she held out on its ribbon.

And then, after his first quick glance, his posture stiffened, and he stared at it.

Sylvie allowed this stranger to study her mother's sweet face: those pale eyes tilted with laughter, the fair hair, the finely drawn bones, the image she had cherished her entire life. The only reminder of the family she had lost. Apart from Claude, Sylvie had never shared this image with anyone until this man who looked at it with wary eyes.

But then the butler's expression transformed. As gradually as winter melts into spring and spring into summer, she saw speculation become uncertainty and—and her breath caught at what this might mean—at last she saw a glimmer of sympathy.

He cleared his throat. Good God, she was surrounded by men who cleared their throats. "May I hold the min—"

"No," Sylvie said the word tersely, but then again, her patience and nerves were frayed. "I hope you understand," she added, conciliatorily. "It is precious to me."

"I suppose I do understand," he said, sounding abstracted now. "May I ask how you came to own this miniature, Mrs.…"

"My name is Sylvie Lamoreux. I've had it always. I'm told it's my mother, Mr.…"

"Bale. My name is Mr. Bale."

He fell quiet. At the curb, the hackney driver cleared his throat.

"*Mon dieu,* have *patience,*" Sylvie snapped over her shoulder.

She turned back to Bale, just in time to see the corner of his mouth twitch. He still seemed thoughtful; he said nothing. She turned the miniature over. "And see, there are words."

"*To Sylvie Hope of her mother Anna,*" Bale read slowly aloud, half to himself. Wonderingly.

Sylvie allowed him to absorb this information. Then she tucked the miniature into her bodice once more while he averted his eyes. Ah, so prim for a man.

"Did the other young ladies who arrived on your doorstep present miniatures, Mr. Bale?" Her tone was lightly acerbic.

The butler looked pensive. "I know nothing of any miniatures of Anna Holt, Mrs. Lamoreux."

"Holt?" Sylvie pounced eagerly on the name. "My mother's name was Anna *Holt*? Sir, I know nothing of her. All my life I have wanted to know..."

Mr. Bale said nothing. His lips worried over each other, folding in, folding out, as he thought.

"Can you tell me please whether Lady Grantham and her husband intended to call upon someone named Claude Lamoreux in Paris?"

The butler was an edifice of silence. As seemingly immovable as the walls of the house he attended.

He was merely being dutiful, Sylvie knew, protecting the privacy of his employers, but at the moment his silence felt unspeakably cruel. But his silence at least spoke of doubt, and the doubt had mercifully eliminated his dreadful patronizing for the moment.

"When will they return? Lady Grantham and her husband?"

"I cannot say, Miss Lamoreux." Flawless, his pronunciation of her name was.

"But can you tell me, *please,* Mr. Bale, does Lady Grantham resemble me?"

"I cannot say."

"Cannot, or *will* not?" she demanded desperately, with growing impatience.

But all at once she comprehended the expression on his face earlier, the source of what appeared to be dawning sympathy.

"She looks like my mother," Sylvie breathed. "Susannah,

Lady Grantham...perhaps *I* do not resemble her, but she *does* resemble the woman in the miniature, yes?"

Sylvie saw the answer in his face, saw him look at her now, as if inventorying her features, trying to draw conclusions. Hope dizzied her.

"Please, Mr. Bale. All of my life, I have wanted to know something of my family. I've had none, you see, and I was told..." She stumbled. "I was told things that I think are not true."

"Miss Lamoreux. I cannot stress enough the significance of the trouble this has caused Lady Grantham. The viscount has in fact arranged for one interloper to be arrested, and has offered a reward to anyone who assists in apprehending impostors. Do you understand my position, Mrs. Lamoreux? I implore you to abandon your charade if you *have* embarked upon a charade."

Do you understand my position? I am alone and penniless and hundreds of miles away from home because I am a headstrong fool.

A silent stalemate ensued.

She imagined saying, "It is *not* a charade," which seemed unproductive. So she tried hauteur instead.

"Will Lady Grantham be angry with you, Mr. Bale, if she discovers you turned her true sister away?"

It worked. He glared at her, clearly torn, frustrated, and wishing she hadn't arrived on *his* doorstep.

"Where will you be staying, Mrs. Lamoreux, while you are in London?" he asked finally, with some resignation.

"I don't know, Mr. Bale," she said bitterly. He deserved the punishment of wondering whether he had done the right thing, she decided unfairly. "Perhaps you should look at the White Lily."

She caught a glimpse of his eyes going wide again as she turned her back and marched down the steps. No royal army had ever retreated more proudly than Sylvie Lamoreux.

"You knew," she accused the hackney driver. "Why did you say nothing?"

"Say nothing? I thought ye knew what ye were about, Miss, and I thought ye'd the look of someone who might verra well 'ave a plan. I mean, ye've a costume, a trunk—ye'd given it all some thought, seemed to me. Thought ye deserved a chance."

He smiled, a hatefully amused gap-toothed smile. "So where shall we go? To visit another relation? To see if the king is in?"

She thought about it for an instant; arrived, suddenly, at what appeared to be her only option. "To the White Lily, please."

The driver's eyebrows shot skyward. "Did you say . . . the White Lily, Miss?"

"Yes." She wasn't certain how to interpret the surprise. "Mr. Tom Shaughnessy will pay my fare." She hoped this was true. Her mind veered to more inventive options she might employ to earn money and immediately batted them away.

"Shaughnessy? *Tommy* Shaughnessy?" All warmth and genuine grins now.

Good God, did *everyone* know Tom Shaughnessy? Perhaps she should have asked the butler whether he knew Tom Shaughnessy to gain an entrée into the viscount's home.

"Mr. Shaughnessy! Well, then! Looking for honest work now then, are ye? The sort of work fer a miss like yerself? Given up the impostor business 'ave ye now?"

"I am *not* a fraud, Mr. . . ."

"Me name's Mick," he said simply.

"I am not looking for 'honest work,' Mr. Mick. Mr. Shaughnessy is . . . is my relation."

The hackney driver's eyes flew open wide. "Your relation?" he said flatly.

"Yes." This man was growing more and more tiresome.

"Tom Shaughnessy is your relation," he repeated. His

mouth began to tremble then, and his eyes grew pink at the rims, and then began watering. Sylvie took a single nervous step backward.

And then as though a dam burst, as though he'd been storing it up all day, he exploded into great gusts of body-buckling laughter.

"Your *relation*!" He howled, and slapped his thigh resoundingly a few times, sending the flesh of it wobbling to and fro in his trousers. "Yer related to everyone in London, are ye now? To viscounts *and* to the likes o' Tom?"

The likes o' Tom? This hardly sounded promising. No doubt, given the luck she was experiencing thus far today, Tom Shaughnessy was a flamboyant criminal of some sort. But she couldn't now ask the hackney driver what the White Lily might be, or who Tom might be, because she imagined it would make him howl even louder, and she didn't think she could bear that.

The storm of laughter finally stuttered out into scattered hiccups, then ended in a deep, satisfied sigh. The hackney driver wiped his eyes, which Sylvie found excessive.

"Oh, all right, Miss. I'll go 'ome poor today, but 'tis your lucky day, as I'm in th' mood fer a lark. Come aboard then."

Chapter Four

◡

The duration of the coach ride merely seemed to emphasize the societal gulf between Grosvenor Square and whatever the White Lily might turn out to be. Through her coach window, Sylvie watched the scenery gradually become darker, narrower, dirtier: well-dressed Englishmen and -women promenading through grand, tailored squares gave way to labyrinthine streets lined with vendors, filthy children crowding them the way mosquitoes swarmed over split fruit. She saw several clearly inebriated people propped against walls, heads lolling.

The great lurid flower swinging on a board over the White Lily's entrance didn't clarify matters for her. Was it a brothel? A tavern? It looked rather like a theater. She doubted a brothel would advertise itself quite so proudly, but then considered she might know less of big cities than she originally thought, and perhaps London was a little different after all.

Perhaps it was a theater. Which would be tremendously ironic, given that nearly her entire life to date had been spent in theaters of some sort, and that she had worked her entire life to avoid spending her days in the sort of theater she suspected this one was.

"Go on, then," the hackney driver coaxed, grinning, still maddeningly amused.

Sylvie was not accustomed to being considered a comedienne. She gave her head a toss and pushed on the door of the White Lily; it gave, and she took a deep breath and stepped inside.

It was empty of people and dim at the moment, but an impression of exaggerated luxury rushed at her, an almost caricature of classicism. Red, the ruby sort, was the predominant theme, seen in the plush carpet and upholstery and the great heavy curtain of velvet that swept across the front of the stage and pooled on the floor of it. There was a pianoforte centered before the stage and room for more musicians on either side of it. Rows of seats sloped upward from where she stood; above them, balconies and tiers traced with gilt and ornate carved plaster gleamed dully, and a few boxes featuring curtains to ensure the occupant's anonymity swelled out from the walls nearest the stage. She tilted her head back and noticed an enormous chandelier—twined brass supporting row upon row of dangling crystal—presided over the subtly domed ceiling. And when she lowered her gaze once again, slowly, she noticed that not a single inch of the walls was bare: murals of gods and goddesses clad—well, "clad" was perhaps too emphatic a word for what they were—diaphanously, chasing and being chased by each other, as was the wont of gods and goddesses.

The place was unabashedly, cheerfully lurid; it was a celebration of sex, the way a man no doubt saw it—necessary, pleasurable, a game perhaps—and made no apologies for it.

"Couldn't stay away, Mademoiselle?" The soft words came from the left of her.

She jumped and turned to find Tom Shaughnessy.

And for a moment she couldn't speak, for the man's face was a fresh shock. It seemed the sort of face that one would always find something new in, its assemblage of angles and shadows. His pale eyes were bright in the dim theater.

When he bent that broad-shouldered frame into a low bow so elegant it nearly mocked, it occurred to her that she hadn't yet spoken, had only gaped, which no doubt gratified the man's vanity.

"Says yer a relation, Tommy." The hackney driver had poked his head in the door. "Ye've a lot of bloody relations, if ye' ask me. All female. But there must 'ave been a male in the lot somewhere t' 'ave spawned all these females."

Tom laughed. "What can I say, Mick? The Shaughnessys must be exceptionally ... fertile."

Mick, the hackney driver, laughed with him. Sylvie suppressed a gusty sigh. If one more man took amusement at her expense, she might very well need to throw something.

And then, and this was the last thing she expected him to say, Tom turned to her and asked, "Are you hungry? Would you like something to eat?"

Sylvie was weary and light-headed and wondered what sort of compensation he intended to extract from her in exchange for paying the hackney driver, and hoped he would say and do nothing untoward, as she wasn't certain she had it in her to employ her knitting needle again when his face was sheer poetry. But no. Though her stomach was empty, it twisted, rebelling at the idea of more food of the sort she'd been given at the coaching inn today.

"No," she said. "I am not hungry, that is. Thank you."

"You ate very little at the inn."

He'd been watching her? Perhaps as aware of her as she'd been aware of him? Difficult to know with one such as he. In her profession, she had known flirts very nearly as skillful as

Tom Shaughnessy. It was a skill they shared generously with nearly every woman, a means to keep it honed.

"Perhaps I require very little, Mr. Shaughnessy."

This made him smile slowly, his way of turning her words into an innuendo. "Oh, I doubt that, Mademoiselle. I expect you require rather a good deal."

She felt the corners of her mouth start to tug up in response, an accomplished flirt's reflexive response to another accomplished flirt; it couldn't quite completely become a smile, however. She was too weary. Too wary. Too angry at herself for leaving herself no other options.

And, though she hated to confess it even to herself . . . simply, quietly afraid.

The hackney driver cleared his throat.

Tom swiveled in his direction. "Oh, of course, Mick. My apologies." Tom fished about in his pockets, came up with a handful of coins, pressed them on Mick. The hackney driver disappeared for a moment and reappeared with her trunk, which he deposited unceremoniously on the floor of the theater. *Clunk.*

"Thank you for looking after her, Mick," he said somberly. "I . . . have her now."

Mick tipped his hat to the two of them; the door swung shut, and suddenly all was silence.

I have her now, Sylvie thought.

"Now . . . I believe you are now in my debt. Shall we discuss how you should repay me?"

Her heart began to trip. She was as interested in the dance of flirtation as in the art of ballet, but her nerves were frayed, and at the moment she felt like a mouse between the paws of a well-dressed cat. He wasn't to know it, however.

"I believe we both know I am now in your debt, Mr. Shaughnessy. Please speak your intent."

Eyebrows up, amused. "All right, then. First, please tell me your name."

"Miss Sylvie..." she hesitated. And then she remembered the butler's warning about the prosecution of those pretending to be Lady Grantham's sister, and considered that someone in London might very well know her name, and thought it best she remain, on the whole anonymous. "Cha...Chapeau."

"Miss Sylvie Chapeau," he repeated flatly.

She nodded weakly.

"You are Miss Sylvie...Hat." He said it almost warningly, as if giving her an opportunity to choose a less ridiculous name.

"Yes," she said, chin hiked.

He nodded thoughtfully. "And you are from..."

"Paris."

"And you are in London because..." he coaxed.

"Because I wished to see it." She wasn't anxious to watch his handsome face become as cynical as the hackney driver's or the butler's when she told him she was, in fact, the sister of Lady Grantham.

He laughed. "Oh, and we were doing so *well* with honesty, Miss Chapeau! Allow me to rephrase my question. Whom precisely are you running from?"

"I am not running from anyone." It was an effort to keep her voice even.

"Running *to,* then," he corrected blithely.

"I believe we were discussing repayment, Mr. Shaughnessy, and not the reasons for my journey." Temper licked at the edges of her words.

"Perhaps I require information about you as payment of your debt."

This seemed reasonable if ungentlemanly, so she remained silent, and began to seethe a little.

"Your English seems improved," he mused suddenly.

"Perhaps because I am no longer..." *Nervous,* she thought, though she reconsidered the wisdom of confessing this to him.

"Running from someone?" he supplied helpfully.

She turned on her heel and made as if to leave. He didn't yet know she had no other place to go, and she suspected he would attempt to lure her back, but it did seem an excellent way to make her point.

"Quite right," he said hurriedly, laughter in his voice. "My apologies for indulging again my curiosity, Miss Chapeau. Very well, I shall ask only questions relevant to your debt. How long do you intend to stay in our fair city?"

She hesitated. "I do not know."

"And do you have any money at all?"

She paused again.

"It's really a simple question, Miss Chapeau." He was beginning to sound impatient. "A 'yes' or 'no' will answer it. You are either here at the White Lily because you have no money and no other options, or because you found me so irresistible that—"

"No," she said quickly.

He grinned, the bloody man. He'd all but cornered her into an admission of her greatest vulnerability: She was currently penniless. It would be wise not to assume she was cleverer than he, despite his too-bright smile and too-bright clothes and this lurid theater. His friends included hackney drivers and highwaymen and only God knew whom else.

"You've no money," he repeated musingly, regarding her unblinkingly. His eyes were so clear it seemed a little unfair, almost, that she could not read the thoughts passing behind them.

The man did have disconcertingly broad shoulders, she noticed absently.

"And do you need a place to stay?"

At this, after another brief hesitation, she merely nodded.

"Do you think you can dance, Miss Chapeau?"

"Of course." The answer was startled from her.

"I didn't mean the waltz."

"Nor did I."

He was quiet a moment, and then, peculiarly, Sylvie thought she saw something like regret darken, just briefly, his face. "How fortunate for you, then, that I, as the owner of this theater, am in a position to employ and lodge you. Your timing could not be better. Come with me."

He pivoted and walked to the back of the theater. Sylvie looked toward the door through which she had entered the White Lily. Outside, it was daylight and an unfamiliar London.

She turned her head back to the theater, where Tom Shaughnessy's broad back and shining head were rapidly moving away from her.

She knew which void she preferred to leap into.

Sylvie scrambled to follow him.

❧

Tom stopped before a door and tapped on it. Behind it she heard giggles and the sound of rustling fabric, familiar sounds to her; the sounds any roomful of women was bound to make, unless they were in mourning. And even then, she'd known a few—

The door swung open to reveal a startlingly lovely woman.

"Good day, Mr. Shaughnessy," she said breathlessly. She dropped a curtsy.

"Good day, Lizzie. May we come in? Are the lot of you fully clothed?" He asked it playfully.

"Would it matter, Mr. Shaughnessy?" She lowered her head and peered up at him through her lashes.

He gave a laugh, which in fact sounded more polite than

flirtatious to Sylvie's ears. And he waited, with a sort of calm authority. As he was the man in charge, after all, the girl stepped aside to allow Tom in, Sylvie behind him.

Sylvie found herself plunged into a veritable nest of girls. The room was windowless but aglow from dozens of small lamps and littered with mirrors and dressing tables and well-worn wooden chairs, and it smelled powerfully, provocatively of female—powder and a stew of different perfumes and soap and stage makeup, kohl and rouge. It was a scent familiar to Sylvie, as she'd dressed in rooms just like this before performances many times before.

A glance over the girls. One was dark-haired and sloe-eyed, another had marble-fair skin and silver-blond hair, another had cheeks warm as hothouse peaches. Each unique but for one shared characteristic: they were all lushly rounded—arms, breasts, hips—in the ways that mattered to men. Sylvie could imagine the flocks of men arriving at the theater night after night for the pleasure of watching—or pursuing, if they had the money to do the pursuing properly—their favorite.

She wondered if Tom Shaughnessy partook of these young ladies as one would a box of sweets.

To a woman, the box of sweets returned her perusal.

"*What* is *that?*" one of the lovelies murmured under her breath, her eyes fixed on Sylvie. A chorus of hushed giggles followed.

Tom either didn't hear the question, or pretended not to hear it, and Sylvie would have wagered the latter.

"Good afternoon. Molly, Rose, Lizzie, Jenny, Sally…"

Sylvie lost track of all the English names and studied the girls instead. Pretty, all of them, some startlingly so.

"Allow me to introduce Miss Sylvie Chapeau, ladies. She will be joining you onstage. Please make her welcome. I trust you will extend the appropriate hospitality? As you know, The

General expects you for rehearsal very shortly. I apologize that I cannot remain longer, Miss Chapeau, to assist with your orientation, but I have an important engagement."

Sylvie glanced at Tom Shaughnessy; his eyes were glinting in fiendish merriment. The silent message in them was: *See if a knitting needle will help you now.*

And then he gave a crisp bow and left Sylvie to the mercy of the girls.

All those pretty eyes, brown and blue and gray, continued to stare at her. Sylvie had seen more hospitality reflected in a row of icicles.

"It's a chicken," the one called Molly mused thoughtfully, answering her own earlier question. "Plucked. With great staring eyes."

Giggles, musical as strummed harp strings and malevolent as cholera, rustled through the room.

Chin up, Sylvie let the giggles wash over her. For her, jealousy was like ants at a picnic…a tiny annoyance that merely confirmed the grandness of the main event.

And Sylvie, of course, was accustomed to being considered the main event.

"Does it 'urt very much?" Molly asked when the giggles had faded away, her brow furrowed in sympathy. Chestnut ringlets, eyes fluffy-lashed spheres of blue, lips a pillow of pink—that was Molly.

Sylvie knew she was clearly being led into a trap of some sort, but apart from feigning deafness, which no dancer could convincingly do, she saw no other option but to respond. She thought she'd try politeness first.

"Forgive me, but does what hurt, Mademoiselle?"

"The rod up your arse. Does it 'urt very much?"

Another rustle of giggles. With a taut little anticipatory edge, now.

"Oh, not so much as jealousy," Sylvie said mildly. "Or so I'm told."

A shocked silence.

And then: *"Oooohhhh,"* one of the dancers breathed in either admiration or terror of what Molly might do, perhaps both.

Scarlet rushed over Molly's smooth face. Sylvie saw the girl's fingers curl a little more tightly around the handle of her hairbrush.

"*Does* jealousy 'urt?" the girl called Rose whispered, sounding genuinely curious. The girl next to her elbowed her hard.

"Why should I be jealous of a plucked chicken?" Molly turned, saw with fresh satisfaction her own incomparable reflection—slightly redder in the face than it had been moments ago, granted. Her shoulders relaxed, confidence restored. She dragged the brush once through her shining length of hair, a little self-caress of reassurance.

Sylvie had just opened her mouth to respond to the chicken remark when a small man—a *very* small man—burst into the room in a blur of brilliant tailoring, and everyone jumped.

"It's five minutes past the hour," he barked. "What the devil are you females—" He saw Sylvie, stopped abruptly, and glared up at her, thick brows knitting into one brow for a moment. "Who are *you*?"

Ah, the White Lily's version of Monsieur Favre, no doubt. "Miss Sylvie Chapeau." She curtsied.

The man didn't bow or introduce himself. He continued frowning and staring as if her presence was so incongruous he could never hope to decipher her purpose here.

"Mr. Shaughnessy hired me," she clarified finally.

"Ah," the little man said. It seemed to Sylvie a more cynical syllable had never been uttered.

His eyes traveled over her shoulders, her torso, returned to her arms, lingered on her face. The scrutiny wasn't entirely without appreciation, but it was more the sort one applied to a potential investment, to a carriage or heifer or silver salver, rather than to a woman. Sylvie was accustomed to being scrutinized dispassionately, as she was a vehicle for the dance in her own way, and a certain amount of dispassion was expected.

Still, this little man didn't know her, and she didn't know him, and she began to feel a little pique.

She gazed evenly back at him—or rather, down at him—and felt her spine go just a little straighter.

And then he reached some sort of conclusion; she saw it in his face, a peculiar sort of guarded thoughtfulness.

"I'll...have a word with Mr. Shaughnessy." He sounded ironic. "Until then, Miss Chapeau, please wait here. Girls, you know what to do. I will join you shortly."

The girls stood and followed The General out of the room, gazes trailing past Sylvie on their way out of the door, sharp as fingernails.

❦

Tom didn't even jump when The General burst into his office, but his papers fluttered up. He patted them down just in time.

"She's a dancer, Tom."

"I know that, Gen. I hired her. Go tell her what to do."

Tom was feeling a trifle impatient. His sleeves were rolled up, and the stack of correspondence—bills, invitations, accounting of expenditures and profits and bribes to Crumstead, the king's man, for looking the other way with regards to the bawdier productions of the White Lily, letters from females pleading for an assignation—awaiting his attention seemed dauntingly tall this morning. Some day he would hire someone to do this—sorting, ordering, responding—for him. In fact, in just an hour or so he would attempt to enthrall a crowd of investors with the plans that might very well make this possible. And once the The Gentleman's Emporium was thriving—

Tom looked up, surprised at The General's assessment. And, quite frankly, at his tone. Warning and ire mixed with a sort of...well, he might have called it *yearning,* if he was of a poetic bent. He was not.

"Did she actually tell you she was a ballerina?"

"No," The General said shortly. And said nothing more.

Tom studied his friend for a bemused moment. He didn't doubt the truth of what The General said. They had been partners for years now, but much of The General's own story remained untold, bits of it came out every now and again. Tom had learned to be patient and not to pry; he rather enjoyed the gradual unfolding of the tale.

"What makes a ballerina a 'real' dancer, Gen?" He said it somewhat irritably. "And there's no money in it. Only the bloody king wants to watch it. And women."

"She'll be trouble, mark my words. It's in that spine of hers," The General said cryptically.

And then Tom couldn't help it: He let a smile take over his face, little by little. "And in everything else of hers, too, I'd warrant."

The General was speechless for a moment. "God, Tommy." His voice cracked. "Tell me you didn't...*smile* at this woman." Tom's smile invariably led to trouble.

"Smiling doesn't work on her, Gen." Tom heard the wistful note in his own voice. "Nothing seems to."

The General squeezed his eyes closed, appeared to count to five, then opened them again. "So that's why you *hired* her? To practice upon her until you find the thing that does work?"

"Oh, for heaven's sake." Tom leaned back in his chair. "Rest easy, Gen. She's a pretty woman. She came looking for a job. I gave her one. And I do not, as you know ... er ... trouble the dancers. You know I have a very strict policy in that regard."

"That's not a pretty woman, Tom. That's a *beautiful* woman. Even worse, possibly an *interesting* woman. Who clearly thinks quite highly of herself. And she hasn't an ounce of spare flesh on her. What on earth will the audience *look* at? If she has breasts at all, I'd be—"

"She'll be different, Gen," Tom said mildly. "And our crowd likes a novelty."

"She'll be trouble," The General said grimly. "She's already trouble. I found the other dancers staring at her like a pack of hounds ready to descend upon a fox."

Tom smiled faintly at this. "I wager she'll hold her own."

"Molly was scarlet, as a matter of fact." The General sounded indignant.

"Was she?" Tom said with genuine interest, wondering what on earth the self-possessed Miss Chapeau might have said to cause Molly, a woman who was soft as a peach on the surface and hard as a cobblestone underneath, to turn colors.

Still, he realized that he had, very likely, quite selfishly and uncharacteristically and utterly on a whim, complicated The General's life, having introduced a rogue element into their little cadre of dancers, thus requiring dances to be rethought, costumes resewn, alliances reshuffled. Usually everyone had plenty of warning before such an event took place, for these very reasons. A new show was planned, discussed, rehearsed. Just the right girl was located and hired after thought and consideration, as the sheer number of girls vying for jobs at the White Lily was boggling. Tom did feel a bit of chagrin.

In truth he'd deliberately installed Sylvie with the dancers, safely out of his own reach. She'd appeared, and buffeted by myriad conflicting and confusing sensations, he'd reacted reflexively, for all the world as though dodging a musket ball or a comet. He wasn't proud of doing it, necessarily; but it was done, and as he was stubborn, he wasn't about to undo it simply to please The General.

"I'm sure you'll cope splendidly, as always, Gen."

And at this, Tom watched with interest as his friend's chest inflated with a deep inhale; then shrank again with an exhale of exaggerated patience that fluttered his cravat as well as the papers stacked on the corner of Tom's desk, as he wasn't very much taller than the desk. Tom patted a hand down over them just in time. He reminded himself to get a paperweight.

"I built a damned castle for you Tom, in a week. I didn't complain. I made sure we had costumes for a bunch of bloody damsels. I didn't complain. And now you've gone and—"

"And they loved it, didn't they? Our audience? The damsels in distress? The song about lances?"

The silence was a concession.

"And you love the sound of coins jingling in your pocket, Gen, am I right?"

"No, I like quiet pockets, Tom."

Tom grinned at this. Such a temper, The General had. Such a gift for sarcasm. But his tone had gone from irate to ironic, and would soon give way to resignation, he knew. So Tom said nothing, just waited for it. Tom could simply exhaust with charm if he so chose.

"You should have consulted me before you hired her, Tom. You usually do."

"I should have," Tom allowed gently. "And I apologize. But by now, I thought you might have learned to trust my instincts."

"Your instincts as a man of business are impeccable, Tom. Your instincts as a *man* get you into duels. And will one day, no doubt, get you killed."

The General stared at him with defiance, and when it was clear that Tom could think of nothing glib to say, the defiance metamorphosed into a sort of satisfaction that had nothing of triumph in it.

"It's a quarter past the hour, Gen," Tom said finally. Cruel, he knew, but it was his only remaining line of defense.

The General jumped and swore and all but bolted from the office.

Tom sighed, half-smiling, then reached back into his stack of mail.

He frowned when he touched one letter.

And then he slowly picked it up, stared down at it. Saw the address upon it, and went very still. Little Swathing, Kent.

He slit it open.

We should be pleased to receive you should you call again.

Cold, formal, polite. But it spoke of pride swallowed, or reservations breached at last, by his own insistent campaign.

He'd made the journey once a week for months now. But today he'd found the occupants of the little cottage in Kent not at home. And now this.

Tom held the letter, staring down at it, not unaware of this irony.

Now that he'd been granted the thing he'd sought out of sheer stubbornness for weeks, he wasn't certain whether in truth he really wanted it.

$\backsim$

Sylvie had been waiting alone in the dressing room a mere ten minutes or so when the girl called Rose appeared, and Sylvie almost smiled. *So Rose was the least thorny of the flowers in this particular theater,* and like the tactician he no doubt was, The

General had decided not to leave Sylvie alone with someone significantly more…challenging, such as Molly, or her sort just yet.

Rose looked at Sylvie with no particular emotion other than a sort of bemused curiosity, which Sylvie suspected was Rose's default expression. It was a pity, because Rose had the sort of beauty that could drop men's jaws—hair and eyes glossy and dark as a crow's wing, a soft natural flush in her ivory cheeks—but she lacked the sort of fire or self-awareness that would fascinate a man to the exclusion of all else. Someday, no doubt, she would be endlessly indulged by a wealthy elderly man seeking an undemanding mistress.

Rose wore her beauty as nonchalantly as her costume, as though she knew this, knew it was only temporary, only part of the show.

"Yer French, then?" Rose asked with barely an inflection to indicate she'd just asked a question, and flung open a large wooden wardrobe. "Truly?"

Yes. No. Maybe. "Yes." It was the simplest answer.

"Well, I suppose The General wants ye to be a fairy today, same as the rest of us, soooo…ye'll need a wand…" When Rose rooted about in the wardrobe, a number of things came tumbling out; a wooden wand topped by a painted star clunked to the floor. Rose plucked it up, set it aside. "It was Kitty's, ye know. Kitty was the girl before ye."

If she stopped to think about it, it would dizzy her, the fact that she was about to dress as a fairy in order to earn her keep. Sylvie decided to ask questions instead.

"The girl before me?"

"The one who left, ye see. A few months ago. They say what Mr. Shaughnessy turned 'er off. Got 'erself in a right…*bind*." Rose whispered the last word meaningfully and cupped her hands meaningfully below her belly."

"So he…'turned 'er off'?" Sylvie repeated, aghast. She

was fairly certain she knew what this particular English turn of phrase meant, given that the girl had gotten herself into a *bind:* He'd sent her away.

"Canna verra well put 'er onstage when she gets big like, can 'e?" Rose observed pragmatically, extending her arms out as though she was encircling an invisible pumpkin. "She was 'ere one day, cryin' and the like, told Molly she'd gone to speak to Mr. Shaughnessy about 'er troubles. An' she was gone the next day. 'Avena seen 'er since."

Rose turned and studied Sylvie for a moment, apparently considering whether to tell Sylvie something that, judging from Rose's expression, was clearly going to be interesting. "Molly says what Mr. Shaughnessy is the papa."

A thrill of horror coiled in Sylvie's stomach.

And Rose nodded once, gratified by the expression on Sylvie's face. "But then, Molly says a *lot,*" Rose added in mild wonder. As though she could scarcely fathom why anyone would want to say more than was necessary.

"You do not believe it?"

Rose hesitated, then shrugged. "Mr. Shaughnessy . . . well, I dinna think 'e would touch a girl what works fer 'im."

"How do you know this?" Sylvie found herself asking.

And whom does he touch instead?

"We've all 'ad a go at it, ye see." Rose grinned at this. "Water off a duck's back, to Mr. Shaughnessy. 'E brooks nooooo nonsense when it comes to the White Lily and those girls what work 'ere. 'E jus' smiles until we give up."

Interesting, given that the man seemed inclined to both frivolity and danger.

"So why would Molly say such a thing?"

"Because 'e willna touch *'er,* though she's tried and tried, and *she* thinks it's because of Kitty. She says Kitty was Mr. Shaughnessy's favorite. We *all* thought Kitty was Mr. Shaughnessy's favorite. 'E *did* seem to like 'er best. 'E . . . laughed wi' 'er, ye see. An' 'e 'asna 'ired a new girl until . . . today. It's been months. An' Molly wants 'im—Mr. Shaughnessy—fer 'erself. Well, and dinna we all?"

No. Yes. Maybe.

Sylvie tactfully ignored the question, which seemed to be rhetorical anyway. And so cheerfully and matter-of-factly said, as if Mr. Shaughnessy's appeal was universal and could be understood and appreciated by any female.

"But Mr. Shaughnessy . . . ever since Kitty left, ye see . . . once a week or so he goes to Kent, I 'eard 'im say t' The General once. But no one knows why. Not even The General. Not even 'Er Majesty."

" 'Her Majesty?' " She had been under the impression that the English were ruled by a king. Perhaps this was another honorary title, like The General.

"Daisy," Rose said laconically, as if this clarified anything. "She's 'er own room to dress in and entertain guests and the like. She doesna share wi' the likes of us. Ye'll see 'er soon enough, no doubt. But she willna speak to the likes of ye."

Ah, a diva. Sylvie was familiar with the sort. As she was something of the sort herself.

"But ladies, they do come to look for Mr. Shaughnessy," Rose hurried to assure Sylvie, as if the fact that he didn't touch his dancers would call his manhood into question. "Cryin' an' beggin' to see 'im, in fact. An' 'usbands are forever callin' 'im out, our Mr. Shaughnessy. Even though 'es not a gentleman, like. It's because 'es such a verra good shot."

"Duels? He fights *duels?*"

"Best shot in London. Shoots the 'eart right out o' the target each time."

Sylvie felt faint. She wondered if duels were any more legal in London than they were in Paris, and doubted it. She remembered the glint of the pistol in Tom Shaughnessy's sleeve as they stood in the clearing among those highwaymen.

"He kills people?"

"Kills?" Rose sounded faintly appalled. Only faintly. Sylvie wondered whether Rose experienced any emotion rather strongly, and given the tempests of her own various passions, felt a slight twinge of envy, wondering what it might be like to drift comfortably through life's dramas.

"Oh, no. They shoot at each other, but everyone seems to miss."

Tom Shaughnessy routinely shot and allowed other people to shoot at him? *Over other men's wives?*

"And The General—he is..." Sylvie paused to think of the word. "In charge of the dancing?"

"'E is, an 'e invents the shows, like, but even 'e answers to Mr. Shaughnessy, an' 'tis Mr. Shaughnessy, oo 'as the *big* ideas. One show a night, every night save Sunday, three acts at least, six or eight songs, usually. Mr. Shaughnessy likes to jumble it up a bit, an 'e seems t'ave a new idea every week. Keeps us busy, 'e does. We've rehearsal every day for as long as The General says. It's a right bit o' work, but it's good pay, and Mr. Shaughnessy, 'e looks after us."

Right bit of work? Sylvie wondered what on earth the dances entailed.

"Do you live here at the theater, Rose?"

"At the theater?" Rose's eyes widened with astonishment. "I've me own rooms up the street. Mr. Shaughnessy pays right well. We all do—'ave our own rooms. The girls, and Poe and Stark, the men what guard the stage door outside, an' Jack, 'oo guards the dressing-room door, an' the boys who work for The General. But there *are* rooms 'ere at the White Lily, up the stairs. Was a grand 'ouse once. Where d'yer live, Sylvie?"

Sylvie didn't know how to respond to that question. She was

spared from answering when the top half of Rose disappeared into the wardrobe and she began fishing about inside it.

She emerged with a gown, a gossamer thing, pale pink over some silvery fabric. It would provide about as much flesh coverage as mist, though in dimmed lights one couldn't *precisely* see through it. Sylvie eyed it askance.

"'Ere. We've five minutes before The General 'as a fit. I'll 'elp wi' yer laces."

Sylvie was accustomed to dressing in front of other girls; modesty was frivolous when one was a dancer preparing to perform. But Sylvie was suddenly profoundly aware of how slight she was, a willow twig compared to these vivid blossoms of girls. It was as if anything superfluous to ballet had melted away from her body, leaving behind only what was necessary to fulfill Monsieur Favre's commands—elegant muscle.

She turned around and presented her back to Rose, and Rose worked the laces on her mourning gown for her. She watched with frank curiosity as Sylvie slipped into the dress.

The dress was too large, hung on her frame loosely, exposing an expanse of chest, stopping just shy of revealing her bosom altogether. And the ribbon from which her miniature hung. Sylvie put her hand up, disguising it.

"The General, 'e won't want ye to wear stays, but ye've not much of a bosom, 'ave ye?"

How on earth did one respond to such a question? Ironically, Sylvie decided. "No, I suppose not."

"Mmm. Stays *will* 'elp wi' the—" Rose covered her own round bosoms with both hands and gave them an illustrative push upward. "Make ye look like ye've a bit more."

Sylvie appreciated that Rose was trying to be helpful, but bosoms had always been about as helpful as ballast in Sylvie's line of work; they got in the way, in other words. She felt herself growing warm in indignation.

And when Rose handed her the big wooden wand, and she turned and got a look at herself in the mirror, the indignity was complete.

But wait. Rose was still rummaging about in the wardrobe, and plucked out a pair of wings, sheer, luminous fabric ingeniously stretched over a frame of wires, fitted with straps. An admirable bit of construction, admittedly. She would admire it more if she weren't required to wear them.

But Rose held them out to her, and Sylvie resignedly took them. She saw loops in the center for her arms. She pushed her slim arms through them. *Voilà!* She was a fairy.

The wings, she had to admit, *were* pretty. They would have done justice to the costumers at the Paris Opera, where some of the finest and most ingenious seamstresses were employed.

"Why did Mr. Shaughnessy take ye on?" Rose wanted to know.

Now that Rose was satisfied that her body was not the typical White Lily body, she apparently could not resist the question.

Sylvie decided that building her own mystique would be a marvelous strategic defense during her stay at the theater.

"Mr. Shaughnessy and I shared a mail coach, which was robbed, and when I kissed a highwayman, they agreed to let us go on."

Rose's dark eyes stared. And then: "*Cor!*" she breathed.

In short, if Sylvie would kiss a highwayman, what *else* might she be capable of?

Sylvie felt absurdly gratified. She might be skinny and dressed inadequately as a fairy, but she could still impress.

"What's funny, it was sudden-like, and 'e always takes 'is time findin' a new girl. Tells us all about it. We thought 'ed never replace Kitty. So ye're a surprise."

I imagine I am.

Chapter Five

The General regarded Sylvie dispassionately: the big dress, the wand, the studiedly stoic expression on her face.

"The costumes will need...significant...altering. How are your skills with a needle, Sylvie?"

"I believe you mean 'Miss Chapeau,'" she said almost reflexively. Perhaps it was a mistake, but she was a tad irritated, as her dignity felt chafed by her costume and by Rose's assessment of her bosom. "My skills with a needle are adequate."

"You may have noticed that we don't stand on ceremony here, Sylvie. Now girls, places please. Sylvie, because of your height, you can stand between *Molly* and *Jenny*—"

"What is *your* name?" Sylvie considered perhaps she should have eaten something when Mr. Shaughnessy offered, as she knew her temper was easier to rouse when her stomach was empty, and it was tempting her now to take risks.

He fixed her with a gaze meant to intimidate, no doubt. "The General," he said evenly. "The. General." He gazed at her with those sharp dark eyes. "Now Josephine, if you'd begin—"

"Your given name is 'The'?" Sylvie said mildly.

Sylvie heard what sounded like a collected sucking of breath. The other girls had done it.

The General turned very slowly and stared up at her wonderingly.

"Then I may call you 'The'?" she pressed on, calmly. Taking a certain perverse, reckless pleasure in it.

"Oh, my, oh my, oh my, oh my," Rose whispered gleefully.

"Don't don't don't don't don't," another girl hissed.

The General muttered something, and Sylvie could have sworn he was taking the name of Tom Shaughnessy in vain. He took in a deep breath, appeared to be counting.

And then he beamed at Sylvie. "Yes. Please do call me 'The.' Or call me cuddlecakes. Call me that 'gorgeous bastard.' I suppose it doesn't matter what you call me when you have need of calling me, as I will more likely need to call *you*, Sylvie. And now, if you would please stand between Molly and Jenny. I assume you can...move to music?"

The last three words were given a special frisson of irony, which puzzled Sylvie just a bit.

"I shall certainly do my very best," she said solemnly.

"Josephine," The General barked.

Josephine, a fair-haired woman who looked astonishingly ordinary in contrast to the rest of the denizens of the theater—as round and pleasant-faced and wholesome as the wife of a country squire—gave a start and landed on the pianoforte, her fingers finding and playing a song with a waltz pattern, tinkling and saucy.

The girls onstage began to sway, arcing their wands to and fro gracefully above their heads.

This presented little challenge; Sylvie managed to master the swaying motion quickly enough.

She noticed The General's eyes on her, and she could have sworn he looked a little amused.

But the swaying motion was pretty in its way, harmless enough, despite the wands and shamelessly gossamer gowns and her pair of wings. She could even imagine how pleasing they all might look beyond the footlights during a performance, all shimmer and beauty.

"Smiles, girls!" The General bellowed.

Rows of pretty teeth were instantly bared. Sylvie suspected hers more closely resembled a grimace, from the feel of things. Still, she curled her lips back.

The music tinkled on for a bar or so, at which point the girls rotated in a circle until their backs faced the audience, all the while twirling their wands in tight circles over their heads. And then they linked arms, a motion Sylvie managed to follow smoothly enough. Sylvie wasn't particularly anxious to touch Molly, but she did it anyhow, and took Jenny's arm, too, and continued to sway to and fro.

This was child's play; she could probably do this and nap at the same time. In fact, a nap was sound—

The row of girls bent double and pushed their fannies up into the air and sang out *"Wheee!"* dragging a startled Sylvie abruptly down with them.

And then they were upright and gently swaying again.

"More derriere next time, Jenny! Get it up there high!" The General ordered, as if commanding troop maneuvers.

They swayed for a bar, twirling their wands, and then, Dear God—

"Wheee!"

They did it again, chins to their knees, derrieres in the air, dragging Sylvie down with them.

When she was upright this time, Sylvie's eyes were wide and nearly watering with horror.

"Ye've scarcely an arse, Sylvie. See the seamstress straightaway and get that dress altered," The General barked over the music. "And the word is '*wheee!*' I want to hear it. *One,* two, three, *one,* two, three, *one,* two, three..."

And suddenly, abruptly, Sylvie unhooked her arm from Molly's and Lizzie's and almost blindly fled down the little stairs of the stage, reflexively fleeing what seemed to her the things she'd devoted her entire life to avoid becoming.

❧

She wasn't quite certain where she was heading, but "away" seemed a sufficient destination at the moment, and her general direction appeared to be the White Lily's door.

She nearly ran headlong into the wall of a linen-clad chest, stopped abruptly and looked up into Tom Shaughnessy's face.

"Tired of dancing so soon, Miss Chapeau?"

"Derrieres...bending...*wheee!*" Sylvie stammered furiously, hands flailing helplessly, unable to convey the horror of it all. "That is *not* dancing, Mr. Shaughnessy."

"You stand there, move about, smile." He was obviously confused. "Of course it's dancing. Audiences pay good money for derrieres and '*whee,*' Miss Chapeau. Does 'dance' mean something else now in French?" And then he frowned in comprehension. "Oh! I believe I see what you are driving at. But I'm afraid no one will pay to see"—Tom paused, as if to give the word a wide mental berth from his other words, and said it gingerly. "*Ballet.* If that's what you're asking. There isn't any money in it."

Sylvie went still for a moment. How on earth would he have known about—

She took a deep breath. "Is there something else I might do to assist here at the theater?" she managed to ask in a steadier voice. "In order to earn my keep."

She hoped, hoped, hoped he wouldn't interpret this question pruriently.

She needn't have worried. "Perhaps you sing?" he asked, his mind clearly ticking away.

"Well—" Sylvie could carry a tune, but more often than not, the tune carried her. It was her body, not her voice, which understood music so well. "Yes." Which was merely a short version of the truth.

"Do you sing... well?" He sounded troubled by the very idea. "You see, we don't want to frighten the audience with... exquisite singing. Most of these men can hear a soprano in any drawing room, you see. They come here to get *away* from sopranos in the drawing room. Sopranos remind them of long evenings with their wives."

"No one will ever invite me to sing in a drawing room," Sylvie told him quite truthfully.

"Would you be willing to sing a bawdy song then?"

She blinked. "A baw—" The words began as a choked laugh and stopped when she noticed there was absolutely nothing of humor in his face. It had been a flat question. He was a businessman deciding how to deploy an asset, and she was the asset.

"A bawdy song," he reiterated impatiently. "Such as..." Tom paused in thought, and then tilted his head back and in a surprisingly decent tenor sang:

"Nell was a young woman so young and so fair
Who cherished her virtue 'til she met Lord Adair
Who took her for a ride in the warm summer air
And gave her a necklace of baubles to wear
Of baubles, of baubles, of baubles to wear,
Oh!
He gave her a necklace of baubles to wear!

He looked at her. "A bawdy song," he concluded briskly.

And now the expression on his face was so distinctly at odds with the content of his song that incredulity warred with hilarity as she decided what to say next.

"Pretty song," she finally said, solemnly. "Perhaps *you* should sing it, instead."

"Oh, I would," Tom assured her in all seriousness, "if I thought anyone would pay to see *me* rouged, or in a shift."

"And are you certain no one would?"

The words were out before she could stop them, because it was precisely the thing any accomplished coquette would have been unable to resist saying in similar circumstances. She regretted them for an instant.

In the next instant, she was surprised to find herself rather breathlessly looking forward to what Tom Shaughnessy might say.

Nothing, as it turned out—for a time, anyway. He regarded her instead, eyes aglow in pure pleasure—he was utterly pleased with *her*—the corner of his mouth quirked upward speculatively, as if deciding what to say next.

"I can sing the French version, too," he said suddenly. "My friend Henri taught the words to me. Would you like to hear it?"

"Have I a choice?"

He ignored her question, and squeezed his eyes closed for a moment in thought, apparently scanning his memory for the lyrics.

At last he opened his eyes, and opened his mouth, and—

Well, the language he used was certainly French.

But the song suddenly had nothing at all to do with Nell and Lord Adair.

Instead, it was all about what a certain man would like to do to a certain woman and what position he'd like to do it *in,* and how certain he was that the woman would enjoy it. Baubles *did* play a role—though they were called something else entirely in this version of the song, as this was French—and the chorus was sung just as enthusiastically.

Perhaps most shockingly, it all rhymed beautifully.

And as he sang: heat. In her cheeks, in the pit of her stomach, sweeping up her arms. *Everywhere* as he sang, the song creating the most specific pictures in her head.

She was certain the bloody man had made the lyrics up on the spot.

For heaven's sake, she'd danced for kings; she couldn't recall the last time she'd conjured a genuine blush. But this man had sent her composure scattering as surely as a cue dashed into a triangle of billiard balls.

When he was done, silence dropped with the ceremony of that great heavy velvet curtain. Tom's face was solemn as a vicar's, but his eyes glinted like the very devil's. He clasped his hands behind his back and waited with wide eyes for her to comment.

Sylvie could not recall words ever deserting her; the traitors, they were doing it now.

"That..." Her voice was a little hoarse. She cleared her throat. "That wasn't the same song, Mr. Shaughnessy."

"No? Wasn't it?" All innocence. "Bother. Henri must have misled me. I'll have a word with him. Perhaps my French is not quite so good as I thought."

She paused. "No," she agreed slowly. " 'Good' is not the word I would have chosen to describe your French, Mr. Shaughnessy." She waited, and her heart beat just a little more quickly in anticipation.

"Wicked, then?" he suggested quickly. "Would you perhaps use 'wicked,' instead?" He sounded as earnest as a schoolboy making a guess at an arithmetic problem.

She couldn't help it; it burbled out of her, a vein of humor struck. She laughed. He'd said precisely what he should have said next in the dance of flirtation, and it delighted her more than it should have, made her breathless the way a well-executed *pas de deux* did.

The laughter, of course, only encouraged him; the wicked grin flashed. "Which part of the song did you like best, Miss Chapeau?"

"The ending," she said quickly, recovering.

He looked at her again, speculatively. "Mmmm," he said, considering this. "That might very well be true, but"—he reached out one finger and dragged it lightly along her flaming jaw—"you should see how attractively pink the *rest* of the song has made you."

She froze. Of all the bold, presumptuous—

He took his hand away and glanced down at it briefly; confusion flickered, his brows dived a little.

And even as outrage flamed in her eyes, even after he took his finger away, his touch echoed through her unnervingly.

An odd silence followed.

"A thought-provoking song, nevertheless, wouldn't you say, Miss Chapeau?" he said, finally.

"It provoked only a longing to hear a *good* tenor, Mr. Shaughnessy." A tart and scrambling effort to impose a distance and gather the shreds of her composure.

Up went his brows. "Did it? My apologies." He sounded genuinely disappointed. "I thought perhaps you understood the lyrics. Clearly you did not, and I have misjudged you, and you are a mere innocent after all."

"I'm not a *mere*—"

White teeth and that crescent-shaped dimple came into view again. "Yes?"

She realized too late how ludicrous it was to defend her honor by declaring she was *not* innocent. Funny, but it had been the word "mere" her temper had reared up against. Sylvie had never been "mere" in any way.

And as she wasn't certain how to ease her way out of this particular corner, she remained silent.

"Mmm. I didn't think you were, somehow," he said idly, and dipped a hand into his pocket and retrieved a watch; it glowed like a tiny planet in the dim theater. He nudged it open with his thumb, and when he saw the time, everything about him became brisk.

"To the subject at hand, Miss Chapeau. I do not operate a charity."

She blinked. It was as though he'd finished a quick afternoon snack and was now pushing himself away from the table to get on with the rest of his day.

"I beg your pardon?" she said.

"It's simple, you see. You may sing a bawdy song of my choosing, or you may dance with the other girls, or you may leave. Those are your choices. And yes, you are passing fair, but you may have noticed beauty is not a rarity, but a requirement, here at the White Lily. Had you been any plainer, I would have sent you packing much earlier. As I said, I cannot afford to offer charity."

Sylvie was speechless. *Passing fair?* When earlier she had been "beautiful"?

"It's called work, Miss Chapeau. *Travailler,* I believe they call it in your language. Or perhaps you're unfamiliar with the concept?"

The weight of the accusation landed full force on her chest, made what felt like a veritable crater in it; indignation and anger sizzled up out of it, robbing her of breath.

Everything she valued in her life—the soft bed she rose from in the morning, the sound of hands put together in applause, the flowers brought to her each night at the end of a performance, the barbs of the girls in the dressing room born of awe and envy, and the quiet adulation of most of Paris and the devotion of a man like Etienne, *everything*—had been forged from discipline and commitment and grim determination. In other words: from work. What could this...this...gilded *street ruffian* possibly know of the sort of sweat and pain required to make people forget themselves as they watched you, to make them soar inside when you danced for them?

She—of the quicksilver, hand-waving, shooting-star temper—was nearly paralyzed by fury.

"You know nothing of me, Mr. Shaughnessy." Her voice was low and taut.

"And whose fault is that, Miss Chapeau?" Pleasantly said. As though the waves of righteous indignation pouring from her were naught but a summer breeze.

She remained incredulously silent.

"Does that mean you *do* know how to work?" He said it patiently, into her silent green glare.

"Yes, Mr. Shaughnessy," she managed ironically. "I warrant I could teach *you* a bit about work."

He gave a short laugh then. "Oh, I'm certain you're quite correct, Miss Chapeau. Consider my work, for instance. It's no trouble at all to order lovely girls about. Mere child's play, in fact. I shall look forward to my lesson about *work* from you. Now: you need to wear what The General tells you to wear, do what he tells you to do, smile, and play nicely with the other girls. Do you think you can manage to do that, or will you be leaving now?"

She listened to his words, but for some reason the words "passing fair" were the ones that scraped away in her mind like a trapped thistle.

Funny, of all the things this man had said, this one for some reason bothered most.

She wondered if he would truly send her packing if she refused; she sensed he wasn't as indifferent to her as he purported to be, and it was tempting to take that risk, to call his bluff.

Passing fair, indeed.

Then again, perhaps he was the sort who trifled idly with novelty and tired of it quickly. A man with his face, even bereft of his...*singular*...charm would certainly be able to view women as offerings on the groaning sideboard of life. Tom Shaughnessy was like a mirror in which the world was reflected backward, different, brand-new, infuriating. Invigorating as a bolted glass of whiskey, and probably just as dangerous and addictive.

All right. So she cherished her pride.

But she *needed* money.

"When will I be paid?"

Was it just the changing light of the day passing through the theater? Or did relief soften his expression briefly?

"When you've performed onstage for our audience, Miss Chapeau. Until then you are an apprentice, and living upon the charity of the White Lily. Will you be staying, then?"

Sylvie Lamoreux, an *apprentice,* living upon *charity?*

"Will you be staying?" There was a faint note of urgency in his voice now. She wondered whether it was concern about her imminent departure or about whatever appointment it seemed she was keeping him from meeting, judging from his one impatient glance at his watch. Perhaps he financed these theaters with the highwaymen's spoils, and he was on his way to meet Biggsy Biggens to sort through his take.

"I shall stay. I shall"—she took a deep breath, and still she couldn't deliver the word with anything other than irony—"dance."

There was a beat of silence before he spoke. Her vanity decided to interpret it as relief.

"Very well, then. And when you return to rehearsal, you may wish to apologize to The General. He predicted that you would be trouble. Perhaps you'll be able to convince him otherwise."

His tone, and the quick grin that accompanied his words, told her he had no confidence whatsoever in her ability to do so.

She didn't disabuse him of that notion.

"And when you are done, Sylvie, please ask Josephine to show you to your room. I've asked her to see that you get something to eat. I won't have you starving."

She stared at him. He stared back at her patiently.

"Thank you," she managed at last with some dignity, and pirouetted neatly to bravely rejoin the hostile little flock of females.

She couldn't help it. She glanced back just once, to see if he was admiring her exit.

But he wasn't. Oddly, he was looking down at his fingers again, and she could have sworn his expression was haunted.

Chapter Six

❧

ombined, they could have financed the English army twice over, yet there was only a title or two among them: Lord Cambry, a baron; George Pinkerton-Knowles, who'd amassed a fortune in shipbuilding; Major William Gordon; Viscount Howath; a few others. They'd inherited the money, or they'd earned it, or they'd all but stolen it through some legal means. But all that mattered to Tom was that they had it, enough of it to ensure that they were often bored and restless and in search of novelty. Enough of it to ensure they had power and status and connections, should it become necessary to call in a few markers in order to achieve his grand goal. And they'd backed him before, taken a risk on the White Lily, perhaps as a lark, and Tom had earned their investment back for them more than three times over. And since he'd done this once, naturally they were interested to hear if he might do it for them again. Tom had been invited to meet with them at Major Gordon's club. From there they would go on to their dinners, and then, very likely, to the White Lily.

Good brandy and better cigars had created the sort of bonhomie necessary for them to loosen their purse strings; the smoke in the air wreathed lamps and full, flushed faces. Pinkerton-Knowles had in fact unbuttoned his coat, and his unfettered belly rested comfortably on his lap. "Talk to us, Shaughnessy," he urged.

It had never occurred to Tom to feel intimidated by any of them. It had never occurred to Tom to want to *be* any of them, which was precisely why they more or less liked him, and more than one of them fancied they wanted to be *him*. He didn't try to be anything he wasn't, and he clearly took such great pleasure in who he was—part Irish, rumored part Gypsy, unapologetically a bastard—that they envied him and enjoyed his company.

He wouldn't be welcome to court their *daughters,* but they envied him and enjoyed his company.

"Gentlemen." Tom rose. Slimmer than all of them, taller than all of them, and far, far better-looking than all of them, their heads craned up. "Thank you for agreeing to meet me today."

"No, thank *you,* Shaughnessy, for my Melinda. And Melinda sends her thanks, as well," the major called out. A chorus of laughter rose up. Melinda had spent some time in the employ of the White Lily before she'd been persuaded to become the major's much-coddled mistress.

Thoughts of Melinda and the major's particular brand of happiness made Tom's thoughts veer to a seemingly innocuous moment at the White Lily, and Miss Sylvie Chapeau. It had been barely a touch, something he'd done out of flirtation so many times before, so easily, so casually. He hadn't expected to find the texture of her skin so... well, *achingly* fine. She'd seemed all pride and steel and fire and wit; perhaps that was why the discovery that her skin was vulnerably soft had been so startling. But the discovery, for some reason, had made him feel strangely awkward and uncertain—which irritated him, as he couldn't recall the last time he'd felt awkward or uncertain about anything.

"Give my regards to the fair Melinda," Tom said with mock solemnity, and reached for his glass to lift. "I'm delighted I could contribute to the happiness of two such fine people."

"To Melinda and the major!" the group roared in unison, and tossed back the balance of their glasses. A series of *thunks* followed, glasses landing on the table again.

"To the business at hand, then," Tom intoned formally. "Gentlemen, I believe it's safe to say that the White Lily has greatly contributed to our collective..." he paused for effect, "...*happiness* and well-being over the past few years. And in light of his earlier confidences, I believe the major, in particular, would concur."

Much rumbled laughter and muttering. "Hear, hear!" the major said with feeling.

"Fine job of it, Shaughnessy. Earned my money back twice over. You've a gift for this sort of thing."

More concurring rumbles.

Tom accepted their tributes with a modest nod. "And no man could ask for better partners in business than yourselves, gentlemen. Which is why I've invited you here this evening. I'd very much like for you to be the first to hear of..." he paused strategically, and lowered his voice a fraction, "...an exclusive opportunity."

Pinkerton-Knowles delicately stifled a belch with a palm. "Opportunity, Shaughnessy? What sort of opportunity?"

"Why, simply an opportunity to participate in one of the boldest, surest, most lucrative endeavors you'll no doubt encounter in your lifetime," he said mildly. "Shall I go on?"

They were silent now and as attentive as hunting dogs, all

bonhomie quenched in favor of the businessman and adventurer in each of them.

"Gentlemen, I give you the"—Tom, a showman to his bones, whisked aside the fringed velvet curtains at the window, and light flooded in, revealing his beautifully rendered sketch propped upon an easel there—" 'Gentleman's Emporium.' A theater, a gentleman's club, a gaming *heaven,* special entertainments . . . all housed on several floors in one elegant building. Imagine, if you will, if the White Lily were wed to White's, if White's were grafted to Gentleman Jackson's, and—if one is an exclusive, private member—where one may dine privately with beautiful women after an evening's entertainment."

"Only 'dine'?" someone repeated, sounding disappointed. A few hoots rose up.

"Only dine." Tom sounded sympathetic. "What you manage to persuade her to do *after* you dine is another thing entirely, of course"—he paused while laughter and teasing jests rippled around the room—"and you will need to find other accommodations for such things, as the Gentleman's Emporium's current plans do not include them."

A diplomatic way of saying, No, he was not opening a brothel.

"Wish I had *your* powers of 'persuasion,' Shaughnessy."

"And *I'm* glad that you do not," Tom shot back.

More laughter. Which then died away, leaving a thoughtful silence as they considered what Tom had just said.

"And the property?" the major barked. "Build or buy?"

A little thrill of excitement spiked in Tom. Specific questions such as these indicated genuine interest. "Buy, renovate, *and* build. I know just the property. Needs a fair amount of work, but behind me"—Tom motioned to the artist's rendering—"you can see how it will look. I invite you to inspect it more closely."

They gathered around the illustration, spent some time in

solemn silence, perusing it, then fired questions at him. About location, and licenses, and time lines, and sopranos (no: no sopranos). He answered them deftly.

And then, when the questions ebbed to a trickle, they resumed their seats, gazing at the drawing, considering. Tom looked levelly at them, patiently awaiting the next and most important question, because if someone asked it, it meant the interest had gone beyond idle; it had taken root. If *he* brought it up, it placed him in a position of vulnerability.

It was the major who spoke. "I might as well be the one to ask it, Shaughnessy. How much do you want from each of us?"

Bravely, Tom told them.

The silence that followed was the sort that follows a kidney punch.

"Good God, Shaughnessy," the major rasped when he'd recovered. "It's a brilliant idea, granted. If anyone can make a go of it, I think it's you. But you don't need to buy a barouche for your wife or send a boy to Eton, or to Oxford, and I do. And the *money*…"

"Your boy is but five years old, is he not, Major?" Tom asked smoothly. "I imagine your investment will have doubled itself by the time he's of Oxford age."

A laugh rose up, amused and gently mocking the major for his lack of fiscal nerve. *Good.* They were beginning to recover from their shock, beginning to hear the faint siren song of a good gamble. And no doubt would be amenable to negotiating now.

"But Tom's boy wouldn't be going to Eton or Oxford even then, would he? You're a lucky bastard, Tommy, no offense. Have to give them a decent start in life, you know, but children are bloody expensive."

More laughter.

Tom was far too comfortable with who he was and what

he'd accomplished to care much what anyone said about him, and it *was* absurd to think that the son of an Irish-Gyspy hybrid bastard might go to Eton and Oxford and muck about with the sons of proper gentlemen.

So he did laugh; a showman, he knew what was necessary to sell his proposal and was willing to do what the moment required. But though it was true, had always been true, he was distantly amused to find that suddenly nothing about the comment amused him.

It was time to seize control of the situation once more, which was part of his strategy. He strode to the curtain, pulled it closed, symbolically and abruptly cutting off the vision of potential riches and pleasant masculine mayhem.

"Gentlemen, thank you for joining me today. I'm looking for a very small and select group of investors, men of vision whom I trust, and naturally I thought first of you. Nothing would please me more than to continue to contribute to your wealth and happiness... not to mention add to my own."

Appreciative laughter.

"But the owner of the property in question shall require an answer from me within a fortnight, as he has others interested in purchasing it. Please do give it some thought, ask any questions you wish—you know where to find me—"

"Follow the trail of women!" someone who'd had a little too much brandy blurted.

"Or look in the arms of Bettina at the Velvet Glove at midnight!"

Tom grinned. "And if I don't hear from you within a fortnight, I'll assume you've decided to invest your money elsewhere. Hope to see you at the White Lily tonight, and"—he lowered his voice—"I'd like you, my friends, to be the first to know that we have the most *extraordinary future* production planned."

In unison, the men leaned forward, grown men all, eager as children.

"Tell, Tommy!"

"I'll give you a hint, gentlemen. Just one word, so remember it." They waited, leaning forward more steeply. He waited a strategic moment, then leaned forward, mouthed it *sotto voce.*

"Venus."

"Veeenusss," someone repeated slowly, sounding awed.

"Spread the word," Tom said. "You've never seen anything like it, and you'll never forget it."

Apart from inventing and singing a naughty French song to Miss Sylvie Chapeau, the day had been one of unrelieved strategic challenges. The moment he returned from his meeting with investors, Tom decided he ought to talk to Daisy, just to get it over with. She often took her supper in her own dressing room before the evening's entertainments—she never joined the girls for rehearsal—so that's where he headed.

How should he approach this? Somberly? Sternly? Brightly? It would be a delicate task, no matter how he went about it, as Daisy was as canny as she was buxom, and they knew each other almost too well. Long years of familiarity, contempt, triumph, and tragedy had created the fabric of their friendship, which was worn and warm as a quilt. Frayed and well used, nibbled about the edges by moths perhaps, but useful and cherished in its way.

"I want to be Venus, Tom." Daisy said it very calmly the moment he set foot in the room.

Damnation. Who on earth would have gotten to her so quickly? How did she *know*? It could not have been The

General. He considered the men in that smoky room he'd exited a mere hour ago and cursed all of them, for clearly one of them had somehow communicated with Daisy. Daisy was shrewd enough to know that the very fact that the show hadn't been mentioned to her meant Tom and The General had something else in mind.

"Oh, now, Daize, don't you think you should give the other girls a chance to shine?"

"Why?" she asked flatly.

The answer to this, as Daisy well knew, was that she was getting older. The flesh beneath her chin was loosening, her posterior was more than a shade wider than ample, her costumes required letting out on a regular basis now, and her majestic bosom was succumbing a little more each day to the tug of gravity. She knew it, Tom knew it, The General knew it, and Daisy, cruelly, wanted Tom to spell it out for her and knew he never, ever would.

Bloody woman.

"Because I need to keep them employed, Daisy, and if I give one or two of them an opportunity to shine, it helps to keep the peace."

This was at least partially true, and Daisy knew this, too. He saw amusement and wry admiration flicker in her eyes.

"Which girl, then? That Molly chit? She 'asn't the *presence* for it."

"Presence"? When had Daisy begun using words like "presence"?

It was time to be stern. "Daisy, the White Lily thrives on novelty, you know that as well as I, and quite simply, using a different girl is a business decision. And should the show fail—"

"It can't fail, Tom," Daisy interrupted firmly. "Which is why I want to be Venus. It's a marvelous idea, and The General is a gen…"

She stopped herself suddenly and swung about to face the mirror, completing a circle of rouge on one cheek, her fingers fussing in her hair, which trailed down over one shoulder.

"The General is what, Daisy?" Tom asked innocently.

"A jester looking for a court."

"Mmm. Odd, I could have sworn you were about to call him a 'genius.'"

"I would no sooner call that wee tyrant a genius than you'd turn Quaker, Tommy."

"Quaker is about the only thing I haven't been, Daisy. I'm thinking of giving it a go."

She smirked at him in the mirror. "Don't change the subject, Tommy. You know I'm perfect for the role of Venus."

Tom knew nothing of the sort. He looked at Daisy and tried to imagine a great oyster shell creaking open to reveal a plump pearl of a dyed redhead instead of the lithe creature Botticelli had painted and that he and The General envisioned. There was no getting around it, really. He couldn't allow it to happen. The fortunes of the theater depended greatly upon it; his own fortunes, and his dream of The Gentleman's Emporium rode greatly upon it.

And besides, he'd promised The General, who doubtless had something tastefully titillating in mind, and only a lithe girl would do.

"Daisy—" he began diplomatically.

"Now listen to me, ye beautiful sod." She whirled on him and wagged her hairbrush at him. Mother-of-pearl-handled, the thing was, had cost a small fortune, as had everything in this room, the plush pink furniture, the soft rugs, the grand gilt mirror, all to please her, to reward her. "Do I need to remind ye of the reason this theater stands 'ere at all?"

"Because I had the good sense to take advantage of your talents?" He gave her a winning smile.

She tried to scowl, but it was clear she couldn't quite force herself to do it in the face of that smile. So she sighed instead. "Come 'ere, Tommy, ye've a thread." She beckoned with a hand and he inched forward obediently; she reached out and wrapped a loose thread hanging from one of his coat buttons around her finger and gave it a yank to snap it. She smoothed his coat down with absent affection.

"Wouldn't want a thing to mar yer perfection now, now, would we, Tommy?" A faint tang of bitterness in her tone now.

He wasn't certain how to deal with this fear and bitterness and pride. He remained silent, and knew she would interpret his silence as sympathy, and would hate it. But Daisy had become a bit comfortable in her diva role, avoiding the other girls or treating them with coolness, arriving late for rehearsals, holding court like a buxom empress in these dressing rooms after the show. Tom was just as familiar with her origins as he was with his own; perhaps, he thought, this was her way of continuing to distance herself from her past, the way owning grand theaters and producing bawdy spectacles and accumulating money was his.

But *he'd* provided a place and the throne for Daisy to blossom into divahood. She'd never abandoned her gutter accent, nor even attempted it, the way he had buffed his own methodically out of existence through listening to gentlemen talk and imitating their inflections, learning their words phonetically, discovering through any means possible what the words meant. Swallowing pride and asking; charming people into teaching him to read. It simply hadn't been necessary for Daisy to make the effort when one possessed a bosom as unforgettable and profitable as hers.

"Ye'll get old, too, Tommy, ye bugger," she said softly. It wasn't an accusation or a threat; it was more like a plea. It made him desperately uncomfortable.

He decided to change the subject. "You'll never guess who I saw, Daisy. Biggsy Biggens."

"Biggsy!" Daisy's eyes widened in surprise. "Good Lord! Where'd yer see 'im? Swingin' 't the end of a rope?" She said it only half-jokingly.

"He was robbing the coach I was aboard, actually."

Daisy snorted. "A good 'eart, but precious little imagination, Biggsy always had. 'E'll come to a bad end yet."

"He asked after you, Daize."

"Yes, well, ye see, Tommy, because even after all of these years, I leave *quite* an impression." She addressed this to the mirror, but her eyes met and held Tom's, pride and defiance . . . and nervousness. He hated the nervousness; Daisy was a peacock, a diva, it was out of place. And it made him feel a cad; he slid his eyes casually away from hers, toward the brandy decanter, then decided he'd already had enough at his investor meeting.

"'E didna shoot ye, apparently? Biggsy?"

"I managed to persuade him not to, for the sake of old times. He required a kiss from one of our passengers, however, as the price of leaving with most of our belongings."

Daisy smiled at this. "I take back what I said about 'is imagination. Did 'e get one?"

Tom paused. "He did. Someone . . . volunteered." Tom saw the image in his mind, Sylvie's slim body, shoulders squared, standing on her toes to reach the highwayman's mouth, Biggsy's near-humble acceptance of the favor proffered, the awe and gratitude lighting the ugly man's face. Tom felt a sharp twinge of something, a pang of indefinable emotion, intriguing but uncomfortable.

Restlessness surged. This conversation with Daisy was taking too long; he decided it was time to be firm. "Daisy, I'd like another girl to play the part of Venus. I haven't decided who it should be. But I have also hired a new girl."

She looked up sharply. "Ye've 'ired a new girl? When?"

"Today."

"Does The General know?"

Ah, but Daisy was shrewd. Tom smiled faintly. "He does now."

Daisy thoughtfully regarded him in the mirror. "'Oo is this girl? She's the replacement for Kitty?"

"She's not a 'replacement' for anyone, Daisy," Tom said sharply. "She's the one from whom Biggsy extracted a kiss."

Daisy's mouth set; however, she looked reluctantly intrigued. "Ye took 'er on out o' pity? Seems unlikely, Tom." She said it dryly.

Tom knew a moment of pique; Daisy perhaps more than anyone had benefited from his pragmatism and good business sense, and he was not without a heart, and she knew it. He ascribed it to her wounded pride, and let it go, and knew the fact that he had let it go would hurt her pride even more. It could not be helped.

"I took her on an impulse." Somehow he thought she would find this a more acceptable answer. He smiled crookedly. "She also jabbed me with a knitting needle when I touched her arm."

Daisy gave a short, surprised laugh, a reluctant little sound. She was intrigued, too. "She's pretty?"

"No, I thought it would be a nice change of pace to hire a homely girl, Daisy."

She snorted at this. "Jus' makin' certain yer still possessed of yer faculties, Tommy. This girl..." She faltered momentarily. "Ye think she's yer Venus?"

Yes. Oh, yes. No. Perhaps.

"I haven't yet decided, Daisy."

"But ye've decided it willna be *me*."

"I'm glad you understand, Daisy," he said briskly.

He saw her jaw drop nearly to her collarbone as he left the

room, but wisely, she said nothing, having known Tom long enough to know when enough was enough.

❧

The General drilled them for three hours, and the seemingly tireless Josephine played the same several tunes again and again. It might have driven another person mad; but Sylvie understood the need for it, having danced over and over to the same tunes for much of her life, having repeated the same motions again and again until they were flawless.

The demands on her body were minor. The demands on her dignity, however, were rigorous.

The other girls did the dances cheerfully, or at least willingly enough, taking it on as matter-of-factly as pushing a broom about the floor, smiling, twirling, hopping, twitching hips, showing a saucy bit of ankle. But Sylvie would never, never, never become accustomed to throwing her derriere up in the air and singing out "whee!"

Molly even sang a bawdy song while the other girls sang a chorus behind her and suggestively wielded their wands— Sylvie now understood the eloquence of that particular prop— and patted their own behinds.

And then, to Sylvie's dismay, they turned to pat the behinds of the girls in front of them.

As it turned out, it was *her* destiny to pat Molly's comfortably plush behind. A rump like a pair of pillows, Molly had.

Good God.

Sylvie became adept rather quickly, as none of it really required the grace or precision of a *grand jeté,* and after the first hour The General only shouted at her once or twice per song. "Get it up there, Sylvie! And don't make that face when you pat Molly! She's a very fine arse! Consider it an honor!"

I can't grow an arse in only three hours, Sylvie felt like grousing to him. *This is all the arse I have.*

Good God. Only three hours and she already sounded like an English street urchin in her thoughts. What sort of word was *"arse"*?

Sylvie had begun to see spots before her eyes from hunger, when rehearsal came to a close with a hearty "Thank you, ladies!" from The General.

The girls drifted away, down the stairs of the stage, filing toward their dressing room to change from fairies into girls again. Sylvie hovered, wondering whether she should follow, then looked up at a touch on her arm. It was Josephine, a bit red-faced and mussed from her energetic turn at the keyboard.

"Mr. Shaughnessy asked me to see to ye, Sylvie, and I think we need to get some food into ye now—ye've gone right peaky. Come wi' me."

She followed Josephine through a narrow corridor, past the dressing room where giggles and squeals came from behind the door, and it occurred to Sylvie that perhaps she should change out of her big fairy dress and put her wand away, and she almost felt excluded from the merriment. She wondered if they would receive her more warmly now that she'd bent and patted derrieres all afternoon.

But then, even in Paris, her status as Prima Ballerina set her apart from the other girls, and there were those who fawned and wanted to be her, and those who plotted and were cold and wanted to be her, or those who were overtly jealous and wanted to be her.

It left her rather as she had been in the mail coach today, with an invisible wall of sorts about her.

She reached her hand up to cover her heart, touched

the miniature of her mother lightly through her fairy dress.
Thought of Susannah, Lady Grantham. *Perhaps this is someone with whom I belong.* She wondered how she would go about
learning when or how Susannah had returned from France.

Josephine saw her glance at the dressing-room door. "Food
first, I think, m'dear. Mr. Shaughnessy willna be pleased if ye faint
away, like. Sets a bad example fer the other girls." She smiled to
show she was teasing. "And I'll show you where ye'll be sleeping."

They traveled the corridor; behind a set of wide doors, much
like those that opened onto a ballroom, Sylvie heard the sounds
of hammers and saws; something dropped with a deafening
clatter, someone swore colorfully, a string of English phrases.
She could have sworn it was The General.

"They're building sets," Josephine confided in a low voice.
"For Venus." She said the word "Venus" with a hushed sort of
reverence.

What on earth was *Venus*?

❧

Josephine took Sylvie up a steep flight of stairs, like the servants' passage, to another corridor lined with rooms, long
and narrow, lit by a small window at the far end; candles were
tucked into simple sconces along the walls. The wicks were
cleanly trimmed; none of them seemed to have been lit recently.

"The White Lily was a bit of a wreck when Mr. Shaughnessy bought it. Turned it into a right beautiful theater," Josephine said as proudly as if he was her own son.

She stopped at the third door from the left in the corridor.
"'Ere's your room, luv. The girls usually take dinner on their own
before the show. We'd the 'ousekeeper bring up summat t' eat."

On the little dressing table Sylvie saw a tray covered by

a cloth; she tentatively plucked at the corner of the cloth and peeked beneath, afraid of the English food she might find. She discovered thickly sliced brown bread, and a yeasty scent still rose from it, so no doubt it was somewhat fresh. Feeling more confident now, she tugged the cloth all the way off and saw slices of cheese—she was a bit worried about English cheese, too, but this was pungent and sharp-smelling and sliced in generous slabs, at least; there were two small rosy apples and a few slices of what appeared to be cold breast of fowl roasted in herbs, if the golden, crusty edge of the meat was any indication. She tugged at a roll of white linen; it proved to be a napkin, and a shiny knife and fork tumbled out. A tiny pot of tea and a cup and saucer completed the setting.

Hunger suddenly took Sylvie so violently her stomach nearly turned in upon itself, and she almost retched. She realized she hadn't slept for nearly a day. And suddenly she was thoroughly weary, so weary she didn't think she could form a sentence or do anything besides satisfy the needs of her body.

She looked around the little room and saw a rectangle of a hooked rug on the swept wood floor, a narrow iron bed made up with white sheets and a coverlet was pushed against the wall, a blue blanket was folded into a rectangle at the foot of it, and at the head two snowy pillows looked almost obscenely plump and welcoming. A wooden stand in the corner held a pitcher and a washbasin. There was no window or fireplace, but there was a small dressing table, and a small oval of a mirror hanging from a ribbon looped over a nail.

It was nothing at all like Claude's small, dark, cluttered apartments in Paris. And it was a world—or at least a continent—away from what she knew her life with Etienne would be, gilded, marbled, gleaming, vast. But something about its size and clean simplicity was soothing in the way she imagined a nun's cell might seem soothing.

And this thought made her nearly laugh aloud. Hunger was making her delusional. Thanks to Etienne, she was most certainly not a nun.

"Chamber pot under the bed," Josephine said matter-of-factly. "Come down to the kitchen later, if ye like. Mrs. Pool is making a tart. Just follow the smell down the stairs. There's some what live 'ere, at the theater. Meself and the 'ousekeeper, Mrs. Pool, and the maids, and there's Mr. Shaughnessy—"

"Mr. Shaughnessy lives here? At the theater?" This surprised Sylvie. She thought for certain he'd have a suite of rooms of his own in London, or a grand town house, rooms as glittering as his appearance.

But then again, she'd met the man in a mail coach. Perhaps his budget was apportioned to silver buttons on his coat.

"Mr. Shaughnessy is a practical man," Josephine said approvingly. "'E lives where 'e works. 'E knows the meaning of economy."

But not, Sylvie thought, *the meaning of restraint.* It was an interesting juxtaposition.

"The General, 'e 'as rooms in town," Josephine volunteered. "And if ye've skill wi' a needle, Sylvie, I've need of some 'elp wi' the costumes for all of it, so when ye're not rehearsin' . . ." Josephine looked hopeful. "It's Mr. Shaughnessy, ye see, and 'is ideas. Always wi' the ideas, and 'e always wants 'em straightaway. So we can sew in the mornings, rehearse in the afternoon, and do a show at night."

Sylvie wondered whether she would be offered any additional money for sewing, then wondered what on earth she might do with the rest of her time here at the White Lily, and decided she might as well sew. She found herself nodding, agreeing.

"*Quelle heure*—" she began, in her fatigue finding the

French words easier to recall than the English. "That is, what is the time now, Josephine, please?"

"Why, time for you to eat m'dear. I'll come and fetch ye before the show, about eight o'clock."

"For the show?" To watch?

"Ye'll be in the show tonight, me dear. Mr. Shaughnessy *did* 'ire ye for that reason. We'll pin yer dress t' fit and alter it tomorrow. The work never ends 'ere a' the White Lily."

She smiled and closed the door, leaving Sylvie to her little feast.

Sylvie was torn between the attractive little heap of food and the soft heap of pillows on the bed.

A moment later, she dived into the food, ignoring the fork, making little shameless moaning sounds as the savory meat and cheese and bread met her tongue. She swallowed, felt it fill her stomach, began to feel human again.

And it probably wasn't wise to sleep on a full stomach, but her body was giving her no choice. She dabbed the corners of her mouth with the napkin and sank backward onto the bed, shifted up until her head found the pillows, sighed, and slept.

Chapter Seven

❧

The tap on the door woke Sylvie with a start, and when she shifted a bit, she realized she was still in her fairy dress, and her legs were tangled in its folds. She gave a few little kicks to free herself; she rolled sleepily over and blinked: A wooden wand was on the pillow next to her.

Ah, so it hadn't been a nightmare induced by coaching inn food, then.

"Sylvie? Time to prepare for the show, m'dear." Josephine's cheery voice came through the door.

Sylvie snatched up her wand, rolled over, fighting a bit with her dress in the attempt, and went for the door.

Josephine eyed her with critical concern.

"Well, there's rouge," she finally said, resignedly, as though the rest of it could not be helped. "And we'll pin yer dress, like, and yer 'air will be down. Ye'll be pretty enough." She sounded as though she'd cheered herself some, if not Sylvie. "Come along wi' me, then."

And so Josephine led Sylvie from her little nun's room back
to what surely must be the opposite of little nun's rooms
everywhere—the dressing room full of buxom girls, giggling
in their shifts, rummaging through cupboards for props and
costumes, exclaiming over the shiny gifts sent by admirers that
littered the little dressing tables. The lamplight burnished their
bare arms pale gold and gleamed on glossy hair and fairy wings.

Lizzie held up a pair of earbobs for all to admire.

"Ooo! Garnets, Lizzie!" Molly peered at them expertly.
"They're meant to dangle."

"Like the bloke 'oo sent 'em," Lizzie said sadly. "'E does
naught but dangle, no matter *wot* I do." She demonstrated by
holding her fairy wand perpendicular to her body for an instant,
then dropping it sadly so that the star pointed at the floor.

An explosion of wicked giggles followed.

And then Molly opened a box and went very still.

"What d'yer 'ave there, Molly?" Lizzie asked.

Molly lifted up a painted ivory-and-silk fan, an exquisite
and nearly excruciatingly tasteful thing and probably worth a
dozen pairs of garnet earrings in cost. She held it almost gingerly. Instantly everyone hovered about her to gasp over it.

"New bloke," Molly said shortly She was reaching for nonchalance but fell short of the mark. "'E asked Poe to send it
in to the... loveliest... girl 'ere." She faltered over the adjec-
tive as though it was not a word she typically included in her
vocabulary, as though she wasn't certain she had a right to it.
But triumph edged her voice. Perhaps it was confirmation of
something she'd long suspected.

Even from the doorway Sylvie could see the fan was a
remarkable little thing. Almost... pointedly singular. A gift

calculated to intrigue and flatter and disarm, and these three things were the first step in seduction, she knew. A wealthy man might send in jewels to a girl such as Molly—Sylvie had been sent more than her share of jewels by admirers—but only a man of breeding and intelligence would have chosen this strategic little fan. Sylvie knew this, because it rather reminded her of the sort of gifts Etienne had sent to her when his wooing had begun. Fine little glittering snowflakes of gifts, which had gradually accustomed her to his attentions, then eased her into expecting them.

Sylvie suddenly felt a peculiar weight in her chest, as though a hand pressed there, limiting her breath. She inhaled deeply, then exhaled, just to prove to herself that she could do it.

Perhaps it was simply because it had been days since she'd danced, days since she'd felt that delicious hard hammering of her heart in her chest from the exertion of it, since she'd worked until a fine sheen of sweat coated her exhausted, exhilarated body. She suspected her body craved the stretch and release of it.

She wondered, a little desperately, when she would have an opportunity to dance again. Ballet, that was. Not... well, whatever it was they did here at the White Lily.

"'Ave ye seen 'im, Molly? Yer new bloke. 'Is 'e 'andsome?" Lizzie asked eagerly.

"I'll know if 'e's 'andsome tonight after the show," Molly said slyly. "'E'll send a carriage fer me after the show. Po told me 'e would."

"Ye've so many admirers," Rose said somewhat resignedly, but without obvious rancor. "'Ope *yer* new one doesna... dangle."

More giggles.

"Willna Belstow and Lassiter and all of the rest of yer admirers be jealous, now, Molly?"

Molly shrugged with one shoulder. "I told Belstow I canna

give 'im more of the time until 'e 'as more of his papa's money, and what Lassiter doesna know willna trouble 'im." She hadn't moved her eyes from the fan.

Molly at last looked up from the fan then and noticed Sylvie and Josephine in the doorway. "Miss Chicken 'as arrived," she said grandly.

"Oh, ye're to be a fairy as soon as tonight, then, Sylvie?" Rose's voice was mildly pleased. "Perhaps ye'll learn to be a damsel tomorrow."

"D'yer really kiss an 'ighwayman, Sylvie?" Jenny, big-eyed, wanted to know. "Rosie said ye did."

"I did," Sylvie confirmed. "He wanted a kiss in exchange for not robbing our coach. And so I kissed him."

"*Ooooh!*" Awed attention swiveled toward Sylvie. But Molly's chestnut head had turned away and was now fixed on a mirror. She was smoothing rouge onto a fair cheek, desperately trying not to look interested.

Sylvie shrugged nonchalantly. She deliberately omitted, "and then the highwayman took all my money and the letter from my sister, forcing me to cast my lot in with the lot of you." She thought perhaps remaining enigmatic might be useful. She shifted her wand into her other hand as Josephine reached beneath her arm.

"Be still now, Sylvie, whilst I pin yer dress." Josephine's mouth was bristling with pins; her large deft hands were plucking at Sylvie's skirt, pinning it closer to her body.

Sylvie dutifully remained motionless until Josephine nudged her this way and that to reach other parts of her dress.

"An' so Mr. Shaughnessy 'ired ye because ye were brave?" Lizzie wanted to know.

Oddly, Sylvie was a little insulted. *No, because I am beautiful.*

But why *did* he hire her? Surely that *was* the reason.

"I do not know," she answered, more or less honestly. With another inscrutable little French shrug. "I needed to work."

"No shrugging," Josephine ordered, plucking a pin from her mouth and poking it into the dress.

And then the door burst open, flinging hard against the wall. The girls shrieked and jumped.

A man stood there: young, handsome but already going to fat, red in the face with fury, breathing as though he'd run for miles. His fists were balled and white with tension, and they were raised, poised to launch.

Sylvie knew danger when she saw it. Her heart raced into her throat. "Get help," she mouthed to Lizzie, who was closest to the door.

Lizzie sidled against the wall behind him and bolted out of the room.

His head swiveled, found Molly. "You," he said flatly, contemptuously. He snatched at the bodice of her dress with one hand and yanked her out of her chair. "Who is he?" he demanded.

"Belstow, I—"

"Tell me who he is!" the man snarled. "Who are you giving your favors to now, you little whore?"

And then, to Sylvie's horror, he struck Molly with the flat of his hand across the face.

A horrible sound, that smack of flesh. Molly cried out.

And when the man lifted his hand over Molly again, Sylvie lunged for him.

❧

Before every performance, while the girls dressed for the show, Tom and The General convened to discuss the particulars of the White Lily's business, and the room they did it in was a snug male fantasy of comfort. Plush chairs sprawled about a hearth like a pride of lazy, sated beasts, and the crackling fire threw light up onto vivid murals, smaller, slightly more lurid versions of the ones that decorated the interior of the theater: satyrs and nymphs, gods and goddesses cavorted in the leaping light of the flames. Ever since he'd learned to read, Tom had loved the unabashed, joyous carnality of Greek myths, the violence and playfulness, the magic and the lessons in them.

There was one character from mythology, however, who never made it up onto the murals: Chiron, the wounded healer. Not an erotic character, Chiron. He lived with pain every day and grew the wiser for it. A teacher, Chiron was. Noble cove.

Tom knew *he* was not a noble cove, and doubted he ever would be. This knowledge did not cost him sleep.

Tom fished a little moon of gold from his pocket, snapped it open, reviewed the time. He could hear through the walls the low cheerful rumble of the gathering crowd of men who nightly enjoyed the entertainments he provided. It was one of his favorite sounds, along with the jingle of shillings and the sounds a woman made in the throes of pleasure.

A pleasant hitch of breath accompanied that last thought, which led to thoughts of one woman in particular. "So how did the new girl fare today, Gen?"

The General pulled a cigar from his mouth and admired the glowing tip. "She has no arse, she's proud and impudent, and I do believe half the girls are wildly jealous of her, thanks to you, and the way you just foisted her upon our cozy little group. How did you think she'd fare, Tom?"

Tom grinned, relishing the description. "But can she dance?"

"She'll do," The General growled.

"Good, then. I'll have a look myself tomorrow, during rehearsals."

"And you . . . broke the news to Daisy about Venus?" The General ventured gingerly.

"Yes," Tom said grimly.

"I expect she took it gracefully?" More stock-in-trade irony from The General.

"Would you *ever* describe Daisy as graceful, Gen?"

There was a curious pause. The General turned away from Tom and studied his cigar again, as though the answer to this question could be found there. "Not the first word that comes to mind," The General finally allowed. Tom would have sworn the words were almost wistful.

Tom studied his friend in bemusement for a moment, frowning slightly.

"I've already had notes from the Major and Lord Cambry. They're in. They want to be a part of The Gentleman's Emporium." His voice was quiet, but triumph infused every note of it.

"Mmm." The General made a little sound of appreciation. "Do you need the whole of that group involved before you go forward with it?"

"If I get at least commitments from all of them this week, I'll buy the property with the capital I have and sign agreements with the builders. You're in, Gen?"

"You need to ask? I want my share in this, too, Tommy. You've all but guaranteed me a prosperous dotage."

"Can you see it now? We'll have—"

Sudden frantic pounding on the door had Tom on his feet in an instant. He flung the door open.

Lizzie stood before him, wild-eyed, breathing hard. "The dressing room—Molly—Mr. Belstow—ye best come—*oh please*—"

Tom took in the scene in the dressing room with a glance: Molly, one arm raised to shield her face; four other girls in various stages of undress cowering in the corner; Belstow standing over Molly, arm lifted, either to protect himself or to strike again.

And next to Belstow Sylvie Chapeau, a starless shard of a wooden wand in her hand, hand raised as if to administer another blow.

Quickly and gently, Tom closed his hand over Sylvie's other arm and tugged her behind him, keeping his fingers closed around her. She resisted him a little, almost reflexively, still bristling with her own anger.

"Where would you like it, Mr. Belstow?" Tom's voice was low and taut. Deceptively polite.

Belstow whirled, startled, frowned in surprise; his hand froze midair.

" 'It'?" he repeated. And for a moment, the bastard looked almost hopeful. As though Tom had come bearing a selection of gifts.

"The knife," Tom clarified slowly. An almost cheery deadliness in his voice. "Through your gullet, across your throat, perhaps . . . ?" Tom gestured casually to his own throat, then swept his coat back idly, just a little, as though it was merely in his way.

Everyone saw the knife tucked there in its sheath at the top of his trousers.

Belstow's face spasmed in disbelief. "You wouldn't *dare*, Shaughnessy. I caught this little whore with another—"

Tom's hand snapped out and seized a fistful of Belstow's shirt and cravat, yanking it taut as a noose, pulling him to the balls of his feet. Belstow teetered on his toes within inches of Tom's face.

"Test me." Tom measured each word out tonelessly, as

though nothing in his life had ever bored him more than the man dangling from his fist.

Tom held him a moment longer, allowing the message in his eyes to penetrate fully.

When Belstow's face went ashen, Tom knew he'd succeeded.

He released him abruptly.

Belstow dropped to his knees, his legs too weak to hold him. And then everyone watched, and no one helped, as Belstow struggled awkwardly, shakily to his feet. He rubbed at his throat.

"When my father hears of this, Shaughnessy—"

"I know your father, Mr. Belstow. I assure you, when I tell him what you've done, you'll be sorry I didn't gut you. I wonder if your father approves of hitting women?"

It was a bluff. Tom didn't know the senior Mr. Belstow from Adam, really; he'd seen him but twice at the theater. But he struck him as a good sort, and Tom's instincts along these lines were typically sharp enough.

His instincts were borne out. Belstow's ashen face took on a lovely undertone of green. Ah. Most weak young men *were* afraid of their fathers.

"I don't think I need to tell you that you're no longer welcome here," Tom added politely. "And I'll leave you to imagine what might happen to you if you *do* choose to show your face here again. Can you leave under your own locomotion, Mr. Belstow, or will you require further assistance?" Tom was all mock solicitousness now.

Belstow's mouth opened and closed. He glared at Tom in quiet fury for another moment.

Tom met his gaze unblinkingly.

Belstow turned, unable to hold the gaze. A moment later, he turned and stalked out the door, without saying another word.

Tom turned and kicked the door closed behind the man.

Breathed in and out, letting air sift through the rage that made it difficult to breathe. He was aware of how quiet the little room was, the way the chatter of birds ceases when a cat is spotted.

Tom turned to Molly. "There now," he said softly. "Come, show it to me."

Molly raised her head up tentatively, keeping one hand shaded over her eye, ashamed, still trembling. Tom gently lifted her hand, and beneath it, her eye was red. It could very well turn a panoply of colors over the next few days. He'd seen enough—too many—blackened eyes on both men and women over the years.

"I...I need the work, Mr. Shaughnessy."

Molly's voice shook, and for good reason. She knew Tom couldn't put a bruised girl onstage—bad for business. She also knew dozens of pretty girls clamored for a job like hers, a job that paid enough for a decent room and clothes and opportunities to meet dozens of wealthy admirers, and required little more of her than following instructions and a willingness to dress in what amounted to little more than her shift.

She was as replaceable as the lamps that lit the room.

Tom looked down at Molly. He still felt the spiky heat of rage on his skin. Diplomacy with Belstow would no doubt have been wiser—he was wealthy, Belstow, in his own right, and connected through that fine webbing of connections the wealthy and privileged enjoyed, and Tom knew both the value and danger of connections.

But he despised cowards who hit women. He'd seen much of that sort of misery when he'd lived in the rookeries, fury and violence brewed by gin and hopelessness. And in the rookeries, one could almost comprehend the source.

But again—Belstow was privileged and wealthy.

Tom felt one of his hands curl into a fist.

"How did he get back here?" he asked everyone in the room curtly. "Where's Jack? Why wasn't he watching the door?"

Silence.

And Tom knew defeat. Knew Jack had probably found the lure of gin more appealing than the lure of a few more bob from Tom Shaughnessy and had left his post for that reason.

Tom didn't look at The General. His own guilt was strong enough without seeing it reflected in The General's face.

Tom dropped his hand from Molly's face, took a deep breath. He supposed there was something to be said for learning sense and caution and judgment the hard way; it was the way he'd learned the most valuable lessons in his own life. Still, the beauty of the White Lily was that Tom had been able to protect any number of people from learning things the hard way, or from learning any more lessons than necessary.

And then suddenly, looking down at Molly, inspiration struck, which was the capricious way of inspiration in general.

"Well, the news is not all bad, Molly. We've decided to introduce a…piratical theme into the show next week. The General will build a ship and we'll have a pirate dance, a song or two. We'll have you in an eye patch if your eye shows a bruise. I wager you'll make a pretty pirate, eh?"

Tom didn't dare look at The General, who would now be required to build some sort of pirate ship and create a dance involving scantily clad female pirates inside a week.

Molly sniffed and gave a tentative little laugh, comforted by the note of flirtation. All around him, he could see shoulders dropping in relief, as the other girls could feel Tom restoring things to order.

But…well, now that Tom thought about it…cutlasses and female pirates…

It was still more genius, frankly. And precisely what they needed to keep the audiences satisfied while the grand work of Venus was under way.

At this conclusion, Tom risked a sideways glance at The General.

The General was glaring incredulous daggers at him.

"Th-thank you, Mr. Shaughnessy." Molly was calmer now.

He looked back at Sylvie. She still held a pointed shard of a wand; he saw the star that belonged on top of it, fallen, severed from its stem, shining on the floor at her feet. She was just as pale as the other girls, but with a difference: Two spots of hectic color sat high on her cheeks, and her eyes were glittery as jewels.

She was furious.

"Every time I see you there's something pointed in your hand," he said to her softly. A jest to ease her temper. She was such a fierce little thing.

And she did smile a little at that. She took her own deep breath.

"Did you hit him?" Tom asked her, gently.

"Not hard enough," she told him fervently.

He couldn't help but smile. "Will he have a bruise in the shape of a star?"

"I hope so."

And then a thought occurred to him. "Did he touch you?" He said it curtly.

"'T'was just a push."

He looked down at her, small and slight; she would come to Belstow's shoulder, and felt a cold kernel of horror in the pit of his gut when he thought of what might have happened to her or to Molly had he not entered the room. She would not retreat, this one, whether or not it was sensible. Her response had been to leap into the fray rather than cower, sensibly, away from it.

Emotion always lit her eyes, he'd noticed during their short acquaintance. She might remain circumspect about the details of her life, but her eyes gave away the woman inside her, what she felt, and they were still hot with a righteous anger. Her hair was unbound, and a few strands of it clung to her flushed face, the rest spilling over her slim shoulders, and she was pinned into her fairy dress. The pale blush color of it suited the high color in her cheeks.

All rose and fire, softness and heat. His fingers gave a little twitch at his side. Having once touched her skin, it seemed they wanted to know if her hair could compete for fineness.

And yet here he stood in a room surrounded by visions of softness.

"He just . . . hit her." Sylvie said it with a sort of helpless, wondering fury. Quietly. As though the words were only for him.

"I know," Tom said gently. "I won't allow it to ever happen again."

He realized then he'd been looking into her eyes, and she'd been looking back for quite some time, and he jerked his head up. The rest of the girls were watching him, their own faces pale, pinched with worry, waiting to hear what he wanted them to do next, trusting him to take care of them as he always had.

Odd for an instant, a dizzying instant, he'd all but forgotten anyone else was in the room.

"'E would 'ave 'it Molly again, Mr. Shaughnessy, but Sylvie came at 'im wi' 'er wand," Rose informed him proudly. Doing her part to build Sylvie's legend. "And then ye came into the room."

Tom released Sylvie's arm.

"Cool water and a rag for the eye, a little brandy for the nerves, Molly. Poe and Stark or someone else will watch the door at all hours from now on. Sylvie, you can take her to our room in the back; get her settled, then come back and finish dressing. Do you think you can dance tonight?"

"Yes," Molly told him quickly.

He glanced at Sylvie, whose face had darkened somewhat. She was watching him strangely. Almost in reproach.

"As for the rest of you . . . come now, we've a show to do." He made it a cheery command. "Don't sit about staring. Where are your wings, girls? Get them on!"

The best way to return everything to normal was to make everything appear as though it had never been anything but normal, he knew.

Happy to be told what to do, everyone scrambled into their wings, plucked up their wands, and prepared to file to the back of the stage.

Chapter Eight

❦

Minutes later, Sylvie was standing backstage in a darkened theater pinned into a gossamer dress, holding a hastily-mended wooden fairy wand in preparation for patting the fannies of similarly dressed girls. All while a great crowd of enthusiastic men looked on. All in the name of a temporary roof over her head.

She teetered between a moment of panic and ironic humor. Her entire life she'd worked to ensure her life was nothing like Claude's, and yet here she was all the same. As though having been raised by an opera dancer, vulgar performance was a drain toward which she must inevitably flow.

She knew another brief moment of dizzying unreality: Everything in her life to date had been planned so carefully. And once Monsieur Favre had discovered a spark of talent in plain Claude Lamoreux's beautiful little girl, Sylvie had given herself to the dance entirely, knowing, perhaps, it was her only chance to be anything other than ordinary. And as she danced, she told herself that every *grand jeté*, every pirouette, every precise and stinging criticism from Monsieur Favre took her further away from sharing the same ultimate fate as Claude Lamoreux: poor, lonely, struggling, with scarcely the energy to be properly bitter. Dance had given Sylvie purpose, and then fame…and then Etienne. And every bit of this had been planned.

This—this cheerful audience at the White Lily, the patting of derrieres—was clearly her reward for a moment of rashness.

But there was still something about the sound of a theater before a performance, regardless of the *nature* of the performance that thrilled her blood. The excited murmur of voices, the squeak of chairs as people shifted their bodies into them, the dimming of lamps, all fed her anticipation, and she couldn't find it within herself to dread it totally. Odd to think it had been nearly two weeks now since she'd danced for an audience. She knew a whimsical urge to *grand jeté* out onto the stage, which no doubt this particular audience would find more shocking than any song about baubles.

And then she simply longed, wistfully, to do anything at all that resembled ballet. She wondered how long it would be before she could dance—truly dance—again.

She peeped out from behind the curtain. A group of other musicians, a violinist, a cellist and, startlingly, someone who appeared to be holding a trumpet that winked a regal gold in the theater lights, had joined Josephine, who sat at the pianoforte, dressed for the occasion in scarlet velvet exposing a grand expanse of chest. Sylvie glanced up, toward those exclusive boxes; she saw the curtains enclosing one of them sway a bit, and knew an extremely wealthy man had come for an evening's entertainment, too. Perhaps Molly's new admirer.

At the top of the aisle near the theater entrance, so close to where she stood onstage she could almost touch them, stood Tom and The General, for all the world like a pair of vivid dukes receiving ball guests. They were dressed in brilliantly striped waistcoats and billowing cravats, and the silver buttons on Tom's coat glinted, bright as a row of eyes inspecting the arriving patrons. Together they were a tableau: Sylvie might have called them *Elegantly Tall and Elegantly Small*.

The audience entered through the wide doors near the stage, then proceeded to their seats. Sylvie took up a nook behind the curtain and watched, listened as Tom warmly greeted nearly every man by name as if he hadn't just threatened to gut someone in a dressing room.

"Good evening, Mr. Pettigrew." Pettigrew: medium build, large comfortable stomach preceding him into the room, conservative evening clothes. *No doubt his wife chooses them,* Sylvie thought. *Wonder if she knows where he is this evening?*

"Shaughnessy, my good man! Sorry I've been away for a few days. My wife insisted upon being entertained as well, and so I've endured a few sopranos for her sake. What do you have for us this evening?"

"If I told you what I had in store for you, Pettigrew, it wouldn't be a surprise then, would it? Don't you care for surprises?" Tom feigned shock.

"I like surprises of the sort *you* provide, Shaughnessy, of course! Those are my very favorite. Very well, I shall prepare to be surprised, then."

"...and the flowers are for?" Pettigrew was holding a paper-wrapped bouquet of vibrant blooms, fresh from a hothouse, from the looks of things. Tom took them.

The man looked a little bashful. "Rose. You'll put in a good word for me, Shaughnessy?" he asked anxiously.

"Of course I'll put in a good word for you," Tom assured Mr. Pettigrew, who, his face now relaxed and lit with hope, went on to find his seat. Tom handed the roses to The General, who handed them to a boy whose job it was to scurry away with the bouquets and bring them to the dressing room to vie for attention with all the other flowers.

Tom waited until Pettigrew was several feet away. "...for him, and for Johnstone, and Mortimer, and Carrick, and Bond, and..." he said to The General.

"Lassiter, too, I think," The General added. "I think you promised to put in a good word for Lassiter."

"I believe Lassiter has transferred his affections to Molly," Tom mused.

"Ah," The General said, as if making a note of it. "I believe Molly is now firmly in the lead in terms of 'good words,' then. Perhaps even beyond Daisy now."

Sylvie turned and whispered to Rose. "You've an admirer. A Mr. Pettigrew. He brought flowers."

"Oh, I've lots of admirers," Rose replied in her own whisper, without a trace of conceit. "But nothing like what Molly 'as."

Molly's eyes caught Sylvie's. She tossed her head and turned away.

She seemed a bit subdued. She hadn't thanked Sylvie for coming to her defense, but perhaps she felt ashamed; no doubt her pride was a bit singed. Sylvie contemplated asking her whether she felt equal to dancing, whether her eye was aching, and then decided Molly wouldn't welcome the question.

Sylvie jerked her head back toward Tom when she heard a bit of a commotion. She peered out, riveted.

A handsome young man, wild-eyed and blond and young enough to have a red spot on his chin, had planted himself in front of Tom and was shouting up at him.

"Name your seconds, Shaughnessy!"

"Now, Tammany—"

"It's my *wife*, damn you, Shaughnessy! My wife! She called your name out in a...in a..." Tammany faltered and lowered his voice almost to a mumble. "...certain moment."

The faltering and mumbling unfortunately rather diminished the injured gravity of his outburst.

"She called out . . . 'Tom Shaughnessy' . . . in a certain moment?" Tom sounded genuinely puzzled. "It seems rather a lot to get out in that *particular* moment. And there are quite a few Toms in the world, are there not?" He turned to The General for confirmation.

"At least a dozen," The General confirmed solemnly.

"She cried out *'Tom!'* " young Tammany clarified indignantly. " '*Tom,*' I tell you! More specifically, '*Oh,* Tom!' I knew it was you she meant. She cannot stop *talking* about you. Thinks you're the most charming bugger this side of . . . of . . . *Byron.* What have you *done* to her? I demand satisfaction!"

There was a pause.

"Have I met his wife?" Tom lowered his voice and said this to The General.

"*Yes,* you damned scoundrel!" Tammany bellowed. Tom winced. "At the shop that sells wooden toys on Bond Street just last week. You met the two of us, and bowed, and said something—"

"Very well." Tom became quickly, resignedly matter-of-fact. "If it means that much to you, The General here will act as one of my seconds as usual and shall we meet—well, why don't we meet at dawn, two days hence? I'll shoot you, and then I suppose I'll console your wife as a favor to you, as she'll no doubt miss you when you're dead. As will I, as you're one of my best patrons, Tammany. One of my very favorites, and truly, I do not exaggerate. Meanwhile, why I would be honored if you took a seat and enjoyed our show one last time. In remembrance of the former warmth of our friendship."

Tom smiled, managing to make it look both warm and gently regretful.

Sylvie, from where she watched through the curtains, put

a hand over her mouth in awe. It was frankly an astonishing performance.

Tammany suddenly looked a little less certain about his grievance. "You can just *apologize,* Shaughnessy, and be done with it," he said huffily.

"I would apologize, Mr. Tammany," Tom said gently, "if I thought I'd done anything requiring an apology."

It struck Sylvie that Tom might be genuinely amused by all of this. There wasn't a shred of fear in his expression, or bearing. He didn't even appear to feel threatened.

Such light talk about shooting one another. She gave an involuntary little shudder. She remembered Rose's words, *Best shot in London.*

Tammany simply glared at Tom, beyond words. And practical considerations—Tom's reputedly extraordinary aim among them—were clearly warring with his pride.

Bateson, the man Tom had deliberately missed just a night earlier, chose that moment to come strolling up the aisle, refreshments in hand, oblivious to the drama taking place.

"Tammany, my good man. You really must ask Mr. Shaughnessy for some pointers at Manton's. He can shoot the heart right out of a target every time!" he volunteered cheerfully. "He's giving me lessons!" He playfully pointed his thumb and forefinger at Tom and strolled on by, and Tom did likewise.

"Boom!" Tom said cheerfully.

"Bateson pulls left," Tom explained solemnly to Tammany. "I nearly shot him last night." Tammany had gone several shades paler. The red spot on his chin now glowed indignantly.

"It's a good show tonight, truly, and we've a new girl. You might wish to cheer her on," Tom coaxed. "She's very pretty, but a bit meek."

Sylvie could have sworn this was for her benefit. She thought she saw Tom Shaughnessy's mouth twitch a little, subtly, as if he knew very well she was listening.

Tammany did some more glaring, but it became less focused as the crowd milled around them, mindless of the little drama, or used to it. Men greeted each other with cheerful familiarity.

"Ho, Tammany!" someone called, and gave a cheery little wave. "Ho, Shaughnessy!"

Tammany managed to curl his lip in response to the greeting.

"Oh, *come* now, Tammany. We've got the girls as fairies tonight," Tom added by way of persuasion. "I know you like the fairies. And you'll *never* believe what we'll have in a week or so."

Tammany glared at him for another few moments, but Tom refused to be anything other than cheerful. So the glare had no place to lock, and thus deprived Tammany of fuel for his ire.

Tammany spun on his heel and stalked up the aisle toward the seats.

Then stopped abruptly, spun about, and stalked back to Tom. "*What* are you having next week?"

Tom dropped an arm over Tammany's shoulder and said it low, making it seem a confidence meant just for Tammany. *"Pirates."*

Tammany's eyes went wide, then slowly glazed with anticipated pleasures. "And Daisy?" Tammany asked, sounding as though he hardly dared hope.

"Captain of the ship," Tom confirmed with a grin.

Tammany's face finally softened and brightened into a blazing grin. "How do you *think* of these things, Shaughnessy?"

Tom shrugged modestly.

And Tammany, whose stride was now considerably less belligerent—it in fact, had a bit of a spring to it—made his way to a seat.

"Don't worry, Gen. He'll want to be alive for the pirates. See? Now aren't you glad I thought of them?"

The General ignored this. "What did you do to his wife, Tom?"

"Hmmm. I honestly don't know. I believe I merely smiled, and she . . ."

"There's no 'merely' about how you smile at women, Tom. There never is."

Tom smiled at this, remembering. "She *was* pretty, now that I recall. And I rarely do more than smile at actual wives. That's why God invented the Velvet Glove."

"I'm not certain it was *God* who invented the Velvet Glove, Tom."

"Mmmm. If not, his name is certainly *invoked* often enough there."

"What is the Velvet Glove?" Sylvie turned to ask Rose in a whisper.

"Brothel," was Rose's laconic reply.

Sylvie nearly sucked in a breath, torn between horror and hilarity.

"You're going to get yourself killed one day, Tom, if you keep toying with these hotheaded lads."

"Can I help it if I'm obliged to defend my honor?" Tom feigned injury.

"If I'm not mistaken, you believe honor is a notion for the rich and bored."

"Oh, it is. I've no use for it. Survival seldom has anything to do with honor. But I consider it my mission in life to entertain the rich and bored."

The General sighed. "Here's another question, Tom: What were you doing in a shop that sells wooden toys?"

"Tammany was mistaken about that bit," Tom said absently. "I must have been introduced to her elsewhere."

The General was silent, but his skepticism was nearly deafening.

"Like church?" he finally said.

"I didn't touch her, Gen, I swear it." Tom sounded defensive.

"Some men settle down with *just one* woman," The General said meaningfully. "They settle down, and they don't continually smile at other people's wives, or get into duels."

"How selfish of you, Gen. I know you think only of your own peace of mind when you say that, and not my happiness." Tom flipped open his watch. "It's time for the show."

A few minutes later, in front of a crowd of enthusiastic men, Sylvie Lamoreux linked arms with a half dozen pretty girls, bent over, thrust her bottom into the air and shouted "whee!"

It was over quickly enough, thankfully. Though no doubt she'd relive it again and again, the way one was haunted by bad meals.

And the response to the show—which, Rose and the other girls had assured her they had already performed dozens of times before—was so warm, appreciative, and boisterous that Sylvie began to wonder why she worked so hard to perfect her own art when it was clearly much easier to please an audience— an audience of men, at least—than she'd ever dreamed.

Though of course pleasing an audience was truly only a small part of why she did what she did.

When it was over, and Molly had sung her own bawdy song—which involved much suggestive wielding of her wand— to rapturous applause, a crew of boys scrambled to push a long, low, carved structure onto the stage, carved in ripples, painted a rich dark green. Seaweed, apparently.

And then Sylvie learned what the trumpet was for.

It sounded, a noble golden peal over the theater, and a hush fell.

Sylvie heard a creaking noise, and looked up. A great, silk-flower-bedecked swing, suspended on a pair of chains, was being lowered from the stage rafters by two sweaty boys. There was an urgent scuffling noise from the wings, and Sylvie saw, to her astonishment, a woman, eye-poppingly buxom, curved, as a matter of fact, as extravagantly as an hourglass, waddling because the bottom half of her was tightly wrapped in a resplendent, sparkly purple mermaid tail. Her hair was long, brilliant with henna, and sparkles no doubt fashioned of paste and streamers of something no doubt meant to be seaweed clung to it.

"'Er Majesty," Rose whispered.

"If she gains even 'alf a stone, that swing will snap like kindling," Molly muttered bitterly.

Ah, so this was Daisy Jones.

Sylvie watched with fascination as they quickly got her settled into her swing—it did make a subtle, if ominous, groaning sound when her posterior was centered on it—and her hands, shiny in gloves that reached her elbows, gripped the chains. The boys then raced to get behind her, scrabbled frantically and in vain for a moment to get enough traction to push her into motion, and then Daisy, rapping out a soft and colorful epithet by way of encouragement, finally gave them a little assist by flapping her tail. The three of them got the swing going to and fro, the chains creaking musically, the trumpet sounded again, and the red velvet curtain swooshed up.

"*DAISY!*" The crowd bellowed in gleeful greeting.

Daisy waved with regal cheer and blew kisses from her fingertips to them, a number of whom pretended to catch them on their own fingers, apply them to their own mouths, and swoon. She gave her tail some vigorous flaps, and soon the swing was soaring above them, and men were trying to get a look underneath it for a glimpse of her magnificent posterior. Daisy's long, dyed-red hair was affixed to the front of her, and her torso was draped in some sort of clever sheer fabric. Her hair flew up tantalizingly, but remained within the bounds of the legal.

Oh, come all ye laddies who e'er set sail and
gather round fer a glimpse of me beautiful tail…

And Daisy's voice, though it reached handily to the rafters, would never be mistaken for "exquisite."

"A mermaid on a swing?" Sylvie said quietly to Rose.

"It's an underwater world, Miss Chapeau." Tom Shaughnessy's voice was a low murmur behind her, and somehow it managed to travel along her spine as though a finger had been dragged lightly there. She felt the gooseflesh rise on the back of her neck. "We create fantasy here at the White Lily. It's a dream, if you will—mermaids playing beneath the waves on swings." He looked out at the crowd, and a satisfied smile curved his mouth. "A *lucrative* dream."

He met her eyes for a moment, then slowly took his gaze away from hers and watched the proceedings—Daisy sailing through the air on a swing that was indeed looking just a bit taxed by her girth—as intently as a scientist or a judge. He glanced below at the audience, his brow crinkling a little, as if wondering how many men would be flattened beneath Daisy should the swing give way.

"Or a nightmare," Sylvie murmured.

Tom turned his head sharply toward her then. And his face became studiously expressionless.

"I suppose it's all in how you view it, Miss Chapeau," he said evenly. "You've earned your wages for tonight. You may collect them from me tomorrow, if you wish."

Once again she saw the gleam of his watch in his hand, and he slipped away to oversee some other aspect of the show.

The show was over, the crowd was gone, and the theater was nearly quiet again. Sylvie watched, as one by one, the girls filtered out the back door of the theater into the night dressed in their own clothes, fairy costumes, wands and wings tucked away in the wardrobes for the evening.

At the side door of the theater, where a small crowd of admirers waited, Sylvie peeped out.

Flanking the door were two enormous men, one missing an eye and not bothering with the formality of a patch; judging from the rest of his attire, perhaps he'd feel overdressed in one. The other man was as wide as he was tall, his mouth pulled up into a permanent half grin by a scar ironically in the shape of a smile itself. Instead of a left hand, he sported a hook, which he lifted in farewell to the girls as they wandered away in pairs, a steely little twin of the slice of moon curving above.

From inside the door, Sylvie watched Molly helped by a footman into a very fine unmarked carriage, saw her slim stocking-covered ankle flash, heard her laugh almost shyly, then she vanished inside to meet the sender of the little fan.

Watching Molly board the fine coach was almost disorienting; Sylvie could almost see herself as she'd been a year ago, when Etienne had begun his pursuit—beautiful, flush with the triumph of that beauty. A fine carriage waiting for her outside the theater, inside it an unimaginably wealthy and important man bearing gifts just for her.

"G'night, Sylvie!" Rose raised her hand in farewell, turned away to trudge off through the streets of London to her own rooms.

"Can I escort ye safely anywhere, Miss?" The man with the shiny curved hand bowed politely. "Ye mus' be the new girl Tommy 'ired." He smiled; the few teeth still embedded in his gums gleamed like skulls in a cave. "Me name's Poe. An' this is Stark."

Stark, the man missing an eye, bowed, too, and said nothing. Sylvie wondered if perhaps Tom had deliberately advertised for men who were missing parts of their bodies.

"Th-thank you, Mr. Poe, but no." She smiled politely, hoping it wasn't impolite to show her full complement of teeth to a man with so few of them, and backed into the theater again.

And into utter silence.

Sylvie availed herself of a candle, but as she began to make her way up the long flights of stairs to the top of the theater, she saw a light burning softly in Tom Shaughnessy's office, which seemed to be a library of sorts; she saw shelves lining the walls. She stopped to peer from the shadows. Through the space made by the open door she was surprised to see Tom, shirtsleeves rolled up, quill in hand, head bent, writing something so slowly and painstakingly he reminded Sylvie of a schoolboy practicing his letters. He glanced up, turned his head to the side in thought, and she watched him massage the fingers of one hand with the other, kneading them methodically, thoughtfully, stretching and fanning the fingers, a half smile on his face at something he'd perhaps been thinking.

She took a moment then to boldly admire the line of his profile, not like Etienne's, which was clean, elegant, refined by centuries of his flawless bloodline the way the sea polishes stones to smoothness. Tom's profile was more difficult to interpret; it offered more interesting places for the eye to land. And despite Tom Shaughnessy's own version of polish, his clothing that bordered on gaudy, she noticed now that he radiated . . . calm. He glittered: his eyes, his smile, those coat buttons . . . but at the core of it was this quiet sort of . . . certainty.

Or perhaps it was ruthlessness.

And then he pressed his palms against his eyes, briefly, and took up his quill once more, dipped it, continued to diligently write. As though he'd given himself an assignment requiring completion tonight.

His memoirs, perhaps, she thought, half-amused. Like *Don Juan,* or *Casanova.* But the tableau, Tom bent over his desk, struck her as odd. Surely London was filled with gaming hells and pubs and places where men like Tom Shaughnessy could find entertainment and feminine company and more women over whom to fight duels. The contrast between the coarse, merry mayhem of hours earlier, the swift violence in the dressing room before the show, and this quiet Tom bending over the desk was incongruous.

She wondered about his mistress. She didn't wonder whether he *had* one; there was no question in her mind that he did. He must. Sylvie wondered who she was. A titled widow? A professional courtesan? Who would appeal to Tom Shaughnessy?

Was he in love with Kitty, the dancer who had disappeared? Or did he really "turn 'er off" for being pregnant to set an example for the other girls? Did he make her pregnant and keep her in Kent, and dutifully visit?

Men like Tom Shaughnessy. She realized, suddenly, that she wasn't certain what this meant.

She'd been too busy to be afraid today, and yet, when she gave it some thought: this was a man who had known highwaymen, whose theater was run by a surly dwarf, whose dancers had no doubt been plucked virtually from the street. Who had, with lightning speed, snatched a burly man up by the cravat and calmly threatened to kill him earlier this evening.

In the moment, Sylvie had believed he would do it. And in the moment, in the flames of her temper, she had to admit that she'd almost hoped he would.

When she'd seen Belstow's hand rise for a blow, as if it had simply been his *right* to strike Molly . . .

Standing in the White Lily's cheerful faux grandeur, she began to wonder whether it had truly been Etienne she'd seen standing at the harbor, or whether her own guilt and nerves had conjured him from some other vision of a tall, broad-shouldered man. Whether it truly had been Etienne's voice she'd heard saying, "I beg your pardon" as he peered into the coach. Had he followed her through Paris to London, somehow?

In the dark of this odd theater, she could almost believe she had imagined him, that it had been some other man entirely, and that only the events inside the White Lily were real.

A dream, Mr. Shaughnessy said. A *lucrative* dream.

Of nearly all of the places she could have landed in Paris, she imagined Etienne was least likely to look for her in an establishment such as this. Etienne's taste in entertainments ran to the rarefied and refined, to the very best of everything. Which had perhaps naturally led him to Sylvie Lamoreux, for she embodied all that was finest of beauty and grace.

It was difficult to believe that she might have hurt Etienne by leaving suddenly. Sylvie wondered whether one truly longed for someone, could truly love, when nothing had ever been denied.

And whether it mattered at all.

Weariness tugged at Sylvie's limbs, her eyelids. She would sleep hard tonight.

And so she climbed the quiet stairs again, counted the doors in the darkened hallway, and thus found her room again.

She knew a moment of gratitude for the place to sleep and the lock on the door, a moment of nervousness about her unusual environment, which strangely had begun to feel more comfortable than she'd almost prefer it to; then, her body, in its wisdom, took her to sleep.

Chapter Nine

⌒

Tom was enjoying the feel of cool morning air—there was mercifully still some damp in it at this hour, some freshness—and the horse he'd hired was a splendidly game animal, taking the road quickly in long smooth strides. Hiring a horse cut the time of the journey to Little Swathing in Kent in half; he wasn't eager to board a mail coach again anytime soon.

Someday he would keep his own carriage. He knew just the one he wanted, just the horses he would choose. Not gray to match the typical English weather, as so many of the titled chose, but something bright, something with a bit of flash: a quartet of bays, perhaps. Or four black geldings, white stars between their eyes or white stockings round their forelegs. He'd even been to Tattersall's, to plan and dream.

He could buy the horses and carriage now and keep them if he chose, for there was a mews behind the White Lily, but Tom was selective about his expenditures. He had decided sometime ago that this particular expenditure could wait, that his journeys about London could take place in hired hackneys and horses and carriages sent by friends. His capital was needed for other things: to pay his employees, for example. To build pirate ships.

To hire beautiful Frenchwomen on a whim.

He half smiled to himself at the thought, but the sudden image of green eyes and flushed cheeks tensed the muscles in his stomach in a way that surprised him. The thought brought a difficult-to-define, distracting pleasure; it carried with it more of an edge than thoughts of beautiful women usually did. He'd watched her last night, smiling and bending and swaying in time with the other girls, and though he could find no fault with her performance, he could not take his eyes from her. She seemed wrong, and yet unimaginably right at the same time.

Odd to think that two such dramatically new things should drop into his life on the same day. Both, in their way, had thrown him ever-so-slightly off course, leaving him, for the first time in years, feeling uncertain of his footing; but both, were perhaps, temporary.

He shook the thought of Sylvie Chapeau away as the cottage came into view. He tethered the horse and pushed open the little white gate, took the flagstones up to the door, to the other new thing.

He'd decided, at last, he should come, at least once, and to do it at once. To ascertain whether in fact it was true.

Mrs. May greeted him at the door. He offered a tense bow to her, and she offered a swift, nearly begrudging, curtsy in return, and polite, stiff words of welcome. Tom imagined there wasn't a good deal written in etiquette books about such occasions, and so he defaulted to quiet politeness for the moment.

Mr. May hovered at the ready, should the infamous Mr. Shaughnessy do anything untoward; Tom saw him out of the corner of his eye, then heard him moving about in another part of the house, making purposeful sounds, picking things up, putting them down, to make his presence known. Somewhere else in the house he heard the voices of older children.

It had taken some very determined coaxing to earn his way over the threshold of this cottage. He'd had the door shut in his face more than once. Mr. May had halfheartedly threatened him with a musket, but Tom had stood his ground; he'd recognized the musket's vintage; it probably had more kick than it did firepower; it would probably harm the shooter more than the target.

And then Tom had come literally hat in hand; he'd come bearing gifts; roses and sweets, and once, in a stroke of originality, a ham.

And then he'd begged.

And really, in the end, very few could withstand a full charm assault from Tom Shaughnessy, which no doubt explained yesterday's letter. Certainly the Mays' pretty daughter Maribeth had scarcely even tried; she'd developed a taste for adventure, a man or two before she landed beneath Tom, and had finally run off with another man entirely. He'd all but forgotten about Maribeth until her letter had arrived a few weeks ago.

"He's yours. You've only to look at him. The hair gives it away."

Ah, romance, Tom thought now, in retrospect.

And when he'd read the letter...he'd gone cold. The blood had left his hands and rushed into his face to heat it. He was tempted just to crumple it and get on with the business of building a bawdy empire.

He did crumple it in fact. Squeezed it in his fist. Where it all but pulsed, the damn thing, as though he'd crushed in his hand a heart.

And so he'd smoothed it out again and stared at it, darkly angry. The anger was strangely unspecific. With himself? With Maribeth? With fate, for casting something in his path that had nothing at all to do with the plans he'd forged from persistence and work and danger and sheer cleverness?

Maribeth had left the boy—Jamie, she'd said his name was—with her parents, who had despaired of their daughter long ago. Her parents were considerably more respectable and conservative than their daughter, if impoverished. They lived in a small cottage in Kent with their other children.

So he'd thought about it. And as a formality, perhaps, Tom sent a letter—polite, formal—requesting to see the boy.

He'd been coldly rebuffed. *"Given your occupation, we think it best for him that you don't see him,"* was the essence of the reply the Mays had sent.

Which is why, in the way of Tom Shaughnessy, seeing Jamie had become a quest.

And in the way of all of Tom's quests to date, he'd been successful.

❧

Mrs. May brought the boy to him in their sitting room, leading him by the hand.

His name was James; he was not yet two years old, Tom had been told. His hair was a silky sheet of copper, his baby-colored eyes already turning gray.

Silver, Jamie's Grammy Shaughnessy would have called them, had she lived to see her grandchild.

Tom, for an instant, couldn't breathe. He could see it. The child looked like him. Just like him, so much smaller, and yet... would grow to be an *entire person* who would look just like him.

The little boy stood and stared back at Tom with bald, unblinking amazement, as surely as though Tom was a dancing bear or a firework. It was both a little flattering and disconcerting, though Tom imagined that everything new that entered Jamie's world was treated to the same stare.

And then Mrs. May released the boy's little hand, and took a seat on one of the two settees that faced each other, each worn, and nearly as curved as a smile from years of being sat upon.

A judge presiding, Tom thought, mordantly amused.

Awkwardly, he remained standing, hat in hand. He couldn't very well *bow* to the child. Or shake his hand. He was…miniature. Everything about him was miniature, the tiny hands and feet, the little ears, that round, delicate head.

So Tom sat down stiffly on the settee, for all the world as if he'd come courting.

What on earth did one *do* with a toddler? And why on earth was he here, after all? The Mays seemed to have it all in hand, and from the sounds heard in the rest of the house, had managed to keep other children alive and fed.

Jamie toddled toward Tom, unable to resist the newness of him.

There was a ball on the braided rug near Tom's feet, a little thing made of leather, a toy. Tentatively, Tom leaned over and rolled it across to the boy.

"Ball!" Jamie bellowed, looking shocked and delighted. He fumbled at it with plump little starfish hands; when he managed to pick it up, a smile scrunched his face nearly in half, as though joy had split it right open.

Jamie tottered over to Tom and generously held out the ball.

After a moment's hesitation, Tom took it. "Why thank you, my good man."

Jamie patted his hands together, pleased to have given a gift. *"Ball!"* he reiterated on a piercing squeal. Tom fought a wince, certain the sound had drilled through his eardrum, fought the impulse to twist one finger in his ear to check.

"Yes, and an *excellent* ball it is, too," Tom agreed. He knew the language of babies, he just wasn't about to speak it, and he wasn't convinced that babies wanted to hear it from adults, either. He admired his gift for a moment, to Jamie's wide-eyed pleasure, then rolled the ball gently across the room for Jamie to wobble after.

Two, three steps, then—oh no!—*splat*. Down he went.

Jamie didn't burst into tears, though he did look surprised, as though he fully hadn't expected his legs to betray him. And then, hands on the floor for leverage, round bottom in the air, he pushed himself upright again and continued his pursuit.

He gets that from me, Tom thought. *Single-minded determination.*

The very thought that anyone—let alone an entire, tiny human being—would have gotten anything at all from him stunned him breathless again.

He watched the boy. *My son,* he thought, trying out the words in his mind to see how they felt. *My son.* Foreign, as it turned out. Two little words, but immense in their implication, like a great mountain he couldn't see around.

He turned suddenly, to find Mrs. May watching him.

It was perhaps even more disconcerting to see the faintest hint of compassion softening her cool, stern vigilance.

This was when he quickly stood again.

"Well, thank you, Mrs. May. I'll just be off then."

He bowed, and left the two of them before she could even rise to her feet, as surely as though hounds were on his heels.

❧

After a breakfast of very good bread and hot tea in the kitchen with Josephine and Mrs. Pool, Sylvie was led back upstairs to a very handsome sitting room. Soft shades of cream and blue were everywhere in the worn but tasteful furniture and the decent rugs and heavy curtains. There was even a little hearth, dark now as the weather was warm and the east-facing window allowed in a good deal of morning sun. Sylvie had abandoned her widow's weeds and was wearing muslin, elegantly cut, subtly striped in a soft shade of willow. A narrow band of lace edged the neckline.

She saw Josephine's eyes widen a bit when she took in the dress. No doubt she had a sense of its cost. But she said nothing; she merely settled Sylvie into the chair across from her and handed across a basket full of snipped-out segments of black flannel.

"Pirate hats," she said matter-of-factly, brandishing one she'd finished with a flourish, to show Sylvie how they should look. "Next we'll do the sashes and pantaloons and cunning little shirts, and dresses for the sea nymphs. Though *those* willna be much more than togas, and I'm thankful fer that, fer Mr. Shaughnessy, 'e does 'ave 'is ideas, one right after t'other, an 'e wants everything done straightaway. First the costumes and song and the sets—and that's The General's bailiwick, ye see, the sets are—and then the lot of ye'll be in rehearsals in two shakes of a lamb's tail. And Mr. Shaughnessy, 'is 'and is in all of it, ye ken. Not that I'm complaining, mind ye," she added hurriedly, "but I'm 'appy fer yer 'elp. And we'll take in all of yer costumes as well, as they're too big for ye."

"Pantaloons?" Sylvie almost breathed the word. "There will be pantaloons?" Even in Paris, pantaloons for women were scandalous.

"They will look like skirts," Josephine said with some relish, "but we'll sew 'em together so that we can 'ave a leg in one side and a leg in the other. They *will* be pantaloons. Mr. Shaughnessy does have 'is ideas," she reiterated admiringly. "And then we'll write a song."

" 'We'll'?" Sylvie repeated.

"Mr. Shaughnessy and I," Josephine clarified benignly, deftly stitching a pirate hat into shape.

Sylvie stared wonderingly at Josephine, who could very well pass for the wife of a curate, with her round cheeks and mild eyes.

Josephine looked up, noticed Sylvie's astonished perusal, and smiled sweetly. "Oh, me 'usband, 'e dinna mind. 'E's known Tom fer simply years, which is 'ow I came into Tom's employ. First wi' the sewing bits, mind ye. Then 'e discovered I'd a bit of a musical flair."

She bent her head again to her sewing, then glanced sideways through her lashes at Sylvie, and said in a humble hush, as though confiding a secret, "and 'tisn't difficult, ye ken, to rhyme things with lance, or joust. It all jus'…comes to me, like. 'Tis a gift."

Tom was relieved to be back again in the White Lily, in his office, among plans of his own making. He knew the way forward from this room—how to make shows, hire and discharge employees. He knew how to talk to a man with a hook for a hand or to a beautiful woman or to a rich investor or to a man threatening to shoot him at dawn.

But he hadn't the faintest idea what to do with the miniature version of himself.

He would write to Mrs. May and thank her for her time, then send money quarterly until the boy was grown, and this would dispatch his duties in this particular situation. Doubtless it wasn't unusual; he was certain more than one man had found himself in similar circumstances.

Somewhat relieved at how tidy this solution felt, Tom turned

to his stack of correspondence gratefully. Mrs. Pool had anticipated his return, and a tray of strong tea, which she had clearly
only recently brewed judging from the heat and aroma of it,
waited for him. He poured a cup of it as he sorted through his
mail, and found wonderful news:

Viscount Howath would be pleased to invest in the Gentleman's Emporium.

And that completed his group of investors. They were all in.

He leaned back in his chair and took a sip of tea, rolling it
about in his mouth as if it were the taste of victory itself, and
the sweet heat and enormity of triumph swelled in him and
momentarily overtook every other concern. He knew a moment
of awe: Tom Shaughnessy, former street urchin, would soon
own one of the largest buildings in London, and the wealthiest
men in London would flock to it in order to be entertained.

Tom allowed himself a moment to dream, to allow the dream
to spiral outward to when the building was renovated and alive
with entertainments, each floor a fantasy of escape and pleasure.

And then he reined his dreams back into the needs of the
present, which included the creation of a song for female
pirates. And he ought to see The General, who no doubt was in
the workshop, begrudgingly supervising the frantic creation of
a pirate ship and a great oyster for Venus to rise up out of, and
swearing and hammering things.

Tom thought it would do him a world of good to hammer
and swear at things for a bit. He would see The General, he
decided, then visit Josephine.

$\backsim$

The little pile of pirate hats had quickly grown. Josephine
wasn't stringent about the needlework; she required only that

Julie Anne Long

Sylvie be swift. They set to work on the pantaloons next, cutting from measurements taken from each girl and refreshed each time a new show was created.

The work was soothing; Josephine wasn't one for talking, and Sylvie felt lulled by the soft sun coming in through the window and the rhythm of her needle passing in and out of the fabric. It had been a very long time since she'd done anything quite so ordinary, and oddly, she found it refreshing. They might be a curate's wife and a curate's daughter, apart from the fact that they were sewing pirate hats and pantaloons.

"Josephine! I'd hoped to find you…"

Sylvie and Josephine looked up abruptly at the voice. Tom Shaughnessy had trailed off when he saw Sylvie perched on a chair opposite Josephine, a basket of sewing demurely on her lap. He looked bemused for an instant, and met her eyes so Sylvie could see it. It was as though he somehow suspected that this version of her, the quiet version dressed in a muslin gown and demurely stitching things, was somehow as wrong as a derriere-patting fairy.

He recovered from his bemusement, but remained in the doorway.

"Oh, so you've given Miss Chapeau something sharp to wield, have you, Josephine? I shall stand over here, Miss Chapeau, at a safe distance, lest your passions become inflamed, and you become tempted to insert me with a needle."

"Should you continue to stand at a…safe distance…Mr. Shaughnessy…I shall not complain," Sylvie replied evenly.

Suspecting that no distance from this man was in truth safe.

This made him laugh, and he came all the way into the room. Fawn trousers today, tall boots, emphasizing those long, long legs. Boots so shiny the light bounced from them as he walked. A coat in a fine mahogany-colored wool. Red-gold hair mussed, falling in loose waves over his brow, as if the wind had just artfully tossed it. The waistcoat was fawn-colored, too, striped in cream, and the buttons on it were, it seemed, brass. Surely they couldn't be gold?

He wandered to where the two ladies sat, then paused when he saw the growing mound of pirate hats. He gazed down at them a moment, then plucked up one of them, fingering it idly, almost delicately, a moment, his expression abstracted.

And then he abruptly put it down again and strode toward the pianoforte.

"Speaking of inflaming passions, Josephine..." Tom struck three or four random keys. "We'll need a new tune for our pirate theme, and we'll need it straightaway, of course. I thought perhaps something to do with... swords?" It was a serious query. "Seems the obvious choice, anyhow."

Josephine became brisk. She abandoned her hats to the chair, a little spill of black felt, and bustled over to Tom to take a seat at the pianoforte.

"I've just the tune, Mr. Shaughnessy." She clasped her fingers together and stretched them out, then positioned them over the keys and struck a hearty, seafaring chanteylike melody.

"Me 'usband was a sailor," she explained over her shoulder to Sylvie. "And when I 'eard about the pirates, I thought to meself, I can jus' *'ear* it now..."

She played a few bars of it while Tom listened attentively.

"Yes, I do think that will do. *Now* all we must do is compose a song that every man who leaves the theater will want to launch into when they're drunk. Perhaps something to do with... *thrusting* swords?" Tom suggested, rubbing his chin in thought.

Josephine tilted her head. "'Ow about..."

Now thrust yer sword laddie, now thrust yer sword...

She paused and looked up at Tom for approval.

"Good, good," he murmured. "It's a beginning." He tilted his head up, searching the ceiling for the next line. "Lord? Bored?"

"Toward?" Josephine suggested, wrinkling her nose to indicate her opinion of her own inspiration. "Snored? Roared?"

"Reward," Sylvie murmured under her breath.

Josephine and Tom swiveled toward her.

There was a brief charged moment of silence.

"What did you say, Miss Chapeau?" Tom asked mildly.

But she'd known this man long enough now to hear the suppressed glee in his voice.

Oh, no. Sylvie kept her face down, jabbing the needle through the flannel, then into her own fingers, and she was forced to bite her lip to keep from squeaking from the pain.

"Come now, dear, do share," Josephine encouraged, as gently as anyone's mother.

Sylvie cleared her throat. "Reward," she said, more loudly this time.

And this time looked Tom evenly in the eye. It was outrageously invigorating to flirt subtly with this man. Still, she could feel heat in her face. Her eyes darted toward the hearth, as though she was tempted to blame it. Deuced thing was dark.

"And, pray tell, how would you use 'reward' in the song?" Tom asked the question with wide-eyed innocence. And then he held up a hand. "I've an idea. Josephine, begin playing the song, if you would. Miss Sylvie Chapeau will complete the line for us at the appropriate time."

"I—" Sylvie began to protest.

But Josephine had already begun playing, her large capable hands jumping over the keys to make the tune spring out.

"Come now, dear!" she urged supportively. "Let's 'ear it!"

And Josephine sang:

Now thrust yer sword, laddie, thrust yer sword

She turned her head over her shoulder to peer at Sylvie, wagging her eyebrows upward encouragingly, her hands bouncing their way through several bars of the tune.

Sylvie flicked a glance at Tom. His eyes had nearly vanished with amusement.

Dear God. Josephine looked so enthusiastic and hopeful, head turned over her shoulder, those encouraging brows uplifted, that Sylvie found she simply could not disappoint her.

So she squeezed her eyes closed and sang, resignedly:

Send me, send me to my reward.

For that, God help her, was precisely what she had been thinking.

❧

Josephine jangled to a halt.

Tom stared at her speechlessly.

Sylvie forced herself to stare back at them with all apparent innocence.

"Your…'reward'?" Tom repeated, finally, in a voice entirely lacking inflection.

Sylvie nodded gingerly.

He wasn't smiling. But still, somehow, his entire face was positively fulsome with unholy, triumphant mirth. It was as if laughter could not possibly do adequate justice to her contribution to the song.

"Hmmm." He paced to and fro before the hearth. "Thrust your sword, laddie, *thrust* your sword." He gave the words a *To be, or not to be* gravity. "Send me, send me to my—" He spun and all but purred the word to her. "—*reward.*"

She suspected her flaming cheeks rather defeated the purpose of her cool stare, which was to make him believe she was entirely unaffected.

Where on earth had the word *come* from? It had just popped right out of her.

Who knew that bawdy songs were contagious?

"Well, I must confess, I think it's bloody brilliant," he said, shaking his head. "It really is. And I do believe I now have the rest, as a result. Josephine? If you would begin again, and we'll sing it together?"

And so Josephine played and sang:

Thrust yer sword, laddie, now thrust yer sword
Send me, send me to my reward,
Whether it takes one thrust or a few
I beg you to

Josephine and Tom completed the last line together, their voices blending skillfully:

Thrust...yer...sword!

"Well then," Tom said crisply, when they were done. "We can have the girls swooning at the 'reward' portion of the song, and clasping their hands in entreaty at the 'I beg you' portion, and at the 'thrust your sword,' part, well—we'll have them thrusting swords." He grinned. "Another fine day's work here at the White Lily, ladies. I'll share the song with Daisy and ask her and The General to come visit you here, Josephine, to learn it. And don't forget, we'll need a song or two for Venus. Think of the possibilities inherent in the word 'pearl.' And I do believe you've earned your keep for the day, Miss Chapeau."

In a quick motion Sylvie was growing to associate with him,

he reviewed the time and turned to move toward the door. But then he paused as surely as though something invisible had tugged him gently back, and wandered back to where Sylvie sat, his tall frame blocking the sunlight from the window.

She looked up at him, felt again that familiar, inconvenient shortness of breath, that needle-sharp spike of awareness that accompanied his closeness.

But he wasn't looking at her. He instead picked up one of the completed pirate hats again and turned the cunning little item about in his hands, shifting it this way and that, his expression oddly reflective, unreadable.

He lowered it back to the chair, slowly, thoughtfully this time. "Do you suppose..." he began. And then he turned to Josephine and continued with a more decisive air. "Do you suppose you could make a very small pirate hat?" He held his hands up and apart, then studied them, and adjusted the space between them to the size of a small melon. "About...this size? By...tomorrow?"

Josephine looked a little puzzled. "Certainly, Mr. Shaughnessy."

"Thank you." He turned to leave. "And I shall see you downstairs in the theater in an hour or so, Miss Chapeau. The General and I have an announcement to make. After rehearsal, do come to see me. Perhaps we can then discuss your...reward."

A grin flashed at them, he bowed once, a gorgeous flourish of a bow, and was gone.

❧

Summoned for Mr. Shaughnessy's special announcement, seven lovely women stood onstage—five young and plush, one young and slender, and one from whom the bloom had fled several seasons earlier, leaving behind a fully blown rose: a lived-in face, hennaed hair, and a rump that many Englishmen insisted that visitors to London should make a point of viewing with deference and awe, the way one viewed the Tower of London or Whitehall. A national treasure, was Daisy Jones's arse, they declared.

Daisy Jones herself stood several feet removed from the lovelies, as if aware of the contrast, or not wanting to dilute her queenly status by breathing the same air as the other girls.

"Jus' look at 'Er Majesty. None too pleased to rub elbows wi' the likes of us," Lizzie murmured.

"'Er bosom is down around 'er elbows, now, anyhow. Wouldna want t' find meself rubbin' *that* by accident, anyway." This was Molly.

An explosion of giggles. High, incensed color rose in Daisy's cheeks, but she neither turned her head nor moved an inch.

"Ladies, you may have heard, thanks to your *many admirers* who cannot seem to stay quiet..." Tom said it teasingly, and the girls giggled. "...of the new production I've planned. It will be a *tour de force,* a thing of beauty and sensu*a*lity..." He gave each syllable the loving, thorough attention of a seducer, weakening the knees of more than one girl onstage. "And it will require just the right girl to make it a success. We are calling it—" Tom paused.

"Venus," all the girls said with a sigh.

Everyone, that is, but Daisy, who remained silent and dark as a thunderhead.

"Quite right. And The General and I will be watching over the next few days to see which of you we believe will personify Venus."

The General whipped his head around at this, seized Tom's arm, and yanked him backward out of earshot of the girls.

"Are you *mad,* Shaughnessy?" he said, his voice low and furious. "They're all going to be *impossible* if they think

they're in competition with each other. I thought we discussed
that Molly would be Venus."

"Or . . . they'll outdo themselves, behave beautifully, perform outrageously onstage, and we'll have crowds in here up
to the rafters night after night this week, at which point we'll
disclose who our Venus will be, a decision that you and I will
make together."

The General glared at Tom.

Tom waited patiently.

"Or . . . a bit of both," The General conceded, slowly, reluctantly, seeing the potential brilliance of the tactic.

Tom grinned. There was a pause.

"Probably Molly," Tom said briskly. The businessman in
Tom said this in a lowered voice. The dreamer in him saw an
entirely different Venus rising up from the sea: a lithe one, with
crackling green eyes and a shard of a wand in her hand, daring
the audience.

"Probably Molly," The General agreed just as briskly, in the
same lowered voice.

This was based more on the size and number of bouquets
sent to her than on anything else at the moment. They were
practical men, and it was a fiscal, not an aesthetic decision.
More men at the moment would probably want to see Molly
rising up out of the sea scantily clad in the shell. She hadn't
Daisy's vocal range, but her voice was clear and her interpreta-
tion of the lyrics was more than convincing; she was fresh, and
had a following of sorts as well as a beautiful bosom. She was
Venus from St. Giles, Molly was.

Whereas Venus of Paris was up there looking uncomfortable in that row of dancers, stoic, proud, staring back at him,
again looking faintly wrong in a damsel costume that required
altering. A bit like a real princess disguised as a princess.

Tom gave The General an encouraging pat on the back.

"Good luck! You *are* giving cutlasses to them, are you not?" He said it almost innocently.

"Cutlasses," The General repeated slowly. "Brilliant! Of course, Tommy. I'll get the crew to work on them today."

"Wait until you hear what I think they should be doing with their *hands* and cutlasses while they sing."

The General grinned, too. "I can already picture it."

"And we've a wonderful new song. Involving swords, of course."

"Good work, Shaughnessy."

Tom grinned. "And now I'm off to see a man about a building, Gen. They're in. They're all in. We'll have our Gentleman's Emporium by next spring. I'll return before rehearsal is over."

Once Mr. Shaughnessy had made his announcement and left them again, The General sent all of them to finish dressing like damsels, which involved the addition of pointed hats and flowing sheer capes trimmed with jewels, which would gleam and twinkle when softly lit, and which apparently were to be flourished provocatively.

Everything was to be done provocatively at the White Lily, Sylvie now knew.

A great wooden castle, complete with turrets and a drawbridge that appeared capable of opening and closing, was pushed onto the stage by the seemingly ever-present crew of young boys. It occurred to Sylvie then that Tom Shaughnessy employed rather a lot of people and kept all of them hopping.

The castle seemed outrageously heavy; the boys were cherry-colored in the face and throwing all of their weight behind it, and the rest of the damsel-clad girls filed onto the stage, Sylvie among them, her body engulfed by the dress and cape. She glanced down glumly. She would need to alter these, too.

"Daisy!" The General bellowed toward the back of the theater. "Get your galleon-sized arse out here or I'll—"

There was an ominous creaking sound; everyone spun.

The boys were slowly lowering the drawbridge of the castle, and it thunked to the floor of the stage, sending up a tiny cloud of dust. The girls coughed and waved at the air.

And there stood Daisy at the entrance of the castle. She struck a pose, arms up and braced in the castle doorway, bosom outthrust, long red tresses tumbling across her shoulders, and waited until she was certain every eye in the place was upon her. The General watched her in smoldering silence as she sashayed across the drawbridge, then Sylvie watched his chin slowly lower until his gaze landed in the vicinity of Daisy's hips and stayed there, as surely as though her hips were the tool of a mesmerist.

There was no denying that Daisy Jones knew how to make an unforgettable entrance. Sylvie suspected that this, for some reason, had been Daisy's point.

She reached the end of the gangplank and paused.

"She gave me a penny to do it!" one of the boys squeaked by way of explanation before dashing offstage, apparently unable to decide who was more fearsome, Daisy or The General.

The General gazed at Daisy at length, inscrutable, no longer glowering. She gazed back at him, faintly defiant, but clearly pleased with herself. The rest of the girls looked on in resentful silence, perhaps knowing they could only dream of making an entrance as majestic.

At last The General cleared his throat. "Josephine—if you would? Sylvie, please, as you did yesterday, just follow along. You're a clever girl. I'm sure you'll catch on."

Again, that frisson of irony. As though something about her privately amused The General.

Josephine clasped her fingers together and stretched them out, then landed them on the pianoforte keyboard. A tune with a faint medieval lilt spilled out.

Daisy plaintively sang, in that voice that reached the rafters, but would never soothe the angels in heaven:

> *"Kind sir, kind sir, we damsels fair*
> *are begging for release*
> *Please wield your lance*
> *Or we've no chance*
> *Of ever finding peace...*

The girls swayed, raised the flat of swooning hands to foreheads, linked arms and...God help her...

Bent double and waved their derrieres in the air.

Again. And Sylvie, sighing inwardly, followed along.

"Get it up there, Sylvie! And if you would *please* not roll your eyes!"

And this, naturally, made Sylvie roll her eyes.

When they'd run through the song a good half dozen times, it seemed, and were upright and turned around to face the audience again, Sylvie saw Tom Shaughnessy at the head of the aisle, his bright eyes fixed rather emphatically on her, walking stick in hand, marking off time almost absently. The expression he wore was strangely...confused. A faint frown hovered between his eyes, as though she was a puzzle he was very close to deciphering.

So he'd returned, then, from whatever business had drawn him briefly away.

Sylvie felt unaccountably, absurdly glad, both at his return, and at the fact that he was clearly watching only her.

When her eyes met his, his faint frown tilted up at the corner and became that smile of acknowledgment, and wicked amusement lit his eyes as surely as if a light had caught them. Reflexively, her own lips turned up slightly, and something else inside her lifted, too.

"Oh!" Pain sliced through her as someone came down hard on the inside of her foot, nearly taking her slipper entirely off. Sylvie teetered briefly, one knee buckling. She righted herself quickly enough, as did the other girls, and danced and smiled through the pain, as she was accustomed to dancing and smiling through pain.

Both The General and Tom Shaughnessy were wearing genuine frowns now, and they were both directed at her. Tom's was puzzled. The General's was censorious.

"Goodness. *So* sorry," Molly murmured to her. Her smile remained in place, her face fixed forward. But her eyes, when Sylvie glanced sideways, her eyes glinted, glass-hard and satisfied.

⁓

He'd told her to find him in his library after rehearsal for her reward, and she knew precisely where this was as she'd seen the light pouring from it last night. As she had essentially spied on him very briefly last night.

She paused in the doorway. Tom Shaughnessy wasn't looking at her, he was sifting a hand through things on his desk, pushing them this way and that, as though he was looking for something in particular. A smile was curving his lips, as though he found the mess immensely satisfying.

Suddenly he froze and his face went dark and taut. With a swift motion he lifted one hand and pressed the thumb of his other hand hard against his palm, sucking in a short, harsh breath.

Sylvie's stomach contracted involuntarily in sympathy. She knew pain when she saw it.

He glanced up, noticing her at last, and his expression shifted instantly, light flooding into it. "Old wound," he explained glibly, lifting up his hand, fanning it out. She saw the scars, white, pulling tightly between thumb and forefinger. "Now and again it sends a humbling reminder through my nerves. Have you come for your...*reward* then, Miss Chapeau?"

She went very still. It was the way he'd said the word. It seemed to have...*dimensions,* the way he'd said it. He'd given it rich levels of innuendo, all of which implied he'd decades of experience rewarding women. He wasn't smiling, but the corners of his mouth were quivering, ready to laugh if she gave him a reason.

Tom Shaughnessy could very likely effortlessly outstrip her in the game of flirtation, she conceded. *She* felt obliged to a certain amount of decorum. Whereas he seemed fearless. And very nearly shameless. Though thankfully, so far, he seemed to be using his fearlessness and shamelessness somewhat judiciously.

"I am here as you requested, Mr. Shaughnessy. Did I earn more for contributing a bit of verse to your...production?" She couldn't resist a bit of irony.

The humor faded from his eyes. "Ah," he said, matching her irony. "I gather you feel our little *productions* lack a certain artistry. But I will tell you this, Miss Chapeau: There's great freedom in not feeling obliged toward respectability."

"I imagine you would know, Mr. Shaughnessy."

It was meant as a jest, albeit a tart one.

He went briefly very still again. His expression was difficult to read, and she considered whether she might have offended him, though it was difficult to see why this would be.

And then he opened up a small wooden box, reached in, and produced a stack of coins, which he settled on the corner of the desk: her wages. An eloquent but silent point made about the rewards of not feeling obliged to respectability.

Sylvie scooped them into her palm. Handed one back to him. "For my room and board."

He handed it back to her. "For the line of verse." They exchanged swift smiles. Tension eased a bit.

"Tell me: Do *you* aspire to respectability, Miss Chapeau?" He asked it idly.

She recognized it for what it was: a gauntlet thrown down, and still she could not resist snapping, "I do not *aspire* to respectability, Mr. Shaughnessy."

"Ah. I see. It is yours already." He was laughing silently at her. "And it was merely the cruel whims of fate that somehow led you to our little den of iniquity. I'm curious then: How does a respectable woman know about . . . rewards?"

"One can be respectable and know about . . . rewards, Mr. Shaughnessy." She heard how absurd the words sounded even as she said them.

"Can one?" he asked mildly. "I suppose that could be true if one is French. I suspect one wouldn't *blurt* the word out with such relish, however."

"I didn't—it wasn't—"

"And as 'respectable' so often means the same thing as 'married,'" he continued, as if she hadn't stammered at all, "and I do not think you are, or have been married, I must conclude that someone's *sword* has been sending you, or has in the past sent you, to your *reward*. So who sends you to your reward, Miss Chapeau? Did you leave a lover behind in France?"

The cutthroat boldness of the question wiped her mind of thought, and for an instant, she froze, unable to react at all. So much for judicious use of fearlessness and shamelessness.

She managed, finally, to produce a disapproving frown. And said nothing.

But this only made him smile, slowly, to demonstrate to her: *I have won this round, Miss Chapeau.*

Sylvie glanced around the room, an attempt to recover her composure. She supposed at one time it might have been used as a small library or sitting room, when the theater, as Josephine had told her, had been a great house; shelves were built into one wall. There were books on them now, which surprised her a little, as Tom Shaughnessy did not strike her as the academic sort—or even, necessarily, the reading sort, though he was certainly well-spoken enough—and all the books looked well thumbed through, too.

On closer inspection, she saw they weren't the sort usually proudly displayed in libraries, philosophical tomes and the like, the kind that are spotless and meant to impress guests. These were novels, for the most part. *Robinson Crusoe* was one of them, the ultimate male adventure. A few horrid novels, it seemed; she recognized them, as she secretly enjoyed them, too, and had read more than one in English. A collection of Greek myths, a large book that she was virtually certain was extravagantly illustrated given the theme of the theater's murals. She imagined they would appeal to his sense of drama and fantasy and whimsy.

But something tucked behind the books surprised her the most: a small wooden horse, a toy. It had a bristly mane and tail, wheels on its feet. She wondered if it had belonged to Tom as a boy, and why on earth such a thing would be tucked into a niche at the White Lily Theater.

And then she remembered the accusation of the man who had called him out: *"At that shop that sells toys."*

Tom had denied being in any such place.

This was intriguing.

She glanced up to meet his eyes on her. He'd been silently watching her peruse his office. Momentarily disconcerted, she glanced down, and saw, unfurled on his desk, a beautiful drawing of a grand building.

"Plans," he said shortly. "For another theater."

"It looks very grand." It did. The building was downright stately, vast; rows of large windows marched across it, a columned entrance greeted guests.

"It will be bloody fantastic," he stated as firmly as if it were already an established fact. "A floor for entertainments, a floor for dining, a floor for..." He trailed off, perhaps imagining it as he recited. And then he looked up at her. "We need a good deal of capital to make it a reality, but we should have the Gentleman's Emporium by next spring. I commissioned this drawing, and I'm working on the plans now." She heard the pride and conviction in his voice as he motioned to the papers spread over his desk. "It will be much like the White Lily...only much more so."

"But why...this sort of thing at all, Mr. Shaughnessy?" She gestured to the theater surrounding them with a wave of her hand. "Why the White Lily?"

He looked surprised at the question, then pretended to mull it quite seriously, head tilted back to look at the ceiling. And then he said suddenly, as though the answer had just then occurred to him: "Sex."

The word hung and pulsed in the air, all soft and crisp consonants, as lurid as the sign that swung over the White Lily's entrance. Long enough for both of them to picture once again what the word meant to each of them.

Long enough for Sylvie to feel distinctly light-headed.

"Very dramatic, Mr. Shaughnessy, but that word won't get any more or less alarming the longer you leave it there. You might as well continue to explain." She was aware that her voice was just a little bit frayed, and hoped that he wouldn't notice.

He threw back his head and laughed, delightedly. "Oh, very well then. It's simple, Miss Chapeau. I began my life with nothing. I wanted much much more than that. I knew a little bit about theater. I know a good deal about men and women, having encountered many kinds of both throughout my life. I followed the momentum of my talents and experience, and here we are. And where's the harm in it?"

"It's..." She waved a hand. *Appalling,* she thought. *Embarrassing. Overt.*

"Fun," he completed with a grin. "Lucrative. Everyone has a wonderful time."

"Including Molly?" she said, perhaps too quickly and sharply.

The grin faded when she said this; he studied her in silence for a moment. And then he inhaled deeply and sat down in his chair, leaned back and continued to study her, as if deciding whether to explain something to a child.

"Do you know what Molly would be doing if I didn't employ her?" he finally asked.

Sylvie was silent as she contemplated this. She could very well guess.

"Do you think she'd make a wonderful governess? Do you think she'd make a splendid scullery maid? Do you think her life would be any better then? Do you want to know where she was living before she came to the theater? What she was doing?"

"I take your point Mr. Shaughnessy. You are a veritable Samaritan."

He grunted a humorless laugh. "Hardly. But I do hire people that many employers would never dream of hiring, people who haven't a prayer of ever working at anything else. People I've encountered throughout my life. It isn't merely charity, Miss Chapeau. Usually I'm richly repaid in loyalty and commitment. But there are times..." he trailed off. "Well, I hired an old

friend to watch the dressing-room door. Jack. And it seems"—
he twisted his quill distractedly in his hand—"that Molly has
paid for my mistake."

He was struggling to disguise the strain in his voice. The
admission, and the event, and the harm to Molly, had cost him,
greatly, Sylvie realized.

She was tempted to apologize. But then he became restless,
glancing down at the work littering his desk. "Perhaps you'd
understand, Miss Chapeau, if you had not been pampered your
entire life."

A deliberate torch touched to the kindling of her temper. It
leaped up instantly.

"I've *never* been—"

"Yes?" He looked up swiftly. His grin was small and
triumphant.

She made it all too easy for him, she realized. But then
everything she felt and thought seemed amplified and very near
the surface when she was near him. As though it was rushing to
be closer to him.

She supposed it was wiser, then, *not* to be near him.

"Do you know a little of work, then?" he pressed. "You did
say you might be able to teach me a thing or two. You might
even find me a willing pupil." Another wicked little grin.

"Yes, I know much about work, and a little about 'nothing,' Mr.
Shaughnessy," she said quietly. "And I, too, intend to never have
nothing again. I have worked all my life to make certain of it."

"So you're an ambitious woman, Miss Chapeau?"

"Aren't all women to some degree? Does life not require it
of us?" She thought she heard a trace of bitterness in her voice.

He fell silent again.

And then he looked down, ran a light hand over the drawing
of the grand building, smoothing it thoughtfully, proprietarily.

"What happened to Molly . . . what happened to Molly

won't happen again. I always learn from my mistakes," he said suddenly, looking up at her again. Holding her eyes. Almost as though he was trying to persuade her of the truth of this. "One might in fact, even say the White Lily originated from a mistake." He grinned swiftly, ruefully, and held up his scarred hand, as if illustrating his point.

"I was ten years old, and I was stealing cheese. The vendor objected and came at me with a knife because boys like me were forever infesting his stalls like little vermin. I fought back, but he got me," Tom said nearly cheerily. "It became septic, and I very nearly died, but an apothecary took pity on me. He made sure I was healthy again, and he knew someone at a tavern at the docks who needed help, and they gave me a job, and that job led to another job at a theater, and..."

He paused, and his eyes lit with some amusement. "I've always just been lucky, I suppose. Particularly in my friends."

Lucky? Sylvie's head spun for a moment with the graphic images; her lungs tightened at the thought of a large man coming at a boy with a knife. Pictured Tom Shaughnessy as small and terrified and wounded and hungry and ill, even dying. It seemed impossible. He seemed...

As though he'd *never* been afraid.

And now she understood that the calm she'd sensed in him had been *earned*... through knowing he could survive the very worst life could conjure.

Sylvie frowned a little. "But your parents—"

"Were dead at the time. I never knew my father."

His smile became faintly cynical when he saw her expression. "Oh, there were thousands of boys just like me, Miss Chapeau. I *was* lucky. It's as simple as that."

She wasn't certain what to say. She wanted to say: *I doubt there were thousands of boys like you. It's impossible to imagine even one other like you.*

"I never knew my parents, either," she found herself saying, instead.

His face changed to something like surprise, whether at the nature of the confession or the fact that she had in fact confessed it, she wasn't certain. He studied her, too, as if adding this information to whatever judgments he'd made of her in his mind.

Sylvie thought she understood something now. The White Lily was the thing Tom Shaughnessy had built to separate him from his old life, in the way ballet was the thing that had lifted her up out of the ordinary.

They were perhaps more alike than different. This she found strangely disturbing.

"Was it yours, when you were a boy?" She said it lightly, and pointed at the horse on the shelf when the silence had shifted into something more intimate, much less familiar to her. And therefore perhaps more dangerous.

He looked at the horse. "It's mine for the moment, anyhow." An answer and not an answer. Ah, inscrutability from Tom Shaughnessy. "I always did want one when I was small."

It was difficult to know whether or not he was serious; the words were glib.

"I always wanted a... *boîte à musique,*" she faltered, almost to herself. She remembered it now; the memory of it returned swiftly, the yearning strangely stirred.

"A music box?" he repeated. He sounded curious. Encouraging, almost.

She fell abruptly silent and straightened her spine, as if pushing away the memory and the moment. There had scarcely been enough money when she was young for what they needed, for Claude never made very much money; there had certainly never been enough for something quite so frivolous as a music box.

Tom Shaughnessy's watch came out then, perhaps inevitably.

"I've a builder to see, Miss Chapeau. I've given your wages to you today, as your employment is only temporary. The other girls are paid weekly. If you intend to stay on, I'll rearrange our budget accordingly. But perhaps we should see how things are . . . day by day."

"Day by day, if that suits you," she found herself saying.

"It suits me," he said softly. He somehow managed to make the words sound like a promise.

Her face grew warm, and she dipped a curtsy and left his office abruptly, her payment for throwing her derriere in the air clutched in her palm.

Chapter Ten

❦

"If you keep swiveling your head about like that, it will fly right off and go careening into those pigeons like a *bocci* ball." Kit Whitelaw, Viscount Grantham, gestured to the little cluster of iridescent birds jostling each other for crumbs near a fountain spraying skyward.

"We're in Paris, not Italy," Susannah reminded him. "I do believe you're as nervous about this as I am."

"Nervous?" Kit scoffed at the very idea. "When I spent a good portion of the war spying upon the enemy, dodging bullets—"

Susannah jerked her arm from his and put her hands over her ears. Trudged on in silence.

Abashed, he walked quietly by her side for a moment, allowing her to make her point.

And then, by way of apology, he gently took her hand from her ear, kissed her palm, and tucked her hand back into his arm, covering it with his own. A silent, symbolic promise: *I will keep you safe always.* It had been thoughtless of him to remind her of the dangers he had survived, on behalf of his country, and on her own behalf not too very long ago. He bore the scars. She'd once jested about those very dangers, about the number of times someone had tried to kill her, and he'd found it intolerable to hear.

"You're forgiven," she said magnanimously, finally.

He smiled.

And then he brought the two of them to a halt and looked up at the window of a flat; bright but wilting flowers trailing out of the window box. The high afternoon sun tinted the walls of the house a soft peach. Unassuming, pleasant, not at all dramatic enough for what it appeared it might be.

"This is the place, Susannah."

Tracking down Claude Lamoreux had proved challenging, but Kit was dogged and experienced and delighted once more to use the skills he'd acquired in service of the crown. The investigation hardly posed the sorts of dangers he'd experienced before—he and Susannah had mostly made the acquaintance of a number of aging former opera dancers, and not one of them had lunged with a knife or pointed a pistol—but the trail had finally led them here, to these apartments on the outskirts of Paris. A little narrow stone staircase led up to them.

It was indeed the same address to which Susannah had directed her letters. What remained for them to discover now was why no one had responded to them.

He could feel her fingers curling a little more tightly into his arm, and she was right. He was nervous on her behalf. They had come so far, and been through so much. He very much wanted Susannah to have the thing she'd dreamed about for so long: a family.

The door was flung open by a housekeeper: gray hair spiraling anarchically out from beneath her cap, a little boomerang of a French nose, tiny, shrewd dark eyes.

An instant later, from behind the housekeeper, from inside the house, a raspy voice said something unspeakably filthy in German.

Susannah had seen Kit's eyes pop, then saw the telltale quivering at the corners of his mouth.

"What did he say?" she hissed.

"I will tell you later," he murmured back. "When you are naked."

That both quieted her and turned her scarlet and completely eradicated her nervousness, which Kit had always been able to do.

"*Pardonnez-moi,* but Guillaume, he over and over says these words, and I know not what it means. I think he is angry." The housekeeper was wringing her hands. "He is making me crazy."

The housekeeper was right. The filthy German words, sounding even more vehement now, were repeated. As if Guillaume were desperate to make a point.

"He is lonely, Guillaume, I think, for Madame Claude."

Kit really had no business knowing, but part of him wanted to meet the person who had such an unabashedly colorful vocabulary. "And who is Guillaume?"

"Guillaume is the parrot of Madame Claude."

This was somehow both disappointing and even better than if Guillaume had been a person.

"So Madame Claude is not at home? We have come from England and hoped to meet her. We believe we have a mutual friend."

"Madame Claude is away. Also Mademoiselle Sylvie. She left me alone here ... with Guillaume," the housekeeper said with dark despair.

The German words wafted toward them again. This time they were a sad, low mutter, sounding nearly as despairing as Madame Gabon did.

"Mademoiselle Sylvie?" Susannah repeated, her voice faint with excitement and hardly dared hope.

Kit took her elbow to steady her, and spoke. "Tell me, Madame"—Kit paused, to allow her to complete the phrase.

"Gabon."

"I am Viscount Grantham, and this is my wife, Lady Grantham. Tell me, Madame Gabon, does Mademoiselle Sylvie look at all like Susannah? Does she resemble Susannah?"

If Madame Gabon thought this was an unusual question, nothing about her betrayed it. She seemed to welcome the little challenge. Madame Gabon peered at Susannah. "You are close in age to Mademoiselle Sylvie, I think, Lady Grantham. I think perhaps your hair?"

"Does Sylvie look like . . . like this woman?" Susannah opened her hand, extended the miniature of her mother, and Madame Gabon squinted at it. Susannah lifted it up a bit higher so the woman could focus upon it more closely.

"Oh no, Mademoiselle. Not so much. Not Sylvie." She looked up. "But you do!" she added hopefully, hating perhaps to disappoint this English nobleman and his wife.

"And Mademoiselle Sylvie is not at home?"

"No. Mademoiselle Sylvie, she left a note for Madame Claude. She is angry, Mademoiselle Sylvie, in the note she is. And they come to see her, Etienne, Monsieur Favre—all angry."

Susannah glanced sideways at Kit. This parade of angry men arriving to see Mademoiselle Sylvie did not sound promising.

"Who is Monsieur Favre?" Kit asked, deciding to begin with that name.

"Mademoiselle Sylvie, she dances for Monsieur Favre. She is very pretty," she added. "Famous. She is famous."

This was better. Or perhaps worse. It was increasingly difficult to know.

"Did Mademoiselle Sylvie travel to the South as well?"

"No, no. To England, the note says. It says…" The housekeeper frowned forbiddingly, as if to narrate the tone of the note. " 'Dear Claude: I have gone to England, and I believe you know why.' "

The housekeeper shrugged then. "*I* know not why, but perhaps Madame Claude, she does. But she is in the South. She is expected to return in two days."

When Guillaume muttered again, it was clear that as far as he was concerned, Madame Claude could not return soon enough.

"Do you know who Mademoiselle Sylvie might have gone to visit in England?" Though Kit suspected he knew the answer. Sylvie's reason was standing right before Madame Gabon at the moment, being gripped by the elbow by Kit.

"I know not. But Madame Claude knows only of a Mrs. Daisy Jones in England. Perhaps it is that Mademoiselle Sylvie is acquainted with her, too. But I do not know, Monsieur, Madame Viscount. But there were letters, too, from England."

"Letters?" Susannah repeated eagerly.

"Only very recently, Madame. Madame Claude burned them when they arrived. All but one, for it arrived but a week ago. Mademoiselle Sylvie, she read the letter. And then *poof*! She is gone to England."

Claude no doubt had burned them to protect Sylvie from the truth of her past; Claude could not possibly have known that all was safe at last. Susannah had not told the entire tale in the letter; she had only sought to know if Claude was indeed the Claude Lamoreux who had adopted one of Anna Holt's daughters.

Anna Holt, accused murderess.

Eagerly: "When did Sylvie leave? Was she alone?"

"Alone? I know not, Madame. I know that Monsieur Etienne did not accompany her. I told him that Sylvie might have gone to see Madame Daisy Jones, for what else might I say?"

"Who is Monsieur Etienne?"

"He is her lover," Madame Gabon said very seriously. "He is a prince. And, *mon dieu,* he is angry."

There was an eloquent pause as Kit and Susannah stood in the Parisian sun and allowed this little bit of information to sink in.

"Your family is proving to be so much more interesting than mine," Kit said enviously.

❧

It was exceptionally early. An hour at which Tom Shaughnessy would have, more typically, been returning from the Velvet Glove to catch an hour or so of uninterrupted sleep in his own cozy room before embarking on the business of his day. Early enough so that damp still clung to the vines tangling the little picket fence, so that sun was seen in the wan gold that touched the flowers and flagstones, but seemed to have gathered no heat yet.

He'd hired a horse again to make the journey quickly, and to be able to return to London quickly, and he tethered the beast at the gate.

The door was already open, for of course the Mays would have seen and heard the hoofbeats of his arrival. Mrs. May stood in the entry, an apron still tied over the well-worn striped muslin of her dress. Her gray-threaded russet hair was scraped back away from her face, and a dot of what appeared to be flour was high on her cheekbone. She'd been at her morning chores then.

"Mr. Shaughnessy."

It was all the greeting she offered, but she didn't sound

surprised. Tom bowed; she dipped a shallow curtsy and stepped aside, allowing him into the house, and held out her hands for his hat and coat. Her face, a worn reminder of Maribeth's, had been all but impassive until she took these things into her hands; her movements slowed, she lingered a bit, as perhaps any woman would, over the fineness of the fabric. He noticed it. He wondered what she thought.

His *behavior* had so far been all that was gentlemanly, glossy appearance notwithstanding. There remained, however, the little matter of his reputation, which followed him like an invisible army into the house each time, he was certain. And he was certain Mrs. May had ideas about what a man of his reputation might do at any minute, and was braced for all of his reprehensibility to come spilling out of him.

"Thank you for allowing me to visit, Mrs. May."

"You're welcome, Mr. Shaughnessy. Have you brought ham, today?"

Tom paused. He could have sworn her eyes sparked for an instant. Then again, it might have been a reflection of the morning light.

So he smiled, to encourage further thawing, if thawing indeed was taking place.

"No, I am afraid not. I brought only . . . these." He held up his hands; in one was the tiny pirate hat; in the other, the wooden horse.

She peered at them for a moment.

"Even better," she said.

⁌

Tiny as the hat was, it still engulfed Jamie's head, but it made him laugh mad, gurgly, contagious laughs and flail his arms about. There passed an hour or so in which they played some combination of pirate and peekaboo, which Tom found surprisingly diverting, and during which Tom taught him to growl "aye, matie!" and to say "Tom!" Jamie was quick, a veritable little parrot, and Tom found it strangely gratifying.

And then Tom got down on his hands and knees and showed Jamie how to pull the horse along. Jamie dragged it briefly, then picked it up by its string and dangled it.

"'Orse!" he told Tom.

Tom looked at Jamie and felt—well, nearly as though a celestial chorus had just sounded.

"Bloody hell—that is—by *God,* it certainly *is* a horse!"

"Buddy hell!" Jamie repeated happily.

Tom felt a little chill of horror. "Oh bloo—" Tom clapped his mouth shut just in time. "Christ. That is—"

"CHRIST!" Jamie bellowed, and grasped the horse by one of its legs and held it up to him.

Mrs. May appeared in the doorway with a tray in her hands. "I thought you might enjoy some—"

"*Christ!*" Jamie roared happily, clutching at the horse with one hand to show her. He toddled over to her and curled one fist into her skirt, looking up at her, offering the horse.

Mrs. Mays had gone utterly still. Her eyes bugged out briefly.

Jamie apparently thought Mrs. May's bulging eyes were funny, because he laughed his gurgly laugh. *"Buddy hell!"* he shouted gleefully, hopping up and down, the horse bouncing in his hand.

Tom squeezed his eyes closed briefly. Apparently "Aye, matie!" wasn't funny enough to repeat to Mrs. May. It certainly didn't make the eyes of adults bulge in that amusing manner. And the child possessed the most remarkable volume. *Everything* became an announcement.

But then again, when almost everything in your world is new, Tom supposed enthusiastic announcements were not untoward.

Mrs. May slowly lifted her head up from Jamie and met Tom's eyes. Tom held her gaze bravely.

There passed an incongruous moment during which little Jamie gleefully hopped about the rug, singing out "buddy hell!" at intervals, while the two adults regarded each other warily.

And then, before Tom's disbelieving eyes, Mrs. May actually, slowly . . .

Well, it was almost a smile. But whatever it was, it changed her face completely, softening and lightening it, and Tom could see the glimmers of Maribeth there.

"They're a challenge, Mr. Shaughnessy. Particularly boys. They hear—and repeat—everything."

Tom cleared his throat. "I fear he most definitely takes after me."

His way of apologizing, and a bit of a risk as far as jests were concerned, since as far as Mrs. May was concerned, he was about as disreputable as they came.

But Mrs. May smiled in earnest at that.

And so Tom knew several milestones had been reached. Jamie had added significantly to his vocabulary, and Tom and Mrs. May had made progress in the warmth of their relationship.

Jamie hopped over to Tom. "'Orse!" he said, and lifted the toy up to him.

Now *he says horse,* Tom thought grimly.

But then, having caught on: "Horse!" Tom echoed delightedly. And made a point of bugging out his eyes.

Jamie clapped his hands. "Aye, matie!"

Tom still didn't know why he had come. He only knew that when he had returned to London, it was as though he brought with him a little invisible strand that bound him to Kent and tugged at him like a string on a bow, pulling him back again.

While Tom was visiting Jamie, Sylvie was learning how to be a pirate. The bawdy female kind, that was.

Josephine and Sylvie and a small crew of hastily recruited seamstresses had been very busy, and now all the girls stood before The General outfitted in pantaloons. Voluminous, nearly skirts, dark in color but sheer in weight, and, if one peered closely, or happened to catch a fortunate glimpse of them in just the right light—and it would be certain that the White Lily and The General would contrive to show them in the right light—deeply scandalous. They wore sashes and grand, ruffled white shirts, and miniature wooden cutlasses hung from their hips. The splendid little pirate hats topped their heads.

And then the results of the hammering and swearing Sylvie had heard behind doors were wheeled out onto the stage, a magnificent, miniature, rather convincing pirate ship, complete with sails of stretched sheets, a flag of skull and crossbones, and a gangplank. A hatch was carved in the hollow middle from which Captain Daisy would burst and sing the bawdy pirate chantey while the girls danced nearby.

Despite the context in which he employed his gifts, Sylvie could not deny that The General was indeed gifted if he had overseen this little masterpiece.

"Ye'll 'ave to make it bigger than that," Molly sniggered, when she saw the hatch.

"Where the bloody hell is Daisy?" The General bellowed.

The woman in question was just now emerging from the long hall that led to her dressing room, bedecked in her own significantly larger version of the pirate clothes, her commanding behind swinging behind her.

"Thank you for gracing us with your presence, Daisy." The General said it mildly, but somehow managed to engrave the sentence in sarcasm.

"Yer welcome, General," she said sweetly.

She swaggered her way up onto the stage, strode up the gangplank, and began to lower herself into the hatch. She was in up to her hips when, for some reason, she stopped lowering.

Daisy went still; her eyes widened in surprise. She twisted to the left. She twisted to the right. Stopped again. Looked confused.

Then alarmed.

"She's wearin' the ship," Molly whispered loud enough for everyone to hear.

A rustle of evil little giggles.

Daisy, a little panicked now, twisted rapidly to the left and right again, and then again, a great redheaded windmill. But she couldn't screw her body any farther into the hold of the small pirate ship.

"*Stuck*...Daisy?" The General asked idly.

Daisy jerked her head violently toward him. Her glare could have melted the windows of the theater.

It *did* rather look as though she were wearing a ship for a skirt, Sylvie noted.

"Jenny, Lizzie, if you would give Miss Jones a hand." The General sounded bored.

Lizzie and Jenny scrambled up the gangplank and knelt to push on Daisy's shoulders. Daisy sank a *bit* lower into the hatch, but her bosom effectively prevented her from going any farther. It lay on the deck in front of her and billowed up around her chin. She peered out from it, eyes bulging and glaring, cheeks scarlet.

"The hatch was cut to the measurements you gave to Josephine last week, Miss Jones," The General informed her.

Daisy's vehement response was muffled by her bosom. She tried to give her head a toss; it was all but immobilized between the pillows of her breasts. So she settled for flapping her arms and making a rude hand gesture.

"One more good push should do it, girls," The General said, and Sylvie could have sworn his eyes had an unholy glint. "Tamp her down in there."

Daisy flailed her arms in vehement objection.

"On second thought, girls, we'd best pull her far enough up again so she can at least sing." The General allowed. "We've lost enough time out of the schedule as it is."

He reviewed his watch while Jenny and Lizzie tugged on Daisy's arms until her entire torso was visible again.

"All right, then! All aboard, maties," The General called, as though the wedging of Daisy was a minor inconvenience. "And I shall demonstrate the dance for you." He brandished a small cutlass. "It's a simple one. It requires a bit of this"—he made an unmistakable gesture with his hand and his sample cutlass, causing giggles—"and a bit of . . . Swordplay." And at this he winked.

More giggles.

Oh, dear God. Sylvie whirled about as though looking for an escape. *I can't do it. I can't,* can't *rub my cutlass like that. I'll sleep on the street.* Surely, please God, she wouldn't be required to—

"Daisy, when the girls have mastered the dance somewhat, *then* we'll do the song."

Just then Sylvie remembered she'd contributed a line of verse to the song. And . . .

Well, damned if there wasn't a small part—a *very* small part—of her that wanted to hear Daisy sing it.

Daisy, a fuming torso popping up from the deck of the ship, would be forced to wait her turn to perform. Sylvie half suspected The General had done this purposely.

"Josephine—the song please," The General ordered.

Josephine lowered her hands, and the merry burst of music sprang through the theater. The General clambered up onstage with the girls, and demonstrated with his own cutlass.

"And a one, and two, and *thrust* your sword and slide, slide, and turn and clash swords with your neighbor and *again*..."

And in this way he and Josephine took them through the song and dance five times. At last he decided to allow them to do it alone. He took a seat and called out the steps from the audience.

"Step, step, and *thrust* your sword—"

Molly thrust her sword right into Sylvie's rear. Sylvie jumped.

"Sorry!" Molly said *sotto voce,* eyes wide and contrite. "So sorry!"

Sylvie gave a shallow, cool nod, and kept up with The General's commands.

"Look lively, girls! And one, two, and turn and *thrust* and—"

Molly poked Sylvie sharply in the arse again, sending Sylvie nearly straight up in the air.

"...one and two and I never said anything about hopping, Sylvie, and *slide* and four..."

"Lud, I *am* sorry!" Molly murmured. "I'll be more careful."

"I. Would. Be. Grateful," Sylvie murmured through a clenched jaw, as she thrust and slid.

"And turn, slide, and *rub* your cutlass, *rub* your cutlass, turn, turn, *thrust*—"

Molly thrust into Sylvie again. "Oh, I'm sor—"

Sylvie whirled around and clubbed Molly across the behind.

Molly shrieked and stumbled forward briefly, then regained her balance and swung her cutlass wildly at Sylvie. But Sylvie was quicker and smaller, and she dodged, bent, took calculated aim at Molly's ankles, and much to her satisfaction, down Molly went.

But Molly proved surprisingly nimble for one so plush. She was upright again in an instant, shrieking her outrage like a scalded parrot and wielding her cutlass like a club, and Sylvie parried expertly. The other girls flocked around them squealing encouragement and wagers.

But with one final parry and a clever and possibly unfair hook of her leg behind Molly's knees, Sylvie had Molly flat on her back and a wooden cutlass pointed at her throat.

They were both breathing like bellows.

"Cor!" Rose breathed.

Josephine had stopped playing the pianoforte long ago. All there was now was silence.

Which stretched as The General regarded the two heaving girls almost curiously, as if they were animals in a menagerie.

"Sylvie," The General drawled, finally. "May I have a word with you, please? Girls, the rest of you are dismissed for now."

Sylvie lifted the tip of her cutlass from Molly's throat and, with a small flourish, tucked it back into its tiny little sewn sheath. With dignity, all eyes upon her, she glided across the stage, trod lightly down the short flight of steps to the floor of the theater, and approached, chin up as if she was in fact the queen granting him an audience.

"Sack her." These were words disguised as a cough, and they came from the stage.

Sylvie followed The General without protest into a room she hadn't seen before, and he closed the door decisively behind the two of them. It was another profoundly masculine room, the theme of the theater condensed in plush overlarge furniture, cigar-and-woodsmoke-permeated air, and lurid murals featuring explicit images of gamboling satyrs and nymphs.

The General halted and turned to her. "Let me begin by saying that I think Tom was dead wrong to hire you."

Sylvie stiffened immediately. "Are you going to..." What was the English term she had just heard? "Sack me?"

" 'Sack you'?" He repeated, darkly amused. "No. That's not for me to do, Sylvie, as Mr. Shaughnessy hired you, and we *all* answer to Tom, ultimately. And he no doubt had his reasons; Tom has flights of brilliance, and flights of insanity, and fortunately the former typically outnumber the latter. I shall reserve judgment on which flight *you* happen to be though I do have my opinion. But you should know, Sylvie, that I'm on to you."

" 'On to me'?" All the casual English expressions were making her more irritable, and were doing nothing to cause her cursed temper to curl up in a quiet corner. She wished the little man would come to his point.

He turned suddenly and paced almost restlessly across the room, a distance away from her. He stopped and idly fingered a tassel on a curtain.

Then spun about so quickly the tails of his coat whipped his legs.

"The Paris Opera, *Le Cygne Noir*." He said it as though accusing her of murder.

Sylvie's heart nearly stopped.

His face went slowly rueful, a little abstracted with awe. "You were magnificent."

Sylvie looked down the mile or so it seemed she needed to see into The General's face, and wondered distantly that there was never anything comic about this man, despite his near-miniature proportions. He never commanded anything other than respect.

She gave a short nod finally, acknowledging his compliment. She knew when she was magnificent, and when she was not, and she knew she *had* been magnificent in the performance he cited. A "thank you" would have sounded condescending, and The General seemed to know it, because he gave his own short nod.

"So what are you doing *here*?" he demanded.

"I came to London in search of a relative. I found them not at home. I hadn't any money or a place to stay. I needed to work."

"Why the false name, Miss Hat? Are you in trouble with the law? Are you running away from someone?"

She remained stubbornly silent.

He studied her a moment longer. "This"—he gestured, apparently to the White Lily, and everything about it—"is not a joke. I believe you greatly underestimate Tom Shaughnessy. He built this—*all* of this—from nothing. He couldn't even *read* when I met him, and he managed to accomplish this. I don't know if you could ever comprehend the kind of nothing Tom came from, but I assure you, what you see here amounts to very nearly a miracle. And if that's a joke, Miss Hat, then it's the sort of joke that keeps a roof over your pretty head and food in your stomach at the moment, isn't it?"

The General was succeeding in making her feel ashamed. He was right. She might not have indulged her temper, she might have tried a little harder to rein it in, she might not have whacked Molly with a cutlass, if he were Monsieur Favre conducting a ballet at the Paris Opera, and not an autocratic dwarf in control of a bawdy theater.

The General didn't seem to require a response from her, regardless. He clearly saw the answer he wanted in her face.

"A theater like this treads a fine line with the authorities; it's a delicate balance. If you endanger it in any way, or call undue attention to it...I shall see that you pay for it."

She looked at him, this man whose head barely reached the pit of her arm, knew a brief moment of indignation and the impulse to protest.

And then she could not help but respect his loyalty and admire it. She nodded shortly, accepting the threat.

"Do you think you can settle your differences with Molly in some fashion other than swordplay and in some other location than the stage during rehearsal?"

Damned if the man wasn't making her cheeks flame in precisely the same way Monsieur Favre was able to. She smiled, a way of collecting her own dignity.

"Mr. Shaughnessy says he is lucky in his friends." An attempt to disarm him.

The General wasn't to be disarmed. "Tom Shaughnessy's friends are lucky in him," he said curtly.

A respectful, if not warm, quiet ensued.

"What were you doing in Paris?" she asked suddenly.

"Drinking," he said grimly.

"Why are *you* here?"

"I like watching pretty girls dancing in very little clothing."

And then he grinned at her, a grin so Tom-like in nature she nearly grinned in response. "And I enjoy making audiences full of wealthy men happy, because it makes *me* wealthy," he added. "There's an art to that, too, Miss Lamoreux, whether or not you believe it."

She fought to keep her eyebrows from dashing upward in rank skepticism.

"There's a room at the top of the theater. Attic room. Spiders and dust in it, no doubt. I'll find a broom for you. And if you should..." He cleared his throat. "If you should care to...use the room when you are not required to rehearse...I shouldn't tell Tom. He would not approve of the waste of your time, as there's no money in it, Miss Lamoreux, and you are his employee. This theater does belong to him, and your time belongs to him as well, at least during the day."

The General was offering her a place to dance, should she care to use it.

He might simply have offered it as an attempt to rein in her artistic temperament and thus make his own life more peaceful.

But she smiled softly at him anyway.

The General, she realized, did not precisely like her. But at his very soul, she suspected he was an artist. He probably understood what this would mean to her.

"Thank you, Mr...."

"General," he said. "The. General."

❧

Tom returned to the White Lily a little later than he would have preferred; still, the sun wasn't entirely high overhead. He expected to find the rehearsal of the pirate show in motion and to add his wisdom to the proceedings, should it be required.

All was silence.

He *did* see the pirate ship on the stage. The General had done a fine job, as usual. It was a magnificent little thing, cobbled together in a tearing hurry though it had been.

And suddenly he pictured, for an instant, what it might be like for a small boy to climb about the rigging and bound about the deck with a small wooden cutlass. How delightful it would be for a *crew* of small boys to—

What a startling thought. A foreign and *unprofitable* thought, and his mind seldom had room for those sorts of thoughts. He dodged it and moved briskly toward his office, when…

Wait. He peered more closely at the pirate ship.

There seemed to be a torso poking up out of the deck of the ship.

An *unmistakable* torso.

"Daisy?" he questioned tentatively.

"Tommy? Yer back, are ye then? They just…*left* me here, Tommy," she said plaintively. "Get me ou' of 'ere!"

He struggled not to laugh. "Are you…*stuck,* Daisy? In the hatch? What *happened*?"

She glared ferocious dark brown daggers at him. Her face was a dangerous shade of pink. "No, it's me new costume, Tommy," she said nastily. "The ship is. Now, ye bugger, get me out of 'ere!"

"Where's The General? Are you being punished? Were you naughty, Daisy? You can tell me." He was laughing silently now.

Then he had a horrible thought. "How long have you *been* there?" He realized any length of time like that would have been too long, so hilarity gave way to sympathy, and he loped up to the stage and took her by her arms, and pulled. Nothing happened, except that she squeaked when he tugged.

"Daisy, luv, I believe you've swelled up a bit. I don't want to hurt you, so we're going to have to cut you out. I'll go fetch a saw. Where's The General?"

"Scolding the new girl. She pinned Molly to the floor with a cutlass."

"*Did* she now?" Tom felt that increasingly familiar, marvelously slow, Sylvie-inspired grin spread across his face. "She can't be trusted with sharp things, you know. I imagine it was provoked."

"Oh, it was. I saw it all. Molly poked 'er in the arse with a cutlass. On purpose, now, mind ye. She 'ad it comin', that Molly did. There was quite a little battle." And Daisy, for the first time in an hour, smiled a bit.

Tom made a quiet mental note to himself; he was probably going to need to apologize to The General for the idea of a competition for Venus. Ah, well.

Wait: A *battle!* A pirate battle! A *female* pirate battle!

The audience would all but swoon for it.

Inspiration *did* arrive in the most unusual ways.

"*I* see the light in yer eyes, Tommy. Ye'd like there to be a battle up onstage." Daisy was watching him. She'd propped her elbows on deck, and propped her face in her hands. "Ye'd be askin' fer trouble, especially with this lot of females."

"You may have a point, but you must admit, Daize, it's a pretty splendid idea. I refuse to abandon it entirely. Now let me fetch a saw to get you out of here. Where have all the boys gone?"

"They scattered, too. Forgot all about me."

Those last four words, the very idea that anyone would forget all about her, Tom knew, was what terrified Daisy the most about the future. He still didn't know precisely how to reassure her; still, he knew reassuring her was tantamount to acknowledging a future without adulation. He gave her a brisk pat on one of her round arms and pushed himself to his feet. "I'll return in a moment, Daize. I promise I shan't forget you."

He leaped down from the ship into the aisle, which is when The General emerged from backstage then, Miss Sylvie Chapeau at his side.

Tom slowed, then stopped, and his eyes . . . feasted. She was dressed like a pirate, a blouse, a sash, those clever, just-shy-of-erotic pantaloons, a warm pink in her cheeks. The flush of the freshly scolded, perhaps. Or perhaps a flush fresh from a vigorous battle with wooden cutlasses.

The General saw Daisy still wedged in the pirate ship, stopped, and stared back at her.

"Happy, ye wee bugger?" she called to him, almost resignedly.

"It suits your eyes, Daisy," The General called in all seriousness. "The ship does. The brown. You should wear it more often."

If Tom was not mistaken...a blush crept in under Daisy's rouge.

"*You*"—The General whirled suddenly on Tom—"owe me an apology for your brilliant idea, Shaughnessy. *This*"—he gestured to Sylvie—"is what results from making Venus a *competition*. Cutlass battles."

"Can't be brilliant all of the time!" Tom confessed cheerfully. "It was worth a try, you must admit."

The General didn't appear to be in the mood to admit anything of the sort.

Tom turned away from the little man's glower and addressed Sylvie instead, as he much preferred to look at her.

"I turn my back for one moment, Miss Chapeau, and what do I hear? You've been brandishing sharp objects yet again." It was meant to be teasing, a crisp scold. He was surprised to hear his own voice emerge as nearly husky.

Sylvie looked swiftly up at him, read his eyes. Responded to what they saw there.

"I shall endeavor to be good, Mr. Shaughnessy." Her tone solemn, her eyes brilliant, her breath held in seeming anticipation.

"I imagine being good will be...a bit of a stretch for you." Never had a sentence been so redolent of innuendo.

And she laughed, a full-throated and feminine laugh, head thrown back.

The laugh splashed over Tom like a sudden burst of sunlight, washed all other thought from his mind. Tom was motionless for a moment. He just watched her with a faint wondering smile on his own face, and felt peculiarly breathless. Peculiarly light.

They both knew he'd not said anything particularly funny.

And then a silence followed that neither Tom nor Sylvie seemed to notice, as they were watching each other.

But The General and Daisy watched the two of them for a moment and then exchanged speaking looks with each other.

"I'll fetch a saw, Tom," The General said firmly. It sounded like a warning.

"A saw?" Tom repeated absently, turning his head with apparent difficulty toward his friend.

Sylvie Chapeau had turned her own head away at last and was now studying the murals, forehead slightly furrowed, as though she was trying to place precisely which gods were which, or was counting them.

"A *saw*, Tom. To free Daisy?" The General repeated patiently. "I'll fetch it. You might wish to know a message arrived for you whilst you were out. You'll find it in your office. And Miss Chapeau, will you please collect the rest of the girls so that we may conclude our rehearsals? That is, if *you've* no objections... Tom?"

More irony from The General.

"No objections," Tom said, cheerily enough.

Without another word, Miss Sylvie Chapeau turned to go. Tom watched her go, those sweetly narrow hips moving beneath her pirate trousers, those slim, elegant shoulders almost militantly squared, the little cutlass thunking at her side.

And when Tom turned for his office, he sang softly under his breath all the way there.

"Thrust your sword laddie, now thrust your sword..."

When Sylvie opened the door to the dressing room, a Tom-Shaughnessy-induced smile still faint on her lips, she saw all the other girls clustered together as if for protection, motionless and utterly silent. At first thought it was because of her, and she was tempted to hold her hands up over her head to show them she was unarmed and came in peace.

But then she noticed they were staring at something on Molly's dressing table, eyes fixed and bulging as if a wild animal had all cornered them in the room. Sylvie stood on her tiptoes to see what it might be. And saw...

Well, they had all received their share of flowers, ranging from flawless hothouse bouquets to sorry clumps purloined from flower boxes in drunken inspiration on the way to the theater. But these were...

Daunting flowers.

Immense roses, red as actual hearts and nearly as large, so vivid they nearly seemed to pulse, twined with lilies and ivy. Standing as high in their vase as a two-year-old child. Drowning the room in scent, as if their intent was to drug all the room's occupants.

"*Cor,* Molly!"

"There's a box! A little box with it!"

Molly snatched it up, slid a small triumphant glance and a matching smile toward Sylvie. Sylvie's dressing table was bare, whereas all the other girls' tables sported at least a trinket or two.

They all crowded snugly around Molly as she lifted the lid, and six pairs of eyes blinked when she did, and there was a collective catch of breath.

Inside was a pair of hair combs, studded with real pearls and sapphires. They were brilliant even in the indifferent lamplight of the dressing room.

Pearls and sapphires. They were the colors, of course, of Molly's fair skin and eyes. She would look like a queen with them tucked into her chestnut hair. The combs were another strategic little gift.

Molly slowly lifted them, held them up to her hair wonderingly, and stared at herself in the mirror. It was clear that her
confidence of a moment ago was shaken; her bravado gone. Sylvie rather knew how she felt. For Etienne's gifts had gradually
increased in expense and glory, until at last she was lifting out
of boxes intricate jewels designed just for her, furred pelisses,
things that so spoke of his wealth and power they managed to
make her feel somehow both immensely important and much
smaller all at once.

Sylvie's hand went up absently then, circling the wrist of
her other hand. She rubbed at it gently. A peculiar reflexive
gesture, as though she wanted to ascertain they weren't bound.
She turned away from Molly's reflection swiftly.

"Yer new bloke sent these, Molly?" Lizzie asked. "When
can we see 'im?"

"'E's only been but twice. But 'e took a box when 'e did,"
Molly said, trying to sound important, but still sounding half-
awed. Even a little subdued. The theater boxes, as they all knew,
were terrifyingly expensive to take, and only very wealthy men
could afford the discretion they provided. And no one was ever
certain precisely when the boxes were taken, for the curtains
were drawn about each one during each show. "'E sends 'is
man to meet me after the show, an' takes me to 'im. An' 'e's not
'alf' 'andsome, I tell ye. 'andsome as Mr. Shaughnessy."

The faces of the girls instantly became skeptical, as if this
was an impossibility.

"'E *could* be a bloody duke," Molly insisted. "And 'e's only
kissed me but once. 'Ere." She pointed to her fair cheek. "'E
jus' asks about everyone 'ere, and asks about my day, and lis-
tens to me talk and talk. Says 'e wants t' court me proper fer a
time."

The room fell silent, as every girl in it wondered what it
would be like for someone to court her proper.

❦

"...send me, send me to my reward, hmm, hmm, hmmm..."

In his office, Tom found the message The General had mentioned centered on the plans for the theater on his desk. He recognized both the seal and the handwriting, and frowned very slightly, a little puzzled but not terribly concerned, as he slid a finger beneath the seal to break it.

The words stopped his singing.

He stared at them, scowled at them a moment, absorbing the small unwelcome shock, breathing through it until it ebbed. He was faintly amused to realize that it ebbed more slowly than it might have a few mere weeks ago; risk was as native to him as breathing, typically, and he recovered from disappointments quickly enough.

It was an admission to himself that more was at stake now.

Specifically, the future of a small boy in Kent.

❦

"The major backed out of the Gentleman's Emporium, Gen."

Outside the walls of the Satyr room, the sounds of men rumbled more thickly than usual, which Tom found comforting. One of the boxes would be occupied this evening, too; a discreet note had been sent to Tom, and he'd arranged for Poe to escort the man in question into the White Lily theater.

"Mmm," The General grunted his own surprise. "Bit late to find another investor now, isn't it? Didn't you commit to the building?"

"He sent his apologies. But no explanation. And he hasn't been to the White Lily of late, has he? And he's been nearly every night for the past year."

"He *knew* he was about to back out, then."

Tom nodded grimly. So the major was avoiding him. Tremendously odd, and he couldn't conceive of a single reason why this should be the case, but it remained manageable as long as the other investors remained. And if Venus proved to be the success he anticipated it would be when they debuted it in a week's time...

Well, it would have to be a *very grand* success now to compensate for the loss of the major's backing.

Tom smiled. He was confident it would be a grand success.

"I peeked in at the workshop again tonight, Gen. The oyster shell for Venus will be smashing. You've outdone yourself."

"And in the footlights, Tom, it will be even more incredible," The General said confidently. "I've found a splendid paint—there's this bloke who has found a way to make it glow just so—a special ingredient, you see. And the fish, we'll have them swimming from the rafters..."

But Tom heard the recitation of The General's vision in terms of a list of expenses. He ticked off in his head the cost of the shell, and the fish, and the splendid paint, not to mention the costumes for the girls, and knew he would need an influx of fresh capital soon, even more than the healthy amount that flowed in nightly from the shows.

The fire leaped up, devouring a log—another expense, there, wood—throwing almost unnecessary heat into the room. But the fixtures and the murals always looked better in the firelight, and Tom and The General tended to keep it lit for that reason. Showmen, the two of them. He wouldn't begin economizing in that regard just yet. He thought he'd change the subject.

"I meant to mention this before, Gen. Veils. Do you think you could do something with veils?"

"Mmmm..." The General said appreciatively, tilting his head back. "Wonderful idea, Shaughnessy. In fact—well, picture this. The girls will be dressed as a harem, and—"

"I have a son," Tom blurted.

The General fell abruptly silent.

Tom didn't look at him. He felt very nearly embarrassed, as though he'd broken wind. He instead took a sip of his brandy, as if the admission had taken something out of him, and he needed to replenish.

A most pronounced gap in the conversation ensued. The General cleared his throat.

"This son. He's in Kent, I take it."

"Yes. Kent."

The exchange of confidences was not what their friendship was based upon; a benign and total acceptance of each other's strengths and flaws and a manly appreciation of all things female comprised the most of it, and an underlying affection based on nothing more than that they suited each other comprised the rest of it. This was new and delicate territory for both of them.

"And he's why you need...money? More than usual? It's not just for the Gentleman's Emporium?" was The General's next careful question.

"Yes. In part. Also, because I prefer to be rich." Tom was sounding a little testy now. The revelation had left him feeling a bit raw.

"A preference I share." The General's mouth quirked, an awkward attempt at humor.

Which led to an awkward silence.

"How did you get a son, Tom?" The General asked suddenly.

"The usual way, Gen," Tom said irritably.

The General laughed. "Sorry. It's just...well, who's the mother? Do you plan to..." The General paused, deciding this next thing needed to be said very, very gingerly. "Do you plan to marry her?"

"I know who she is. I just don't know *where* she is. She left him with her parents." Answering yet not answering The General's question.

Another silence fell.

Tom cleared his throat. "He's almost two years old now. And I find..."

He inhaled, and stood up, restlessly paced over to the hearth and stared up at the mural on the way. Satyrs having their way with nymphs, who showed every indication of enjoying themselves as well.

"I find that I want him to go to *Eton*," he said, half-wonderingly, incredulously. He gave a short laugh. "I want him to go to Oxford. For God's sake, I want him to sit in bloody Parliament. I was in that room with the investors, those men the other day, some of them smug, all of them wealthy and comfortable and ordinary. And now I think... I want my son to grow up to have a chance to be one of those smug men, I honestly do. I can make it possible if I have enough money. But... if the world knows I'm his father, his road will be difficult."

The General inhaled deeply, exhaled, taking in these words.

And not denying the truth of them.

"You're a good man, Tom," he finally said. It was inadequate, but it was about all that could be said.

Tom looked at The General wryly. "Hardly, Gen."

"I mean it. You're the best *I've* ever known, anyhow."

"Now that I can believe."

The General snorted softly, a laugh of sorts. And then he took a long draught of his tea, his own form of replenishment, and shifted his legs up onto a plump ottoman. Tea was the strongest brew he took since the days Tom had found him slumped against the wall outside the Green Apple Theater. He in fact took it so strongly that Tom could smell it from where he stood, even through cigar smoke and the wood being consumed by the fire.

"I've noticed there have been fewer duels lately, Tom. Smiling less?" Slyly said.

Tom gave him a sharp look. "Busy," he said curtly.

"Or just smiling *more* . . . at one particular woman?" As though Tom had said nothing at all.

At this Tom threw a sharp warning glance at The General. The little man was a bit too observant.

"You do know it's unwise, Tom," The General said. "For too many reasons to enumerate. The other dancers, for instance, would perhaps expire from jealousy or heartbreak. You could confidently anticipate a mutiny."

"I know it's unwise." Tom smiled crookedly. "My whole life has been an exercise in the unwise."

"But perhaps . . . well, you might make things easier for yourself if you . . ."

Tom looked at him expectantly.

"Oh, bloody hell. Never mind." The General sighed.

Tom absently worked his stiff fingers, bending them. Too much writing lately had made the old wound complain, even occasionally waking him up in the middle of the night, but there were plans and inquiries and ideas and permissions to be obtained before the dream of the Gentleman's Emporium could take tangible shape. Securing the backing of his investors was only a very small part of it all.

Odd how soft and amorphous-sounding the word "dream" was. So many practical things, bits and pieces, tangible things, nails, wood and pound notes and people, went into the making of dreams.

He rather liked all of it, the dreams, and the bits and pieces. He liked making it all look effortless. He liked giving jobs to people.

"He's too young to know who I am, Gen. The boy. And sometimes...well, I've begun to think I should just settle some money on him and quietly step aside."

The General rolled his eyes. "Ah, yes. That sounds like you. Someone who would 'quietly step aside.'" The General pointed at Tom's hand. "Tell me again how you got the scar? This theater?"

Tom stopped working his fingers, glanced down at them.

"This is different," he said shortly.

The General apparently didn't believe he was qualified to argue this particular point. He was quiet, and after a moment he simply said, "So...harems, eh?" and stood, reaching for his coat.

"Have you heard of the story of Scheherazade, Gen?" Tom reached for his own coat.

And the two of them, immensely relieved to be talking of business again, prepared to plunge into the theater to greet their guests.

After the evening's performance, back in the dark of the theater, Sylvie saw the girls take off out the door; saw the fine carriage taking Molly away, and turned once more to go up to her little room.

But she saw a light shining in Tom's office. Once again she couldn't resist the urge to peer in.

Tom lifted his head a little, frowned, then leaped to his feet, hand on what she knew to be his knife, and peered out.

She jumped back, hand over her mouth.

He went very still when he saw her. And said nothing for a moment, only dropped his hand from his knife. "You were peeking, Miss Chapeau."

"I wasn't," she said quickly. She was beginning to be tremendously sorry she'd given such a ridiculous name. She suspected he enjoyed using it for that very reason, and would have otherwise called her Sylvie the way everyone else did.

"You *were*," he disagreed firmly. "You did"—Tom broadly mimed furtively peering around a corner, then ducked back and put a coy hand over his mouth, eyes wide—"this. I saw you."

She tried, she did. But it proved impossible not to laugh.

"And did you see anything you liked while you were peeking?" he asked with all evidence of politeness.

Really, if a contest for flirting were ever held, Tom Shaughnessy had a duty to represent England.

"I saw a light, and wondered who it might be," she told him coolly.

"This is my library. It's where I work. You perhaps expected to see someone else in my place?"

He waited, and apparently decided just this once perhaps to not corner her into a response that would amuse him further. He sat back down at his desk and became brisk instead. "I've noticed that you and The General seemed to have reached a sort of détente. He doesn't like you, but he doesn't really like anyone, except perhaps me. And Daisy."

"One would think he likes Daisy least of all."

"One would think." His smile was enigmatic and swiftly gone.

There was a silence while they regarded each other. And then Tom made a self-conscious little gesture, smoothing a hand over his hair, pushing it away from his face. She found it oddly touching. Though he obviously reveled and took advantage of his splendid looks, it was clear he wasn't a slave to them. This little bit of vanity was clearly for her benefit, and it pleased her.

"Well? Will you sit down then?" He said it impatiently, in a rush, as though he'd actually issued an invitation and she'd been standing there mulling it in silence.

No, she thought. *Because that would be foolish, foolish, foolish.*

"All right," she said evenly, softly.

She looked back at him for a moment. His fingers were stained with ink, his shirtsleeves rolled up to expose strong and corded forearms. Long fingers, tapered, hands blue-veined and strong and tanned, that scar across one, white, drawn tightly at the edges. His shirt was open at the throat a few buttons, cravat dispensed with entirely, and she struggled to keep her eyes from peering at the opening to see whether his chest might be smooth, or whether, as on Etienne, hair curled there. Regardless, his chest was certainly broad and in the lamplight, a lovely shade of gold, a sort of tea with a hint of milk. Whether it was the quiet of the evening, the dark of the theater, the lack of other things to occupy her senses, everything about him, all the little details suddenly stood out in stark relief. The scar on his hand, his lashes, the faintest, faintest of lines beneath his eyes.

He noticed her regard, and she looked up sharply to meet his eyes.

"Who are you *really,* Miss Chapeau?" He said it winningly, coaxingly, with a grin. As if the sheer outpouring of charm would flood the answer right from her.

And this made her laugh. "I am merely a visitor to England, Mr. Shaughnessy, who was unfortunate enough to lose all of her money."

"When you first arrived, The General suggested you might be a...ballet dancer." He said the words the way he might have said "a native of Borneo."

She tensed a little with wariness, knowing The General had promised not to reveal her identity. Gave a pretty little laugh. "I wonder why he would think such a thing?"

Tom leaned back in his chair and regarded her for a disconcertingly long moment, hands linked behind and above his head, which only served to emphasize how very broad his chest was. She managed to look back at him evenly, eventually choosing to focus on his left eye, lest she go cross-eyed. She had the distinct sensation he was doing the very same thing to her that she was to him a moment earlier: inventorying her features.

And in the end, he looked more puzzled and a little uncomfortable more than anything else, which wasn't terribly flattering.

"Do you know how I met The General?" he said, unexpectedly.

"I cannot begin to guess."

"There's a theater in the East End—the Green Apple. Right rough little place. Perhaps you know of it?"

She gave a tight little smile. He grinned in response.

"No? Well, I got my start in theater there, you see, at the Green Apple. I'd worked at a pub by the docks, and met a fellow who ran a theater, and . . . well, anyhow I decided to create a show, pretty girls dancing. Dressed as flowers. Daisy petals round their heads." Tom circled the air around his face with a finger, illustrating. "Very clever, if I do say so myself. No one else had done anything quite like it, at least in the East End. And frankly, I very much enjoy pretty girls dancing.

"And, well, the first night of it, men came to the show, but not enough of them—the theater wasn't full. And the next time it was the same. The Green Apple's owner—well, he was right miffed, since he'd backed the show and was losing money. And I was getting right *nervous,* since the owner was a mad cove who would happily slit my gullet for losing his money."

He said this matter-of-factly, and Sylvie tried not to flinch. Just when Tom Shaughnessy had begun to seem human, he demonstrated yet again that he hailed from an almost entirely different universe from hers. A universe where one did business with gullet-slitters.

"Well, I stepped outside the theater when the show was over, and I was leaning against the wall, wondering whether to smoke a cigar, my very last one, and wondering what the devil I was going to do, you see, as I hadn't any money left, either.

"And then I heard this voice from somewhere down around my ankles. A drunk, *slurry* voice. And it said—well, I *thought* it said; *'Organza.'*

"Of all things! So I looked down toward the voice and saw a...little man, slumped there against the wall. He was only about as big as a child, thin, but with a full beard. Filthy bugger. And he smelled like a gin still—like he'd been soaked in the brew and tossed there against the wall. One spark from a tinderbox would have sent him up in flames.

"So I said to this filthy bugger, 'I *beg* your pardon?' Because I'm polite, you see."

"Of course," Sylvie said, mouth twitching.

"And so the little blighter says, from down around my ankles"—and here Tom adopted slurry, surly tones. " 'I said *organza,* you bloody idiot! Hangs better, and you can nearly see through it in the...in the"—Tom hiccuped for effect—"*lamp-light.* You've got all those girls in *muslin,* you damn fool. You *deserve* to fail.' "

Imitation concluded, Tom looked at Sylvie. "And then, after he'd said these *most* inflammatory things, this nasty little bastard slumped back against the wall. And I was certain he'd blacked right out, and I was about to go on my way.

"And then while I was staring at him, damned if he didn't stir and try to struggle to his feet. Rolling a bit, thrashing. It was taking him a good long while, so I found myself helping him up by the elbow."

Sylvie laughed, and yet something in her was surprisingly, oddly moved. She could imagine the contempt of another man for a small drunken man; she imagined most men would not have listened, would have walked away out of disgust. She wondered whether it was innate curiosity or a streak of mischief that caused Tom to do it. She imagined it was the sort of thing that would get him into trouble as often as it would prove lucky.

And strangely she found herself thinking: Etienne would never be subjected to such a situation in his life. Etienne would never have to make such a choice.

"So I help him to his feet, and the thanks I get is this. 'And if they're *flowers,* you bloody idiot,' he says to me when he's on his feet, swaying like a damn flower himself, 'they need to dance like flowers. *Erotic* flowers.'" He slurred the word extravagantly. "And I swear to you, Sylvie, right there, before my eyes...this little man begins to dance like—like—an erotic flower. Staggering about, waving his arms in the air." Tom waved his arms about in wide loops.

Sylvie burst into laughter; she couldn't help it.

Tom looked at her, smiling, savoring the sound, it seemed. "But even then..." He sat back in his chair. "Even then I could see what he was driving at." He said it wonderingly, as though even now he marveled at it.

"So I took this little man by the arm, which he didn't seem to like, as he kicked me in the ankles a few times, but his aim was poor, you see, because he was full of gin, and he missed more often than he struck home. And then I picked him up—Good God, but I cannot begin to tell you how the man stank—and he wriggled quite a bit. But I was able to hold him out from my body, seeing as how he's small and was very thin at the time, not at all the sturdy fellow you see now, and so he didn't manage to kick me in the baubles, though I assure you, he *did* try. And I got him back to my rooms, which were very near the Green Apple, and locked him into one, and let him dry out. Which wasn't pretty at all," Tom said grimly. "He kicked. He ranted. Said a lot of foul things about someone or something named 'Beetle' or 'Beedle' or some such."

"Did you say...Beedle?" This was intriguing. Sylvie knew of a Mr. Beedle, and if the Mr. Beedles were one and the same, this went a long way toward answering a few questions about The General.

"Beedle," Tom confirmed. "Never heard such swearing, not even during the war. But when The General was cleaned up and sober, he proved to be a right decent chap. Knew quite a bit about *organza,* in fact, and a lot more. He knew specific things—how to design costumes, beautiful ones. How to build sets. How to make wonderfully entertaining dances. As it so happened, our talents and tastes rather complemented each other. The Green Apple show became a great success with a quick change of costume and a few changes here and there to the dance. We had our erotic flowers. I gave him some of the money from the show. And he never took another drink."

She was quiet for a moment. "Kind of you to do that for him," Sylvie said softly.

"Perhaps," he mused. "I think it was more luck and curiosity than kindness. But then, as I've said, I've always been lucky in my friends."

"Friends like Biggsy the highwayman?" she couldn't help but say acerbically.

"I warrant most of the other passengers on the coach would consider it rather lucky that I knew him," he said with equanimity. "And Mick managed to drive *you* to the White Lily theater, didn't he? Though I haven't yet decided whether I consider that lucky."

He smiled at her; she narrowed her eyes.

"Which brings me to my point, Miss Chapeau. I've known The General for a good many years, and during that time I've learned to rely upon his decidedly singular body of knowledge. So if he believes that you're a ballet dancer..." He paused again. "I'm inclined to think his opinion has merit."

"Based simply upon his opinion?"

"That, and because, Miss Chapeau, you're *clearly* not a lady."

She was struck silent.

"I beg your pardon?" She nearly choked out the words.

He continued, seemingly oblivious to her outrage. "I've known many women..." He paused, tilted his head back as though they were parading across the ceiling, and a faint smile turned up his lips. "...*many* women," he confirmed, wryly and emphatically. "Women from all walks of life. Some with titles, many without. And you are neither a lady nor in service. You are accustomed to being looked at and to getting your way, and you haven't the air of a married woman, because you haven't the air of someone accustomed to being... well, looked after."

As this was startlingly true, Sylvie was rendered speechless.

"You've a different sort of confidence. Something explains this, and I'm not certain what it is. So I've told you a bit about me... why don't you tell me why you're in London."

"I have come to London to visit... a relative," she offered finally, tentatively. He deserved that much, she supposed. "I found my relative unexpectedly not at home."

"Ah. So the... Chapeau... family was called away suddenly on urgent affairs? Perhaps they've gone to visit your cousins, the Pelisse family of Shropshire?" He asked it innocently.

She was tempted to laugh. Tom Shaughnessy was cleverer than she wanted him to be. She considered whether to confide in him: *My sister is married to a viscount, and apparently every opportunist in the land is claiming to be her sister, and, by the way, there's a large, grand reward for the apprehension of these opportunists. You might have heard, as the rest of London seems to have. And didn't you mention you needed a good deal of capital for your new theater?*

"Their house was dark, there were no servants about, no one to allow you in?" he pressed. "No one expected you?"

"No," she said shortly. "No servants."

"And you will leave the White Lily when your relative returns?"

She hesitated. "Yes."

He was quiet for a moment. "You don't trust me. I was hoping you would."

"No," she said shortly, with a little smile.

And to his credit, after a moment, he smiled too. "Perhaps you shouldn't."

The flirtation was back in his words, but faintly, as though he was forcing it there to make her feel more comfortable. An odd little silence passed by. He cleared his throat.

"If you are in any danger, Miss Chapeau, you can tell me. I shan't let you come to harm."

He said it almost gently. But with absolute quiet conviction. And she understood now that this sentence, this offer, had been the entire point of his interrogation.

"Thank you," she said finally. Feeling nearly shy.

Tom was watching her, his light eyes serious. "Your lover is a fool," he said swiftly.

"He is *not* a—"

"Yes?"

Sylvie squeezed her eyes closed, infuriated. And then something fought up in her: a reluctant amusement at and admiration for his ability to find precisely the right places in her pride and temper to prod in order to get her to confess things. She suspected it was his particular talent. She preferred not to think of it as her particular weakness.

She opened her eyes, found him watching her, but strangely, not smiling. "Your temper, Miss Chapeau, may one day be the death of you. But it makes you truthful, I believe. And your lover . . ."

He waited, to give her one more opportunity to deny the existence of a love. She wouldn't give him the pleasure of it.

"And your lover can't be a very good one."

She should have been outraged.

Instead: *Why?* she wanted to ask. *Is there something about me that betrays this? Are there different kinds of lovers? What makes a good lover? Do they scramble your wits and make you laugh one moment and furious the next and make you want to feast with your eyes upon the details of their faces?*

Or do they take you, then fall asleep leaving you unsatisfied more often than not, and tell you they love you as often as they remark about the weather and promise everything you've always wanted? Safety and peace and wealth and comfort?

She decided to call his bluff. "What on earth makes you think so, Mr. Shaughnessy?" Her voice was light, nearly inviting.

The candle guttered in its glass globe. It changed the shadows in the room ever so slightly, made Sylvie aware that she had been sitting alone with him for perhaps too long.

"Because you are here with me right now and not with him."

The logic of this seemed unassailable when delivered in a voice low and soft, nearly husky. He sounded gently patient. As though he'd been waiting for her to arrive at the answer on her own.

And then she tore her eyes away from his and took a deep breath, and the spell he'd managed to weave with his soft voice drifted away.

"I told you why I am in London, Mr. Shaughnessy. It has naught to do with him. Or with you."

Another silence, as Tom seemed to be contemplating his next question.

"You admit you are an ambitious woman, Miss Chapeau."

"Yes," she said tersely.

"And your lover—"

"Will give me what I need," she completed firmly for him.

Tom dropped his chin once, almost a nod, as if taking this in. He took up his quill, twirled it absently between his fingers. And then he looked up, and his voice was dangerously gentle.

"But what do you *want,* Miss Chapeau?"

Such a simple question. And yet, for a moment, it shocked her motionless.

Finally, she laughed shortly. "There's no place in my life for 'want' in and of itself, Mr. Shaughnessy. And I have... earned... *everything* I need."

"And *everyone* you need?" he said ironically.

She stood quickly. "I should retire and leave you to your... your work."

"Very well, Miss Chapeau. But wait—" He frowned suddenly. "There's something..."

She paused, hovered, uncertain, sat again.

"You've... a mark of some sort on your cheek." He narrowed his eyes, as if trying to ascertain just what it might be. "...allow me to..."

He leaned over the desk toward her, suddenly. She held her breath, willing herself not to turn her head as those silver eyes came closer, knowing this was a dare. And yet her eyelashes fluttered, her eyes began to close, then did close. Her speeding heart made her breath come short, and each breath took in the scent of warm man, and each breath scrambled her senses just a little more. She waited.

"I was mistaken," his voice came to her, softly, after what seemed an eternity. So close it seemed to be coming from somewhere inside her own body. The breath of his words brushed her cheek. "Perhaps... it was just a shadow."

Her eyes opened again in time to watch his long body lean slowly back in his chair.

She had expected him to be wearing a faintly victorious smile.

Instead, he looked just as unsettled as she felt; his face had gone strangely taut. His eyes were darker now. Slate.

Sylvie was conscious that her shoulders were moving more rapidly with her breathing. The pierce of anticipation ebbed, leaving behind a peculiarly acute disappointment. As though a gift proffered had been yanked away.

"I believe you've crushed your quill, Mr. Shaughnessy."

Tom glanced down at the mangle of feathers in his hand. And for a moment he looked genuinely puzzled.

And then he deposited his broken quill almost tenderly on his desk.

"Good night, Sylvie," he said softly. "And it might be wise to keep in mind that I'm not a gentleman. I'm not obliged to play fair."

Sylvie stood and whipped about so quickly that her skirts nearly tripped her. She took a swift step toward the door.

"And Sylvie—"

She paused but didn't turn around.

"Sometimes . . . sometimes they're one and the same."

She knew he meant want and need.

And oddly, it sounded as though it was a revelation to him, too.

Chapter Eleven

◌

For Tom, days had always passed quickly, but with the addition of visits to Kent to his week as well as preparations for the Venus show—they now had a song, there was a dance for the girls to rehearse, and the oyster was nearly complete and required his opinion—the rest of the week was a bit of a blur.

He saw Sylvie Chapeau every day, stoically smiling and patting fannies, learning to be a water nymph. He kept a safe distance, at the foot of the aisle, considering what it meant to *him* to want and need.

Toward the end of the week as Tom was ensconced in his office, poring over expenditures for The Gentleman's Emporium and planning new ones, another message arrived.

He eyed it warily, but knew he had no choice but to open it: He broke the seal.

Lord Cambry offered his apologies, but regretted he could no longer invest in The Gentleman's Emporium.

The words struck like an adder bite.

He'd scarcely had time to register them when he looked up and saw a woman dressed not as a fairy or a pirate or a water nymph, but in a walking dress, a rather nice one, and it took him a moment to recognize Molly. It wasn't the sort of dress one could afford to have made on her salary unless one saved for a good, long time. He wondered, briefly, if the bordering-on-demure, well-cut gown meant that yet another girl had acquired a wealthy protector or a willing husband and had decided to retire from the White Lily.

The timing would be inconvenient regardless, given the role they planned for Molly in the Venus show. But Tom philosophically began considering alternatives—none of them Daisy Jones—even before he spoke.

"You've arrived early today, Molly, haven't you?" he managed cheerily enough.

"Josephine needed 'elp wi' the sewing, an' so I offered to come in."

Molly had never struck Tom as the type to volunteer for extra work. He frowned a little, bemused. "She needs additional help? Isn't Sylvie helping her with the sewing? All the costumes have been sewn—it's only mending, is it not?"

"Well, that's just it, Mr. Shaughnessy. Sylvie ought to 'elp, but now she goes off to meet 'er lover midday of late, so Josephine asked fer me help."

Time stopped. Tom's breathing stopped as well.

"Sylvie goes off to meet her lover?" he managed to repeat levelly.

Molly fingered the corner of his desk. "Every day, middle o' th' day, Josephine says. Past few days." Molly was the very picture of innocence. "All of a sudden, like. She leaves early, and comes back mussed and red in the face, like, and she looks…'appy. *Real* 'appy."

"Thank you, Molly." Tom breathed in, breathed out, to get his lungs, his heart moving again. He didn't want to hear any more. "This is interesting."

She looks 'appy.

"Yer own needs bein' met, Mr. Shaughnessy?" Molly asked frankly.

"Mr. Shaughnessy?" she repeated, when he didn't answer her.

He did manage to get his mouth to turn up, but the motion was painful, seemed as unnatural as bending in half backward. "Your concern is touching, Molly, but I haven't any complaints in that regard."

"My concern *is*...touching, Mr. Shaughnessy," she said quite seriously, with a duck of her head. She trailed a hand provocatively across her collarbone, then, very casually, down across one full breast.

He was a man, after all; he watched the hand's entire journey. The trouble was, it all looked rather like choreography to him now.

"Thank you for considering my needs, Molly, and I *am* flattered. But I believe you know my policy." He said the words firmly, with a small smile to soften them.

Leave, he thought. He wanted her to leave so he could be alone with the alien sensation pressing inside his chest. If he didn't know better, he would have called it an ache.

He kept his voice level. "You said you believe Sylvie creeps off to see her lover rather than doing the work she was hired to do? And this is why you've decided to pay me a visit?"

"Oh, yes," Molly said somberly. "Right about this time o' day."

The top half of the White Lily was divided into two spaces: one, the attic room in which Tom felt most comfortable, because smaller spaces made him feel more secure somehow. And the other, a room that hadn't been used for decades for anything other than storage.

When he arrived, he discovered the determined sunlight filtering through the dust-caked windows, creating a sort of twilight in the room; the floor, he noticed, had been swept, barrels and crates pushed aside to create a clearing. A stage.

Tom hovered behind in the dark hallway as she left her room, closed the door behind her, and furtively, hurriedly took the stairs up a flight toward the attic room, her feet touching the stairs lightly as a cat. Inexplicably, as the day was warm and the heat had risen to fill the upper rooms with a sultry density, she had covered herself in a cloak. A disguise?

Or did she spread the cloak over the floor so she could lie upon it with her lover?

His hands squeezed closed into involuntary fists, echoing what his heart had done at the thought.

Still, he followed her, taking the stairs as lightly as he could, and keeping his head down. What did he intend to do? Leap out and cry *"A-ha!"*

He should leave.

He couldn't leave.

And then, at last, the foreign tightness in his chest eased a little when all he saw was Sylvie.

She was standing in the middle of the room, head down, shoulders back, arms curved out from her body as though she cradled a great invisible heart between them, the fingertips of each hand just shy of meeting below her belly. Her feet were pointed out, her hair pulled back, combed smooth and pinned so tightly the sun glanced off it as though the surface was mirrored—sable with a sheen of fire.

The cloak had been folded neatly and set aside; he saw it. And she wore a dress that, scandalously, remarkably, exquisitely, exposed a length of elegant ankle and calf. The reason for the disguise, he supposed. Fragile, the skirt of it seemed to hover like mist above her calves, looking ready to flutter up should she move or breathe.

Her throat was long and white, so fair he could see the faint blue trace of a vein in it. It should have made her seem vulnerable; instead, everything about how she held her body at the moment spoke of power and intent.

And for a moment, it seemed, he couldn't know for certain whether the light radiated from her or came through the window, or if it was merely an agreed-upon exchange between Sylvie and the sun.

And then he noticed the smile. Faint, but so privately, confidently joyous Tom could nearly *feel* it. Nearly. It was both bitter and sweet, taut and rich, like the first bite of a plum, because he was certain he'd never worn that kind of smile, felt that kind of joy.

It was very like the smile one would give a longtime lover, he imagined.

The smile became softly inviting; she stretched her arms out toward some invisible partner, and balanced—floated—it seemed, on one leg.

Then she swiftly gathered her limbs together and pirouetted, rising all the way up on her toes, and like a dandelion caught in a breeze, covered the distance of that rough floor with leaping steps and turns, before stopping to arch backward, one knee drawn up, her body lithe as a ribbon. And he saw now that her dress was less a costume than very nearly a pair of wings, for it merely enhanced the sense that he was watching a creature of flight.

Mesmerized, Tom watched her, pressed back against the

stairwell, breathing all but suspended, the better to hear, to feel her dance. He'd seen paintings of ballerinas before, but the dance itself never interested him; he'd considered it a conceit for those at court. And, of course, there wasn't any money in it.

But now, something like awe and panic warred inside him, and amused him distantly. Truly, he felt as though he'd stumbled, sober, across an actual fairy, the sort his Irish mother had so fervently believed in and feared, not the sort that he and The General swarmed the stage with to ribald acclaim. Sylvie no longer seemed to belong to the same species as he did; she didn't seem crafted of flesh and bone. Rather, suddenly she was made of fire or water, something that burned or flowed.

And Good God—just look at that. She could bend nearly in *half.*

Backward.

The prurient possibilities of this did not escape him.

He could almost hear the music Sylvie moved to in his head, could feel the story of it as she danced. He sensed, even through the pleasure on her face, that she was meticulously counting the steps off in her head, each placement of her foot precise and calculated as it thumped lightly on the floor in satin slippers, or left the floor to sail through the air briefly, though to the viewer it would all seem entirely artless. She hadn't mirrors to follow her movements; he wondered if she missed them. She must know from the way her body felt to her that the movements were correct, the way Josephine could play a song from feel.

And as he watched Sylvie's arms floating upward, rippling, her delicate neck tilted back, he knew this was beautiful; he in fact knew that "beautiful" was an inadequate word for it. This was artistry, and in a way he resented it. For in watching it he felt every bit of his own roughness, the roughness he had ruthlessly wrestled into submission.

And at the same time, he knew learning to dance like this

would have required pain and sacrifice and endless practice, a superhuman determination. The determination of someone who was resolved to be something, anything other than ordinary.

A determination, in fact, rather similar to his own.

The pieces fell into place: the source of this woman's confidence, and her determination, perhaps, to move out of the shadows of the *demi-monde*. Perhaps she, like he, was beginning to understand the limitations of the shadowy place within society they occupied. And perhaps this was the reason she had taken a lover, no doubt a wealthy one.

He will give me what I need, she'd said.

Somehow, Tom had known from the moment she'd landed in his lap in the mail coach that this woman was far, far from ordinary. And now he realized why watching her wield cutlasses and pat derrieres . . . was rather like watching a unicorn pulling a plow.

Then again, he rather liked seeing Sylvie in her fairy wings. He rather liked seeing her dressed as a pirate and patting derrieres. Somehow, they all seemed simply aspects of her: the delicate, the ethereal, the magical. The dangerous, the wicked, the fearless.

Although he'd begun to suspect he'd rather like seeing her dressed in anything at all.

Tom watched, and knew the longer he watched, the greater the risk she would see him. And now he almost wished he hadn't followed her, for he knew the image of her dancing, of that smile, would haunt him. He felt nearly as conflicted as if he'd actually caught her with a lover.

And in a way, he knew, he had.

She looks . . .'appy.

He backed slowly, carefully, down the stairs, wondering why he should feel guilty, why he should feel as though he'd been intruding, when everything in this theater belonged to him, including the room she'd cleared to become her own private stage. His own determination and passion had made it so.

He'd forgotten the final step that had always creaked just a little. And it made no exception for him this time.

❧

Sylvie stopped dancing, turned, swiftly alert, when the stair creaked.

And she froze, her throat stopped, when she saw just a flash of bright hair and an unmistakable pair of shoulders vanishing from sight.

❧

Sylvie arrived a bit late to rehearsal, shedding her ballet slippers and dress in her room in a frantic hurry, dressing in an empty dressing room, scrambling just in time to join the other girls onstage, her cutlass thumping against her hip as she ran.

The General had wanted to rehearse the pirates today, as he wasn't satisfied with them just yet. Everyone was already in place aboard the great pirate ship, and with a warning disciplinary frown at Sylvie for her tardiness, The General waved a hand at Josephine. The music began.

This was when Sylvie noticed Tom Shaughnessy standing at the foot of the aisle. Stern-faced, distracted. Determined, it seemed, to pass judgment. Sylvie suspected she knew why, and her heart lurched in her chest, making her feel, perhaps appropriately, just a little seasick.

The girls all clambered aboard the little ship and prepared

to walk down the gangplank, brandishing their cutlasses. The General had wisely separated Sylvie and Molly, and though he lamented the slightly uneven row of girls—as Sylvie was just an inch or so shorter than Molly—he was more committed to keeping relative peace. Daisy had already squeezed down into the hatch—today, thanks to skillful sawing, she only needed a little surreptitious assistance from two of the girls, who tamped down on her ample shoulders with the balls of their feet until Daisy's great pirate hat finally disappeared from view—and Josephine began playing the bawdy sea chantey.

Two bars into the song, Daisy's pirate hat and enormous bosom popped out of the hatch, and, using her hands and struggling just a little, she hoisted the rest of herself out onto the deck more or less gracefully and launched into the tune, which was only enhanced by the fact that she was breathing a little heavily from her exertions.

> *Now, thrust your sword, laddie, now thrust your sword!*
> *Send me, send me to my reward!*

Meanwhile, Sylvie, with the rest of the piratesses, dutifully pointed and thrust and rubbed her cutlass.

Given the gaiety of the onstage entertainment, Tom Shaughnessy's stern face glaring up from the foot of the aisle was tremendously jarring. Sylvie found herself unable to turn her lips up into the requisite smile. Grimly, she felt as though she were dancing before her executioner.

The General had taken one of the front-row seats to observe; his feet were draped over the seat in front of him.

But even he jumped when Tom gave a sudden thump with his walking stick.

"Josephine," Tom barked.

Startled, Josephine and everyone onstage stumbled to a halt.

All eyes were on him, wide and expectant, waiting for the suggestion or reprimand.

"*She*—" Tom pointed with the gold top of his walking stick at Sylvie.

"Sylvie?" The General queried carefully, staring at Tom as if he'd gone mad.

"Sylvie needs to be smiling."

In contrast to his orders, Sylvie found herself glaring at Tom. Who was studiously avoiding her gaze.

"It's really not that difficult, Sylvie." The General jammed two of his fingers into the corners of his mouth, pushing it upward. "It looks like *this,* a smile does. Give it a try. I assure you, the gentlemen who attend our entertainments don't want to see a...a...glowering stick."

Giggles tinkled, as surely as if Josephine had run a brisk hand over the pianoforte's upper registers.

"Nor do they want to see a pack of females entirely bereft of grace."

This came from Tom, and so sharply it surprised everyone, including The General, if the abrupt elevation of his eyebrows was any indication. The girls onstage froze in astonishment, whirled as one to stare at him, all lower lips dropped wonderingly.

And Tom wasn't finished. "Some of you have decided you needn't try anymore." He landed a distinctly uncharitable gaze on Molly.

It occurred to Sylvie, with a peculiar warming of her cheeks, that the man had, in the span of a minute, singled her out for a picayune criticism, then promptly and vehemently come to her defense at the expense of someone else.

And he was still studiously refusing to look at her.

Tom Shaughnessy was *rattled.*

"Wot's '*beref*'?" Rose whispered to the girl next to her.

" 'Avin' none," Lizzie clarified on a hiss.

"As in, 'Mr. Shaughnessy is nivver beref' of someone to warm 'is bed,' " Jenny elaborated, to show off her vocabulary skills.

More giggles.

Not from Molly, however. Molly was absolutely rigid—and magenta—with outrage at Tom's implied reprimand.

The General silenced all the girls with a potent saturnine glare.

"You are pirates, ladies, dangerous and *desirable* pirates. And capable of dancing without colliding with each other or otherwise disgracing me." Tom's voice entirely lacked the glib lilt it normally had. He sounded decidedly peevish. "I've seen you do it. Please do it again."

He turned toward Josephine, who was watching him with mouth dropped. "Josephine?"

Josephine gave a start and all but fell on the pianoforte, fingers flying with more than her usual vigor, as if the rare reprimand from Tom Shaughnessy had been all for her.

The girls obediently glided down the gangplank brandishing their cutlasses, snarling charmingly, hips swaying.

Tom lingered for a moment, watching; he lowered his walking stick to the ground, twisted it idly about. Looking at, but not seeing, the stage. He gave one absent, halfhearted sort of thump, then stopped, as if his mind was too full to allow him to both thump and think at the same time. He lingered a moment longer.

And then he turned abruptly and strode toward his office.

Through the pianoforte music they all heard the sound of a door being shut a bit harder than necessary.

Sylvie could scarcely get through the rest of rehearsal without thoughts of what Tom Shaughnessy might do. Would he…"turn 'er off"? Would he "sack her" and leave her to her own devices in London? Would she have the nerve to blame The General?

And so when The General gave them leave to go, she lagged behind, watching the other girls vanish into the dressing room. She saw Molly cast a glance over her shoulder, toss her head again, murmur something to Lizzie.

And then, her heart thumping as surely as if Tom Shaughnessy were marking time with his walking stick, Sylvie made her decision.

She turned and marched stoically toward Tom's office.

He was shaking off his coat when she appeared in the doorway. He froze midmotion, one arm in a sleeve, one arm out, when he saw her. His cravat had already been tossed over the globe in the corner, as though he'd entered the office and violently rid himself of a noose at once.

It occurred to her then, very suddenly: *He wears a costume, too.* The man she saw leaning over his desk at night, shirtsleeves rolled up, two buttons open to free his movements—the stripped-to-essentials Tom was the real Tom Shaughnessy.

They stared at each other, frozen in an indecipherable moment, trying in vain to ascertain what the other was thinking.

"I saw you."

They both said it at once, in a rush. Both faintly accusatory. Faintly apologetic.

Tom's face was difficult to read. He turned from her and finished getting out of his coat, draped it over his chair carefully. Absently unbuttoned the cuffs of his shirt, then rolled them up, and she watched every motion, and watching him reveal his arms seemed somehow as intimate as watching him undress completely. It wasn't at all what a gentleman would have done in front of her during the day. She could not for a moment imagine Etienne rolling up his sleeves in front of her, though she had of course seen every inch of Etienne uncovered.

Tom looked down. He fumbled with the papers on his desk, then appeared to realize he was fumbling and stopped. He let his eyes wander over to the window, over to the bookshelves, back to the desk.

In other words, to anywhere she wasn't.

"Well, then. Did you come to see me for a reason, Sylvie?" Stiffly said, and formally. It sounded like a foreign language coming from him.

She watched him, unfamiliar with whatever this mood happened to be. She sensed he was unfamiliar with it, too.

"Are you...angry?" It was at least a place to begin asking questions.

He looked toward the bookshelf and appeared to consider this. As though he was having difficulty deciding precisely *what* he was.

"No," he finally said. To the bookshelves, not to her.

An awkward silence.

"All right," she said softly. "I'll go."

"There's no money in it," he said quickly. Abruptly. Almost as though trying to convince himself of something.

She remained where she was.

Which was when he did finally look at her. He nearly blinked when their eyes met, as though receiving a tiny shock. His expression was oddly...defiant. Uncertain. As though, for heaven's sake, he was being required to defend himself and didn't know quite how to go about it.

In short, Tom Shaughnessy was for some reason decidedly *uncomfortable*.

Not angry. Not glib. Not amused.

Not even flirting.

Sylvie stared at him, fascinated. She'd watched him

gracefully and adeptly field highwaymen and earls and frightened women and incensed husbands with scarcely a ripple in his authority and good humor. And now...

Me, she thought. *I did this to him.* With her dancing, her own form of brilliance, she'd shifted his balance. She'd made Tom Shaughnessy feel...

Vulnerable. Ah, yes, that was it.

It pleased her inordinately. Particularly since this was a man who had made the ground beneath her feet feel nearly as wobbly as the deck of that ship that brought her across the Channel. From the very moment she'd clapped eyes upon him.

She suspected her eyes began to glow a bit, because that's when his eyes went dark and something like firm resolve crossed his face. He took two decisive steps toward her.

Which made her suck in a nearly audible breath and take an almost imperceptible step back.

Which made his mouth twitch just a little.

It took every bit of her courage to hold her ground as he slowly closed the distance that remained between them, until he stood so close that the heat of his body and the singular scent of him wound her in a cocoon. She should have known a man this wicked would smell like paradise: tobacco and soap and some hint of spice. Sweat, just a little. Clean linen.

And the unmistakable, most singular, subtle scent of all— desire. She knew the scent. For she was not, as he had guessed right from the start, an innocent.

It was the first time, however, that she had gloried in this.

Words. I need words. Words to parry with and to build a net of safety with. "Do you see something on my cheek, Mr. Shaughnessy?"

The words were, unfortunately, a nearly breathless rush of sound. Her speeding heartbeat was making her blood ring in her ears.

It didn't appear as though he'd even heard the question.

"I believe I mentioned that I'm not obliged to play fair, Sylvie." He said it softly, his voice low and level. It was a warning. An apology.

And a dare.

And it was the last that made her determined to stand her ground.

Even with her speeding heart sending the blood whooshing in her ears and all but freezing her lungs. Even as the intent became very clear in the set of his jaw, in the heat of his eyes. Even as the want in her rose so fiercely that she thought she would simply die if this time he didn't...if he didn't...

And now he was so close she could see the facets of silver in his eyes, the fine creases at the corners of them, like the rays of stars.

But when his lips touched hers she saw nothing more. Her eyes closed as the kiss detonated in her.

So very nearly painful in its sweetness. As though she'd been cracked gently open, only to discover she was full of nothing but brilliant light.

And then it was over. Her eyes fluttered open to discover why.

She saw that Tom had taken a step back from her. His silver eyes had gone pewter-dark, stunned. For an instant, they were motionless together. Assessing. Reassessing.

For with one near-chaste kiss both had managed to strip themselves of pretense and combat and flirtation and all the other little things they used to defend themselves against each other. They were suddenly equal. And equally uncertain.

A moment later, one of them became certain, and naturally it was Tom.

He stepped swiftly toward her; his hands came up, held her face lightly. A statement of intent. And like this, for the span of several breaths, he waited. *Not obliged to play fair,* he'd said to her. And even now, she knew he wasn't playing fair: For he was forcing her to choose.

And she could have twisted away from his touch, or taken a step back. It would have been such a simple thing to do, a wise thing, perhaps.

Instead, when his face at last came to hers again, she exhaled softly, in relief or pleasure, she knew not, and angled her head to meet his lowering lips with her own.

Sylvie hadn't known a kiss could begin like this: as scarcely more than a sigh of a touch, as another pair of lips brushed soft as breath across her own. But this was how they learned the shape and texture of each other; this was how, this was why, little by little, her bones became molten, and she murmured his name.

And then Tom nipped very softly at the lush curve of her bottom lip, brushed, lightly, lightly, with his lips, the corners of her mouth. Mesmerized, caught up in the delicacy of it, Sylvie at first allowed him to lead this dance, to caress her with his lips only, until the tension in her pulled tight as a crossbow, and she could no longer bear it. It was she who parted her lips, who touched her tongue to his lips, inviting him in.

He made a sound low in his throat when she did, and his hands stroked over her cheekbones, trembling, coaxing her head back just a little so he could take the kiss deeper, the pads of his fingertips rough, his touch gentle against the skin of her jaw. Dizzying, the taste of him, the textures of him, the heat and velvet of his tongue and lips. She fumbled for fistfuls of his shirt for balance, pulled herself closer; beneath her hands his hard chest rose and fell swiftly, and she felt against her thighs the hard, hard swell of his erection. She shifted herself to fit herself tightly against him, heard the sharp intake of his breath when she did. Excitement spiraled drunkenly in her, demanding appeasement. She was of a mind to satisfy it; she thought, in that moment, she would have done anything at all to satisfy it.

It was then the kiss grew fierce, each of them battling to give and take more. Tom's palm drifted down from her cheek, spread wide; brushed against her breast, lightly, lightly across her already achingly taut nipple. His touch split through her like lightning. She arced from it, her breath caught, jagged in her throat.

And as though they had both just received confirmation of potential grave danger, they went still. His hand risked nothing more; he dropped it to his side. And the kiss ended. Not abruptly, but as though it had come to its choreographed conclusion.

Leaving behind the harsh rush of breathing, the musk of desire fanned, interrupted. Confusion.

In silence they regarded each other across this new and treacherous terrain they had created. And they didn't speak, but Sylvie wasn't conscious of the stretch of time; it could have been an eternity; it could have been mere minutes. The kiss had upended the universe, and she seemed no longer ruled by time at all.

"You have another rehearsal, Sylvie," Tom's voice was a little hoarse. He cleared his throat, and added, "If your legs will hold you up."

Said as if mundane words could restore things to the way they had been.

She could still only gaze dumbly back at him. Rendered entirely new by one kiss, she had no language yet with which to speak.

When she said nothing, his faint smile faded completely, and he ducked his head, looked at the floor. His shoulders were still moving, his breathing still unsettled, as surely as if they had indeed danced a whole ballet together. She watched him, bereft of speech, both gratified and a little frightened that he was so clearly shaken, too, this man who had no doubt partaken of a veritable pageant of lovers from all walks of life from the time he'd been able to...thrust his sword.

It merely proved there was something between them that would demand resolution, regardless of what was wise or safe.

And then Tom looked up, as though he'd found a decision on the floor.

"My room is at the top of the theater, Sylvie, as you know. You'll find me there...most nights."

And he turned and left her, closing the door quietly behind him, as if to leave her alone with those words.

Most nights. The words sank home.

And when they did, she almost laughed. She almost cried.

If she'd had something to throw, she might have thrown it at the door.

And this was Tom Shaughnessy, forever causing her to feel everything she possibly could feel all at once, and in so doing making her feel more alive, somehow, than she'd ever felt before. It infuriated her, because she didn't want to feel...*alive*.

She needed, in the end, to feel safe.

And nothing, *nothing* about this man was safe.

Most nights.

She almost cursed him for leaving the choice in her hands. A fine time for Tom Shaughnessy to pretend he was a gentleman.

Chapter Twelve

ylvie didn't sleep. She tossed this way and that in her narrow bed, marveling, resenting the fact that her body seemed to be mutinying against the discipline she'd imposed upon it for years. It wanted something that made no sense and had no order or purpose.

He would shoot the heart right out of a target, he knew how to use a knife for something more sinister than slicing cheese, he might very well be keeping a mistress named Kitty in Kent. *What does it matter?* Her body wheedled. *What does any of that matter? Take him. Take him. Take him.* Her body wanted Tom Shaughnessy's hands and lips upon her skin, wanted his body covering hers. It was as simple as that.

And so she but sleepwalked through the rehearsals the following morning, smiling, bending, patting bums without feeling them, eliciting The General's approval for once. "Thank you for not pulling a face when you pat Molly, Sylvie!"

She'd joined Josephine for an hour or so to repair fairy dresses and gossamer clothes for nymphs and pantaloons for pirates, driving needles into them to stitch their wounds closed, and absently wished the solution to her own troubles was quite so simple. A wound had not been opened in her by the kiss. It was more like a portal. She didn't know where it led, she hadn't known it was there, and she couldn't close it again. Her choices were to walk away from it, knowing always it stood behind her, missed.

Or to walk through it.

Or to lose herself in dance, where everything was choreographed and planned and made perfect sense, where discipline was required to make beauty, and not consider it for an afternoon.

She excused herself from Josephine early, offering no explanation, and left for her attic room to dance away her thoughts, if she could.

And now Sylvie stretched and balanced, arms floating out straight like wings aloft on a current of wind, one leg outstretched. A perfect—no: nearly perfect—arabesque. She could almost hear Monsieur Favre's voice in her head. *Mon dieu, you are dancing, not pulling a plow, Sylvie.*

She arched her back a fraction of an inch, extended her arms forward aaaand . . . *there*. That was perfect. She could feel it.

"What do you call *that*?"

Sylvie congratulated herself on not toppling over. She nearly flinched, but when she heard the voice, she was proud she managed to do nothing more than blink.

"Ballet," she said simply, to Molly. As though she'd been expecting to see her all along.

Sylvie drew her arms down, dropped her leg, curved her arms above her head and dipped into a *plié* to stretch her muscles. Her body knew the position from feel, could create the movements of a dance the way a musician's fingers could find a song by memory. Still, she wished for a mirror and a barre. She almost wished for Monsieur Favre.

Mostly she wished—though this was probably the most futile wish of all—that God would roll back time to the point just before Molly had discovered that Sylvie danced at the top of the theater, and then perhaps knock her unconscious.

She imagined Molly had followed her here, just the same as Tom had. Soon the bloody attic would boast as much traffic as the bottom of the theater.

"'Oo would want to watch ye...squat?" Surprisingly, Molly didn't sound entirely scornful.

"Princes," Sylvie said idly. "Kings." She moved her feet and arms into fourth position. *Relevé*. Still, her heart was beating a little harder than usual with the effort to sound nonchalant.

Molly snorted.

It was the snort that made Sylvie do it. She stood *en demi-pointe* and thrust her arms up over her head, then spun in a dazzlingly effortless series of *ronde de jambe* turns across the room, the room blurring in circles before her eyes. She concluded *en attitude croissé,* then arched her back and sank into a kneel; her body, she knew, looked as soft as folding velvet.

She rose once more, her face expressionless, and assumed third position.

A moment later she flicked a glance at Molly.

She saw in Molly's face longing, and an impotent sort of fury. A helpless admiration that no barbs or amount of pride could ever hope to disguise.

Sylvie knew a deep shame. It had been unworthy of her, unfair, her cocky demonstration of something that had taken her years of sacrifice and work to render effortless. Her own pride had made her momentarily cruel.

Molly was flushed. She swallowed and looked toward the window, studying it. "Wants cleaning," she muttered.

"Mmmm," Sylvie responded. She returned to her exercises.

She lifted one arm over her head in a gentle arc, raised the other lightly across her waist. From fourth position she would—

"Why . . . why do ye do it? So men will admire ye?"

Sylvie paused and looked at Molly, who was struggling for understanding through her own pride. The question was asked in all seriousness.

"Because . . . No. So that *I* will admire me." It was an answer, but only in part.

Molly was quiet again.

"And is ballet why ye've got no—" Molly gestured with her finger to her breasts, one at a time "—t' speak of?"

It was an entirely serious question. Sylvie didn't know whether to laugh or sigh.

"It might be," she allowed at last. "Did you follow me here, Molly?"

Molly said nothing for a moment. "I thought . . ." She turned, didn't complete the sentence. She instead wandered across the room, found something fascinating about an old barrel, studied it with her back to Sylvie.

"Why do you dislike me?" Sylvie thought it might disarm her to be direct.

Molly turned to her, and Sylvie was slightly amused that she didn't deny it, and Molly had a half-admiring tilt to her mouth. She actually seemed to be giving the question some thought. As though she wanted to give precisely the correct answer.

"'E looks at ye. *Really* looks." Molly looked away from Sylvie as she said this. "'E doesna see the rest of us. Never 'as," she added, half-bitterly, half-amused.

"Who?" Sylvie asked. Though she suspected she knew, and something inside her gave another grand leap.

"*Who?*" Molly scoffed. She might as well have added, "you fool," for that was precisely her tone.

She didn't complete the sentence. Sylvie didn't ask her to.

Molly studied Sylvie. There was a resigned twist to her mouth, and wry pain, suppressed, in her voice. "'E's the best man I've ever known."

Sylvie was struck silent. It would never have occurred to her to describe Tom Shaughnessy in quite that way.

"What of your lover?" Sylvie asked gently. "The one who is as handsome as a duke?"

Molly paused, and then her mouth twisted again. "'E's a man." A lift of the shoulder. And the faintest hint of scorn, for herself, or for her lover, Sylvie wasn't certain. "Even 'e asked about ye. Said ye looked . . . wrong." She looked half-pleased, half-troubled by this assessment. "'E wondered why ye were 'ere at the White Lily at all. I told 'im ye'd a lover right 'ere at the White Lily, that was why," Molly said half-casually, half-spitefully. And tossed a glance over her shoulder again.

Uncomfortable, suddenly, with the drift of the conversation, unwilling to engage in any sort of confirmation or combat, Sylvie touched her hand to a barrel for balance and dipped into a *plié*. She allowed Molly to watch her. She imagined she did look wrong onstage, despite her best efforts to sway and bend and pat derrieres. Odd, but she was a little stung by the criticism.

"Is it difficult to learn?" Molly said. She said it casually. "This way of dancing?"

Brutally difficult. It takes everything from you, it requires all you have, it will make your feet ugly and your body thin and powerful and you will never know a moment when a part of you does not physically ache. Only a very few are truly wonderful, and I am the best, the very best, and I worked to be the best.

Molly sought the answer in Sylvie's face.

And Sylvie thought she saw the faintest traces of a bruise remaining below her eye on that fair, smooth skin, the mark left by Belstow's hand. It was the price Molly had paid for living so men would admire her.

And then Sylvie understood then that her answer to Molly had been almost unfairly untruthful.

For she had committed her whole self to the dance in order to have a life other than ordinary. In order, in many ways, to attract a man like Etienne, who would give her a future so different from the one Claude now lived out, with its careful, spartan economies, tawdry memories, resigned to the loneliness and bitterness of living out her days in the twilight of society in a tiny apartment with an intelligent, foul-mouthed parrot.

In short: Sylvie had done it so men *would* admire her. She had grown to love the dance, but the reasons she had committed herself to it were twofold and inextricable from each other.

Still: She knew to own such a skill was to own magic and power.

She gazed at Molly and couldn't believe what she was about to say.

"Would you like me to show you how?"

Chapter Thirteen

Amidst his plans for the Gentleman's Emporium was correspondence from the man who was to provide mirrors for the dressing rooms, and that afternoon, while Sylvie danced in the attic Tom fished it out, smiling to himself. He had a marvelous idea. It involved mirrors.

And then he saw another missive centered on the plan in the middle of his desk. A different seal, a different handwriting.

But Tom knew what it would say even before he opened it, and the smile disappeared.

"Viscount Howath backed out," Tom told The General before the evening's show. "He sent a message today."

It was odd, this one-by-one backing out by his investors. Like death by little cuts, and highly uncharacteristic of this group of men, who had been friends and patrons for some time now. And *none* had been to the theater lately. He hadn't seen them about town.

Which could only mean they were avoiding him.

It was the sort of thing he found maddening. He could persuade, he could cajole, he could convince with facts and charm. He would happily—perhaps not happily, but at least logically—accept a reason for backing out at a very inconvenient moment. He could deal with *anything* directly.

But he loathed the quiet and evasion. He considered it cowardly, and there was nothing he could do to combat it. It was inexplicable, and it was difficult not to attempt to ascribe it to a single cause.

And yet he couldn't think of one.

He was distantly amused. Not since he was a small boy had everything in his world seemed so precarious. And odd how that even as one dream took shape, began to crumble in his hands, caused him to scramble to salvage it, something else presented itself, and it was this, too, that made his world seem more precarious than usual.

He'd thought to solve this yesterday, with a kiss. He'd kissed women before, naturally, and enjoyed it; kisses were typically preliminaries to very pleasant foregone conclusions. He'd imagined, before he kissed Sylvie Chapeau, that kissing her might at last restore balance to his world. Desire, once indulged, inevitably faded, and curiosity, once indulged, ceased to plague. She had been both—curiosity and desire—since she'd landed on his lap and poked him with a knitting needle.

He hadn't known that from the moment he'd idly touched her that touching would simply never be enough. And he hadn't known a single kiss could become howling, impatient hunger that robbed him of sleep and also made him want to lay the moon at her very feet.

Well, if he couldn't bring down the moon for her, he would

begin with...mirrors. He smiled a little. She would see them soon enough.

"Have you ever been in love, Gen?"

The General's head snapped toward him. An irritated dent appeared between his eyes.

"Good God, Tom, how much of that brandy have you consumed? Are we going to do this every evening now, like a pair of girls? Exchanging our 'hopes and dreams'?" he mocked in a girlish voice. "I want none of it."

Tom laughed silently. "I want to know, Gen."

"Are you wondering whether *you're* in love, Tom, is that it?" The General said slyly. "Why don't you just say it?"

Tom stared at him evenly. "*I* found you filthy, drunk, lying on the street—"

The General shot him a black look. "Good God, but you play dirty, Shaughnessy."

Tom shrugged cheerfully.

The General sighed. "All right. Yes. I've been in love."

"And?"

"It makes you feel ridiculous, helpless, awkward, glorious, and immortal." The General sounded downright surly, and as though he was ticking off a list. "Happy now?"

"And?" Tom urged.

A long pause.

"She thought I was too short." He said it lightly.

Tom felt the words as surely as if a tiny knife had twisted right into his own heart.

"You're the biggest man *I've* ever known, Gen." He made sure he said the words lightly, too.

"And that doesn't surprise *me* in the least."

Tom laughed. Smoothly, he said, "So shall we do a harem bit in a week or so? I think Daisy might make a splendid centerpiece for the harem bit."

"Daisy might make a splendid Christmas ham," The General muttered darkly.

"Oh, you might be right. Pink, and plump, and warm, and succulent..." Tom mused, drawing each word out, mischievously, deliberately.

Tom noticed that The General's ears went decidedly pinker with each word.

A day away from an incendiary kiss and a good night's sleep after last evening's show made Sylvie feel much stronger. It in fact seemed downright possible not to think about Tom Shaughnessy for entire minutes at a time.

Until she arrived that afternoon in the attic.

She stopped at the top of the stairs, nearly blinded by the dazzle. It took her a moment to realize why.

Mirrors. A series of mirrors had been propped along one wall, each tall and rectangular.

And the sun came through brilliant now, nearly blinding, striking light from them.

The windows of the little-used room had been scrubbed clean, both inside and out. One of them had even been pried open, and a breeze had pushed its way in. As this was London's East End, a number of unidentifiable and objectionable smells came in with it. But a breeze would be lovely on the back of her neck as she danced.

Sylvie put her hand to her cheek; her heart gave a sudden *grand jeté* of sweet, strange joy. She was breathless with the surprise of it and didn't know why. She'd been given gifts before. Etienne showered her with gifts. Most of them jeweled or scented or lushly crafted of silk or fur or velvet.

But when she looked, she saw her awe reflected in Tom's gift to her, those mirrors.

Six of them, spanning one side of the room. It was perhaps the first gift she'd ever received that was specific to her, that some other woman would not have been just as happy to have.

And she studied her face, for it was an expression she'd never before seen on it, and it was like seeing a vivid, joyous stranger who might just be related to her. And it made her wonder about Susannah. Whether living a different life would have given her sister different eyes, whether they would be bright with curiosity and joy, or dull with complacency. Whether they would be more or less knowing than Sylvie's, more or less kind.

More or less awed by a simple, perfect gift from a beautiful, dangerous man.

There's no money in it. Tom Shaughnessy, gaudy on the surface, shrewd penny-squeezer who slept in an attic beneath, had decided to indulge her gift, anyhow.

There was a creak on the stairs, and her heart lurched. She whirled.

Somehow, she didn't want to see him just yet. And somehow it seemed unlikely he would seek her here to witness a response. She wanted to be alone with the fullness of her thoughts, to decide what it was she wanted.

Wanted. Simply to take something because she wanted it seemed a foreign concept, and her mind fumbled at it like a child attempting to pick up a toy too big for its hands.

Sylvie turned toward the stairs and saw nobody. But still the footsteps creaked up. Slowly, steadily up.

Which is when she realized it must be The General if she couldn't yet see the top of his head.

And it was.

"Well," he said, when he saw the mirrors.

The word was full and eloquent. The General was no fool,

naturally. She would not have been able to obtain those mirrors and haul them into the White Lily on her own.

She gazed at him, eyebrows lifted, waiting for the next words.

"You've transformed the room quite a bit since I saw it last," he said finally. "You...hadn't mirrors." Again, meaningfully.

"No," she said carefully. Waiting for the next, more specific question. The one she didn't want to answer. "I hadn't mirrors."

The General's eyes, she decided, were decidedly too shrewd, too knowing. She suddenly realized she knew how to deflect that gaze.

"Do you happen to know a Mr. Beedle, General?"

Ah, and the result of that question was deeply gratifying. Those sharp eyes flew wide. Hectic color flooded his cheeks. He blinked rapidly several times.

Then all of it disappeared—the blinking, the color, the wide eyes—as he gathered his composure.

"Why?" he demanded curtly. And then: "Do you ask?" he completed, as if this would make the question more polite.

She drifted across the room, viewing herself in yet another of those mirrors. She felt as though she wanted to see herself in each one.

"Because I once knew of a Mr. Beedle, an English choreographer, very talented. He visited the Paris Opera, and we danced for him. He married one of his ballerinas, I believe. Maria Bellacusi. She was quite gifted, too. I lately heard he worked in the English court. But ballet is not so popular here in England."

"No." The General narrowed his eyes. "Not so popular."

"Just at court. For the king."

"Yes. Just at court. For the king."

Sylvie smiled at him and tilted her head. "You love ballet, perhaps. But not...ballerinas."

The General let out a startled bark of laughter.

And then he paced a bit across the room, almost as if taking the measure of it, the bright sun counting off the shiny buttons on his coat. He turned to look at her.

"It was more, Miss Lamoreux . . . that a ballerina did not love me."

Honored and startled by the confidence, Sylvie was quiet for just a moment, but made certain to speak before he felt awkward.

"Did you come to pay me a social call, General, or to tell me I am needed somewhere else in the theater?" she said to him.

He clasped his hands behind his back. "I came, Miss Lamoreux, because I have an idea."

He said this with all appearance of dignity, but she could see the anxiety in the clasping of those hands. And what very much looked like . . . hope . . . taut in his face.

"An idea?"

"For a . . ." he cleared his throat. "For a ballet."

❧

"I meant only to protect her."

Claude Lamoreux and Guillaume the parrot had been reunited. From a perch on her shoulder, Guillaume every now and then gave loving nibbles to Claude's ear. Claude sat, pale and distraught, dabbing at the corners of her eyes, across from the Viscount and Lady Grantham. Her hair was dark, with threads of silver running through it at the temples. Eyes very large, very dark, puffs of fatigue bulging beneath. Grooves were worn into her face on either side of her nose. Time was drawing her face downward; she would, in a few years, Susannah could see, have laps of skin on either side of her mouth.

It looked as though life had not been easy, on the whole, for Claude Lamoreux, who had never truly been pretty and who had never married.

"I feared what would become of Sylvie if she knew the truth of her life. If Etienne, her lover, knew the truth of her life."

Susannah knew she should be more worldly, but really, the use of the word "lover," as though it were "settee" or "teapot," would take a bit of getting accustomed to.

"He wants to marry her, you know, and she will have a good life, a much better life than ever I had or could ever give her. He is a prince. Of the House of Bourbon."

Claude could not entirely disguise a very small bit of smugness in this. A prince certainly outranked a viscount.

"So I burned the letters you sent, Lady Grantham. I am sorry, Lady Grantham. I was afraid, both for Sylvie and for myself."

Susannah had been torn between wanting to depart for England immediately in search of her sister and wanting to wait for Claude, but the shipping schedule ultimately made their decision for them. It would be days before a ship could take them home. And so they sat now in the room in which Sylvie, her sister, had lived for almost her entire life. Small as a closed fist, the apartment seemed, careful years of economy epitomized in the plain worn furniture and carpets, with one bright window letting light into the parlor, landing a beam on Guillaume's perch. He clearly had the run of the place, as Susannah could see feathers and fluff scattered about. No doubt they were the bane of Madame Gabon's existence.

Susannah reached out and covered Claude's hand with her own. "Thank you for caring for her all these years. I know what a risk it was."

"I danced a bit at the Green Apple long ago, you see, which is where I met Anna, and Daisy Jones. I learned through Daisy

of your…plight…and when I returned home to France I…I
brought Sylvie with me to raise as my own. And as no one ever
heard from Anna again…I never told Sylvie about her, as there
never seemed a need to trouble her with it. I never knew what
became of the other little girls—of you, Lady Grantham, or
Sabrina. And it was wisest not to write of it to anyone, for the
danger was…the danger was…"

Guillaume murmured an English obscenity tenderly and
gave Claude another nibble.

Claude looked up apologetically. "He belonged to a sailor
once, long ago," she said. "He has a remarkable vocabulary."

Remarkable did not begin to describe Guillaume's
vocabulary.

Susannah gave her a weak smile. Kit held her hand in his,
and squeezed it. He, she suspected, was trying not to laugh.

"I'm sorry, Susannah." Claude's voice thickened again, and
she dabbed at her eyes.

"Oh, Claude, I am not angry," Susannah told her, "for I
likely would have burned the letters, too, for someone I love.
You told us that Sylvie's letter said that she went to England. Do
you know where she might have gone when she arrived?"

"I do not know. I am sorry. Daisy Jones is my only English
friend, you see. But I do not believe that Sylvie knew of her."

Claude sniffed. "I am worried. As you can see, our life is
not grand, and it was not easy when she was very young. But
Sylvie…she is now the finest ballerina in Paris. Everyone
knows she has gone. Monsieur Favre…Madame Gabon tells
me is very angry."

"Sylvie is a ballerina?" Kit repeated, fascinated.

And Susannah was instantly a wee bit jealous, because it *did*
seem like a fascinating thing to be.

And then she was a wee bit proud, because it was fascinating to be related to a ballerina.

Who had a *lover*.

Claude took a deep breath, steadying herself. "If you find her...when you return...will you tell her I am sorry? I never meant to hurt her. She is very disciplined, my Sylvie. It is so unlike her just to run. But, oh, she has a temper, and I fear this time impulse sent her across the sea, and possibly she will not be safe on her own."

Susannah saw Kit glance sideways at her.

So Sylvie was not the only one in the Holt family to possess a temper. Somehow, Susannah was pleased to hear it, and felt closer to her sister already.

❧

Because Tom and The General loved drama, that afternoon they positioned the girls as well as Daisy in the audience, a view they seldom enjoyed. Almost like little girls being brought on an outing, they were quiet and wide-eyed, perhaps tense with anticipation, well behaved. No giggles or murmurs.

For they knew why Tom and The General had gathered them here.

Sylvie slid a sidelong glance at Molly, only to find it intercepted by Molly's sidelong glance. After their conversation in the attic yesterday, Sylvie knew Molly was certain that Sylvie would be appointed Venus.

A portentous thumping noise, sliding, a few crashes and some swearing were heard from behind the red velvet curtains.

"The day you've been waiting for has arrived, ladies," Tom announced grandly.

And then the curtains shimmied up.

"Cor!" Rose breathed, perhaps predictably.

An enormous oyster sat on the stage, glowing softly. In the

dim light of the theater, they could barely see a series of long, dark ropes attached to it, painted to disappear into the darkness when the lights were lowered. A crew of rough little boys stood at the ready to tug on them, to open the great creature's maw.

"It will look lovelier at night," The General assured them. "We shall surround it by waving seaweed and floating fish..." With his hands in the air, he sketched the picture of them, and the girls' eyes followed his hands, envisioning it.

"Venus," Tom told them, from where he stood onstage, "will have the honor of waiting inside the oyster and being revealed, slowly, to a breathlessly waiting audience. She will truly be the pearl in the oyster, and she'll rise, gracefully, and sing a song recently composed by our beloved Josephine."

Josephine nodded graciously.

Sylvie immediately thought: *Pearl, girl...*

What had this place *done* to her?

"And since I know all of *you* are breathlessly waiting to be told who she will be..." Tom continued.

They *were* breathless.

Sylvie was breathless, in particular, hoping, praying, it would *not* be her. And in truth, she hadn't the faintest idea what to expect from Tom Shaughnessy, whether he would consider such a thing a gift... or whether it would amuse him to put her in the shell when he would know she so clearly didn't want to be there. She supposed she could protest, but he still provided the roof over her head for the time being.

No: He was a practical man, and she would make a dreadful Venus.

He allowed the silence to gain in momentum, drawing it out the way an orchestra conductor draws out the violins, perhaps.

"Molly," Tom Shaughnessy said quietly. "Would you please step forward?"

The exhale of breath from the girls in the audience nearly lifted up the curtains.

"*Ohhhh . . .* Molly . . ." Congratulatory murmurs rose up. Mostly unsurprised murmurs, as Molly's supremacy was all but unquestioned. Mostly, to their credit, pleased murmurs.

Molly, as though it were her very own coronation, rose, and all but floated toward the stage.

And when she turned around again, her smug smile could have lit the entire theater at night.

"Let's applaud Molly, shall we, ladies?" Tom said with appropriate gravity.

Gracious applause fluttered from the seats, and Molly basked as The General and Tom flanked her.

And Daisy Jones lifted herself up from her seat and quietly, with dignity, made her way toward the back of the theater, toward her velvety pink room, like a storm retreating in the face of the advancing sun.

Sylvie watched her go. The woman had never spoken to her directly; Sylvie had never seen her speak to any of the girls directly. Daisy kept a precise boundary between herself and those she perhaps considered beneath her.

She looked up, saw Tom smiling down at the girls. But The General was watching the majesty of Daisy's retreat, his expression difficult to fathom.

⟳

The next hour or so was devoted to Molly's learning how to fold herself into the oyster shell and rise from inside it as it slowly, slowly opened. Every girl wanted a turn at it, which took a bit of time, and The General, flush with his success, indulged them just this once while Tom solemnly discussed with the boys the timing of the pulleys, the angle and speed at which to tug the ropes to most gracefully reveal Venus. He demonstrated this himself.

Sylvie peered closer at the huge oyster, ran her fingers over the satin of the inside, admiring the sheer whimsical brilliance of the craftsmanship, and the very idea that had spawned it. It was lined in rippling, pillowy pale pink satin, as befitted the throne of an undersea queen. It would gleam in the footlights softly, reflecting Molly's fair skin. It was, indeed, the ideal setting for a pearl.

The seed for it, the mind that had seen the potential for the beauty and whimsy and sensuality of it, had been Tom Shaughnessy's.

Sylvie thought of Tom as a boy in the rookeries, stealing to eat. Hiding from those who might drag him off to the authorities, as though he was merely something to be disposed of, like a feral cat. Learning to fight and to survive with the tools at his disposal.

Lucky in my friends, he'd said.

And as she caressed the inside of that absurdly beautiful, magnificently silly oyster, she knew it might as well have been Tom himself she was touching.

She glanced up, knowing somehow his eyes would find her.

He was still discussing the mechanics of the pulleys with the boys, and he noticed, perhaps, the shift in her posture, and it was but a glance, a swift hold of her gaze. His eyes darkened even then. And then he returned to the business at hand.

Most nights.

Chapter Fourteen

The next day, Molly arrived in the attic shortly after Sylvie did. But she wasn't alone. She'd brought the rest of the girls with her.

And all of them stopped and stared, wide-eyed and silent, at Sylvie, who stood with her hair pulled tightly back, the lovely exotic dress she wore to practice her dancing floating about her calves.

Molly finally spoke. "I told them about the ballet, and the princes and kings." Her chin was up.

"And you would all like to learn to dance this way?" Sylvie asked them.

She had never before taught a roomful of girls, though she had advised younger students about form, and every now and then wiped away Monsieur-Favre-instigated tears.

"Can ye show us?"

Sylvie looked at those lovely girls, with their round bodies accustomed to very little work at all apart from, perhaps, the sort that took place on a mattress or the sort that took place on the White Lily's stage. And wondered how they would cope with the pain and discipline, the nuance and complexity—

But she needn't tell them it was difficult, or painful, or that few really excelled at it. She would show them, and they could decide for themselves whether or not they found it so.

"Yes. I will teach you."

They looked back at her, and shy smiles were exchanged.

But Molly's expression shifted as something occurred to her. "The mirrors...ye'd no mirrors before." She looked almost accusingly at Sylvie.

But before Sylvie would respond she heard more creaking on the stairs.

They all froze, and Sylvie saw for an instant a stricken expression flicker over Molly's face. *She thinks it is Tom coming to meet me,* Sylvie thought.

But Sylvie recognized the step of The General, for she had invited him to meet them here.

"They would like to learn the ballet," Sylvie told him very calmly.

The General stared at the six girls, six very beautiful and very different women reflected in the mirrors of this cramped little room, the context so different from the White Lily's stage.

And at first, the faintest hint of incredulity shadowed his brow. Or perhaps it was bemusement.

And then...a glimmer of inspiration dawned in his shiny dark eyes. It was a familiar gleam. A nearly *fanatic* gleam.

She'd seen it in Monsieur Favre's eyes before.

"Will you work hard and do what I say and not complain? I will only ask once, and if you complain even once, I shall refuse to work with you."

This he directed to everyone except Sylvie.

Five heads ducked up and down. No harm in agreeing, no

doubt they imagined. They had no true idea what was in store for them.

"Well, then. Shall we begin?"

❧

It was to be a night of pirates, fairies, damsels and a mermaid on a swing, and the girls, after their first simple lessons in the ballet earlier in the day, settled down at their tables to the task of becoming fairies first of all. All was, as usual, noisy chatter, and the air was nearly clouded with powder, complaints, and exclamations over gifts that had been delivered by the ever-present crew of little boys.

Sylvie arrived in the dressing room to find her little table to prepare herself for the performance, and slowed when she saw what was atop it—a little box.

"Oh, look! Ye've an admirer, Sylvie!" Rose said encouragingly. The unspoken words were: *at last.*

Compared to the gaudy things that arrived on their little dressing tables each night, the clusters of blooms and baubles, the gift on Sylvie's table seemed exceedingly modest. She stared at it, wondering, half-bemused, how on earth she would respond to an admirer from the White Lily's audience.

Just then, Molly lifted a silk shawl out of its wrappings, the latest of her gifts from her anonymous admirer, the one who watched the shows from the private box and intended to court her "proper." It was a thing of limp, luminous beauty, and a collective sigh went up when it was revealed. The girls flocked to it. They all wanted to touch it and wrap it about their own shoulders, and Sylvie and her tiny gift were instantly forgotten.

She approached the box almost cautiously, as though it might turn into a great moth and fly at her, and took it up gingerly in her hand. It was of wood, and it fit neatly into her palm, with a heft that belied its petite size.

And then she saw, painted, very delicately across the top: a ballerina, her dress floating like a cloud about her, her arms stretched overhead, her face rapt.

Sylvie felt the first rushes of heat in her cheeks, the sort of heat that always stole her breath, made her heart feel like a tiny sun in her chest.

Attached to the box by a thin gold cord was a petite gold key.

With trembling hands, Sylvie fumbled the lid of the box to reveal the shining drum that would turn to spill the music out. For it was indeed a *boîte à musique*.

A music box.

She fitted the key into the slot, not unaware that the very act of inserting a key into a slot to create music had a certain poetry and prurience to it. A certain symbolism, given who had left this box for her, and somehow she doubted it had been lost upon him.

What do you want, *Sylvie?*

And so she turned the key. And a little tune began softly, scarcely audible in the roomful of laughter and chatter. Playing just for her.

Later, after they'd been pirates and fairies and were waiting to be damsels behind the curtain, watching Daisy in the swing and taking wagers on whether it would hold, Sylvie felt Tom stand behind her briefly. Over the top of their heads he watched Daisy in the swing. He didn't look at Sylvie at all, or speak to her or Molly or Rose, nor did Sylvie turn to meet his eyes. He was distracted and alert, overseeing his show from every angle, just as he did each night.

But when he turned to leave, his hand brushed against her back, a light, seemingly accidental drag of fingers. Scarcely even a touch.

And then he was gone, off to see to the Earl of Rawden, the famous poet earl, who had just arrived with the gust of authority he always brought with him and was swiveling his head about looking for Tom, and off to pay the king's man, Crumstead, who had arrived for the show and for his bribe.

Scarcely even a touch. It might even have been construed as accidental. Certainly the other girls had noticed nothing, for they were still peering out at the audience from where they stood next to her, whispering comments she'd ceased listening to.

But this was Tom Shaughnessy after all, who did have a certain talent for timing and drama. The touch had been deliberate, she knew. A message, a fleeting moment enclosing the two of them in a silent understanding:

I want you.

In that instant, joy and fierce desire battled with anger, and with the fear of all that she felt. And there was resentment that she should feel it at all, when all her life she'd channeled her passions so effectively, when everything in her life had been as choreographed as the dance, and she knew the next step she should take, and the next.

But with mirrors and a music box and secret proprietary touches, Tom Shaughnessy was wooing her with an intuition and a subtlety at odds with everything he appeared to be, and in so doing had somehow managed to sink through the walls of her reason as water sank into hard earth, undaunted by the challenge.

Made for the challenge, in fact.

And then she wryly corrected a word in her mind. He wasn't wooing her. He was seducing her. The ends were altogether different.

'E doesna touch the dancers. She heard Rose's words again. The theater was everything to Tom, and he wasn't a foolish man. He used his own appeal skillfully with his employees while maintaining a sensible distance, aware of the delicacy required to keep everyone happy, everything running smoothly. And because Sylvie knew how important the theater and everyone in it were to him, she knew the sheer subtlety of his campaign meant he had not undertaken it lightly.

The implications of this made her breathless.

She had felt often that Etienne's wooing had been more or less ceremonial, that the outcome had never been in question for him.

But here ... here she had a choice.

And though she had at first resented Tom for leaving the choice in her hands ... she now saw it as the most splendid of his gifts.

❧

Later, Sylvie, once again in muslin, rouge rubbed from her cheeks, hair twisted once again into a sedate knot, watched the girls leave for the evening, and waved her good-byes. She lifted a hand to Poe at the door. He lifted a hook in return.

And when everyone was gone, she turned away, availed herself of a lit candle, and took the stairs up to her room. But before she did, she glanced for a light in the depths of the theater; the door to his office was closed, and no light shone from beneath the door.

The evening had been long and raucous. Invitations had been issued to Tom; she'd heard them as he'd greeted the guests near the door and as they'd said their farewells. The Velvet Glove had been suggested to him more than once.

Most nights.

She went up to her room. She unpinned her hair, and brushed it smooth. She stepped out of her dress, untied her stockings, rolled them down, and lifted her night rail in her hands, preparing to drop it over her head.

But then she paused and saw her reflection in the mirror. And she thought about life as choreography, and about mirrors, and a music box. At the top of the White Lily there was a proud, beautiful man who wanted her. But with these small gifts, he'd shown her that he *knew* her, too. The gifts told her so much more about him than he realized.

She set the night rail aside, laying it carefully on the bed. She dropped the dress over her head again, took her cloak from the hook on the wall, and wrapped herself in it. And then she took up the candle again.

c

It wasn't until he heard the creak of a light step on the stairs to his room that he admitted to himself that he'd been waiting to hear it for days now. That he'd lain awake for nights desperate for it, every one of his senses honed to razor alertness, hoping for it. Denied invitations, conducted a campaign of quiet seduction so unlike him it unnerved and distantly even amused him. Never had he wanted anything more, it seemed. Never had he been so uncertain about getting it.

Tom sat up in his bed, struck the flint to light the lamp next to his bed, and the tiny room glowed in the warm light. His hands shook, for God's sake, even as he did it. His heart had set up a drumming in his chest.

He saw the light of her candle quiver against the wall first, then the shadow of her, and finally the woman herself. Her cloak was wrapped around her; beneath the hem, he saw light muslin.

Her hair was down, a sheet of silky darkness burnished by the dueling lights of her candle and his lamp. He could scarcely breathe. When she saw his lit lamp, she lifted her own candle with hands that trembled, and puffed it out.

He couldn't speak.

In silence, he watched her drop the cloak. Saw, in the shadows, the outline of her lithe body through her dress, her long legs, slim waist. And in silence he watched as matter-of-factly she reached for her dress, and pulled it—*Oh God*—right over her head.

The sight of her body completely bare to him all at once was an exquisite physical shock. He stopped breathing.

She began to fold the dress. He remembered to breathe again in order to speak.

"For the love of God, Sylvie, leave the dress." His voice was low, hoarse.

She dropped it and laughed then, a soft, shaky little laugh. Lifted her hand to push back the long mass of hair, and he watched, mesmerized, the lift of her small, perfect breast when her arm rose, then the waterfall sheen of the hair spilling behind her.

A woman who had been nude in front of a man before—not coy, not ashamed, and yet not wanton, either. A woman who understood the purpose of bodies. A woman who knew, no doubt, how to use her body for work, and for art...and for pleasure.

And at this last thought, a peculiar current of jealousy arced through Tom's excitement. Someone else, at this moment, somewhere, was perhaps missing her. Had touched her. Someone else no doubt felt he had the right to her, and Tom knew he should entertain guilt or regret.

But she was *here* now.

Lover or no lover waiting for her somewhere else, she had crossed the theater tonight, candle in hand, climbed each creaking stair to be with him.

❧

She sat down on the edge of the bed near him, curled her legs up beneath her.

"Sylvie." A whisper. Nearly rueful.

Tom shifted slightly, and his light blanket slipped away from his chest, folding to his waist. He pushed it impatiently aside, and there before her, inches away from her touch, she saw the broad line of his smooth shoulders, the hard muscles cut into his chest, the slim waist. And curving up against his flat belly, the evidence of how badly he wanted her. Her senses flooded; she could scarcely believe she was here.

His hand extended, hovered an instant so close to her, deciding. Then, delicately, he rested the backs of his fingers against her ribs, as though testing the temperature of water, wondering if it perhaps would scald him.

And the entire surface of her skin began to glow like something gently set aflame.

She turned her head from the expression in his eyes. Somehow it was too much to take in all at once.

Tom's hand moved then; she could hear his breath catch as he slid it up slowly, slowly, over her ribs, leaving a trail of sensation behind. He tipped his fingers up to cup her breast; the rough pad of his thumb dragged over her nipple. Shocking, the serrated pleasure suddenly everywhere in her. She closed her eyes. It stilled the breath in her lungs; she heard the ragged catch in her own breath.

"Small," she whispered roughly, self-consciously.

"Soft," he said at once, like a correction, his voice low and rough. As erotic as his touch.

His hand slowly dropped away; he seemed to sense her tension.

And together for a time they sat in silence so thick and heated it was like another entire body between them.

"Show me then, love, how you'd like it to be," he said softly.

Sylvie opened her eyes and inhaled deeply, and took in with her breath the musk of his desire, the warmth of his skin, and it was potent, harsh and sweet; it was wine, it was opium. It dissolved what remained of her ability to think, but this seemed almost a relief; she had come here for one reason only, after all, and thinking had nothing at all to do with it.

Sylvie leaned forward and looped her arms loosely around his neck. Rested them against the warmth of his bare skin. Her mouth nearly touched his; her nipples just brushed the skin of his chest, sending a swift scorch of pleasure through her. His breathing was shallow and swift, and she could feel it against her mouth, and yet still he merely watched her, thoughtfully. His eyes never moving from hers, his hands waiting, curling into the blanket at his sides.

And then she leaned back, her weight pulling him slowly down with her. He came down over her; heat and smooth muscle covering her; she wrapped her legs around the furrowed contours of his thighs, cradling him, capturing him with her body, slid her ugly dancer's feet down his hard calves in a caress. Shifted so that the hard length of his arousal fit perfectly against her. Saw his eyes darken when he sensed she was ready for him even now.

They breathed in and out, swiftly, their bodies so close their ribs moved together in time; it seemed they drew in, exhaled the same breath. His mouth was a tense line.

Tom searched her eyes for doubt or surrender or intent, perhaps; she truly didn't know what he would find there. *Want,* was all her mind and body said. *Want.*

"No mercy, then," he whispered.

His mouth fell hard upon hers; she felt his low groan vibrate through her as they tasted each other again at last.

There were few preliminaries; she needed none, for it seemed necessary to take him in all at once, like an antidote. She arched her hips up against him to take him inside her, and she took him as equally as he took her, nearly crying out her pleasure when they were joined.

He propped himself up over her and gazed down. And continued to gaze.

"Tom—*s'il tu plait*—fast—*vite*—"

He stared down at her, his eyes still so dark, his mouth curved up. She could feel the sweat starting over her own skin. And still he didn't move.

Her voice became a rasp of urgency. "Tom—you must—I want—"

"No."

Sylvie felt the breath of his word against her lips. She opened her eyes; his face almost touching hers. He'd managed to make his refusal sound nonchalant, but the perspiration gathering, gleaming on his chest, the muscles trembling beneath her fingers, made a liar of him.

"I need—"

"Beg me, Sylvie."

"*Please,* I beg of you—"

"Hush, love. You should never, never beg."

She half laughed, half groaned. *"Tu est un bête."*

"A beast, am I?" She heard soft laughter in his voice. He drew his hips back from her, slowly, so slowly, allowing both of them to feel every inch of each other, the sensation exquisite, too much, too much. "Is it this..." He swiftly thrust, once, twice. Stopped. Hovered over her, again, his arms propping his body above her. "Is it this you want, Sylvie?"

She tried to swear; English or French, it would not have mattered, but God help her, she could only moan her assent. *Bloody man.*

He dipped his head then, brought his mouth to her ear and confided in a whisper: "It's what I want, too."

She nearly laughed; it became a shameless moan instead, when he moved inside her at last.

Eyes locked with his, she clung, conscious of the blanket scraping against her back as she arched up to meet his thrusts, of the squeak as they taxed the springs of the narrow bed, the chafe of his whiskers exquisite against the skin of her throat as he ducked his head to kiss her arched neck. Of her hands sliding over his sweat-slick back and the low roar of swift, mingled breathing, and their mouths finding and losing each other again in the ferocity of their coupling. And then her nails biting into his shoulder blades for purchase and the primal sound of bare skin meeting bare skin swiftly and hard as urgency drove them toward release.

Too soon it had Sylvie in its teeth; and then all at once it engulfed her, shocking, total, a pleasure indescribable.

"Tom—"

She would have screamed it, but he covered her lips with his, took his own name into his mouth as she came apart beneath him, the pleasure savage, seismic. Her body bowed up from the force of it, and still he moved in her, and moved, until his eyes closed and his body stilled as the consuming pleasure of his own release took him.

Tom lowered himself slowly, careful not to crush her; his breath was hot, rough, in the crook of her neck.

A peace like nothing she'd ever felt cupped Sylvie inside

it. She listened to his breathing, floated on the sound of it, as though it was soft music. After a moment, she wrapped a spiral of his hair around one finger, pulled it straight, released it to watch it snap back into its loose wave.

She felt him smile against her throat.

Languidly, he lifted his head, as though the effort cost every bit of his strength, and gazed down at her, studying her as if seeing her for the first time. For so long and so quietly she began to feel uneasy.

"Your mouth…" he began.

But then he shook his head once and kissed her instead. And this kiss was all softness. All tenderness that silenced her, made her shy.

He stopped, and they lay in peaceful silence for a moment.

And then he propped himself up on his elbow. "And now may I show you how I'd like it to be?" Eyes serious, the question solemn.

Feeling breathless, she hesitated. Then nodded. And waited.

His head lowered; his lips brushed hers again, very softly.

And though they were places he had been planning to kiss her from the moment he'd seen her, a way of stating his intent to discover every corner of her, he kissed her. Her earlobe. Her temple. The base of her throat. Her collarbone. As if every place on her was precious, worthy of exploration. She discovered the places along with him, felt them all but sing beneath the touch of his lips.

"When I saw you dancing, Sylvie, it was like watching a… flame. And yet, here is your body, as solid, as strong as… as strong as an ox…" He dragged his fingers, softly up the curve of one slim thigh, moved his face there to kiss a tiny mole on the silky skin between them.

"An *o-ox?*" The last word began as indignant and ended as a gasp when his tongue dipped into her navel.

"An ox," he repeated firmly. "I am not a poet. So strong...so fine..." He flattened a hand over her taut belly, traced outward to the sharp corners of her hip, then kissed the smooth curve of it and turned his cheek so she could feel his whiskers against her tender skin. Gooseflesh swept over her.

"I'd never seen anything so...so beautiful, Sylvie." His voice grew thicker.

He dragged his lips lower, and lower, into the silky dark triangle between her legs.

She gasped when his tongue reached its destination. Dipping into the wet heat of her, a deliberate, skillful caress.

"Is it good?" his voice low and taut.

"Dieu." She breathed it.

"It will get even better." His voice low and dark with promise.

With tongue and lips and breath, he proved it.

And it was difficult, for this was a different kind of surrender, this allowing him to give to her. This opening up of herself to this searching, skillful lover, who made love to her as though he wanted to know every bit of her. And even as her body wanted to submit, surrender, lose itself to him entirely, a part of her resisted, was very nearly afraid, and she could not have said why.

And he knew.

"It's all right, love," he murmured. "I have you. I have you. It's all right to let go."

And inexorably, little by little, fear gave way beneath his fingertips, his tongue, his breath, his lips, and the word dissolved until it was comprised only of his touch and her body's response to it. She moved with him, at first learning how to take, then learning how to demand, with sighs.

"So beautiful," he murmured. And he gave more, until she thought she could no longer bear it.

Lost.

It wracked her when it came, her release, a great wave that rippled from somewhere inside her, and it seemed to go on and on, tossing her with it.

"I want to be inside you again, Sylvie." Tom's voice came to her distantly, a hoarse demand.

"Yes." It was the only word she knew at the moment.

He lifted her hips and guided himself into her, slowly, slowly, and she took fresh pleasure, fresh awe, in watching him lose himself in her. He moved rhythmically until she saw the cords of his neck draw tight and his eyes close. And with a ragged gasp, he spilled into her, his body jerking.

He withdrew, sank down next to her, and held her loosely against him. And for a long time they lay like that, two sated bodies, damp with sweat. His hands moved in her hair, stroking out the tangles, as though he had all the time in the world to do just that.

Her hair was long and fine, a skein of silk. It tangled so easily.

"He didn't ask before he took you, did he, Sylvie? This... lover...of yours."

Her breath nearly stopped.

It was the tone of his voice. She didn't like it...and she did. A tight, low band of sound. Gentleness shot through with veins of fury.

She couldn't answer him, any more than she could seem to stop the tears that astonished her. They spilled slowly, large and cold. Old tears. As though they'd been inside her for a very long time.

She impatiently brushed them away. "I was a grown woman. I did not refuse him."

"Ah. That makes it all right, then." Ironic now, and harder.

She heard his breathing grow rougher, but his hand was still gentle. Tracing the lines of her, the sharp blades of her shoulders, the fine strong muscles of her back created from the magic of the dance, which allowed her to continue to make such magic. The small even bumps of her spine. Gently, gently. Stripping her down to nothing with this relentless, searching, tenderness.

"How did it happen?"

"Does it matter?"

His silence told her he realized that it did not. "But it did. Happen, that is. He just...took."

Sylvie closed her eyes and tried to focus on the path of his hand over her.

She remembered Etienne's charm, his words; she'd been flattered and overwhelmed and an accomplished coquette, and so she had found his pursuit exhilarating, a game, even as she recognized the dangers inherent in it. She remembered the day: He'd stolen a kiss, as he had a half dozen times before. And then she'd been in his arms, up against the wall, his mouth hot against hers, and she had returned his kisses with ardor and skill, because it was thrilling, and part of the game.

And then his hands were beneath her skirt, and it had felt... interesting, and new. She sensed rather than saw him open his trousers. Too afraid to deny him, half-enamored of her own worldliness, too proud, in a way, to protest what she knew was about to happen and what did happen.

She'd realized when it was over that she hadn't been worldly at all.

He had smoothed down her skirt and promised her the next time would be better. That he'd been overcome and perhaps hasty. He'd been all apologies and charm and flowers and gifts. And...it *had* gotten better. She had learned to take pleasure as well as to please.

But no, there had never been any asking. He had never given her a choice.

Had never assumed that she might want one.

And he had been her very first.

"He loves me. He wants to marry me."

Tom's hand stilled on her. Sylvie was glad for the moment for the chance to gather herself. And glad when it resumed moving over her again, because for a moment she'd feared he no longer wanted to touch her.

"Do you love him?" He asked it gruffly.

The truth was she didn't really know. "He is a prince."

She felt Tom's body go utterly still. "Metaphorically speaking, or an *actual* prince?"

"Meta..." Not an English word she knew.

"Is he truly a prince?" he clarified for her. "A real prince?"

"He is truly a prince," she confirmed. In such a way that Tom knew that she meant it.

There was a beat of silence. "Christ, Sylvie." He actually sounded darkly amused.

He sat up abruptly and swung his legs off the edge of the bed. Though she doubted he'd be going anywhere, since he was naked and his clothing was on the other side of the room and this *was* his room, after all.

❧

"Do you love him?" he had asked her. In truth, she really didn't know. What did she really know of love? Etienne promised her safety and permanence and status and all of the things she had wanted for so long. A long future of comfort. Of certainty.

But oh, it was nothing, nothing like this.

She was tempted to call this love, this savage, tender want for Tom Shaughnessy, but she wasn't entirely sure it was; she was afraid to think that it might be, and what she would then be giving up when she left him. Easier to call it desire, for such a thing could ostensibly be appeased, spent.

She felt shy, suddenly, admiring the broad spread of his back in the lamplight, the smooth golden ridges of muscle on either side of his spine. Utterly unself-conscious in his nudity, his hair poking up in odd peaks and horns created from sweat and passion and her hands rummaging through it, his small white buttocks looking oddly vulnerable, both comical and uncompromisingly masculine somehow as he sat there at the edge of the narrow bed.

He suddenly seemed a stranger, this strong, clever, beautiful man. A complicated man, for all of that.

She supposed it could be love, this surprising ache that spread through her, and seemed to need...all that he was...to ease it. The dazzle, the temper, the roughness, the tenderness, the pragmatism, the passion. But how could it be love after so short a time?

Perhaps a better question was: How could such a short time seem like forever?

And yet Tom Shaughnessy had nothing at all to do with the life she wanted and needed. She had taken him, and he had taken her. And perhaps that was all this could be.

A moment later she inched toward him, wrapped her arms around his back, pressed her body against him, held him loosely. Little by little, she felt the tension leave him as he relaxed into her. And oddly, nothing had ever made her feel more powerful than the knowledge that she could give comfort as well as pleasure to this man.

"Come to sleep," she murmured.

He turned and looked at her over his shoulder. "Stay with me?"

She nodded. He turned and slid into bed, lifting the blanket for her, and she slid next to him.

He wrapped an arm around her. She waited for him to sleep before she allowed herself to do so.

e~

Tom was awakened the following morning in what he was certain was the very best way any man on the planet could hope to wake:

A soft hand was sliding down his thigh, and silky hair was dragging behind the hand.

"Sylvie?" he murmured sleepily.

He opened one eye; he didn't see her on the pillow next to him. He fumbled a hand down beneath the blankets and found his hand tangling in her soft hair. "Good morni—*God.* Oh God."

Her tongue had just slid down his shaft, which was immediately more than alert.

She paused. "Good morning to you," she said politely, somewhat muffled from beneath the blanket. And then giggled.

"*Unh,*" he gasped in response.

She laughed again, a low rumble against his sensitive flesh, and the sound was painfully arousing.

She took the length of him into her mouth, slowly, gently at first, and he sucked in breath, and stirred, opened his legs wider. And then he slid his fingers from her hair to pull the blanket back, because he wanted to watch.

He surrendered languidly to the skills of her mouth and hands, hot and delicate on the insides of his thighs, clever and insistent over the length of his shaft, and in so doing she took him from lazy, floating bliss to the gasping, knife-edge of release.

He grasped her hair in his hands to stop her.

"Sylvie." He gasped out the word. "I want you."

She looked up, saw his face, and came into his arms, because she knew that's what he meant.

He rolled her over so he could slip inside her. Gently he tipped the two of them so they were lying side by side. So he could kiss her mouth, and watch her eyes as he moved in her, feel her breasts chafe against his chest. Beautiful eyes. Her eyelids heavy with pleasure, slit with it; her dark lashes quivering; he watched the flush rush over her cheeks and throat as they clung and rocked together, slowly this time. His hands brushing over the silk of her lithe back, of her legs, tangling in her hair. Their lips brushed against each other, taking small kisses, murmuring unintelligible things, endearments, sensual requests.

"Je t'aime," he thought he heard her sigh against his lips.

"Say it again," he demanded in a whisper.

She didn't. But she did say his name when she came shuddering in his arms, and she'd made it sound very nearly the same.

Chapter Fifteen

Sylvie threw her dress on over her head, smoothed her riotous hair out, with Tom's help, and got it twisted into a more decorous knot, and then sat on the edge of his bed and watched him get into his clothes. She studied every move of it—the buttoning of trousers, the tying of the cravat—fascinated, for some reason, as if the very act of dressing was something wondrous and new.

It was only because *he* was doing the dressing, she knew.

And when he caught her watching, he froze and smiled, and then sat down next to her. Her breath hitched. And this, this sharp thing inside her chest, sharp and brilliant, felt quite a bit like joy.

He cradled the back of her head in one hand, and his fingers, briefly, tangled in her hair, touched, lightly, the nape of her neck. He looked down at her for a moment, his silver eyes looking every bit as bemused as she felt. And then, kissed her, and it was warm and lingering and thorough.

And this was how their day began—with no conversation,

just a kiss. She preceded him out of the attic room, and he followed her, and with a smile over her shoulder, she went to her rehearsal, and he went to his library, or to wherever he needed to be. She didn't ask.

‧ ⁀ᵔ

Did it show, she wondered, as she arrived in the dressing room? The night she'd spent in the arms of Tom Shaughnessy? Not a single girl in this room was a virgin, not by far. Could they tell from the faint traces of blue fatigue beneath her eyes, by her kiss-swollen lips, by her eyes that looked at all of them but somehow saw only last night before them, like a waking dream?

Regardless, everyone chattered just the same, and stripped out of their day dresses to get dressed as water nymphs, and no one seemed to notice that she didn't say a word, unless it was Molly, who always seemed peripherally aware of her, regardless.

" 'Ello, everyone."

The voice was soft, but the laughter and chatter in the dressing room stopped as abruptly as if someone had struck a gong. They swiveled as one toward the entrance.

The girl standing there was beautiful even by the White Lily's standards. Fine silvery blond hair coiled up off her face, a few spirals of it touching her cheeks and forehead; a sprinkle of pale freckles across her nose and delicate cheekbones. Brandy gold eyes, doe-sized and luminous. Her clothes were well made, even expensive, suited to her coloring; a walking dress in sarcenet, a bonnet lined in a rich red-brown, matching ribbons tied beneath her chin.

But it wasn't the girl that riveted everyone's attention. It was the small bundle she held in her arms.

Tiny reddish fists popped out of it. And then it made a mewling sound.

The air in the dressing room immediately all but combusted with the collective rabid curiosity.

"Does it 'ave ginger 'air?" one of the girls whispered.

Sylvie felt faint. *Kitty.* This was Kitty, Tom's favorite, ostensibly. The mysterious disappearing girl. Right here in the doorway.

And there was a baby in her arms.

"Kitty!" Rose was the one who rose to kiss the girl on the cheek. "H'it's a *looovely* babe! And ye're in splendid looks. Ye've been missed."

" 'E's a boy," Kitty said proudly, not to the room, but gazing down at the bundle. "Strong an' loud. I'm right lucky 'e's sleepin' now. Must be all of these women. 'E's playin' possum, like. 'E knows we rule the world."

She smiled softly at the baby and made little clucking sounds.

"D'yer name 'im Tom— *Ow!*" Rose was elbowed by the girl next to her.

Kitt looked up dreamily. "I should 'ave done." She looked down again with a soft smile.

An excruciatingly *enigmatic* smile to just about everyone in the room.

Rose peered into the bundle. " 'E's got *no* 'air," she announced meaningfully to the room.

Kitty seemed oblivious to the silent turmoil she'd caused. She was protected by a bubble of new motherhood, and nothing that didn't directly affect her infant could touch her now.

"Then what *d'yer* name 'im?" Rose asked.

Kitty looked up and smiled impishly then. "The General."

And at the collective dropping of jaws, Kitty laughed merrily, which made her little son protest with baby noises. And the laughter lit her face and eyes, and made it clear that she was more than beautiful, she was unique.

Sylvie felt the fear sink through her. *Tom's favorite.*

And Sylvie remembered the toy horse on his shelf: there and then gone.

"I just wanted to see all of ye. I thought ye might 'ave worried over me. But we're doing wonderfully well."

It almost sounded defiant; it felt rather like a final good-bye, and no doubt it was. Kitty had perhaps come to take a look at her old life, perhaps to prove something to everyone in that room, perhaps to prove something to herself.

She turned and left.

"Someone go an' ask 'er."

"She willna tell, that one. Mum's the word, 'er."

"Ask 'er if she lives in Kent. Go, go!"

"*You* go."

And more such whispers rustled.

Sylvie noticed how strangely pale Molly had become. Silent, too.

Sex, Tom Shaughnessy had said. What the White Lily was about, what it celebrated. What she and Tom had celebrated together last night, this morning. It wasn't as if she hadn't known all along, she told herself. It wasn't as though he'd betrayed her in any sense, or promised her a thing. She'd taken her pleasure, and pleasure had been taken from her, and this must be the cost: the plummeting feeling in her stomach, the ice that settled in there, and she couldn't begin to explain why this would be.

She waited an interval, silent. And then moved out of the dressing room, with the thought of perhaps blindly seeking refuge, perhaps in her little room. To breathe through the pain, or walk it off, as though she'd simply twisted an ankle.

And camouflaged by the chatter, she made her way out of the room, still in her day dress.

Tom had his gloves and hat and walking stick in hand and was hurriedly moving toward the door from his office.

"Sylvie." He stopped when he saw her. She saw the memory of last night in his eyes and in his smile, and she was suddenly warm everywhere from it, even as uncertainty and her own pride made her cool to him.

"You are off to visit your family, then?"

He looked shocked. "My...family?"

"To Kent?" Sylvie said. Perhaps he was shocked that she knew.

"My family," he repeated. Staring at her oddly. And then he made a little sound of wondering incredulity. "Well, I suppose I am. But...how do you..."

"And so you take them with you now...Kitty and the baby?"

"With Kitty and the—" And now he seemed utterly baffled. "What on earth are you running on about? What do you know of Kitty? Does—"

"Kitty was here with the baby," she said flatly.

"Kitty was here?" He sounded mildly surprised. "Is she still here? Is she well? And the baby? I imagine Poe or Stark must have let her into the building."

How could he be so cavalier about this? Unless..."They are both well," she said cautiously.

"Good, then." He smiled at her.

She couldn't return the smile. She frowned slightly, looked up at him, and said nothing, utterly tangled in this conversation, not to mention her own thoughts and emotions.

And then she turned to leave.

He closed a quick hand around her arm, stopping her. "Sylvie, what the bloody hell is troubling you?"

She saw the rest of the girls filing out of the dressing room;

a few heads turned, then paused, lowering their voices to talk as they saw them.

She wasn't certain Tom saw the other dancers. For he gently, slowly, released her arm. Made the release somehow a caress.

She had no right to say it, to think it, to demand any sort of clarification from him. She had no right or reason to expect he was anything other than what he appeared to be.

"They say..." She paused. "The girls say..." She cleared her throat. "They say you... They say Kitty..."

He frowned a little. And then his head went back slightly as understanding dawned, came down in a short nod of comprehension.

"Do 'they' now?" Ironically drawled.

She lifted her eyes up swiftly, tried looking into his eyes, but found it difficult somehow. So she looked down at his boots instead. Shiny. She could see her face in them, and what she saw chafed her pride, for she could see that she was feeling hurt, and that meant he could see it, too.

"Tell me truthfully, Sylvie: Would it trouble you if the things 'they' say are true?" His expression was careful now.

It should not trouble her. It should not even surprise her. She certainly hadn't a right to feel any particular way about it at all.

She did look up then.

He was fussing uncomfortably with his walking stick, twisting and twisting it in one gloved hand. Using it to help him think, perhaps. Watching her, his own face tense.

Still, she said nothing.

And then he breathed in deeply, exhaled deeply, either in resignation or like someone gathering courage.

"I would be pleased if you would accompany me to Kent, Sylvie. Will you come?"

The invitation sounded awkward, nearly formal.

"With Kitty and the—"

"No."

She frowned a little, confused, and feeling stubborn now. "The sewing—"

"Will wait."

"Rehearsal—"

"Sylvie." The impatient word stopped her. "I employ everyone here."

Meaning: If he chose, he could order her to accompany him.

A man like Tom Shaughnessy. She remembered thinking that the night she arrived. What he seemed to be warring with, what she felt him to be.

She sensed something waited in Kent that would finally, definitively tell her what this truly meant.

"I will come with you."

❧

He was witty and entertaining on the ride there. He taught her another bawdy song having to do with pirates, one deemed far too risqué for the White Lily's show. But he didn't touch her, or kiss her, or speak of the previous evening, and a hired closed carriage seemed the *ideal* environment in which to dally. Certainly, Etienne had taken liberties in closed carriages.

"We're visiting the May family of Little Swathing," is all he told her. "And you're my cousin," he said to her, as they reached their destination.

This made her snap her head around.

He was laughing silently. "For the sake of Mrs. May. She already finds me scandalous, so you're my cousin for the afternoon. I doubt she'll be fooled, but it's a lie she can be comfortable pretending to believe, I think."

The Mays' cottage was small and worn and comfortable

looking from the outside, wrapped around by a flower-and-vine-tangled picket fence. Mrs. May, a solemn-faced woman, greeted them at the door, and even before introductions had been exchanged, a little boy toddled from behind her and flung his arms up toward Tom.

"*Tah!*"

Tom bent down and scooped the boy up and plopped him down on his shoulders, which made the little boy giggle and curl his hands into Tom's hair.

"Owwww!" Tom's howl was especially for the child's benefit, and it worked a treat, as Jamie laughed. Tom reached up and gently loosened ten little fingers from his hair. "Not so tightly, thank you, my good man."

And then Tom turned and met Sylvie's eyes, and her heart nearly stopped. Two faces looked back at her:

Tom and a little twin of Tom. One pair of eyes wide and wondering and innocent; the other pair searching, a little guarded. Decidedly not innocent.

And unapologetic.

"He says that now, Mr. Shaughnessy," Mrs. May said. "I think he's saying 'Tom.' He asks for you."

And when Mrs. May said that, a confluence of emotions raced over Tom's face. Startled pleasure, Sylvie would have said. Or startled pain. It was difficult to know the difference, for the moment was fleeting.

Mrs. May had all but completely succumbed to Tom Shaughnessy's charm, and had over the past few weeks become something approximating warm, which had some to do with the fiscal contributions Tom made to their household, and much to do with Tom himself.

Or so Tom flattered himself into thinking.

"Clever boy," Tom said, lowering his son to the ground. "What else does he say now?"

"Ball!" Jamie hollered, as if in answer, and squirmed to be lowered to the ground. His father obliged him. And then Jamie reached for his ball, and he toddled over to Sylvie and offered it to her.

Sylvie couldn't speak. Little James was a walking, miniature imprint of his father. Not a shy child, either, she could see; he was all joy and curiosity and restless energy. She supposed the Mays were in part responsible for the joy. But she wondered if Tom saw those qualities in Jamie, and whether he recognized them as his own.

She leaned forward to take the ball from him. Jamie dropped it in favor of seizing her nose in one small hand and squeezing it hard.

"Nose!" Jamie bellowed gaily.

"Unnnh…" Sylvie's eyes began to water with the effort not to scream in pain.

"He says 'nose' now, too," Mrs. May said.

Tom was laughing helplessly, if silently, the bloody man. He knelt and gently removed the pincers of his little boy's fingers from Sylvie's nose.

Sylvie reached up to feel if her nose was still in place. It was on fire.

She had very little experience with children. She knew they made loud noises, emitted noxious smells, and were often effortlessly enchanting. Even as her nose burned, Jamie's face split into that smile that took up nearly his entire face, and she was moved.

"I've often been tempted to do that, myself." Tom said this half to Sylvie, half to Jamie, mostly for his own amusement. "It's a fine nose."

And then he swooped Jamie up and bounced him back up onto his shoulders.

"What word of Maribeth?" Tom asked of Mrs. May, quietly.

"None, I fear."

And they began to talk of Jamie, while Sylvie watched and listened—his words, how tall he was getting, what he was eating and refusing to eat. What else he might need in a few weeks time—clothes, shoes. As matter-of-factly as Tom discussed costumes and bawdy songs.

Sylvie listened, fascinated, and watched as little Jamie delved about in Tom's hair with his hands, and kicked at Tom's chest once or twice with a small foot, while Tom absently jounced him a bit, and absently but firmly removed Jamie's fingers when they probed into his ear. He somehow looked as natural with a small boy at his head as he did when he greeted the guests arriving at the White Lily.

"Mr. Shaughnessy, I'm afraid he's named the horse…" Mrs. May lowered her voice to a whisper, and turned a shade of pink. "Bloody Hell." She sounded faintly accusatory.

"I'm terribly, terribly sorry, Mrs. May." Tom was struggling not to laugh. "Perhaps he'll grow out of the horse and forget all about it."

"He's growing so quickly. I thought…" Mrs. May paused and cleared her throat. "I thought you might like to take him for a day, Mr. Shaughnessy. You should hate to miss any new words."

It wasn't a dramatic change in expression, really. But Sylvie noticed the shift. Tom's lighthearted pleasure became a mask over something careful.

"Perhaps," he said lightly, and lowered Jamie to the ground. "Perhaps we'll discuss it."

⁓

"Why did you not tell me about him on the way here?" Sylvie asked him when the carriage was once again pulling them home.

"I wanted you to see him first. Before you judged me," he said.

For of course he knew she ultimately would be judging him. She understood his point, even as she hadn't enjoyed the suspense.

"Who is his mother?"

He cleared his throat. "Maribeth May was an adventuress of the first order." Tom smiled wryly. "She and I enjoyed each other on several occasions"—he gave the word "enjoy" an accent of irony—"and then she left for…oh, I believe it was Shropshire, word had it…with another man, one who doubtless had more money or perhaps prospects than she assumed I had. She was ambitious, Maribeth was, and one could scarcely blame her. I was not heartbroken, nor was I terribly surprised, given what I knew of her. I was informed of Jamie's existence by letter."

As he spoke Tom absently, slowly, worked the fingers of his scarred hand with the other fingers. "I imagine she found him an inconvenience, perhaps financially. Or perhaps she found him a…a hindrance to her pleasures." The last words seemed difficult for him to say.

They both fell silent for a moment.

"I have no doubts he is my son," he added.

No one who laid eyes on the boy could ever have any doubts, either, Sylvie knew. She simply nodded. "He is beautiful," she said gently.

Tom looked up quickly, some emotion flaring in his eyes. And then he gave her a swift smile, teasing her, knowing she'd just complimented him, too. "You haven't asked about Kitty."

"And Kitty?" Sylvie obliged him.

"Kitty was…" Tom smiled faintly. "Quick-witted, more so than the other girls. Lovely. I did like Kitty. But then she came to me and told me she was pregnant. She was afraid I would be angry and let her go, and it was a valid fear: I would have *had* to let her go, regardless. I can't put a pregnant girl onstage, God knows. Her man had no employment at the time, and so I...I gave her some money. Enough for them to marry. To find their own rooms in town. I made some inquiries and found a position for her husband.

"But this..." He paused. "This was after I learned of Jamie."

Telling her, quite frankly, that his Jamie had perhaps changed the way he viewed the world. That perhaps his generosity toward Kitty had a little something to do with his own guilt.

"Give your hand to me," Sylvie said quietly.

Tom looked up, surprised.

"Give your hand—" But then she stopped and simply took his hand in hers.

She skillfully began working his fingers, kneading between them, stretching them, gently rubbing the joints. She was an expert at this since it was a necessity to do this to her feet after rehearsals, after performances. She knew intimately the little universe of bone and muscle and sinew in her own feet.

"Good?" she asked.

He nodded. But his expression was guarded, a little bemused. As though struggling with or suppressing something, and so he couldn't speak. She thought of the ways in which Tom Shaughnessy had always looked after those around him, including her, in his way. She wondered if anyone had ever truly looked after him. It was almost as though he didn't know how to allow someone to do it.

"He's your only child," she said, half statement, half question.

"The only one I know about."

Ironically said. And no doubt something that could be said for nearly any man, even—perhaps especially—someone like Etienne.

Finally, Tom sighed and closed his eyes slightly, leaned back against the carriage wall, accepting her ministrations.

What a pair we are, she thought half-ruefully. *I rushed across the Channel from the arms of one lover to learn about my past, to learn who I am. Never dreaming I'd land in the arms of another lover.*

And finally, she stopped massaging Tom's hand and simply held it for a moment, drew her fingers lightly over the lines in his palm, daring a caress. He opened his eyes then, and slowly withdrew his hand from hers, lifted it to her face. With his thumb, he traced, very lightly, the line of her jaw. She turned her cheek into his hand; for a moment he cradled it.

And she thought he might kiss her, but she wasn't certain whether she wanted him to kiss her just now. She wanted to sit quietly and absorb this matter-of-factly recited tale of a casual liaison with a woman that had resulted in a beautiful bastard child, and to picture how Tom had looked a moment ago when he held that child.

And to remember the look in his eyes when he hovered over her, moved inside her. When he had kissed her for the very first time. The stunned darkness in his eyes.

And when she did, like a wave it swept through her, the desire, fierce and complete, spinning her head.

She wondered if today's journey was his way of warning her away. *This is who I am.*

Or whether, in showing her Jamie, he had just shown her the inside of his heart and was waiting for her to tell him what she thought of it.

He didn't kiss her. He took his hand away from her cheek, then turned his head toward the window. He remained silent for the rest of the journey.

When the White Lily's brilliantly ostentatious sign was once again in view, the coach stopped.

Tom reached out a hand and helped her down from the hackney, then paid the hackney driver, counting out coins and seeing him off with the lift of a hand.

Sylvie shook out her skirts and looked for Tom.

He wasn't looking at her; his head was pointed toward the center of London, squinting in the sunlight. He had the abstracted air of one looking through a telescope, attempting to bring something very far away into focus.

She noticed he was standing very still, lightly tapping his walking stick absently into the ground.

"Your prince...is he very wealthy, Sylvie?"

"Yes," she answered, after a hesitation.

"Can he give you a life of comfort and certainty?"

She watched him, attempting to gauge his mood. She frowned a little. Reluctantly—as though she didn't want him to arrive at whatever conclusion he seemed to be seeking, she answered: "Yes." Her heart had begun knocking strangely.

"And he loves you."

It was a statement; he already knew the answer to the question, for she had told him the night before. He seemed to be adding all of this up in an equation of sorts in his mind.

Suddenly, Tom looked at his hat, as though he'd just remembered he was holding it, and then placed it on his head. Ruefulness in the gesture, as though he knew a real gentleman would not have forgotten to replace it once removed.

"Then you'd be foolish not to marry him."

He looked at her evenly when he said this.

And when she didn't speak, because she couldn't speak in the aftermath of those words, he nodded shortly, as though she'd answered some sort of silent question.

He turned and pushed open the door to the theater, and she watched the White Lily swallow him up.

❦

The note was in The General's handwriting, and was succinct, as befitted the gravity of it. It had been placed under the paperweight that Tom had finally, wisely, acquired, given The General's penchant for gusty sighs.

Pinkerton-Knowles backed out. That's the last of them.

Tom didn't swear. Or toss the note down. Tom simply held it, felt some cold sensation wash over the back of him. The wave of disappointment, followed by the wave of inspiration, which would normally have followed such a total defeat—it wasn't as though he'd never known defeat—had given way instead to a peculiar quiet fury.

Something was amiss, and he couldn't begin to guess what that might be. When the enthusiasm had been so uniform and total, when the idea was so good, when all of it had been taking shape so splendidly. When his days were spent marshaling builders and making plans.

When he had already committed all of his own spare capital to it. And now, in the absence of a strong dose of capital from some other source very soon...he would be swiftly ruined.

❦

It started as just a tiny spark, a spark that resulted, she supposed from striking his words over and over again in the tinderbox of her temper.

Then you'd be foolish not to marry him. Then you'd be

foolish not to marry him. Then you'd be foolish not to marry him.

They played in her head beneath the words of the silent music she danced to as she taught the girls the steps to the ballet that afternoon. She heard them in her mind as she praised their form, laughed with them. She heard them in her mind as she argued with The General over what the next step in their dance should be.

And then the spark grew when she applied the little puff of her pride to it. She supposed she wanted to be the one to tell Tom, "Oh no, this could never be. I am promised to another. Thank you for the moments of pleasure." Sylvie Lamoreux, the much-desired queen of the Paris ballet, had taken a lover, a ruffian of a lover, as a lark, and now it was over. She had sampled something she wanted, and now it was over.

But Tom Shaughnessy, the name purred most often on female lips throughout London, or so it was said, had tired of her after one evening of sensual pleasure. She told herself this to see if perhaps it felt true, to see if this was why she was so furious, so that then she could spend her uncomfortable anger on it and have it be done.

But no. This didn't feel true, either. So she probed about in her mind for whatever it was that seemed to be feeding her temper, flushing her skin until it felt burned.

And then realized she should be probing about in her heart instead.

And that was where she found the answer.

And that was when she became well and truly furious.

She flung open the door to his office, heedless of who might see her enter, slammed it again, glanced about, seized his paperweight, and heaved it at him.

It would have struck him square in the chest, but Tom caught it just in time, looking startled and very briefly impressed, either with his own reflexes or with her aim.

"What the bloody he—"

"Tu est un lâche!" Sylvie reached for a book and hurled that.

But Tom was a quick study. He nimbly dodged it, backed away from her around the desk.

"*What* am I?" He was genuinely befuddled, backing away from her. "What the devil are you—"

She stalked him around the desk. And finally, in the flames of her temper, she found the English word and spat it:

"Coward."

She saw it happen, the instant and terrifying transformation: his eyes go the color of slate, his mouth become a tight, white line. She'd made him furious.

"Explain yourself."

Any sensible person would have been frightened and backed away. She'd witnessed his temper, and knew it was easily the equal of her own. But she was too angry to be sensible.

" 'Then you'd be foolish not to marry him,' " she mimicked nastily. "Coward! You are just afraid because . . . because . . ."

" 'Because'?" he snapped.

"Because you are in the love with me."

Tom blinked as if the words had struck him between the eyes.

Silence fell, guillotine-swift.

Then Sylvie became aware of the sound of quick breathing, her fury mingled with his.

His eyes never left her face. His hands remained tensed at his sides, at the ready to defend himself if she intended to throw anything else.

And this struck her as somewhat comical, even as Sylvie

was aware that neither of them had blinked for an unnatural amount of time.

And then—and then—the bloody man's mouth slowly tilted up at the corners. And as usual, anything approximating a smile transformed his face.

" 'In the love with' you?" he repeated softly.

She squeezed her eyes closed. *Damn.* Her cursed temper had made smithereens of her English. She took a deep breath, soothing her mind, recovering her dignity.

"*In* love," she corrected quietly. "*In* love with me."

She watched the rest of his anger leave him. And somehow, the silence had gone from fraught . . . to velvet.

"Well, *I* think," Tom countered finally, softly, "that you are 'in the love with' *me,* Sylvie."

Neither of them confirmed or denied a thing.

Simply watched. Simply breathed.

But finally, this silent stubbornness of his was enough to stir the cinders of her temper again.

"And because you are afraid"—Sylvie waved her hand abruptly, in helpless frustration—"this is why you push me away."

He stared at her wonderingly. The beginnings of a frown creased his forehead.

And then he drew in a breath so deep it was as though he was trying to suck patience from the very air. He sat down hard in his chair at the desk.

"Listen to me. You saw that child today, Sylvie."

She nodded, though she knew he didn't require it.

His words were careful, and they almost had the sound of a recital. She imagined he'd rehearsed them in his head during their silent ride back to London.

"I never knew my own father. My mother and I were always desperately poor, and she died when I was very young. Much of what I did to survive—*most* of it—I would never boast about, or even wish to describe to you. I did what I needed to, and to this day I count myself bloody lucky that I'm not in Newgate, or didn't end up swinging from a gallows. I suppose," he said almost wryly, "if I were to reflect, I could arrive at a *few* regrets. But they wouldn't include Jamie, and they wouldn't include..." He looked up at her, seemed to lose his words for a moment. "They wouldn't include you," he concluded quietly.

"But I also know now it would be bloody... *unconscionable* to subject someone to the uncertainty of my life, of my reputation, when something so much better can be had for them."

She wasn't certain about the word "unconscionable," but she was virtually positive it meant "wrong."

"And Sylvie, this doesn't make me a—what was your word?"

"Lâche?" she supplied.

"Yes. It doesn't make me a *lâche*. If you truly understood how... if you knew you would..." He dragged impatient hands over his hair. "You would know that it makes me... it probably makes me a..." He paused, as a revelation flickered over his face. "A damned *hero*."

He ground out the last words, oddly, darkly amused, bemused. Clearly it was the last thing he'd ever, ever expected to be.

She considered them.

"It makes you bloody stupid," she said flatly.

His head jerked toward her.

And then in one smooth startling motion he stood up, crossed the room, and grasped her chin in his hand.

She gasped when he tipped her face sharply up to him, tried to jerk her chin away. He held it firmly.

"Tell me, Sylvie, and answer me honestly for once: are you angry with *me*... or with yourself?"

"I—"

But then his mouth was on hers, hard.

It was a kiss that infuriated, confirmed, stirred, and then somehow . . . despite everything . . . became all she'd always needed, suspected she would ever need, which infuriated her all over again.

And it felt entirely final.

And then he stopped, released her chin. He closed his eyes briefly.

They were both breathing roughly. When he opened his eyes again, she saw the iron resolve in them.

"So stop blaming *me,* Miss *Chapeau.* It's simply how things must be. If you gave it a moment's thought instead of indulging your temper, you would realize that I'm right. And it's just your own bloody misfortune to love two men."

"I don't—"

"Yes?" he said swiftly. His face tense. Waiting.

But when she said nothing, he nodded once, curtly.

"Tell me now who's 'bloody stupid,' Sylvie. Tell me now who's a coward."

She looked at him. And for a moment she forgot his words, and simply looked, fell into the beauty of his hard, elegant face, the character and wear of it. Looking for a reason to hate him.

Finding only that it resembled her own heart. And this brought with it a quiet sort of terror.

"Don't feel you need to stay," he said softly. Ironically.

She turned abruptly.

And to spite him, because she knew he was looking for passion . . . she closed the door quietly behind her.

Chapter Sixteen

꩜

It was so dark in her little nun's cell of a room; her eyes remained open, and still it was as though she was looking at the inside of her eyelids. She'd found it comforting before, and snug. Tonight, somehow, it seemed to mock her mood. Shame was not nearly as comfortable a bed partner as a warm, passionate man.

A quick temper was her curse; she relived throwing things earlier today, the shouting, and put her hands up to her cheeks. *Mon dieu.* She wondered if her sister had a temper. It would be lovely to have someone with whom to commiserate about a family trait.

I think you are in the love with me, Sylvie.

Are you angry with me, or with yourself?

She knew how to be with Etienne, knew what to expect. Knew how the days of her life would play out. And she knew a moment of regret for ever leaving him, for now she was all too aware of the places in her he would never be able to stir.

And more aware than ever of the things he could offer her that someone like Tom Shaughnessy could not.

Indeed, *had* not.

This was the trouble, she realized, with surrendering to want.

And as she'd left his library today, she'd glanced down and seen the note that had been tucked beneath the paperweight she'd hurled:

Pinkerton-Knowles backed out. That is the last of them.

She knew what this meant: Tom had lost all of his investors, and thus all of his capital, too. His future was now nearly as uncertain as it had been when he was a child, stealing cheese. She felt it on his behalf, the winds of the abyss whistling at her ankles. She had fought too long, her entire life, to dance away from that abyss.

Sylvie stood and lit a candle, pushed open her trunk, unfolded the miniature of her mother from where she kept it wrapped, hidden, in a soft cotton shift. And stared down at it, holding the candle away from it so the wax would not drip down.

I will tell him who I am, she thought.

It was something she wanted to give to him, a gift in parting—an apology, and her trust. To tell him he was right about everything after all—this was all it could be, and that she understood that this interlude was indeed over, and she would no doubt be gone soon.

To thank him. The gratitude didn't seem specific. Perhaps she simply meant to thank him for being.

Her heart knocking, she traveled the dark hallway and found the stairs leading to his portion of the attic.

The room was dark. She hovered near the last step, listened for breathing, and heard none.

"Tom?" she whispered. She took the last step, lifted her candle.

The bed was tightly, neatly made. He hadn't slept in it.

You can find me in it... most nights.

The pain was savage and instant and utterly shocking, and for a moment, it hurt to breathe, as though her lungs were suddenly made of rough-edged glass. She simply stood there on the step and stared at Tom's made bed, in a room that smelled and felt so strongly of him it seemed impossible he wasn't in it.

And this was when she admitted to herself that she hadn't come to apologize for her temper. That she hadn't come to tell him who she truly was. Or to tell him he was right about everything.

Though she *might* have done those things after they had made love again and again.

A clock somewhere bonged 3:00 a.m.

So she left, no less ashamed than when she had set out to find him.

Chapter Seventeen

❧

Down the hall girls were dressing for the show in nymph-like togas, shimmering organza to match the shimmer of the grand oyster, smoothing rouge onto their cheeks, while Tom and The General discussed the final details of Venus. For tonight was the night: In the absence of all of his investors, the success of Venus was the pivot upon which Tom's future turned.

"We need to make a damned fortune on this show, or we're sunk." Tom managed to say the words easily. This, in itself, did not come easily.

"We'll make the damned fortune." The General was quietly confident.

Tom shifted restlessly in his chair, patted his hand on the arm of it for a moment. "Gen...I had an inspiration."

"Mmm?" The General looked up alertly.

"Well...what if I made the Gentleman's Emporium a... Family Emporium."

"A *what?*" The General sounded alarmed.

"Family Emporium."

"Family," The General repeated slowly, lingering over the word as if he'd never heard the word before in his life. "Emporium."

"That *is* what I said, Gen," Tom said irritably. "I thought, perhaps, there could be a floor for mothers to take tea together, and then a floor for fathers to drink with other fathers, we'll have cards and games, a place to get ices and cakes, a floor for entertainment that men can bring their wives to, a place for children to play together on little pirate ships, and in castles, and..."

He trailed off at the look on The General's face. As if he wanted to test Tom's forehead for fever.

"Things of that sort," Tom finished uncomfortably.

The General seemed to be searching for diplomatic words, which was highly unlike him.

"You have an area of expertise, Tommy..." he began slowly.

"Area*s*," Tom corrected testily.

"Very well, then," The General humored him. "Areas. Which is why you're rich now."

"Was rich," Tom corrected. "Now every spare penny I had is in that building across town, and as I said, if we don't make a fortune tonight..."

The General waved that away impatiently. "*This*...is what you know. Venus..." The General said the word lovingly— neither one of them could say the word with any other sort of intonation—"is what you know. They resulted from your instincts, and following your instincts has made you a success."

"It doesn't mean I can't develop other areas of expertise," Tom said irritably.

"No," The General agreed. Sounding as though he was humoring him.

"And it's not a bad idea, though, is it?" Tom insisted. "A Family Emporium?"

The General shrugged. Which was something of a concession.

Tom fell into a near-brooding silence. Which was highly unlike *him*. "She called me a coward and threw things at me." It was becoming a habit, it seemed, this exchange of confidences.

The General was quiet for a moment.

"The French," he finally said, shaking his head in commiseration.

It amused Tom distantly that The General knew precisely who he was talking about, but perhaps he shouldn't have been surprised.

Then The General's head snapped toward Tom. "Wait. She called *you* a coward?"

"A *lâche,* more specifically."

"And she's still alive?"

Tom grunted a laugh.

"Should I ask *why* she called you a coward? And does this mean . . . do you mean to say . . . are you confessing that you did . . . *finally* . . . touch a dancer, Tom?" The General's lips were pressed together, as if he was struggling not to laugh.

"I touched a dancer, Gen." Tom sounded surly. "And she *is* a real dancer, as you said."

"Mmm." The General's way of agreeing. His gaze drifted then, as if he didn't want to look Tom in the eye. He sipped at his tea.

"The dance," Tom began. "She . . . It's . . ." He struggled for a word.

"Beautiful?" The General said.

"Yes," Tom said, sounding defeated.

"So you saw it?"

"Yes." He paused. "But there's no money in it," he added hurriedly.

"Mmm," The General said. His gaze drifted again.

"Have you noticed that all the girls seem to be getting just a little thinner, Gen?" Tom peered hard at The General. "Almost as if they've been getting more exercise."

"Hadn't, really," The General said, still looking elsewhere. "So...she threw things and called you a coward because..."

"A wealthy French nobleman apparently wants to marry her. I told her she should marry him. That she'd be foolish not to."

He looked at The General, whose face, at the moment, was completely unreadable.

The General continued to stare at him. And then he frowned a little, looking oddly puzzled. His eyes scoured the murals searchingly, as if looking for the answer to whatever question was silently plaguing him. "Tom?"

"What is it?" Tom said curtly.

"Who's that noble cove you told me about from the Greek myths, when we were having the murals painted? The one who lives with a wound, or some such, and suffered every day, and grew wiser for it?"

"Chiron?" Tom supplied, confused.

"Right. Chiron. Here's the rub: *You,* Tom Shaughnessy, are *not* a noble cove. Not even close. It's just not your nature, that martyr bit. That"—he pointed to Tom's hand, and Tom stopped rubbing—"and this"—he made an eloquent circle with his hand to encompass the theater—"is *your* nature. You *fight*. You fight dirty, if you have to, for what you want. You like a little drama. All of which are benefits of *not* being a gentleman. You don't"— he drawled the words mockingly—"'quietly back away.'"

Tom considered this. "This is different, Gen," he said ungraciously.

The General stared at him, those intense dark eyes bright beneath those thick brows, which then dived nearly to a point at the top of his nose.

Tom matched him glower for glower.

"Well I'll be damned," The General finally said, wonderingly. He gave a short incredulous laugh. Then he reached for his watch from his coat, peeked at the time. He stood and stubbed out his cigar.

"What?" Tom snapped.

The General slipped into his coat, headed for the door, and said the words over his shoulder.

"She was right."

❧

Seats creaked and coats rustled, a few throats rumbled to clear, then silence dropped, heavy as the velvet curtain that obscured the evening's promised delights. And as raucousness, not silence, typically reigned at the White Lily, right up to and during the show, this silence underscored the momentousness of the occasion, built upon itself until the anticipation in the audience was so palpable it could almost be beaten like a drum.

Tom looked out from the back of the theater: row upon row of heads were upturned, pointed raptly at the stage. Behind that curtain, in the wings, a crew of boys were poised to fan the fish and pull open the oyster; the girls dressed as water nymphs were poised to drift out when Molly began her song.

Tom's gut tightened in a way it hadn't since the owner of the Green Apple Theater had threatened to slit his gullet for losing money on a show. So much rested on this single evening.

Josephine's head, pale in the darkness, was turned over her shoulder, watching for his signal; at last, he lifted a finger, and she nodded and dragged her fingers across the pianoforte in a long glissando. The velvet curtain lurched up.

Tom heard the collective gasp with satisfaction, and exhaled his relief.

All the while the liquid notes of the sonata poured caressingly through the theater, as Josephine dutifully played on.

"DO. SOMETHING," Tom commanded in a growl to The General.

The General bolted toward the back of the stage.

For a moment, all was quiet. The oyster remained still, glowing its soothing, glorious nacre colors, while the sonata delicately scented the air, and the audience waited, primed now: Tom could sense it.

And then the shell inched open. *Creeeeeeak.*

The audience inhaled in anticipation.

Abruptly the shell clapped shut again. *Clack.*

A collective exhale.

The shell inched open again. *Creeeeeeak.*

Another inhale of anticipation.

Then clapped shut again. *Clack.*

It looked like—dear God—

"I think it's *chewing* her! It looks like it's chewing her!" someone in the crowd marveled.

Like that.

The laughter became utterly helpless then. There really was no hope for it. Great roars of it ripped up the rows, a conflagration of mirth. Men began thrashing in their chairs, and the percussion of knees and backs slapped joined it.

"Bloody brilliant!" someone bellowed. "Shaughnessy, you're a bloody *genius!*"

The oyster *creeeeeeaked* open again. Steadily this time: an inch, then six inches, then a foot, and then three feet.

The audience settled somewhat, leaned forward, eagerly waiting.

Until it finally opened enough to reveal Daisy. Disheveled, wild-eyed, a grin pasted on her mouth. Tentatively she began to raise her arms into the air in a pose; at the same time, she cautiously peered back over her shoulder at the shell.

It clapped shut abruptly and she vanished.

The audience roared.

Josephine, clearly at a loss for what else she might do, dutifully continued to play the sonata. From where he stood, Tom could see the perspiration gleaming on her face, too.

The delicate music was all but drowned out beneath the stamp of feet and roars of men.

The shell creaked open again. Slowly, slowly, slowly.

Daisy, her optimism clearly spent, was curled up in the center of it, her arms wrapped protectively over her head.

But when the shell remained open, she lifted her head up, peeped cautiously over her shoulder at it. Wildly mussed strands of her ruddy hair were puffing out around her ruddy face.

"It wants you for dinner, Daize!" an audience member bellowed. "Run! Run while you can!"

"You can be the pearl in my oyster any day, Daisy Jones!"

The shell remained open. Cautiously, tentatively, Daisy rose to her knees, facing the audience. She peered suspiciously over her shoulder at her nemesis, the oyster.

"Harpoon the beast!" someone suggested in a bellow. "Kill it before it eats you, Daize!"

More gusts of wild laughter.

One of Daisy's enormous breasts had nearly freed itself from her gracefully wrapped toga in the tussle, and now, as she began to rise, it glowed in the footlights, a luminous, miniature twin of the oyster from which she'd emerged.

"Oh . . . my . . . *God!*" someone howled in helpless mirth.

Daisy took a visibly deep breath, her bosom cresting and falling like a tidal wave, and gave her toga a twist to recapture the breast.

And finally, when it became clear the top of the shell would remain aloft, Daisy flung her arms triumphantly into the air and crooked a knee.

The lascivious, buxom, grinning antithesis of Botticelli's Venus.

"Bravo! Bravo!"

The applause was thunderous; hands had never beat together so violently before, and the theater resounded with stamps and cheers. Suddenly the air was filled with glittering things: coins raining toward the stage. Then a hail of flowers. Then cravats and shoes and watch fobs.

All was spectacularly successful mayhem.

From where Tom stood in the back of the theater, he could see the wild look slowly fade from Daisy's eyes, and little by little her desperate smile made the subtle transformation from panic...to uncertainty...

To triumph.

Ah, well. Daisy was a diva. It was perhaps the way of divas to prevail.

The General had returned, looking considerably more sweaty and disheveled. "The damn boys with the pulleys have disappeared."

"Sack them if you ever see them again," Tom said flatly. "Why was the oyster chewing her?"

"I tried—several times—but when *I* pulled on the pulley, I only dangled. Couldn't get it to open far enough." He said this matter-of-factly, accustomed to the myriad trivial inconveniences of his size. "Several of the girls helped me get it open."

They both took a moment to watch Daisy basking in the waves of applause.

"That bloody woman is going to do that exactly the same way every night this week," Tom said with grim satisfaction.

The congratulatory crowds had finally cleared away from Daisy's dressing room, leaving her alone amidst a veritable forest of flowers. She considered whether to call a carriage to take her home. Alone. Perhaps she should stop in to see Tom before she did.

It wasn't a conversation she looked forward to having.

A tap sounded on her dressing room door, surprising her. She quickly blotted her eyes and huffed out the nearest lamp. In the shadows, she hoped it would be difficult to see how red they had become.

"Come in," she sang out, hoping her voice didn't sound as thick to the person on the other side of the door as it did to her.

The door opened. The General stood in the doorway.

He said nothing at all. Merely regarded her with those intense dark eyes. She returned his stare.

"Well?" she all but snapped, finally.

"You've been crying," he accused.

She turned away from him and began fussing with the petals of one of the flower arrangements. Hothouse flowers, which is what one earned when one was feted by dukes and earls. They'd been brought to her for years, a consequence of her notoriety. She wondered how much longer she could expect them.

The General, of course, was empty-handed. "You were an enormous success this evening," he began.

"Ha," Daisy said this to the mirror. " 'Enormous' is the word."

He said nothing.

She tried not to, but she did anyway: she sniffed. *Bloody hell.* And so now he knew for certain that she *had* been crying.

"I suppose I should apologize to Tom," she said tentatively.

"Oh, I think Tom has forgiven you," The General said with faint irony.

No one said anything for a time.

"I paid 'er a guinea. Molly," Daisy confessed.

"I should have thought Molly could be bought much cheaper."

Daisy almost smiled at that. "I just thought it would be so... pretty," she said wistfully. "I wanted it to be me. All the girls were so damned...they gloated about it."

As this was true, and partially Daisy's fault for being such a diva, The General remained silent.

"I'm sorry I ruined yer beautiful show." She meant it.

He gave a one-shouldered shrug. "They loved it, the crowd did. They loved you."

"But not fer the reasons I wanted them to love it."

He conceded this with silence. "Perhaps it's for the best."

Daisy knew this meant that perhaps her future featured comic roles and not roles for a youthful siren, and that she might as well become accustomed to it now.

"I'm not pretty anymore, am I, Gen?"

"Oh, Daisy. You were never pretty."

She whipped her head toward him, her eyes enormous with horrified astonishment.

He rapidly closed the distance between them then. And to her amazement, reached out, and with his thumb gently dabbed a tear on her cheek.

"Don't ever use words like 'pretty' to describe yourself, Daisy Jones," he said, softly, but firmly and unapologetically, too. "Pretty is far, far too tepid a word for what you are. And no one will *ever* forget you, you know."

And suddenly Daisy Jones, who had sported with dukes and earls atop her cherished nearby pink velvet settee, who'd been feted and showered with gifts by the richest men in London, felt as shy as a girl before the message she saw written in The General's dark eyes.

Gently, without hesitation, he lifted her chin up to touch his lips to hers. And then he proceeded to kiss her in a way that stripped away all her years and experience, all notions or cynicism about romance, and left only the two of them alone.

"You know I love you, don't you?" he said softly when he was done.

"I do know." She sounded as breathless as a girl.

"And?"

"And I love ye, too, ye wee bugger."

"That works out nicely for the both of us then, doesn't it?" he said gruffly. "And speaking of that guinea, Daize... I know of a better investment than Molly. And it has to do with Tom."

⁂

Tom kept to his word. Every night that week, Daisy climbed in the beautiful oyster shell, struggled to free herself from it, was chewed, nearly lost a breast out of her toga, and in the end was cheered wildly. She was also supposed to sing a bawdy song, but occasionally the cheering made it all but impossible.

The theater was filled to the rafters day after day, so they added shows, keeping Daisy exceptionally busy. And Tom began to breathe a little more easily. He had no investors, he was in debt up to his eyes, but his coffers were refilling just a little, and another few weeks of this kind of roaring success would buy him enough time to rally more investors before the costs of building the Gentleman's Emporium dragged him under, and with it the White Lily and everyone who depended upon it... and him.

But Daisy's Venus so warmed up the crowds that nearly

anything they would have put onstage after it would have elicited howls of approval. Fairies, pirates, damsels—it would not have mattered if he had dressed all the girls as horses and trotted them out.

An equestrian theme!

It just demonstrated that inspiration was always just one thought away.

But then he thought of a wooden horse named Bloody Hell that could be pulled on a string. And suddenly he pictured how much small boys would enjoy playing with other small boys on hobbyhorses. How much they might enjoy a *show* featuring hobbyhorses.

Or maybe puppets...

She was right, The General had said.

You fight, he'd said. *Dirty, if you have to.*

There simply had to be a way to have everything he wanted, for he always had.

And so his thoughts warred with accepting that he might not be able to have the things he wanted and grappling and rejecting ways to get them.

ᶜ⁓

For a few nights, he waited until his eyes were raw from lack of sleep for the creak of footsteps on the stairs.

But he saw her only onstage: a fairy, a pirate, a damsel, game but reluctant, fiery and proud.

Other nights he left looking for other female company, other arms, other hands, that could do things to and with him to remind him how easily passion could make one forget, and how much pleasure could be had from one's own body without complications. Without involving anything other than the body.

But he'd always lost the will halfway to the Velvet Glove, where they had no doubt become lonely for his company, and instead spent an evening staring at the building he intended to transform into the Gentleman's Emporium, sipping at a flask of whiskey and making plans. And thinking, mordantly amused, about the flawed things he suspected he loved. A dwarf choreographer and an aging diva and a little boy with a wooden horse named Bloody Hell and a beautiful, bad-tempered, achingly tender ballerina who made love as though she were both dancing and fighting for her life.

It wasn't as though he didn't know where she slept. As if he couldn't have made a meal of his own pride and gone to see her.

But it was for the best, he told himself. She would be leaving, and life as he knew it would resume without her.

Augustus Beedle hadn't aged well, but The General found to his surprise he didn't look upon this with any particular satisfaction. His hair, once a leonine sweep, now began much farther back on his head, leaving an expanse of lined forehead; five lines, he counted, evenly spaced, like a staff of music awaiting the notes of a composition. His waistcoat bulged just a little. *How about that,* The General thought. The famously lean Beedle now sported a wee paunch.

Given the missing hair and the forehead lines, The General suspected that being married to a temperamental ballerina was perhaps more challenging than Augustus Beedle had expected.

And at this thought, The General *did* experience a twinge of satisfaction.

They exchanged bows. Once upright again, they took a quiet moment to eye each other, assessing. The General saw Beedle whisk a look over his clothes, trace their genus to Weston, and do the math of their cost in his head, for his face ultimately reflected a begrudging approval.

What he lacked in height, The General had always made up for in flair. Beedle had never been able to compete in that regard, at least.

"You've been missed," he said finally. "Your gift for sets has been unsurpassed, and your eye for choreography—"

"It's been a very long time, Beedle," The General said wryly. In other words, doubting the sincerity of all of this.

Beedle smiled wryly, acknowledging the little jab. "Your talent was exceptional, and I did enjoy working with you. Should you need a—"

"I'm happy where I am." The General thought of Daisy for a moment: warm, round, loud, honest, kind, proud Daisy. "Very happy."

Beedle cleared his throat. "I should like to say that I'm grateful for this opportunity to apologize for our misunderstanding."

"Maria was not a 'misunderstanding,' Beedle."

The General had forgiven Beedle, for despite the friendship between the two men, it wasn't precisely Beedle's fault that Maria had chosen not to love a short man and that The General had chosen to drown his broken heart in all manner of liquor in every major city on the Continent. But The General's strategy required keeping the other man off-balance and feeling guilty and uncomfortable for the time being.

In other words, he needed him in the proper condition to do a favor. For this was his sole mission today. It was a mission, coincidentally, that Tom Shaughnessy knew nothing about. And the mission was entirely for Tom's sake.

"She is well?" he asked solicitously. Keeping his voice ever-so-slightly strained. Brave-sounding. "Maria?"

Beedle smiled tiredly. "Yes."

"Very good." Again, just a hint, a crucial hint, of noble strain in his voice.

The General allowed the silence to stretch until it was officially awkward. And then:

"You're familiar with the White Lily, Augustus?"

A small, appreciative smile. "Yes. Tom Shaughnessy's theater. Beautiful girls."

"I thought you might be interested to know, Augustus, that I've formed my own *corps de ballet,* very talented dancers, all. And they were all employed by the White Lily."

Augustus Beedle's eyes went gratifyingly wide. "Where can I see them?"

"Well, that's just it, Augustus. They will be featured as part of a new, grand entertainment center. A...Family Emporium."

"Shaughnessy's idea?"

"Yes."

"Then no doubt it will be wildly successful."

"No doubt," The General said. "And I'd like to beg a favor of you, Augustus."

"Anything," Beedle promised.

"We could also use a blessing from an exalted source. Specifically, a very well-known patron of the ballet."

It took Beedle but a moment.

And then he smiled. "That, my friend, should not be difficult."

⁓

Sylvie was sitting quietly with Josephine in the sunny room, next to where all the hammering and swearing normally took place, stitching a rent in a fairy wing, when the housekeeper, Mrs. Pool, interrupted them.

"Ladies, a Viscount Grantham and a Lady Grantham are downstairs."

Sylvie stood so abruptly that her fairy wing tumbled from her lap and lay upside down on the floor, like a big butterfly shot from the sky.

"They are looking for a girl named Sylvie Lamoo…Lamo-something. A right fancy name. They thought she might have come to the White Lily." Mrs. Pool gave a merry laugh at the absurdity of the very idea. "Mr. Shaughnessy sent me up to find you. Shall I send them away?"

"I—" It was an airless squeak. Sylvie gaped for a moment at the housekeeper. Then she turned and gaped at Josephine.

Then she smoothed her hands nervously over her hair, and nervously down her skirt, then gave up on the grooming and simply bolted down the stairs.

⸎

Near the door of the theater, near the stage, three people stood. Two men, one very tall and fair-haired, an air of easy importance and casual danger, rather the sort of air Tom Shaughnessy wore like a coat. This must be Viscount Grantham.

The other man was Tom. His face was quiet, oddly pensive. He didn't smile when he saw her. Simply watched her, standing very still. She felt his eyes on her, physical as hands drawing her to him.

But it was the third person, the small person, the woman, who riveted Sylvie.

She slowed, then stopped a few paces away from her, and stared, folded her hands into her skirt in front of her.

She's pretty. She doesn't look quite like me. Dear God, she looks like Mama. Look at her beautiful dress. She is my family. My family. My sister.

The thoughts collided in Sylvie's head, competing for expression and attention, ultimately making speech impossible. Mouth parted slightly, she gaped at Susannah Whitelaw, née Holt. Lady Grantham. Her hand went up to her mouth in sheer wonder. Tears stung her eyes.

Luckily, Susannah was doing all of the very same things at very nearly the same time, so she needn't have feared she would be considered rude.

It was Sylvie who finally managed the curtsy. And her sister, Susannah, Lady Grantham, gave a short giddy laugh and curtsied, too.

They approached each other slowly, tentatively, as if they each feared the other would evaporate. They each reached out their hands; their fingers met and clung. *My flesh and blood,* Sylvie thought wonderingly, holding her sister's cool palms.

"You look just like her," Sylvie finally said breathlessly.

"*You* don't," Susannah said just as breathlessly, just as wonderingly.

"I must look like *him,*" Sylvie told her.

They laughed together, giddily, though nothing was funny. Joy. The sound of joy and disbelief.

Then silence, slightly awkward, slightly awed.

Tom broke it. "Why don't you take your sister to your room upstairs, Miss Lamoreux?"

And Sylvie did start at the sound of her name, her real name, from Tom's lips.

"Thank you," she said softly, trying to give the words every meaning possible. She held his eyes for a moment.

And she took Susannah by the arm and led her upstairs.

Susannah and Sylvie sat together, a pair of shy strangers who were not strangers. In their hands they held their miniatures of their mother. It was a family reunion, of sorts.

"Your maid—" Susannah began.

"Madame Gabon?"

"Yes. She said you were a dancer, Sylvie. She said you were famous."

"I am a ballerina," Sylvie confirmed. "And I *am* famous," she said with an utter lack of conceit. "In Paris, at least. And I am known in other countries."

"Oh, my," her sister, wife of a viscount, breathed. "It seems everyone in the family is a dancer, except me. Unless you include the waltz."

"We must *always* include the waltz," Sylvie said somberly.

Her sister laughed, and this was grand, as Sylvie suspected Susannah loved to laugh and would do it easily.

"Sabrina is our other sister?"

"Yes. We must find her, too."

"I wonder if she's a dancer, too."

"Miss Daisy Jones said she thought she might have been raised by a curate."

"Miss Daisy Jones?" Sylvie looked at her sister blankly. "Why would Miss Jones know about Sabrina?"

"Daisy knew our mother! Didn't you know?" Susannah was astonished.

This was stunning news. "Miss Jones does not speak to the other dancers here at the White Lily."

And here was something that Sylvie half understood, and wasn't certain that Susannah would: why Daisy would keep her distance from the other dancers. Having no doubt come such a great distance in life, Daisy wanted to keep a safe distance between herself and her past. For a distance reminded her of how far she had come, and kept her safe from the gravity such a past might exert.

"I shall speak to Daisy, soon," was all she said.

A lull, for they were still discovering the rhythm of being sisters.

"Your housekeeper said you were beautiful," Susannah said gently. "When you danced."

"I am," Sylvie said firmly.

Susannah laughed delightedly. "Now I *know* we're related."

They exchanged proud, smug, amused glances, perhaps their first of sisterly solidarity.

And Sylvie squeezed Susannah's hand, and hers was squeezed in return. Lovely to take for granted this exchange of warmth.

But she had a pressing question.

"Do you...do you have a temper?" Sylvie wanted to know.

"I *slapped* a man once in a fit of temper," Susannah confessed shamefacedly. "I threatened a man with a vase when he tried to take my dresses."

Sylvie felt immensely relieved. "So it is not only me. *Mon dieu,* it plagues me, I fear."

"Daisy says Mama had—has—a temper."

When Susannah stumbled over the verb tense, they both fell quiet for a moment.

"Do you think she's alive?" Susannah finally dared to ask.

"I think, even when I was very small and alone with Claude...somehow I didn't believe she was dead when Claude told me so. Mr. Bale said there had been a...trial?" she ventured.

And so Susannah told Sylvie, who drank it in thirstily, the extraordinary tale of their mother and father: Anna Holt, who had been blamed for their father's murder and forced to flee, leaving her daughters behind, and of Richard Lockwood, their handsome—naturally—and much-beloved politician father. Of Thaddeus Morley, another politician who now moldered in the

Tower, waiting to learn whether he would swing for the crime of the murder of Richard Lockwood.

"Do you think we will find her?" Sylvie dared the question.

"We will try," Susannah said firmly, and Sylvie nodded, approving of Susannah's resolve. Not a pair of milquetoasts, not the Holt sisters.

"And what of your husband, Susannah?"

A lovely, soft pink slowly flooded Susannah's cheeks, and she went quiet.

Sylvie laughed. "Ah, so you are in *love* with your husband!"

"He's..." She stopped and shook her head, as if she could never complete that sentence to her own satisfaction. She cleared her throat.

"And you...you have a lo-lover." Susannah stumbled over the word, trying to look nonchalant about it, which amused Sylvie. "Etienne. Your housekeeper said his name is Etienne."

"Madame Gabon told you about *Etienne*?" Sylvie would need to have a word with the garrulous housekeeper. "She is too talkative."

"Madame Gabon said he came to find you, and she told him you had gone to England. He wasn't happy to find you gone." There was a pause. "Are you in *love* with *him*?" Susannah asked shyly.

Sylvie laughed to deflect the question. "He is very handsome."

Susannah was no fool. She tilted her head and studied Sylvie curiously, which was disconcerting. And Sylvie began to comprehend that sisters might very well come with some disconcerting features, too. It was lovely to be cared for, and lovely to be scrutinized, even as it wasn't entirely comfortable.

"When did you know you were in love with Kit?" Sylvie braved the question. She'd never before had a woman to ask such a question of.

Susannah's head went back a bit in thought. "I don't think there was a *when* I knew, necessarily. It almost felt...as if it always was. He seemed all wrong, at first. He was not what I expected, I suppose. But..." She gave a little self-conscious laugh. "He was everything I needed. He was like...air." She blushed again. "I cannot explain. I'm sorry."

Sylvie was silent, and simply admired her sister for a moment. She was very pretty. She was absurdly pleased to have a pretty sister, who seemed clever, too.

"Mr. Shaughnessy is very handsome," Susannah said idly.

"Do you think so?" Sylvie turned away, traced a little square pattern with her finger on the counterpane.

"Oh, yes. I remember when I met him. He took away my breath. Even as Kit stood next to me."

Sylvie looked up swiftly at her sister. Then looked away just as swiftly.

"And it's not just how Mr. Shaughnessy looks. It's..." She paused. "Something about him reminds me of Kit."

And by the silence that followed, she knew her sister was studying her. Sylvie was both pleased and irritated, and imagined this was the way of sisters, too, the feeling pleased and irritated all at once.

"Will you come to stay with us, or will you want to stay here at the White Lily?" Susannah sounded shy about it.

Sylvie finally looked up and ceased worrying the counterpane.

How tempting it was to stay, when there was a little attic room at the top of the stairs with a man who might or might not be sleeping in it at night. She considered its dangerous lure, and how the very thought of its being empty at night ached as if a hole had been driven through her.

Most nights.

No; it would be absurd to stay. Pointless, dangerous, foolish.

"May I stay with you?" she asked Susannah, just as shyly. In fact, she was rather looking forward to greeting Mr. Bale the butler again. Perhaps sticking her tongue out at his back.

"Oh, yes, please!"

They reached for each other and enjoyed their first of no doubt many, many hugs as sisters.

And so with a hug sealing their bargain, Susannah tripped gaily down the stairs to tell Kit the news about their new guest, leaving Sylvie to pack for her departure from the White Lily.

She lifted the lid of her trunk and saw her mourning dress folded there, lurking like a stowaway. *Her disguise.* Tom Shaughnessy had seen through it straightaway, but then again, he *was* rather an expert at costumes.

She stood and reached for her cloak, hanging from the peg in the wall. For a moment, she lifted it, allowed the weight of it to drape from her hands, and indulged in the memory of how she'd wrapped it around herself when she'd made that journey from this little room to Tom's.

She would never forget the look in his eyes when she had dropped the cloak. As though she, Sylvie, was a gift he'd never, ever dared hope to receive.

"You could have told me. Sylvie Lamoreux. Or is it Sylvie Holt?"

The voice made her jump. Sylvie whirled to find Tom in the doorway, his broad shoulders filling it completely. Her heart skipped, lightly, painfully, a stone cast across water.

It was odd, incongruous, to see him here in this prim little room, this vivid man she associated with every wicked pleasure.

His words hadn't been an accusation, precisely. They had almost been conversational. Almost teasing. His smile was slight, and oddly, his posture almost diffident.

"I wanted to tell you," she faltered. "I did go to—"

She stopped. She wouldn't tell him that she had gone to his room that evening...only to find it empty.

And how it had felt to wonder whether he had gone from her arms to another's.

Her chin went up instead; she sought refuge in her pride. "Would you have seen me differently?" she asked him instead. "If I had told you at first?"

"That you were a famous ballerina in Paris and related to a viscount?" Faint irony in his words.

"I feared you might believe I was yet another impostor, someone posing as Lady Grantham's sister. I didn't want you to believe that of me."

"And you thought I might turn you in for a reward." He said it wryly.

She flushed.

"You'd make a terrible impostor, Sylvie. Everything you are is always in your eyes. I would never have thought it of you."

He said it quietly, almost vehemently.

And the words both thrilled her strangely and made her powerfully sad, too. Confused, she looked down and finished folding her cloak, to give her hands something to do.

"Your sister is delighted that you'll be staying with her."

Sylvie felt her cheeks grow warm with pleasure at that; she smiled softly. "I'm delighted to have a sister."

Tom watched her for a moment, as if simply enjoying her pleasure. "I'm glad," he said gently, finally.

She knelt quickly and placed the cloak in the trunk, to avoid looking into that gentleness, to avoid considering how it made her feel.

"Were you running from him when you came to England?" he asked suddenly.

Her head went up in surprise. "Etienne?"

He smiled a little at that. "Yes."

He'd done it again: surprising her into somehow revealing more than she intended, this time the name of her lover. Tom *did* have a point: She'd probably make a terrible impostor.

"I suppose I...I did not want to hurt him, and I didn't want him to persuade me not to come to England, so I did not tell him I was leaving."

It was only part of the truth. She still wasn't certain what the entire truth was; it still hovered somewhere, out of reach of her thoughts. Or perhaps she'd skillfully tucked it away in her mind because she was afraid to reach for it. She'd known only one truth for so long.

"Ah," was all Tom said. His face went closed, and he looked away from her then, but the room offered very little for a wandering eye accustomed to gaudy things, and so his gaze inevitably returned to her.

"And you will go back to him?" he asked it almost lightly. "After you spend time with your sister?"

She looked at him. "Yes." *If he will take me.* She supposed this was the truth, anyhow.

Tom inhaled and nodded. And then he straightened, reached into his pocket for his watch. A busy man as usual, Tom Shaughnessy.

"The show tonight. I came up to see if you would be leaving it, or if you would consent to stay for the remainder of the week." Brisk now.

She smiled faintly. "For you, I will be a fairy, a pirate, and a damsel for the rest of the week."

He didn't smile. "That's how I see you, you know. As all of those things."

Startled, she gave a short laugh.

And surprising her even more, he reached out and with his finger slowly traced the line of her jaw, deliberate as a cartographer.

Her eyes closed of their own accord, as if to allow her skin to remember the feel of his touch upon it this one last time.

"Good-bye. I wish you the very best, Sylvie Lamoreux."

And then he turned and was gone.

Chapter Eighteen

⁓

On Friday evening, the end of the week of Venus, just as the doors had been flung open and a few audience members had begun to filter into the White Lily to be greeted warmly by Tom and The General, the king's man, Crumstead, appeared at the entrance. He looked distinctly ill at ease.

Three men Tom had never before seen hovered behind him, looking just as ill at ease. And faintly resolved.

"Crummy!" Tom greeted him. "Back so soon? Didn't we just pay you?"

"We're shutting you down, Shaughnessy." Crumstead said the words in a slurry rush, as though they were so distasteful he wanted them to leave his mouth as quickly as possible.

Tom froze. He shot a questioning frown at The General, who normally made sure Crumstead got his bribe. The General shrugged in confusion.

Tom returned his attention to Crumstead. "You're jesting, are you not?"

"I'm dreadfully sorry, Shaughnessy, but it's the order of the law. We need to shut down the White Lily." He squared his shoulders, as if he needed all of his strength to deliver the news.

Tom gave a short humorless laugh. "Come now, Crummy. If you want more money, you've only to ask. We're friends."

Crumstead mumbled something.

"I didn't hear you, Crumstead," Tom snapped.

He cleared his throat. "Indecency. We're shutting you down for indecency."

Crumstead did have the decency to look ashamed about it. For the White Lily was not the worst of London's theaters by far. Simply the most popular, the most successful, and certainly the most inventive.

Tom glared at Crumstead. And Crumstead said nothing more, as he knew anything else he might say would be absurd. He glanced nervously down at Tom's hand, folding into a fist, then up into Tom's face. Tom could feel the heat of anger begin to flush his skin.

"Tom, if you don't close the doors and stop the shows, we'll..." He cleared his throat. "Have to a-arrest you."

"*Arrest* me?" Tom barked. Crumstead took a step back.

"You won't shoot me, will you, Shaughnessy?" Crumstead was not the world's most courageous fellow.

"Oh, for God's sake...Crumstead...what is this about? Tell me, and we shall take care of it as we always have. This is ridiculous, and you know it."

Crumstead looked miserable. "I wish I could tell you, Tommy, I honestly do. I don't know. I only know that those were my orders. Please. I need to close you down. God knows I don't want to drag you in."

The faces of the men standing behind Crumstead echoed this—nervous determination to do what they had been ordered to do.

And Tom suddenly realized this lot had been sent to take him in if he resisted.

The look Tom turned upon Crumstead made the man blanch, but Tom wasn't actually seeing Crumstead. He was held motionless by a white fury and an extraordinary realization. He now understood that someone had encouraged—no doubt, *threatened,* rather—his investors to withdraw, and when that didn't appear to ruin him...had deliberately arranged to have the White Lily closed. He could only imagine the little web of connections required for something like this to take place— only someone with great wealth and power, the kind of power with infinite reach would be able to discover precisely how to ruin Tom Shaughnessy in particular. It had been a breathtakingly personal campaign.

But who on earth would have taken the trouble? Tom couldn't think of a soul he would call an enemy.

"Closed for how long?" Tom snapped.

"I imagine that will be up to the courts."

Nothing escaped the torpor of the courts of England before years had passed.

The dancers, aware of the tumult below, had moved from the wings and gathered on the lip of the stage, and now stood before the curtains in a row to watch.

Tom looked up, saw the row of white faces. Saw Sylvie hovering behind Molly. Saw her vivid eyes even from where he stood.

He imagined he would never be able to stand within a few feet of her without that pierce of awareness.

Crumstead sighed. "Tom, can I trust you to shut the doors, or will we have to take you with us?"

Tom's mind worked rapidly, sorting through possibilities, abandoning them, taking them up again.

"Tom, I really don't want to—"

"I'll shut the doors," he said tersely.

"I'm sorry, Shaughnessy. You don't know *how* sorry. Give

my regards to Molly?" he added sadly. Because he knew the English courts as well as anyone, and understood it could quite simply be an eternity before he ever saw Molly again.

Crumstead and the men he'd brought with him finally slunk away.

And when he did, behind them stood a man Tom had never before seen. Tall, as tall as Tom, nearly, his face obscured in shadows until he took two steps into the White Lily, and stopped, a few feet away from where Tom stood.

He regarded Tom, quiet triumph and a faint contempt passing over his features.

The man's breeding surrounded him almost like a nimbus; the kind saints wore in medieval paintings. So pronounced it nearly hummed. He was darkly handsome and sleekly clothed, so sleekly that it almost seemed as though nothing, no dust, no harm, could ever possibly cling to him. He was the sort of man, Tom realized, who would never hope to be unobtrusive, and probably never wanted to be.

Rather like himself.

And suddenly Tom realized who this must be.

But he was older than Tom had imagined him. There was a weariness about his eyes, a hardness in his face that comes from living perhaps too much. Or perhaps from seeing or hearing of relatives go to the guillotine.

Because he *was* a French nobleman, after all.

The answer came definitively from Sylvie, as a shocked intake of breath: *"Etienne."*

But there was an echo of the name, too, another feminine voice. Stunned, Tom turned to its source:

Molly.

Molly's eyes met his, widened; she gave her head a little shake, and her hands went up to her face. She turned her head away.

Etienne's gaze landed only briefly on Molly. Tom understood that she was merely the implement he'd used to learn what he'd needed to learn, after all; he'd no doubt wooed her with trinkets and lovely walking dresses, intimidated and awed her with his manners, and then had skillfully extracted information from her, information about Tom and Sylvie and the White Lily. And she was no longer useful.

Etienne's eyes swept impatiently over the girls until he found Sylvie: took in her costume, the wand and the dress and the wings.

And then Etienne's expression...

With a shock, Tom realized: *This man loves her.*

If he was a prince, no doubt he could have anything and anyone he wanted. But even being a prince couldn't protect this man from the humbling vicissitudes of love. From all of those things on The General's list.

And he imagined that Etienne resented being humbled at the hands of a dancer, even if she was a glorious dancer, the magnificent Sylvie Lamoreux. And no doubt Etienne couldn't believe that *anyone,* let alone the mongrel part-Irish, part-Gypsy, part–God knows who else—though ultimately all English—owner of a bawdy theater might have presumed to *touch* what he considered rightfully his.

And so he had set out to ruin Tom. To teach the dancer a lesson? Or to teach the English mongrel a lesson?

Whatever had flickered over Etienne's face when he saw Sylvie finally settled into a sort of petulant anger. It was this expression that lingered.

Sylvie stared back at him, as if she simply couldn't look away. "How did you..."

"You could have told me you were leaving, Sylvie," he said. Nearly flawless English. Scarcely even a hint of his nationality. "And it was a simple thing to follow you, my love." He said it almost condescendingly. "Across Paris, and then to this... place."

Tom knew an impulse to seize the man by the cravat and give him a good choking.

The crowd was thickening at the door, wondering why a single man seemed to be blocking the doorway of their beloved theater. Tom saw Bateson's face. And behind Bateson... Belstow. The man who had dangled from Tom's fist just a few short weeks ago. Another man who thought it was his right to do as he pleased to women. He suspected Belstow had done his part to assist Etienne in the destruction of Tom.

"You would have stopped me, Etienne, from coming to London," Sylvie said. "And I wanted to know the truth of me and my family. That is all."

Etienne regarded her for a moment, his features unreadable, not denying the truth of this.

"I forgive you," he finally said. "We shall discuss it when we return."

Tom saw Sylvie's hand tighten around her wand and wondered if she intended to hurl it.

This was the man who had... taken Sylvie. As if it had simply been his right. As if she wasn't something precious and rare and beautiful, worth winning, worth fighting for. Something to be worthy *of.*

And now he was here to take her back, again, as if it was his right.

You fight. Dirty, if you have to.

Suddenly everything was elegantly simple.

"Name your seconds, Etienne."

A gasp went up. The showman in Tom was distantly gratified, even as he could hardly believe he'd uttered the words he'd heard so many times before. In truth, it wasn't even his right to utter them, as he wasn't, in fact, a gentleman.

But he saw now the uses of honor. He had also, quickly, as he was Tom Shaughnessy after all, derived a plan to fight dirty in the *guise* of honor.

Etienne's mouth curved faintly, condescendingly. His brows might have lifted a fraction, but other than that his expression was bland. As though nothing here could possibly touch him. "You are challenging me to a duel, Shaughnessy? I can't imagine why you feel you'd have the right."

"Since your English has thus far been splendid, I'm rather surprised you need clarification now. But yes, I am challenging you to a duel."

"Tom, for God's sake..." The General murmured. "You'll kill him. I mean you really will kill him. He *will* kill you," The General said, as if in concern, to Etienne.

Etienne's head swung toward the sound of The General's voice, then lowered his head to find the man who'd actually said the words. He frowned a little, puzzled by him, too, then returned his eyes to Tom.

A throat cleared. "He's really a marvelous shot, Etienne," Belstow allowed.

London, granted, would be much less interesting if Tom Shaughnessy were to be shot dead. Not even Belstow seemed eager to see it done.

"You've no true right to call me out, Mr. Shaughnessy," Etienne said calmly. "Duels are for..." He delicately trailed off, as if it would be ungentlemanly to point out that Tom was patently not a gentleman. "And what on earth would my transgression be, if you please?"

Tom looked at him. The room, and everyone in it, had gone eerily silent.

"You're afraid of me, aren't you, your Highass?"

Not his best attempt at humor, but then again, he'd just

called someone out for the first time, and he was wildly, coldly, furious. Tom forgave himself.

Etienne stiffened then. His elegant jaw set. "Oh, come, Shaughnessy. You'll *hang* for killing me."

"But you'll be just as dead as I am, only sooner, as I assure you I'm a *flawless* shot."

"Shoots the heart out of the target every time." Bateson, who was hovering on the periphery of the small crowd, volunteered, voice quavering just a little.

Coldly now, Etienne said, "If men choose not to invest in your endeavors, if the authorities choose to take away your right to this travesty of a theater—"

"...bit more than a suggestion, from what I hear," someone muttered.

"...said he'd tell Pinkerton-Knowles's wife he liked to go to the theater to watch pretty girls," another muttered.

"—then that's their choice," Etienne concluded.

"*You* did this, Etienne?" Sylvie's voice was faint with bewilderment. "*You* closed the White Lily?"

Etienne turned his head toward her, opened his mouth slightly, as if to reply, then apparently decided a reply was unnecessary. He turned back to Tom.

Tom saw Sylvie's eyes become green flints.

"Name your seconds," Tom repeated calmly.

The two men locked eyes for a moment, and Tom saw a flicker of panic flash there in the depths of Etienne's dark ones, even as his features remained immobile.

"Etienne—" Molly said.

Etienne flicked her a look of such contempt that her face went white. "I'm sorry," she choked out, meeting Tom's eyes. "Mr. Shaughnessy...I..."

"Stop," Sylvie said, her voice low, thrumming with panic and fury. "Both of you."

"I shall stop," Tom said evenly, "if Etienne agrees to apologize for what he has done."

Etienne's lip curled condescendingly. "This is business, Shaugh—"

"No, Etienne." Tom's voice was as deadly and precise as his aim. "This is *not* business. I meant that you should apologize to Sylvie. This is about Sylvie. And I think you know why."

Etienne was silent. Hatred, flat and dark, dulled his eyes as he regarded Tom. Measuring him, and not arriving at conclusions he liked.

"Please," Sylvie's voice came again. Thin, taut. "Please stop."

Tom turned to her. "Very well, then. Tell me that you don't love me, Sylvie, and there will be no duel."

Sylvie stared at him, eyes glittering in her stark face. All the heads of the dancers were pointed at her, riveted, lovely mouths dropped open.

"Tell me you don't love me, Sylvie," Tom repeated calmly. "Look me in the eye and tell me, in front of these witnesses, that you don't love me, and there will be no duel, and you can return to Paris with Etienne."

And then he saw her square her shoulders, just a little shift of a motion, preparing herself just the way he'd seen her do right before she'd kissed Biggsy the highwayman.

She looked him evenly in the eye.

"I don't love you."

And her voice scarcely even trembled.

Four words. Each given equal weight. As somber, and as permanent sounding, as a sentence handed down by a judge.

Tom held her eyes evenly with his. Daring her to look away.

"Now tell me you love Etienne. Look me in the eye, in front of all these witnesses, and tell me you love *him,* and there will be no duel."

No color in her cheeks or lips. Her hands, he could see, were shaking, and surreptitiously she pressed them into her dress. Her chin went up.

"I love Etienne."

Tom stared at her. And finally he dropped his head into his chest with a nod.

Then looked up again at the prince. "I'll see you at dawn, Etienne. My seconds shall arrange it with yours."

"But—" The shocked protest came from Sylvie.

"I lied," Tom said, not looking at her.

Etienne made an exasperated sound, turned his noble palm up in apparent confusion. "Come now, Shaughnessy. You've nothing at all to prove. You might as well forgo the drama. She doesn't want you; she just said as much herself. And I'd hate to waste a perfectly good bullet on a mongrel."

Tom nodded along as Etienne spoke, as if this was all very fascinating. "But you've taken away all I have, including Sylvie, who has told everyone here she does not love me, so now I have nothing left to lose, do I, Etienne? Why should I care whether I live or die?" Tom's voice was level. He made it sound like a philosophical conundrum, something worthy of idle discussion over brandies.

"Because I knew there was more pleasure to be had in ruining you than killing you," Etienne said simply. "And you've no right to her. You've never had a right to her."

Tom furrowed his brow a little. "I see. So now that you've ruined *me* . . . Sylvie will love you?" He made it sound as though he was genuinely baffled by the logic. "Because it's clear from all the effort you've gone through to ruin me that you don't believe that she truly does. Or ever will. Despite what she says."

Tom watched with satisfaction as the color drained from Etienne's face, leaving him white with fury.

"You heard her," Etienne said coldly. "She doesn't want you, Shaughnessy."

"I heard her." Tom gave him an enigmatic little smile.

Etienne's breath came quickly now, along with his words, staccato and furious. "Very well. Since you want killing so badly, I will shoot you at dawn."

"Splendid. As I said, my seconds shall arrange it with yours."

Tom turned on his heel and made for the mural room, past Sylvie, past all the other staring faces, through the gasps and murmurs, without looking at any of them.

❧

"You're really going through with it?"

The General simply watched, as he had so many times before, as Tom got out his pistols. He hadn't lit a cigar. Just being practical. There wasn't time, of course, to smoke it down satisfactorily, since dawn was a mere hour away.

Tom pried his pistol from its velvet nest. *Inspecting it for perhaps the last time,* he thought mordantly. "Yes."

"Are you going to shoot him?"

"I am," Tom said, hefting the pistol in his hand, "going to do my level best. Should it come to that."

Quiet in this cozy room once more. Kit Whitelaw, Viscount Grantham, was outside speaking with Belstow; he'd volunteered to be Tom's other second. The discussion was a mere formality, for the duel would be as they always were: in the clearing at the edge of St. John's Wood, with pistols, at dawn, just as the light began to dilute the dark.

"And your son?"

"Will know his father wasn't a coward—if anyone remembers me and tells him. I assume that will be you."

The General gave a lift of the shoulder: *Of course*.

Tom looked at him. "You aren't going to remind me that you told me she'd be trouble, are you?"

The General shook his head to and fro. "She might even be worth it," The General said.

Suddenly The General's head jerked toward him. "Wait: 'Should it come to that,' you just said. Does this mean you have a plan?"

"Don't I always, Gen?" Tom grinned.

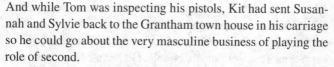

And while Tom was inspecting his pistols, Kit had sent Susannah and Sylvie back to the Grantham town house in his carriage so he could go about the very masculine business of playing the role of second.

In the Grantham parlor, over tea laced with whiskey, Susannah held Sylvie's hand.

Sylvie was dimly aware she was still dressed as a fairy.

"I remember this," Susannah said softly. "I remember another dark night, long ago. And it was you who held my hand."

"You were crying," Sylvie said softly. "I remember, too."

And she remembered she'd scarcely cried since, if ever. She wasn't crying now. She could not. She felt numb clear through. She was made of ice, she breathed ice. Her heart might be beating, but she could scarcely feel it.

"Well, I'm glad I can hold your hand now."

Sylvie said nothing.

"Somehow I knew it would be exciting to have a sister," Susannah added.

Sylvie managed a faint laugh at this. "I think we are doomed to be exciting, given the story of our mother's life."

"Sometimes men have duels and deliberately miss. Kit shot his best friend over a woman when he was just seventeen, and he deliberately missed." Susannah's way of offering comfort.

"Etienne won't miss," Sylvie said dully. "He won't try to miss. His temper... And Tom..." Her voice broke over the word. "Tom won't try to miss, either."

Susannah was very quiet. And still. Sylvie could feel her almost vibrating with alertness. "Mr. Shaughnessy is very handsome. Ow."

Sylvie had squeezed Susannah's hand a little too tightly. "I am sorry, Susannah."

Another deafening silence.

"You just called him Tom," Susannah added softly.

And a trifle, if Sylvie was being honest, insistently. Which began to penetrate the ice in her mind and heart.

Safety, certainty. These were the things she'd always wanted. Or thought she wanted. The things that Etienne promised, a future that should have seemed enormous and comfortable, a future beyond the *demi-monde*.

Why then, when then, did the idea of it become stifling? Even frightening? *Were you running from him when you came to England?* Tom had asked. And she had known he'd meant Etienne.

She realized then: she'd known he'd meant Etienne, because she *had* been running from Etienne as well as trying to discover her past.

Her breathing began to quicken. Etienne claimed to love her, but Tom's words returned to her now: *So now that you've ruined me... Sylvie will love you?*

It wasn't so much that Etienne loved her. Etienne felt *entitled* to her.

And then Sylvie thought about what Susannah had said: That Kit had felt like... air. Like everything she had always needed. But he was not at all what she expected.

She thought of Tom Shaughnessy, and how even as he glittered, and even as he reveled in all things bawdy and some things deadly, and even as he took her to what surely must be sinful bliss with his hands and mouth, there was something about him that made her feel…

Safe.

It wasn't so much about what he did, or what he owned. It was simply a part of him, that core of strength, of confidence, of—

Oh, this would amuse him:

Of goodness.

He was the best man she had ever known.

"Susannah, call the carriage! Now!" Sylvie yanked her sister to her feet.

"Oh Good *God,* I was afraid you were never going to say that." Susannah stumbled after her.

❧

It was nearly as familiar to Tom as Manton's now, this clearing at the edge of the park. Half a bright moon hung overhead, tangled in shreds of clouds. Dawn was encroaching; the deep purple of the sky was softening, gradually, to mauve.

Two carriages hung on the edge of the park, horses calm in their traces, nipping at the grass, unaffected by the various madnesses of men. They no doubt would scarcely flinch when the shots were fired in a few minutes.

The air was sharp; it was the brink of autumn, after all. An impatient wind gusted, getting in hair, lifting coats, tugging at the carriage reins.

The seconds had loaded the pistols; the surgeon, called from his bed, rubbed at his eyes and stood quietly next to Kit and The General, and Tom and Etienne had counted off.

They now stood the appropriate number of killing paces apart from each other, arms raised, pistols pointed.

Then everyone heard the clatter of hooves, a carriage being driven at breakneck speed, pulled by a team of dark horses. The door burst open before it even came to a complete halt.

"Stop!"

A blur of dark flying hair and cloak hurtled out of the coach and planted itself between the two men, undecided, it seemed, as to which way to turn.

"I've heard of this sort of thing happening," The General muttered.

And at first, there was a stunned silence, for the *Code Duello* didn't particularly address women bursting in upon the proceedings.

"Sylvie," Etienne's voice finally cracked in the silence. "Don't be a fool. Step aside. Leave us."

She whirled on Etienne decisively. "Lower the pistol, Etienne, or I will shoot you myself."

And by God, she did have a pistol, which she raised. Who would have given her a pistol? Her *sister*?

Susannah's head was just now peeking out of the coach. The viscount turned and glared at his wife, who made a small "eep" sound and pulled her head back in.

"Susannah," Kit growled.

Ah, apparently so.

"I'm afraid I have to agree with Etienne to some extent, Sylvie," Tom said calmly. "Please don't point that at an armed and angry man."

Sylvie turned to Tom; her eyes caught the early light; she clenched the fist that wasn't holding the gun against her billowing skirts.

"Have they changed the rules for these things?" Kit murmured to The General. "There are usually only *two* armed parties."

"Sylvie—" Etienne's voice was dark with warning.

She turned back to him, and her voice rose so that everyone present could hear it, furious, aching with the need to confess. "I lied! I lied. Damn both of you, but I *lied*."

"What sort of lie did you tell, Miss Chapeau?" Tom encouraged almost conversationally.

She whirled on him, glaring, breeze whipping her hair out behind her, then across her face, like those shreds of clouds in the sky.

And then she spun back to Etienne. Her voice softened just a little, but the words were firm with resolve.

"I am sorry, Etienne. When *I* said I loved you, I only meant to stop the duel. But since you are *both* idiots, and *must* duel..."

Suddenly the fury went out of her. She caught her hair in her fist to keep it from blowing about her face. "I did lie, Etienne. I do not want to be with you. I do not love you. It is...it is not you I love."

Tom doubted any man in the clearing truly gloated, for it was clear from Etienne's stance, the frozen posture, that she might just as well have shot him.

It was quiet, except for a horse whickering softly.

"When Molly said...when she said she thought she heard you throwing things at him..." Etienne lowered his pistol, handed it to Belstow. He gave a short laugh, a sound half pain, half disgust. "I suppose I knew."

His way of attempting to seize a little dignity from the occasion.

Sylvie was silent, gazing defiantly at Etienne. Watching him, daring him to do anything further.

And everyone, for the moment, was utterly still, apart from the rude wind buffeting coats and whipping hair.

And then Etienne nodded, lifted a hand, either in surrender or farewell or dismissal. He walked away, stepped into the coach. Belstow followed a moment later and pulled the door shut behind them.

Everyone watched until the horses lurched and pulled the carriage away.

Tom cleared his throat.

Sylvie turned suddenly. Gazed at him from a distance, very still. And then she knelt so she could gently place the borrowed pistol on the ground. Took two steps toward him. And stopped.

Tom obligingly handed his pistol to Kit.

Then Sylvie broke into a run and flung herself into his arms. He wrapped her tightly, buried his face in her hair, and forgot there was anyone else in the world in the sheer relief of holding her.

"I lied," she murmured again.

"So you said. Pity you lack faith in my aim." His voice was thick. "You thought he would kill me. You wanted to save me."

"I lied because I love *you*," she said indignantly.

"Oh yes, I know that, too. But *you* didn't know."

He held her. Gently touched the rough tip of his finger to the one tear shining on her cheek. Pressed his lips where the tear had once been.

"Well?" she demanded, looking up at him. "And?"

"Oh. Hmm. Well, I suppose if this isn't love, then love doesn't exist."

"Tom." The word was a warning and a command.

"Oh, very well. I love you, too."

He said it quickly. Trying to be glib. But he'd never said the words before, to anyone, in his entire life, and they instantly turned him inside out. He was suddenly glad she was there, warm in his arms, because though he was no coward, he suddenly felt very exposed.

And she knew. Smiled softly up at him.

And the first kiss in the aftermath of "I love you" was

different from any other kiss he'd known. He kissed her then, pulled her close into his body, tightly against him, and took her lips with his, knowing he would never grow tired of the soft perfection of that lower lip of hers, of the sweet singular taste of her, hadn't tasted her nearly enough.

He lifted his head.

"Do you see how clever I was?" he congratulated himself. "You thought Etienne would shoot me dead, and there I would be on the ground, the life bleeding out of me. And I knew you would come and stop the proceedings because you couldn't let me go to my death without saying you lo*mmph*—"

She'd clapped a hand over his mouth, very much not wanting to hear the rest of it.

And then, when she realized what he'd been saying, she frowned. And went very still in his arms. And pulled away a little.

"You . . . carried through with a duel so that I would come here and make a scene?"

He refused to release her. Not when he'd just told her he loved her. "Of course. How else would you know that you *really* loved me if I hadn't? How else would you find the courage to take what you really want, Sylvie? And if I hadn't followed through with it, how else would you know that I loved you, too? You might have gone home with Etienne simply to save my life."

She considered this, then narrowed her eyes at him. "That was a risky game."

He smiled faintly. "It certainly was. I've some experience with risk, however."

He noticed her expression and the dangerous little sparks in her eyes, visible even by the waning moonlight, anger stiffening her arms.

"All's fair in love and war, Sylvie."

He *had* fought dirty, of course. But not with Etienne—with Sylvie.

Who was still glaring silently.

"Are you going to begin throwing things, Sylvie? If so, can you begin by throwing your body at me again?"

This won a smile. And so he ran his hands up her bare arms, chilled now, pulled her back into his chest, wrapped his arms around her, and she pressed her cheek against his heart. Held her for a moment.

He noticed, distantly, that Kit and The General had melted away to a polite distance, out of hearing range of declarations of love.

Over near the carriage, Tom saw a distant point of light: the tip of The General's cigar.

"I am sorry," Sylvie said after a moment. "I *was* bloody stupid."

"Quite all right," he said magnanimously.

"Do you need a wife?" she murmured against his chest.

"Are you proposing to me, Miss Sylvie Lamoreux?"

"I believe that I am."

"I'm but a penniless bastard, and you, apparently, are some sort of ballet royalty related to a bloody viscount."

"Not so penniless," she murmured.

"You should have had the decency to allow me to do the proposing," he added.

"Forgive me." She sounded contrite. "How would you have done it? With a bawdy song?"

"Like this, the man of economy that I am: Will you be my wife?"

He knew a brief moment of terror when the words were out of his mouth, and she was silent, still in his arms. It was a dizzying moment, where his world tilted on its axis, and he knew in the next instant, nothing would ever be the same.

"Mmm," she said softly against his throat, nuzzling him shamelessly there. "Yes, I believe I am quite willing to do that."

Ridiculous, awkward, helpless, glorious, immortal.

It called for another kiss, the first one after a proposal of marriage. And this one was different, too. Full of wonder and promise.

"Wait," he said suddenly. "What did you mean by 'not so penniless'?"

She looked up almost guiltily. But her eyes rivaled the rising sun for glow. "The General and I have something to tell you."

ᐯ

They decided to divide the party into two carriages for the journey home, and Susannah and Kit were very understanding—more than understanding, if all the raised brows and meaningful smiles and manly pats on the back (for Tom) were any indication—when Sylvie asked whether they minded if she stayed, just for the evening, with her fiancé, Mr. Tom Shaughnessy. It was all in the family, anyhow: The surgeon was no doubt too sleepy to spread the scandalous tale of Tom Shaughnessy and his fiancée, and Kit and Susannah most decidedly didn't care, having done their own share of scandalous things.

And so Kit and Susannah and The General and the sleepy surgeon all boarded one carriage, and the other carriage took Sylvie and Tom.

He pulled her instantly into his arms, across his lap, and he pulled the cloak around the two of them, each warming the other.

"Are you still dressed as a fairy?" he murmured, suddenly.

"Mmm."

And then his mouth was at the base of her throat, hot against her chilled flesh, and his hands were fumbling up her dress. The aftermath of fear and near violence, relief and completion, fueled urgency, and Sylvie helped him, just as desperate for him. Swiftly, awkwardly, the dress was raised sufficiently, trousers unbuttoned. He brought his mouth to hers, covered her breasts with his hands, but still they took each other swiftly and gracelessly, half-laughing in wonder at the sheer raw hurry of it, release coming for both of them in harsh exultant cries minutes later.

Followed by peace.

Tom held her, pulled the cloak more tightly around her. Tucked his head between her shoulder and her chin, in that soft fragrant place. Placed his lips against her beating heart there.

"By the way, Sylvie, I know," he murmured.

She went still. "What do you know?" She tried for innocence.

He laughed softly. "Didn't you notice there were six mirrors? One for each girl. I sensed you might rather take matters into your own hands when it came to the ballet."

A silence. "Clever, aren't you."

"Mmm."

"But there is something you might not know, Tom." And now she was smug.

"Is there?"

"There *is* money in it."

And she told him of their plans.

London was filled with towers and bridges and other high places, and rumor had it that the day Tom Shaughnessy married Sylvie Lamoreux women flew so thickly from them it was like watching confetti fall from the sky. But then again, exaggeration and spectacle had always followed Tom Shaughnessy wherever he went. Tom, in fact, did his part to encourage the rumor, because it amused him, even as his wife appreciated it somewhat less.

It was, in fact, spectacle enough, some said, to see the formerly infamous Tom Shaughnessy strolling the floors of his outrageously popular Family Emporium, his arm linked with that of his beautiful wife, Sylvie Holt Lamoreux Shaughnessy, a small copper-haired child atop his shoulders.

And the Family Emporium was outrageously popular in large part because Tom Shaughnessy had always been lucky in his friends.

Once Augustus Beedle learned of the Family Emporium from The General, he not only roused the interest of a number of wealthy investors, he persuaded His Majesty, King George IV, to pay a visit to watch a new *corps de ballet* comprised of beautiful girls named Molly, Lizzie, Jenny, Sally, Rose, and Sylvie performing a ballet crafted by The General himself.

Called, naturally: *Venus.*

His Majesty had not required undue persuasion. Few men did where beautiful women were concerned.

"The least I could do for you, Tom," The General told him.

On every floor something delightful took place: Plays for children to watch and wonderful things for them to climb upon, horses and castles and pirate ships; on other floors, places for men and women to enjoy the company of each other separately and together, over tea or cigars or cards.

Watching the ballet was something they did together, primarily because everyone knew the king had done it.

But it *was* clear to everyone that Tom Shaughnessy, having acquired a beautiful wife and a beautiful child—for Jamie had come to live with him—had abandoned his wicked ways for good.

But every night, in a snug little room in a snug little bed, his wife insisted he remind her how very, very wicked he could be.

Fall in love with more books
from Julie Anne Long!

About the Author

Julie Anne Long is a *USA Today* bestselling author and RITA®
Award winner whose books have been translated into fifteen
languages, and readers around the world have called her books
"dazzling," "brilliant," and "impossible to put down." She lives
in Northern California.

You can learn more at:
    JulieAnneLong.com
    Twitter @JulieAnneLong
    Facebook.com/AuthorJulieAnneLong

*Looking for more historical romances?
Get swept away by handsome rogues and clever
ladies from Forever!*

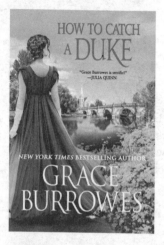

HOW TO CATCH A DUKE
by Grace Burrowes

Miss Abigail Abbott needs to disappear—permanently—and the only person she trusts to help is Lord Stephen Wentworth, heir to the Duke of Walden. Stephen is brilliant, charming, and absolutely ruthless. So ruthless that he proposes marriage to keep Abigail safe. But when she accepts his courtship of convenience, they discover intimate moments that they don't want to end. Can Stephen convince Abigail that their arrangement is more than a sham and that his love is real?

NOT THE KIND OF EARL YOU MARRY
by Kate Pembrooke

When William Atherton, Earl of Norwood, learns of his betrothal in the morning paper, he's furious that the shrewd marriage trap could affect his political campaign. Until he realizes that a fake engagement might help rather than harm...Miss Charlotte Hurst may be a wallflower, but she's no shrinking violet. She would never attempt such an underhanded scheme, especially not with a man as haughty or sought-after as Norwood. And yet...the longer they pretend, the more undeniably real their feelings become.

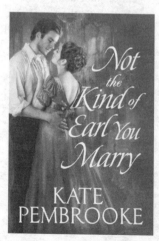

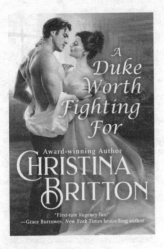

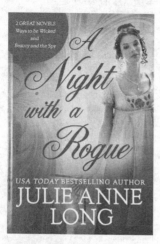

A NIGHT WITH A ROGUE
(2-in-1 edition)
by Julie Anne Long

Enjoy these two stunning, sensual historical romances! In *Beauty and the Spy*, when odd accidents endanger London darling Susannah Makepeace, who better than Viscount Kit Whitelaw, the best spy in His Majesty's secret service, to unravel the secrets threatening her? In *Ways to Be Wicked*, a chance to find her lost family sends Parisian ballerina Sylvie Lamoureux fleeing across the English Channel—and into the arms of the notorious Tom Shaughnessy. Can she trust this wicked man with her heart?

A ROGUE TO REMEMBER
by Emily Sullivan

After five Seasons turning down every marriage proposal, Lottie Carlisle's uncle has declared she must choose a husband, or he'll find one for her. Only Lottie has her own agenda—namely ruining herself and then posing as a widow in the countryside. But when Alec Gresham, the seasoned spy who broke Lottie's heart, appears at her doorstep to escort her home, it seems her best-laid plans appear to have been for naught…and it soon becomes clear that the feelings between them are far from buried.

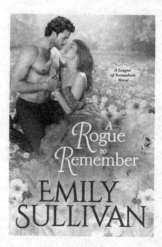

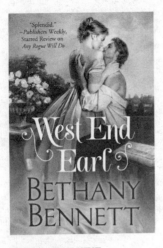

WEST END EARL
by Bethany Bennett

While most young ladies attend balls and hunt for husbands, Ophelia Hardwick has spent the past ten years masquerading as a man. As the land steward for the Earl of Carlyle, she's found safety from the uncle determined to kill her and the freedoms of which a lady could only dream. Ophelia's situation would be perfect—if she wasn't hopelessly attracted to her employer...

HOW TO SURVIVE A SCANDAL
by Samara Parish

Benedict Asterly never dreamed that saving Lady Amelia's life would lead to him being forced to wed the hoity society miss. He was taught to distrust the aristocracy at a young age, so when news of his marriage endangers a business deal, Benedict is wary of Amelia's offer to help. But his quick-witted, elegant bride defies all his expectations...and if he's not careful, she'll break down the walls around his guarded heart.

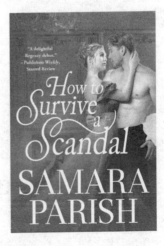